THE
UNCANNY
READER

Also by Marjorie Sandor

The Late Interiors:
A Life Under Construction

Portrait of My Mother, Who Posed Nude in Wartime:
Stories

The Night Gardener:
A Search for Home

A Night of Music:
Stories

THE UNCANNY READER

Stories from the Shadows

Edited by

Marjorie Sandor

 St. Martin's Griffin ⚓ New York

THE UNCANNY READER. Copyright 2015 by Marjorie Sandor. All rights reserved. Printed in the United States of America. For information, address St. Martin's Press, 175 Fifth Avenue, New York, N.Y. 10010.

www.stmartins.com

Designed by Molly Rose Murphy

For copyright acknowledgments, see page 557.

Library of Congress of Cataloging-in-Publication Data

The uncanny reader : stories from the shadows / edited by Marjorie Sandor. — First U.S. edition.

    pages cm

ISBN 978-1-250-04171-5 (trade paperback)

ISBN 978-1-4668-3868-0 (e-book)

1. Horror tales. 2. Paranormal fiction. 3. Fantasy fiction. 4. Uncanny, The (Psychoanalysis), in literature. I. Sandor, Marjorie, editor.

PN6071.H727U53 2015

808.83'8738—dc23

2014034217

St. Martin's Griffin books may be purchased for educational, business, or promotional use. For information on bulk purchases, please contact the Macmillan Corporate and Premium Sales Department at 1-800-221-7945, extension 5442, or write to specialmarkets@macmillan.com.

First Edition: February 2015

10 9 8 7 6 5 4 3 2 1

For Rory Watson,
Poet and Professor Emeritus, University of Stirling, Scotland,
with gratitude

CONTENTS

THE
UNCANNY
READER

UNRAVELING: AN INTRODUCTION

A few years ago, a friend and I stayed the night in an English farmhouse rich in ghost stories. As our host led us around, I found myself shadowed by my childhood reading self: that devourer of supernatural tales, that reader with her forbidden flashlight, lost in the story but dimly aware of—and pleased by—the little circle of light and the way it boldly resisted the dark. And so I roamed the thousand-year-old house as if it were a book. I peered into the old closet on the landing, where once a young housemaid read her own forbidden book and left her candle's scorch mark on the ceiling. I stepped cautiously around the boggy shoreline of the small lake where, we were told, the figure of that young maid had been known to appear.

I left unhaunted.

Or so I thought. Back home in America, feeling curiously bereft, I started looking—in stories of the supernatural old and new—for my old reading self and her simple pleasures. She was long gone, but someone else began to show up. A reader who inclined toward stories fractured and stippled with uncertainty; stories set in entirely recognizable, earthly places and whose language undid the ordinary, button by button, then kept on going, until every last thread of the safe-and-the-known was unraveled. Sometimes these stories were set in romantic old houses far from home. But the newer stories took place in familiar cities and suburbs, in apartment buildings, commuter trains, and back gardens. Their strange acid dissolved the lines between public and private, animate and inanimate. Between the living and the dead.

In these stories—and increasingly in the newspaper, on the radio, and especially on the Internet—this reader was aware of a word that kept cropping up; everywhere she turned, there it was.

"Uncanny."

Old and homely and volatile, this word. Old Scots/Northern English, it's been traced as far back as 1593. In its simplest current usage, you'll find such slim definitions as "seemingly supernatural" and "mysterious." But then again, *seemingly*. Already a door has opened. Something is uncertain. We have stepped over the threshold into a haunted word, a way of perceiving, a way of saying. In fact, if you look back to its origins, you discover that the word "canny"—Scots-Gaelic for "cunning" and "knowledge"—also meant, very early on, "supernaturally wise." You might say that from the get-go "canny" had a shadow self, a doppelgänger waiting to emerge.

Why am I telling you this at the beginning of an anthology of short stories? Because it was this capacity in the word itself that led me to collect thirty-one stories that do not fit neatly into one literary category—ranging as they do from the darkly obsessive to the subversively political, from the ghostly to the satirical.

By the late eighteenth century, the word "uncannie" can be found burrowing into stories and poems with homely force. Read the "Country Dreams and Apparitions" of Scots writer James Hogg or the poems of Robert Fergusson and you'll find it there, a small lantern light held over someone—or something—close to home but not home-like: a shepherd with the second sight, or two little children whispering about murder at bedtime. In some of these stories, the word hovers close to the exposure of a suppressed crime or socially taboo act within the intimate confines of family or village.

Over the course of the nineteenth century the uncanny migrates from rural to urban, from village and glen to the crowded cities with their factories, their soot-blackened tenements and jails. The railroad and its stations, its signal booths and waiting rooms. We are moving faster and faster, and as we do we bury our old buildings and their histories under new ones. We replace our old rituals, our language itself. We forget who we were. But something remembers. Something wants to speak from beneath the rubble.

The modern experience of alienation has come of age, and throughout the nineteenth century artists and thinkers—Karl Marx and Friedrich Nietzsche among them—begin to reflect on it, to explore its sources, its peculiar traits and expressions, its possible consequences. Think—in the world of fiction—of Henry James' 1898 novella, *The Turn of the Screw*, in which a story of "general uncanny ugliness and horror and pain" is offered up as a country-fireside Christmas tale. The story has been locked in a desk drawer in London for twenty years. It must be sent away for and unwrapped—the story we hear has been "transcribed" from the original, which was written in "the beautiful hand" of a woman long dead. Most disturbing of all: the gathered audience rubs its collective hands at the prospect of a tale of two children—not merely one—being the victims of a haunting. It has "the utmost price." We want the story, and we will pay for it. But it is not "ours," we tell ourselves. Our hands are clean.

It was Sigmund Freud's 1919 essay *Das Unheimliche*, translated into English as *The Uncanny*, that revealed the word's capacity to speak to what unsettles us now. (It's hard, these days, to find a place where the term hasn't found a home. Nicholas Royle, in his 2003 study, *The Uncanny,* finds it "transforming the concerns of art, literature, film, psychoanalysis, philosophy, science and technology, religion, history, politics, economics, autobiography and teaching.")

When Freud wrote his essay, he was following up on the work of another German psychologist, Ernst Jentsch, whose short essay "On the Psychology of the Uncanny" is well worth reading. But the Freud essay, driven by an impulse to be exhaustive, is a carnival ride of weirdness. Among other things, he gets drawn into the sticky web of the German word *heimlich,* which is just as capacious and unstable as "canny." For our purposes here, it's enough to note that like the old Scots word "canny," the word *heimlich* contained, among its early synonyms, not only "belonging to the house," but also "private," "secret," and "concealed."

Is it any wonder that the concept of the uncanny, emerging from a pair of words with such complex histories, would infuse the literature of the twentieth and twenty-first centuries? If ambiguity and uncertainty live in the very root of the word—a word that itself touches on all that we think most safe and familiar—then there's no end to its linguistic and dramatic potential, its capacity to reflect us and our times. As Royle declares, "the uncanny is a 'province' still before us, awaiting our examination."

Here are a handful of the experiences Freud catalogued as capable of causing the sensation of the uncanny. I include them, in a roughly paraphrased improvisation, here at the threshold of this cabinet of curiosities, to suggest just how tricky—how full of nooks and crannies and trapdoors—the uncanny-in-fiction really is. It's just a bare glimpse but might give you a sense of the full and glorious range of possibilities for uncanny effects, whether in a story by Ambrose Bierce or Franz Kafka or any of the contemporary writers included here.

> *When something that should have remained hidden has come out into the open.*
> *When we feel as if something primitive has occurred in a modern and secular context.*

When we feel uncertainty as to whether we have encountered a human or an automaton.

When the inanimate appears animate. Or when something animate appears inanimate.

When something familiar happens in an unfamiliar context.

Conversely, when something strange happens in a familiar context.

When we find ourselves noticing a repetition—such as the number 17 appearing three times in one day, in different contexts. Or when we catch ourselves involuntarily repeating a word, for instance the word "uncanny." Or the word "word."

When we see someone who looks like us—that is, our double.

The fear of being buried alive.

When we feel as if there is a foreign body inside our own. When we become foreign to ourselves.

There are many more uncanny-inspiring occasions listed in Freud's compendium—too many to include here. Suffice it to say that they all, in some way or another, speak to the uninvited exposure of something so long repressed—whether by individuals or by whole cultures—that we hardly recognize it as ours. That may be why the sensation, at its core, makes us anxious about the stability of those persons, places, and things in which we have placed our trust, our deepest sense of identity and belonging.

Is that why so many of the stories here take place in dwelling places? The uncanny likes to let the lamplight fall a different way on a perfectly ordinary silver picture frame. Above all, it seeks out a recollected or half-neglected *physical place* to inhabit: childhood houses, houses under construction, houses revised by later occupants.

Maybe, too, this lean toward dwelling places—and the personal and secret lives held within them—accounts for the prevalence of first-person narrations in this anthology or, if not first-person, then a third-person voice that holds tight to the consciousness of one character. Because as

Henry James—and Sigmund Freud—understood so well, the uncanny is nothing if not idiosyncratic. It happens to one person at a time and isolates that person, heightening the terror or the exaltation.

Not all of Freud's examples will speak to you. But the marvelous thing about his essay is that for a good stretch of it he turned to a piece of fiction as a base from which to explore what was, in his day, a neglected corner of psychology. He sounds a bit wistful near the essay's end, as he remarks: "The uncanny that we find in fiction—in creative writing, imaginative literature—actually deserves to be considered separately. It is above all much richer than what we know from experience." Later he goes a bit further: ". . . In a sense, then, [the fiction writer] betrays us to a superstition we thought we had 'surmounted'; he tricks us by promising us everyday reality and then going beyond it. We react to his fictions as if they had been our own experiences."

The story Freud chose as his focus is Ernst Theodor Amadeus Hoffmann's 1817 tale "The Sand-man," which you will find at the beginning of this anthology. Every reader—Freud included—will be distressed by something slightly different in it. But perhaps its most universal feature is the childhood fear of the legendary figure gone real. The terrifying Sand-man is at first the boy's proudly imagined creation and, in that way, stands in for creativity itself. It's when the *real* Sand-man shows up—the advocate Coppelius, a friend of young Nathanael's father, with his creepy hair-bag and habit of touching the children's favorite foods with his hairy hands—that the real terror sets in. A terror entirely earthly and one that threatens to foul childhood's last pure sanctuary: the creative imagination itself, that place from which we learn to perceive the world.

❧

E. T. A. Hoffmann and his contemporaries (among them Heinrich von Kleist, Jean Paul, and Ludwig Tieck) called their stories *Kunstmärchen*—art fairy tales—and revolutionized literary fiction by setting their tales in the market squares and coffeehouses, at the homely firesides and sleeping alcoves of their own towns and cities, and then, like crazed chemists, injecting a trace of the extraordinary into those known places, sending their heroes and the reading public on a journey into the unmapped terrains of our own minds. A new sort of fictional hero emerges: a flawed, rather sensitive figure—often an artist or student—a young idealist, a morose dreamer. The grown-up Nathanael, the student-poet at the heart of "The Sand-man," cannot reconcile his inner vision with that of the world. His vulnerability—however foolishly he behaves—is heartbreaking and spookily contemporary.

It is that irreconcilable feeling, as it expresses itself from 1817 to the present, that binds these thirty-one stories together. As I followed the trail of authors chronologically from Hoffmann to the most recently born, I tried to honor the tradition of the *Kunstmärchen* and, whenever possible, listened for the expression of something from Freud's catalogue. As a result, most of the stories you'll find here take place in a recognizable world, in which something, or someone, begins to go unfamiliar. And because the German word *unheimlich* and the Scots word "uncanny" come from far away, I aimed for as international—and geographically diverse—an atmosphere as I could. So you will find here writers from Egypt, France, Germany, Japan, Poland, Russia, Scotland, England, Sweden, the United States, Uruguay, and Zambia—although their birthplaces are not always the terrains they plumb in their stories, nor do they confine themselves to their own eras.

From E. T. A. Hoffmann we move on to Edgar Allan Poe, Ambrose Bierce, and Guy de Maupassant, all of whom were in some way influenced by the writers of *Kunstmärchen* and all of whom have their own distinctive ways of showing us just how unknown we are to ourselves. The narrator of Edgar Allan Poe's "Berenice" has, like Nathanael, a rising terror of his own slipping consciousness as he sits in his library, wondering how that "little box . . . of no remarkable character" made it to his lamp table. In "One of Twins," Ambrose Bierce takes us to the night streets of San Francisco and into our fear of doppelgängers and their sinister acts. Acts that might—or might not—be attributed to us. Or are they ours? In Guy de Maupassant's "On the Water," a local fisherman finds his beloved home river transformed overnight as he sits trapped in his boat, its anchor held fast by a mysterious weight from below.

And because I don't think of the uncanny as a literary genre so much as a genre buster, a kind of viral strain, I have included here a story of Anton Chekhov's with nothing remotely supernatural about it. The Russians—through early-twentieth-century critic Viktor Shklovsky—have a word for what Chekhov does in "Oysters"—*ostranenie,* "to make strange," to defamiliarize. This aesthetic principle lies at the heart of this anthology: Every writer in this collection strips away the armor of familiar, overused language. They pass through walls; they silence the numbing din out there; they make us *see* and *hear* anew.

As we make our way across the border of the twentieth century, the uncanny burrows deeper into that sacred institution called home. Edith Wharton traces the fragile path of a new marriage haunted by an old one, just as the new century roars in with its telephones and motorcars, its "devouring blaze of lights." The perfect marriage and the perfect house go suspect in Marjorie Bowen's "Decay." H. P. Lovecraft leads us into a warren of old Paris and up under the eaves of an ancient apartment house; only then can an impossible music begin to haunt the listener. Our megalomania and our dreams of safe escape play themselves out on increasingly dream-like stages: in the Schulzian universe a father is slowly turning the family home into an aviary, while Kafka tugs us, along with his adolescent hero, ever deeper into "the uncertain hold of a ship moored to the coast of an unknown continent."

***

It's been said that what is frightening to one generation will not be to the next. Virginia Woolf put it thus in her essay "The Supernatural in

Fiction." "If you wish to guess what our ancestors felt when they read *The Mystery of Udolpho*, you cannot do better than read *The Turn of the Screw*." So it's no wonder that the nearer we get to our own age, the more the shapes and shadows of uncanniness reflect our contemporary fears. It gets harder to locate the source of the disturbance. Who is our "Sandman"? and where is he hiding? For like Nathanael, we still feel watched by a force much larger than ourselves and we still ask, Did I have something to do with its dark making? That feeling—of being watched, listened in on, followed all the way home—is timelessly rendered in Shirley Jackson's "Paranoia," while Joan Aiken's "The Helper" takes us into the haunted space of a grief shadowed by an unshakable sense of deliberate menace. Our bodies go uncanny to us as we discover, with Felisberto Hernández's lonely young theater usher, a disturbing physical power over which we have no control. Robert Aickman's northern train station—a place we hope will provide a moment's rest and haven from the chaos without—is only waiting until the deep solitude of a winter's night, and a solitary, undefended guest, to bring a warm hearth glow and a forgotten horror back to life.

By Virginia Woolf's time we were no longer afraid of "ruins, or moonlight, or ghosts," and her question "But what is it we are afraid of?" is one that shifts with every hour in the twenty-first century. Let's just say that the uncanny-in-literature has the power to reflect—and allow us to reflect on—our increasingly unstable sense of home. How do we cope with the contradiction of technologies designed to improve our communications, but which seem to isolate and alienate us further, technologies that proliferate beyond our control? Are we fracking ourselves to pieces, turning our planet *unheimlich*?

The late-twentieth-century stories included here speak to our new anxieties in a variety of forms and in a variety of voices. Dwelling places continue to seduce us with their promises of safety, then begin to show

how fragile they are, how haunted by the histories repressed by their inhabitants—by us, with our unrelenting drive to contain, improve, and control. The foundations of apartment buildings whisper of state-sanctioned horrors more vast and more thoroughly concealed than those beneath Aickman's waiting room, and we must strain all the harder to catch the past trapped in the groomed and genteel borderlands between twin suburban mansions. And strain we do: we listen to our town's phantoms until they are more alive than we are. Grief and loss send us back to old childhood places—to islands and underwater caves and the edges of legendary mountains—but what we find there speaks more to the present and the future than the past. And sometimes, the terrain in which we grope and search to find ourselves is a place purely of the mind: no less real—and no less labyrinthine—than the passages of a ship's hold or the lost streets of Paris.

Train compartments reveal us to ourselves, as do streets slated for demolition. The uncanny takes us into the tightest of spots, both meta-phorically and physically; thus you may find yourself negotiating the terrifying darkness of a death camp chimney. Travel to postcolonial Zambia, where a child witnesses the ghostliness of race and class in her own family.

And if earthly places go unfamiliar here, so do voices. Think of "The Sand-man" as a Pandora's box of voices, out from which has emerged a mad host of urgent storytellers, from the voice of a whole town gradu-ally revealing its secret self to a handful of desperate letter writers, one of whom is a little marionette. Obsessed narrators abound: Some con-fess; some bear witness. Some are secret puppeteers themselves, conceal-ing their subversive intent in playful satire, in acts of ventriloquism, and by hiding inside the very language of institutions.

We go uncanny to each other, breathtakingly so, in adolescence and adulthood; public spaces go unnervingly intimate, and our bodies cry out when they should have remained silent. Keep a wary eye on fathers—and the friends of fathers. Beware the aged advocate, the optician with too many coat pockets. Beware uncommonly beautiful women who seem eager to know you; beware their daughters. The odd policeman, the stranger who looks oddly familiar. The spectacular antique automaton placed just so on a couch. Beware the carrot shaped like a hand; beware the stone rabbits by the front door. Worry about the mysterious self-destructive behavior of tigers in the forest. Come home again and ask yourself, Am I trying too hard to create a perfect body, a perfect home? A perfect world?

We turn to stories to slow ourselves down, to experience the thrill and dislocation of our world transformed. To experience, if only for an instant, what Bruno Schulz meant when he described his work as an expression of rebellion "against the kingdom of the quotidian, that fixing and delimiting of all possibilities, the guarantee of secure borders."

Therefore, dear reader, get out your flashlight and read in the dark. Read and, for a little time, let those borders dissolve.

THE SAND-MAN

Ernst Theodor Amadeus Hoffmann

Translated by J. T. Bealby

NATHANAEL TO LOTHAIR

I know you are all very uneasy because I have not written for such a long, long time. Mother, to be sure, is angry, and Clara, I dare say, believes I am living here in riot and revelry, and quite forgetting my sweet angel, whose image is so deeply engraved upon my heart and mind. But that is not so; daily and hourly do I think of you all, and my lovely Clara's form comes to gladden me in my dreams, and smiles upon me with her bright eyes, as graciously as she used to do in the days when I went in and out amongst you. Oh! How could I write to you in the distracted state of mind in which I have been, and which, until now, has quite bewildered me! A terrible thing has happened to me. Dark forebodings of some awful fate threatening me are spreading themselves out over my head like black clouds, impenetrable to every friendly ray of sunlight. I must now tell you what has taken place; I must, that I see well enough, but only to think upon it makes the wild laughter burst from my lips. Oh! My dear, dear Lothair, what shall I say to make you feel, if only in an inadequate way, that that which happened to me a few days ago could thus really exercise such a hostile and disturbing influence upon my life? Oh that you were here to see for yourself! But now you will, I suppose, take me for a superstitious ghost-seer. In a word, the terrible thing which I have experienced, the fatal effect of which I in vain exert every effort to shake off, is simply that some days ago, namely, on the 30th October, at twelve o'clock at noon, a dealer in weather-glasses came into my room and wanted to sell me one of his wares. I bought nothing, and threatened to kick him downstairs, whereupon he went away of his own accord.

You will conclude that it can only be very peculiar relations— relations intimately intertwined with my life—that can give significance to this event, and that it must be the person of this unfortunate hawker which has had such a very inimical effect upon me. And so it really is. I will summon up all my faculties in order to narrate to you calmly and patiently as much of the early days of my youth as will suffice to put matters before you in such a way that your keen sharp intellect may grasp everything clearly and distinctly, in bright and living pictures. Just as I am beginning, I hear you laugh and Clara say, "What's all this childish nonsense about!" Well, laugh at me, laugh heartily at me, pray do. But, good God! My hair is standing on end, and I seem to be entreating you to laugh at me in the same sort of frantic despair in which Franz Moor entreated Daniel to laugh him to scorn. But to my story.

Except at dinner we, *i.e.*, I and my brothers and sisters, saw but little of our father all day long. His business no doubt took up most of his time. After our evening meal, which, in accordance with an old custom, was served at seven o'clock, we all went, mother with us, into father's room, and took our places around a round table. My father smoked his pipe, drinking a large glass of beer to it. Often he told us many wonderful stories, and got so excited over them that his pipe always went out; I used then to light it for him with a spill, and this formed my chief amusement. Often, again, he would give us picture-books to look at, whilst he sat silent and motionless in his easy-chair, puffing out such dense clouds of smoke that we were all as it were enveloped in mist. On such evenings mother was very sad; and directly it struck nine she said, "Come, children! Off to bed! Come! The 'Sand-man' is come I see." And I always did seem to hear something trampling upstairs with slow heavy steps; that must be the Sand-man. Once in particular I was very much frightened at this dull trampling and knocking; as mother was leading us out of the room I asked her, "O mamma! But who is this nasty Sand-man who always sends us away from papa? What does he look like?" "There is no Sand-man, my dear child," mother answered; "when I say the Sand-man is come, I only mean that you are sleepy and can't keep your eyes open, as if somebody had put sand in them." This answer of mother's did not satisfy me; nay, in my childish mind the thought clearly unfolded itself that mother denied there was a Sand-man only to prevent us being afraid,—why, I always heard him come upstairs. Full of curiosity to learn something more about this Sand-man and what he had to do with us children, I at length asked the old woman who acted as my youngest sister's attendant what sort of a man he was— the Sand-man? "Why, 'thanael, darling, don't you know?" she replied. "Oh! He's a wicked man, who comes to little children when they won't go to bed and throws handfuls of sand in their eyes, so that they jump out of their heads all bloody; and he puts them into a bag and takes them to the half-moon as food for his little ones; and they sit there in the nest and have hooked beaks like owls, and they pick naughty little boys' and girls' eyes out with them." After this I formed in my own mind a horrible picture of the cruel Sand-man. When anything came blundering upstairs at night I trembled with fear and dismay; and all that my mother could get out of me were the stammered words "The Sand-man! the Sand-man!" whilst the tears coursed down my cheeks. Then I ran into my bedroom, and the whole night through tormented myself with the terrible apparition of the Sand-man. I was quite old enough to perceive that the old woman's tale about the Sand-man and his little ones' nest in the half-moon couldn't be altogether true; nevertheless the Sand-man continued to be for me a fearful incubus, and I was always seized with terror—my blood always ran cold, not only when I heard anybody come up the stairs, but when I heard anybody noisily open my father's room door and go in. Often he stayed away for a long season altogether; then he would come several times in close succession.

This went on for years, without my being able to accustom myself to this fearful apparition, without the image of the horrible Sand-man growing any fainter in my imagination. His intercourse with my father began to occupy my fancy ever more and more; I was restrained from asking my father about him by an unconquerable shyness; but as the years went on the desire waxed stronger and stronger within me to fathom the mystery myself and to see the fabulous Sand-man. He had been the means of disclosing to me the path of the wonderful and the adventurous, which so easily find lodgment in the mind of the child. I liked nothing better than to hear or read horrible stories of goblins, witches, Tom Thumbs, and so on; but always at the head of them all stood the Sand-man, whose picture I scribbled in the most extraordinary and repulsive forms with both chalk and coal everywhere, on the tables, and cupboard doors, and walls. When I was ten years old my mother removed me from the nursery into a little chamber off the corridor not far from my father's room. We still had to withdraw hastily whenever, on the stroke of nine, the mysterious unknown was heard in the house. As I lay in my little chamber I could hear him go into father's room, and soon afterwards I fancied there was a fine and peculiar smelling steam spreading itself through the house. As my curiosity waxed stronger, my resolve to make somehow or other the Sand-man's acquaintance took deeper root. Often when my mother had gone past, I slipped quickly out of my room into the corridor, but I could never see anything, for always before I could reach the place where I could get sight of him, the Sand-man was well inside the door. At last, unable to resist the impulse any longer, I determined to conceal myself in father's room and there wait for the Sand-man.

One evening I perceived from my father's silence and mother's sadness that the Sand-man would come; accordingly, pleading that I was excessively tired, I left the room before nine o'clock and concealed myself in a hiding-place close beside the door. The street door creaked, and slow, heavy, echoing steps crossed the passage towards the stairs. Mother hurried past me with my brothers and sisters. Softly—softly—I opened father's room door. He sat as usual, silent and motionless, with his back towards it; he did not hear me; and in a moment I was in and behind a curtain drawn before my father's open wardrobe, which stood just inside the room. Nearer and nearer and nearer came the echoing footsteps. There was a strange coughing and shuffling and mumbling outside. My heart beat with expectation and fear. A quick step now close, close beside the door, a noisy rattle of the handle, and the door flies open with a bang. Recovering my courage with an effort, I take a cautious peep out. In the middle of the room in front of my father stands the Sand-man, the bright light of the lamp falling full upon his face. The Sand-man, the terrible Sand-man, is the old advocate *Coppelius* who often comes to dine with us.

But the most hideous figure could not have awakened greater trepidation in my heart than this Coppelius did. Picture to yourself a large broad-shouldered man, with an immensely big head, a face the colour of yellow-ochre, grey bushy eyebrows, from beneath which two piercing, greenish, cat-like eyes glittered, and a prominent Roman nose hanging over his upper lip. His distorted mouth was often screwed up into a malicious smile; then two dark-red spots appeared on his cheeks, and a strange hissing noise proceeded from between his tightly clenched teeth. He always wore an ash-grey coat of an old-fashioned cut, a waistcoat of the same, and nether extremities to match, but black stockings and buckles set with stones on his shoes. His little wig scarcely extended beyond the crown of his head, his hair was curled round high up above his big red ears, and plastered to his temples with cosmetic, and a broad closed hair-bag stood out prominently from his neck, so that you could see the silver buckle that fastened his folded neck-cloth. Altogether he was a most disagreeable and horribly ugly figure; but what we children detested most of all was his big coarse hairy hands; we could never fancy anything that he had once touched. This he had noticed; and so, whenever our good mother quietly placed a piece of cake or sweet fruit on our plates, he delighted to touch it under some pretext or other, until the bright tears stood in our eyes, and from disgust and loathing we lost the enjoyment of the tit-bit that was intended to please us. And he did just the same thing when father gave us a glass of sweet wine on holidays. Then he would quickly pass his hand over it, or even sometimes raise the glass to his blue lips, and he laughed quite sardonically when all we dared do was to express our vexation in stifled sobs. He habitually called us the "little brutes"; and when he was present we might not utter a sound; and we cursed the ugly spiteful man who deliberately and intentionally spoilt all our little pleasures. Mother seemed to dislike this hateful Coppelius as much as we did, for as soon as he appeared her cheerfulness and bright and natural manner were transformed into sad, gloomy seriousness. Father treated him as if he were a being of some higher race, whose ill-manners were to be tolerated, whilst no efforts ought to be spared to keep him in good-humour. He had only to give a slight hint, and his favourite dishes were cooked for him and rare wine uncorked.

As soon as I saw this Coppelius, therefore, the fearful and hideous thought arose in my mind that he, and he alone, must be the Sand-man; but I no longer conceived of the Sand-man as the bugbear in the old nurse's fable, who fetched children's eyes and took them to the half-moon as food for his little ones—no! but as an ugly spectre-like fiend bringing trouble and misery and ruin, both temporal and everlasting, everywhere wherever he appeared.

I was spell-bound on the spot. At the risk of being discovered, and, as I well enough knew, of being severely punished, I remained as I was, with my head thrust through the curtains listening. My father received Coppelius in a ceremonious manner. "Come, to work!" cried the latter, in a hoarse snarling voice, throwing off his coat. Gloomily and silently my father took off his dressing-gown, and both put on long black smock-frocks. Where they took them from I forgot to notice. Father opened the folding-doors of a cupboard in the wall; but I saw that what I had so long taken to be a cupboard was really a dark recess, in which was a little hearth. Coppelius approached it, and a blue flame crackled upwards from it. Round about were all kinds of strange utensils. Good God! As my old father bent down over the fire how different he looked! His gentle and venerable features seemed to be drawn up by some dreadful convulsive pain into an ugly, repulsive Satanic mask. He looked like Coppelius. Coppelius plied the red-hot tongs and drew bright glowing masses out of the thick smoke and began assiduously to hammer them. I fancied that there were men's faces visible round about, but without eyes, having ghastly deep black holes where the eyes should have been. "Eyes here! Eyes here!" cried Coppelius, in a hollow sepulchral voice. My blood ran cold with horror; I screamed and tumbled out of my hiding-place into the floor. Coppelius immediately seized upon me. "You little brute! You little brute!" he bleated, grinding his teeth. Then, snatching me up, he threw me on the hearth, so that the flames began to singe my hair. "Now we've got eyes—eyes—a beautiful pair of children's eyes," he whispered, and, thrusting his hands into the flames he took out some red-hot grains and was about to strew them into my eyes. Then my father clasped his hands and entreated him, saying, "Master, master, let my Nathanael keep his eyes—oh! Do let him keep them." Coppelius laughed shrilly and replied, "Well then, the boy may keep his eyes and whine and pule his way through the world; but we will now at any rate observe the mechanism of the hand and the foot." And therewith he roughly laid hold upon me, so that my joints cracked, and twisted my hands and my feet, pulling them now this way, and now that. "That's not quite right altogether! It's better as it was!——the old fellow knew what he was about." Thus lisped and hissed Coppelius; but all around me grew black and dark; a sudden convulsive pain shot through all my nerves and bones. I knew nothing more.

I felt a soft warm breath fanning my cheek; I awakened as if out of the sleep of death; my mother was bending over me. "Is the Sand-man still there?" I stammered. "No, my dear child; he's been gone a long, long time; he'll not hurt you." Thus spoke my mother, as she kissed her recovered darling and pressed him to her heart. But why should I tire you, my dear Lothair? Why do I dwell at such length on these details, when there's so much remains to be said? Enough——I was detected in my eavesdropping, and roughly handled by Coppelius. Fear and terror had brought on a violent fever, of which I lay ill several weeks. "Is the Sand-man still there?" These were the first words I uttered on coming to myself again, the first sign of my recovery, of my safety. Thus, you see, I have only to relate to you the most terrible moment of my youth for you to thoroughly understand that it must not be ascribed to the weakness of my eyesight if all that I see is colourless, but to the fact that a mysterious destiny has hung a dark veil of clouds about my life, which I shall perhaps only break through when I die.

Coppelius did not show himself again; it was reported he had left the town.

It was about a year later when, in pursuance of the old unchanged custom, we sat around the round table in the evening. Father was in very good spirits, and was telling us amusing tales about his youthful travels. As it was striking nine we all at once heard the street door creak on its hinges, and slow ponderous steps echoed across the passage and up the stairs. "That is Coppelius," said my mother, turning pale. "Yes, it is Coppelius," replied my father in a faint broken voice. The tears started from my mother's eyes. "But, father, father," she cried, "must it be so?" "This is the last time," he replied; "this is the last time he will come to me, I promise you. Go now, go and take the children. Go, go to bed—good-night."

As for me, I felt as if I were converted into cold, heavy stone; I could not get my breath. As I stood there immovable my mother seized me by the arm. "Come, Nathanael! Do come along!" I suffered myself to be led away; I went into my room. "Be a good boy and keep quiet," mother called after me; "get into bed and go to sleep." But, tortured by indescribable fear and uneasiness, I could not close my eyes. That hateful, hideous Coppelius stood before me with his glittering eyes, smiling maliciously down upon me; in vain did I strive to banish the image. Somewhere about midnight there was a terrific crack, as if a cannon were being fired off. The whole house shook; something went rustling and clattering past my door; the house door was pulled to with a bang. "That is Coppelius," I cried, terror-struck, and leapt out of bed. Then I heard a wild heartrending scream; I rushed into my father's room; the door stood open, and clouds of suffocating smoke came rolling towards me. The servant-maid shouted, "Oh! My master! My master!" On the floor in front of the smoking hearth lay my father, dead, his face burned black and fearfully distorted, my sisters weeping and moaning around him, and my mother lying near them in a swoon. "Coppelius, you atrocious fiend, you've killed my father," I shouted. My senses left me. Two days later, when my father was placed in his coffin, his features were mild and gentle again as they had been when he was alive. I found great consolation in the thought that his association with the diabolical Coppelius could not have ended in his everlasting ruin.

Our neighbours had been awakened by the explosion; the affair got talked about, and came before the magisterial authorities, who wished to cite Coppelius to clear himself. But he had disappeared from the place, leaving no traces behind him.

Now when I tell you, my dear friend, that the weather-glass hawker I spoke of was the villain Coppelius, you will not blame me for seeing impending mischief in his inauspicious reappearance. He was differently dressed; but Coppelius's figure and features are too deeply impressed upon my mind for me to be capable of making a mistake in the matter. Moreover, he has not even changed his name. He proclaims himself here, I learn, to be a Piedmontese mechanician, and styles himself Giuseppe Coppola.

I am resolved to enter the lists against him and revenge my father's death, let the consequences be what they may.

Don't say a word to mother about the reappearance of this odious monster. Give my love to my darling Clara; I will write to her when I am in a somewhat calmer frame of mind. Adieu, &c.

CLARA TO NATHANAEL

You are right, you have not written to me for a very long time, but nevertheless I believe that I still retain a place in your mind and thoughts. It is a proof that you were thinking a good deal about me when you were sending off your last letter to brother Lothair, for instead of directing it to him you directed it to me. With joy I tore open the envelope, and did not perceive the mistake until I read the words, "Oh! my dear, dear Lothair." Now I know I ought not to have read any more of the letter, but ought to have given it to my brother. But as you have so often in innocent raillery made it a sort of reproach against me that I possessed such a calm, and, for a woman, cool-headed temperament that I should be like the woman we read of—if the house was threatening to tumble down, I should, before hastily fleeing, stop to smooth down a crumple in the window-curtains—I need hardly tell you that the beginning of your letter quite upset me. I could scarcely breathe; there was a bright mist before my eyes. Oh! my darling Nathanael! what could this terrible thing be that had happened? Separation from you—never to see you again, the thought was like a sharp knife in my heart. I read on and on. Your description of that horrid Coppelius made my flesh creep. I now learnt for the first time what a terrible and violent death your good old father died. Brother Lothair, to whom I handed over his property, sought to comfort me, but with little success. That horrid weather-glass hawker Giuseppe Coppola followed me everywhere; and I am almost ashamed to confess it, but he was able to disturb my sound and in general calm sleep with all sorts of wonderful dream-shapes. But soon—the next day—I saw everything in a different light. Oh! do not be angry with me, my best-beloved, if, despite your strange presentiment that Coppelius will do you some mischief, Lothair tells you I am in quite as good spirits, and just the same as ever.

I will frankly confess, it seems to me that all that was fearsome and terrible of which you speak existed only in your own self, and that the real true outer world had but little to do with it. I can quite admit that old Coppelius may have been highly obnoxious to you children, but your real detestation of him arose from the fact that he hated children.

Naturally enough the gruesome Sand-man of the old nurse's story was associated in your childish mind with old Coppelius, who, even though you had not believed in the Sand-man, would have been to you a ghostly bugbear, especially dangerous to children. His mysterious labours along with your father at night-time were, I daresay, nothing more than secret experiments in alchemy, with which your mother could not be over well pleased, owing to the large sums of money that most likely were thrown away upon them; and besides, your father, his mind full of the deceptive striving after higher knowledge, may probably have become rather indifferent to his family, as so often happens in the case of such experimentalists. So also it is equally probable that your father brought about his death by his own imprudence, and that Coppelius is not to blame for it. I must tell you that yesterday I asked our experienced neighbour, the chemist, whether in experiments of this kind an explosion could take place which would have a momentarily fatal effect. He said, "Oh, certainly!" and described to me in his prolix and circumstantial way how it could be occasioned, mentioning at the same time so many strange and funny words that I could not remember them at all. Now I know you will be angry at your Clara, and will say, "Of the Mysterious which often clasps man in its invisible arms there's not a ray can find its way into this cold heart. She sees only the varied surface of the things of the world, and, like the little child, is pleased with the golden glittering fruit, at the kernel of which lies the fatal poison."

Oh! my beloved Nathanael, do you believe then that the intuitive prescience of a dark power working within us to our own ruin cannot exist also in minds which are cheerful, natural, free from care? But please forgive me that I, a simple girl, presume in my way to indicate to you what I really think of such an inward strife. After all, I should not find the proper words, and you would only laugh at me, not because my thoughts were stupid, but because I was so foolish as to attempt to tell them to you.

If there is a dark and hostile power which traitorously fixes a thread in our hearts in order that, laying hold of it and drawing us by means of it along a dangerous road to ruin, which otherwise we should not have trod—if, I say, there is such a power, it must assume within us a form like ourselves, nay, it must be ourselves; for only in that way can we believe in it, and only so understood do we yield to it so far that it is able to accomplish its secret purpose. So long as we have sufficient firmness, fortified by cheerfulness, to always acknowledge foreign hostile influences for what they really are, whilst we quietly pursue the path pointed out to us by both inclination and calling, then this mysterious power perishes in its futile struggles to attain the form which is to be the reflected image of ourselves. It is also certain, Lothair adds, that if we have once voluntarily given ourselves up to this dark physical power, it often reproduces within us the strange forms which the outer world throws in our way, so that thus it is we ourselves who engender within ourselves the spirit which by some remarkable delusion we imagine to speak in that outer form. It is the phantom of our own self whose intimate relationship with, and whose powerful influence upon our soul either plunges us into hell or elevates us to heaven. Thus you will see, my beloved Nathanael, that I and brother Lothair have well talked over the subject of dark powers and forces; and now, after I have with some difficulty written down the principal results of our discussion, they seem to me to contain many really profound thoughts. Lothair's last words, however, I don't quite understand altogether; I only dimly guess what he means; and yet I cannot help thinking it is all very true. I beg you, dear, strive to forget the ugly advocate Coppelius as well as the weather-glass hawker Giuseppe Coppola. Try and convince yourself that these foreign influences can have no power over you, that it is only the belief in their hostile power which can in reality make them dangerous to you. If every line of your letter did not betray the violent excitement of your mind, and if I did not sympathise with your condition from the bottom of my heart, I could in truth jest about the advocate Sand-man and weather-glass hawker Coppelius. Pluck up your spirits! Be cheerful! I have resolved to appear to you as your guardian-angel if that ugly man Coppola should dare take it into his head to bother you in your dreams, and drive him away with a good hearty laugh. I'm not afraid of him and his nasty hands, not the least little bit; I won't let him either as advocate spoil any dainty tit-bit I've taken, or as Sand-man rob me of my eyes.

My darling, darling Nathanael,
Eternally your, &c. &c.

NATHANAEL TO LOTHAIR

I am very sorry that Clara opened and read my last letter to you; of course the mistake is to be attributed to my own absence of mind. She has written me a very deep philosophical letter, proving conclusively that Coppelius and Coppola only exist in my own mind and are phantoms of my own self, which will at once be dissipated, as soon as I look upon them in that light. In very truth one can hardly believe that the mind which so often sparkles in those bright, beautifully smiling, child-like eyes of hers like a sweet lovely dream could draw such subtle and scholastic distinctions. She also mentions your name. You have been talking about me. I suppose you have been giving her lectures, since she sifts and refines everything so acutely. But enough of this! I must now tell you it is most certain that the weather-glass hawker Giuseppe Coppola is not the advocate Coppelius. I am attending the lectures of our recently appointed Professor of Physics, who, like the distinguished naturalist, is called Spalanzani, and is of Italian origin. He has known Coppola for many years; and it is also easy to tell from his accent that he really is a Piedmontese. Coppelius was a German, though no honest German, I fancy. Nevertheless I am not quite satisfied. You and Clara will perhaps take me for a gloomy dreamer, but nohow can I get rid of the impression which Coppelius's cursed face made upon me. I am glad to learn from Spalanzani that he has left the town. This Professor Spalanzani is a very queer fish. He is a little fat man, with prominent cheekbones, thin nose, projecting lips, and small piercing eyes. You cannot get a better picture of him than by turning over one of the Berlin pocketalmanacs and looking at Cagliostro's portrait engraved by Chodowiecki; Spalanzani looks just like him.

Once lately, as I went up the steps to his house, I perceived that beside the curtain which generally covered a glass door there was a small chink. What it was that excited my curiosity I cannot explain; but I looked through. In the room I saw a female, tall, very slender, but of perfect proportions, and splendidly dressed, sitting at a little table, on which she had placed both her arms, her hands being folded together. She sat opposite the door, so that I could easily see her angelically beautiful face. She did not appear to notice me, and there was moreover a strangely fixed look about her eyes, I might almost say they appeared as if they had no power of vision; I thought she was sleeping with her eyes open. I felt quite uncomfortable, and so I slipped away quietly into the Professor's lecture-room, which was close at hand. Afterwards I learnt that the figure which I had seen was Spalanzani's daughter, Olimpia, whom he keeps locked in a most wicked and unaccountable way, and no

man is ever allowed to come near her. Perhaps, however, there is after all
something peculiar about her; perhaps she's an idiot or something of
that sort. But why am I telling you all this? I could have told you it all
better and more in detail when I see you. For in a fortnight I shall be
amongst you. I must see my dear sweet angel, my Clara, again. Then the
little bit of ill-temper, which, I must confess, took possession of me after her fearfully sensible letter, will be blown away. And that is the reason why I am not writing to her as well to-day. With all best wishes, &c.

Nothing more strange and extraordinary can be imagined, gracious
reader, than what happened to my poor friend, the young student Nathanael, and which I have undertaken to relate to you. Have you ever
lived to experience anything that completely took possession of your
heart and mind and thoughts to the utter exclusion of everything else?
All was seething and boiling within you; your blood, heated to fever
pitch, leapt through your veins and inflamed your cheeks. Your gaze
was so peculiar, as if seeking to grasp in empty space forms not seen of
any other eye, and all your words ended in sighs betokening some mystery. Then your friends asked you, "What is the matter with you, my
dear friend? What do you see?" And, wishing to describe the inner pictures in all their vivid colours, with their lights and their shades, you in
vain struggled to find words with which to express yourself. But you felt
as if you must gather up all the events that had happened, wonderful,
splendid, terrible, jocose, and awful, in the very first word, so that the
whole might be revealed by a single electric discharge, so to speak. Yet
every word and all that partook of the nature of communication by intelligible sounds seemed to be colourless, cold, and dead. Then you try
and try again, and stutter and stammer, whilst your friends' prosy questions strike like icy winds upon your heart's hot fire until they extin-
guish it. But if, like a bold painter, you had first sketched in a few audacious
strokes the outline of the picture you had in your soul, you would then

easily have been able to deepen and intensify the colours one after the other, until the varied throng of living figures carried your friends away, and they, like you, saw themselves in the midst of the scene that had proceeded out of your own soul.

Strictly speaking, indulgent reader, I must indeed confess to you, nobody has asked me for the history of young Nathanael; but you are very well aware that I belong to that remarkable class of authors who, when they are bearing anything about in their minds in the manner I have just described, feel as if everybody who comes near them, and also the whole world to boot, were asking, "Oh! what is it? Oh! do tell us, my good sir?" Hence I was most powerfully impelled to narrate to you Nathanael's ominous life. My soul was full of the elements of wonder and extraordinary peculiarity in it; but, for this very reason, and because it was necessary in the very beginning to dispose you, indulgent reader, to bear with what is fantastic—and that is not a little thing—I racked my brain to find a way of commencing the story in a significant and original manner, calculated to arrest your attention. To begin with "Once upon a time," the best beginning for a story, seemed to me too tame; with "In the small country town S—— lived," rather better, at any rate allowing plenty of room to work up to the climax; or to plunge at once *in medias res*, "'Go to the devil!' cried the student Nathanael, his eyes blazing wildly with rage and fear, when the weather-glass hawker Giuseppe Coppola"—well, that is what I really had written, when I thought I detected something of the ridiculous in Nathanael's wild glance; and the history is anything but laughable. I could not find any words which seemed fitted to reflect in even the feeblest degree the brightness of the colours of my mental vision. I determined not to begin at all. So I pray you, gracious reader, accept the three letters which my friend Lothair has been so kind as to communicate to me as the outline of the picture, into which I will endeavour to introduce more and more colour as I proceed with my narrative. Perhaps, like a good portrait-painter, I may succeed in depicting more than one figure in such wise that you will recognise it as a good likeness without being acquainted with the original, and feel as if you had very often seen the original with your own bodily eyes. Perhaps, too, you will then believe that nothing is more wonderful, nothing more fantastic than real life, and that all that a writer can do is to present it as a dark reflection from a dim cut mirror.

In order to make the very commencement more intelligible, it is necessary to add to the letters that, soon after the death of Nathanael's father, Clara and Lothair, the children of a distant relative, who had likewise died, leaving them orphans, were taken by Nathanael's mother into her own house. Clara and Nathanael conceived a warm affection for each other, against which not the slightest objection in the world could be urged. When therefore Nathanael left home to prosecute his studies in G——, they were betrothed. It is from G—— that his last letter is written, where he is attending the lectures of Spalanzani, the distinguished Professor of Physics.

I might now proceed comfortably with my narration, did not at this moment Clara's image rise up so vividly before my eyes that I cannot turn them away from it, just as I never could when she looked upon me and smiled so sweetly. Nowhere would she have passed for beautiful, that was the unanimous opinion of all who professed to have any technical knowledge of beauty. But whilst architects praised the pure proportions of her figure and form, painters averred that her neck, shoulders, and bosom were almost too chastely modelled, and yet, on the other hand, one and all were in love with her glorious Magdalene hair, and talked a good deal of nonsense about Batoni-like colouring. One of them, a veritable romanticist, strangely enough likened her eyes to a lake by Ruisdael, in which is reflected the pure azure of the cloudless sky, the beauty of woods and flowers, and all the bright and varied life of a living landscape. Poets and musicians went still further and said, "What's all this talk about seas and reflections? How can we look upon the girl without feeling that wonderful heavenly songs and melodies beam upon us from her eyes, penetrating deep down into our hearts, till all becomes awake and throbbing with emotion? And if we cannot sing anything at all passable then, why, we are not worth much; and this we can also plainly read in the rare smile which flits around her lips when we have the hardihood to squeak out something in her presence which we pretend to call singing, in spite of the fact that it is nothing more than a few single notes confusedly linked together." And it really was so. Clara had the powerful fancy of a bright, innocent, unaffected child, a woman's deep and sympathetic heart, and an understanding clear, sharp, and discriminating. Dreamers and visionaries had but a bad time of it with her; for without saying very much—she was not by nature of a talkative disposition—she plainly asked, by her calm steady look, and rare ironical smile, "How can you imagine, my dear friends, that I can take these fleeting shadowy images for true living and breathing forms?" For this reason many found fault with her as being cold, prosaic, and devoid of feeling; others, however, who had reached a clearer and deeper conception of life, were extremely fond of the intelligent, childlike, large-hearted girl. But none had such an affection for her as Nathanael, who was a zealous and cheerful cultivator of the fields of science and art. Clara clung to her lover with all her heart; the first clouds she encountered in life were when he had to separate from her. With what delight did she fly into his arms when, as he had promised in his last letter to Lothair, he really came back to his native town and entered his mother's room! And as Nathanael had foreseen, the moment he saw Clara again he no longer thought about either the advocate Coppelius or her sensible letter; his ill-humour had quite disappeared.

Nevertheless Nathanael was right when he told his friend Lothair that the repulsive vendor of weather-glasses, Coppola, had exercised a fatal and disturbing influence upon his life. It was quite patent to all; for even during the first few days he showed that he was completely and entirely changed. He gave himself up to gloomy reveries, and moreover acted so strangely; they had never observed anything at all like it in him before. Everything, even his own life, was to him but dreams and presentiments. His constant theme was that every man who delusively imagined himself to be free was merely the plaything of the cruel sport of mysterious powers, and it was vain for man to resist them; he must humbly submit to whatever destiny had decreed for him. He went so far as to maintain that it was foolish to believe that a man could do anything in art or science of his own accord; for the inspiration in which alone any true artistic work could be done did not proceed from the spirit within outwards, but was the result of the operation directed inwards of some Higher Principle existing without and beyond ourselves.

This mystic extravagance was in the highest degree repugnant to Clara's clear intelligent mind, but it seemed vain to enter upon any attempt at refutation. Yet when Nathanael went on to prove that Coppelius was the Evil Principle which had entered into him and taken possession of him at the time he was listening behind the curtain, and that this hateful demon would in some terrible way ruin their happiness, then Clara grew grave and said, "Yes, Nathanael. You are right; Coppelius is an Evil Principle; he can do dreadful things, as bad as could a Satanic power which should assume a living physical form, but only— only if you do not banish him from your mind and thoughts. So long as you believe in him he exists and is at work; your belief in him is his only power." Whereupon Nathanael, quite angry because Clara would only grant the existence of the demon in his own mind, began to dilate at large upon the whole mystic doctrine of devils and awful powers, but Clara abruptly broke off the theme by making, to Nathanael's very great disgust, some quite commonplace remark. Such deep mysteries are sealed books to cold, unsusceptible characters, he thought, without being clearly conscious to himself that he counted Clara amongst these inferior natures, and accordingly he did not remit his efforts to initiate her into these mysteries. In the morning, when she was helping to prepare breakfast, he would take his stand beside her, and read all sorts of mystic books to her, until she begged him—"But, my dear Nathanael, I shall have to scold you as the Evil Principle which exercises a fatal influence upon my coffee. For if I do as you wish, and let things go their own way, and look into your eyes whilst you read, the coffee will all boil over into the fire, and you will none of you get any breakfast." Then Nathanael hastily banged the book to and ran away in great displeasure to his own room.

Formerly he had possessed a peculiar talent for writing pleasing, sparkling tales, which Clara took the greatest delight in listening to; but now his productions were gloomy, unintelligible, and wanting in form, so that, although Clara out of forbearance towards him did not say so, he nevertheless felt how very little interest she took in them. There was nothing that Clara disliked so much as what was tedious; at such times her intellectual sleepiness was not to be overcome; it was betrayed both in her glances and in her words. Nathanael's effusions were, in truth, exceedingly tedious. His ill-humour at Clara's cold prosaic temperament continued to increase; Clara could not conceal her distaste of his dark, gloomy, wearying mysticism; and thus both began to be more and more estranged from each other without exactly being aware of it themselves. The image of the ugly Coppelius had, as Nathanael was obliged to confess to himself, faded considerably in his fancy, and it often cost him great pains to present him in vivid colours in his literary efforts, in which he played the part of the ghoul of Destiny. At length it entered into his head to make his dismal presentiment that Coppelius would ruin his happiness the subject of a poem. He made himself and Clara, united by true love, the central figures, but represented a black hand as being from time to time thrust into their life and plucking out a joy that had blossomed for them. At length, as they were standing at the altar, the terrible Coppelius appeared and touched Clara's lovely eyes, which leapt into Nathanael's own bosom, burning and hissing like bloody sparks. Then Coppelius laid hold upon him, and hurled him into a blazing circle of fire, which spun round with the speed of a whirlwind, and, storming and blustering, dashed away with him. The fearful noise it made was like a furious hurricane lashing the foaming sea-waves until they rise up like black, white-headed giants in the midst of the raging struggle. But through the midst of the savage fury of the tempest he heard Clara's voice calling, "Can you not see me, dear? Coppelius has deceived you; they were not my eyes which burned so in your bosom; they were fiery drops of your own heart's blood. Look at me, I have got my own eyes still." Nathanael thought, "Yes, that is Clara, and I am hers forever." Then this thought laid a powerful grasp upon the fiery circle so that it stood still, and the riotous turmoil died away rumbling down a dark abyss. Nathanael looked into Clara's eyes; but it was death whose gaze rested so kindly upon him.

Whilst Nathanael was writing this work he was very quiet and sober-minded; he filed and polished every line, and as he had chosen to submit himself to the limitations of metre, he did not rest until all was pure and musical. When, however, he had at length finished it and read it aloud to himself he was seized with horror and awful dread, and he screamed, "Whose hideous voice is this?" But he soon came to see in it again nothing beyond a very successful poem, and he confidently believed it would enkindle Clara's cold temperament, though to what end she should be thus aroused was not quite clear to his own mind, nor yet what would be the real purpose served by tormenting her with these dreadful pictures, which prophesied a terrible and ruinous end to her affection.

Nathanael and Clara sat in his mother's little garden. Clara was bright and cheerful, since for three entire days her lover, who had been busy writing his poem, had not teased her with his dreams or forebodings. Nathanael, too, spoke in a gay and vivacious way of things of merry import, as he formerly used to do, so that Clara said, "Ah! now I have you again. We have driven away that ugly Coppelius, you see." Then it suddenly occurred to him that he had got the poem in his pocket which he wished to read to her. He at once took out the manuscript and began to read. Clara, anticipating something tedious as usual, prepared to submit to the infliction, and calmly resumed her knitting. But as the sombre clouds rose up darker and darker she let her knitting fall on her lap and sat with her eyes fixed in a set stare upon Nathanael's face.

He was quite carried away by his own work, the fire of enthusiasm coloured his cheeks a deep red, and tears started from his eyes. At length he concluded, groaning and showing great lassitude; grasping Clara's hand, he sighed as if he were being utterly melted in inconsolable grief, "Oh! Clara! Clara!" She drew him softly to her heart and said in a low but very grave and impressive tone, "Nathanael, my darling Nathanael, throw that foolish, senseless, stupid thing into the fire." Then Nathanael leapt indignantly to his feet, crying, as he pushed Clara from him, "You damned lifeless automaton!" and rushed away. Clara was cut to the heart, and wept bitterly. "Oh! he has never loved me, for he does not understand me," she sobbed.

Lothair entered the arbour. Clara was obliged to tell him all that had taken place. He was passionately fond of his sister; and every word of her complaint fell like a spark upon his heart, so that the displeasure which he had long entertained against his dreamy friend Nathanael was kindled into furious anger. He hastened to find Nathanael, and upbraided him in harsh words for his irrational behaviour towards his beloved sister. The fiery Nathanael answered him in the same style. "A fantastic, crack-brained fool," was retaliated with, "A miserable, common, everyday sort of fellow." A meeting was the inevitable consequence. They agreed to meet on the following morning behind the garden-wall, and fight, according to the custom of the students of the place, with sharp rapiers. They went about silent and gloomy; Clara had both heard and seen the violent quarrel, and also observed the fencing master bring the rapiers in the dusk of the evening. She had a presentiment of what was to happen. They both appeared at the appointed place wrapped up in the same gloomy silence, and threw off their coats. Their eyes flaming with the bloodthirsty light of pugnacity, they were about to begin their contest when Clara burst through the garden door. Sobbing, she screamed, "You savage, terrible men! Cut me down before you attack each other;

for how can I live when my lover has slain my brother, or my brother slain my lover?" Lothair let his weapon fall and gazed silently upon the ground, whilst Nathanael's heart was rent with sorrow, and all the affection which he had felt for his lovely Clara in the happiest days of her golden youth was awakened within him. His murderous weapon, too, fell from his hand; he threw himself at Clara's feet. "Oh! can you ever forgive me, my only, my dearly loved Clara? Can you, my dear brother Lothair, also forgive me?" Lothair was touched by his friend's great distress; the three young people embraced each other amidst endless tears, and swore never again to break their bond of love and fidelity.

Nathanael felt as if a heavy burden that had been weighing him down to the earth was now rolled from off him, nay, as if by offering resistance to the dark power which had possessed him, he had rescued his own self from the ruin which had threatened him. Three happy days he now spent amidst the loved ones, and then returned to G——, where he had still a year to stay before settling down in his native town for life.

Everything having reference to Coppelius had been concealed from the mother, for they knew she could not think of him without horror, since she as well as Nathanael believed him to be guilty of causing her husband's death.

<hr />

When Nathanael came to the house where he lived he was greatly astonished to find it burnt down to the ground, so that nothing but the bare outer walls were left standing amidst a heap of ruins. Although the fire had broken out in the laboratory of the chemist who lived on the groundfloor, and had therefore spread upwards, some of Nathanael's bold, active friends had succeeded in time in forcing a way into his room in the upper storey and saving his books and manuscripts and instruments. They had carried them all uninjured into another house, where they engaged a room for him; this he now at once took possession of. That he lived opposite Professor Spalanzani did not strike him particularly, nor did it occur to him as anything more singular that he could, as he observed, by looking out of his window, see straight into the room where Olimpia often sat alone. Her figure he could plainly distinguish, although her features were uncertain and confused. It did at length occur to him, however, that she remained for hours together in the same position in which he had first discovered her through the glass door, sitting at a little table without any occupation whatever, and it was evident that she was constantly gazing across in his direction. He could not but confess to himself that he had never seen a finer figure. However, with Clara mistress of his heart, he remained perfectly unaffected by Olimpia's stiffness and apathy; and it was only occasionally that he sent a fugitive glance over his compendium across to her—that was all.

He was writing to Clara; a light tap came at the door. At his summons to "Come in," Coppola's repulsive face appeared peeping in. Nathanael felt his heart beat with trepidation; but, recollecting what Spalanzani had told him about his fellow-countryman Coppola, and what he had himself so faithfully promised his beloved in respect to the Sand-man Coppelius, he was ashamed at himself for this childish fear of spectres. Accordingly, he controlled himself with an effort, and said, as quietly and as calmly as he possibly could, "I don't want to buy any weather-glasses, my good friend; you had better go elsewhere." Then Coppola came right into the room, and said in a hoarse voice, screwing up his wide mouth into a hideous smile, whilst his little eyes flashed keenly from beneath his long grey eyelashes, "What! Nee weather-gless? Nee weather-gless? 've got foine oyes as well—foine oyes!" Affrighted, Nathanael cried, "You stupid man, how can you have eyes?—eyes—eyes?" But Coppola, laying aside his weather-glasses, thrust his hands into his big coat-pockets and brought out several spy-glasses and spectacles, and put them on the table. "Theer! Theer! Spect'cles! Spect'cles to put 'n nose! Them's my oyes—foine oyes." And he continued to produce more and more spectacles from his pockets until the table began to gleam and flash all over. Thousands of eyes were looking and blinking convulsively, and staring up at Nathanael; he could not avert his gaze from the table. Coppola went on heaping up his spectacles, whilst wilder and ever wilder burning flashes crossed through and through each other and darted their blood-red rays into Nathanael's breast. Quite overcome, and frantic with terror, he shouted, "Stop! stop! you terrible man!" and he seized Coppola by the arm, which he had again thrust into his pocket in order to bring out still more spectacles, although the whole table was covered all over with them. With a harsh disagreeable laugh Coppola gently freed himself; and with the words "So! went none! Well, here foine gless!" he swept all his spectacles together, and put them back into his coat-pockets, whilst from a breastpocket he produced a great number of larger and smaller perspectives. As soon as the spectacles were gone Nathanael recovered his equanimity again; and, bending his thoughts upon Clara, he clearly discerned that the gruesome incubus had proceeded only from himself, as also that Coppola was a right honest mechanician and optician, and far from being Coppelius's dreaded double and ghost. And then, besides, none of the glasses which Coppola now placed on the table had anything at all singular about them, at least nothing so weird as the spectacles; so, in order to square accounts with himself, Nathanael now really determined to buy something of the man. He took up a small, very beautifully cut pocket perspective, and by way of proving it looked through the window. Never before in his life had he had a glass in his hands that brought out things so clearly and sharply and distinctly. Involuntarily he directed the glass upon Spalanzani's room; Olimpia sat at the little table as usual, her arms laid upon it and her hands folded. Now he saw for the first time the regular and exquisite beauty of her features. The eyes, however, seemed to him to have a singular look of fixity and lifelessness. But as he continued to look closer and more carefully through the glass he fancied a light like humid moonbeams came into them. It seemed as if their power of vision was now being enkindled; their glances shone with ever-increasing vivacity. Nathanael remained standing at the window as if glued to the spot by a wizard's spell, his gaze rivetted unchangeably upon the divinely beautiful Olimpia. A coughing and shuffling of the feet awakened him out of his enchaining dream, as it were. Coppola stood behind him. "Tre zechini" (three ducats). Nathanael had completely forgotten the optician; he hastily paid the sum demanded. "Ain't 't? Foine gless? foine gless?" asked Coppola in his harsh unpleasant voice, smiling sardonically. "Yes, yes, yes," rejoined Nathanael impatiently; "adieu, my good friend." But Coppola did not leave the room without casting many peculiar side-glances upon Nathanael; and the young student heard him laughing loudly on the stairs. "Ah well!" thought he. "He's laughing at me because I've paid him too much for this little perspective—because I've given him too much money—that's it." As he softly murmured these words he fancied he detected a gasping sigh as of a dying man stealing awfully through the room; his heart stopped beating with fear. But to be sure he had heaved a deep sigh himself; it was quite plain. "Clara is quite right," said he to himself, "in holding me to be an incurable ghost-seer; and yet it's very ridiculous—ay, more than ridiculous—that the stupid thought of having paid Coppola too much for his glass should cause me this strange anxiety; I can't see any reason for it."

Now he sat down to finish his letter to Clara; but a glance through the window showed him Olimpia still in her former posture. Urged by an irresistible impulse he jumped up and seized Coppola's perspective; nor could he tear himself away from the fascinating Olimpia until his friend and brother Siegmund called for him to go to Professor Spalanzani's lecture. The curtains before the door of the all-important room were closely drawn, so that he could not see Olimpia. Nor could he even see her from his own room during the two following days, notwithstanding that he scarcely ever left his window, and maintained a scarce interrupted watch through Coppola's perspective upon her room. On the third day curtains even were drawn across the window. Plunged into the depths of despair,—goaded by longing and ardent desire, he hurried outside the walls of the town. Olimpia's image hovered about his path in the air and stepped forth out of the bushes, and peeped up at him with large and lustrous eyes from the bright surface of the brook. Clara's image was completely faded from his mind; he had no thoughts except for Olimpia. He uttered his love-plaints aloud and in a lachrymose tone, "Oh! my glorious, noble star of love, have you only risen to vanish again, and leave me in the darkness and hopelessness of night?"

Returning home, he became aware that there was a good deal of noisy bustle going on in Spalanzani's house. All the doors stood wide open; men were taking in all kinds of gear and furniture; the windows of the first floor were all lifted off their hinges; busy maid-servants with immense hair-brooms were driving backwards and forwards dusting and sweeping, whilst within could be heard the knocking and hammering of carpenters and upholsterers. Utterly astonished, Nathanael stood still in the street; then Siegmund joined him, laughing, and said, "Well, what do you say to our old Spalanzani?" Nathanael assured him that he could not say anything, since he knew not what it all meant; to his great astonishment, he could hear, however, that they were turning the quiet gloomy house almost inside out with their dusting and cleaning and making of alterations. Then he learned from Siegmund that Spalanzani intended giving a great concert and ball on the following day, and that half the university was invited. It was generally reported that Spalanzani was going to let his daughter Olimpia, whom he had so long so jealously guarded from every eye, make her first appearance.

Nathanael received an invitation. At the appointed hour, when the carriages were rolling up and the lights were gleaming brightly in the decorated halls, he went across to the Professor's, his heart beating high with expectation. The company was both numerous and brilliant. Olimpia was richly and tastefully dressed. One could not but admire her figure and the regular beauty of her features. The striking inward curve of her back, as well as the wasp-like smallness of her waist, appeared to be the result of too-tight lacing. There was something stiff and measured in her gait and bearing that made an unfavourable impression upon many; it was ascribed to the constraint imposed upon her by the company. The concert began. Olimpia played on the piano with great skill; and sang as skilfully an *aria di bravura*, in a voice which was, if anything, almost too sharp, but clear as glass bells. Nathanael was transported with delight; he stood in the background farthest from her, and owing to the blinding lights could not quite distinguish her features. So, without being observed, he took Coppola's glass out of his pocket, and directed it upon the beautiful Olimpia. Oh! then he perceived how her yearning eyes sought him, how every note only reached its full purity in the loving glance which penetrated to and inflamed his heart. Her artificial *roulades* seemed to him to be the exultant cry towards heaven of the soul refined by love; and when at last, after the *cadenza*, the long trill rang shrilly and loudly through the hall, he felt as if he were suddenly grasped by burning arms and could no longer control himself,—he could not help shouting aloud in his mingled pain and delight, "Olimpia!" All eyes were turned upon him; many people laughed. The face of the cathedral organist wore a still more gloomy look than it had done before, but all he said was, "Very well!"

The concert came to an end, and the ball began. Oh! to dance with her—with her—that was now the aim of all Nathanael's wishes, of all his desires. But how should he have courage to request her, the queen of the ball, to grant him the honour of a dance? And yet he couldn't tell how it came about, just as the dance began, he found himself standing close beside her, nobody having as yet asked her to be his partner; so, with some difficulty stammering out a few words, he grasped her hand. It was cold as ice; he shook with an awful, frosty shiver. But, fixing his eyes upon her face, he saw that her glance was beaming upon him with love and longing, and at the same moment he thought that the pulse began to beat in her cold hand, and the warm life-blood to course through her veins. And passion burned more intensely in his own heart also, he threw his arm round her beautiful waist and whirled her round the hall. He had always thought that he kept good and accurate time in dancing, but from the perfectly rhythmical evenness with which Olimpia danced, and which frequently put him quite out, he perceived how very faulty his own time really was. Notwithstanding, he would not dance with any other lady; and everybody else who approached Olimpia to call upon her for a dance, he would have liked to kill on the spot. This, however, only happened twice; to his astonishment Olimpia remained after this without a partner, and he failed not on each occasion to take her out again. If Nathanael had been able to see anything else except the beautiful Olimpia, there would inevitably have been a good deal of unpleasant quarrelling and strife; for it was evident that Olimpia was the object of the smothered laughter only with difficulty suppressed, which was heard in various corners amongst the young people; and they followed her with very curious looks, but nobody knew for what reason. Nathanael, excited by dancing and the plentiful supply of wine he had consumed, had laid aside the shyness which at other times characterised him. He sat beside Olimpia, her hand in his own, and declared his love enthusiastically and passionately in words which neither of them understood, neither he nor Olimpia. And yet she perhaps did, for she sat with her eyes fixed unchangeably upon his, sighing repeatedly, "Ach! Ach! Ach!" Upon this Nathanael would answer, "Oh, you glorious heavenly lady! You ray from the promised paradise of love! Oh! what a profound soul you have! my whole being is mirrored in it!" and a good deal more in the same strain. But Olimpia only continued to sigh, "Ach! Ach!" again and again.

Professor Spalanzani passed by the two happy lovers once or twice, and smiled with a look of peculiar satisfaction. All at once it seemed to Nathanael, albeit he was far away in a different world, as if it were growing perceptibly darker down below at Professor Spalanzani's. He looked about him, and to his very great alarm became aware that there were only two lights left burning in the hall, and they were on the point of going out. The music and dancing had long ago ceased. "We must part— part!" he cried, wildly and despairingly; he kissed Olimpia's hand; he bent down to her mouth, but ice-cold lips met his burning ones. As he touched her cold hand, he felt his heart thrilled with awe; the legend of "The Dead Bride" shot suddenly through his mind. But Olimpia had drawn him closer to her, and the kiss appeared to warm her lips into vitality. Professor Spalanzani strode slowly through the empty apartment, his footsteps giving a hollow echo; and his figure had, as the flickering shadows played about him, a ghostly, awful appearance. "Do you love me? Do you love me, Olimpia? Only one little word— Do you love me?" whispered Nathanael, but she only sighed, "Ach! Ach!" as she rose to her feet. "Yes, you are my lovely, glorious star of love," said Nathanael, "and will shine for ever, purifying and ennobling my heart." "Ach! Ach!" replied Olimpia, as she moved along. Nathanael followed her; they stood before the Professor. "You have had an extraordinarily animated conversation with my daughter," said he, smiling; "well, well, my dear Mr. Nathanael, if you find pleasure in talking to the stupid girl, I am sure I shall be glad for you to come and do so." Nathanael took his leave, his heart singing and leaping in a perfect delirium of happiness.

During the next few days Spalanzani's ball was the general topic of conversation. Although the Professor had done everything to make the thing a splendid success, yet certain gay spirits related more than one thing that had occurred which was quite irregular and out of order. They were especially keen in pulling Olimpia to pieces for her taciturnity and rigid stiffness; in spite of her beautiful form they alleged that she was hopelessly stupid, and in this fact they discerned the reason why Spalanzani had so long kept her concealed from publicity. Nathanael heard all this with inward wrath, but nevertheless he held his tongue; for, thought he, would it indeed be worthwhile to prove to these fellows that it is their own stupidity which prevents them from appreciating Olimpia's profound and brilliant parts? One day Siegmund said to him, "Pray, brother, have the kindness to tell me how you, a sensible fellow, came to lose your head over that Miss Wax-face—that wooden doll across there?" Nathanael was about to fly into a rage, but he recollected himself and replied, "Tell me, Siegmund, how came it that Olimpia's divine charms could escape your eye, so keenly alive as it always is to beauty, and your acute perception as well? But Heaven be thanked for it, otherwise I should have had you for a rival, and then the blood of one of us would have had to be spilled." Siegmund, perceiving how matters stood with his friend, skilfully interposed and said, after remarking that all argument with one in love about the object of his affections was out of place, "Yet it's very strange that several of us have formed pretty much the same opinion about Olimpia. We think she is—you won't take it ill, brother?—that she is singularly statuesque and soulless. Her figure is regular, and so are her features, that can't be gainsaid; and if her eyes were not so utterly devoid of life, I may say, of the power of vision, she might pass for a beauty. She is strangely measured in her movements, they all seem as if they were dependent upon some wound-up clock-work. Her playing and singing has the disagreeably perfect but insensitive time of a singing machine, and her dancing is the same. We felt quite afraid of this Olimpia, and did not like to have anything to do with her; she seemed to us to be only acting *like* a living creature, and as if there was some secret at the bottom of it all." Nathanael did not give way to the bitter feelings which threatened to master him at these words of Siegmund's; he fought down and got the better of his displeasure, and merely said, very earnestly, "You cold prosaic fellows may very well be afraid of her. It is only to its like that the poetically organised spirit unfolds itself. Upon me alone did her loving glances fall, and through my mind and thoughts alone did they radiate; and only in her love can I find my own self again. Perhaps, however, she doesn't do quite right not to jabber a lot of nonsense and stupid talk like other shallow people. It is true, she speaks but few words; but the few words she does speak are genuine hieroglyphs of the inner world of Love and of the higher cognition of the intellectual life revealed in the intuition of the Eternal beyond the grave. But you have no understanding for all these things, and I am only wasting words." "God be with you, brother," said Siegmund very gently, almost sadly, "but it seems to me that you are in a very bad way. You may rely upon me, if all— No, I can't say any more." It all at once dawned upon Nathanael that his cold prosaic friend Siegmund really and sincerely wished him well, and so he warmly shook his proffered hand.

Nathanael had completely forgotten that there was a Clara in the world, whom he had once loved—and his mother and Lothair. They had all vanished from his mind; he lived for Olimpia alone. He sat beside her every day for hours together, rhapsodising about his love and sympathy enkindled into life, and about psychic elective affinity—all of which Olimpia listened to with great reverence. He fished up from the very bottom of his desk all the things that he had ever written—poems, fancy sketches, visions, romances, tales—and the heap was increased daily with all kinds of aimless sonnets, stanzas, canzonets. All these he read to Olimpia hour after hour without growing tired; but then he had never had such an exemplary listener. She neither embroidered, nor knitted; she did not look out of the window, or feed a bird, or play with a little pet dog or a favourite cat, neither did she twist a piece of paper or anything of that kind round her finger; she did not forcibly convert a yawn into a low affected cough—in short, she sat hour after hour with her eyes bent unchangeably upon her lover's face, without moving or altering her position, and her gaze grew more ardent and more ardent still. And it was only when at last Nathanael rose and kissed her lips or her hand that she said, "Ach! Ach!" and then "Good-night, dear." Arrived in his own room, Nathanael would break out with, "Oh! what a brilliant—what a profound mind! Only you—you alone understand me." And his heart trembled with rapture when he reflected upon the wondrous harmony which daily revealed itself between his own and his Olimpia's character; for he fancied that she had expressed in respect to his works and his poetic genius the identical sentiments which he himself cherished deep down in his own heart in respect to the same, and even as if it was his own heart's voice speaking to him. And it must indeed have been so; for Olimpia never uttered any other words than those already mentioned. And when Nathanael himself in his clear and sober moments, as, for instance, directly after waking in a morning, thought about her utter passivity and taciturnity, he only said, "What are words—but words? The glance of her heavenly eyes says more than any tongue of earth. And how can, anyway, a child of heaven accustom herself to the narrow circle which the exigencies of a wretched mundane life demand?"

Professor Spalanzani appeared to be greatly pleased at the intimacy that had sprung up between his daughter Olimpia and Nathanael, and showed the young man many unmistakable proofs of his good feeling towards him; and when Nathanael ventured at length to hint very delicately at an alliance with Olimpia, the Professor smiled all over his face at once, and said he should allow his daughter to make a perfectly free choice. Encouraged by these words, and with the fire of desire burning in his heart, Nathanael resolved the very next day to implore Olimpia to tell him frankly, in plain words, what he had long read in her sweet loving glances,—that she would be his forever. He looked for the ring which his mother had given him at parting; he would present it to Olimpia as a symbol of his devotion, and of the happy life he was to lead with her from that time onwards. Whilst looking for it he came across his letters from Clara and Lothair; he threw them carelessly aside, found the ring, put it in his pocket, and ran across to Olimpia. Whilst still on the stairs, in the entrance-passage, he heard an extraordinary hubbub; the noise seemed to proceed from Spalanzani's study. There was a stamping—a rattling—pushing—knocking against the door, with curses and oaths intermingled. "Leave hold—leave hold—you monster— you rascal—staked your life and honour upon it?—Ha! ha! ha! ha!— That was not our wager—I, I made the eyes—I the clock-work.—Go to the devil with your clock-work—you damned dog of a watch-maker—be off—Satan—stop—you paltry turner—you infernal beast!—stop— begone—let me go." The voices which were thus making all this racket and rumpus were those of Spalanzani and the fearsome Coppelius. Nathanael rushed in, impelled by some nameless dread. The Professor was grasping a female figure by the shoulders, the Italian Coppola held her by the feet; and they were pulling and dragging each other backwards and forwards, fighting furiously to get possession of her. Nathanael recoiled with horror on recognising that the figure was Olimpia. Boiling with rage, he was about to tear his beloved from the grasp of the madmen, when Coppola by an extraordinary exertion of strength twisted the figure out of the Professor's hands and gave him such a terrible blow with her, that he reeled backwards and fell over the table all amongst the phials and retorts, the bottles and glass cylinders, which covered it: all these things were smashed into a thousand pieces. But Coppola threw the figure across his shoulder, and, laughing shrilly and horribly, ran hastily down the stairs, the figure's ugly feet hanging down and banging and rattling like wood against the steps. Nathanael was stupefied,—he had seen only too distinctly that in Olimpia's pallid waxed face there were no eyes, merely black holes in their stead; she was an inanimate puppet. Spalanzani was rolling on the floor; the pieces of glass had cut his head and breast and arm; the blood was escaping from him in streams. But he gathered his strength together by an effort.

"After him—after him! What do you stand staring there for? Coppelius—Coppelius—he's stolen my best automaton—at which I've worked for twenty years—staked my life upon it—the clock-work—speech—movement—mine—your eyes—stolen your eyes—damn him—curse him—after him—fetch me back Olimpia—there are the eyes." And now Nathanael saw a pair of bloody eyes lying on the floor staring at him; Spalanzani seized them with his uninjured hand and threw them at him, so that they hit his breast. Then madness dug her burning talons into him and swept down into his heart, rending his mind and thoughts to shreds. "Aha! aha! aha! Fire-wheel—fire-wheel! Spin round, fire-wheel! merrily, merrily! Aha! wooden doll! spin round, pretty wooden doll!" and he threw himself upon the Professor, clutching him fast by the throat. He would certainly have strangled him had not several people, attracted by the noise, rushed in and torn away the madman; and so they saved the Professor, whose wounds were immediately dressed. Siegmund, with all his strength, was not able to subdue the frantic lunatic, who continued to scream in a dreadful way, "Spin round, wooden doll!" and to strike out right and left with his doubled fists. At length the united strength of several succeeded in overpowering him by throwing him on the floor and binding him. His cries passed into a brutish bellow that was awful to hear; and thus raging with the harrowing violence of madness, he was taken away to the madhouse.

Before continuing my narration of what happened further to the unfortunate Nathanael, I will tell you, indulgent reader, in case you take any interest in that skilful mechanician and fabricator of automata, Spalanzani, that he recovered completely from his wounds. He had, however, to leave the university, for Nathanael's fate had created a great sensation; and the opinion was pretty generally expressed that it was an imposture altogether unpardonable to have smuggled a wooden puppet instead of a living person into intelligent tea-circles,—for Olimpia had been present at several with success. Lawyers called it a cunning piece of knavery, and all the harder to punish since it was directed against the public; and it had been so craftily contrived that it had escaped unobserved by all except a few preternaturally acute students, although everybody was very wise how and remembered to have thought of several facts which occurred to them as suspicious. But these latter could not succeed in making out any sort of a consistent tale. For was it, for instance, a thing likely to occur to any one as suspicious that, according to the declaration of an elegant beau of these tea-parties, Olimpia had, contrary to all good manners, sneezed oftener than she had yawned? The former must have been, in the opinion of this elegant gentleman, the winding up of the concealed clock-work; it had always been accompanied by an observable creaking, and so on. The Professor of Poetry and Eloquence took a pinch of snuff, and, slapping the lid to and clearing his throat, said solemnly, "My most honourable ladies and gentlemen, don't you see then where the rub is? The whole thing is an allegory, a continuous metaphor. You understand me? *Sapienti sat.*" But several most honourable gentlemen did not rest satisfied with this explanation; the history of this automaton had sunk deeply into their souls, and an absurd mistrust of human figures began to prevail. Several lovers, in order to be fully convinced that they were not paying court to a wooden puppet, required that their mistress should sing and dance a little out of time, should embroider or knit or play with her little pug, &c., when being read to, but above all things else that she should do something more than merely listen—that she should frequently speak in such a way as to really show that her words presupposed as a condition some thinking and feeling. The bonds of love were in many cases drawn closer in consequence, and so of course became more engaging; in other instances they gradually relaxed and fell away. "I cannot really be made responsible for it," was the remark of more than one young gallant. At the tea-gatherings everybody, in order to ward off suspicion, yawned to an incredible extent and never sneezed. Spalanzani was obliged, as has been said, to leave the place in order to escape a criminal charge of having fraudulently imposed an automaton upon human society. Coppola, too, had also disappeared.

When Nathanael awoke he felt as if he had been oppressed by a terrible nightmare; he opened his eyes and experienced an indescribable sensation of mental comfort, whilst a soft and most beautiful sensation of warmth pervaded his body. He lay on his own bed in his own room at home; Clara was bending over him, and at a little distance stood his mother and Lothair. "At last, at last, O my darling Nathanael; now we have you again; now you are cured of your grievous illness, now you are mine again." And Clara's words came from the depths of her heart; and she clasped him in her arms. The bright scalding tears streamed from his eyes, he was so overcome with mingled feelings of sorrow and delight; and he gasped forth, "My Clara, my Clara!" Siegmund, who had staunchly

stood by his friend in his hour of need, now came into the room. Nathanael gave him his hand— "My faithful brother, you have not deserted me." Every trace of insanity had left him, and in the tender hands
of his mother and his beloved, and his friends, he quickly recovered his
strength again. Good fortune had in the meantime visited the house;
a niggardly old uncle, from whom they had never expected to get anything, had died, and left Nathanael's mother not only a considerable
fortune, but also a small estate, pleasantly situated not far from the
town. There they resolved to go and live, Nathanael and his mother, and
Clara, to whom he was now to be married, and Lothair. Nathanael was
become gentler and more childlike than he had ever been before, and
now began really to understand Clara's supremely pure and noble character.

None of them ever reminded him, even in the remotest degree, of
the past. But when Siegmund took leave of him, he said, "By heaven,
brother! I was in a bad way, but an angel came just at the right moment
and led me back upon the path of light. Yes, it was Clara." Siegmund
would not let him speak further, fearing lest the painful recollections of
the past might arise too vividly and too intensely in his mind.

The time came for the four happy people to move to their little
property. At noon they were going through the streets. After making
several purchases they found that the lofty tower of the town-house was
throwing its giant shadows across the market-place. "Come," said Clara,
"let us go up to the top once more and have a look at the distant hills."
No sooner said than done. Both of them, Nathanael and Clara, went up
the tower; their mother, however, went on with the servant-girl to her
new home, and Lothair, not feeling inclined to climb up all the many
steps, waited below. There the two lovers stood arm-in-arm on the top-
most gallery of the tower, and gazed out into the sweet scented wooded
landscape, beyond which the blue hills rose up like a giant's city.

"Oh! do look at that strange little grey bush, it looks as if it were
actually walking towards us," said Clara. Mechanically he put his hand

into his sidepocket; he found Coppola's perspective and looked for the bush; Clara stood in front of the glass. Then a convulsive thrill shot through his pulse and veins; pale as a corpse, he fixed his staring eyes upon her; but soon they began to roll, and a fiery current flashed and sparkled in them, and he yelled fearfully, like a hunted animal. Leaping up high in the air and laughing horribly at the same time, he began to shout, in a piercing voice, "Spin round, wooden doll! Spin round, wooden doll!" With the strength of a giant he laid hold upon Clara and tried to hurl her over, but in an agony of despair she clutched fast hold of the railing that went round the gallery. Lothair heard the madman raging and Clara's scream of terror: a fearful presentiment flashed across his mind. He ran up the steps; the door of the second flight was locked. Clara's scream for help rang out more loudly. Mad with rage and fear, he threw himself against the door, which at length gave way. Clara's cries were growing fainter and fainter,—"Help! save me! save me!" and her voice died away in the air. "She is killed—murdered by that madman," shouted Lothair. The door to the gallery was also locked. Despair gave him the strength of a giant; he burst the door off its hinges. Good God! there was Clara in the grasp of the madman Nathanael, hanging over the gallery in the air; she only held to the iron bar with one hand. Quick as lightning, Lothair seized his sister and pulled her back, at the same time dealing the madman a blow in the face with his doubled fist, which sent him reeling backwards, forcing him to let go his victim.

Lothair ran down with his insensible sister in his arms. She was saved. But Nathanael ran round and round the gallery, leaping up in the air and shouting, "Spin round, fire-wheel! Spin round, fire-wheel!" The people heard the wild shouting, and a crowd began to gather. In the midst of them towered the advocate Coppelius, like a giant; he had only just arrived in the town, and had gone straight to the market-place. Some were going up to overpower and take charge of the madman, but Coppelius laughed and said, "Ha! ha! wait a bit; he'll come down of his own accord"; and he stood gazing upwards along with the rest. All at once

Nathanael stopped as if spell-bound; he bent down over the railing, and perceived Coppelius. With a piercing scream, "Ha! foine oyes! foine oyes!" he leapt over.

When Nathanael lay on the stone pavement with a broken head, Coppelius had disappeared in the crush and confusion.

Several years afterwards it was reported that, outside the door of a pretty country house in a remote district, Clara had been seen sitting hand in hand with a pleasant gentleman, whilst two bright boys were playing at her feet. From this it may be concluded that she eventually found that quiet domestic happiness which her cheerful, blithesome character required, and which Nathanael, with his tempest-tossed soul, could never have been able to give her.

BERENICE

Edgar Allan Poe

Dicebant mihi sodales, si sepulchrum amicæ visitarem,
curas meas aliquan tulum forelevatas.
—*Ebn Zaiat*

Misery is manifold. The wretchedness of earth is multiform. Over-reaching the wide horizon as the rainbow, its hues are as various as the hues of that arch—as distinct too, yet as intimately blended. Over-reaching the wide horizon as the rainbow! How is it that from beauty I have derived a type of unloveliness?—from the covenant of peace, a simile of sorrow? But, as in ethics, evil is a consequence of good, so, in fact, out of joy is sorrow born. Either the memory of past bliss is the anguish of to-day, or the agonies which *are,* have their origin in the ec-stasies which *might have been.*

My baptismal name is Egæus; that of my family I will not mention. Yet there are no towers in the land more time-honored than my gloomy, gray, hereditary halls. Our line has been called a race of visionaries; and in many striking particulars—in the character of the family mansion—in the frescos of the chief saloon—in the tapestries of the dormitories—in the chiselling of some buttresses in the armory—but more especially in the gallery of antique paintings—in the fashion of the library chamber—and, lastly, in the very peculiar nature of the library's contents—there is more than sufficient evidence to warrant the belief.

The recollections of my earliest years are connected with that chamber, and with its volumes—of which latter I will say no more. Here died my mother. Herein was I born. But it is mere idleness to say that I had not lived before—that the soul has no previous existence. You deny it?—let us not argue the matter. Convinced myself, I seek not to convince. There is, however, a remembrance of aërial forms—of spiritual and meaning eyes—of sounds, musical yet sad—a remembrance which will not be excluded; a memory like a shadow—vague, variable, indefinite, unsteady; and like a shadow, too, in the impossibility of my getting rid of it while the sunlight of my reason shall exist.

In that chamber was I born. Thus awaking from the long night of what seemed, but was not, nonentity, at once into the very regions of fairy land—into a palace of imagination—into the wild dominions of monastic thought and erudition—it is not singular that I gazed around me with a startled and ardent eye—that I loitered away my boyhood in books, and dissipated my youth in reverie; but it *is* singular that as years rolled away, and the noon of manhood found me still in the mansion of my fathers—it *is* wonderful what stagnation there fell upon the springs of my life—wonderful how total an inversion took place in the character of my commonest thought. The realities of the world affected me as visions, and as visions only, while the wild ideas of the land of dreams became, in turn, not the material of my every-day existence, but in very deed that existence utterly and solely in itself.

Berenice and I were cousins, and we grew up together in my paternal halls. Yet differently we grew—I, ill of health, and buried in gloom—she, agile, graceful, and overflowing with energy; hers, the ramble on the hill-side—mine the studies of the cloister; I, living within my own heart, and addicted, body and soul, to the most intense and painful meditation—she, roaming carelessly through life, with no thought of the shadows in her path, or the silent flight of the raven-winged hours. Berenice!—I call upon her name—Berenice!—and from the gray ruins of memory a thousand tumultuous recollections are startled at the sound! Ah, vividly is her image before me now, as in the early days of her light-heartedness and joy! Oh, gorgeous yet fantastic beauty! Oh, sylph amid the shrubberies of Arnheim! Oh, Naiad among its fountains! And then—then all is mystery and terror, and a tale which should not be told. Disease—a fatal disease, fell like the simoon upon her frame; and, even while I gazed upon her, the spirit of change swept over her, pervading her mind, her habits, and her character, and, in a manner the most subtle and terrible, disturbing even the identity of her person! Alas! the destroyer came and went!—and the victim—where is she? I knew her not—or knew her no longer as Berenice!

Among the numerous train of maladies superinduced by that fatal and primary one which effected a revolution of so horrible a kind in the moral and physical being of my cousin, may be mentioned as the most distressing and obstinate in its nature, a species of epilepsy not unfrequently terminating in *trance* itself—trance very nearly resembling positive dissolution, and from which her manner of recovery was in most instances, startlingly abrupt. In the meantime my own disease—for I have been told that I should call it by no other appellation—my own disease, then, grew rapidly upon me, and assumed finally a monomaniac character of a novel and extraordinary form—hourly and momently gaining vigor—and at length obtaining over me the most incomprehensible ascendancy. This monomania, if I must so term it, consisted in a morbid irritability of those properties of the mind in metaphysical science termed the *attentive*. It is more than probable that I am not understood; but I fear, indeed, that it is in no manner possible to convey to the mind of the merely general reader, an adequate idea of that nervous *intensity of interest* with which, in my case, the powers of meditation (not to speak technically) busied and buried themselves, in the contemplation of even the most ordinary objects of the universe.

To muse for long unwearied hours, with my attention riveted to some frivolous device on the margin, or in the typography of a book; to become absorbed, for the better part of a summer's day, in a quaint shadow falling aslant upon the tapestry or upon the floor; to lose myself, for an entire night, in watching the steady flame of a lamp, or the embers of a fire; to dream away whole days over the perfume of a flower; to repeat, monotonously, some common word, until the sound, by dint of frequent repetition, ceased to convey any idea whatever to the mind; to lose all sense of motion or physical existence, by means of absolute bodily quiescence long and obstinately persevered in: such were a few of the most common and least pernicious vagaries induced by a condition of the mental faculties, not, indeed, altogether unparalleled, but certainly bidding defiance to anything like analysis or explanation.

Yet let me not be misapprehended. The undue, earnest, and morbid attention thus excited by objects in their own nature frivolous, must not be confounded in character with that ruminating propensity common to all mankind, and more especially indulged in by persons of ardent imagination. It was not even, as might be at first supposed, an extreme condition, or exaggeration of such propensity, but primarily and essentially distinct and different. In the one instance, the dreamer, or enthusiast, being interested by an object usually *not* frivolous, imperceptibly loses sight of this object in a wilderness of deductions and suggestions issuing therefrom, until, at the conclusion of a day-dream *often replete with luxury*, he finds the *incitamentum*, or first cause of his musings, entirely vanished and forgotten. In my case, the primary object was *invariably frivolous*, although assuming, through the medium of my distempered vision, a refracted and unreal importance. Few deductions, if any, were made; and those few pertinaciously returning in upon the original object as a centre. The meditations were *never* pleasurable; and, at the termination of the reverie, the first cause, so far from being out of sight, had attained that supernaturally exaggerated interest which was the prevailing feature of the disease. In a word, the powers of mind more particularly exercised were, with me, as I have said before, the *attentive,* and are, with the day-dreamer, the *speculative.*

My books, at this epoch, if they did not actually serve to irritate the disorder, partook, it will be perceived, largely, in their imaginative and inconsequential nature, of the characteristic qualities of the disorder itself. I well remember, among others, the treatise of the noble Italian, Cœlius Secundus Curio, "*De Amplitudine Beati Regni Dei*"; St. Austin's great work, the "City of God"; and Tertullian's "*De Carne Christi,*" in which the paradoxical sentence "*Mortuus est Dei filius; credible est quia ineptum est: et sepultus resurrexit; certum est quia impossibile est,*" occupied my undivided time, for many weeks of laborious and fruitless investigation.

Thus it will appear that, shaken from its balance only by trivial things, my reason bore resemblance to that ocean-crag spoken of by Ptolemy Hephestion, which steadily resisting the attacks of human violence, and the fiercer fury of the waters and the winds, trembled only to the touch of the flower called Asphodel. And although, to a careless thinker, it might appear a matter beyond doubt, that the alteration produced by her unhappy malady, in the *moral* condition of Berenice, would afford me many objects for the exercise of that intense and abnormal meditation whose nature I have been at some trouble in explaining, yet such was not in any degree the case. In the lucid intervals of my infirmity, her calamity, indeed, gave me pain, and, taking deeply to heart that total wreck of her fair and gentle life, I did not fail to ponder, frequently and bitterly, upon the wonder-working means by which so strange a revolution had been so suddenly brought to pass. But these reflections partook not of the idiosyncrasy of my disease, and were such as would have occurred, under similar circumstances, to the ordinary mass of mankind. True to its own character, my disorder revelled in the less important but more startling changes wrought in the *physical* frame of Berenice—in the singular and most appalling distortion of her personal identity.

During the brightest days of her unparalleled beauty, most surely I had never loved her. In the strange anomaly of my existence, feelings with me, *had never been* of the heart, and my passions *always were* of the mind. Through the gray of the early morning—among the trellised shadows of the forest at noonday—and in the silence of my library at night—she had flitted by my eyes, and I had seen her—not as the living and breathing Berenice, but as the Berenice of a dream; not as a being of the earth, earthy, but as the abstraction of such a being; not as a thing to admire, but to analyze; not as an object of love, but as the theme of the most abstruse although desultory speculation. And *now*—now I shuddered in her presence, and grew pale at her approach; yet, bitterly lamenting her fallen and desolate condition, I called to mind that she had loved me long, and, in an evil moment, I spoke to her of marriage.

And at length the period of our nuptials was approaching, when, upon an afternoon in the winter of the year—one of those unseasonably warm, calm, and misty days which are the nurse of the beautiful Halcyon,[1]—I sat, (and sat, as I thought, alone,) in the inner apartment of the library. But, uplifting my eyes, I saw that Berenice stood before me.

Was it my own excited imagination—or the misty influence of the atmosphere—or the uncertain twilight of the chamber—or the gray draperies which fell around her figure—that caused in it so vacillating and indistinct an outline? I could not tell. She spoke no word; and I—not for worlds could I have uttered a syllable. An icy chill ran through my frame; a sense of insufferable anxiety oppressed me; a consuming

---

1 For as Jove, during the winter season, gives twice seven days of warmth, men have called this clement and temperate time the nurse of the beautiful Halcyon.—*Simonides*

curiosity pervaded my soul; and sinking back upon the chair, I remained for some time breathless and motionless, with my eyes riveted upon her person. Alas! its emaciation was excessive, and not one vestige of the former being lurked in any single line of the contour. My burning glances at length fell upon the face.

The forehead was high, and very pale, and singularly placid; and the once jetty hair fell partially over it, and overshadowed the hollow temples with innumerable ringlets, now of a vivid yellow, and jarring discordantly, in their fantastic character, with the reigning melancholy of the countenance. The eyes were lifeless, and lustreless, and seemingly pupilless, and I shrank involuntarily from their glassy stare to the contemplation of the thin and shrunken lips. They parted; and in a smile of peculiar meaning, *the teeth* of the changed Berenice disclosed themselves slowly to my view. Would to God that I had never beheld them, or that, having done so, I had died!

The shutting of a door disturbed me, and, looking up, I found that my cousin had departed from the chamber. But from the disordered chamber of my brain, had not, alas! departed, and would not be driven away, the white and ghastly *spectrum* of the teeth. Not a speck on their surface—not a shade on their enamel—not an indenture in their edges—but what that period of her smile had sufficed to brand in upon my memory. I saw them *now* even more unequivocally than I beheld them *then*. The teeth!—the teeth!—they were here, and there, and everywhere, and visibly and palpably before me; long, narrow, and excessively white, with the pale lips writhing about them, as in the very moment of their first terrible development. Then came the full fury of my *monomania*, and I struggled in vain against its strange and irresistible influence. In the multiplied objects of the external world I had no thoughts but for the teeth. For these I longed with a frenzied desire. All other matters and all different interests became absorbed in their single contemplation. They—they alone were present to the mental eye, and they, in their sole individuality, became the essence of my mental life. I held them in every light. I turned them in every attitude. I surveyed their characteristics. I dwelt upon their peculiarities. I pondered upon their conformation. I mused upon the alteration in their nature. I shuddered as I assigned to them in imagination a sensitive and sentient power, and even when unassisted by the lips, a capability of moral expression. Of Mademoiselle Salle it has been well said, "*Que tous ses pas etaient des sentiments*," and of Berenice I more seriously believed *que toutes ses dents etaient des idees. Des idees!*—ah here was the idiotic thought that destroyed me! *Des idees!*—ah *therefore* it was that I coveted them so madly! I felt that their possession could alone ever restore me to peace, in giving me back to reason.

And the evening closed in upon me thus—and then the darkness came, and tarried, and went—and the day again dawned—and the mists of a second night were now gathering around—and still I sat motionless in that solitary room—and still I sat buried in meditation—and still the *phantasma* of the teeth maintained its terrible ascendancy, as, with the most vivid hideous distinctness, it floated about amid the changing lights and shadows of the chamber. At length there broke in upon my dreams a cry as of horror and dismay; and thereunto, after a pause, succeeded the sound of troubled voices, intermingled with many low moanings of sorrow or of pain. I arose from my seat, and throwing open one of the doors of the library, saw standing out in the ante-chamber a servant maiden, all in tears, who told me that Berenice was—no more! She had been seized with epilepsy in the early morning, and now, at the closing in of the night, the grave was ready for its tenant, and all the preparations for the burial were completed.

I found myself sitting in the library, and again sitting there alone. It seemed that I had newly awakened from a confused and exciting dream. I knew that it was now midnight, and I was well aware, that since the setting of the sun, Berenice had been interred. But of that dreary period which intervened I had no positive, at least no definite comprehension. Yet its memory was replete with horror—horror more horrible from being vague, and terror more terrible from ambiguity. It was a fearful page in the record my existence, written all over with dim, and hideous, and unintelligible recollections. I strived to decipher them, but in vain; while ever and anon, like the spirit of a departed sound, the shrill and piercing shriek of a female voice seemed to be ringing in my ears. I had done a deed—what was it? I asked myself the question aloud, and the whispering echoes of the chamber answered me,—*"what was it?"*

On the table beside me burned a lamp, and near it lay a little box. It was of no remarkable character, and I had seen it frequently before, for it was the property of the family physician; but how came it *there,* upon my table, and why did I shudder in regarding it? These things were in no manner to be accounted for, and my eyes at length dropped to the open pages of a book, and to a sentence underscored therein. The words were the singular but simple ones of the poet Ebn Zaiat:—*"Dicebant mihi sodales si sepulchrum amicæ visitarem, curas meas aliquantulum forelevatas."* Why then, as I perused them, did the hairs of my head erect themselves on end, and the blood of my body become congealed within my veins?

There came a light tap at the library door—and, pale as the tenant of a tomb, a menial entered upon tiptoe. His looks were wild with terror, and he spoke to me in a voice tremulous, husky, and very low. What said he?—some broken sentences I heard. He told of a wild cry disturbing the silence of the night—of the gathering together of the household—of a search in the direction of the sound; and then his tones grew thrillingly distinct as he whispered me of a violated grave—of a disfigured body enshrouded, yet still breathing—still palpitating—*still alive!*

He pointed to garments;—they were muddy and clotted with gore. I spoke not, and he took me gently by the hand: it was indented with the impress of human nails. He directed my attention to some object against the wall. I looked at it for some minutes: it was a spade. With a shriek

I bounded to the table, and grasped the box that lay upon it. But I could not force it open; and in my tremor, it slipped from my hands, and fell heavily, and burst into pieces; and from it, with a rattling sound, there rolled out some instruments of dental surgery, intermingled with thirty-two small, white and ivory-looking substances that were scattered to and fro about the floor.

ONE OF TWINS

Ambrose Bierce

❧

A LETTER FOUND AMONG THE PAPERS OF THE LATE MORTIMER BARR

You ask me if in my experience as one of a pair of twins I ever observed anything unaccountable by the natural laws with which we have acquaintance. As to that you shall judge; perhaps we have not all acquaintance with the same natural laws. You may know some that I do not, and what is to me unaccountable may be very clear to you.

You knew my brother John—that is, you knew him when you knew that I was not present; but neither you nor, I believe, any human being could distinguish between him and me if we chose to seem alike. Our parents could not; ours is the only instance of which I have any knowledge of so close resemblance as that. I speak of my brother John, but I am not at all sure that his name was not Henry and mine John. We were regularly christened, but afterward, in the very act of tattooing us with small distinguishing marks, the operator lost his reckoning; and although I bear upon my forearm a small "H" and he bore a "J," it is by no means certain that the letters ought not to have been transposed. During our boyhood our parents tried to distinguish us more obviously by our clothing and other simple devices, but we would so frequently exchange suits and otherwise circumvent the enemy that they abandoned all such ineffectual attempts, and during all the years that we lived together at home everybody recognized the difficulty of the situation and made the best of it by calling us both "Jehnry." I have often wondered at my father's forbearance in not branding us conspicuously upon our unworthy brows, but as we were tolerably good boys and used our power of embarrassment and annoyance with commendable moderation, we escaped the iron. My father was, in fact, a singularly good-natured man, and I think quietly enjoyed Nature's practical joke.

Soon after we had come to California, and settled at San Jose (where the only good fortune that awaited us was our meeting with so kind a friend as you), the family, as you know, was broken up by the death of both my parents in the same week. My father died insolvent, and the homestead was sacrificed to pay his debts. My sisters returned to relatives in the East, but owing to your kindness John and I, then twenty-two years of age, obtained employment in San Francisco, in different quarters of the town. Circumstances did not permit us to live together, and we saw each other infrequently, sometimes not oftener than once a week. As we had few acquaintances in common, the fact of our extraordinary likeness was little known. I come now to the matter of your inquiry.

One day soon after we had come to this city I was walking down Market Street late in the afternoon, when I was accosted by a well-dressed man of middle age, who after greeting me cordially said: "Stevens, I know, of course, that you do not go out much, but I have told my wife about you, and she would be glad to see you at the house. I have a notion, too, that my girls are worth knowing. Suppose you come out to-morrow at six and dine with us, *en famille;* and then if the ladies can't amuse you afterward I'll stand in with a few games of billiards."

This was said with so bright a smile and so engaging a manner that I had not the heart to refuse, and although I had never seen the man in my life I promptly replied: "You are very good, sir, and it will give me great pleasure to accept the invitation. Please present my compliments to Mrs. Margovan and ask her to expect me."

With a shake of the hand and a pleasant parting word the man passed on. That he had mistaken me for my brother was plain enough. That was an error to which I was accustomed and which it was not my habit to rectify unless the matter seemed important. But how had I known that this man's name was Margovan? It certainly is not a name that one would apply to a man at random, with a probability that it would be right. In point of fact, the name was as strange to me as the man.

The next morning I hastened to where my brother was employed and met him coming out of the office with a number of bills that he was to collect. I told him how I had "committed" him and added that if he didn't care to keep the engagement I should be delighted to continue the impersonation.

"That's queer," he said thoughtfully. "Margovan is the only man in the office here whom I know well and like. When he came in this morning and we had passed the usual greetings some singular impulse prompted me to say: 'Oh, I beg your pardon, Mr. Margovan, but I neglected to ask your address.' I got the address, but what under the sun I was to do with it, I did not know until now. It's good of you to offer to take the consequence of your impudence, but I'll eat that dinner myself, if you please."

He ate a number of dinners at the same place—more than were good for him, I may add without disparaging their quality; for he fell in love with Miss Margovan, proposed marriage to her and was heartlessly accepted.

Several weeks after I had been informed of the engagement, but before it had been convenient for me to make the acquaintance of the young woman and her family, I met one day on Kearney Street a handsome but somewhat dissipated-looking man whom something prompted me to follow and watch, which I did without any scruple whatever. He turned up Geary Street and followed it until he came to Union Square. There he looked at his watch, then entered the square. He loitered about the paths for some time, evidently waiting for someone. Presently he was joined by a fashionably dressed and beautiful young woman and the two walked away up Stockton Street, I following. I now felt the necessity of extreme caution, for although the girl was a stranger it seemed to me that she would recognize me at a glance. They made several turns from one street to another and finally, after both had taken a hasty look all about—which I narrowly evaded by stepping into a doorway—they entered a house of which I do not care to state the location. Its location was better than its character.

I protest that my action in playing the spy upon these two strangers was without assignable motive. It was one of which I might or might not be ashamed, according to my estimate of the character of the person finding it out. As an essential part of a narrative educed by your question it is related here without hesitancy or shame.

A week later John took me to the house of his prospective father-in-law, and in Miss Margovan, as you have already surmised, but to my profound astonishment, I recognized the heroine of that discreditable adventure. A gloriously beautiful heroine of a discreditable adventure I must in justice admit that she was; but that fact has only this importance: her beauty was such a surprise to me that it cast a doubt upon her identity with the young woman I had seen before; how could the marvelous fascination of her face have failed to strike me at that time? But no—there was no possibility of error; the difference was due to costume, light and general surroundings.

John and I passed the evening at the house, enduring, with the fortitude of long experience, such delicate enough banter as our likeness naturally suggested. When the young lady and I were left alone for a few minutes I looked her squarely in the face and said with sudden gravity:

"You, too, Miss Margovan, have a double: I saw her last Tuesday afternoon in Union Square."

She trained her great gray eyes upon me for a moment, but her glance was a trifle less steady than my own and she withdrew it, fixing it on the tip of her shoe.

"Was she very like me?" she asked, with an indifference which I thought a little overdone.

"So like," said I, "that I greatly admired her, and being unwilling to lose sight of her I confess that I followed her until—Miss Margovan, are you sure that you understand?"

She was now pale, but entirely calm. She again raised her eyes to mine, with a look that did not falter.

"What do you wish me to do?" she asked. "You need not fear to name your terms. I accept them."

It was plain, even in the brief time given me for reflection, that in dealing with this girl ordinary methods would not do, and ordinary exactions were needless.

"Miss Margovan," I said, doubtless with something of the compassion in my voice that I had in my heart, "it is impossible not to think you the victim of some horrible compulsion. Rather than impose new embarrassments upon you I would prefer to aid you to regain your freedom."

She shook her head, sadly and hopelessly, and I continued, with agitation:

"Your beauty unnerves me. I am disarmed by your frankness and your distress. If you are free to act upon conscience you will, I believe, do what you conceive to be best; if you are not—well, Heaven help us all! You have nothing to fear from me but such opposition to this marriage as I can try to justify on—on other grounds."

These were not my exact words, but that was the sense of them, as nearly as my sudden and conflicting emotions permitted me to express it. I rose and left her without another look at her, met the others as they re-entered the room and said, as calmly as I could: "I have been bidding Miss Margovan good evening; it is later than I thought."

John decided to go with me. In the street he asked if I had observed anything singular in Julia's manner.

"I thought her ill," I replied; "that is why I left." Nothing more was said.

The next evening I came late to my lodgings. The events of the previous evening had made me nervous and ill; I had tried to cure myself and attain to clear thinking by walking in the open air, but I was oppressed with a horrible presentiment of evil—a presentiment which I could not formulate. It was a chill, foggy night; my clothing and hair were damp and I shook with cold. In my dressing-gown and slippers before a blazing grate of coals I was even more uncomfortable. I no longer shivered but shuddered—there is a difference. The dread of some impending calamity was so strong and dispiriting that I tried to drive it away by inviting a real sorrow—tried to dispel the conception of a terrible future by substituting the memory of a painful past. I recalled the death of my parents and endeavored to fix my mind upon the last sad scenes at their bedsides and their graves. It all seemed vague and unreal, as having occurred ages ago and to another person. Suddenly, striking through my thought and parting it as a tense cord is parted by the stroke of steel—I can think of no other comparison—I heard a sharp cry as of one in mortal agony! The voice was that of my brother and seemed to come from the street outside my window. I sprang to the window and threw it open. A street lamp directly opposite threw a wan and ghastly light upon the wet pavement and the fronts of the houses. A single policeman, with upturned collar, was leaning against a gatepost, quietly smoking a cigar. No one else was in sight. I closed the window and pulled down the shade, seated myself before the fire and tried to fix my mind upon my surroundings. By way of assisting, by performance of some familiar act, I looked at my watch; it marked half-past eleven. Again I heard that awful cry! It seemed in the room—at my side. I was frightened and for some moments had not the power to move. A few minutes later—I have no recollection of the intermediate time—I found myself hurrying along an unfamiliar street as fast as I could walk. I did not know where I was, nor whither I was going, but presently sprang up the steps of a house before which were two or three carriages and in which were moving lights and a subdued confusion of voices. It was the house of Mr. Margovan.

You know, good friend, what had occurred there. In one chamber lay Julia Margovan, hours dead by poison; in another John Stevens, bleeding from a pistol wound in the chest, inflicted by his own hand. As I burst into the room; pushed aside the physicians and laid my hand upon his forehead he unclosed his eyes, stared blankly, closed them slowly and died without a sign.

I knew no more until six weeks afterwards, when I had been nursed back to life by your own saintly wife in your own beautiful home. All of that you know, but what you do not know is this—which, however, has no bearing upon the subject of your psychological researches—at least not upon that branch of them in which, with a delicacy and consideration all your own, you have asked for less assistance than I think I have given you:

One moonlight night several years afterward I was passing through Union Square. The hour was late and the square deserted. Certain memories of the past naturally came into my mind as I came to the spot where I had once witnessed that fateful assignation, and with that unaccountable perversity which prompts us to dwell upon thoughts of the most painful character I seated myself upon one of the benches to indulge them. A man entered the square and came along the walk toward me. His hands were clasped behind him, his head was bowed; he seemed to observe nothing. As he approached the shadow in which I sat I recognized him as the man whom I had seen meet Julia Margovan years before at that spot. But he was terribly altered—gray, worn and haggard. Dissipation and vice were in evidence in every look; illness was no less apparent. His clothing was in disorder, his hair fell across his forehead in a derangement which was at once uncanny and picturesque. He looked fitter for restraint than liberty—the restraint of a hospital.

With no defined purpose I rose and confronted him. He raised his head and looked me full in the face. I have no words to describe the ghastly change that came over his own; it was a look of unspeakable terror—he thought himself eye to eye with a ghost. But he was a courageous man. "Damn you, John Stevens!" he cried, and lifting his trembling arm he dashed his fist feebly at my face and fell headlong upon the gravel as I walked away.

Somebody found him there, stone-dead. Nothing more is known of him, not even his name. To know of a man that he is dead should be enough.

ON THE WATER

Guy de Maupassant

Translated by Edward Gauvin

Last summer, I rented a little cottage on the banks of the Seine, several leagues from Paris, to which I retired nightly. After a few days, I came to know one of my neighbors. He could have been anywhere between thirty and forty, and was quite the strangest fellow I had ever laid eyes on. An old hand at boating, he was really quite fanatical about it—always down by the water, on the water, in the water. He must have been born in a boat, and when the time comes, it is in a boat that he will meet his end.

One evening, as we were strolling by the Seine, I asked him to regale me with a few tales from his life on the water. All of a sudden the good gentleman lit up, wouldn't you know—was transfigured, waxed eloquent, almost poetic. In his heart was a great passion, a devouring, irresistible passion: the river.

"Ah!" said he, "how many memories I have of the river you see flowing along beside us! You city dwellers with your streets simply have no idea what the river is. But hear how a fisherman utters the word. To a fisherman, the river is that mysterious thing—profound, uncharted, a land of mirages and phantasmagoria, where by night one sees things that are not, hears noises that one knows not, shivers without reason, as when passing through a graveyard: indeed, it is that most sinister of graveyards, where not a single grave is to be found.

"To a fisherman the earth is bounded, and in the shadows of a moonless night, the river is limitless. A sailor hardly feels the same thing out at sea. Harsh and wicked as it is, howl and scream as it may, the open sea is honest and true, but the river is silent and perfidious. It never roars; it always flows without a sound, and this eternal movement of water is more terrifying to me than the high ocean waves.

"Dreamers claim the sea hides in its bosom vast bluish lands where the drowned toss and turn amidst giant fish in strange forests and crystalline grottoes. The river's only depths are black and rotten with mud. Yet how beautiful the river is when it shimmers in the rising sun and laps gently at its banks rife with murmuring reeds.

"The great Hugo said, speaking of the Ocean:

> *O tides, how many tearful tales you know!*
> *Fathomless tides, your stories whispering,*
> *You drive the fearful mothers to their prayer*
> *And give the waves their voices of despair*
> *As rising you draw near in evening.*

Well, if you ask me, the stories those slender reeds whisper ever so sweetly in their little voices are surely more sinister still than the tearful tragedies told by the roaring of the waves.

"But since you've asked me for a few memories, I shall tell you of a singular adventure that befell me here, about ten years ago.

"At the time I was living, as I still do today, at old Mother Lafon's place, and one of my best friends, Louis Bernet, who has since given up boating and his wild, carefree ways in favor of a seat on the Council of State, had set himself up in the village of C., two leagues away. We dined together every night, sometimes at his place, sometimes at mine.

"One night, as I was coming home alone, fairly tired, laboriously lugging my big boat behind me, a twelve-foot skiff I always used at night, I stopped for a few moments to catch my breath by that headland of reeds—over there, about two hundred yards before the railroad bridge. The weather was wonderful: the moon shining brightly, the river brilliant, the air calm and mild. This serenity was so tempting. What a nice spot, I thought, for a few puffs on my pipe. No sooner had this thought crossed my mind than I was grabbing my anchor and tossing it into the river.

"My boat, borne back downstream on the current, ran out its chain to the end, and stopped. I settled in the stern on my sheepskin as comfortably as I could. There was not a sound to be heard, not a single sound—except now and then I thought to discern a gentle, almost imperceptible lapping of water against the shore, and I could make out the taller stands of reeds, which took on surprising shapes and seemed, at times, to move.

"The river was perfectly serene, but I felt moved by the extraordinary silence around me. Every creature—frogs and toads, those carolers of the night marsh—was quiet. Suddenly, to my right, as if to cross me, a frog croaked; I gave a start. It fell silent. I heard nothing now, and decided to keep smoking a bit to take my mind off. Now I've cured my share of pipes in my day, but it was no use. By the second puff I felt sick to my stomach, and quit. I started humming, but found the sound of my own voice hard to bear, so I stretched out in the bottom of the boat and gazed at the skies. For a few moments, I was at peace, but soon the slight swaying of the boat began to unsettle me. It seemed to be yawing violently from side to side, touching either riverbank in turn; then I fancied some being or invisible force was tugging it gently to the very depths before lifting it again and letting it fall. I was tossed about as if by a storm; I heard noises all around; I leapt to my feet. The water lay glittering, utterly calm.

"I knew my nerves were a bit shot, and so I decided to move on. I pulled on my chain. The boat began to move, and then I felt some resistance. I pulled harder; the anchor wouldn't give. It had caught on something in the depths and I couldn't lift it; I began tugging again, but to no avail. I took up my oars, turned the boat, and brought it upstream to change the anchor's position. No good: it still wouldn't budge. I grew furious and wrathfully rattled the chain. Nothing stirred. I sat down, discouraged, and began to think about my predicament. There was no way I could break the chain, nor separate it from the boat, for it was massive and fastened to the bow in a piece of wood bigger than my arm. But since the weather was still quite wonderful, I thought it wouldn't be long before some other fisherman came along to rescue me. My misadventure had settled my nerves; I sat down and found that I could smoke my pipe at last. I had a bottle of rum. After two or three glasses, my situation seemed comic. It was very warm, so warm that if I had to, I could spend the night outside without any harm.

"Suddenly, a little bump sounded against the hull. I leapt up, and a cold sweat chilled me from head to toe. The sound was probably some bit of wood carried on the current, but it was enough: once more, I was overcome by a strange nervous agitation. I seized the chain and pulled on it with all my might in another desperate attempt. The anchor held. I sat down again, exhausted.

"Bit by bit, a thick white mist had crept across the river, low over the low water, such that when I stood up I could no longer see the river, or my feet, or even the boat, but only the tips of the reeds and, in the distance, the fields completely pale by the light of the moon, with great black patches rising into the sky, formed by stands of Lombardy poplars. It was as if I were buried to the waist in a woolen layer of singular whiteness, and the wildest fantasias occurred to me. I imagined that someone was trying to board the boat I could no longer see; that the river, hidden in impenetrable fog, must be full of strange creatures swimming around me. I felt a terrible malaise, a tightening around my temples, my heart was hammering so hard I couldn't breathe; just then, I lost my head and thought to save myself by swimming away. The very next moment, that idea made me shudder with fear. I saw myself lost, flailing about in this thick fog, thrashing amidst the inevitable weeds and reeds, gasping with fright, unable to see the banks or find my boat, and I seemed to feel myself being dragged by my feet down into the depths of that black water.

"In fact, as I would have had to swim upstream for at least five hundred yards before finding a stretch free of weeds and rushes where I could get a foothold, odds were nine out of ten I'd lose my way in the fog and drown, as strong a swimmer as I was.

"I tried to reason with myself. Firmly resolved though I was not to feel afraid, there was something else inside me besides my resolve, and that something else was afraid. I wondered what it was I feared; the brave me mocked the cowardly one. Never have I so clearly understood as on that night the struggle between the two beings which live within us, one desiring, the other resisting, each by turns taking the upper hand.

"This dumb, inexplicable fear grew ever greater and soon became terror. I remained unmoving, eyes wide, ears alert, waiting . . . for what? I had no idea, but it must have been terrible. Had it occurred to a fish to so much as leap from the water, as often happens, it would surely have sufficed to send me reeling floorward in a dead faint.

"And yet, through some violent effort, I finally managed to regain control of my fleeing wits. I took hold of my bottle of rum once more and downed a few great gulps. Then I had an idea, and began hollering at the top of my lungs toward all four corners of the compass, one after the next. When my throat froze up completely, I listened . . . In the distance, a dog howled.

"I drank some more, and lay down on my back in the bottom of the boat. I stayed that way an hour, maybe two, eyes wide open, not sleeping, nightmares all around. I didn't dare get up, though I desperately wanted to. I kept putting it off from one minute to the next. 'Here we go, on your feet!' I'd tell myself, then be afraid to make a move. At last, with infinite care, I got up slowly as if my life depended on every slightest sound I made, and looked overboard.

"I was dazzled by the most marvelous, most astonishing sight it is possible to imagine. It was one of those phantasmagorias from fairyland, one of those visions travelers tell of who have returned from far-off climes, and whom we listen to without believing.

"The fog, which, two hours earlier, was still floating o'er the water, had withdrawn bit by bit and gathered on the shore, leaving the river absolutely clear. On either bank it had formed an unbroken hill, twenty feet high, which shone in the moonlight with the splendor of snow. Such that nothing could be seen but the river a-glitter with fire between those two white mountains, while on high, overhead, full and wide, a great moon unfurled its light in a blue-tinged, milky sky.

"All the creatures of the water had woken; the frogs were croaking furiously, while every now and then, sometimes from the right, sometimes from the left, I caught the short, sad, monotonous note that toads fling starward in coppery tones. Oddly enough, I was no longer afraid; I stood in so extraordinary a landscape that even the strangest, most singular things could not have surprised me.

"How long it lasted I have no idea, for in the end I nodded off. When I opened my eyes, the moon had set; the sky was full of clouds. The water lapped gloomily at boat and shore. A wind had risen; it was cold, and the darkness was complete.

"I drank what remained of my rum and then, shivering, listened to the rustle of the reeds and the sinister sound of the river. I tried, but could not make out my boat, or even my own hands, which I brought to my face.

"And yet little by little, the darkness grew less dense. Suddenly I thought I sensed a shadow gliding by beside me; I let out a cry, and a voice replied: a fisherman. I called out to him; he drew near, and I told him of my misadventure. He pulled his boat up alongside mine, and together we pulled on the chain. The anchor wouldn't move. Day broke—somber, rainy, freezing, gray—one of those days that bring you only sorrow and misfortune. I saw another boat; we waved him down. The man on board joined his efforts with our own, and then, bit by bit, the anchor gave way. It came up, but slowly, ever so slowly, and burdened with a considerable weight. At last we made out a black mass, and hauled it aboard.

"It was the corpse of an old woman with a great stone tied round her neck."

OYSTERS

Anton Chekhov

❦

Translated by Constance Garnett

I need no great effort of memory to recall, in every detail, the rainy autumn evening when I stood with my father in one of the more frequented streets of Moscow, and felt that I was gradually being overcome by a strange illness. I had no pain at all, but my legs were giving way under me, the words stuck in my throat, my head slipped weakly on one side . . . It seemed as though, in a moment, I must fall down and lose consciousness.

If I had been taken into a hospital at that minute, the doctors would have had to write over my bed: *Fames,* a disease which is not in the manuals of medicine.

Beside me on the pavement stood my father in a shabby summer overcoat and a serge cap, from which a bit of white wadding was sticking out. On his feet he had big heavy goloshes. Afraid, vain man, that people would see that his feet were bare under his goloshes, he had drawn the tops of some old boots up round the calves of his legs.

This poor, foolish, queer creature, whom I loved the more warmly the more ragged and dirty his smart summer overcoat became, had come to Moscow, five months before, to look for a job as copying-clerk. For those five months he had been trudging about Moscow looking for work, and it was only on that day that he had brought himself to go into the street to beg for alms.

Before us was a big house of three storeys, adorned with a blue signboard with the word "Restaurant" on it. My head was drooping feebly backwards and on one side, and I could not help looking upwards at the lighted windows of the restaurant. Human figures were flitting about at the windows. I could see the right side of the orchestrion, two oleographs, hanging lamps. . . . Staring into one window, I saw a patch of white. The patch was motionless, and its rectangular outlines stood out sharply against the dark, brown background. I looked intently and made out of the patch a white placard on the wall. Something was written on it, but what it was, I could not see . . .

For half an hour I kept my eyes on the placard. Its white attracted my eyes, and, as it were, hypnotised my brain. I tried to read it, but my efforts were in vain.

At last the strange disease got the upper hand.

The rumble of the carriages began to seem like thunder, in the stench of the street I distinguished a thousand smells. The restaurant lights and the lamps dazzled my eyes like lightning. My five senses were over-strained and sensitive beyond the normal. I began to see what I had not seen before.

"Oysters . . ." I made out on the placard.

A strange word! I had lived in the world eight years and three months, but had never come across that word. What did it mean? Surely it was not the name of the restaurant-keeper? But signboards with names on them always hang outside, not on the walls indoors!

"Papa, what does 'oysters' mean?" I asked in a husky voice, making an effort to turn my face towards my father.

My father did not hear. He was keeping a watch on the movements of the crowd, and following every passer-by with his eyes. . . . From his eyes I saw that he wanted to say something to the passers-by, but the fatal word hung like a heavy weight on his trembling lips and could not be flung off. He even took a step after one passer-by and touched him on the sleeve, but when he turned round, he said, "I beg your pardon," was overcome with confusion, and staggered back.

"Papa, what does 'oysters' mean?" I repeated.

"It is an animal . . . that lives in the sea."

I instantly pictured to myself this unknown marine animal. . . . I thought it must be something midway between a fish and a crab. As it was from the sea they made of it, of course, a very nice hot fish soup with savoury pepper and laurel leaves, or broth with vinegar and fric- assee of fish and cabbage, or crayfish sauce, or served it cold with horse-radish. . . . I vividly imagined it being brought from the market, quickly cleaned, quickly put in the pot, quickly, quickly, for everyone was hungry . . . awfully hungry! From the kitchen rose the smell of hot fish and crayfish soup.

I felt that this smell was tickling my palate and nostrils, that it was gradually taking possession of my whole body. . . . The restaurant, my father, the white placard, my sleeves were all smelling of it, smelling so strongly that I began to chew. I moved my jaws and swallowed as though I really had a piece of this marine animal in my mouth . . .

My legs gave way from the blissful sensation I was feeling, and I clutched at my father's arm to keep myself from falling, and leant against his wet summer overcoat. My father was trembling and shivering. He was cold . . .

"Papa, are oysters a Lenten dish?" I asked.

"They are eaten alive . . ." said my father. "They are in shells like tortoises, but . . . in two halves."

The delicious smell instantly left off affecting me, and the illusion vanished. . . . Now I understood it all!

"How nasty," I whispered, "how nasty!"

So that's what "oysters" meant! I imagined to myself a creature like a frog. A frog sitting in a shell, peeping out from it with big, glittering eyes, and moving its revolting jaws. I imagined this creature in a shell with claws, glittering eyes, and a slimy skin, being brought from the market. . . . The children would all hide while the cook, frowning with an air of disgust, would take the creature by its claw, put it on a plate, and carry it into the dining-room. The grown-ups would take it and eat it, eat it alive with its eyes, its teeth, its legs! While it squeaked and tried to bite their lips. . . .

I frowned, but . . . but why did my teeth move as though I were munching? The creature was loathsome, disgusting, terrible, but I ate it, ate it greedily, afraid of distinguishing its taste or smell. As soon as I had eaten one, I saw the glittering eyes of a second, a third . . . I ate them too. . . . At last I ate the table-napkin, the plate, my father's goloshes, the white placard . . . I ate everything that caught my eye, because I felt that nothing but eating would take away my illness. The oysters had a terrible look in their eyes and were loathsome. I shuddered at the thought of them, but I wanted to eat! To eat!

"Oysters! Give me some oysters!" was the cry that broke from me and I stretched out my hand.

"Help us, gentlemen!" I heard at that moment my father say, in a hollow and shaking voice. "I am ashamed to ask but—my God!—I can bear no more!"

"Oysters!" I cried, pulling my father by the skirts of his coat.

"Do you mean to say you eat oysters? A little chap like you!" I heard laughter close to me.

Two gentlemen in top hats were standing before us, looking into my face and laughing.

"Do you really eat oysters, youngster? That's interesting! How do you eat them?"

I remember that a strong hand dragged me into the lighted restaurant.

A minute later there was a crowd round me, watching me with curiosity and amusement. I sat at a table and ate something slimy, salt with a flavour of dampness and mouldiness. I ate greedily without chewing, without looking and trying to discover what I was eating. I fancied that if I opened my eyes I should see glittering eyes, claws, and sharp teeth.

All at once I began biting something hard, there was a sound of a scrunching.

"Ha, ha! He is eating the shells," laughed the crowd. "Little silly, do you suppose you can eat that?"

After that I remember a terrible thirst. I was lying in my bed, and could not sleep for heartburn and the strange taste in my parched mouth. My father was walking up and down, gesticulating with his hands.

"I believe I have caught cold," he was muttering. "I've a feeling in my head as though someone were sitting on it. . . . Perhaps it is because I have not . . . er . . . eaten anything to-day. . . . I really am a queer, stupid creature. . . . I saw those gentlemen pay ten roubles for the oysters. Why didn't I go up to them and ask them . . . to lend me something? They would have given something."

Towards morning, I fell asleep and dreamt of a frog sitting in a shell, moving its eyes. At midday I was awakened by thirst, and looked for my father: he was still walking up and down and gesticulating.

POMEGRANATE SEED*

Edith Wharton

━━❧━━

I

Charlotte Ashby paused on her doorstep. Dark had descended on the brilliancy of the March afternoon, and the grinding, rasping street life of the city was at its highest. She turned her back on it, standing for a moment in the old-fashioned, marble-flagged vestibule before she inserted her key in the lock. The sash curtains drawn across the panes of the inner door softened the light within to a warm blur through which no details showed. It was the hour when, in the first months of her marriage to

---

* Persephone, daughter of Demeter, goddess of fertility, was abducted and taken to Hades by Pluto, the god of the underworld. Her mother begged Jupiter to intercede, and he did so. But Persephone had broken her vow of abstinence in Hades by eating some pomegranate seeds. She was therefore required to spend a certain number of months each year—essentially the winter months —with Pluto.

Kenneth Ashby, she had most liked to return to that quiet house in a street long since deserted by business and fashion. The contrast between the soulless roar of New York, its devouring blaze of lights, the oppression of its congested traffic, congested houses, lives, minds and this veiled sanctuary she called home, always stirred her profoundly. In the very heart of the hurricane she had found her tiny islet—or thought she had. And now, in the last months, everything was changed, and she always wavered on the doorstep and had to force herself to enter.

While she stood there she called up the scene within: the hall hung with old prints, the ladder-like stairs, and on the left her husband's long shabby library, full of books and pipes and worn armchairs inviting to meditation. How she had loved that room! Then, upstairs, her own drawing room, in which, since the death of Kenneth's first wife, neither furniture nor hangings had been changed, because there had never been money enough, but which Charlotte had made her own by moving furniture about and adding more books, another lamp, a table for the new reviews. Even on the occasion of her only visit to the first Mrs. Ashby—a distant, self-centered woman, whom she had known very slightly—she had looked about her with an innocent envy, feeling it to be exactly the drawing room she would have liked for herself; and now for more than a year it had been hers to deal with as she chose—the room to which she hastened back at dusk on winter days, where she sat reading by the fire, or answering notes at the pleasant roomy desk, or going over her stepchildren's copybooks, till she heard her husband's step.

Sometimes friends dropped in; sometimes—oftener—she was alone; and she liked that best, since it was another way of being with Kenneth, thinking over what he had said when they parted in the morning, imagining what he would say when he sprang up the stairs, found her by herself and caught her to him.

Now, instead of this, she thought of one thing only—the letter she might or might not find on the hall table. Until she had made sure whether or not it was there, her mind had no room for anything else.

The letter was always the same—a square grayish envelope with "Kenneth Ashby, Esquire," written on it in bold but faint characters. From the first it had struck Charlotte as peculiar that anyone who wrote such a firm hand should trace the letters so lightly; the address was always written as though there were not enough ink in the pen, or the writer's wrist were too weak to bear upon it. Another curious thing was that, in spite of its masculine curves, the writing was so visibly feminine. Some hands are sexless, some masculine, at first glance; the writing on the gray envelope, for all its strength and assurance, was without doubt a woman's. The envelope never bore anything but the recipient's name; no stamp, no address. The letter was presumably delivered by hand—but by whose? No doubt it was slipped into the letter box, whence the parlormaid, when she closed the shutters and lit the lights, probably extracted it. At any rate, it was always in the evening, after dark, that Charlotte saw it lying there. She thought of the letter in the singular, as "it," because, though there had been several since her marriage—seven, to be exact—they were so alike in appearance that they had become merged in one another in her mind, become one letter, become "it."

The first had come the day after their return from their honeymoon— a journey prolonged to the West Indies, from which they had returned to New York after an absence of more than two months. Re-entering the house with her husband, late on that first evening—they had dined at his mother's—she had seen, alone on the hall table, the gray envelope. Her eye fell on it before Kenneth's, and her first thought was: "Why, I've seen that writing before"; but where she could not recall. The memory was just definite enough for her to identify the script whenever it looked up at her faintly from the same pale envelope; but on that first day she would have thought no more of the letter if, when her husband's glance lit on it, she had not chanced to be looking at him. It all happened in a flash—his seeing the letter, putting out his hand for it, raising it to his shortsighted eyes to decipher the faint writing, and then abruptly withdrawing the arm he had slipped through Charlotte's, and moving away to the hanging light, his back turned to her. She had waited—waited for a sound, an exclamation; waited for him to open the letter; but he had slipped it into his pocket without a word and followed her into the library. And there they had sat down by the fire and lit their cigarettes, and he had remained silent, his head thrown back broodingly against the armchair, his eyes fixed on the hearth, and presently had passed his hand over his forehead and said: "Wasn't it unusually hot at my mother's tonight? I've got a splitting head. Mind if I take myself off to bed?"

That was the first time. Since then Charlotte had never been present when he had received the letter. It usually came before he got home from his office, and she had to go upstairs and leave it lying there. But even if she had not seen it, she would have known it had come by the change in his face when he joined her—which, on those evenings, he seldom did before they met for dinner. Evidently, whatever the letter contained, he wanted to be by himself to deal with it; and when he reappeared he looked years older, looked emptied of life and courage, and hardly conscious of her presence. Sometimes he was silent for the rest of the evening; and if he spoke, it was usually to hint some criticism of her household arrangements, suggest some change in the domestic administration, to ask, a little nervously, if she didn't think Joyce's nursery governess was rather young and flighty, or if she herself always saw to it that Peter— whose throat was delicate—was properly wrapped up when he went to school. At such times Charlotte would remember the friendly warnings she had received when she became engaged to Kenneth Ashby: "Marrying a heartbroken widower! Isn't that rather risky? You know Elsie Ashby absolutely dominated him"; and how she had jokingly replied: "He may be glad of a little liberty for a change." And in this respect she had been right. She had needed no one to tell her, during the first months, that her husband was perfectly happy with her. When they came back from their protracted honeymoon the same friends said: "What have you done to Kenneth? He looks twenty years younger"; and this time she answered with careless joy: "I suppose I've got him out of his groove."

But what she noticed after the gray letters began to come was not so much his nervous tentative faultfinding—which always seemed to be uttered against his will—as the look in his eyes when he joined her after receiving one of the letters. The look was not unloving, not even indifferent; it was the look of a man who had been so far away from ordinary events that when he returns to familiar things they seem strange. She minded that more than the faultfinding.

Though she had been sure from the first that the handwriting on the gray envelope was a woman's, it was long before she associated the mysterious letters with any sentimental secret. She was too sure of her husband's love, too confident of filling his life, for such an idea to occur to her. It seemed far more likely that the letters—which certainly did not appear to cause him any sentimental pleasure—were addressed to the busy lawyer than to the private person. Probably they were from some tiresome client—women, he had often told her, were nearly always tiresome as clients—who did not want her letters opened by his secretary and therefore had them carried to his house. Yes; but in that case the unknown female must be unusually troublesome, judging from the effect her letters produced. Then again, though his professional discretion was exemplary, it was odd that he had never uttered an impatient comment, never remarked to Charlotte, in a moment of expansion, that there was a nuisance of a woman who kept badgering him about a case that had gone against her. He had made more than one semiconfidence of the kind—of course without giving names or details; but concerning this mysterious correspondent his lips were sealed.

There was another possibility: what is euphemistically called an "old entanglement." Charlotte Ashby was a sophisticated woman. She had few illusions about the intricacies of the human heart; she knew that there were often old entanglements. But when she had married Kenneth Ashby, her friends, instead of hinting at such a possibility, had said: "You've got your work cut out for you. Marrying a Don Juan is a sinecure to it. Kenneth's never looked at another woman since he first saw Elsie Corder. During all the years of their marriage he was more like an unhappy lover than a comfortably contented husband. He'll never let you move an armchair or change the place of a lamp; and whatever you venture to do, he'll mentally compare with what Elsie would have done in your place."

Except for an occasional nervous mistrust as to her ability to manage the children—a mistrust gradually dispelled by her good humor and the children's obvious fondness for her—none of these forebodings had come true. The desolate widower, of whom his nearest friends said that only his absorbing professional interests had kept him from suicide after his first wife's death, had fallen in love, two years later, with Charlotte Gorse, and after an impetuous wooing had married her and carried her off on a tropical honeymoon. And ever since he had been as tender and lover-like as during those first radiant weeks. Before asking her to marry him he had spoken to her frankly of his great love for his first wife and his despair after her sudden death; but even then he had assumed no stricken attitude, or implied that life offered no possibility of renewal. He had been perfectly simple and natural, and had confessed to Charlotte that from the beginning he had hoped the future held new gifts for him. And when, after their marriage, they returned to the house where his twelve years with his first wife had been spent, he had told Charlotte at once that he was sorry he couldn't afford to do the place over for her, but that he knew every woman had her own views about furniture and all sorts of household arrangements a man would never notice, and had begged her to make any changes she saw fit without bothering to consult him. As a result, she made as few as possible; but his way of beginning their new life in the old setting was so frank and unembarrassed that it put her immediately at her ease, and she was almost sorry to find that the portrait of Elsie Ashby, which used to hang over the desk in his library, had been transferred in their absence to the children's nursery. Knowing herself to be the indirect cause of this banishment, she spoke of it to her husband; but he answered: "Oh, I thought they ought to grow up with her looking down on them." The answer moved Charlotte, and satisfied her; and as time went by she had to confess that she felt more at home in her house, more at ease and in confidence with her husband, since that long coldly beautiful face on the library wall no longer followed her with guarded eyes. It was as if Kenneth's love had penetrated to the secret she hardly acknowledged to her own heart—her passionate need to feel herself the sovereign even of his past.

With all this stored-up happiness to sustain her, it was curious that she had lately found herself yielding to a nervous apprehension. But there the apprehension was; and on this particular afternoon—perhaps because she was more tired than usual, or because of the trouble of finding a new cook or, for some other ridiculously trivial reason, moral or physical—she found herself unable to react against the feeling. Latchkey in hand, she looked back down the silent street to the whirl and illumination of the great thoroughfare beyond, and up at the sky already aflare with the city's nocturnal life. "Outside there," she thought, "skyscrapers, advertisements, telephones, wireless, airplanes, movies, motors, and all the rest of the twentieth century; and on the other side of the door something I can't explain, can't relate to them. Something as old as the world, as mysterious as life. . . . Nonsense! What am I worrying about? There hasn't been a letter for three months now—not since the day we came back from the country after Christmas. . . . Queer that they always seem to come after our holidays! . . . Why should I imagine there's going to be one tonight!"

No reason why, but that was the worst of it—one of the worst!—that there were days when she would stand there cold and shivering with the premonition of something inexplicable, intolerable, to be faced on the other side of the curtained panes; and when she opened the door and went in, there would be nothing; and on other days when she felt the same premonitory chill, it was justified by the sight of the gray envelope. So that ever since the last had come she had taken to feeling cold and premonitory every evening, because she never opened the door without thinking the letter might be there.

Well, she'd had enough of it: that was certain. She couldn't go on like that. If her husband turned white and had a headache on the days when the letter came, he seemed to recover afterward; but she couldn't. With her the strain had become chronic, and the reason was not far to seek. Her husband knew from whom the letter came and what was in it; he was prepared beforehand for whatever he had to deal with, and master of the situation, however bad; whereas she was shut out in the dark with her conjectures.

"I can't stand it! I can't stand it another day!" she exclaimed aloud, as she put her key in the lock. She turned the key and went in; and there, on the table, lay the letter.

II

She was almost glad of the sight. It seemed to justify everything, to put a seal of definiteness on the whole blurred business. A letter for her husband; a letter from a woman—no doubt another vulgar case of "old entanglement." What a fool she had been ever to doubt it, to rack her brains for less obvious explanations! She took up the envelope with a steady contemptuous hand, looked closely at the faint letters, held it against the light and just discerned the outline of the folded sheet within. She knew that now she would have no peace till she found out what was written on that sheet.

Her husband had not come in; he seldom got back from his office before half-past six or seven, and it was not yet six. She would have time to take the letter up to the drawing room, hold it over the tea kettle which at that hour always simmered by the fire in expectation of her return, solve the mystery and replace the letter where she had found it. No one would be the wiser, and her gnawing uncertainty would be over. The alternative, of course, was to question her husband; but to do that seemed even more difficult. She weighed the letter between thumb and finger, looked at it again under the light, started up the stairs with the envelope—and came down again and laid it on the table.

"No, I evidently can't," she said, disappointed.

What should she do, then? She couldn't go up alone to that warm welcoming room, pour out her tea, look over her correspondence, glance at a book or review—not with that letter lying below and the knowledge that in a little while her husband would come in, open it and turn into the library alone, as he always did on the days when the gray envelope came.

Suddenly she decided. She would wait in the library and see for herself; see what happened between him and the letter when they thought themselves unobserved. She wondered the idea had never occurred to her before. By leaving the door ajar, and sitting in the corner behind it, she could watch him unseen. . . . Well, then, she would watch him! She drew a chair into the corner, sat down, her eyes on the crack, and waited.

As far as she could remember, it was the first time she had ever tried to surprise another person's secret, but she was conscious of no compunction. She simply felt as if she were fighting her way through a stifling fog that she must at all costs get out of.

At length she heard Kenneth's latchkey and jumped up. The impulse to rush out and meet him had nearly made her forget why she was there; but she remembered in time and sat down again. From her post she covered the whole range of his movements—saw him enter the hall, draw the key from the door and take off his hat and overcoat. Then he turned to throw his gloves on the hall table, and at that moment he saw the envelope. The light was full on his face, and what Charlotte first noted there was a look of surprise. Evidently he had not expected the letter— had not thought of the possibility of its being there that day. But though he had not expected it, now that he saw it he knew well enough what it contained. He did not open it immediately, but stood motionless, the color slowly ebbing from his face. Apparently he could not make up his mind to touch it; but at length he put out his hand, opened the envelope, and moved with it to the light. In doing so he turned his back on Charlotte, and she saw only his bent head and slightly stooping shoulders. Apparently all the writing was on one page, for he did not turn the sheet but continued to stare at it for so long that he must have reread it a dozen times—or so it seemed to the woman breathlessly watching him. At length she saw him move; he raised the letter still closer to his eyes, as though he had not fully deciphered it. Then he lowered his head, and she saw his lips touch the sheet.

"Kenneth!" she exclaimed, and went on out into the hall.

The letter clutched in his hand, her husband turned and looked at her. "Where were you?" he said, in a low bewildered voice, like a man waked out of his sleep.

"In the library, waiting for you." She tried to steady her voice: "What's the matter! What's in that letter? You look ghastly."

Her agitation seemed to calm him, and he instantly put the envelope into his pocket with a slight laugh. "Ghastly? I'm sorry. I've had a hard day in the office—one or two complicated cases. I look dog-tired, I suppose."

"You didn't look tired when you came in. It was only when you opened that letter—"

He had followed her into the library, and they stood gazing at each other. Charlotte noticed how quickly he had regained his self-control; his profession had trained him to rapid mastery of face and voice. She saw at once that she would be at a disadvantage in any attempt to surprise his secret, but at the same moment she lost all desire to maneuver, to trick him into betraying anything he wanted to conceal. Her wish was still to penetrate the mystery, but only that she might help him to bear the burden it implied. "Even if it *is* another woman," she thought.

"Kenneth," she said, her heart beating excitedly, "I waited here on purpose to see you come in. I wanted to watch you while you opened that letter."

His face, which had paled, turned to dark red; then it paled again. "That letter? Why especially that letter?"

"Because I've noticed that whenever one of those letters comes it seems to have such a strange effect on you."

A line of anger she had never seen before came out between his eyes, and she said to herself: "The upper part of his face is too narrow; this is the first time I ever noticed it."

She heard him continue, in the cool and faintly ironic tone of the prosecuting lawyer making a point: "Ah, so you're in the habit of watching people open their letters when they don't know you're there?"

"Not in the habit. I never did such a thing before. But I had to find out what she writes to you, at regular intervals, in those gray envelopes."

He weighed this for a moment; then: "The intervals have not been regular," he said.

"Oh, I dare say you've kept a better account of the dates than I have," she retorted, her magnanimity vanishing at his tone. "All I know is that every time that woman writes to you—"

"Why do you assume it's a woman?"

"It's a woman's writing. Do you deny it?"

He smiled. "No, I don't deny it. I asked only because the writing is generally supposed to look more like a man's." Charlotte passed this over impatiently. "And this woman—what does she write to you about?"

Again he seemed to consider a moment. "About business."

"Legal business?"

"In a way, yes. Business in general."

"You look after her affairs for her?"

"Yes."

"You've looked after them for a long time?"

"Yes. A very long time."

"Kenneth, dearest, won't you tell me who she is?"

"No. I can't." He paused, and brought out, as if with a certain hesitation: "Professional secrecy."

The blood rushed from Charlotte's heart to her temples. "Don't say that—don't!"

"Why not?"

"Because I saw you kiss the letter."

The effect of the words was so disconcerting that she instantly repented having spoken them. Her husband, who had submitted to her cross-questioning with a sort of contemptuous composure, as though he were humoring an unreasonable child, turned on her a face of terror and distress. For a minute he seemed unable to speak; then, collecting himself, with an effort, he stammered out: "The writing is very faint; you must have seen me holding the letter close to my eyes to try to decipher it."

"No; I saw you kissing it." He was silent. "Didn't I see you kissing it?"

He sank back into indifference. "Perhaps."

"Kenneth! You stand there and say that—to me?"

"What possible difference can it make to you? The letter is on business, as I told you. Do you suppose I'd lie about it? The writer is a very old friend whom I haven't seen for a long time."

"Men don't kiss business letters, even from women who are very old friends, unless they have been their lovers, and still regret them."

He shrugged his shoulders slightly and turned away, as if he considered the discussion at an end and were faintly disgusted at the turn it had taken.

"Kenneth!" Charlotte moved toward him and caught hold of his arm.

He paused with a look of weariness and laid his hand over hers. "Won't you believe me?" he asked gently.

"How can I? I've watched these letters come to you—for months now they've been coming. Ever since we came back from the West Indies—one of them greeted me the very day we arrived. And after each one of them I see their mysterious effect on you, I see you disturbed, unhappy, as if someone were trying to estrange you from me."

"No, dear; not that. Never!"

She drew back and looked at him with passionate entreaty. "Well, then, prove it to me, darling. It's so easy!"

He forced a smile. "It's not easy to prove anything to a woman who's once taken an idea into her head."

"You've only got to show me the letter."

His hand slipped from hers and he drew back and shook his head.

"You won't?"

"I can't."

"Then the woman who wrote it is your mistress."

"No, dear. No."

"Not now, perhaps. I suppose she's trying to get you back, and you're struggling, out of pity for me. My poor Kenneth!"

"I swear to you she never was my mistress."

Charlotte felt the tears rushing to her eyes. "Ah, that's worse, then—that's hopeless! The prudent ones are the kind that keep their hold on a man. We all know that." She lifted her hands and hid her face in them.

Her husband remained silent; he offered neither consolation nor denial, and at length, wiping away her tears, she raised her eyes almost timidly to his.

"Kenneth, think! We've been married such a short time. Imagine what you're making me suffer. You say you can't show me this letter. You refuse even to explain it."

"I've told you the letter is on business. I will swear to that too."

"A man will swear to anything to screen a woman. If you want me to believe you, at least tell me her name. If you'll do that, I promise you I won't ask to see the letter."

There was a long interval of suspense, during which she felt her heart beating against her ribs in quick admonitory knocks, as if warning her of the danger she was incurring.

"I can't," he said at length.

"Not even her name?"

"No."

"You can't tell me anything more?"

"No."

Again a pause; this time they seemed both to have reached the end of their arguments and to be helplessly facing each other across a baffling waste of incomprehension.

Charlotte stood breathing rapidly, her hands against her breast. She felt as if she had run a hard race and missed the goal. She had meant to move her husband and had succeeded only in irritating him; and this error of reckoning seemed to change him into a stranger, a mysterious incomprehensible being whom no argument or entreaty of hers could reach. The curious thing was that she was aware in him of no hostility or even impatience, but only of a remoteness, an inaccessibility, far more difficult to overcome. She felt herself excluded, ignored, blotted out of his life. But after a moment or two, looking at him more calmly, she saw that he was suffering as much as she was. His distant guarded face was drawn with pain; the coming of the gray envelope, though it always cast a shadow, had never marked him as deeply as this discussion with his wife.

Charlotte took heart; perhaps, after all, she had not spent her last shaft. She drew nearer and once more laid her hand on his arm. "Poor Kenneth! If you knew how sorry I am for you—"

She thought he winced slightly at this expression of sympathy, but he took her hand and pressed it.

"I can think of nothing worse than to be incapable of loving long," she continued, "to feel the beauty of a great love and to be too unstable to bear its burden."

He turned on her a look of wistful reproach. "Oh, don't say that of me. Unstable!"

She felt herself at last on the right tack, and her voice trembled with excitement as she went on: "Then what about me and this other woman? Haven't you already forgotten Elsie twice within a year?"

She seldom pronounced his first wife's name; it did not come naturally to her tongue. She flung it out now as if she were flinging some dangerous explosive into the open space between them, and drew back a step, waiting to hear the mine go off.

Her husband did not move; his expression grew sadder, but showed no resentment. "I have never forgotten Elsie," he said.

Charlotte could not repress a faint laugh. "Then, you poor dear, between the three of us—"

"There are not—" he began; and then broke off and put his hand to his forehead.

"Not what?"

"I'm sorry; I don't believe I know what I'm saying. I've got a blinding headache." He looked wan and furrowed enough for the statement to be true, but she was exasperated by his evasion.

"Ah, yes; the gray envelope headache!"

She saw the surprise in his eyes. "I'd forgotten how closely I've been watched," he said coldly. "If you'll excuse me, I think I'll go up and try an hour in the dark, to see if I can get rid of this neuralgia."

She wavered; then she said, with desperate resolution: "I'm sorry your head aches. But before you go I want to say that sooner or later this question must be settled between us. Someone is trying to separate us, and I don't care what it costs me to find out who it is." She looked him steadily in the eyes. "If it costs me your love, I don't care! If I can't have your confidence I don't want anything from you."

He still looked at her wistfully. "Give me time."

"Time for what? It's only a word to say."

"Time to show you that you haven't lost my love or my confidence."

"Well, I'm waiting."

He turned toward the door, and then glanced back hesitatingly. "Oh, do wait, my love," he said, and went out of the room.

She heard his tired step on the stairs and the closing of his bedroom door above. Then she dropped into a chair and buried her face in her folded arms. Her first movement was one of compunction; she seemed to herself to have been hard, unhuman, unimaginative. "Think of telling him that I didn't care if my insistence cost me his love! The lying rubbish!" She started up to follow him and unsay the meaningless words. But she was checked by a reflection. He had had his way, after all; he had eluded all attacks on his secret, and now he was shut up alone in his room, reading that other woman's letter.

III

She was still reflecting on this when the surprised parlormaid came in and found her. No, Charlotte said, she wasn't going to dress for dinner; Mr. Ashby didn't want to dine. He was very tired and had gone up to his room to rest; later she would have something brought on a tray to the drawing room. She mounted the stairs to her bedroom. Her dinner dress was lying on the bed, and at the sight the quiet routine of her daily life took hold of her and she began to feel as if the strange talk she had just had with her husband must have taken place in another world, between two beings who were not Charlotte Gorse and Kenneth Ashby, but phantoms projected by her fevered imagination. She recalled the year since her marriage—her husband's constant devotion; his persistent, almost too insistent tenderness; the feeling he had given her at times of being too eagerly dependent on her, too searchingly close to her, as if there were not air enough between her soul and his. It seemed preposterous, as she recalled all this, that a few moments ago she should have been accusing him of an intrigue with another woman! But, then, what—

Again she was moved by the impulse to go up to him, beg his pardon and try to laugh away the misunderstanding. But she was restrained by the fear of forcing herself upon his privacy. He was troubled and unhappy, oppressed by some grief or fear; and he had shown her that he wanted to fight out his battle alone. It would be wiser, as well as more generous, to respect his wish. Only, how strange, how unbearable, to be there, in the next room to his, and feel herself at the other end of the world! In her nervous agitation she almost regretted not having had the courage to open the letter and put it back on the hall table before he came in. At least she would have known what his secret was, and the bogy might have been laid. For she was beginning now to think of the mystery as something conscious, malevolent: a secret persecution before which he quailed, yet from which he could not free himself. Once or twice in his evasive eyes she thought she had detected a desire for help, an impulse of confession, instantly restrained and suppressed. It was as if he felt she could have helped him if she had known, and yet had been unable to tell her!

There flashed through her mind the idea of going to his mother. She was very fond of old Mrs. Ashby, a firm-fleshed clear-eyed old lady, with an astringent bluntness of speech which responded to the forthright and simple in Charlotte's own nature. There had been a tacit bond between them ever since the day when Mrs. Ashby Senior, coming to lunch for the first time with her new daughter-in-law, had been received by Charlotte downstairs in the library, and glancing up at the empty wall above her son's desk, had remarked laconically: "Elsie gone, eh?" adding, at Charlotte's murmured explanation: "Nonsense. Don't have her back. Two's company." Charlotte, at this reading of her thoughts, could hardly refrain from exchanging a smile of complicity with her mother-in-law; and it seemed to her now that Mrs. Ashby's almost uncanny directness might pierce to the core of this new mystery. But here again she hesitated, for the idea almost suggested a betrayal. What right had she to call in anyone, even so close a relation, to surprise a secret which her husband was trying to keep from her? "Perhaps, by and by, he'll talk to his mother of his own accord," she thought, and then ended: "But what does it matter? He and I must settle it between us."

She was still brooding over the problem when there was a knock on the door and her husband came in. He was dressed for dinner and seemed surprised to see her sitting there, with her evening dress lying unheeded on the bed.

"Aren't you coming down?"

"I thought you were not well and had gone to bed," she faltered.

He forced a smile. "I'm not particularly well, but we'd better go down." His face, though still drawn, looked calmer than when he had fled upstairs an hour earlier.

"There it is; he knows what's in the letter and has fought his battle out again, whatever it is," she reflected, "while I'm still in darkness." She rang and gave a hurried order that dinner should be served as soon as possible—just a short meal, whatever could be got ready quickly, as both she and Mr. Ashby were rather tired and not very hungry.

Dinner was announced, and they sat down to it. At first neither seemed able to find a word to say; then Ashby began to make conversation with an assumption of ease that was more oppressive than his silence. "How tired he is! How terribly overtired!" Charlotte said to herself, pursuing her own thoughts while he rambled on about municipal politics, aviation, an exhibition of modern French painting, the health of an old aunt and the installing of the automatic telephone. "Good heavens, how tired he is!"

When they dined alone they usually went into the library after dinner, and Charlotte curled herself up on the divan with her knitting while he settled down in his armchair under the lamp and lit a pipe. But this evening, by tacit agreement, they avoided the room in which their strange talk had taken place, and went up to Charlotte's drawing room.

They sat down near the fire, and Charlotte said: "Your pipe?" after he had put down his hardly tasted coffee.

He shook his head. "No, not tonight."

"You must go to bed early; you look terribly tired. I'm sure they overwork you at the office."

"I suppose we all overwork at times."

She rose and stood before him with sudden resolution. "Well, I'm not going to have you use up your strength slaving in that way. It's absurd. I can see you're ill." She bent over him and laid her hand on his forehead. "My poor old Kenneth. Prepare to be taken away soon on a long holiday."

He looked up at her, startled. "A holiday?"

"Certainly. Didn't you know I was going to carry you off at Easter? We're going to start in a fortnight on a month's voyage to somewhere or other. On any one of the big cruising steamers." She paused and bent closer, touching his forehead with her lips. "I'm tired, too, Kenneth."

He seemed to pay no heed to her last words, but sat, his hands on his knees, his head drawn back a little from her caress, and looked up at her with a stare of apprehension. "Again? My dear, we can't; I can't possibly go away."

"I don't know why you say 'again,' Kenneth; we haven't taken a real holiday this year."

"At Christmas we spent a week with the children in the country."

"Yes, but this time I mean away from the children, from servants, from the house. From everything that's familiar and fatiguing. Your mother will love to have Joyce and Peter with her."

He frowned and slowly shook his head. "No, dear; I can't leave them with my mother."

"Why, Kenneth, how absurd! She adores them. You didn't hesitate to leave them with her for over two months when we went to the West Indies."

He drew a deep breath and stood up uneasily. "That was different."

"Different? Why?"

"I mean, at that time I didn't realize—" He broke off as if to choose his words and then went on: "My mother adores the children, as you say. But she isn't always very judicious. Grandmothers always spoil children. And sometimes she talks before them without thinking." He turned to his wife with an almost pitiful gesture of entreaty. "Don't ask me to, dear."

Charlotte mused. It was true that the elder Mrs. Ashby had a fearless tongue, but she was the last woman in the world to say or hint anything before her grandchildren at which the most scrupulous parent could take offense. Charlotte looked at her husband in perplexity.

"I don't understand."

He continued to turn on her the same troubled and entreating gaze. "Don't try to," he muttered.

"Not try to?"

"Not now—not yet." He put up his hands and pressed them against his temples. "Can't you see that there's no use in insisting? I can't go away, no matter how much I might want to."

Charlotte still scrutinized him gravely. "The question is, *do* you want to?"

He returned her gaze for a moment; then his lips began to tremble, and he said, hardly above his breath: "I want—anything you want."

"And yet—"

"Don't ask me. I can't leave—I can't!"

"You mean that you can't go away out of reach of those letters!"

Her husband had been standing before her in an uneasy half-hesitating attitude; now he turned abruptly away and walked once or twice up and down the length of the room, his head bent, his eyes fixed on the carpet.

Charlotte felt her resentfulness rising with her fears. "It's that," she persisted. "Why not admit it? You can't live without them."

He continued his troubled pacing of the room; then he stopped short, dropped into a chair and covered his face with his hands. From the shaking of his shoulders, Charlotte saw that he was weeping. She had never seen a man cry, except her father after her mother's death, when she was a little girl; and she remembered still how the sight had frightened her. She was frightened now; she felt that her husband was being dragged away from her into some mysterious bondage, and that she must use up her last atom of strength in the struggle for his freedom, and for hers.

"Kenneth—Kenneth!" she pleaded, kneeling down beside him. "Won't you listen to me? Won't you try to see what I'm suffering? I'm not unreasonable, darling, really not. I don't suppose I should ever have noticed the letters if it hadn't been for their effect on you. It's not my way to pry into other people's affairs; and even if the effect had been different—yes, yes, listen to me—if I'd seen that the letters made you happy, that you were watching eagerly for them, counting the days between their coming, that you wanted them, that they gave you something I haven't known how to give—why, Kenneth, I don't say I shouldn't have suffered from that, too; but it would have been in a different way, and I should have had the courage to hide what I felt, and the hope that someday you'd come to feel about me as you did about the writer of the letters. But what I can't bear is to see how you dread them, how they make you suffer, and yet how you can't live without them and won't go away lest you should miss one during your absence. Or perhaps," she added, her voice breaking into a cry of accusation—"perhaps it's because she's actually forbidden you to leave. Kenneth, you must answer me! Is that the reason? Is it because she's forbidden you that you won't go away with me?"

She continued to kneel at his side, and raising her hands, she drew his gently down. She was ashamed of her persistence, ashamed of uncovering that baffled disordered face, yet resolved that no such scruples should arrest her. His eyes were lowered, the muscles of his face quivered; she was making him suffer even more than she suffered herself. Yet this no longer restrained her.

"Kenneth, is it that? She won't let us go away together?"

Still he did not speak or turn his eyes to her; and a sense of defeat swept over her. After all, she thought, the struggle was a losing one. "You needn't answer. I see I'm right," she said.

Suddenly, as she rose, he turned and drew her down again. His hands caught hers and pressed them so tightly that she felt her rings cutting into her flesh. There was something frightened, convulsive in his hold; it was the clutch of a man who felt himself slipping over a precipice. He was staring up at her now as if salvation lay in the face she bent above him. "Of course we'll go away together. We'll go wherever you want," he said in a low confused voice; and putting his arm about her, he drew her close and pressed his lips on hers.

IV

Charlotte had said to herself: "I shall sleep tonight," but instead she sat before her fire into the small hours, listening for any sound that came from her husband's room. But he, at any rate, seemed to be resting after the tumult of the evening. Once or twice she stole to the door and in the faint light that came in from the street through his open window she saw him stretched out in heavy sleep—the sleep of weakness and exhaustion. "He's ill," she thought, "he's undoubtedly ill. And it's not overwork; it's this mysterious persecution."

She drew a breath of relief. She had fought through the weary fight and the victory was hers—at least for the moment. If only they could have started at once—started for anywhere! She knew it would be useless to ask him to leave before the holidays; and meanwhile the secret influence—as to which she was still so completely in the dark—would continue to work against her, and she would have to renew the struggle day after day till they started on their journey. But after that everything would be different. If once she could get her husband away under other skies, and all to herself, she never doubted her power to release him from the evil spell he was under. Lulled to quiet by the thought, she too slept at last.

When she woke, it was long past her usual hour, and she sat up in bed surprised and vexed at having overslept herself. She always liked to be down to share her husband's breakfast by the library fire; but a glance at the clock made it clear that he must have started long since for his office. To make sure, she jumped out of bed and went into his room, but it was empty. No doubt he had looked in on her before leaving, seen that she still slept, and gone downstairs without disturbing her; and their relations were sufficiently lover-like for her to regret having missed their morning hour.

She rang and asked if Mr. Ashby had already gone. Yes, nearly an hour ago, the maid said. He had given orders that Mrs. Ashby should not be waked and that the children should not come to her till she sent for them. . . . Yes, he had gone up to the nursery himself to give the order. All this sounded usual enough, and Charlotte hardly knew why she asked: "And did Mr. Ashby leave no other message?"

Yes, the maid said, he did; she was so sorry she'd forgotten. He'd told her, just as he was leaving, to say to Mrs. Ashby that he was going to see about their passages, and would she please be ready to sail tomorrow?

Charlotte echoed the woman's "Tomorrow," and sat staring at her incredulously. "Tomorrow—you're sure he said to sail tomorrow?"

"Oh, ever so sure, ma'am. I don't know how I could have forgotten to mention it."

"Well, it doesn't matter. Draw my bath, please." Charlotte sprang up, dashed through her dressing, and caught herself singing at her image in the glass as she sat brushing her hair. It made her feel young again to have scored such a victory. The other woman vanished to a speck on the horizon, as this one, who ruled the foreground, smiled back at the reflection of her lips and eyes. He loved her, then—he loved her as passionately as ever. He had divined what she had suffered, had understood that their happiness depended on their getting away at once, and finding each other again after yesterday's desperate groping in the fog. The nature of the influence that had come between them did not much matter to Charlotte now; she had faced the phantom and dispelled it. "Courage—that's the secret! If only people who are in love weren't always so afraid of risking their happiness by looking it in the eyes." As she brushed back her light abundant hair it waved electrically above her head, like the palms of victory. Ah, well, some women knew how to manage men, and some didn't—and only the fair—she gaily paraphrased—deserve the brave! Certainly she was looking very pretty.

The morning danced along like a cockleshell on a bright sea—such a sea as they would soon be speeding over. She ordered a particularly good dinner, saw the children off to their classes, had her trunks brought down, consulted with the maid about getting out summer clothes—for of course they would be heading for heat and sunshine—and wondered if she oughtn't to take Kenneth's flannel suits out of camphor. "But how absurd," she reflected, "that I don't yet know where we're going!" She looked at the clock, saw that it was close on noon, and decided to call him up at his office. There was a slight delay; then she heard his secretary's voice saying that Mr. Ashby had looked in for a moment early, and left again almost immediately. . . . Oh, very well; Charlotte would ring up later. How soon was he likely to be back? The secretary answered that she couldn't tell; all they knew in the office was that when he left he had said he was in a hurry because he had to go out of town.

Out of town! Charlotte hung up the receiver and sat blankly gazing into new darkness. Why had he gone out of town? And where had he gone? And of all days, why should he have chosen the eve of their suddenly planned departure? She felt a faint shiver of apprehension. Of course he had gone to see that woman—no doubt to get her permission to leave. He was as completely in bondage as that; and Charlotte had been fatuous enough to see the palms of victory on her forehead. She burst into a laugh and, walking across the room, sat down again before her mirror. What a different face she saw! The smile on her pale lips seemed to mock the rosy vision of the other Charlotte. But gradually her color crept back. After all, she had a right to claim the victory, since her husband was doing what she wanted, not what the other woman exacted of him. It was natural enough, in view of his abrupt decision to leave the next day, that he should have arrangements to make, business matters to wind up; it was not even necessary to suppose that his mysterious trip was a visit to the writer of the letters. He might simply have gone to see a client who lived out of town. Of course they would not tell Charlotte at the office; the secretary had hesitated before imparting even such meager information as the fact of Mr. Ashby's absence. Meanwhile she would go on with her joyful preparations, content to learn later in the day to what particular island of the blest she was to be carried.

The hours wore on, or rather were swept forward on a rush of eager preparations. At last the entrance of the maid who came to draw the curtains roused Charlotte from her labors, and she saw to her surprise that the clock marked five. And she did not yet know where they were going the next day! She rang up her husband's office and was told that Mr. Ashby had not been there since the early morning. She asked for his partner, but the partner could add nothing to her information, for he himself, his suburban train having been behind time, had reached the office after Ashby had come and gone. Charlotte stood perplexed; then she decided to telephone to her mother-in-law. Of course Kenneth, on the eve of a month's absence, must have gone to see his mother. The mere fact that the children—in spite of his vague objections—would certainly have to be left with old Mrs. Ashby, made it obvious that he would have all sorts of matters to decide with her. At another time Charlotte might have felt a little hurt at being excluded from their conference, but nothing mattered now but that she had won the day, that her husband was still hers and not another woman's. Gaily she called up Mrs. Ashby, heard her friendly voice, and began: "Well, did Kenneth's news surprise you? What do you think of our elopement?"

Almost instantly, before Mrs. Ashby could answer, Charlotte knew what her reply would be. Mrs. Ashby had not seen her son, she had had no word from him and did not know what her daughter-in-law meant. Charlotte stood silent in the intensity of her surprise. "But then, where *has* he been?" she thought. Then, recovering herself, she explained their sudden decision to Mrs. Ashby, and in doing so, gradually regained her own self-confidence, her conviction that nothing could ever again come between Kenneth and herself. Mrs. Ashby took the news calmly and approvingly. She, too, had thought that Kenneth looked worried and over-tired, and she agreed with her daughter-in-law that in such cases change was the surest remedy. "I'm always so glad when he gets away. Elsie hated traveling; she was always finding pretexts to prevent his going anywhere. With you, thank goodness, it's different." Nor was Mrs. Ashby surprised at his not having had time to let her know of his departure. He must have been in a rush from the moment the decision was taken; but no doubt he'd drop in before dinner. Five minutes' talk was really all they needed. "I hope you'll gradually cure Kenneth of his mania for going over and over a question that could be settled in a dozen words. He never used to be like that, and if he carried the habit into his professional work he'd soon lose all his clients. . . . Yes, do come in for a minute, dear, if you have time; no doubt he'll turn up while you're here." The tonic ring of Mrs. Ashby's voice echoed on reassuringly in the silent room while Charlotte continued her preparations.

Toward seven the telephone rang, and she darted to it. Now she would know! But it was only from the conscientious secretary, to say that Mr. Ashby hadn't been back, or sent any word, and before the office closed she thought she ought to let Mrs. Ashby know. "Oh, that's all right. Thanks a lot!" Charlotte called out cheerfully, and hung up the receiver with a trembling hand. But perhaps by this time, she reflected, he was at his mother's. She shut her drawers and cupboards, put on her hat and coat and called up to the nursery that she was going out for a minute to see the children's grandmother.

Mrs. Ashby lived nearby, and during her brief walk through the cold spring dusk Charlotte imagined that every advancing figure was her husband's. But she did not meet him on the way, and when she entered the house she found her mother-in-law alone. Kenneth had neither telephoned nor come. Old Mrs. Ashby sat by her bright fire, her knitting needles flashing steadily through her active old hands, and her mere bodily presence gave reassurance to Charlotte. Yes, it was certainly odd that Kenneth had gone off for the whole day without letting any of them know; but, after all, it was to be expected. A busy lawyer held so many threads in his hands that any sudden change of plan would oblige him to make all sorts of unforeseen arrangements and adjustments. He might have gone to see some client in the suburbs and been detained there; his mother remembered his telling her that he had charge of the legal business of a queer old recluse somewhere in New Jersey, who was immensely rich but too mean to have a telephone. Very likely Kenneth had been stranded there.

But Charlotte felt her nervousness gaining on her. When Mrs. Ashby asked her at what hour they were sailing the next day and she had to say she didn't know—that Kenneth had simply sent her word he was going to take their passages—the uttering of the words again brought home to her the strangeness of the situation. Even Mrs. Ashby conceded that it was odd; but she immediately added that it only showed what a rush he was in.

"But, mother, it's nearly eight o'clock! He must realize that I've got to know when we're starting tomorrow."

"Oh, the boat probably doesn't sail till evening. Sometimes they have to wait till midnight for the tide. Kenneth's probably counting on that. After all, he has a level head."

Charlotte stood up. "It's not that. Something has happened to him."

Mrs. Ashby took off her spectacles and rolled up her knitting. "If you begin to let yourself imagine things—"

"Aren't you in the least anxious?"

"I never am till I have to be. I wish you'd ring for dinner, my dear. You'll stay and dine? He's sure to drop in here on his way home."

Charlotte called up her own house. No, the maid said, Mr. Ashby hadn't come in and hadn't telephoned. She would tell him as soon as he came that Mrs. Ashby was dining at his mother's. Charlotte followed her mother-in-law into the dining room and sat with parched throat before her empty plate, while Mrs. Ashby dealt calmly and efficiently with a short but carefully prepared repast. "You'd better eat something, child, or you'll be as bad as Kenneth. . . . Yes, a little more asparagus, please, Jane."

She insisted on Charlotte's drinking a glass of sherry and nibbling a bit of toast; then they returned to the drawing room, where the fire had been made up, and the cushions in Mrs. Ashby's armchair shaken out and smoothed. How safe and familiar it all looked; and out there, somewhere in the uncertainty and mystery of the night, lurked the answer to the two women's conjectures, like an indistinguishable figure prowling on the threshold.

At last Charlotte got up and said: "I'd better go back. At this hour Kenneth will certainly go straight home."

Mrs. Ashby smiled indulgently. "It's not very late, my dear. It doesn't take two sparrows long to dine."

"It's after nine." Charlotte bent down to kiss her. "The fact is, I can't keep still."

Mrs. Ashby pushed aside her work and rested her two hands on the arms of her chair. "I'm going with you," she said, helping herself up.

Charlotte protested that it was too late, that it was not necessary, that she would call up as soon as Kenneth came in, but Mrs. Ashby had already rung for her maid. She was slightly lame, and stood resting on her stick while her wraps were brought. "If Mr. Kenneth turns up, tell him he'll find me at his own house," she instructed the maid as the two women got into the taxi which had been summoned. During the short drive Charlotte gave thanks that she was not returning home alone. There was something warm and substantial in the mere fact of Mrs. Ashby's nearness, something that corresponded with the clearness of her eyes and the texture of her fresh firm complexion. As the taxi drew up she laid her hand encouragingly on Charlotte's. "You'll see; there'll be a message."

The door opened at Charlotte's ring and the two entered. Charlotte's heart beat excitedly; the stimulus of her mother-in-law's confidence was beginning to flow through her veins.

"You'll see—you'll see," Mrs. Ashby repeated.

The maid who opened the door said no, Mr. Ashby had not come in, and there had been no message from him.

"You're sure the telephone's not out of order?" his mother suggested; and the maid said, well, it certainly wasn't half an hour ago; but she'd just go and ring up to make sure. She disappeared, and Charlotte turned to take off her hat and cloak. As she did so her eyes lit on the hall table, and there lay a gray envelope, her husband's name faintly traced on it. "Oh!" she cried out, suddenly aware that for the first time in months she had entered her house without wondering if one of the gray letters would be there.

"What is it, my dear?" Mrs. Ashby asked with a glance of surprise.

Charlotte did not answer. She took up the envelope and stood staring at it as if she could force her gaze to penetrate to what was within. Then an idea occurred to her. She turned and held out the envelope to her mother-in-law.

"Do you know that writing?" she asked.

Mrs. Ashby took the letter. She had to feel with her other hand for her eyeglasses, and when she had adjusted them she lifted the envelope to the light. "Why!" she exclaimed; and then stopped. Charlotte noticed that the letter shook in her usually firm hand. "But this is addressed to Kenneth," Mrs. Ashby said at length, in a low voice. Her tone seemed to imply that she felt her daughter-in-law's question to be slightly indiscreet.

"Yes, but no matter," Charlotte spoke with sudden decision. "I want to know—do you know the writing?"

Mrs. Ashby handed back the letter. "No," she said distinctly.

The two women had turned into the library. Charlotte switched on the electric light and shut the door. She still held the envelope in her hand.

"I'm going to open it," she announced.

She caught her mother-in-law's startled glance. "But, dearest—a letter not addressed to you? My dear, you can't!"

"As if I cared about that—now!" She continued to look intently at Mrs. Ashby. "This letter may tell me where Kenneth is."

Mrs. Ashby's glossy bloom was effaced by a quick pallor; her firm cheeks seemed to shrink and wither. "Why should it? What makes you believe— It can't possibly—"

Charlotte held her eyes steadily on that altered face. "Ah, then you *do* know the writing?" she flashed back.

"Know the writing? How should I? With all my son's correspondents. . . . What I do know is—" Mrs. Ashby broke off and looked at her daughter-in-law entreatingly, almost timidly.

Charlotte caught her by the wrist. "Mother! What do you know? Tell me! You must!"

"That I don't believe any good ever came of a woman's opening her husband's letters behind his back."

The words sounded to Charlotte's irritated ears as flat as a phrase culled from a book of moral axioms. She laughed impatiently and dropped her mother-in-law's wrist. "Is that all? No good can come of this letter, opened or unopened. I know that well enough. But whatever ill comes, I mean to find out what's in it." Her hands had been trembling as they held the envelope, but now they grew firm, and her voice also. She still gazed intently at Mrs. Ashby. "This is the ninth letter addressed in the same hand that has come for Kenneth since we've been married. Always these same gray envelopes. I've kept count of them because after each one he has been like a man who has had some dreadful shock. It takes him hours to shake off their effect. I've told him so. I've told him I must know from whom they come, because I can see they're killing him. He won't answer my questions; he says he can't tell me anything about the letters; but last night he promised to go away with me—to get away from them."

Mrs. Ashby, with shaking steps, had gone to one of the armchairs and sat down in it, her head drooping forward on her breast. "Ah," she murmured.

"So now you understand—"

"Did he tell you it was to get away from them?"

"He said, to get away—to get away. He was sobbing so that he could hardly speak. But I told him I knew that was why."

"And what did he say?"

"He took me in his arms and said he'd go wherever I wanted."

"Ah, thank God!" said Mrs. Ashby. There was a silence, during which she continued to sit with bowed head, and eyes averted from her daughter-in-law. At last she looked up and spoke. "Are you sure there have been as many as nine?"

"Perfectly. This is the ninth. I've kept count."

"And he has absolutely refused to explain?"

"Absolutely."

Mrs. Ashby spoke through pale contracted lips. "When did they begin to come? Do you remember?"

Charlotte laughed again. "Remember? The first one came the night we got back from our honeymoon."

"All that time?" Mrs. Ashby lifted her head and spoke with sudden energy. "Then—yes, open it."

The words were so unexpected that Charlotte felt the blood in her temples, and her hands began to tremble again. She tried to slip her finger under the flap of the envelope, but it was so tightly stuck that she had to hunt on her husband's writing table for his ivory letter opener. As she pushed about the familiar objects his own hands had so lately touched, they sent through her the icy chill emanating from the little personal effects of someone newly dead. In the deep silence of the room the tearing of the paper as she slit the envelope sounded like a human cry. She drew out the sheet and carried it to the lamp.

"Well?" Mrs. Ashby asked below her breath.

Charlotte did not move or answer. She was bending over the page with wrinkled brows, holding it nearer and nearer to the light. Her sight must be blurred, or else dazzled by the reflection of the lamplight on the smooth surface of the paper, for, strain her eyes as she would, she could discern only a few faint strokes, so faint and faltering as to be nearly undecipherable.

"I can't make it out," she said.

"What do you mean, dear?"

"The writing's too indistinct. . . . Wait."

She went back to the table and, sitting down close to Kenneth's reading lamp, slipped the letter under a magnifying glass. All this time she was aware that her mother-in-law was watching her intently.

"Well?" Mrs. Ashby breathed.

"Well, it's no clearer. I can't read it."

"You mean the paper is an absolute blank?"

"No, not quite. There is writing on it. I can make out something like 'mine'——oh, and 'come.' It might be 'come.'"

Mrs. Ashby stood up abruptly. Her face was even paler than before. She advanced to the table and, resting her two hands on it, drew a deep breath. "Let me see," she said, as if forcing herself to a hateful effort.

Charlotte felt the contagion of her whiteness. "She knows," she thought. She pushed the letter across the table. Her mother-in-law lowered her head over it in silence, but without touching it with her pale wrinkled hands.

Charlotte stood watching her as she herself, when she had tried to read the letter, had been watched by Mrs. Ashby. The latter fumbled for her glasses, held them to her eyes, and bent still closer to the outspread page, in order, as it seemed, to avoid touching it. The light of the lamp fell directly on her old face, and Charlotte reflected what depths of the unknown may lurk under the clearest and most candid lineaments. She had never seen her mother-in-law's features express any but simple and sound emotions—cordiality, amusement, a kindly sympathy; now and again a flash of wholesome anger. Now they seemed to wear a look of fear and hatred, of incredulous dismay and almost cringing defiance. It was as if the spirits warring within her had distorted her face to their own likeness. At length she raised her head. "I can't—I can't," she said in a voice of childish distress.

"You can't make it out either?"

She shook her head, and Charlotte saw two tears roll down her cheeks.

"Familiar as the writing is to you?" Charlotte insisted with twitching lips.

Mrs. Ashby did not take up the challenge. "I can make out nothing—nothing."

"But you do know the writing?"

Mrs. Ashby lifted her head timidly; her anxious eyes stole with a glance of apprehension around the quiet familiar room. "How can I tell? I was startled at first. . . ."

"Startled by the resemblance?"

"Well, I thought—"

"You'd better say it out, mother! You knew at once it was *her* writing?"

"Oh, wait, my dear—wait."

"Wait for what?"

Mrs. Ashby looked up; her eyes, traveling slowly past Charlotte, were lifted to the blank wall behind her son's writing table.

Charlotte, following the glance, burst into a shrill laugh of accusation. "I needn't wait any longer! You've answered me now! You're looking straight at the wall where her picture used to hang!"

Mrs. Ashby lifted her hand with a murmur of warning. "Sh-h."

"Oh, you needn't imagine that anything can ever frighten me again!" Charlotte cried.

Her mother-in-law still leaned against the table. Her lips moved plaintively. "But we're going mad—we're both going mad. We both know such things are impossible."

Her daughter-in-law looked at her with a pitying stare. "I've known for a long time now that everything was possible."

"Even this?"

"Yes, exactly this."

"But this letter—after all, there's nothing in this letter—"

"Perhaps there would be to him. How can I tell? I remember his saying to me once that if you were used to a handwriting the faintest stroke of it became legible. Now I see what he meant. He *was* used to it."

"But the few strokes that I can make out are so pale. No one could possibly read that letter."

Charlotte laughed again. "I suppose everything's pale about a ghost," she said stridently.

"Oh, my child—my child—don't say it!"

"Why shouldn't I say it, when even the bare walls cry it out? What difference does it make if her letters are illegible to you and me? If even you can see her face on that blank wall, why shouldn't he read her writing on this blank paper? Don't you see that she's everywhere in this house, and the closer to him because to everyone else she's become invisible?" Charlotte dropped into a chair and covered her face with her hands. A turmoil of sobbing shook her from head to foot. At length a touch on her shoulder made her look up, and she saw her mother-in-law bending over her. Mrs. Ashby's face seemed to have grown still smaller and more wasted, but it had resumed its usual quiet look. Through all her tossing anguish, Charlotte felt the impact of that resolute spirit.

"Tomorrow—tomorrow. You'll see. There'll be some explanation tomorrow."

Charlotte cut her short. "An explanation? Who's going to give it, I wonder?"

Mrs. Ashby drew back and straightened herself heroically. "Kenneth himself will," she cried out in a strong voice. Charlotte said nothing, and the old woman went on: "But meanwhile we must act; we must notify the police. Now, without a moment's delay. We must do everything—everything."

Charlotte stood up slowly and stiffly; her joints felt as cramped as an old woman's. "Exactly as if we thought it could do any good to do anything?"

Resolutely Mrs. Ashby cried: "Yes!" and Charlotte went up to the telephone and unhooked the receiver.

THE STOKER

Franz Kafka

❦

Translated by Michael Hofmann

As the seventeen-year-old Karl Rossmann, who had been sent to America by his unfortunate parents because a maid had seduced him and had a child by him, sailed slowly into New York harbour, he suddenly saw the Statue of Liberty, which had already been in view for some time, as though in an intenser sunlight. The sword in her hand seemed only just to have been raised aloft, and the unchained winds blew about her form.

"So high," he said to himself, and quite forgetting to disembark, he found himself gradually pushed up against the railing by the massing throng of porters.

A young man with whom he had struck up a slight acquaintance during the crossing said to him in passing: "Well, don't you want to get off yet?" "I'm all ready," said Karl laughing to him, and in his exuberance and because he was a strong lad, he raised his suitcase on to his shoulder. But as he watched his acquaintance disappearing along with the others, swinging a cane, he realized that he had left his umbrella down in the ship. So he hurriedly asked his acquaintance, who seemed less than overjoyed about it, to be so good as to wait by his suitcase for a moment, took a quick look around for his subsequent orientation, and hurried off. Below deck, he found to his annoyance that a passage that would have considerably shortened the way for him was for the first time barred, probably something to do with the fact that all the passengers were disembarking, and so he was forced instead to make his way through numerous little rooms, along continually curving passages and down tiny flights of stairs, one after the other, and then through an empty room with an abandoned desk in it until, eventually, only ever having gone this way once or twice previously, and then in the company of others, he found that he was totally and utterly lost. Not knowing what to do, not seeing anyone, and hearing only the scraping of thousands of human feet overhead and the last, faraway wheezings of the engine, which had already been turned off, he began without thinking to knock at the little door to which he had come on his wanderings. "It's open!" came a voice from within, and Karl felt real relief as he opened the door. "Why are you banging about on the door like a madman?" asked an enormous man, barely looking at Karl. Through some kind of overhead light-shaft, a dim light, long since used up in the higher reaches of the ship, fell into the wretched cabin, in which a bed, a wardrobe, a chair and the man were all standing close together, as though in storage. "I've lost my way," said Karl. "I never quite realized on the crossing what a terribly big ship this is." "Well, you're right about that," said the man with some pride, and carried on tinkering with the lock of a small suitcase, repeatedly shutting it with both hands to listen to the sound of the lock as it snapped shut. "Why don't you come in," the man went on, "don't stand around outside." "Aren't I bothering you?" asked Karl. "Pah, how could you bother me?" "Are you German?" Karl asked to reassure himself, as he'd heard a lot about the dangers for new arrivals in America, especially coming from Irishmen. "Yes, yes," said the man. Still Karl hesitated. Then the man abruptly grabbed the door handle, and pulling it to, swept Karl into the room with him. "I hate it when people stand in the corridor and watch me," said the man, going back to work on his suitcase, "the world and his wife go by outside peering in, it's quite intolerable." "But the passage outside is completely deserted," said Karl, who was standing squeezed uncomfortably against the bedpost. "Yes, now," said the man. "But now is what matters," thought Karl. "He is an unreasonable man." "Lie down on the bed, you'll have more room that way," said the man. Karl awkwardly clambered on to the bed, and had to laugh out loud about his first vain attempt to mount it. No sooner was he on it, though, than he cried: "Oh God, I've quite forgotten all about my suitcase!" "Where is it?" "Up on deck, an acquaintance is keeping an eye on it for me. What was his name now?" And from a secret pocket that his mother had sewn into the lining of his jacket for the crossing, he pulled a calling-card: "Butterbaum, Franz Butterbaum." "Is the suitcase important to you?" "Of course." "Well then, so why did you give it to a stranger?" "I forgot my umbrella down below and went to get it, but I didn't want to lug my suitcase down with me. And now I've gone and gotten completely lost." "Are you on your own? There's no one with you?" "Yes, I'm on my own." I should stay by this man, thought Karl, I may not find a better friend in a hurry. "And now you've lost your suitcase. Not to mention the umbrella," and the man sat down on the chair, as though Karl's predicament was beginning to interest him. "I don't think the suitcase is lost yet." "Think all you like," said the man, and scratched vigorously at his short, thick, black hair. "But you should know the different ports have different morals. In Hamburg your man Butterbaum might have minded your suitcase for you, but over here, there's probably no trace of either of them any more." "Then I'd better go back up right away," said Karl and tried to see how he might leave. "You're staying put," said the man, and gave him a push in the chest, that sent him sprawling back on the bed. "But why?" asked Karl angrily. "There's no point," said the man, "in a little while I'll be going up myself, and we can go together. Either your suitcase will have been stolen and that's too bad and you can mourn its loss till the end of your days, or else the fellow's still minding it, in which case he's a fool and he might as well go on minding it, or he's an honest man and just left it there, and we'll find it more easily when the ship's emptied. Same thing with your umbrella." "Do you know your way around the ship?" asked Karl suspiciously, and it seemed to him that the otherwise attractive idea that his belongings would be more easily found on the empty ship had some kind of hidden catch. "I'm the ship's stoker," said the man. "You're the ship's stoker," cried Karl joyfully, as though that surpassed all expectations, and propped himself up on his elbow to take a closer look at the man. "Just outside the room where I slept with the Slovak there was a little porthole, and through it we could see into the engine-room." "Yes, that's where I was working," said the stoker. "I've always been terribly interested in machinery," said Karl, still following a particular line of thought, "and I'm sure I would have become an engineer if I hadn't had to go to America." "Why did you have to go to America?" "Ah, never mind!" said Karl, dismissing the whole story with a wave of his hand. And he smiled at the stoker, as though asking him to take a lenient view of whatever it was he hadn't told him. "I expect there's a good reason," said the stoker, and it was hard to tell whether he still wanted to hear it or not. "And now I might as well become a stoker," said Karl. "My parents don't care what becomes of me." "My job will be going," said the stoker, and coolly thrust his hands into his pockets and kicked out his legs, which were clad in rumpled, leather-like iron-grey trousers, on to the bed to stretch them. Karl was forced to move nearer to the wall. "You're leaving the ship?" "Yup, we're off this very day." "But what for? Don't you like it?" "Well, it's circumstances really, it's not always whether you like something or not that matters. Anyway you're right, I don't like it. You're probably not serious about saying you could become a stoker, but that's precisely how you get to be one. I'd strongly advise you against it myself. If you were intending to study in Europe, why not study here. Universities in America are incomparably better." "That may be," said Karl, "but I can hardly afford to study. I did once read about someone who spent his days working in a business and his nights studying, and in the end he became a doctor and I think a burgomaster, but you need a lot of stamina for that, don't you? I'm afraid I don't have that. Besides, I was never especially good at school, and wasn't at all sorry when I had to leave. Schools here are supposed to be even stricter. I hardly know any English. And there's a lot of bias against foreigners here too, I believe." "Have you had experience of that too? That's good. Then you're the man for me. You see, this is a German ship, it belongs to the Hamburg America Line, everyone who works on it should be German. So then why is the senior engineer Rumanian? Schubal, his name is. It's incredible. And that bastard bossing Germans around on a German ship. Don't get the idea"—he was out of breath, and his hands flapped—"don't you believe that I'm complaining for the hell of it. I know you don't have any influence, and you're just a poor fellow yourself. But it's intolerable." And he beat the table with his fist several times, not taking his eyes off it as he did so. "I've served on so many ships in my time"—and here he reeled off a list of twenty names as if it was a single word, Karl felt quite giddy—"and with distinction, I was praised, I was a worker of the kind my captains liked, I even served on the same clipper for several years"—he rose, as if that had been the high point of his life—"and here on this bathtub, where everything is done by rote, where they've no use for imagination—here I'm suddenly no good, here I'm always getting in Schubal's way, I'm lazy, I deserve to get kicked out, they only pay me my wages out of the kindness of their hearts. Does that make any sense to you? Not me." "You mustn't stand for that," said Karl in agitation. He had almost forgotten he was in the uncertain hold of a ship moored to the coast of an unknown continent, that's how much he felt at home on the stoker's bed. "Have you been to see the captain? Have you taken your case to him?" "Ah leave off, forget it. I don't want you here. You don't listen to what I say, and then you start giving me advice. How can I go to the captain?" And the stoker sat down again, exhausted, and buried his face in his hands.

"But it's the best advice I know," Karl said to himself. And it seemed to him that he would have done better to fetch his suitcase, instead of offering advice which was only ignored anyway. When his father had given the suitcase into his possession, he had mused in jest: I wonder how long you'll manage to hang on to it for? And now that expensive suitcase might already be lost in earnest. His only consolation was the fact that his father couldn't possibly learn about his present fix, even if he tried to make inquiries. The shipping company would only be able to confirm that he had reached New York safely. But Karl felt sad that there were things in the suitcase that he had hardly used, although he should have done, he should have changed his shirt for example, some time ago. He had tried to make false economies; now, at the beginning of his career, when he most needed to be in clean clothes, he would have to appear in a dirty shirt. Those were fine prospects. Apart from that, the loss of his suitcase wasn't so serious, because the suit he was wearing was better than the one in the suitcase, which was really nothing better than a sort of emergency suit, which his mother had even had to mend just before his departure. Then he remembered there was a piece of Verona salami in the suitcase as well, which his mother had given him as a last-minute gift, but of which he had only been able to eat a tiny portion, since for the whole crossing he had had very little appetite and the soup that was doled out in the steerage had been plenty for him. Now, though, he would have liked to have had the salami handy, to make a present of it to the stoker, because his sort are easily won over by some small present or other. Karl knew that from the example of his father who won over all the junior employees he had to deal with by handing out cigars to them. Now the only thing Karl had left to give was his money, and if he had indeed already lost his suitcase, he wanted to leave that untouched for the moment. His thoughts returned to the suitcase, and now he really couldn't understand why, having watched it so carefully for the whole crossing that his watchfulness had almost cost him his sleep, he had now permitted that same suitcase to be taken from him so simply. He recalled the five nights during which he had incessantly suspected the little Slovak, who was sleeping a couple of places to his left, of having intentions on his suitcase. That Slovak had just been waiting for Karl, finally, sapped by exhaustion, to drop off for one instant, so that he could pull the suitcase over to himself by means of a long rod which he spent his days endlessly playing or practising with. That Slovak looked innocent enough by day, but no sooner did night fall than he would get up time and again from his bed and cast sad looks across at Karl's suitcase. Karl saw this quite clearly, someone, with the natural apprehensiveness of the emigrant, was forever lighting a little lamp somewhere, even though that was against the ship's regulations, and trying by its light to decipher the incomprehensible pamphlets of the emigration agencies. If there happened to be one such light close by, then Karl would be able to snooze a little, but if it was some way off, or even more if it was dark, then he had to keep his eyes open. His efforts had exhausted him, and now it seemed they might have been in vain. That Butterbaum had better look out, if he should ever run into him somewhere.

At that moment, the complete silence that had so far prevailed was broken by the distant sound of the pattering of children's feet, that grew louder as it approached, and then became the firm strides of men. They were obviously walking in single file, in the narrow passage, and a jangling as of weapons became audible. Karl, who was almost on the point of stretching out on the bed and falling into a sleep freed of all worries about suitcase and Slovaks, was startled up and nudged the stoker to get his attention at last, because the head of the column seemed to have reached the door. "That's the ship's band," said the stoker. "They've been playing up on deck, and now they're packing up. That means everything's done, and we can go. Come on." He took Karl by the hand, at the last moment removed a picture of the Virgin from the wall over the bed, crammed it into his top pocket, picked up his suitcase and hurriedly left the cabin with Karl.

"Now I'm going to the purser's office to give those gents a piece of my mind. There's no one left, no point in hanging back any more." This the stoker repeated with variations in various ways and he also attempted to crush a rat that crossed their path with a sideways swipe of his boot, but he only succeeded in propelling it into its hole which it had reached just in time. He was generally slow in his movements, for if his legs were long they were also heavy.

They came to a part of the kitchen where a few girls in dirty aprons—which they were spattering on purpose—were cleaning crockery in large vats. The stoker called out to one Lina, put his arm around her hip, and walked with her for a few steps, as she pressed herself flirtatiously against him. "We're just off to get paid, do you want to come?" he asked. "Why should I bother, just bring me the money yourself," she replied, slipped round his arm and ran off. "Where did you get the good-looking boy from?" she added, not really expecting an answer. The other girls, who had stopped their work to listen, all laughed.

They for their part carried on and reached a door that had a little pediment above it, supported on little gilded caryatids. For something on a ship, it looked distinctly lavish. Karl realized he had never been to this part of the ship, which had probably been reserved for the use of first- and second-class passengers during the crossing, but now the separating doors had been thrown open prior to the great ship's cleaning. They had in fact encountered a few men carrying brooms over their shoulders who greeted the stoker. Karl was amazed at all the bustle, between decks where he had been he had had no sense of it at all. Along the passages ran electrical wires, and one continually heard the ringing of a little bell.

The stoker knocked respectfully on the door, and when there was a shout of "Come in" he motioned Karl to step in and not be afraid. Karl did so too, but remained standing in the doorway. Through the three windows of the room he could see the waves outside and his heart pounded as he watched their joyful movement, as though he hadn't just spent the last five days doing nothing else. Great ships kept crossing paths, and yielded to the motion of the waves only insofar as their bulk allowed. If you narrowed your eyes, the ships seemed to be staggering under their own weight. On their masts were long, but very narrow flags, which were pulled tight by their speed through the air, but still managed to be quite fidgety. Greeting shots rang out, probably from warships, the guns of one such ship not too far away and quite dazzling with the sun on its armour, seemed soothed by the safe and smooth, if not entirely horizontal movement. The smaller ships and boats could only be seen if they were some distance away, at least from the doorway, multitudes of them running into the gaps between the big ships. And behind it all stood New York, looking at Karl with the hundred thousand windows of its skyscrapers. Yes, you knew where you were in this room.

Seated at a round table were three men, one a ship's officer in a blue marine uniform, the two others were port officials dressed in black American uniforms. On the table lay a pile of various documents, which were perused first by the officer with his pen in hand and then passed on to the other two, who would read, copy and file them away in their briefcases whenever one of them, making an almost incessant clicking noise with his teeth, wasn't dictating something in protocol to his colleague.

At a desk by the window, his back to the door, sat a smaller man who was doing something with great ledgers that were lined up in front of him, at eye level, on a stout bookshelf. Beside him was an open cash till, which at first glance anyway appeared to be empty.

The second window was untenanted and afforded the best views. But in the proximity of the third stood two gentlemen, conducting a muffled conversation. One of them was leaning beside the window, he too in ship's uniform, toying with the handle of a sabre. His collocutor was facing the window and by occasional movements revealed some part of a row of medals on the other's chest. He was in a civilian suit and had a thin bamboo cane, which, as he had both hands on his hips, stood out like a sabre as well.

Karl had little time to take in all of this, because a servant soon approached the stoker and, frowning, as though he didn't belong there, asked him what he was doing. The stoker replied, as quietly as he could, that he wanted a word with the chief cashier. The servant declined this wish with a movement of his hand but, nevertheless, on the tips of his toes, and giving the round table a wide berth, went up to the man with the ledgers. The man—it was quite evident—froze at the servant's words, then finally turned to face the man who wanted to speak to him, but only in order to make a vehement gesture of refusal to the stoker, and then, to be on the safe side, to the servant as well. Whereupon the servant went back to the stoker and in a confiding sort of tone said: "Now get the hell out of here!"

On hearing this reply the stoker looked down at Karl, as if he were his own heart, to whom he was making silent plaint. Without any more ado, Karl broke away, ran right across the room actually brushing the officer's chair on his way, the servant swooped after him with arms outspread, like a ratcatcher, but Karl was first to the chief cashier's table, and gripped it with both hands in case the servant should attempt to haul him away.

Naturally, with that the whole room suddenly sprang to life. The ship's officer leapt up from the table, the men from the port authority looked on calmly and watchfully, the two men by the window drew together, while the servant, who believed it was not his place to carry on when his superiors were themselves taking an interest, withdrew. Standing by the door, the stoker waited nervously for the moment at which his assistance might become necessary. Finally the chief cashier swung round to the right in his swivel chair.

Karl reached into his secret pocket, which he had no fear of revealing to the eyes of these gentlemen, and pulled out his passport which he opened and laid out on the table, by way of an introduction. The chief cashier seemed unimpressed by the document, flicking it aside with two fingers, whereupon Karl, as though this formality had been satisfactorily concluded, pocketed his passport once more. "I should like to say," he began, "that in my opinion the stoker here has been the victim of an injustice. There is a certain Schubal who oppresses him. He himself has served, to complete satisfaction, on many ships, which he is able to name to you. He is industrious, good at his work and it's really hard to understand why, on this of all ships, where the work isn't excessively onerous, the way it is for instance on clipper ships, he should let anyone down. There can only be some slander that is in the way of his advancement, and is robbing him of the recognition he should otherwise certainly not lack for. I have kept my remarks general, let him voice his particular complaints himself." Karl had addressed all the men in the office, because they were all listening, and the odds that one of their number should prove just were much better than that the chief cashier should be the man. Cunningly, Karl had failed to say that he had only known the stoker for a short time. He would have spoken far better if he hadn't been confused by the red face of the man with the cane, whom he could see properly, really for the first time, from his new position.

"Every word he says is true," said the stoker before anyone could ask, even before anyone looked at him. Such precipitateness on the stoker's part might have cost him dear, had not the man with the medals, who, as it dawned on Karl, must be the captain, already decided for himself that he would listen to the stoker's case. He put out a hand and called out: "Come here!" in a voice so firm you could have beaten it with a hammer. Now everything depended on the conduct of the stoker, for Karl had no doubt as to the rightness of his cause.

Happily, it became clear that the stoker was well versed in the ways of the world. With exemplary calmness he plucked from his little case a bundle of papers and a notebook, and, completely ignoring the chief cashier as though there was no question of doing anything else, went straight to the captain, and laid out his evidence on the window-sill. The chief cashier had no option but to join them there himself. "That man is a well-known querulant," he explained. "He spends more time in the office than in the engine-room. He has driven that easy going man Schubal to a state of despair. Listen, you!" he turned to the stoker, "You're really taking your importunity a stage too far. The number of times you've been thrown out of the accounts offices, quite rightly, with your completely and utterly, and with no exception, unjustified claims! The number of times you've come from there straight to the head office here! The number of times we've taken you aside and quietly reminded you that Schubal is your immediate superior, that you work to him and must deal directly with him! And now you barge in here in the presence of the captain himself, and you start pestering him, you've even had the neck to bring with you this well-rehearsed spokesman for your stale grudges, in the form of this little chap here, whom I've never even seen before."

Karl had to restrain himself forcibly. But there was the captain, saying: "Let's just listen to the man, shall we. Schubal's been getting a little too independent for my liking lately, which isn't to say that I accept your case." This last remark was meant for the stoker, it was only natural that he couldn't take his part at once, but things seemed to be going well. The stoker embarked on his explanations, and right at the outset he even managed to refer to Schubal as "Mr. Schubal". What joy Karl felt, standing by the chief cashier's now deserted desk, repeatedly pushing down a little pair of scales, for sheer delight. Mr. Schubal is unjust. Mr. Schubal favours the foreigners. Mr. Schubal dismissed the stoker from the engine-room and made him clean lavatories, which was surely not part of his job as stoker. On one occasion, the diligence of Mr. Schubal was alleged to be more apparent than real. At that point Karl fixed the captain as hard as he could, frankly, as if he were his colleague, lest he be influenced by the stoker's somewhat clumsy way of expressing himself. Because, though he said much, nothing of substance was revealed, and while the captain went on looking straight ahead, showing in his expression his determination to hear the stoker out for once, the other men were becoming restless and the stoker's voice was now no longer in sole command of the room, which did not bode well. First of

all, the man in the civilian suit activated his cane, and began softly tap-
ping it on the floor. Of course the other men couldn't help looking in
his direction now and again. The men from the port authority, obviously in a hurry, reached for their files and went back to looking through
them, though in a slightly distant manner; the ship's officer moved back
to his table; and the chief cashier, scenting victory, heaved a deep and
ironic sigh. The only one unaffected by the general air of distraction
that was setting in was the servant, who had some sympathy with the
sufferings of the underdog at the hands of the powerful, and nodded
earnestly at Karl as though to assure him of something.

In the meantime the life of the harbour was going on outside the
windows. A flat barge carrying a mountain of barrels, which must have
been miraculously laden so as not to start rolling, passed by and plunged
the room into near-darkness. Little motorboats, which Karl would have
been in good position to examine if he'd had the leisure, pursued their
dead straight courses, responsive to every twitch of the hands of the men
standing at their wheels. Strange floats surfaced occasionally from the
turbulent water, only to become swamped again and sink astonishingly
from sight. Boats from the great liners were rowed ashore by toiling
sailors, full of passengers who obediently kept their places and sat quietly and expectantly, even though a few couldn't refrain from turning
their heads this way and that to look at the change of scene. All was
endless movement, a restlessness communicated by the restless element
to the helpless men and their works.

Everything enjoined haste, precision, clarity of representation—and
what was the stoker doing? He was talking himself into a lather, his
trembling hands could no longer hold the papers by the window-sill. He
was deluged with complaints about Schubal that came to him from every
direction, and one of which in his opinion would have sufficed to completely bury Schubal, but all he could put across to the captain was just
a mishmash of all of them. The man with the bamboo cane had begun
whistling quietly up at the ceiling, the men from the port authority had

the officer at their table again, and showed no sign of relinquishing him, the chief cashier was obviously only constrained by the calm of the captain from the intervention he was all too eager to make. The sergeant was waiting at attention for an imminent order from the captain regarding the stoker.

At that Karl could no longer stand idly by. He walked slowly up to the group, rapidly considering how best to approach the affair. It was really high time to stop. Much more of it and the two of them might easily find themselves slung out of the office. The captain was a good man and he might at that very moment have some particular grounds, so Karl thought, to show himself to be a fair master, but for all that he wasn't a musical instrument to be played into the ground—which was precisely how the stoker was treating him, albeit from a soul that was illimitably indignant.

So Karl said to the stoker: "You'll have to explain it all much more clearly and simply, the captain can't respond to what you're telling him now. In order to be able to follow your account, he would have to know the first and last names of every single machinist and errand boy. Put your complaints in order, say the most important thing first, and then go through the others in order of decreasing importance, perhaps you won't even be called upon to mention most of them that way. You always explained it so clearly to me." If America was the sort of place where they stole suitcases then the occasional lie was permissible, he thought in extenuation.

If only it had helped! But was it not already too late? The stoker broke off the moment he heard the familiar voice, but with eyes dimmed with the tears of offended male honour, of frightful memories and the dire need of the moment, he barely even recognized Karl. How could he, Karl suddenly thought as the two of them silently confronted one another, how could he suddenly change his whole manner of speaking, it must seem to him that he had already said all there was to say, without anything to show for it, and, conversely, that he had said nothing at all, and he couldn't presume that the gentlemen would willingly listen to everything. And at such a moment, his solitary supporter, Karl, comes along wanting to give him a piece of advice, but instead only shows that all is lost.

"If only I'd come earlier, instead of looking out of the window," Karl said to himself, he lowered his gaze before the stoker, and smacked his hands against his trouser seams in acknowledgement that all hope was gone.

But the stoker misunderstood him, he probably sensed some veiled reproach from Karl and hoping to reason him out of it, he now, to cap everything, began quarrelling with Karl. Now: with the gentlemen at the round table incensed at the pointless noise which was interrupting them in their important work, with the chief cashier increasingly baffled by the captain's patience and on the point of erupting, with the servant once more back in the camp of his masters, wildly eyeing the stoker, and finally, even the man with the little bamboo cane, to whom the captain sent friendly looks from time to time, seeming completely indifferent to the stoker, yes, even disgusted by him, and pulling out a little notebook, and clearly engaged with something entirely different, continually looking between the notebook and Karl.

"I know, I know," said Karl, who had difficulty in warding off the tirade which the stoker now directed at him, but still keeping a friendly smile on his face. "You're right, you're right, I never doubted that." He felt like grasping the gesticulating hands of the other, for fear of being hit, even better he would have liked to go into a corner with him and whisper one or two quiet soothing words into his ear, that none of the others needed to hear. But the stoker was out of control. Karl even started to draw comfort from the thought that in an emergency the stoker, with strength born of desperation, could vanquish all the other seven men in the room. Admittedly, on the desk there was, as he saw at a glance, a centrepiece with far too many electrical buttons on it. Simply pressing a hand down on that could turn the whole ship against them, and fill its corridors with their enemies.

Then the so entirely uninvolved man with the bamboo cane stepped up to Karl and asked, not loudly, but quite audibly over the stoker's shouting: "What is your name please?" At that moment, as though it had been a cue for someone behind the door there was a knock. The servant glanced at the captain, who nodded. So the servant went over to the door and opened it. Outside, in an old frogged coat, stood a man of medium build, not really suited, to go by his appearance, to working with machines, and yet—this was Schubal. If Karl hadn't known it from looking at everyone's eyes, which showed a certain satisfaction—from which even the captain himself was not exempt—he must have learned it from the stoker who, to his alarm, tensed his arms and clenched his fists, as though that clenching was the most important thing to him, something for which he would willingly give all the life in his body. All his strength, even what kept him on his feet, was invested there.

So there was the enemy all sprightly and snug in his Sunday suit, with an account book under his arm, probably the wages and work record of the stoker, looking round into the eyes of all those present, one after the other, quite shamelessly gauging the mood of each one of them. All seven were his friends, for even if the captain had entertained, or had seemed to entertain, certain reservations about him before, after what the stoker had put him through, Schubal probably seemed free from any stain. One couldn't be too hard on a man like the stoker, and if Schubal was guilty of anything, then it was the fact that he hadn't been able to break the rebellious spirits of the stoker in time to prevent him from daring to appear before the captain today.

It was perhaps still reasonable to expect that the confrontation between the stoker and Schubal would have much the same effect before this company as before a higher assembly, because even if Schubal was a skilful dissembler, he surely couldn't keep it up right to the end. Just a quick flash of his wickedness would be enough to make it apparent to the gentlemen, and Karl wanted to provoke it. He was already acquainted with the respective acuity, the weaknesses and the moods of the company, so, at least from that point of view, his time here hadn't been wasted. If only the stoker had been in better shape, but he seemed completely out of commission. If Schubal had been dangled in front of him, he would probably have been able to split his hated skull open with his bare fists like a nut in a thin shell. But even to walk the few paces to reach him seemed to be beyond him. Why had Karl failed to predict the wholly predictable eventuality, that Schubal would at some stage present himself in person, either under his own steam, or else summoned by the captain. Why hadn't Karl formulated a precise plan of attack with the stoker on their way here instead of turning up hopelessly unprepared, thinking it was enough to step through the door? Was the stoker even still capable of speech, could he say yes and no under a cross-examination, which itself would only become necessary in the most favourable circumstances. He stood there, feet apart, knees slightly bent, head a little raised, and the air coming and going through his open mouth, as though he had no lungs in him with which to breathe.

Karl for his part felt stronger and more alert than he had ever done at home. If only his parents could see him, fighting for a good cause in a strange land before distinguished people, and while he hadn't won yet, he was absolutely ready for the final push. Would they change their minds about him? Sit him down between them and praise him? For once look into his eyes that shone with devotion to them? Doubtful questions, and hardly the time to start asking them now!

"I have come because I believe the stoker is accusing me of some dishonesty or other. One of the kitchen maids told me she had seen him on his way here. Captain, gentlemen, I'm prepared to refute any accusation against me with the help of these written records, and, if need be, by the evidence of some impartial and unprejudiced witnesses, who are waiting outside the door." Thus Schubal. It was the clear speech of a man, and to judge by the change in the expressions of the listeners, it was as though they had heard human sounds for the first time in a long while. What they failed to realize was that even that fine speech was full of holes. Why was "dishonesty" the first important word to occur to him? Perhaps the charges against him should have begun with that, rather than with national bias? A kitchen maid had seen the stoker on his way to the office, and straightaway drawn the right conclusion? Was it not guilt sharpening his understanding? And he had come with witnesses, and impartial and unprejudiced witnesses at that? It was a swindle, one big swindle, and the gentlemen stood for it and thought it was a proper way to behave? Why had he almost certainly allowed so much time to elapse between the maid's report and his arrival here, if not for the purpose of letting the stoker so tire everybody out that they lost their power of judgement, which was what Schubal would have good reason to fear? Had he not been loitering behind the door for a long time and only knocked when that one gentleman's irrelevant question suggested to him that the stoker was finished?

It was all so clear, and in spite of himself Schubal only confirmed it, but the gentlemen still needed to have it put to them even more unambiguously. They needed shaking up. So, Karl, hurry up and use the time before the witnesses appear and muddy everything.

Just at that moment, though, the captain motioned to Schubal "enough," and he—his affair for the moment put back a little—promptly walked off and began a quiet conversation with the servant, who had straightaway allied himself with him, a conversation not without its share of sidelong glances at the stoker and Karl, and gestures of great conviction. It seemed that Schubal was rehearsing his next big speech.

"Didn't you want to ask the young man here a question, Mr. Jakob?" said the captain to the man with the bamboo cane breaking the silence.

"Indeed I did," he replied, thanking him for the courtesy with a little bow. And he asked Karl again: "What is your name please?"

Karl, believing it was in the interest of the principal cause to get the stubborn questioner over with quickly, replied curtly and without, as was his habit, producing his passport, which he would have had to look for first, "Karl Rossmann."

"But," said the man addressed as Jakob, taking a step backwards with a smile of near-disbelief. The captain too, the chief cashier, the ship's officer, even the servant clearly displayed an excessive degree of surprise on hearing Karl's name. Only the gentlemen from the port authority remained indifferent.

"But," repeated Mr. Jakob and rather stiffly walked up to Karl, "then I'm your Uncle Jakob, and you're my dear nephew. Didn't I know it all along," he said to the captain, before hugging and kissing Karl, who submitted quietly.

"What's your name?" asked Karl, once he felt he had been released, very politely but quite unmoved, and trying to see what consequences this new turn of events might have for the stoker. For the moment there was at least no suggestion that Schubal could draw any advantage from it.

"Don't you see you're a very lucky young man," said the captain, who thought the question might have hurt the dignity of Mr. Jakob who had gone over to the window, obviously in order to keep the others from seeing the emotion on his face, which he kept dabbing at with a handkerchief. "The man who has presented himself to you as your uncle is the state councillor Edward Jakob. You now have a glittering career ahead of you, which you surely cannot have expected. Try to understand that, though it isn't easy, and pull yourself together."

"I do indeed have an Uncle Jakob in America," said Karl to the captain, "but if I understood you correctly, it was the state councillor's surname that was Jakob."

"That's correct," said the captain expectantly.

"Well, my Uncle Jakob, who is my mother's brother, is Jakob by his first name, while his surname is of course the same as my mother's maiden name which is Bendelmayer."

"Gentlemen, I ask you," cried the state councillor, returning from his restorative visit to the window, with reference to Karl's explanation.

Everyone, with the exception of the port officials, burst out laughing, some as though moved, others more inscrutably.

But what I said wasn't so foolish, thought Karl.

"Gentlemen," reiterated the state councillor, "without your meaning to, or my meaning you to, you are here witnessing a little family scene, and I feel I owe you some explanation, seeing as only the captain here"—an exchange of bows took place at this point—"is completely in the picture."

"Now I really must pay attention to every word," Karl said to himself, and he was glad when he saw out of the corner of his eye that animation was beginning to return to the figure of the stoker.

"In the long years of my stay in America—although the word stay hardly does justice to the American citizen I have so wholeheartedly become—in all those years I have lived completely cut off from my relatives in Europe, for reasons that are firstly not relevant here, and secondly would distress me too much in the telling. I even dread the moment when I shall be compelled to relate them to my nephew, when a few home truths about his parents and their ilk will become unavoidable."

"He really is my uncle, no question," Karl said to himself, as he listened. "I expect he's just had his name changed."

"My dear nephew has simply been got rid of by his parents—yes, let's just use the phrase, as it describes what happened—simply got rid of, the way you put the cat out if it's making a nuisance of itself. It's not my intention to gloss over what my nephew did to deserve such treatment— glossing over isn't the American way—but his transgression is such that the mere naming of it provides an excuse."

That sounds all right, thought Karl, but I don't want him to tell them all. How does he know about it anyway? Who would have told him? But let's see, maybe he does know everything.

"What happened," the uncle went on, resting his weight on the little bamboo cane and rocking back and forth a little, which robbed the

matter of some of the unnecessary solemnity it would certainly have
otherwise had—"what happened is that he was seduced by a maidser-
vant, one Johanna Brummer, a woman of some thirty-five years of age.
In using the word seduced, I have no wish to insult my nephew, but it's
difficult to think of another word that would be applicable."

Karl, who had already moved quite close to his uncle, turned round
at this point to see what impact the story was having on the faces of the
listeners. There was no laughter from any of them, they were all listening quietly and gravely: it's not done to laugh at the nephew of a state
councillor at the first opportunity that comes along. If anything, one
might have said that the stoker was smiling very faintly at Karl, but, in
the first place, that was encouraging as a further sign of life on his part,
and, in the second place, it was excusable since back in the cabin Karl
had tried to keep secret a matter that was now being so openly aired.

"Well, this Brummer woman," the uncle continued, "went on to have
a child by my nephew, a healthy boy who was christened Jakob, I suppose with my humble self in mind, because even my nephew's no doubt
passing references to me seem to have made a great impression on the
girl. Just as well too, let me say. For the parents, to avoid paying for the
child's upkeep or to avoid being touched by the scandal themselves—I
must state that I am not acquainted either with the laws of the place,
or with the circumstances of the parents, of whom all I have are two
begging letters that they sent me a long time ago, to which I never replied, but which I was careful to keep and which now constitute the
only, one-sided, written communications between us in all these years—to
resume then, the parents, to avoid scandal and paying maintenance, had
their son, my dear nephew, transported to America with, as you may see,
lamentably inadequate provision—thus leaving the boy, saving those
miracles that still happen from time to time and particularly here in
America, entirely to his own devices, so that he might easily have met his
death in some dockside alleyway on his arrival, had not the maid written to me, which letter, after lengthy detours, came into my possession

only the day before yesterday, and acquainted me with the whole story, together with a personal description of my nephew, and, very sensibly, also with the name of the ship on which he was travelling. Now, if it were my purpose at this point to entertain you, gentlemen, I might well read out some choice passages from this letter"——he pulled from his pocket two enormous, closely written pages, and waved them around—— "It would certainly make a hit, written as it is with a certain low, but always well-intentioned, cunning and with a good deal of affection for the father of her child. But neither do I want to amuse you more than is necessary, nor do I want to injure any tender feelings possibly still entertained by my nephew, who may, if he cares to, read the letter for himself in the privacy of his own room, which already awaits him."

Actually, Karl had no feelings for the girl. In the crush of an ever-receding past, she was sitting in the kitchen, with one elbow propped on the kitchen dresser. She would look at him when he went into the kitchen for a glass of water for his father, or to do an errand for his mother. Sometimes she would be sitting in her strange position by the dresser, writing a letter, and drawing inspiration from Karl's face. Sometimes she would be covering her eyes with her hand, then it was impossible to speak to her. Sometimes she would be kneeling in her little room off the kitchen, praying to a wooden cross, and Karl would shyly watch her through the open door as he passed. Sometimes she would be rushing about the kitchen, and spin round, laughing like a witch whenever Karl got in her way. Sometimes she would shut the kitchen door when Karl came in, and hold the doorknob in her hand until he asked her to let him out. Sometimes she would bring him things he hadn't asked for, and silently press them into his hands. Once, though, she said "Karl!" and led him——still astonished at the unexpected address——sighing and grimacing into her little room, and bolted it. Then she almost throttled him in an embrace, and, while asking him to undress her she actually undressed him, and laid him in her bed, as though she wanted to keep him all to herself from now on, and stroke him and look after him until the end of the world. "Karl, O my Karl!" she said as if she could see him and wanted to confirm her possession of him, whereas he couldn't see anything at all, and felt uncomfortable in all the warm bedding which she seemed to have piled up expressly for his sake. Then she lay down beside him, and asked to hear some secret or other, but he was unable to tell her any, then she was angry with him or pretended to be angry, he wasn't sure which, and shook him, then she listened to the beating of his heart and offered him her breast for him to listen to, but Karl couldn't bring himself to do that, she pressed her naked belly against his, reached her hand down, it felt so disgusting that Karl's head and neck leapt out of the pillows, down between his legs, pushed her belly against his a few times, he felt as though she were a part of him, and perhaps for that reason he felt seized by a shocking helplessness. He finally got to his own bed in tears, and after many fond goodnights from her. That had been all, and yet the uncle had managed to turn it into a big deal. So the cook had thought of him, and informed his uncle that he was arriving. That was nice of her, and one day he would like to pay her back.

"And now," said the Senator, "I want to hear from you loud and clear, whether I am your uncle or not."

"You are my uncle," said Karl and kissed his hand, and was kissed on the forehead in return. "I'm very glad I've met you, but you're mistaken if you think my parents only say bad things about you. But there were a few other mistakes in what you said, I mean, not everything happened the way you described it. But it's difficult for you to tell from such a distance and anyway I don't think it matters if the gentlemen here have been given an account that's inaccurate in a few points of detail, about something that doesn't really concern them."

"Well spoken," said the Senator, and took Karl over to the visibly emotional captain, and said, "Haven't I got a splendid fellow for a nephew?"

The captain said, with a bow of the kind that only comes with military training, "I am delighted to have met your nephew, Senator. I am particularly honoured that my ship afforded the setting for such a reunion. But the crossing in the steerage must have been very uncomfortable, you never know who you've got down there. Once, for instance, the first-born son of the highest Hungarian magnate, I forget his name and the purpose of his voyage, travelled in our steerage. I only got to hear about it much later. Now, we do everything in our power to make the voyage as pleasant as possible for steerage passengers, far more than our American counterparts, for example, do, but we still haven't been able to make a voyage in those conditions a pleasure."

"It did me no harm," said Karl.

"It did him no harm!" repeated the Senator, with a loud laugh.

"Only I'm afraid I may have lost my suitcase—" and with that he suddenly remembered all that had taken place, and all that still remained to be done, and looked around at all those present, standing in silent respect and astonishment. None of them had moved and all were looking at him. Only in the port officials, inasmuch as their stern and self-satisfied faces told one anything, could one see regret that they had come at such an unsuitable time; the wristwatch they had laid out in front of them was probably more important to them than anything that had happened, and that might yet happen, in the room.

The first man, after the captain, to express his pleasure was, extraordinarily, the stoker. "Hearty congratulations," he said and shook Karl by the hand, also wanting to show something like admiration. But when he approached the Senator with the same words, the latter took a step back, as though the stoker had taken things too far, and he stopped right away.

But the others saw what had to be done, and they crowded round Karl and the Senator. Even Schubal offered Karl his congratulations in the confusion, which he accepted with thanks. When things had settled down again, the last to appear were the port officials who said two words in English, and made a ridiculous impression.

To make the most of such a pleasant occasion, the Senator went on to describe, for the benefit of himself and everyone else present, various other, lesser moments, which weren't only tolerated but listened to with interest. He pointed out, for instance, that he had copied down in his notebook some of Karl's distinguishing features as they were described in the cook's letter, in case they should prove useful to him. During the stoker's intolerable tirade he had taken out the notebook for no other purpose than to amuse himself, and for fun tried to match the cook's less than forensically accurate descriptions with Karl's actual appearance. "And so a man finds his nephew," he concluded, as though expecting a further round of congratulations.

"What's going to happen to the stoker now?" asked Karl, ignoring his uncle's latest story. It seemed to him that in his new position he was entitled to say whatever was on his mind.

"The stoker will get whatever he deserves," said the Senator, "and whatever the captain determines. But I'm sure the company will agree we've had enough and more than enough of the stoker."

"But that's not the point, it's a question of justice," said Karl. He was standing between the captain and his uncle, and perhaps influenced by that position, he thought the decision lay in his hands.

But the stoker seemed to have given up hope. He kept his hands half tucked into his belt, which his excited movements had brought into full view along with a striped shirt. That didn't trouble him in the least, he had made his complaint, let them see what rags he wore on his back, and then let them carry him off. He thought the servant and Schubal, the two lowliest persons present, should do him that final service. Then Schubal would have peace and quiet, no one to drive him to the brink of despair, as the chief cashier had said. The captain would be able to engage a crew of Rumanians, everyone would speak Rumanian, and maybe everything would go better. There would be no more stoker to speechify in the office, only his last tirade might live on fondly in their memories because, as the Senator had stated, it had led indirectly to the recognition of his nephew. That very nephew had tried to help him several times before that, and so he didn't owe him anything for his help in having made him recognized; it never occurred to the stoker to ask anything more of him now. Anyway, Senator's nephew he might be, but he wasn't a captain, and it was the captain who would be having the final say in the affair— So the stoker wasn't really trying to catch Karl's eye, only, in a room filled with his enemies, there was nowhere else for him to look.

"Don't misunderstand the situation," said the Senator to Karl, "it may be a question of justice, but at the same time it's a matter of discipline. In either case, and especially the latter, it's for the captain to decide."

"That's right," muttered the stoker. Anyone who heard him and understood smiled tightly.

"Moreover, we have kept the captain from his business for long enough, which must be particularly onerous at the moment of arrival in New York. It's high time we left the ship, lest our completely unnecessary intervention may turn this trifling squabble between a couple of engineers into a major incident. I fully understand your behaviour, dear nephew, but that's precisely what gives me the right to lead you swiftly from this place."

"I'll have them get a boat ready for you right away," said the captain, astonishing Karl by not offering the slightest objection to the uncle's self-deprecating words. The chief cashier hurried over to the desk and telephoned the captain's order to the boatswain.

"Time is pressing," Karl said to himself, "but without offending them all there is nothing I can do. I can't leave my uncle who's only just found me. The captain is being polite, but really nothing more. When it's a matter of discipline, his kindness will come to an end, I'm sure uncle was right about that. I don't want to talk to Schubal, I'm even sorry I shook hands with him. And everyone else here is just chaff."

So thinking, he walked slowly over to the stoker, pulled his right hand out of his belt, and held it playfully in his own. "Why don't you say anything?" he asked. "Why do you let them get away with it?"

The stoker furrowed his brow, as though looking for words for what he wanted to say. He looked down at his hand and Karl's.

"You've suffered an injustice, more than anyone else on the ship, I'm convinced of that." And Karl slipped his fingers back and forth between those of the stoker, whose eyes were shining and looking around as though feeling inexpressible bliss and at the same time daring anyone to take it away from him.

"You must stand up for yourself, say yes and no, otherwise people will never learn the truth. I want you to promise me to do that, because I'm very much afraid that soon I won't be able to help you any more." Karl was crying as he kissed the stoker's cracked and almost lifeless hand, holding it and pressing it to his cheek, like some dear thing from which he had to be parted. His uncle the Senator appeared at his side, and, ever so gently, pulled him away. "The stoker seems to have put you under his spell," he said, and looked knowingly across to the captain over Karl's head. "You felt abandoned, then you found the stoker, and you're showing your gratitude to him, it's all very laudable. But please for my sake don't overdo it, and learn to come to terms with your position."

Outside the door, there was a commotion, shouting, and it even seemed as though someone was being viciously pushed against it. A rather wild-looking sailor came in, wearing a girl's apron. "There's people outside," he said, pumping his elbows as though still in the crowd. Finally he came to his senses, and was about to salute the captain, when he noticed his girl's apron, tore it off, threw it on the ground, and said: "That's disgusting, they've tied a girl's apron on me." Then he clicked his heels together and saluted. Someone stifled a laugh, but the captain said sternly: "Enough of these high jinks. Who is it who's outside?" "They are my witnesses," said Schubal stepping forward, "I'd like to apologize for their behaviour. At the end of a long sea voyage, they sometimes get a little unruly." "Call them in right away," ordered the captain, and turning quickly to the Senator, he said kindly but briskly:

"Would you be so kind now, my dear Senator, as to take your nephew and follow the sailor who will escort you to your boat? I can't say what happiness and honour your personal acquaintance has brought me. I only wish I may have another opportunity soon of resuming our discussion of the American Navy, and then perhaps to be interrupted as pleasantly as we were today." "One nephew's enough for me for the moment," said the uncle laughing. "And now please accept my thanks for your kindness, and farewell. It's by no means out of the question that we"—he pressed Karl affectionately to himself—"might spend a little longer in your company on the occasion of our next visit to Europe." "I should be delighted," said the captain. The two gentlemen shook hands, Karl took the captain's hand quickly and silently because he was then distracted by about fifteen people who had come into the office, a little chastened but very noisily still, under Schubal's leadership. The sailor asked the Senator to let him go first, and cleared a way for him and Karl, who passed quite easily through the crowd of bowing people. It seemed these cheerful souls thought the quarrel between Schubal and the stoker was a joke that even the captain was being permitted to share. Among them Karl spotted Line the kitchen maid, who winked merrily at him as she tied on the apron which the sailor had thrown down, because it was hers.

With the sailor leading the way, they left the office and went out into a little passage, which after a few steps took them to a small door, after which a short flight of steps led them down to the boat which had been prepared for them. The sailors in the boat—into which their escort leapt with a single bound—rose to salute them. The Senator was just telling Karl to be careful as he climbed down, when Karl started sobbing violently on the top step. The Senator took Karl's chin in his right hand, hugged him tight, and stroked him with his left hand. They went down together, one step at a time, and in a tight embrace got into the boat where the Senator found Karl a good seat directly facing him. At a signal from the Senator, the sailors pushed off from the ship, and straightaway were rowing hard. Barely a few metres from the ship, Karl discovered to his surprise that they were facing the side of the ship where the head office looked out. All three windows were occupied by Schubal's witnesses, shouting goodbye and waving cheerfully, the uncle even waved back and one sailor managed to blow a kiss without interrupting the rhythm of his rowing. It really was as though there was no stoker. Karl examined his uncle a little more closely—their knees were almost touching—and he wondered whether this man would ever be able to replace the stoker for him. The uncle avoided his eye, and looked out at the waves, which were bobbing around the boat.

DECAY

Marjorie Bowen

I want to write it down at once, to get it 'out of my head' as they say, though why one should suppose these things are in one's head I don't know—they seem to me all about us, flavouring the food we eat, colouring the sky.

Of course I've got the journalist's habit of scribbling too, it is so much easier to jot things down than explain them by speech.

To us, at least.

And you are so far away it is a good excuse to send 'newsy' letters. Only, I've got a feeling that in Lima this will read, well, *queer*.

Still you *must* be interested and I must write, no, I forestall your objection, it won't do for 'copy.' I'm not spoiling a good 'scoop.'

What I have got to say can never be published.

Nor written to anyone but yourself—and you won't speak of it, I know.

Good Lord, you won't *want* to.

You'll remember the people as they would you—we were all in the same 'set' together for so long—I think you were the first to break away when you got this Lima job, weren't you?

And soon after that came the marriage of Cedric Halston.

You heard all about it, I sent you the 'cuttings' written by our own colleagues—you were rather fond of Halston, I think.

So was I.

Of course we were rather prejudiced by his being called Cedric and writing poetry, but it was such good stuff and he was such a decent sort and, of course, being so palpably ruined in Fleet Street! Much too good for what was too good for the rest of us, wasn't he?

And rather more poverty-stricken than anyone ought to be it seemed to me.

Lord! The sheer sordidness of Halston, 'hard-upishness'!

He couldn't write his stuff for grind and worry and despair—but the little bits that struggled through as it were, were jolly fine.

Even the old Die-hards that 'slam the door in the face of youth,' etc., etc., said he was—well, the right stuff.

None of your crazy, mazy, jig-saw, jazzy poets, poison green and liver yellow, but the 'real thing.'

Like Keats.

Of course there ought to have been money in a stunt like that, being the real thing, I mean, and starving, but poor old Halston never could work it, could he? He just—starved.

Not very picturesquely.

Till he met Jennifer Harden.

(Did you ever think how *wrong* that 'Jennifer' was? I'd never seen the name before except signing one of those articles that begin, 'It's *ever* so crowded on the Riviera now, and oh my dear'—you know the patter—and the people who write it!)

You know they married—one rather wanted to jeer, but couldn't—we all sat back and looked humble.

It was so tremendous you could only describe it in terms of claptrap, 'Abelard and Heloise,' a 'grande passion' and 'immortal love,' 'eternal devotion,' 'twin souls' and all the rest of the good old frayed symbols, old chap, but they are getting worn—I'm thinking.

You remember I sent you her photo? One of those misty affairs looking like—well, *not* like Jennifer Harden.

Still, she was beautiful, but out of drawing—lots of money, lots of taste, not too young, by any means—and then the 'love of a lifetime' thrown in.

She didn't mind using that phrase about him—publicly, in the woman's club she ran, and where she had met him—lured to gas on 'Truth in relation to Modesty' by the bribe of a good dinner. She also said she worshipped him—I admired her for that—you know they take a bit of saying, those sort of things now-a-days!

And he raved about her—got the rose-coloured spectacles firmly fixed and took her on as she was, 'Jennifer' and all—dashed into poetry and spread himself out over ivory pomegranates, roses, and all the rest of the irrelevant stuff we drag in to say a woman's a *woman*. Do you remember the old Italian who saw his beloved at the fountain and said:

'She alone of all the world is worthy to be called a woman'?

That is the prettiest compliment I know of.

Well, to return to the Halstons, they were married and I don't suppose you ever heard any more of them.

It is three years ago.

You know how lucky we all thought him—she really had such a lot of money.

And money had always been just what Halston wanted.

Of course they were very wonderful about it: he was 'so humble in his great happiness, he could not let paltry pride stand in the way,' and she only 'valued her fortune in that it could minister to his genius'—a pity how all these fine sentiments slip into 'clichés.'

I suppose someone believes them, or means them, sometimes.

I wonder?

Well, they cleared out. She bought a place in Herts and called it 'Enchantment.' Why not, after all? You might really feel that, I suppose.

Well, they shut themselves in this Paradise—never came to town, hardly ever wrote—sometimes a few 'choice' poems from him, the kind that goes with handmade paper and silk ties and you keep reading over feeling sure that it means much more than it possibly could—and sometimes letters from her to 'privileged' friends (they really thought they were), letters that are like screams of happiness.

Of course we all thought it rather wonderful that they could stay shut up like that and enjoy it—it was quite a blow for the real cynics.

'A case in a million' was all they could say.

He never wrote to anyone and there was not one of us who would not have thought it cheek to write to him, we even sank to seriously thinking of him as 'a God-sent genius.'

Well, here comes what I must set down—only to you, Lorimer.

Halston and I knew you best of all in the old days and you are the only person I can tell.

Forgive the preamble, but I have a sense of your being so far away—I imagine you saying: 'Who is Halston?'

I haven't mentioned him for so long—there was nothing to mention—'Happy nations,' etc. Here is the story.

I was sent down to Hertford town a few weeks ago to investigate some ghost story, you know what a rage that sort of thing is with us just now, all of us shouting things you can hardly say in a whisper and trying to disprove what no one can prove.

The case was interesting and kept me some time—the day before I was due back in London I met Halston in the High Street. He seemed very cordial and prosperous, had a good car waiting, was rather too well dressed in uncommon kind of clothes—sort of peasant handicraft and Savile Row combined. But I did not think he looked well, strained, aged and thin—but this he explained by the fact that he was writing an Epic.

(Why do you smile, Lorimer, people *have* written Epics, you know.)

That was why he had been shut away all the time—that great work might grow under the beautiful ministrations of his wife ... Jennifer, I gathered, was really running a little Paradise for his special benefit ... she had just snatched him away from all that was ugly or crude or mean or distressing and lapped him in Love and Beauty and Service ...

Of course I grinned ... but I was ashamed of grinning.

Halston did not seem to notice; he actually asked me over to 'Enchantment' to stay a few days.

Being a free lance I could accept and did—you can imagine my curiosity—a vulgar thing to admit to, but don't you think it will be our first emotion if we ever step into Heaven?

Imagine the relish of being able to settle those questions—'What is God really like?' and 'those robes and crowns?' and the 'many mansions?'— and little private pet queries of your own.

That was how I felt as I motored over to 'Enchantment,' which was known to the outsider as a very delightful Tudor Farm House, completely brought up to date, that had formerly been called Eversley Lodge and run by a city gentleman, whose reputation was more noted for lustre than solidity. I found the place (which was isolated, a great way from the station, a good way from the road) perfect.

Rather like the 'Ideal Homes' they make so much of just now, still they *are* ideal, aren't they?

Well, here it all was, 'pleasance,' 'pleached walk,' sunk ponds, statues, peacock, arbours, box hedges, astrolabes, sundials—all the bag of tricks and inside everything done by electricity and servants so efficient you forgot they were there. Wonderfully comfortable.

Everything right—flowers, pictures, furniture, food—the last word in little contrivances for ease and luxury—three cars, I think, electric bells disguised as lanthorns and telephones concealed in sedan chairs, wood fires to 'look nice' and steam heating. Elzivirs to tone with the walls and modern books slipped into brocade covers to read, you know the kind of thing!

But really perfect!

Halston had a wing built on specially for himself—specially for the Epic, I ought to say, perhaps.

The most marvellous writing-room and library. I don't know what he hadn't got.

It was all 'choice'; I hate the word but no other will do.

All really 'choice' and as I was gaping round, in came Jennifer.

And she was 'choice' too.

Just a rough silk dress, a girdle of queer stones no one else would have liked, leather shoes simply asserting they were hand-made—and a manner.

She was gracious—sweeter than anyone need or ought to be, I thought, but I hadn't quite got the atmosphere.

'Our first guest,' she murmured, holding out both hands. 'How strange Cedric should meet you. He so seldom goes to the town, or ever leaves the house. He doesn't care to,' she added with a thrill in her voice.

She looked at him and he looked at her and murmured, 'Jennifer.'

While we had dinner—all excellent—that evening I observed her; she absolutely fascinated me and I want to describe her to you, Lorimer.

She is tall, with wide shoulders and a full Rossetti sort of neck, and a head rather nicely set, dark waved hair gathered in a knot at her nape and good forehead and dark rather flat eyes—then the nose tight, the lips hard and crooked, the complexion harsh and grained with red and the chin too small, running with a bad line into the Rossetti throat.

She lisped a little and showed more of her teeth than her lips when she talked.

Graceful enough she somehow gave an impression as I have said of beauty; she had a still yet enthusiastic manner and an air of almost incredible fastidiousness and refinement.

The conversation was delicately 'high-brow,' and afterwards she played to us (yes, it was a Scriabin, and someone else, unknown to me who makes even Scriabin seem old-fashioned!), then he played and she stood behind him and rested her hands on his shoulders, and when it was over raised his face with slow fingers and kissed him.

There was a lot of this sort of thing; she, Jennifer, looked through me, with a sort of 'divine pity'—but she was kind, very kind.

I soon learnt that Halston's 'sanctum' was 'just for writing,' upstairs they shared the same room; he hadn't a corner, not even in the 'sanctum,' for she would glide in there and sit in place of the banal secretary who could not have been tolerated in 'Enchantment.'

Not a corner—the woman pervaded the whole house—but why not?

You don't want corners in Paradise.

There was a day or two of this; I don't know why I stayed save that I was really rather fascinated.

Wanting to pick holes and not able to—you know.

I'm not sneering when I say again that it was really perfect.

Comfort, beauty, ease, leisure—every book, picture, magazine you could think of, the exquisite garden, the marvellous service (the servants were all in some quarters of their own, I believe, so seldom did one see them). And always Jennifer in tasteful gowns, in pretty poses moving lightly about doing useless beautiful things.

And always Cedric in his good quiet clothes with his fountain pen and his smile, and his running his fingers through his hair and his one or two dropped words that she understood so perfectly and took up with that bright brave smile 'one soul signalling to another along the ramparts of eternity'—that was Jennifer's smile.

She knew it and so did I; but I wished she had prettier teeth.

Of course, I should not have been noticing teeth, or the way she whitened her rather red throat, or the quick glitter of her eyes so out of harmony with her slow speech . . . but I still had not quite got the atmosphere.

Of course also there were no callers or callings, the mere thought was like a blasphemy, the isolation was as complete as the rarefied air . . . it was really rather wonderful how they did it.

You will have guessed there were no children, what an intrusion children would have been in such a life!

One rather wondered ... it is always the important things one mustn't touch on, isn't it? The things that matter most, that fill our souls, our minds, even our eyes ... I'm always amazed at our eternal reticences ... well, there were no children and I am queer in my views on marriage without children, it is a tricky business this mating ... one knows too much ... you've got to be jolly careful the people you marry to each other or, well, sometimes I've felt nauseated.

Anyhow, here were two carrying it off beautifully—all grossness purged away, they would tell you, the souls in perfect communion—all lovely and delicate, serving Art—beauty, nature, God. Yes, but why didn't she give the poor devil a corner to himself?

I don't believe he was alone for five minutes of the day or night—she used to speak of '*our* bedroom' and carry up flowers and fountain pens and biscuits, for the table beside *their* bed ... ugh! I became uneasy at meeting his glance, I don't know why.

Then ... I was coming in from the garden the fourth evening she was playing as usual, in a white gown that didn't suit her, and he was seated on his pure coloured chair with a Danish book of poetry.

As I entered the room I was assailed by a smell, so creeping, so foetid I could hardly forbear an exclamation—yet this was so obviously bad manners that I was silent.

I thought of course of drains or even dead birds in the chimney and that the discomfortable thing would be marked and removed. But neither of them noticed it and it died away presently.

Still, though it hung round us the whole evening now faint, now stronger ... always indescribably awful.

It was not in my own room, yet I woke up in the night drenched with it, sick and shuddering with the horror of it ... potent as a live thing it filled the lovely chamber. Lord! what a smell ... I was retching as I staggered out to shut the window.

But it was in the house for the closed window made no difference . . . I passed a night of torment . . . by the morning it was gone.

I won't bore you with my next day's work, which was to trace that smell.

Quite fruitless.

The garden, the drains, the kitchens, all furtively examined were in perfect order.

How could one suspect anything else in such a house?

Yet with evening . . . that loathsome terror again.

It so saturated the rooms that everything seemed tainted with it, like a fog dirties and dims, so this smell blighted and smeared every lovely thing in the place.

And there were lovely things, I'd envied some of them really.

But it was all spoilt for me now—even when the ghastly odour wasn't there everything reminded me of it . . . I was in a state of perpetual nausea.

Naturally I resolved to clear out.

But it couldn't be done at less than a couple of days' notice, for I had come for a fortnight.

I mentioned the smell, actually dared to Jennifer (I shall always think of her as that, never as 'Mrs Halston,' I know) and she was so distantly sweet about it that I felt I had been very impertinent.

'Of course there is nothing,' she said kindly. 'Cedric is so particular about—perfumes—sensitive people are, are they not? Perhaps you have fancies? Cedric used to . . . that is where I was able to . . . help him.'

Again the little thrill on the last two words: 'help him!' poor brute. Yes she has helped him all right . . . but where to.

I could do nothing but agree.

Jennifer gazed at me and I could see she meant to be very soothing.

'I banished everything ugly out of Cedric's life . . . Someday you will meet a woman who will do that for you—' then, with that natural brightness she used to mask her sacred emotions, 'Will you come and look at the rose bushes? I *think* I have got some teeny weeny buds for you to see—'

Yes, she had and must needs pick me one and give it me gravely . . . as a symbol of something or other, I'm sure. But it was no good; her 'teeny weeny' buds *stank*, my God, Lorimer, that is the only word for it stank to Heaven.

That day it was awful, the smell I mean. I took two long walks to get rid of it, the countryside was sweet and clean enough . . . the abomination was in the house, clinging to everything.

After dinner I asked them if they meant to live this life always, asked it bluntly, I suppose.

'Dear friend,' said Jennifer, 'you don't quite understand, does he, Cedric? This is . . . just home . . . ours . . .'

'Home?' I was worse than blunt, but the smell was torturing me. 'What have you got in it?'

They both looked at me.

'Each other, haven't we, Cedric?' Her smile was transcendent.

'Oh, yes,' I echoed, 'you've got each other—one can see that—feel it—sm—'

I stopped; what was I going to say?—what was slipping out?

I bit my tongue; but now I knew and it rather frightened me.

I cleared . . . I remember she said: 'And the Epic,' but I just cleared out into the garden like a lunatic and walked as I was into Hertford to the hotel where they knew me.

Do you see it, Lorimer? It was all dead, love, ambition, kindness, the souls themselves, shut in, stagnant, he sold for money, his comforts, she sold for her satisfied lusts, each exacting the price . . . each *hating* the other—no children, nothing let in, nothing going on—putrid, rotten . . . each caged and caught by the other—and, Lorimer, *stinking themselves to Hell.*

THE MUSIC OF ERICH ZANN

H. P. Lovecraft

I have examined maps of the city with the greatest care, yet have never again found the Rue d'Auseil. These maps have not been modern maps alone, for I know that names change. I have, on the contrary, delved deeply into all the antiquities of the place, and have personally explored every region, of whatever name, which could possibly answer to the street I knew as the Rue d'Auseil. But despite all I have done, it remains an humiliating fact that I cannot find the house, the street, or even the locality, where, during the last months of my impoverished life as a student of metaphysics at the university, I heard the music of Erich Zann.

That my memory is broken, I do not wonder; for my health, physical and mental, was gravely disturbed throughout the period of my residence in the Rue d'Auseil, and I recall that I took none of my few acquaintances there. But that I cannot find the place again is both singular and perplexing; for it was within a half-hour's walk of the university and was distinguished by peculiarities which could hardly be forgotten by anyone who had been there. I have never met a person who has seen the Rue d'Auseil.

The Rue d'Auseil lay across a dark river bordered by precipitous brick blear-windowed warehouses and spanned by a ponderous bridge of dark stone. It was always shadowy along that river, as if the smoke of neighboring factories shut out the sun perpetually. The river was also odorous with evil stenches which I have never smelled elsewhere, and which may some day help me to find it, since I should recognize them at once. Beyond the bridge were narrow cobbled streets with rails; and then came the ascent, at first gradual, but incredibly steep as the Rue d'Auseil was reached.

I have never seen another street as narrow and steep as the Rue d'Auseil. It was almost a cliff, closed to all vehicles, consisting in several places of flights of steps, and ending at the top in a lofty ivied wall. Its paving was irregular, sometimes stone slabs, sometimes cobblestones, and sometimes bare earth with struggling greenish-grey vegetation. The houses were tall, peaked-roofed, incredibly old, and crazily leaning backward, forward, and sidewise. Occasionally an opposite pair, both leaning forward, almost met across the street like an arch; and certainly they kept most of the light from the ground below. There were a few overhead bridges from house to house across the street.

The inhabitants of that street impressed me peculiarly. At first I thought it was because they were all silent and reticent; but later decided it was because they were all very old. I do not know how I came to live on such a street, but I was not myself when I moved there. I had been living in many poor places, always evicted for want of money; until at last I came upon that tottering house in the Rue d'Auseil kept by the paralytic Blandot. It was the third house from the top of the street, and by far the tallest of them all.

My room was on the fifth story; the only inhabited room there, since the house was almost empty. On the night I arrived I heard strange music from the peaked garret overhead, and the next day asked old Blandot about it. He told me it was an old German viol-player, a strange dumb man who signed his name as Erich Zann, and who played evenings in a cheap theatre orchestra; adding that Zann's desire to play in the night after his return from the theatre was the reason he had chosen this lofty and isolated garret room, whose single gable window was the only point on the street from which one could look over the terminating wall at the declivity and panorama beyond.

Thereafter I heard Zann every night, and although he kept me awake, I was haunted by the weirdness of his music. Knowing little of the art myself, I was yet certain that none of his harmonies had any relation to music I had heard before; and concluded that he was a composer of highly original genius. The longer I listened, the more I was fascinated, until after a week I resolved to make the old man's acquaintance.

One night as he was returning from his work, I intercepted Zann in the hallway and told him that I would like to know him and be with him when he played. He was a small, lean, bent person, with shabby clothes, blue eyes, grotesque, satyr-like face, and nearly bald head; and at my first words seemed both angered and frightened. My obvious friendliness, however, finally melted him; and he grudgingly motioned to me to follow him up the dark, creaking and rickety attic stairs. His room, one of only two in the steeply pitched garret, was on the west side, toward the high wall that formed the upper end of the street. Its size was very great, and seemed the greater because of its extraordinary barrenness and neglect. Of furniture there was only a narrow iron bedstead, a dingy washstand, a small table, a large bookcase, an iron music-rack, and three old-fashioned chairs. Sheets of music were piled in disorder about the floor. The walls were of bare boards, and had probably never known plaster; whilst the abundance of dust and cobwebs made the place seem more deserted than inhabited. Evidently Erich Zann's world of beauty lay in some far cosmos of the imagination.

Motioning me to sit down, the dumb man closed the door, turned the large wooden bolt, and lighted a candle to augment the one he had

brought with him. He now removed his viol from its moth-eaten covering, and taking it, seated himself in the least uncomfortable of the
chairs. He did not employ the music-rack, but, offering no choice and
playing from memory, enchanted me for over an hour with strains I had
never heard before; strains which must have been of his own devising.
To describe their exact nature is impossible for one unversed in music.
They were a kind of fugue, with recurrent passages of the most captivating quality, but to me were notable for the absence of any of the weird
notes I had overheard from my room below on other occasions.

Those haunting notes I had remembered, and had often hummed
and whistled inaccurately to myself, so when the player at length laid
down his bow I asked him if he would render some of them. As I began
my request the wrinkled satyr-like face lost the bored placidity it had
possessed during the playing, and seemed to shew the same curious
mixture of anger and fright which I had noticed when first I accosted
the old man. For a moment I was inclined to use persuasion, regarding
rather lightly the whims of senility; and even tried to awaken my host's
weirder mood by whistling a few of the strains to which I had listened
the night before. But I did not pursue this course for more than a moment; for when the dumb musician recognized the whistled air his face
grew suddenly distorted with an expression wholly beyond analysis, and
his long, cold, bony right hand reached out to stop my mouth and silence the crude imitation. As he did this he further demonstrated his
eccentricity by casting a startled glance toward the lone curtained window, as if fearful of some intruder—a glance doubly absurd, since the
garret stood high and inaccessible above all the adjacent roofs, this window being the only point on the steep street, as the concierge had told
me, from which one could see over the wall at the summit.

The old man's glance brought Blandot's remark to my mind, and
with a certain capriciousness I felt a wish to look out over the wide and
dizzying panorama of moonlit roofs and city lights beyond the hilltop,
which of all the dwellers in the Rue d'Auseil only this crabbed musician

could see. I moved toward the window and would have drawn aside the nondescript curtains, when with a frightened rage even greater than before, the dumb lodger was upon me again; this time motioning with his head toward the door as he nervously strove to drag me thither with both hands. Now thoroughly disgusted with my host, I ordered him to release me, and told him I would go at once. His clutch relaxed, and as he saw my disgust and offense, his own anger seemed to subside. He tightened his relaxing grip, but this time in a friendly manner, forcing me into a chair; then with an appearance of wistfulness crossing to the littered table, where he wrote many words with a pencil in the labored French of a foreigner.

The note which he finally handed me was an appeal for tolerance and forgiveness. Zann said that he was old, lonely, and afflicted with strange fears and nervous disorders connected with his music and with other things. He had enjoyed my listening to his music, and wished I would come again and not mind his eccentricities. But he could not play to another his weird harmonies, and could not bear hearing them from another; nor could he bear having anything in his room touched by another. He had not known until our hallway conversation that I could overhear his playing in my room, and now asked me if I would arrange with Blandot to take a lower room where I could not hear him in the night. He would, he wrote, defray the difference in rent.

As I sat deciphering the execrable French, I felt more lenient toward the old man. He was a victim of physical and nervous suffering, as was I; and my metaphysical studies had taught me kindness. In the silence there came a slight sound from the window—the shutter must have rattled in the night wind, and for some reason I started almost as violently as did Erich Zann. So when I had finished reading, I shook my host by the hand, and departed as a friend.

The next day Blandot gave me a more expensive room on the third floor, between the apartments of an aged money-lender and the room of a respectable upholsterer. There was no one on the fourth floor.

It was not long before I found that Zann's eagerness for my company was not as great as it had seemed while he was persuading me to move down from the fifth story. He did not ask me to call on him, and when I did call he appeared uneasy and played listlessly. This was always at night—in the day he slept and would admit no one. My liking for him did not grow, though the attic room and the weird music seemed to hold an odd fascination for me. I had a curious desire to look out of that window, over the wall and down the unseen slope at the glittering roofs and spires which must lie outspread there. Once I went up to the garret during theatre hours, when Zann was away, but the door was locked.

What I did succeed in doing was to overhear the nocturnal playing of the dumb old man. At first I would tip-toe up to my old fifth floor, then I grew bold enough to climb the last creaking staircase to the peaked garret. There in the narrow hall, outside the bolted door with the covered keyhole, I often heard sounds which filled me with an indefinable dread—the dread of vague wonder and brooding mystery. It was not that the sounds were hideous, for they were not; but that they held vibrations suggesting nothing on this globe of earth, and that at certain intervals they assumed a symphonic quality which I could hardly conceive as produced by one player. Certainly, Erich Zann was a genius of wild power. As the weeks passed, the playing grew wilder, whilst the old musician acquired an increasing haggardness and furtiveness pitiful to behold. He now refused to admit me at any time, and shunned me whenever we met on the stairs.

Then one night as I listened at the door, I heard the shrieking viol swell into a chaotic babel of sound; a pandemonium which would have led me to doubt my own shaking sanity had there not come from behind that barred portal a piteous proof that the horror was real—the awful, inarticulate cry which only a mute can utter, and which rises only in moments of the most terrible fear or anguish. I knocked repeatedly at the door, but received no response. Afterward I waited in the black hallway, shivering with cold and fear, till I heard the poor musician's feeble effort to rise from the floor by the aid of a chair. Believing him just conscious after a fainting fit, I renewed my rapping, at the same time calling out my name reassuringly. I heard Zann stumble to the window and close both shutter and sash, then stumble to the door, which he falteringly unfastened to admit me. This time his delight at having me present was real; for his distorted face gleamed with relief while he clutched at my coat as a child clutches at its mother's skirts.

Shaking pathetically, the old man forced me into a chair whilst he sank into another, beside which his viol and bow lay carelessly on the floor. He sat for some time inactive, nodding oddly, but having a paradoxical suggestion of intense and frightened listening. Subsequently he seemed to be satisfied, and crossing to a chair by the table wrote a brief note, handed it to me, and returned to the table, where he began to write rapidly and incessantly. The note implored me in the name of mercy, and for the sake of my own curiosity, to wait where I was while he prepared a full account in German of all the marvels and terrors which beset him. I waited, and the dumb man's pencil flew.

It was perhaps an hour later, while I still waited and while the old musician's feverishly written sheets still continued to pile up, that I saw Zann start as from the hint of a horrible shock. Unmistakably he was looking at the curtained window and listening shudderingly. Then I half fancied I heard a sound myself; though it was not a horrible sound, but rather an exquisitely low and infinitely distant musical note, suggesting a player in one of the neighboring houses, or in some abode beyond the lofty wall over which I had never been able to look. Upon Zann the effect was terrible, for, dropping his pencil, suddenly he rose, seized his viol, and commenced to rend the night with the wildest playing I had ever heard from his bow save when listening at the barred door.

It would be useless to describe the playing of Erich Zann on that dreadful night. It was more horrible than anything I had ever overheard, because I could now see the expression of his face, and could realize that this time the motive was stark fear. He was trying to make a noise; to ward something off or drown something out—what, I could not imagine, awesome though I felt it must be. The playing grew fantastic, delirious, and hysterical, yet kept to the last the qualities of supreme genius which I knew this strange old man possessed. I recognized the air—it was a wild Hungarian dance popular in the theatres, and I reflected for a moment that this was the first time I had ever heard Zann play the work of another composer.

Louder and louder, wilder and wilder, mounted the shrieking and whining of that desperate viol. The player was dripping with an uncanny perspiration and twisted like a monkey, always looking frantically at the curtained window. In his frenzied strains I could almost see shadowy satyrs and Bacchanals dancing and whirling insanely through seething abysses of clouds and smoke and lightning. And then I thought I heard a shriller, steadier note that was not from the viol; a calm, deliberate, purposeful, mocking note from far away in the West.

At this juncture the shutter began to rattle in a howling night wind which had sprung up outside as if in answer to the mad playing within. Zann's screaming viol now outdid itself emitting sounds I had never thought a viol could emit. The shutter rattled more loudly, unfastened, and commenced slamming against the window. Then the glass broke shiveringly under the persistent impacts, and the chill wind rushed in, making the candles sputter and rustling the sheets of paper on the table where Zann had begun to write out his horrible secret. I looked at Zann, and saw that he was past conscious observation. His blue eyes were bulging, glassy and sightless, and the frantic playing had become a blind, mechanical, unrecognizable orgy that no pen could even suggest.

A sudden gust, stronger than the others, caught up the manuscript and bore it toward the window. I followed the flying sheets in desperation, but they were gone before I reached the demolished panes. Then I remembered my old wish to gaze from this window, the only window in the Rue d'Auseil from which one might see the slope beyond the wall, and the city outspread beneath. It was very dark, but the city's lights always burned, and I expected to see them there amidst the rain and wind. Yet when I looked from that highest of all gable windows, looked while the candles sputtered and the insane viol howled with the night-wind, I saw no city spread below, and no friendly lights gleamed from remembered streets, but only the blackness of space illimitable; unimagined space alive with motion and music, and having no semblance of anything on earth. And as I stood there looking in terror, the wind blew out both the candles in that ancient peaked garret, leaving me in savage and impenetrable darkness with chaos and pandemonium before me, and the daemon madness of that night-baying viol behind me.

I staggered back in the dark, without the means of striking a light, crashing against the table, overturning a chair, and finally groping my way to the place where the blackness screamed with shocking music. To save myself and Erich Zann I could at least try, whatever the powers opposed to me. Once I thought some chill thing brushed me, and I screamed, but my scream could not be heard above that hideous viol. Suddenly out of the blackness the madly sawing bow struck me, and I knew I was close to the player. I felt ahead, touched the back of Zann's chair, and then found and shook his shoulder in an effort to bring him to his senses.

He did not respond, and still the viol shrieked on without slackening. I moved my hand to his head, whose mechanical nodding I was able to stop, and shouted in his ear that we must both flee from the unknown things of the night. But he neither answered me nor abated the frenzy of his unutterable music, while all through the garret strange currents of wind seemed to dance in the darkness and babel. When my hand touched his ear I shuddered, though I knew not why—knew not why till I felt the still face; the ice-cold, stiffened, unbreathing face whose glassy eyes bulged uselessly into the void. And then, by some miracle, finding the door and the large wooden bolt, I plunged wildly away from that glassy-eyed thing in the dark, and from the ghoulish howling of that accursed viol whose fury increased even as I plunged.

Leaping, floating, flying down those endless stairs through the dark house; racing mindlessly out into the narrow, steep, and ancient street of steps and tottering houses; clattering down steps and over cobbles to the lower streets and the putrid canyon-walled river; panting across the great dark bridge to the broader, healthier streets and boulevards we know; all these are terrible impressions that linger with me. And I recall that there was no wind, and that the moon was out, and that all the lights of the city twinkled.

Despite my most careful searches and investigations, I have never since been able to find the Rue d'Auseil. But I am not wholly sorry; either for this or for the loss in undreamable abysses of the closely written sheets which alone could have explained the music of Erich Zann.

THE BIRDS

Bruno Schulz

⁘

Translated by John Curran Davis

Yellow and filled with boredom, the winter days were here. A threadbare and patchy, too-short mantle of snow was spread over the reddened earth. It was too meagre for the many roofs, which remained black or rust coloured, slatted roofs and arches, concealing within them the smoke-blackened expanses of attics—charred-black cathedrals bristling with ribs of rafters, purlins and joists, dark lungs of the winter gales. Each dawn uncovered new vent pipes and chimney stacks, sprung up in the night, blown out by the nocturnal gale—black pipes of the Devil's organs. The chimney sweeps could not drive away the crows that perched in the evenings like living black leaves on the branches of the trees by the church, which rose up again, flapping, finally to cling once more, each to its own place on its own branch, while at daybreak they took to the air in vast flocks, clouds of soot, flecks of undulating and fantastic lampblack, smearing with their twinkling cawing the dull-yellow streaks of dawn. The days hardened in the cold and boredom, like last year's bread loaves. They were cut with blunt knives, without appetite, in idle sleepiness.

Father no longer left the house. He lit the stoves and studied the never-to-be-fathomed essence of fire. He savoured the salty, metallic taste and smoky aroma of the winter flames, a cool caress of salamanders, licking at the shiny soot in the throat of the chimney.

He undertook with enthusiasm in those days all of the repairs in the loftier regions of the parlour. He could be seen at any time of day, squatting at the top of a stepladder as he tinkered at something close to the ceiling, around the cornices of the tall windows or the counterweights and chains of the hanging lamps. As house painters do, he used his stepladder like enormous stilts, and he felt happy in that bird's-eye perspective, close to the ceiling's painted sky, its arabesques and birds. He took himself further and further away from the affairs of practical life. Should Mother, filled with anxiety and concern about his condition, attempt to draw him into a conversation about the business, about the bills due at the end of the month, he would listen to her distractedly, utterly vexed, twitches affecting his absent face. He would occasionally interrupt her with a sudden, imploring gesture of the hand, to scurry into a corner and press his ear to a chink between the floorboards, and—with the index fingers of both hands upraised to indicate the supreme importance of the investigation—to listen. We had not yet come to understand the lamentable background to these eccentricities, the gloomy complex that was ripening in the depths.

Mother held no influence over him; though upon Adela he bestowed much reverence and attention. When she swept his chamber it was a great and momentous ceremony to him, one that he never neglected to witness, following Adela's every movement with a mixture of fear and a shudder of delight. He ascribed to her every action some deeper, symbolic meaning, and when the girl pushed a long-handled brush across the floor, with youthful and bold thrusts, it was almost beyond his endurance. Tears streamed from his eyes then; his face was choked up with silent laughter and his body shook with a pleasurable spasm of orgasm. His ticklishness bordered on madness. Adela had merely to point a finger at him, with a motion that suggested tickling, and he would fly through room after room in a wild panic, fastening their doors behind him, finally to collapse in the last, on his stomach on the bed, twisting in convulsions of laughter provoked by that singular inner vision he could least endure. Because of this, Adela held almost unlimited authority over Father.

At that time, we first began to notice Father's passionate interest in animals. In the early stages, it was the passion of a hunter and an artist combined. It was also, perhaps, one creature's deeper, zoological affinity with kindred and yet so different forms of life, experimentation in the unexplored registers of being. It was not until a later stage that the affair took that peculiar, embroiled and profoundly sinful turn against nature that it would be better not to bring to the light of day.

It all began with the incubation of birds' eggs.

With a considerable outlay of effort and expense, Father obtained—from Hamburg, Holland and African zoological stations—fertilised birds' eggs, and he set enormous Belgian hens to the task of incubating them. It was a process that I too found highly absorbing, that hatching out of nestlings, real anomalies of shape and colouration. One could scarcely have envisioned in those monsters, their enormous, fantastic beaks yawning wide open the moment they were born, hissing voraciously in the abysses of their throats—those salamanders with the frail and naked bodies of hunchbacks—the peacocks, pheasants, wood grouse and condors they were to become. Consigned to baskets, in cotton wool, that dragon brood lifted up on thin necks their blind and walleyed heads, squawking voicelessly from their mute throats. My father walked along his shelves in a green apron, like a gardener along his cactus frames, and coaxed from nothingness those blind blisters pulsating with life, those clumsy abdomens taking in the external world only in the form of food, those excrescences of life, scrabbling gropingly toward the light. And when, some weeks later, those blind buds of life finally did burst into the light, the rooms were all filled with colourful chirruping, the twinkling twittering of their new inhabitants. They perched on the wooden pelmets and the mouldings on the wardrobes. They nested in the thicket of the tin branches and arabesques of the many-armed hanging lamps.

As Father studied his huge ornithological compendiums, browsing through their coloured plates, those fledged phantasms seemed to come flying out of them, filling the room with colourful fluttering, slivers of crimson, shreds of sapphire, verdigris and silver. At feeding time, they comprised a varicoloured, surging patch on the floor, a living carpet that was torn to pieces upon anyone's incautious entry, rent asunder into animated flowers, fluttering into the air, to perch at last in the loftier regions of the parlour. A certain condor especially remains in my memory, an enormous bird with a bare neck, its face wrinkled and rank with excrescences. It was a gaunt ascetic, a Buddhist lama with impassive dignity in its whole demeanour, comporting itself in accordance with the strict etiquette of its illustrious tribe. As it sat opposite Father, unmoving in its monumental posture of the ancient Egyptian gods, its eye clouding over with a white film, which spread from the edge to the pupil, enclosing it entirely in contemplation of its venerable solitude—and with its stone hard profile—it seemed to be an older brother of my father: the same substance of its body, its tendons and its wrinkled, hard skin; the same dried up, bony face with those same deep and horny sockets. Even Father's long and thin hands, hardened into nodules and ending in his curling nails, had their analogon in the condor's talons. Seeing it asleep, I could not resist the impression that I was looking at a mummy—the mummy, shrunken by desiccation, of my father. Nor, as I suspected, had this astonishing resemblance escaped Mother's notice; although we never pursued the topic. Characteristically, both the condor and my father used the same chamber pot.

Not confining himself to incubating ever younger specimens, my father arranged ornithological weddings. He dispatched matchmakers and tethered the enticing, ardent betrothed in the gaps and hollows of the attic. And he succeeded, in fact, in turning the roof of our house—an enormous, shingled span-roof—into a veritable bird's inn, a Noah's ark to which feathered creatures of all kinds flocked from faraway places. Even long after the avian farm had been liquidated, that tradition regarding our house continued to be observed in the aerial realm, and come the period of the springtime migrations, whole hosts of cranes, pelicans, peacocks and birds of all kinds would alight on our roof.

But by and by, after its brief magnificence, the venture took a sad turn. It soon proved necessary to translocate Father to two rooms in the attic, which had served for lumber rooms, and from that time onward the mingled, early dawn clamour of the birds' voices reached us from there. Augmented by the resonance of the roof's expanse, those wooden boxes of attic rooms rang throughout with uproar, fluttering and crowing, hoots and gurgles. Father was lost to our sight throughout several weeks. He came down to the apartment only occasionally, and only then could we perceive that he was somewhat diminished; that he had lost weight and shrunk. Sometimes, in his forgetfulness, he would start up from his seat at table and let out long hoots, beating his arms like wings as a cloud of leucoma rose to his eyes. But afterward, in his embarrassment, he laughed along with us and tried to make a joke of the incident.

One day, during her general housework, Adela appeared without warning in Father's ornithological kingdom. Standing in the doorway, she wrung her hands at the stench rising in the air, at the heaps of excrement that coated the floor, the tables and the chairs. With hasty decisiveness, she threw the window open, and with her long brushes she set the whole mass of birds whirling. An infernal storm-cloud of feathers, wings and screeches flew up, in the midst of which Adela—looking like a furious mænad, half-obscured by the spinning of her thyrsus—danced a dance of destruction. My father flapped his arms in horror and tried to raise himself into the air together with his flock of birds. Gradually, the winged storm-cloud thinned, until at last on the battlefield there stood only Adela, exhausted and breathing hard, and my father, with an air of distress and shame, ready to capitulate on any terms.

A moment later, my father descended the stairway of his dominion, a broken man, an exiled king who had lost his throne and his reign.

THE USHER

Felisberto Hernández

❧

Translated by Luis Harss

As soon as I grew up, I went to live in a big city. The city's downtown—
where everyone rushed around among tall buildings—was near a river.

I was an usher at a movie theater, but the rest of the time I, too, scur-
ried around like a mouse in old furniture. I knew holes everywhere with
unexpected connections through which to reach my favorite places. And
it gave me just as much pleasure to imagine the parts of the city I didn't
know.

I had the late-afternoon shift at the theater. I rushed into my dressing room, polished my gold buttons, slipped my green tail coat on over
my gray vest and trousers, and took up my post in the left aisle of the
orchestra, where the gentlemen handed me the seat numbers and then
fell in behind the ladies who followed my sinking steps down the red
carpet. At each stop I did a minuet turn, bowed and put out my hand. I
always expected to be surprised by the tip and knew how to bow at once
with respect and contempt. I didn't care if people weren't aware of my

superiority: I felt like an old rake with a flower in his buttonhole, wise to the ways of the world. I was happy watching the ladies in their different dresses and enjoyed the moment of confusion there was each time the screen lit up and the house darkened. Then I hurried back to the dressing room to count my tips, and afterward I set out to explore the city.

I got in tired, but on my way to my room, up stairs and along hallways, I hoped to see more sights through half-open doors. As soon as I turned on the light, the flowers of the wallpaper gave out a blaze of color: they were red and blue, on a black background. The ceiling light had been lowered on its cord until it almost touched the foot of the bed. I lay right under it to read, using a newspaper as a shade to block some of the glare and to dim the flowers a bit. At the head of the bed stood a table with bottles and other objects I watched for hours on end. Afterward I stayed awake with the light off until the sound of bones being sawed and hacked came in the window and I heard the butcher cough.

Twice a week a friend took me to a dining room where I could get a free meal. You went through an entrance hall that was almost as large as a theater lobby, into the silent luxury of the dining room. It belonged to a man who was going to go on offering those meals for as long as he lived because of a promise he had made when his daughter was saved from the river. The diners were foreigners sunk in memories. Each had the right to bring a friend twice a week. Once a month the host ate with them. He made a grand entry, like a conductor when the orchestra is ready to start playing, but the only thing he conducted was the silence. At eight o'clock sharp, a wing of the huge white double door at the far end of the room swung open on the dark emptiness of a neighboring room, and out of the darkness stepped a tall figure in black tails, his head cocked to the right and a hand raised to indicate we should remain seated. All faces turned toward him, but with blank stares, their eyes still on the thoughts inhabiting them at that moment. The conductor nodded a greeting as he sat and the players bent over their plates and sounded their instruments, each a professor of silence playing to himself. At first you heard pecking silverware, but then the noise took off and you no longer noticed it. To me it was just a meal, but to my friend, who was like the others, it meant the chance to spend a few moments remembering his country. Suddenly I felt confined to a circle the size of my plate, as if I had no thoughts of my own, surrounded by sleepers eating in concert, watched over by the servants. We knew we were finished with a plate when it was whisked away; soon we were cheered by the next one. Sometimes we had to divide our surprise between the plate and the neck of a bottle that came enveloped in a white napkin. At other times we were surprised at how the dark stain of the wine seemed to grow in the air, suspended in its crystal glass.

After a few such meals I had gotten used to the objects on the table and learned to play the instruments to myself alone, but the remoteness of the guests still troubled me. When the "conductor" made his appearance on the second month I no longer believed his generosity was because his daughter had been saved: I insisted on supposing she had drowned. In my wayward thoughts, a couple of long, nebulous steps carried me down the few blocks that separated us from the river, where I pictured the girl floating just below the surface. A yellowish moon shone on her but at the same time her gorgeous dress and the skin of her arms and face were all bright white—a privilege due perhaps to her father's wealth and his untold sacrifices on her behalf. I imagined the guests across the table from me, with their backs to the river, had also drowned: they hovered over their plates as if they were trying to come up to the surface from the bottom of the river. Those of us eating on my side of the table bowed in their direction but did not reach out to them.

Once during the meal I heard some words. A very fat guest said: "I'm dying," and immediately his head rolled forward, into his soup, as if he were trying to drink it without a spoon. All the other heads swiveled to look at the one served up in the soup plate, and all the silverware stopped clicking. Then there was the sound of scraping chair legs, the servants carried the dead man into the hat room and made the phone ring to call the doctor, and before the body was cold everyone was back in place clicking and pecking again.

In those days I had begun to slow down at my job, sick with silence. I was sinking into myself the way you sink into a swamp. My colleagues at work kept bumping into me—I had become an aimless obstacle. The only thing I did well was polish my gold buttons. Once I heard a colleague say: "Move it, hippo!" The word fell into my swamp, stuck to me, and sank in. It was followed by other insults that piled up in my mind like dirty dishes. By then everyone avoided me, changing direction to stay out of my swamp.

Some time later I was fired and my foreign friend got me another job in a less elegant theater. Here the women dressed badly and there were no big tippers. Still, I tried to hang on.

But on one of my most miserable days something appeared before my eyes that made up for all my ills. I had been catching glimpses of it now and then. One night I woke up in the dark silence of my room and, on the wall papered with purple flowers, I saw a light. I suspected at once that something extraordinary was happening to me and I was not frightened. I moved my eyes sideways and the spot of light shifted with them. It was like the spot you see in the dark when you put out a lamp, but it lasted longer and you could see through it. I lowered my eyes to the table and saw my bottles and other objects. There could be no doubt: the light was coming from my eyes and had been developing for some time. I stared at the back of my hand and saw my open fingers. Soon I felt tired: the light dimmed and I closed my eyes. In a minute I opened them again to make sure I was not imagining things. I looked at the electric lightbulb and it lit up with my light—so I was convinced. I smiled to myself: who else in the world saw with his own eyes in the dark?

The light grew stronger every night. In the daytime I stuck nails all over the wall and at night I hung glass and porcelain objects—the ones I could see best—from them. In a small cabinet engraved—before my time—with my initials I kept goblets with strings tied to their stems, bottles with strings around their necks, frilly saucers with looped edges, teacups with gold lettering, and so on. One night I was seized by a terror that almost drove me mad. I had gotten up to see if there was anything left in the cabinet, and, before I could turn on the electric light, I saw my face and eyes in the mirror, lit with my own light. I fainted, and when I woke up my head was under the bed and I saw the metal frame as if I were under a bridge. I swore never again to look at that face of mine with its otherworldly eyes. They were greenish yellow eyes in which some unknown disease gleamed triumphant: glowing round holes in a face broken into pieces no one could put together or understand.

I stayed awake until the sound of the bones being sawed and hacked came in the window.

The next day I remembered that as I had made my way up the shadowy orchestra aisle a few nights before, a woman had caught my eye with a frown. On another night my foreign friend had made fun of my eyes, saying they shone like cat eyes. Now I began to watch for my face in dark store windows, where I could ignore the objects behind the windows. After much thought, I had decided I ought to use my light only when I was alone.

At one of the free dinners, before the host appeared in the white doorway, I saw the darkness through the half-open door and felt like penetrating it with my eyes. So I began planning a way to get into that room, where I had already detected glass cases loaded with objects that intensified the light in my eyes.

The hall leading from the street into the dining room was actually the back entrance to a house that stretched clear across the block and had its main entrance on another street. The only person you ran into in the back entrance at that time of day—by now I had seen him more than once on my walks up and down the street—was the butler, who had an apelike way of lumbering toward you with bow legs and flap arms, although seen from the side in his stiff tails he looked more like a stuffed bird. One afternoon, before dinner, I dared to address him. He watched me from under thick brows as I said:

"There's something I'd like to discuss with you. But I must ask you to keep it to yourself."

"At your pleasure, sir."

"It's just that"—now he waited, staring at his feet—"I have a light in my eyes that allows me to see in the dark."

"Indeed, sir, I understand."

"How could you understand?" I was annoyed. "You can't ever have met anyone capable of seeing in the dark."

"I said I understood your words, sir. But of course I find them amazing."

"Well, listen: if we go into that room—the hat room—and close the door, you can take any object from your pocket and put it on the table and I'll tell you what it is."

"But what if someone comes in, sir?"

"If by someone you mean the host, you have my permission to tell him everything. Do me the favor: it will only take a minute."

"But what for?"

"You'll soon find out. Put anything you want on the table when I close the door and I'll tell you . . ."

"Just make it quick, sir, please . . ."

He hastened in, straight to the table. I closed the door. The next moment, I said:

"That's only your open hand!"

"Alright, you've proved your point, sir."

"Now pull something from your pocket."

He produced his handkerchief and I laughed and said:

"What a dirty handkerchief!"

He laughed, too—but suddenly let out a squawk and made for the door. When he opened it he had a hand over his eyes and was trembling.

I realized then he had seen my face—a possibility I had not anticipated. He was pleading;

"Go away, sir! Go away!"

And he started across the dining room, which was already lit but empty.

The next time the host ate with us I borrowed my friend's place near the head of the table, where the host sat: it was the area served by the butler, who would not be able to avoid me. In fact, when he was bringing in the first dish he felt my eyes on his, and his hands began to shake. While knives and forks made the silence throb, I kept up my pressure on him. Afterward I ran into him in the hall. He began:

"Please, sir, you'll ruin me."

"I certainly will if you don't listen to me."

"But what does the gentleman want of me?"

"Only that you let me see, and I mean only see—you can search me when I come out—the glass cases in the room next to the dining room."

He gestured and grimaced wildly before he could get a word out. Finally he managed to say:

"Consider my years of service in this house, sir . . ."

I felt sorry for him, and disgusted at myself for being sorry. My craving to see made me regard him as a complicated obstacle. He was telling me the story of his life, explaining why he could not betray his master. I interrupted him to threaten:

"Save your breath—he'll never find out. But I'll scramble your brains if you don't obey, and then you really might do something you'd regret. Wait for me at two o'clock tonight. I'll be in that room until three."

"Scramble my brains, sir, kill me . . ."

"It'll be worse than death for you unless you do as I say."

As I left I repeated:

"Tonight, at two. I'll be at the door."

On my way out, trying to find an excuse for my behavior, I said to myself, "When he sees that nothing bad happens he won't suffer any more." I wanted to be let in that same night because it was the night when I ate there and the food and the wine excited me and made my light brighter.

During dinner the butler was not as nervous as I expected, and I thought he would not open the door, but when I went back at two o'clock he did. Following him and his candelabrum across the dining room I had the sudden notion that he had caved in under the mental torture of my threat and told the host everything and they had set a trap for me. The minute we were in the room with the glass cases I looked at him. He was staring at his feet, expressionless. So I said:

"Bring me a mattress. I can see better from the floor and I want my body to be comfortable."

He hesitated, hanging on to the candelabrum, but went out. Alone in the room, I started to look around me and it was like being in the center of a constellation. Then I remembered it might be a trap: the butler was taking his time. But he wouldn't have needed long to trap me. Finally he came in dragging a mattress with one hand, holding the candelabrum up with the other. In a voice too loud for a room full of glass cases he said:

"I'll be back at three."

At first I was afraid to see myself reflected in the huge mirrors or in the glass cases, but lying on the floor I was outside their range. Why had the butler seemed so calm? My light wandered over the universe of things around me but I felt no pleasure. After daring so much, I had no courage left to calm down. I could look at an object and make it mine by holding it for a while in my light, but only if I was at ease and knew I had the right to look at it. I decided to focus on a small area near my eyes. There was a missal in a tortoise-shell binding with a streaked surface like burnt sugar, except for a filigree in one corner, on which a flower had been pressed. Next to it, like a coiled reptile, lay a rosary of precious stones. Spread above those two objects were fans that looked like dancing girls flaring out their skirts. My light wavered a bit when it went over several with sequins and stopped on one showing a Chinaman with his face made of mother-of-pearl, his robe of silk. Only that Chinaman could stand being there alone in endless space: his impassiveness was as mysterious as stupidity. Yet he was the one thing I was able to make mine that night. As I left I tried to give the butler a tip, but he refused it saying:

"I'm not doing this for money, sir. You're obliging me to do it."

During the second session I focused on some jasper miniatures, but when I was scanning a small bridge with elephants crossing over it I realized there was another light in the room besides mine. I turned my eyes before turning my head and saw a woman in white advancing toward me with a blazing candelabrum. She had come out of the depths of the wide avenue bordered with glass cases. I felt my temples quiver and the quivers run like sleepy streams down my cheeks, then wrap around my head like a turban, and finally creep down my thighs and knot at my knees. The woman advanced slowly, her head rigid. I expected her to scream when her mantle of light touched my mattress. Every now and then she stopped and, before she started up again, I thought of escaping, but I couldn't move. In spite of the spots of shadow on her face I could tell she was beautiful: she seemed to have been made by hand after having been outlined on paper. She was coming too near, but I had decided to lie still to the end of time. She stopped by the edge of the mattress and then proceeded with one foot on the mattress and the other on the floor. I was like a dummy stretched out in a store window while she went by with one foot on the curb and the other in the street. I stayed there without blinking, although her light flickered strangely. On her way back she wove a winding path among the glass cases, the tail of her gown gently tangling in their legs. I had the feeling I had been asleep for a moment before she reached the door at the far end of the room. She had left it open when she came in and she went out without closing it. Her light had not completely faded when I became aware of another light behind me. Now I was able to get up. I grabbed the mattress by a corner and dragged it out after me. The butler was waiting, his whole body and his candelabrum shaking. I couldn't understand what he said because his dentures were chattering.

At the next session I knew she would return and I couldn't concentrate on anything, all I could do was wait for her. But when she appeared I calmed down. Everything happened just as before: she had the same trancelike stare in her hollow eyes; and yet, in some way I couldn't fathom, each night had been different. At the same time, she was already a fond habit I cherished. When she reached the foot of the mattress I had a moment of anxiety. I realized she was not going to walk along the edge but pass over me. Again I was terrified thinking she would scream. She had stopped by my feet, and now her first step came down on the mattress, another on my knees—which shuddered and parted, making her foot slip—the next, with the other foot, on the mattress, another on the pit of my stomach, then one more on the mattress, followed by a bare foot that landed on my throat. And then I lost all sense of what was happening in the delicate rustling of her perfumed gown as its tail brushed over my face.

After that the nights blurred together. Although I had different feelings each time, the events were so much alike that in the end they fused in my mind, as if they had happened in just a few nights. The tail of her gown erased guilty memories, sweeping me into space on airs as gentle as the ones stirred long ago by childhood bedsheets. Sometimes the tail settled on my face for a moment and then I dreaded losing touch with her, under the threat of an unknown present, but when the airy feeling returned and I had cleared the abyss I thought of the interruption as an affectionate joke and breathed in as much of the tail as I could before it was whisked away.

Sometimes the butler would say:

"Haven't you seen everything by now, sir?"

But I would head back to my room, slowly brush down my black suit at the knees and waist, and then go to bed to think of her. I had forgotten about my own light—and would have given every bit of it to remember her more clearly in her mantle of candlelight. I went over her steps and imagined that one night she would stop and kneel by me and then it would not be her gown I'd feel but her hair and lips. I rehearsed the scene in different ways. Sometimes I put words in her mouth: "My darling, I've been lying to you . . ." But the words did not seem to fit her, and I would have to go back and start all over again. The rehearsals kept me awake and even found their way into my dreams. Once I dreamed she was going up the nave in church. There was the glow of candlelight against a background of red and gold. The brightest light fell on her wedding gown with the long train she slowly drew after her. She was about to get married but walked alone, with one hand clasped in the other. I was a woolly dog, shiny black, lying on her train. She dragged me along proudly, and I seemed to be asleep. At the same time I was being swept up in the crowd that followed the bride and the dog. In this version of myself I had feelings and ideas my mother could have had, and I tried to get as close to the dog as possible. He sailed along as calmly as if he were asleep on a beach, waking from time to time, wrapped in spray. I had transmitted an idea to him which he received with a smile. It was: "Let yourself go, but think of something else."

Then, at dawn, I would hear the meat being sawed and hacked.

One night, with few tips coming my way, I left the theater and went down to the street that ran along the river. My legs were tired but my eyes were aching to see. When I paused at a stall that sold used books I saw a foreign couple go by. He was dressed in black with a French beret; she wore a Spanish mantilla and spoke German. We had been walking in the same direction, but they were in a hurry and they left me behind. When they reached the corner, however, they bumped into a child who was selling candy, and spilled his merchandise. She laughed and helped the boy pick up his goods and gave him some coins before moving on—and when she turned for a last look back at him I recognized my woman in white and felt myself sinking into a hole in the air. I followed the couple anxiously and also barged into someone—a fat woman who said:

"Watch where you're going, you idiot!"

By then I was running and on the point of crying. They reached a seedy movie theater and while he bought the tickets she turned and looked at me with some insistence because of my frantic haste but did not recognize me. I was certain about her, though. I went in and sat a few rows ahead of them, and one of the times I looked back at her she must have seen my eyes in the dark because she whispered nervously in the man's ear. After a while I turned back again and again they exchanged a few words, out loud this time, then immediately got up and left, and I ran out after them. I was chasing her without knowing what I would do. She had not recognized me—besides, she was running off with someone else. I had never been so excited and—though I suspected it would end badly—I couldn't stop myself. I was convinced it was all a case of misplaced persons and lives, yet the man holding her arm had pulled his cap down over his ears and walked faster every minute. It was as if all three of us were plunging into the danger of a fire: I was catching up without a thought for what might happen. They stepped off the sidewalk and started to run across the street. I was going to do the same when another man in a beret stopped me from his car, honking and swearing at me. As soon as the car was gone I saw the couple approach a policeman. Without losing a beat I swung off in another direction. When I looked back after a few yards there was no one following me, so I started to slow down and return to the everyday world. I had to watch my step and do a lot of thinking. I realized I was going to be in a black mood and went into a dimly lit tavern where I could be alone with myself. I ordered wine and started to spend the tips I had been saving to pay for my room. The light shining on the street through the bars of an open window lit up the leaves of a tree that stood on the curb. I made an effort to concentrate on what had been happening to me. The floorboards were old planks full of holes. I was thinking the world in which she and I had met was inviolable, she could not just step out of it after all the times she had passed the tail of her gown over my face: it was a ritual governed by some fateful design. I would have to do something—or perhaps await some signal from her on one of our nights together. Meantime she seemed unaware of the danger of being awake and out in the street at night, in violation of the design guiding her steps when she walked in her sleep. I was proud to be nothing but a poor usher sitting in a dingy tavern and yet the only one to know—because even she did not know it—that my light had penetrated a world closed to everyone else. When I left the tavern I saw a man with a beret, then several others. I decided men with berets were everywhere but had nothing to do with me. I got on a trolley thinking I would carry a hidden beret with me the next time we met among the glass cases and suddenly show it to her. A fat man dropped his bulk into the seat next to me, and I couldn't think any more.

I took the beret into the next session, not knowing whether I would use it. But the moment she appeared in the depths of the room I whipped it out and waved it as if I were signaling with a dark lantern. Suddenly she stopped and, instinctively, I put the cap away; but when she started up I took it out and signaled her again. When she paused by the edge of the mattress I was afraid and threw the cap at her. It hit her on the chest and landed at her feet. It took her another few seconds to let out a scream. She dropped the candelabrum, which fell with a clatter and went out. Then I heard her body fall with a soft thud, followed by the louder sound of what must have been her head. I stood and reached out as if feeling for one of the glass cases, but just then my light came on and focused on her. She had fallen as if ready to slip into a happy dream, with half-open arms, her head to one side and her face modestly hidden under her waves of hair. I ran my light up and down her body like a thief searching her with a flashlight. I was surprised to find what looked like a large rubber stamp by her feet: it turned out to be my beret. My light not only lit her up but stripped something from her. I was pleased at the thought that the cap lying next to her belonged to me and to no one else. But suddenly my eyes began to see her feet turn a greenish yellow, like my face the night I had seen it in my wardrobe mirror. The color brightened in some parts of the feet and darkened in others, and soon I noticed little white bony shapes that reminded me of the bones of toes. By then horror was spinning in my head like trapped smoke. I ran my light over her body again and it looked changed, completely fleshless. One of her hands had strayed and lay across her groin: it was nothing but bones. I didn't want to go on looking and I tried to clamp my eyes shut, but they were like two worms turning and twisting in their holes until the light they projected reached her head. She had lost her hair and the bones of her face had the spectral glow of a far-off star seen through a telescope. And then suddenly I heard the butler's heavy step: he was switching on the lights and babbling frantically. She had recovered her full shape, but I could not bear to look at her. The host burst through a door I hadn't noticed before and ran to pick up his daughter. He was on his way out with her in his arms when another woman appeared. As they all left together the butler kept shouting:

"It was his fault, it's that fiendish light in his eyes. I didn't want to do it, he made me . . ."

Alone for a moment, I realized I was in serious trouble. I could have left, but I waited for the host to return. At his heel was the butler who said:

"You still here?"

I began to work on an answer, which would have gone something like this: "I'm not someone to just walk out of a house. Besides, I owe my host an explanation." But it took me too long—and I considered it beneath my dignity to respond to the butler's charges.

By then I was facing the host. He had been running his fingers through his hair, frowning as if in deep thought. Now he drew himself up to his full height and, narrowing his eyes, he asked:

"Did my daughter invite you into the room?"

His voice seemed to come out of a second person inside him. I was so startled that all I could say was:

"No, it's just that ... I'd be in here looking at these objects ... and she'd walk over me ..."

He had opened his mouth to speak but words failed him. Again he ran his fingers through his hair. He seemed to be thinking: "An unforeseen complication."

The butler was carrying on again about my fiendish light and all the rest of it. I felt nothing in my life would ever make sense to anyone else. I tried to recover my pride and said:

"You'll never understand, my dear sir. If it makes you feel better, call the police."

He also stood on his dignity:

"I won't call the police because you have been my guest. But you have betrayed my trust. I leave it to your honor to make amends."

At that point I began to think of insults. The first one that came to mind was "hypocrite." I was looking for something else when one of the glass cases burst open and a mandolin fell out. We all listened attentively to the clang of the box and strings. Then the host turned and headed for his private door. The butler, meantime, had gone to pick up the mandolin. It was a moment before he could bring himself to touch it, as if he thought it might be haunted, although the poor thing looked as dried-out as a dead bird. I turned as well and started across the dining room with ringing steps: it was like walking inside a sound box.

The next several days I was very depressed and lost my job again. One night I tried to hang my glass objects on the wall, but they looked ridiculous. And I was losing my light: I could barely see the back of my hand when I held it up to my eyes.

THE WAITING ROOM

Robert Aickman

❦

Against such interventions of fate as this, reflected Edward Pendlebury, there was truly nothing that the wisest and most farsighted could do; and the small derangement of his plans epitomised the larger derangement which was life. All the way from Grantham it had been uncertain whether the lateness of the train from King's Cross would not result in Pendlebury missing the connection at York. The ticket inspector thought that "they might hold it"; but Pendlebury's fellow passengers, all of them businessmen who knew the line well, were sceptical, and seemed to imply that it was among the inspector's duties to soothe highly-strung passengers. "This is a Scarborough train," said one of the businessmen several times. "It's not meant for those who want to go further north." Pendlebury knew perfectly well that it was a Scarborough train: it was the only departure he could possibly catch, and no one denied that the time table showed a perfectly good, though slow, connection. Nor could anyone say why the express was late.

It transpired that the connection had not been held.

"Other people want to get home besides you," said the man at the barrier, when Pendlebury complained rather sharply.

There were two hours to wait; and Pendlebury was warned that the train would be very slow indeed. "The-milk-and-mail we call it," said his informant.

"But it does go there?"

"In the end."

Already it was late at night; and the Refreshment Room was about to close. The uncertainty regarding the connection had made Pendlebury feel a little sick; and now he found it difficult to resume reading the Government publication the contents of which it was necessary for him to master before the next day's work began. He moved from place to place, reading and rereading the same page of technicalities: from a draughty seat under a light to a waiting room, and, when the waiting room was invaded by some over-jolly sailors, to the adjoining hotel, where his request for coffee seemed to be regarded as insufficient.

In the end it was long before the train was due when he found his way to the platform from which his journey was to be resumed. A small but bitterly cold wind was now blowing through the dark station from the north; it hardly sufficed to disturb the day's accumulation of litter, but none the less froze the fingers at a touch. The appearance of the train, therefore, effected a disproportionate revival in Pendlebury's spirits. It was composed of old stock, but none the less comfortable for that; the compartment was snugly heated, and Pendlebury sat in it alone.

The long journey began just in time for Pendlebury to hear the Minster clock clanging midnight as the train slowly steamed out. Before long it had come to rest again, and the bumping of milk churns began, shaking the train as they were moved, and ultimately crashing, at stately intervals, to the remote wayside platforms. Observing, as so many late travellers before him, that milk seems to travel from the town to the country, Pendlebury, despite the thuds, fell asleep, and took up the thread of anxiety which he so regularly followed through the caves of the night. He dreamed of the world's unsympathy, of projects hopefully begun but soon unreasonably overturned, of happiness alone, it was beautiful and springtime; until suddenly a bitter wind descended upon him from no-where, and he awoke, hot and cold simultaneously.

"All change."

The door of the compartment was open, and a porter was address-ing him. "Where are we?"

"Casterton. Train stops here."

"I want Wykeby."

"Wykeby's on the main line. Six stations past."

"When's the next train back?"

"Not till six-thirty."

The guard had appeared, stamping his feet.

"All out please. We want to go to bed."

Pendlebury rose to his feet. He had cramp in his left arm, and could not hold his suitcase. The guard pulled it out and set it on the platform. Pendlebury alighted and the porter shut the door. He jerked his head to the guard, who clicked the green slide of his lantern. The train slowly steamed away.

"What happens to passengers who arrive here fast asleep?" asked Pendlebury. "I can't be the first on this train."

"This train's not rightly meant for passengers," replied the porter. "Not beyond the main line, that is."

"I missed the connection. The London train was late."

"Maybe," said the porter. The northerner's view of the south was implicit in his tone.

The train could be seen coming to rest in a siding. Suddenly all its lights went out.

"Casterton is quite a big place, I believe?"

"Middling," said the porter. He was a dark featured man, with a saturnine expression.

"What about a hotel?"

"Not since the Arms was sold up. The new people don't do rooms. Can't get the labour."

"Well, what *am* I to do?" The realisation that it was no business of the porter to answer this question made Pendlebury sound childish and petulant.

The porter looked at him. Then he jerked his head as he had done to the guard and began to move away. Picking up his suitcase (the other hand was still numb and disembodied), Pendlebury followed him. Snow was beginning to fall, not in flakes but in single stabbing spots.

The porter went first to a small office, lighted by a sizzling Tilley lamp, and heated to stuffiness by a crackling coke stove. Here he silently performed a series of obscure tasks, while Pendlebury waited. Finally he motioned Pendlebury out, drew the fire, extinguished the light, and locked the door. Then he lifted from its bracket the single oil lamp which illuminated the platform and opened a door marked "General Waiting Room." Once more he jerked his head. This time he was holding the light by his dark face, and Pendlebury was startled by the suddenness and violence of the movement. It was a wonder that the porter did not injure his neck.

"Mind you, I'm not taking any responsibility. If you choose to spend the night, it's entirely your own risk."

"It's not a matter of choice," rejoined Pendlebury.

"It's against the regulations to use the waiting rooms for any purpose but waiting for the company's trains."

"They're not the company's trains any more. They're supposed to be *our* trains."

Presumably the porter had heard that too often to consider it worth reply.

"Thank you," said Pendlebury. "What about a fire?"

"Not since before the war."

"I see," said Pendlebury. "I suppose you're sure there's nowhere else?"

"Have a look if you want to."

Through the door Pendlebury could see the drops of snow scudding past like icy shrapnel.

"I'll stay here. After all, it's only a few hours." The responsibilities of the morrow were already ranging themselves around Pendlebury, ready to topple and pounce.

The porter placed the lamp on the polished yellow table.

"Don't forget it's nothing to do with me."

"If I'm not awake, I suppose someone will call me in time for the six-thirty?"

"Yes," said the porter. "You'll be called."

"Goodnight," said Pendlebury. "And thank you."

The porter neither answered, nor even nodded. Instead he gave that violent twist or jerk of his head. Pendlebury realised that it must be a twitch; perhaps partly voluntary, partly involuntary. Now that he had seen it in the light, its extravagance frightened him. Going, the porter slammed the door sharply; from which Pendlebury deduced also that the lock must be stiff.

As well as the yellow table the waiting room contained four long seats stoutly upholstered in shiny black. Two of these seats were set against the back wall, with the empty fireplace between them; and one against each of the side walls. The seats had backs, but no arms. There were also two objects in hanging frames: one was the address of the local representative of an organisation concerned to protect unmarried women from molestation when away from home; the other a black and white photograph of the Old Bailey, described, Pendlebury observed, as The New Central Criminal Court. Faded though the scene now was, the huge blind figure which surmounted the dome still stood out blackly against the pale sky. The streets were empty. The photograph must have been taken at dawn.

Pendlebury's first idea was to move the table to one side, and then bring up one of the long seats so that it stood alongside another, thus making a wider couch for the night. He set the lamp on the floor, and going around to the other end of the table began to pull. The table remained immovable. Supposing this to be owing to its obviously great weight, Pendlebury increased his efforts. He then saw, as the rays of the lantern advanced towards him across the dingy floorboards, that at the bottom of each leg were four L-shaped metal plates, one each side, by which the leg was screwed to the floor. The plates and the screws were dusty and rusty, but solid as a battleship. It was an easy matter to confirm that the four seats were similarly secured. The now extinct company took no risks with its property.

Pendlebury tried to make the best of a single bench, one of the pair divided by the fireplace. But it was both hard and narrow, and curved sharply upwards to its centre. It was even too short, so that Pendlebury found it difficult to dispose of his feet. So cold and uncomfortable was he that he hesitated to put out the sturdy lamp. But in the end he did so. Apart from anything else, Pendlebury found that the light just sufficed to fill the waiting room with dark places which changed their shape and kept him wakeful with speculation. He found also that he was beginning to be obsessed with the minor question of how long the oil would last.

With his left hand steadying the overcoat under his head (most fortunately he had packed a second, country one for use if the weather proved really cold), he turned down the small notched flame with his right; then lifting the lamp from the table, blew it out. Beyond the waiting room it was so dark that the edges of the two windows were indistinct. Indeed the two patches of tenuous foggy greyness seemed to appear and disappear, like the optical illusions found in Christmas crackers. If there was any chance of Pendlebury's eyes "becoming accustomed to the light," it was now dissipated in drowsiness. Truly Pendlebury was very tired indeed.

Not, of course, that he was able to sleep deeply or unbrokenly. Tired as he was, he slept as all must sleep upon such an unwelcoming couch. Many times he woke, with varying degrees of completeness: sometimes it was a mere half-conscious adjustment of his limbs; twice or thrice a plunging start into full vitality (he noticed that the wind had begun to purr and creak in the choked-up chimney); most often it was an intermediate state, a surprisingly cosy awareness of relaxation and irresponsibility, when he felt an extreme disinclination for the night to end and for the agony of having to arise and walk. Pendlebury began to surmise that discomfort, even absurd discomfort, could recede and be surmounted with no effort at all. Almost he rejoiced in his adaptability. He seemed no longer even to be cold. He had read (in the context of polar expedition) that this could be a condition of peculiar danger, a lethal delusion. If so, it seemed also a happy delusion, and Pendlebury was surfeited with reality.

Certainly the wind was rising. Every now and then a large invisible snowflake (the snow seemed no longer to be coming in bullets) slapped against one of the windows like a gobbet of paste; and secret little draughts were beginning to flit even about the solidly built waiting room. At first Pendlebury became aware of them neither by feeling nor by hearing; but before long they were stroking his face and turning his feet to ice (which inconvenience also he proved able to disregard without effort). In a spell of wakefulness, still surprisingly unattended with discomfort, he began to speculate upon the stormy windswept town which no doubt surrounded the lifeless station; the yeomanry slumbering in their darkened houses, the freezing streets paved with lumpy granite setts, the occasional lover, the rare lawbreaker, both withdrawn into deep doorways. Into such small upland communities until two or three centuries ago wolves had come down at night from the fells when snow was heavy. From these reflections about a place he had never seen, Pendlebury drew a curious contrasting comfort.

Suddenly the wind loosened the soot in the chimney; there was a rustling rumbling fall, which seemed as if it would never end; and Pendlebury's nostrils were stuffed with dust. Horribly reluctant, he dragged himself upwards. Immediately his eyes too were affected. He could see nothing at all; the dim windows were completely gone. Straining for his handkerchief, he felt the soot even on his hands. His clothes must be smothered in it. The air seemed opaque and impossible to breathe. Pendlebury began to cough, each contraction penetrating and remobilising his paralysed limbs. As one sinking into an icepack, he became conscious of deathly cold.

It was as if he would never breathe again. The thickness of the air seemed even to be increasing. The sooty dust was whirling about like a sandstorm, impelled by the draughts which seemed to penetrate the stone walls on all sides. Soon he would be buried beneath it. As even his coughing began to strangle in his throat, Pendlebury plunged towards the door. Immediately he struck the heavy screwed-down table. He stumbled back to his bench. He was sure that within minutes he would be dead.

But gradually he became aware that again there was a light in the waiting room. Although he could not tell when it had passed from imperception to perception, there was the tiniest faintest red glow, which was slowly but persistently waxing. It came from near the floor, just at the end of Pendlebury's bench. He had to crick his neck in order to see it at all. Soon he realised that of course it was in the fireplace. All this time after the commencement of the war, once again there was a fire. It was just what he wanted, now that he was roused from his happy numbness into the full pain of the cold.

Steadily the fire brightened and sparkled into a genial crepitation of life. Pendlebury watched it grow, and began to feel the new warmth lapping at his fingers and toes. He could see that the air was still thick with black particles, rising and falling between floor and ceiling, and sometimes twisting and darting about as if independently alive. But he had ceased to choke and cough, and was able again to sink his head upon the crumpled makeshift pillow. He stretched his legs as life soaked into them. Lethargy came delightfully back.

He could see now that the dust was thinning all the time; no doubt settling on the floor and hard, resisting furniture. The fire was glowing ever more strongly; and to Pendlebury it seemed in the end that all the specks of dust had formed themselves into the likeness of living writhing Byzantine columns, which spiralled their barley-sugar whorls through the very texture of the air. The whorls were rapidly losing density, however, and the rosy air clearing. As the last specks danced and died Pendlebury realised that the waiting room was full of people.

There were six people on the side bench which started near his head; and he believed as many on the corresponding bench at the opposite side of the room. He could not count the number on the other bench, because several more people obscured the view by sitting on the table. Pendlebury could see further shadowy figures on the bench which stood against his own wall the other side of the fireplace. The people were of both sexes and all ages, and garbed in the greatest imaginable variety. They were talking softly but seriously to one another. Those nearest the fire sometimes stretched a casual hand toward the flames, as people seated near to a fire usually do. Indeed, except perhaps for the costume of some of them (one woman wore a splendid evening dress), there was but one thing unusual about these people ... Pendlebury could not precisely name it. They looked gentle and charming and in every way sympathetic, those who looked rich and those who looked poor. But Pendlebury felt that there was about them some single uncommon thing which, if he could find it, would unite and clarify their various distinctions. Whatever this thing was Pendlebury was certain that it was shared by him with the people in the waiting room, and with few others. He then reflected that naturally he was dreaming.

To realise that one is dreaming is customarily disagreeable, so that one strains to awake. But than this dream Pendlebury wanted nothing better. The unexpected semi-tranquility he had before at times felt in the comfortless waiting room was now made round and complete. He lay back with a sigh to watch and listen.

On the side bench next to him, with her shoulder by his head, was a pretty girl wearing a black shawl. Pendlebury knew that she was pretty although much of her face was turned away from him as she gazed at the young man seated beside her, whose hand she held. He too had looks in his own way, Pendlebury thought. About both the clothes and the general aspect of the pair was something which recalled a nineteenth century picture by an Academician. None the less it was instantly apparent that each lived only for the other. Their love was like a magnifying glass between them.

On the near corner of the bench at the other side of the fire sat an imposing old man. He had a bushel of silky white hair, a fine brow, a commanding nose, and the mien of a philosopher king. He sat in silence, but from time to time smiled slightly upon his own thoughts. He too seemed dressed in a past fashion.

Those seated upon the table were unmistakably of to-day. Though mostly young, they appeared to be old friends, habituated to trusting one another with the truth. They were at the centre of the party, and their animation was greatest. It was to them that Pendlebury most wanted to speak. The longing to communicate with these quiet happy people soon reached a passionate intensity which Pendlebury had never before known in a dream, but only, very occasionally, upon awaking from one. But now, though warm and physically relaxed, almost indeed disembodied, Pendlebury was unable to move; and the people in the waiting room seemed unaware of his presence. He felt desperately shut out from a party he was compelled to attend.

Slowly but unmistakably the tension of community and sociality waxed among them, as if a loose mesh of threads weaving about between the different individuals was being drawn tighter and closer, further isolating them from the rest of the world, and from Pendlebury: the party was advancing into a communal phantasmagoria, as parties should, but in Pendlebury's experience seldom did; an *ombre chinoise* of affectionate ease and intensified inner life. Pendlebury so plainly belonged with them. His flooding sensation of identity with them was the most authentic and the most momentous he had ever known. But he was wholly cut off from them; there was, he felt, a bridge which they had crossed and he had not. And they were the select best of the world, from different periods

and classes and ages and tempers; the nicest people he had ever known—
were it only that he could know them.

And now the handsome woman in evening dress (Edwardian evening dress, Pendlebury thought, décolleté but polypetalous) was singing, and the rest were hushed to listen. She was singing a drawing-room
ballad, of home and love and paradise; elsewhere doubtless absurd, but
here sweet and moving, made so in part by her steady mezzo-soprano
voice, and soft intimate pitch. Pendlebury could see only her pale face
and bosom in the firelight, the shadow of her dark hair massed tight on
the head above her brow, the glinting and gleaming of the spirit caught
within the large jewel at her throat, the upward angle of her chin; but
more and more as she sang it was as if a broad knife turned round and
round in his heart, scooping it away. And all the time he knew that he
had seen her before; and knew also that in dreams there is little hope of
capturing such mighty lost memories.

He knew that soon there would be nothing left, and that it was necessary to treasure the moments which remained. The dream was racing
away from him like a head of water when the sluice is drawn. He wanted
to speak to the people in the waiting room, even inarticulately to cry
out to them for rescue; and could feel that the power, hitherto cut off,
would soon be once more upon him. But all the time the rocks and debris of common life were ranging themselves before him as the ebbing
dream uncovered them more and more. When he could speak, he knew
that there was no one to speak to.

In the doorway of the waiting room stood a man with a lantern.

"All right, sir?"

The courtesy suggested that it was not the porter of the previous
night.

Pendlebury nodded. Then he turned his face to the wall, out of the
lantern's chilly beam.

"All right, sir?" said the man again. He seemed to be sincerely concerned.

Pendlebury, alive again, began to pick his way from lump to lump across the dry but muddy watercourse.

"Thank you. I'm all right."

He still felt disembodied with stiffness and numbness and cold.

"You know you shouted at me? More like a scream, it was. Not a nice thing to hear in the early morning." The man was quite friendly.

"I'm sorry. What's the time?"

"Just turned the quarter. There's no need to be sorry. So long as you're all right."

"I'm frozen. That's all."

"I've got a cup of tea brewed for you in the office. I found the other porter's note when I opened up this morning. He didn't ought to have put you in here."

Pendlebury had forced both his feet to the floor, and was feebly brushing down his coat with his congealed hands.

"There was no choice. I missed my station. I understand there's nowhere else to go."

"He didn't ought to have put you in here, sir," repeated the porter.

"You mean the regulations? He warned me about them."

The porter looked at Pendlebury's dishevelled mass on the hard dark bench.

"I'll go and pour out that tea." When he had gone, Pendlebury perceived through the door the first frail foreshadowing of the slow northern dawn.

Soon he was able to follow the porter to the little office. Already the stove was roaring.

"That's better, sir," said the porter, as Pendlebury sipped the immensely strong liquor.

Pendlebury had begun to shiver, but he turned his head towards the porter and tried to smile.

"Reckon anything's better than a night in Casterton station waiting room for the matter of that," said the porter.

He was leaning against the high desk, with his arms folded and his feet set well apart before the fire. He was a middle-aged man, with grey eyes and the look of one who carried responsibilities.

"I expect I'll survive."

"I expect you will, sir. But there's some who didn't."

Pendlebury lowered his cup to the saucer. He felt that his hand was shaking too much for dignity. "Oh," he said. "How was that?"

"More tea, sir?"

"I've half a cup to go yet."

The porter was regarding him gravely. "You didn't know that Casterton station's built on the site of the old gaol?"

Pendlebury tried to shake his head.

"The waiting room's on top of the burial ground."

"The burial ground?"

"That's right, sir. One of the people there is Lily Torelli, the Beautiful Nightingale. Reckon they hadn't much heart in those times, sir. Not when it came to the point."

Pendlebury said nothing for a long minute. Far away he could hear a train. Then he asked: "Did the other porter know this?"

"He did, sir. Didn't you notice?"

"Notice what?"

The porter said nothing, but simply imitated the other porter's painful and uncontrollable twitch.

Pendlebury stared. Terror was waxing with the cold sun.

"The other porter used to be a bit too partial to the bottle. One night he spent the night in that waiting room himself."

"Why do you tell me this?" Suddenly Pendlebury turned from the porter's grey eyes.

"You might want to mention it. If you decide to see a doctor about the trouble yourself." The porter's voice was full of solicitude but less full of hope. "Nerves, they say. Just nerves."

PARANOIA

Shirley Jackson

Mr. Halloran Beresford, pleasantly tired after a good day in the office, still almost clean-shaven after eight hours, his pants still neatly pressed, pleased with himself particularly for remembering, stepped out of the candy shop with a great box under his arm and started briskly for the corner. There were twenty small-size gray suits like Mr. Beresford's on every New York block, fifty men still clean-shaven and pressed after a day in an air-cooled office, a hundred small men, perhaps, pleased with themselves for remembering their wives' birthdays. Mr. Beresford was going to take his wife out to dinner, he decided, going to see if he could get last-minute tickets to a show, taking his wife candy. It had been an exceptionally good day, altogether, and Mr. Beresford walked along swiftly, humming musically to himself.

He stopped on the corner, wondered whether he would save more time by taking a bus or by trying to catch a taxi in the crowd. It was a long trip downtown and Mr. Beresford ordinarily enjoyed the quiet half

hour on top of a Fifth Avenue bus, perhaps reading his paper. He disliked the subway intensely, and found the public display and violent
exercise necessary to catch a taxi usually more than he was equal to.
However, tonight he had spent a lot of time waiting in line in the candy
store to get his wife's favorite chocolates, and if he were going to get
home before dinner was on the table he really had to hurry a little. Mr.
Beresford went a few steps into the street, waved at a taxi, said "Taxi!" in
a voice that went helplessly into a falsetto, and slunk back, abashed, to
the sidewalk while the taxi went by uncomprehending. A man in a light
hat stopped next to Mr. Beresford on the sidewalk and for a minute, in
the middle of the crowd, he stared at Mr. Beresford and Mr. Beresford
stared at him as people sometimes do without caring particularly what
they see. What Mr. Beresford saw was a thin face under the light hat, a
small mustache, a coat collar turned up. Funny-looking guy, Mr. Beresford thought, lightly touching his clean-shaven lip. Perhaps the man
thought Mr. Beresford's almost unconscious gesture was offensive; at
any rate he frowned and looked Mr. Beresford up and down before he
turned away. Ugly customer, Mr. Beresford thought.

The Fifth Avenue bus Mr. Beresford usually took came slipping up
to the corner and Mr. Beresford, pleased not to worry about a taxi,
started for the stop. He had reached out his hand to take the rail inside
the bus door when he was roughly elbowed aside and the ugly customer
in the light hat shoved on ahead of him. Mr. Beresford muttered and
started to follow, but the bus door closed on the packed crowd inside
and the last thing Mr. Beresford saw as the bus went off down the street
was the man in the light hat grinning at him from inside the door.

"*There's* a dirty trick," Mr. Beresford told himself, and settled his
shoulders irritably in his coat. Still under the influence of his annoyance, he ran a few steps out into the street and waved again at a taxi, not
trusting his voice, and was almost run down by a delivery truck. As Mr.
Beresford skidded back to the sidewalk the truck driver leaned out and
yelled something unrecognizable at Mr. Beresford and when Mr. Beres-

ford saw the people around him on the corner laughing he decided to start walking downtown; in two blocks he would reach another bus stop, a good corner for taxis, and a subway station; much as Mr. Beresford disliked the subway, he might still have to take it, to get home in any sort of time. Walking downtown, his candy box under his arm, his gray suit almost unaffected by the crush on the corner, Mr. Beresford decided to swallow his annoyance and remember it was his wife's birthday; he began to hum again as he walked.

He watched the people as he walked along, his perspective sharpened by being a man who has just succeeded in forgetting an annoyance; surely the girl in the very high-heeled shoes, coming toward him with a frown on her face, was not so able to put herself above petty trifles, or maybe she was frowning because of the shoes; the old lady and man looking at the shop windows were quarrelling. The funny-looking guy in the light hat coming quickly through the crowd looked as though he hated someone . . . the funny-looking guy in the light hat; Mr. Beresford turned clean around in the walking line of people and watched the man in the light hat turn abruptly and start walking downtown, about ten feet in back of Mr. Beresford. What do you know about that, Mr. Beresford marvelled to himself, and began to walk a little quickly. Probably got off the bus for some reason, wrong bus maybe. Then why would he start walking uptown instead of catching another bus where he was? Mr. Beresford shrugged and passed two girls walking together and talking both at once.

Halfway from the corner he wanted, Mr. Beresford realized with a sort of sick shock that the man in the light hat was at his elbow, walking steadily along next to him. Mr. Beresford turned his head the other way and slowed his step. The other man slowed down as well, without looking at Mr. Beresford.

Nonsense, Mr. Beresford thought, without troubling to work it out any further than that. He settled his candy box firmly under his arm and cut abruptly across the uptown line of people and into a shop, a souvenir and notion shop, he realized as he came through the door. There were two or three people inside—a woman and a little girl, a sailor— and Mr. Beresford retired to the far end of the counter and began to fuss with an elaborate cigarette box on which was written "Souvenir of New York City," with a trylon and a perisphere painted beneath.

"Isn't this cute?" the mother said to the little girl, and they both began to laugh enormously over the match holder made in the form of a toilet; the matches were to go in the bowl, and on the cover, Mr. Beresford could see, was a trylon and a perisphere, with "Souvenir of New York City" written above.

The man in the light hat came into the shop and Mr. Beresford turned his back and busied himself picking up one thing after another from the counter; with half his mind he was trying to find something that did not say "Souvenir of New York City" and with the other half of his mind he was wondering about the man in the light hat. The question of what the man in the light hat wanted was immediately subordinate to the question of *whom* he wanted; if his lighthatted designs were against Mr. Beresford they must be nefarious, else why had he not announced them before now? The thought of accosting the man and demanding his purpose crossed Mr. Beresford's mind fleetingly, and was succeeded, as always in an equivocal situation, by Mr. Beresford's vivid recollection of his own small size and innate cautiousness. Best, Mr. Beresford decided, to avoid this man. Thinking this, Mr. Beresford walked steadily toward the doorway of the shop, intending to pass the man in the light hat and go out and catch his bus home.

He had not quite reached the man in the light hat when the shop's clerk came around the end of the counter and met Mr. Beresford with a genial smile and a vehement "See anything you like, Mister?"

"Not tonight, thanks," Mr. Beresford said, moving left to avoid the clerk, but the clerk moved likewise and said, "Got some nice things you didn't look at."

"No, thanks," Mr. Beresford said, trying to make his tenor voice firm.

"Take a look at it," the clerk insisted. This was unusually persistent even for such a clerk; Mr. Beresford looked up and saw the man in the light hat on his right, bearing down on him. Over the shoulders of the two men he could see that the shop was empty. The street looked very far away, the people passing in either direction looked smaller and smaller; Mr. Beresford realized that he was being forced to step backward as the two men advanced on him.

"Easy does it," the man in the light hat said to the clerk. They continued to move forward slowly.

"See here now," Mr. Beresford said, with the ineffectuality of the ordinary man caught in such a crisis; he still clutched his box of candy under his arm. "See *here*," he said, feeling the solid weight of the wall behind him.

"Ready," the man in the light hat said. The two men tensed and Mr. Beresford, with a wild yell, broke between them and ran for the door. He heard a sound more like a snarl than anything else behind him and the feet coming after him. I'm safe on the street, Mr. Beresford thought as he came through the door into the line of people, as long as there are lots of people they can't do anything to me. He looked back, walking downtown between a fat woman with many packages and a girl and a boy leaning on one another's shoulders, and he saw the clerk standing in the door of the shop looking after him; the man with the light hat was not in sight. Mr. Beresford shifted the box of candy so that his right arm was free and thought, Perfectly silly. It's still broad daylight. How they ever hoped to get away with it . . .

⚬⚬

The man in the light hat was on the corner ahead, waiting. Mr. Beresford hesitated in his walk and then thought, It's preposterous, all these people watching. He walked boldly down the street; the man in the light hat was not even watching him, but was leaning calmly against a building lighting a cigarette. Mr. Beresford reached the corner, darted quickly into the street, and yelled boisterously, "Taxi!" in a great voice he had never suspected he possessed until now. A taxi stopped as though not daring to disregard that great shout, and Mr. Beresford moved gratefully toward it. His hand was on the door handle when another hand closed over his and Mr. Beresford was aware of the light hat brushing his cheek.

"Come on if you're coming," the taxi driver said; the door was open and Mr. Beresford, resisting the push that urged him into the taxi, slipped his hand out from under the other hand and ran back to the sidewalk. A crosstown bus had stopped on the corner and Mr. Beresford, no longer thinking, hurried into it, dropped a nickel into the coin register, and went to the back of the bus and sat down. The man in the light hat sat a little ahead, between Mr. Beresford and the door. Mr. Beresford put his box of candy on his lap and tried to think. Obviously the man in the light hat was not carrying a grudge all this time about Mr. Beresford's almost unconscious gesture toward the mustache, unless he were peculiarly sensitive. In any case, there was the clerk in the souvenir shop; Mr. Beresford realized suddenly that the clerk in the souvenir shop was a very odd circumstance indeed. He set the clerk aside to think about later and went back to the man in the light hat. If it was not the insult to the mustache, what was it? And then another thought caught Mr. Beresford breathless: how long, then, had the man in the light hat been following him? He thought back along the day: he had left his office with a group of people, all talking cheerfully, all reminding Mr. Beresford that it was his wife's birthday; they had escorted Mr. Beresford to the candy shop and left him there. He had been in his office all day except for lunch with three fellows in the office; Mr. Beresford's mind leaped suddenly from the lunch to his first sight of the man in the light hat at the bus stop; it seemed that the man in the light hat had been trying to push him *on* the bus into the crowd, instead of pushing in ahead. In that case, once he was on the bus . . . Mr. Beresford looked around. In the bus he was riding on now there were only five people left. One was the driver, one Mr. Beresford, one the man in the light hat, sitting slightly ahead of Mr. Beresford. The two others were an old lady with a shopping bag and a man who looked as though he might be a foreigner. Foreigner, Mr. Beresford thought, while he looked at the man, foreigner, foreign plot, spies. Better not rely on any foreigner, Mr. Beresford thought.

The bus was going swiftly along between high dark buildings. Mr. Beresford, looking out of the window, decided that they were in a factory district, remembered that they had been going east, and decided to wait until they got to one of the lighted, busy sections before he tried to get off. Peering off into the growing darkness, Mr. Beresford noticed an odd thing. There had been someone standing on the corner beside a sign saying "Bus Stop" and the bus had not stopped, even though the dim figure waved its arms. Surprised, Mr. Beresford glanced up at the street sign, noticed that it said "E. 31 St." at the same moment that he reached for the cord to signal the driver he wanted to get off. As he stood up and went down to the aisle, the foreign-looking man rose also and went to the door beside the driver. "Getting off," the foreign man said, and the bus slowed. Mr. Beresford pressed forward and somehow the old lady's shopping bag got in his way and spilled, sending small items—a set of blocks, a package of paper clips—spilling in all directions.

"Sorry," Mr. Beresford said desperately as the bus doors opened. He began to move forward again and the old lady caught his arm and said, "Don't bother if you're in a hurry. I can get them, dear." Mr. Beresford tried to shake her off and she said, "If this is your stop don't worry. It's perfectly all right."

A coil of pink ribbon was caught around Mr. Beresford's shoe; the old lady said, "It was clumsy of me, leaving my bag right in the aisle."

As Mr. Beresford broke away from her the doors closed and the bus started. Resigned, Mr. Beresford got down on one knee in the swaying bus and began to pick up paper clips, blocks, a box of letter paper that had opened and spilled sheets and envelopes all over the floor. "I'm so sorry," the old lady said sweetly. "It was all my fault, too."

Once, over his shoulder, Mr. Beresford saw the man in the light hat sitting comfortably. He was smoking and his head was thrown back and his eyes were shut. Mr. Beresford gathered together the old lady's shopping as well as he could, and then made his way forward to stand by the driver. "Getting off," Mr. Beresford said.

"Can't stop in the middle of the block," the driver said, not turning his head.

"The next stop, then," Mr. Beresford said.

The bus moved rapidly on. Mr. Beresford, bending down to see the streets out the front window, saw a sign saying "Bus Stop."

"Here," he said.

"What?" the driver said, going past.

"Listen," Mr. Beresford said. "I want to get off."

"It's O.K. with me," the driver said. "Next stop."

"You just passed one," Mr. Beresford said.

"No one waiting there," the driver said. "Anyway, you didn't tell me in time." Mr. Beresford waited. After a minute he saw another bus stop and said, "O.K."

The bus did not stop, but went past the sign without slowing down.

"Report me," the driver said.

"Listen, now," Mr. Beresford said, and the driver turned one eye up at him; he seemed to be amused.

"Report me," the driver said. "My number's right here on this card."

"If you don't stop at the next stop," Mr. Beresford said, "I shall smash the glass in the door and shout for help."

"What with?" the driver said. "The box of candy?"

"How do you know it's—" Mr. Beresford said before he realized that if he got into a conversation he would miss the next bus stop. It had not occurred to him that he could get off anywhere except at a bus stop; he saw lights ahead and at the same time the bus slowed down and Mr. Beresford, looking quickly back, saw the man in the light hat stretch and get up.

The bus pulled to a stop in front of a bus sign; there was a group of stores.

"O.K.," the bus driver said to Mr. Beresford, "you were so anxious to get off." The man in the light hat got off at the rear door. Mr. Beresford, standing by the open front door, hesitated and said, "I guess I'll stay on for a while."

"Last stop," the bus driver said. "Everybody off." He looked sardonically up at Mr. Beresford. "Report me if you want to," he said. "My number's right on that card there."

Mr. Beresford got off and went directly up to the man in the light hat, standing on the sidewalk. "This is perfectly ridiculous," he said emphatically. "I don't understand any of it and I want you to know that the first policeman I see—"

He stopped when he realized that the man in the light hat was looking not at him but, bored and fixedly, over his shoulder. Mr. Beresford turned and saw a policeman standing on the corner.

"Just you wait," he said to the man in the light hat, and started for the policeman. Halfway to the policeman he began to wonder again: what did he have to report? A bus that would not stop when directed to, a clerk in a souvenir shop who cornered customers, a mysterious man in a light hat—and why? Mr. Beresford realized suddenly that there was nothing he could tell the policeman: he looked over his shoulder and saw the man in the light hat watching him, and then Mr. Beresford bolted down a subway entrance. He had a nickel in his hand by the time he reached the bottom of the steps, and he went right through the turnstile; to the left it was downtown and he ran that way.

He was figuring as he ran: he'll think if I'm very stupid I'd head downtown, if I'm smarter than that I'd go uptown, if I'm really smart I'd go downtown. Does he think I'm middling smart or very smart?

The man in the light hat reached the downtown platform only a few seconds after Mr. Beresford and sauntered down the platform, his hands in his pockets. Mr. Beresford sat down on the bench listlessly. It's no good, he thought, no good at all, he knows just how smart I am.

The train came blasting into the station, Mr. Beresford ran in the door and saw the light hat disappear into a door of the next car. Just as the doors were closing Mr. Beresford dived, caught the door, and would have been out except for a girl who seized his arm and shouted, "Harry! Where in God's name are you going?"

The door was held halfway by Mr. Beresford's body, his arm left inside with the girl, who seemed to be holding it with all her strength. "Isn't this a fine thing," she said to the people in the car, "he sure doesn't want to see his old friends."

A few people laughed; most of them were watching.

"Hang on to him, sister," someone said.

The girl laughed and tugged on Mr. Beresford's arm. "He's gonna get away," she said laughingly to the people in the car and a big man stepped to her with a grin and said, "If you gotta have him that bad, we'll bring him in for you."

Mr. Beresford felt the holding grasp on his arm turn suddenly to an irresistible force which drew him in through the doors, and they closed behind him. Everyone in the car was laughing at him by now, and the big man said, "That ain't no way to a treat a lady, chum."

Mr. Beresford looked around for the girl but she had melted into the crowd somewhere and the train was moving. After a minute the people in the car stopped looking at him and Mr. Beresford smoothed his coat and found that his box of candy was still intact.

The subway train was going downtown. Mr. Beresford, who was now racking his brains for detective tricks, for mystery-story dodges, thought of one that seemed infallible. He stayed docilely on the train, as it went downtown, and got a seat at Twenty-third Street. At Fourteenth he got off, the light hat following, and went up the stairs and into the street. As he had expected, the large department store ahead of him advertised "Open till 9 tonight" and the doors swung wide, back and forth, with people going constantly in and out. Mr. Beresford went in. The store bewildered him at first—counters stretching away in all directions, the lights much brighter than anywhere else, the voices clamoring. Mr. Beresford moved slowly along beside a counter; it was stockings first, thin and tan and black and gauzy, and then it was handbags, piles on sale, neat solitary ones in the cases, and then it was medical supplies, with huge almost human figures wearing obscene trusses, standing right there on the counter, and people coming embarrassedly to buy. Mr. Beresford turned the corner and came to a counter of odds and ends. Scarves too cheap to be at the scarf counter, postcards, a bin marked "Any item 25¢," dark glasses. Uncomfortably, Mr. Beresford bought a pair of dark glasses and put them on.

He went out of the store at an entrance far away from the one he had used to go in; he could have chosen any of eight or nine entrances, but this seemed complicated enough. There was no sign of the light hat, no one tried to hinder Mr. Beresford as he stepped up to the taxi stand, and, although debating taking the second or the third car, finally took the one that was offered him and gave his home address.

⚭

He reached his apartment building without mishap, stole cautiously out of the taxi and into the lobby. There was no light hat, no odd person watching for Mr. Beresford. In the elevator, alone, with no one to see which floor button he pressed, Mr. Beresford took a long breath and began to wonder if he had dreamed his wild trip home. He rang his apartment bell and waited; then his wife came to the door and Mr. Beresford, suddenly tired out, went into his home.

"You're *terribly* late, darling," his wife said affectionately, and then, "But what's the matter?"

He looked at her; she was wearing her blue dress and that meant she knew it was her birthday and expected him to take her out; he handed her the box of candy limply and she took it, hardly noticing in her anxiety over him. "What on *earth* has happened?" she asked. "Darling, come in here and sit down. You look terrible."

He let her lead him into the living room, into his own chair where it was comfortable, and he lay back.

"Is there something wrong?" she was asking anxiously, fussing over him, loosening his tie, smoothing his hair. "Are you sick? Were you in an accident? What *has* happened?"

He realized that he seemed more tired than he really was, and was glorying in all this attention. He sighed deeply and said, "Nothing. Nothing wrong. Tell you in a minute."

"Wait," she said. "I'll get you a drink."

He put his head back against the soft chair as she went out. Never knew that door had a key, his mind registered dimly as he heard it turn. Then he was on his feet with his head against the door listening to her at the telephone in the hall.

She dialled and waited. Then: "Listen," she said, "listen, he came here after all. I've got him."

THE HELPER

Joan Aiken

Paris in the rainy morning: like a series of triangles cut from pewter. The wet grey streets met one another at acute angles, shutters peered down slit-eyed, the town reflected a murky, watery sky. It was unfriendly, repulsing. Hostile.

Frost, consulting the professor's letter again—Charles-Edouard Aveyrand, Academician, 48 rue Lecluse—saw that he would not need to take a taxi or the metro; it would be an easy walk from the Gare St. Lazare. And he could do with a walk; he was hungry, stiff, and chilled to the bone from the night journey.

He ought to have remembered that address. And as he walked towards it, he did begin to remember.

"Knowing you to be an official of the British Patent Office," the professor had written in his formal stiff English, "and remembering our agreeable association of some years ago, I made bold to invite your assistance in this matter. My finances in these days are a matter of some anxiety, otherwise I would not have troubled you. My daughter Menispe invites herself to be recollected by you and regrets a lack of correspondence between the families since the sad death of your charming daughter."

Striding along the chilly canyon of a street, between high narrow grey houses and motorbikes that continually snarled at his elbow, Frost thought of Menispe Aveyrand. There was little need for her self-invitation, he thought. Only too easily could he summon up the image of the girl who, for five successive years, had come to stay *en famille* with the Frosts, learn English, and be, virtually, an adopted sister for Louise. Both girls had been only children; the arrangement, initiated through a school club, had proved so successful that when Menispe was not spending holidays in England, Louise went to the Aveyrand apartment in Paris.

Menispe at age nine had been a skinny waiflike little creature, all pale freckles and bony, sharp features, with an unexpectedly engaging triangular grin, a mobile face, never still for a moment, stringy fair hair, and shrewd hazel-green eyes. She was witty even then, *méchante*, but also touching; deprived of a mother since the age of six, she attached herself to the Frost family with passionate, starved affection, like a stray kitten offered its first bowl of warm milk. She and Louise had been inseparable, written each other immense weekly letters during the school terms, counted the days to each reunion. Frost and his wife had been "*chère tante Josephine*" and "*gentil oncle Frank*" in dozens of polite, dutiful breadand-butter letters always signed "*affectueusement, votre belle-fille,* Menispe."

The last visit, of course, had been that of Louise to the Paris apartment; after which, nothing more had been heard from Menispe.

Frost wondered, detachedly, how she had turned out. There had been a boyfriend, hadn't there, Lucien; what had become of him?

Perhaps she had married him.

The apartment house in which Professor Aveyrand lived was high, colourless, forbidding, with a mansard roof and so much exterior embellishment in the way of shutters, ironwork, lanterns, balconies, that there seemed hardly enough wall to sustain them. Inside, Frost remembered the varicose-veined marble and brown flock wallpaper, and the terrifyingly slow lift, with a heavy glass door, and room for only two persons inside, which creaked its way up from floor to floor.

It was in that lift that he had first been alone with his daughter Louise after the final visit, when he had come, to fetch her home. She had gazed away over his shoulder as if he did not exist, although they were obliged to stand almost pressed together. When he said, "I wonder what our chances are of getting a taxi?" she looked at him with the same total boredom as if he had speculated on the chances of the Tory candidate in the Stockton-on-Tees council elections.

Numero Onze, in trailing metal script on the door; the bell inside clanged at some distance, harshly, as he stood waiting in the close, windowless passage, only elbow-width, and lit by what appeared to be a three-watt bulb.

After a longish pause the door was opened by Professor Aveyrand himself. He had aged immensely since Frost's last visit; was gnarled, shaky, dwarfish, and stooped, like some ancient Nibelung creeping out of his crevice on the scent of gold. And that, Frost told himself sharply, was a thoroughly unfair judgment. The professor had always been the most abstracted, unworldly figure, plunged in the past and his studies; money was of no importance to him. Indeed, if he had not been so oblivious to what went on about him, of what his daughter was up to, at the time of that last visit, Frost might have been alerted a bit sooner, the calamity might never have happened . . . Enough of that.

By now the professor had gingerly, hesitantly, ushered him in. They were sitting on two upright chairs upholstered in hard brown velvet, facing one another across an empty marble hearth closed by a steel shutter. The apartment smelt dreadful—unaired, dusty, with a hint of something decaying—perhaps the plumbing needed attention, or a mouse had died in the pantry; it did not look as if the place ever, nowadays, received the attentions of a maid.

"...since I retired had sufficient time to pursue my hobby," the professor was explaining—one thing, he had got down to business right away, no beating about the bush, there was that much to be said for him, thought Frost. Well, so much the better; who would want to spend an extra minute in this dank, depressing place with its horrible associations? "My family, of course...," the professor went on. "Interested in these matters for generations... Indeed an ancestor of mine in the sixteenth century... treatise on solar and planetary energy... as a matter of fact, he narrowly escaped execution for heresy..."

Frost dutifully returned the old man's thin smile as he added, "Fortunately his patron was Cardinal Richelieu—the affair was smoothed over. He had to burn his books, of course, but... Before that... twelfth-century Sieur d'Aveyrand... brought back books on alchemy and physics from the East—and a wife too, a Moorish astrologer..."

"Indeed," Frost commented, politely concealing irritation and boredom. Now he remembered Menispe, aged twelve, airily boasting, "Of course I was named after a Saracen princess that one of our ancestors brought back from the Crusades. Don't you think it's rather *parvenu* not to know your family history?" "Snobbish little thing," he had teased her. "*Non, ce n'est pas snobbisme, oncle Frank, c'est pratique!*"

"What a very commendable record of your ancestors you have kept, Professor;" he remarked. "I'm afraid in our family we can hardly trace our forebears beyond a pork butcher in 1893; but perhaps that is just as well. I daresay they were nothing to brag about."

The professor's pained, reluctant acknowledgment of this pleasantry made it evident that his views on the subject were widely divergent from those of Frost; he said, "Well, it is true... must be admitted that there are advantages... but now, let me show you my specifications."

He levered himself out of his chair—his arms looked as frail as celery stalks—and limped as fast as he was able to an Empire escritoire beside a lace-curtained window which looked into a dark interior well.

The desk was piled high with papers which were plainly in no sort of order; it took the professor a little while to find what he wanted.

"Here, now—these, you see, are my diagrams—and these are the figures—it is all clear, I think, but my English is not adequate for the technical language—I do not know the proper terms for 'Unified Field theory' or 'planetary wave particle duality'—" He had fallen into French, which Frost read and understood well, though he did not speak it with great fluency.

"Yes, I see, Professor. I don't think there will be any problem about that. Look, I have brought over some blank application forms. You fill them in like this—here, see—I will of course take care of the registration, and so forth—you will need a clear diagram of course; yes, this one should serve perfectly well. Put your name at the beginning, 'I, Charles-Edouard Aveyrand—'"

"De Froissart Aveyrand," put in the professor fussily.

"'Being a subject of the French Republic, do hereby declare the invention, for which I pray that a patent be granted to me, and the method by which it is to be performed, to be particularly described in and by the following statement—' Incidentally, do you have a madeup model of the—of your invention?"

"Naturally, Monsieur Frost, naturally I have."

To Frost's considerable surprise, he then lifted up his voice and called, "Carloman! Allo, Carloman!

"I have programmed it to respond to my voice frequencies," he explained. "Of course, for another person, it would only be needed to slip in a different tape. All that is entered in the specification. I thought it most practical. I am, you see, sometimes very stiff with my rheumatic trouble, hardly able to rise from my chair; it is so with many of my age, I daresay: but the voice is always at command. *Bien,* here it comes; like its inventor, it does not move very fast."

A shuffling tread could now be heard in the corridor, and soon, round the open door, appeared a smallish figure, rather less than five foot high.

Frost could not repress a start of surprise at the sight of it, for it appeared to be a knight in fourteenth-century armour. It moved slowly into the room and carefully positioned itself in the exact centre of a small threadbare rug about six feet away from the professor.

"Carloman, change the lights," ordered Aveyrand, and the model accordingly proceeded to shuffle slowly round the room altering the illumination; first it switched on various table lamps by pulling down their strings with its mailed hand; after this it turned off the switch by the door which governed the overhead light, encountering a little difficulty in getting its metal fingers on to the target; finally it switched off the standard lamp beside the professor's chair by pressing a floor switch with its mailed foot. Then it returned to the centre of the rug and stood, apparently awaiting further orders.

"Remarkable," said Frost. "Will it do anything else?"

"Oh, *bien sûr*, but that is all I have programmed it for at present. Later it could be instructed to make beds, use the vacuum cleaner . . . But I thought, do you see, how useful for people who are afraid of thieves . . . I must confess I am often in anxiety about brigands breaking into this place and stealing my valuables when I am out." He glanced, almost apologetically, over his shoulder. "One can leave the model, you see, with instructions to go round at irregular intervals of time, changing all the lights, so that it must appear some living person is there. A time switch could not be so irregular. Whereas I could give Carloman a random series of changes which would continue for one hundred days without repeating."

"Is it plugged into the mains? Or run off a battery?"

"Neither, monsieur; wholly self-contained. The planetary influence is sufficient to power it indefinitely on its present programme."

"Very clever indeed," said Frost. "I should certainly think you could find a ready market for such an invention."

"Oh, my dear sir! Without doubt! There are so many people who, like myself, fear thieves, fear to go away and leave their possessions."

Frost could not help being somewhat struck by the irony of this; looking round the dismal apartment he wondered what in it was worth taking? In any case, surely the professor was almost always at home?

"Tell me, why are you applying first for a British patent? Why not begin in your own country?"

The professor gave a classic Gallic shrug. "There is too much corruption here. I should have to grease too many palms. I cannot afford it. And otherwise, it would not be achieved in my lifetime, I would not reap the benefit... Although I am a sick old man, I still have some things left to offer the world—to render my name historic—this is only one of the uses of planetary energy which I propose."

A somewhat febrile glitter came into his eyes; he began muttering about Mars, Venus, and Saturn, until he was interrupted by a fit of coughing and obliged to stop, holding a soiled handkerchief to his lips. When the paroxysm went on and on, Frost, feeling that he ought to make some attempt at assistance, went into the next room, an indescribably sordid and untidy kitchenette. The sink was piled high with dirty dishes and there seemed nothing fit to eat or drink—not even a bottle of Evian water. However, the professor called out, "Coffee! Coffee!" in a feeble voice amid his eructations, and so Frost heated up a pan which contained mostly grounds and some discoloured liquid over the tiny gas stove, and brought a cupful of the stuff back to the old man. How could Louise have been so happy to spend so many holidays here? he wondered in amazed disgust, glancing round him. But of course that had been years ago, when the professor was still teaching at the Institute of Astronomy; there had been money enough for a *bonne* to help out in those days.

After drinking the gritty coffee, the professor in due course recovered sufficiently to complete the patent-application forms, which Frost then slipped into his briefcase.

"What do you call it, by the way? The invention has to have some sort of a title."

"I call it *l'Assistant*—the Helper."

"Would there be any chance of taking a—a specimen?" Frost then inquired. "To England, I mean? It might facilitate—speed up the process, you know—if I could present a model as well as the drawings. Do you, perhaps, have others?"

"Other models? *Non, non*—Carloman *seulement*," the professor replied, after looking vaguely round the room, as if there might possibly be another, somewhere, only just at present his memory failed him regarding its whereabouts. He added, after a moment, "I suppose you might perhaps take that one; doubtless I could construct another without too much trouble."

"Why did you make it in the form of a crusader?" Frost asked. He looked with dislike at the motionless figure on the rug; it filled him with a slight, uneasy feeling of repugnance. He had always been annoyed by phoney antiquity, cigarette lighters in the shape of jousting knights, mock-baronial coalscuttles—he found Carloman in decidedly poor taste.

"Why in that shape? Oh, merely because I happened to have the armour. There were various pieces left from the collection in our family château—now sold, alas, to foreigners. But possessing the armour already saved me some tedious construction work. Also it is convenient—*regardez*—" Aveyrand flipped up Carloman's visor and revealed a mass of wires and connections where the face should have been. He added absently, "I do have other pieces of armour, *bien sûr*, I would be able to construct another model. It is just that I am so pressed for time." He reflected. "Carloman is not too heavy. We could, I daresay, pack him into a golf bag. Somewhere, I will recollect in a moment, there used to be such an article. Thus you might carry it back to England."

"Perhaps I could help you find the bag?"

Frost glanced around the overfurnished room. The sooner he was out of this dreary place, the better.

"*Merci, mon ami.*" The professor rubbed his forehead uncertainly. "It might be on top of the armoire in my bedroom . . . You forgive that I do not accompany you? I have to husband my strength these days."

Passing a couple of rooms rammed to the ceiling with the accretions of years—from which he nervously averted his eyes—Frost searched in the bedroom's dusty disorder, and did, after a while, manage to unearth the golf bag among a stack of photographic equipment, rucksacks, telescopes, botanical specimen cases, and aged wicker luggage. On a chiffonier he was disconcerted to encounter a photograph of his daughter Louise and her friend Menispe, arm in arm, laughing and squinting into the sunshine of a Paris street; from this he hastily averted his eyes. He left the bedroom and carried the bag back into the salle.

Aided rather ineffectually by the professor, who, by the end of the interview, very evidently had little energy to spare, Frost managed to pack the armour-suited model into the golf bag, wadding it with copies of *Le Monde* and *France Soir*. "What about the programming?" he thought to ask. "It will need your voice, won't it?"

"There is a tape built in—no problem. You merely move the switch to the second position—*voilà*—to re-record."

"Yes, yes, of course. Well, I will say good-bye, Professor—I'm sure I have tired you long enough. It has been extremely interesting—"

"I regret infinitely that I cannot offer you *déjeuner*—but the resources of my kitchen these days are so limited, I go out so seldom—"

"No, no, my dear sir—don't think of such a thing—" Frost suppressed a shudder as he thought of that kitchen.

"I am deeply sorry, also, that my daughter Menispe did not return in time to see you again."

"Menispe? You mean that she is still living here?" Frost was not sure why this information startled him so. Menispe had not seemed the kind of daughter who would remain under the parental roof a day longer than she was obliged to. He recalled that last occasion; her all-too-evident boredom and scorn . . .

"But of course she still lives here!" The professor seemed quite shocked. "Who, if not she, my daughter, would look after me and charge herself with my errands?"

Although Frost entertained no very kind feelings towards Menispe, he could not avoid a shiver at this calm statement by her father. What a fate for the wretched girl, he thought, and he asked, "Did she not marry, then? What became of her fiancé—Lucien, was it?"

"Ah, Lucien? Poor young man, he died, some years ago. He contracted an unfortunate addiction—"

Like Louise. Frost found himself inquiring dispassionately, "Menispe herself never did so?"

"No, monsieur. Menispe is not liable to such habits."

No. She merely observes the results of them in her friends, Frost thought, but Aveyrand continued, "She has problems, though, she will not eat enough—sometimes I am very disquieted about her. Ah, but—*à la bonheur*—there she comes now!" he exclaimed in a tone of triumph as the outer door rattled.

Frost let out a silent, heartfelt oath. In all the world the last person he wanted to see was Menispe Aveyrand; if only he had cut short his visit by five minutes, this encounter could have been avoided.

Now she came strolling in with a faint smile, lifting her chin, staring at him impudently under lowered sandy eyelashes; they might have met five minutes before, instead of seven years. She was wet through from the rain which was beating down in earnest now, but seemed unaware of the fact; she did not remove her outer clothes for she had none to take off, her garments consisting of worn jeans, thong sandals, and a draggled Indian shirt. Her hair was close-cropped, and her face resembled that of some starving waterbird—she was skeleton-thin, seemed smaller, if possible, than in those bygone days when she had come to stay in Wimbledon.

"Menispe!"

He could not be cordial, his tongue refused the hypocritical forms of greeting, all that he could muster, lamely enough, was, "Fancy seeing you again."

"Monsieur Frost—what a surprise!" Her tone was ironic, she did not seem in the least surprised. She slung a leg over the scrolled end of a dusty green velvet chaise-longue, and sat watching him with a slight smile as he gathered together the handles of the golf bag.

"What, you are taking away our poor Carloman? Kidnapping him? Shall we never see him again?"

"It is very kind of Monsieur Frost to interest himself in our affairs," her father said repressively. "Considering—"

"Considering?" Menispe lit a thin brown cigarette and blew a smoke-ring. "Considering that his wife and daughter are dead? Monsieur Frost probably has time on his hands."

"Menispe! Monsieur Frost kindly undertakes the English patent for us."

"So; soon, then, we shall be rich?"

"I hope so," Frost said coldly. "Of course you can never tell whether these things will get taken up by manufacturers."

Now he was overcome by weary distaste for the whole project. Why should he take any pains to enrich this hateful pair? In any case, Avey-rand looked to be at death's door, would probably go off within the next year or so, while his daughter seemed like a cadaver as it was. And then—to remember Louise. With all her happy intelligence, her bright promise cut short—

"I will write to you from London as soon as I have any news," Frost said hastily to the professor, and manoeuvred himself and his burden awkwardly out of the door.

"Do not let Carloman get rusty!" Menispe called after him.

Going down in the lift—he had to hold Carloman vertically in order to fit him in—Frost was reminded again of Louise by the question of whether he would be able to find a taxi.

⁂

Back at his cottage in Essex—for he had left Wimbledon after the death of Louise and his wife's subsequent suicide—he did not immediately unpack the bag containing Aveyrand's model. There was plenty to do after a three-day absence—the house needed cleaning, the lawn had grown shaggy. And on the following morning at the Patent Office, he found his desk piled high with accumulated work which would require several days to clear.

Nevertheless, it was not the outcome of will, of premeditated plan, his slowness to take action on Aveyrand's behalf. He had sincerely meant to respond to the old man's appeal for help. When he decided to go to Paris, his intentions had been disinterested and benevolent; he felt it was not his business to make judgments or withhold professional advice when it was requested.

But now... All he could feel was a profound lethargy and reluctance. No doubt the profits from the manufacture and marketing of Carloman's issue would in time earn the old man—and Menispe—a considerable amount of money. What would they do with it? That was no affair of Frost's.

He asked himself once or twice why he did not simply turn the professor's application over to a colleague to deal with—that would be the rational solution to his problem. But still, day after day, he let the papers lie on his desk, and for some weeks Carloman remained zipped into the golf bag under the copies of *France Soir*.

Nearly four months after his trip to Paris, Frost received an Eiffel Tower card addressed to him in a familiar looped untidy black handwriting.

"My father has asked me to inquire if there is any news of his patent," wrote Menispe—no "*cher oncle* Frank" this time. "He grows discouraged at your long silence and would be pleased to receive a letter from you."

Prompted by this, guilty and resentful, Frost unpacked the model and set it up. Winter had come with the promise of snow, and several lights were burning in his cottage. Following the professor's instructions, Frost re-recorded the tape, slotted it back into the visor, and then clearing his throat, feeling somewhat foolish, he ordered the model:

"Carloman, change the lights."

Obediently the model began moving about Frost's living room, switching on any lights that were off, and turning off those that were already on; evidently this was its all-purpose programme if not provided with more specific instructions. Its movements were slow, fumbling and hesitant, as it worked over this new course, but thorough. When the lights were all changed, it returned to the spot where it had first stood, and took up its position there, motionless, waiting.

"All right, Frankenstein, that's enough," muttered Frost, with a slight shiver—there was something disagreeably like Aveyrand himself about the model's uncertain, cautious movements—and he hastily clicked off the master switch on the breastplate.

"I'll put the application in today," he resolved.

That day was unusually harassed, though; and on the following morning he received a long letter from a friend in Australia, a distant cousin of his wife, who by some mischance had never been informed of her death and proposed visiting England next month; that necessitated a long letter going through, yet again, the whole miserable story of how, following the death of Louise from an overdose, Mary had sunk into such a deep depression that one night when Frost was kept late at the office by a rush of work she had decided to end it all . . .

By the time he had finished his letter, Frost was feeling so bitterly hostile towards the Aveyrand family that he deliberately decided to put aside the professor's application for another month. He could not, he simply *could not* take an action about it just at present. Why should he be the one to act for them? Let them wait a little longer.

And a month later his eye was caught by a small paragraph in the *Times* as he travelled home one evening: "French Academician dies. Charles-Edouard Aveyrand, for many years Professor in Astrophysics at the Paris Faculté des Sciences . . . author of *La Révolution Astrophysique, Opuscules Astronomiques, Employant Vénus et Saturne,* etc., etc. . . . holder of the following academic honours and decorations . . . was found dead in his

Paris apartment yesterday. He lived alone, having been predeceased by his daughter, who had died in hospital of anorexia nervosa two weeks before. By a sad piece of irony, the professor, too, it is thought, died of undernourishment and hypothermia. Neighbours were alerted to his fate because the lights in his apartment remained on day and night for a week."

So: he never made that second model, thought Frost, after a blank, shocked moment. If he had, perhaps the neighbours would not have found him yet; Carloman II would still be stumping about the apartment, switching lights on and off at random intervals.

He re-read the paragraph, waiting for guilt and remorse to bite. But all he felt was a kind of dreary satisfaction; even guilt seemed wasted on that pair. Aveyrand would hardly have lasted much longer, with all the wealth in the world; nor would Menispe, and it was unlikely that anybody regretted her passing.

But what, now, should he do with Aveyrand's invention? Enter the patent in his own name and give the proceeds to charity? Search for other family connections? Or—his strongest impulse—do nothing, smash the model to smithereens with a hatchet?

The train pulled up at his station. He put the *Times* in his briefcase, got out, and walked up the long and muddy lane towards his cottage.

Yes: a hatchet might be the best solution to Carloman. On the other hand—he might just keep the model, which was proving quite useful. There had been a number of burglaries lately in the district; he had formed the habit of leaving Carloman switched on, to create the effect of human activity in the house.

Indeed the lights changed as Frost approached the cottage: the kitchen window went dark and, after a short interval, the bedroom was illuminated. Handy though the model was, Frost thought, opening the gate, it was hard to conquer the slight unease of entering the house, aware that somewhere inside this mindless but human-seeming object was plodding slowly around, carrying out its programmed tasks.

Then, glancing through the window of the ground-floor bedroom, Frost was startled to observe that, this evening, Carloman had performed a task for which he had not yet been programmed: he was just moving away from the bed, having, with his gauntleted hands, twitched back the covers.

With a suddenly accelerated heart, and a dry mouth, Frost opened the front door, which led straight into the dining room. The table was laid for two.

Now he could hear slow, thudding steps as the model negotiated the short passage from bedroom to hall. Soon the thing came in sight, moving deliberately with its slow, swaying gait. The closed bars of the visor looked straight ahead: blind, expressionless. But inside them—Frost was visited by a mad notion—inside, if he were to lift the visor, he believed that he would reveal not a random-seeming mass of wires and terminals but the mocking, hostile features of Menispe Aveyrand.

THE JESTERS

Joyce Carol Oates

He said, "Do you hear—"

She listened. She'd just come to join him on the terrace at the rear of the house.

It was dusk: the calls of birds close about the house were subsiding. A flock of glossy-black-winged birds had taken over a hilly section of the lawn for much of that day, but had now departed. At the lake a quarter mile away, not visible from their terrace, Canada geese and other waterfowl were emitting the random querulous cries associated with nighttime.

At first, she heard nothing except the waterfowl. Then, she began to hear what sounded like voices, at a distance.

"Our neighbors. Must be on West Crescent Drive."

The husband spoke matter-of-factly. It was not like him to take notice of neighbors unless in annoyance—which was rare, in Crescent Lake Farms. He seemed bemused and not annoyed.

They had never seen these neighbors. Whoever lived on the far side of the wooded area were strangers to them. There was no occasion for the husband and the wife to drive on West Crescent Drive, which wasn't easily accessible from the cul-de-sac at the end of East Crescent Drive, where they lived: this would involve a circuitous twisting route to Juniper Road, which traversed the rural-suburban "gated community" called Crescent Lake Farms, an approximate half mile north on that road, and then a turn into the interior of the development and, by way of smaller, curving roads, onto West Crescent Drive.

Like a labyrinth, it was! Crescent Lake Farms was not a residential area hospitable to strangers. Easily one could become lost in a maze of drives, lanes, "ways," and "circles," for the gated community had been designed to discourage aimless driving.

Their three-acre property did not include frontage on the man-made ovoid Crescent Lake. But a small stream meandered through it, to empty into the lake a short distance away.

"They sound *young*."

The wife heard what sounded like low thrilled throaty laughter. There was a strange unsettling intimacy to this laughter, as if their neighbors on West Crescent Drive were very near and not a quarter mile away, at the very least.

You stared at the massed trees, expecting to see human figures there.

"Yes. And happy."

The wife had brought drinks for her husband and herself: whiskey and water for the husband, lemon-flavored sparkling water for the wife. And a little silver bowl of the husband's favorite nuts, pistachios.

Hungrily, noisily the husband chewed pistachios. Yet his attention was riveted to the dark cluster of trees which the sounds of voices and laughter teasingly penetrated.

It wasn't unlike hearing voices through a wall. Intimate, tantalizing. You heard the musical cadences but not distinct words.

Drinks outside on the terrace behind their house was their ritual before dinner, in warm weather. Though he wasn't any longer making his forty-minute commute to Investcorp International, Inc., in Forrestal Village, on Route 1, where the husband had directed the applied math and computational division of the company for the past seventeen years, the husband and the wife had not changed their before-dinner ritual.

They had lived in this sprawling five-bedroom shingleboard house in Crescent Lake Farms for nearly thirty years and in that time, very little had changed in the gated community which was one of the oldest and most prestigious in northern New Jersey.

There was a waiting list of would-be homeowners. Elsewhere, properties were difficult to sell, but not in Crescent Lake Farms.

The wife thought, *We are protected here. We are very happy here.*

Thoughtfully, his head cocked in the direction of the massed trees, the husband finished his whiskey-and-water. The voices continued— softly, teasingly. A sudden squawking squabble among geese in the near distance, and the gentler sounds were drowned out.

In any case it was time to go inside for dinner which was more or less ready to be served—in a warm oven, and in a microwave. And on the kitchen counter a lavish green salad in a gleaming wooden bowl with feta cheese, arugula, avocado, cherry tomatoes—the husband's favorite salad.

"I think they must have gone inside. Over there."

Shyly the wife touched the husband's hand. He did not, as he'd used to do, turn his hand to grasp hers, instinctively; but he did not brush her hand away as he sometimes did, not rudely, not impolitely, but half-mindedly.

It appeared to be so: their neighbors' voices had faded. All you could hear was the quarrelsome sound of waterfowl and, startlingly near at their stream, the excited miniature cries of spring peepers.

She said, "Will you come inside, darling? It's late."

Airy and melodic the laughter, summer evenings.

Almost, the husband and the wife could hear through the woods a delicate tinkle of glassware from time to time—wine glasses? And cutlery.

The *neighbors-through-the-trees* frequently dined outside. Their voices were low and murmurous and no words were distinct but the sounds were happy sounds, unmistakably.

"Oh—is that a baby? D'you think?"

The wife heard something a little different, one evening in June. A sweet cooing sound—was it? Just barely discernible beyond the nocturnal cries of the waterfowl on Crescent Lake and low guttural bullfrog grunts in their grassy lawn.

The husband listened, paused in his pistachio-chewing.

"Maybe."

"Though we haven't heard a baby crying, ever. "

The wife sounded wistful. Her own babies had grown and departed the house at 88 East Crescent Drive, years ago.

The wife was thinking *They are dining by candlelight probably. Their faces reflected in a glass-topped wrought-iron table on a flagstone terrace like ours.*

If the *husband-through-the-trees* brushed the hand of the *wife-through-the-trees*, the wife could not observe. If the *wife-through-the-trees* paused to take up the baby in her arms, to kiss him on his little snub nose, the wife could not observe.

"A baby *would cry.* So maybe it isn't a baby."

Yet, the soft cooing sound persisted. And adult voices, and throaty laughter. The husband and the wife listened acutely, sitting very still on their terrace.

It was their custom now to eat outside. In the past, the husband had not liked to eat outside which he'd thought too *picnicky.*

The wife did not mind the extra effort of carrying things from the kitchen and back again. The wife quite enjoyed the romance of mealtimes on the rear terrace, in the company, at a little distance, of their mysterious *neighbors-through-the-trees*.

For often, since his retirement, the husband was very quiet. The wife felt lonely even as she told herself *Don't be ridiculous! You are not lonely.*

It was strange that, in the past, they'd had no particular awareness of these neighbors. Possibly, a new family had moved into the house on West Crescent Drive?

Other, nearer neighbors, who lived on East Crescent Drive, were more visible of course and more annoying, at times; there were frequently large summer lawn parties, children's birthday parties with balloons tied to mailboxes, political fund-raisers involving vehicles parked on both sides of the narrow road. But over all, Crescent Lake Farms was a quiet place. In the Crescent Lake Farms homeowners' manual *disturbing the peace and privacy of our neighbors* was expressly forbidden.

And the properties were large: a minimum of three acres. So your neighbors weren't inescapable, as in an urban setting.

Now the wife recalled: at Easter, on an unseasonably warm Sunday afternoon when their daughter Ellen had come to visit with her two small children, and they were walking in the back lawn, the wife had heard an unusual sound through the thicket of trees—a woman's voice, it might have been, so melodic as to seem like music, but indistinct, and soon fading. At the time she hadn't known what it was, assumed it was coming from their neighbors at 86 East Crescent Drive, and had paid no particular attention to it.

The husband hadn't noticed this female voice, at the time. Their daughter, distracted by her young children, hadn't noticed.

Ellen said, "This is a lovely house. I have such good memories of this house. It's a shame, you will probably be selling it . . ."

Selling it? The wife reacted with dismay, and did not glance at the husband, knowing that the husband would be upset by their daughter's careless remark.

"...I mean, since it's so large. And it must be so expensive to maintain especially in the winter..."

The husband had walked stiffly on, headed for the edge of the property, where there was a gate, rarely used, that opened onto a no-man's-land—a densely wooded area that belonged not to any private landowner but to Hecate Township.

The wife was embarrassed by the husband's rudeness. But she, too, was offended by the question and did not want to think that their other children were speculating about their future.

The wife remained with their daughter and lively grandchildren, talking of other things.

Now, the wife recalled that awkward episode. And the way their daughter had lifted one of the children into her arms, with such familiarity, and such confidence, and joy. Listening to the neighbors' cooing baby weeks later, she was feeling a pang of loss.

Inwardly protesting to her daughter *But we are so happy here! Whyever would we want to move?*

⚜

"What is *that*?"—the husband was baffled.

The wife listened: a soft blunted sound as of wood striking wood, she was sure she'd never heard before.

It was a morning in mid-June. The wife and the husband were outside on the deck reading the Sunday newspaper that fluttered in the breeze. A part of the paper had gotten loose from the husband's grasp and had been blown into shrubbery close by, which the wife would retrieve.

"Is it coming from—*over there*?"

"I think so, yes."

"Some sort of—repair work? A kind of hammer striking wood?"

"Not a hammer. I don't think so."

They listened. Again the blunted sound came, a near-inaudible *crack.*

They were staring at the trees. Pine trees, deciduous trees whose names they didn't know—beech? Oak? Beyond their six-foot wire fence was a dense jungle of bushes, scrub trees, mature trees. However deep the woods was, whether a quarter mile or less, it was as opaque to their eyes by day as by night.

The wife had to suppose that not one but two fences separated their property from that of the *neighbors-through-the-trees.* For the other property would be fenced-off as well.

In the land owned by Hecate Township there was a median strip kept mowed in the summer, probably no more than fifty feet across, where power lines had been installed.

The husband and the wife had never walked along the median. The wife had a vague recollection of stubbled weeds, marshy soil. Nothing like the fastidiously tended suburban lawns of Merion bluegrass, the preferred grass for Crescent Lake Farms.

Years ago when they'd walked more frequently, often hand-in-hand, they'd walked in parks, or along hiking trails; they had never explored the area behind their house which did not seem hospitable to strolling couples.

The wife assumed that there were signs posted in the woods behind their house, as elsewhere in Crescent Lake Farms, forbidding *trespassing, hunting with gun or bow.*

White-tailed Virginia deer dwelt in the woods of Crescent Lake Farms. Occasionally, no matter how vigilant homeowners were, no matter how high their fences, deer would manage to slip through, to ravage gardens in the night.

It had happened, the wife's roses had been decimated, years before. Her carefully tended little vegetable garden, even her potted geraniums.

But the husband had had the fence repaired, and no deer had set foot on the property since.

Crack!—a light glancing sound.

It was utterly baffling, what this sound might be. At once sharp, yet muffled. A *playful* sort of sound, the wife thought.

The husband had ceased reading the newspaper. The politics of the day infuriated him: even when power lay with the politicians he supported, and the opposition appeared to be failing, so much in the political sphere seemed to him vile, vulgar, meretricious, inane—he threatened that he wouldn't be voting at all.

The husband, whose professional life had been involved with the most complex algorithms and equations, knew to distrust the sort of crude polls you saw reported in the media, and "statistical studies." The husband made the droll joke that *roughly forty percent* of what was printed in the *New York Times* in such quasi-scientific or economic terms was fabricated by researchers.

"Only naïve people take polls seriously. The publication of a poll is a stratagem of *persuasion*."

After degrees from Harvard the husband had begun his career at a mathematical research center in Cambridge, Mass. Then, he'd been recruited by a medical science research center in White Plains, New York. Then, by a pharmaceutical manufacturer in Princeton, New Jersey, where he'd developed algorithms brilliantly forecasting consumer purchases. By the time he'd moved to Investcorp International, Inc., his work in mathematical computation was so complex, the wife had virtually no knowledge of what her husband did, or how it was related to the *actual world*.

"What is it that Dad *does*?"—so the children would ask one by one.

The wife recalled when her young husband had talked excitedly of his work to anyone who would listen. But in recent years, never.

She no longer made inquiries. Much of his life was separate from hers as if each was on an ice floe, drifting in the same direction and yet drifting inevitably apart.

"Something hitting against something else—that's what we're hearing. It sounds like wood."

"Croquet?"

The husband was impressed, the wife had solved the mystery.

"Yes of course! Such a civilized lawn game—*croquet.*"

They did not mind the glancing *crack* of the mallet against the croquet ball, for the sound was diminished at a distance, like their neighbors' voices and laughter.

"I've never played croquet, have you?"

"Oh, long ago. At my grandparents' house on Nantucket."

The wife spoke wistfully. The husband spoke nostalgically.

"D'you think they have guests? They're playing croquet with guests?"

They listened. It was impossible to tell from the near-inaudible murmuring voices.

The wife half-closed her eyes. In twilight figures clothed elegantly in white were gracefully wielding mallets, striking painted wooden balls and driving them forward in the grass beneath little wire hoops.

The woman or the women wore long skirts. The men, white coats and trousers.

"I'd like to play croquet again. Would you?"

"Yes. I'd love to play croquet with you."

They smiled at each other. The wife felt an impulse to take up her husband's hand and kiss it.

On the backs of her husband's hands, bruises the hue of grapes. His blood was thin: he bled easily, beneath his skin. This was to correct for high blood pressure.

"We could order a set online, maybe. I doubt there are croquet sets for sale in town."

"Yes. Let's!"

They realized that the croquet game through-the-trees must have ended, when they'd been talking. It was past dark by now: fully night.

The trees beyond their property were a solid block of darkness like a gigantic mouth.

High overhead, a blurred moon that cast a blurred light.

$$\maltese$$

"Darling? Come here."

The wife called excitedly to the husband, who was working in his *home office* on the first floor facing the front of the house.

Though there was no longer an office at Investcorp International, Inc., yet the husband's office at home remained his *home office*.

"Hurry, darling! Please."

It was midday. Strains of music were penetrating the trees at the rear of their property, sweetly delicate, captivating. At first, the wife had assumed that the exquisite sound was the singing of an unusual species of bird but when she'd listened closely, and determined that the sound was coming through the trees, she realized that this was no bird.

"I think someone is playing the violin over there. I mean—it isn't a recording or a radio, it's an actual person."

The husband had come outside, frowning. He seemed irritable at having been interrupted at his desk yet he leaned over the railing, listening.

"Maybe a child? Practicing his lesson?"

The husband frowned, cocking his head.

"I'm not sure that I hear anything. I think you're imagining a *violin*."

They listened, intently. There came, from the roadway in front of the house, a sudden blaring of rock music: from one of the damned tradesmen's vans, or delivery vans, so prevalent in the neighborhood.

"I'm sure that I heard—something. . . . It wasn't ordinary music but something special."

The wife knew: it was household protocol never to interrupt her husband when he was working in his *home office*. The children had never dared.

Apologetically the wife said she might have been mistaken. She was sorry to have called the husband and she knew that if she admitted her error at once, the husband would not be angry with her.

He was saying, petulantly, "I didn't hear a thing. Certainly not any *violin*."

The husband returned to the house. The wife continued to listen, in a trance of expectation.

But she heard no more "violin" notes. Maybe the sound had been a bird's song after all.

Or blood pulsing in her ears. Beating in her heart.

That was what she'd been hearing—was it?

༄

They had been married for nearly forty years. Not an hour, had they ceased to be married in forty years.

The husband had been "unfaithful" to the wife—probably. On those business trips. On company "retreats" to Palm Beach, Key West, Bermuda and St. Bart's, Costa Rica and Mexico, to which wives had not been invited.

But these trips were of the past. The last one had been several years ago. The wife had ceased to think of these humiliations as one ceases to think of an illness, painful but not lethal, of long-ago.

The husband would be a domestic animal now, confined to the household and to the wife. And to his online life, in his *home office.*

The wife had not been unfaithful to the husband. Not with any man—any individual.

In her heart. In the mysterious and uncharitable way of the heart.

But I love him. That will never change.

༄

"Listen! A dog."

Not often but from time to time, when the *neighbors-through-the-trees* appeared to be in their backyard, or on their deck, adults and a child, or children, there came the sound of a dog barking—not protracted, not disturbing, just two or three short barks, then silence.

A dignified dog, the wife thought. A German shepherd, or a border collie. One of those elegant long-haired dogs she'd always fantasized owning—an Afghan.

"I think we should get a dog, darling. Everyone says . . ."

"Dogs are too needy, and demanding. Dogs have to be walked twice a day."

"Once a day, I think."

"Twice."

"It might depend upon the breed."

"*Twice.* And I don't have time."

You are retired. You have all the time in the world.

"A dog would be lovely company for us both. And a watch-dog."

The husband laughed, the way the wife said *watch-dog.*

"Oh, what's so funny?"

The wife wanted to laugh with him but the husband had turned his gaze to somewhere beyond the trees and had not seemed to hear her.

"Listen! Is it—Satie?"

This time there was no mistaking, they were hearing music through the trees: piano music.

Acutely they listened, on the terrace.

"Definitely, piano music. It seems remarkably near."

"An actual piano, being played. But not by a child—this would be an adult. Someone who has played for years."

The wife-through-the-trees, the wife thought. She herself had had ten years of piano lessons, as a girl, but had not seriously played for more than twenty years.

Delightful music! Just audible, at dusk.

Mixed with the sounds of waterfowl at the lake, frogs and nocturnal insects in the grass.

The poetic stately notes of Erik Satie. The wife was deeply moved—this was *her music*, she'd played with such eager pleasure for her piano teacher at college.

She'd had talent, her teacher had said. Beyond his words the subtle admonition she must not acknowledge, for fear of embarrassing them both—*Only not just enough talent.*

She knew, she'd understood and she'd accepted. *You have gone as far as you can go, very likely. You must not delude yourself, you will only be disappointed.*

Her life since that time had been a systematic avoidance of *delusion.* She had thought this was maturity, clear-mindedness. She had married her husband knowing that he could not love her as much as she loved him, for it was not in the man's nature to love generously and without qualification, as it was in hers. In matters of emotion, he had *gone as far as he could go.*

Yet, she would love him, and she would certainly marry him. For she was eager to be married. She did not want to be not-married. She did not want to be conspicuously *alone.* And whatever followed from that decision, she vowed she would not regret.

Three children, whom she loved (unevenly). For no mother can help loving one child above others, as no child can help loving one parent more than the other.

Before she'd married her husband, at the age of twenty-three, she'd had her single great emotional adventure, that would last her lifetime. This memory had crystallized inside her as a secret, insoluble as mineral. Her self had seemed to form around it, encasing it. And never would she reveal it.

The music of Satie reminded her. Tears shimmered in her eyes, the husband would not notice.

Gnossiennes. Gymnopédies.

The composer's annotations in the compositions were original, curious—*du bout de la pensée, sur la langue, postulez en vous-même, sans orgueil, ouvrez la tête, très perdu.*

How strange that had seemed to her, a girl: *très perdu.*

" 'Quite lost!' "

She'd spoken aloud. The husband glanced at her, in mild curiosity.

When the husband was not critical of her, the husband was bemused by her. Their marriage had not been a marriage of equals.

Through the trees, the piano music ceased; then, after a moment, began again, what seemed to be a new composition by Satie, that differed from its predecessor only subtly.

Composed in the 1880s the piano music of Erik Satie sounded contemporary. It was eerily simple, beautiful. It was unhurried as time relentlessly passing second by second and it was seemingly without emotion even as it evoked, in the listener, the most intense sorts of emotion—melancholy, sorrow, loss.

A rebuff to Romantic music perhaps, with its many cascading notes and emotional excess, or to Baroque music, the fierce precision of clockwork.

"Isn't that something you used to play?"—the husband seemed only now to recall.

She said, laughing, "Yes. But not so well—I'd never played the music so well."

In fact she'd played Satie quite well. Her teacher and others had praised her, and they had not exaggerated.

The wife and the husband had not had an easy week, this week: there had been doctors' appointments, scheduling for "tests" and more appointments, stretching into the summer.

The husband's tenderness with the wife was just unusual enough to leave her shaken and uncertain. She knew it was his apprehension of the future—their future.

He is afraid. But I must not be.

The *neighbors-through-the-trees* lived in a house that mirrored their own, the wife presumed. Possibly, it was an identical house: artificially weathered shingleboard with dark red shutters, a steep roof, several stone chimneys. A three-car garage. Not a new house, for Crescent Lake Farms was not a new subdivision, but an attractive house, you might say a beautiful house. And expensive.

The wife had not driven by the house at 88 West Crescent Drive but she'd studied the Crescent Lake Farms map and saw how precisely the lots were positioned, three- and four-acre properties on each side of the man-made lake and each with its replica like halves of the human brain.

The property at 88 West Crescent Drive was three acres, like their own. It was equidistant from the man-made lake less than a mile to the east.

The wife had been fascinated, as an undergraduate, by human anatomy as well as by music. She'd thought—perhaps—she might apply to medical school—but requirements like organic chemistry and molecular biology had dampened her enthusiasm.

Yet, she remained (secretly) fascinated by illustrations of the human body, its labyrinthine yet symmetrical interior. The brain was the most complex of all organs.

Cortex, cerebellum, spinal cord.

Frontal lobe, parietal lobe, occipital lobe, temporal lobe.

She was fascinated with the possibility of "dissection"—the human body opened up, its secrets labeled. Yet, she could not bear to look upon an actual human corpse. She certainly could not bear to see a human corpse dissected.

The mere sight of blood caused her to feel weak, faint. Even the thought of blood. It was an involuntary reflex like gagging.

"Hello? What are you thinking about?"

The husband was staring at her, smiling.

"I—wasn't thinking. I was listening to the music."

She'd forgotten where she was, for the moment. The pristine piano notes of Erik Satie had faded and in their place were the raucous cries of Canada geese, flapping their wings and squabbling on the lake.

⁕

" *'Seul, pendant un instant'*—'alone, for a moment.' "

At the piano she'd neglected for most of her adult life she was playing—attempting to play—Satie. Inside the piano bench she'd found the yellowing photocopied pages she had annotated many years ago, precise instructions from her music teacher.

She did not want to think *Mr. Krauss must be dead. A long time now, dead.*

She'd loved him, at one time. How desperately, how helplessly—and yet, in secret. For he'd never known.

Her fingers had absorbed his interest. The sounds that leapt from her fingers. Of her, he'd had but a vague awareness, and very little interest.

He'd been at least thirty years her senior. And married.

He'd hummed with her piano playing, when she was playing well. Half-consciously he'd hummed, like Glenn Gould. But when she struck a wrong note, or faltered, the humming ceased abruptly.

She'd begun now with the simplest *Gnossienne.* Her fingering was awkward, she struck wrong notes. The very clarity of the music was a rebuke to her clumsiness but she continued, she returned to the beginning of the piece and continued through to the end; and, at the end, she returned again to the beginning and continued through to the end, with fewer mistakes. She did this several times before moving on to the second *Gnossienne.* She began to feel a small hesitant satisfaction—rising, almost, to elation—joy! *I haven't forgotten. The music is in my fingers.*

For ninety minutes she remained at the piano, playing the music of Erik Satie. Her shoulders ached. Her fingers ached. She was having difficulty reading the notes that seemed to her smaller than she recalled. But she persevered. She was quite happy, even with her fumbling fingers.

Someone came to stand in the doorway, to listen. Her heart reacted, she was startled. Though knowing it could only be the husband.

She waited for him to speak. He might say *Hey—that's pretty good.*

Or—*Hey, is that the music we were hearing through-the-trees?*

Or—*The piano needs tuning, eh?*

But when she turned, there was no one in the doorway.

She closed up the keyboard. She was strangely excited, and apprehensive. She foresaw returning to all her piano music, the many old and yellowed books and photocopied sheets, like an excavation of the past it would be, digging back into time.

The music is in my fingers. Any time I want to retrieve it.

<hr />

"Listen!"

It was just past 6 P.M. The midsummer sun was far from the treeline. The husband was on the deck at the rear of the house, for something had attracted him there.

He'd brought a drink with him. Earlier each evening he was leaving his *home office* until, this evening, he'd left to come out onto the porch before 6 P.M.

The wife came to join the husband, distracted. She'd heard him calling to her and hadn't realized at first where he was. There had been a telephone call from her oncologist—she'd had to call back, and to wait several long minutes.

It will be a simple procedure. A biopsy with a local anesthetic, a needle.

The husband had left the terrace and was standing in the fresh-mowed grass. He stood approximately fifty feet from the fence at the property line.

He was listening to—what?—the wife heard what seemed to her familiar voices, through the trees. A ripple of laughter.

But there were unfamiliar voices as well. The wife was sure she'd never heard these voices before.

These were dissonant sounds, somewhat jarring. The laughter loud and sharp and a dog's barking commingled with the laughter, distorted through the trees.

A party? A picnic?

There were children's voices as well, and shouts. And the dog barking excitedly as they'd never heard it bark before.

"They sound happy."

"They sound *drunk*."

The wife wanted to protest, this was unfair. She understood that the husband felt envious. It had been a long time since they'd hosted a party at their house . . .

An odor of barbecue, wafting through the woods. Fatty ground meat on a grill. Salsa, raw onion. Beer.

They had friends—of course. Numerous friends, and yet more friendly acquaintances. But their friends were *like themselves*—their political prejudices, children and grandchildren, homeowners' complaints, experiences in travel, physical ailments. Like mirror-reflections these friends were, and not flattering.

And their older friends were fading, irrevocably. Some of them had retired to the southwest, or to Florida. Some were mysteriously ill. A few had died—it was always a small shock, to realize *But she isn't alive any longer. There is no way I can reach her.*

The wife had accompanied the husband to his fortieth reunion at Harvard the previous year. The husband had arranged to meet old classmates, a former roommate, "friends" he'd maintained, to a degree, over the course of decades, though the men had rarely seen one another in the interim. The wife had liked these men—to a degree—and she'd liked their wives, who were making a special effort to be friendly with one another, under the strain of the college reunion which was tightly scheduled, boisterous, and exhausting. And on the drive home, when the wife said how good it was to see the husband with such old friends, one or two of the men "like brothers," clearly enjoying himself, the husband had listened in silence and not until they were home, preparing for bed, the husband brooding, slump-shouldered, and the flaccid flesh at his waist and belly pale as unbaked bread dough, did he say, in a flat cold voice, without meeting the wife's startled gaze, "Frankly, I don't care if I ever see any of them again."

Yet, hearing the festive sounds of the party *through-the-trees*, clearly the husband felt envy, as well as disapproval; he had to be thinking, the wife surmised, that since retiring from Investcorp, he saw relatively few people, from day to day and from week to week. (Was it possible, the husband's Investcorp colleagues/friends were forgetting him? Those frequent email invitations sent to a set group of individuals had ceased to show up in the husband's inbox, he'd only just begun to realize. And his emails to his former colleagues/friends were not being returned.)

The husband had only recently wielded *such power*—in his division at Investcorp. And now . . .

The husband said, "That sounds like—what?—furniture being dragged on the terrace?"

They listened. Through the trees came a sound very like furniture—heavy, wrought-iron terrace furniture—being dragged along a terrace.

More voices, laughter. Raucous laughter, and braying laughter. The wife was shocked, their *neighbors-through-the-trees* had not seemed like such—well, gregarious people. Until now they had seemed like an ideal family, well-bred, private.

The husband said, "Maybe it's a political fund-raiser. It sounds *large*."

The husband detested noisy "fund-raisers" in the neighborhood. The husband had grown so contemptuous of politicians, even "conservative" politicians for whom he felt obliged to vote, in the effort of maintaining his accumulated investments and savings, the wife avoided bringing the subject up to him.

"I don't think it's that large. I think it's just—another family or two. An outdoor barbecue, in summer. I think they're just having *fun*."

Not just one dog was barking, but at least two. And now came amplified music, some sort of rock, or—was it "rap"?

The husband turned away in disgust, and stomped back into the house. The wife remained for a few minutes, indecisive, listening.

How loud they are. But how happy-sounding.

⁂

"The Jesters."

The husband must have been thinking aloud. For he hadn't addressed the wife, who was standing a few feet away, gardening implements in her gloved hands.

"What do you mean—'the Jesters'?"

"That's their name: 'Jester.'"

"I don't understand. Whose name?"

"Our neighbors through the trees."

The husband gestured in disgust, in the direction of the woods. Already, on this weekday morning, though it wasn't yet noon, there was a barrage of noise coming through the trees: lawn mower, leaf blower, chain saw.

The wife said, faltering, "But—everyone in Crescent Lake has lawn work done. We have our lawn mowed and serviced. How is this different?"

"It is different. It is God-damned *louder*."

The wife recoiled, the husband was being irrational. Surely the decibel level of the chain saw through the trees was no higher than that of the chain saws the husband had hired to trim away dead limbs from their own trees? (Of course, when the lawn crew was working on their large, sloping lawn, the husband and the wife made certain that they weren't at home.)

In any case it was too noisy, the wife had to concede, for she was trying to avoid a migraine headache, and nausea from medication, for her to work outside in the rose garden, which had suffered an onslaught of

Japanese beetles and badly needed her care. She had wanted, too, to remove those tough little tendril-weeds from the terrace that poked up between the flagstones, giving it a shabby look.

Too noisy for the sensitive husband to remain on the terrace where he'd brought some of his *home office* work—his laptop, investment accounts, sheets of yellow paper on which he penciled notes.

(When the wife asked the husband about their finances, the husband tended to reply curtly. She understood that they had "lost some money" in stocks, but then—who in Crescent Farms had not? The wife did not dare to ask more of the husband who would interpret such questions as a critique of his ability to handle their finances, thus of his manhood.)

The husband who'd been restless in his *home office* now returned to the house. The wife shut all the windows, and turned on the air conditioning. And a ceiling fan in the husband's office that made a gentle whirring sound.

"The lawn crew won't be there much longer, I'm sure. Then I'll help you move outside again."

The husband waved her away with a look of commingled disgust and dismay that pierced the wife to the heart.

"Those damned Jesters! What did I tell you!"

This day, mid-morning, a lovely day in late June, there came what sounded like raw adolescent voices, boys' voices, through the trees. And barking. (Two dogs: one with a deep-throated growling bark, the other a petulant miniature, a high-pitched excruciating yipping.)

And there came too as the husband and the wife listened in fascinated horror, a harsh sound of slapping against pavement. Slap-slap-*slap*.

"A basketball? They have one of those damned portable baskets in their driveway so their sons can practice basketball."

"So soon!"

"What do you mean, 'so soon'?"

The wife wasn't sure what she had meant. The words had sprung from her lips. Faltering she said, "They'd just been young children, it seemed. So recently."

She was thinking *What has happened to the croquet set?*

She was thinking *We forgot entirely about it! Croquet.*

No longer could the husband linger on the terrace after breakfast where it was his habit to read the newspaper that so infuriated him but which he could not seem to resist—the *New York Times.*

(The wife knew, the husband sent angry emails to the *Times* editorial page, at least once a week. The subjects of the emails ranged from politics to global warming, from taxes, "earmarks," the President and the President's wife, to "sick cultures" in the Middle East and in the Far East.)

(The wife knew, the husband had sent angry complaints to the Crescent Lake Farms Homeowners Association. He had tried to call, but there was only voice-mail, which was never answered. And the email complaints were answered automatically, with a promise of "looking into the situation.")

Often then in the days following, intermittently and unpredictably through the day, there came the sound of teenagers practicing basketball, playing amplified rap music, exchanging shouts. It seemed clear that the Jester children had visitors—the shouts were various, at times the several young voices were quite distinct.

No words, only just sounds. Raw brash crude sounds.

And the dogs' nonstop barking, that continued after the young people left, often into the night.

(Were the dogs tied outside? Were no other neighbors disturbed? How could the *neighbors-through-the-trees* fail to hear and be disturbed, themselves?)

(Wasn't it cruelty to animals, to keep dogs tied outside? Ignoring their barking in the night?)

It was astonishing to the wife and the husband, how loud these noises were; how *close-seeming*.

"It's like they're just outside our house. They couldn't be any louder if they were inside our house."

"Maybe—we should go away. Sooner than August."

They'd planned two weeks on Nantucket Island, in August: in a rented house on the ocean, to which they'd been returning for decades. But the husband was furious at the suggestion of being *driven out of his own house, by neighbors.*

"I wouldn't want to give them the satisfaction."

"But they don't know anything about us—they don't know *us*."

"They know that they have neighbors. They know that their noise must carry through the trees. And what of their neighbors on West Crescent Drive? You'd think that they would have complained by now."

"Maybe they have. Maybe nothing came of it."

"Listen!"—the husband lifted his hand.

For now, there was the sound of a younger child, crying. Or screaming. Sobbing, screaming, crying.

Other childish voices, shouts. The teenagers' raw-voiced shouts. Must have been a game of some kind involving physical contact.

And the dogs' barking. Louder.

The husband and the wife left their house, earlier than they'd planned for dinner in town. The husband could barely eat his food, the ignominy of being *driven away* from his own house was intolerable to him.

At least when they returned, the noise through the trees had abated.

Only nocturnal birds, bullfrogs and insects in the grass. And high overhead, a quarter-moon curved like a fingernail.

In gratitude and exhaustion, the husband and the wife slept that night, in their dreams twined in each other's arms.

———— ❧ ————

"Listen!"—the husband threw down his newspaper, and heaved himself to his feet.

There came a child's cries, another time. Quite clearly, a girl's cries. Amid the coarser sound of boys' voices, laughter. And the barking dogs.

"But—where are you going?"

"Where do you think I'm going? Over there."

"But—there's no way to get through. Is there?"

"It sounds like a child is being harassed. Or worse. I'm not going to just sit here on my ass, for Christ's sake."

The wife followed close behind the husband. She had not seen him so agitated, so *activated*, in a long time.

They were descending the lawn, in the direction of the gate. The grass had been cut recently, not in horizontal rows but diagonally across the width of the lawn. The air smelled sweetly of mown grass, that had been taken away by the lawn crew.

Rarely opened, the gate was stuck in grass and dirt, and had to be shaken hard.

The husband was very excited. The wife felt light-headed with excitement, and dread.

For this was a violation of Crescent Farms protocol. No one ever approached a neighbor's house from the rear. It was rare that anyone "visited" a neighbor's house uninvited.

"There's a girl who's hurt. And that hysterical barking. Something is terribly wrong over there."

"We should call 911."

"We don't know their house number."

"The police would find it. We could tell them the situation— approximately where the Jesters live . . ."

" 'Jesters' is not their name."

"I *know that*. Of course, 'Jesters' is not their name. We don't know their name."

"And we don't know their address. We can't even describe their house."

"But we know—"

The husband had managed to get the gate open. It was a surprise to see that, like the fence, it was badly rusted.

They made their way then into the thicket of trees, onto township property. Here were scrubby little trees and bushes and coarse weeds, thigh-high. And there was the median, where the power lines were, that looked as if it hadn't been mowed for weeks.

Somewhat hesitantly the husband and the wife made their way into the woods on the other side of the median. Here, there were many trees that appeared to be just partially alive, or wholly dead; there had been much storm damage, broken limbs and other debris heaped every-where.

There were no paths into the woods, that they could discover. No one ever walked here. No children played here. It was not the habit of Crescent Farms children to wander in such places, as the generation of their grandparents had once done.

About fifty feet into the thicket, they encountered a fence. The six-foot fence belonging to their *neighbors-through-the-trees*.

They were panting, very warm. They peered through the fence but could see nothing except trees.

The noises from their neighbors had abated, mostly. The girl had ceased crying. The other voices had vanished. Only a dog continued to bark, less hysterically.

"Maybe we'd better go back? We don't want to get lost."

"*Lost!* We can't possibly get lost."

The husband laughed incredulously. A swarm of gnats circled his damp face, his eyes glared at the wife like the eyes of a man sinking in quicksand.

"The fence is like our own. Unless we've gone in a circle, and it is our own fence. . . ."

"This isn't our fence, don't be ridiculous. Our property is behind us, on the other side of the median."

"Yes, but . . ."

The fence did resemble their own fence. It was (possibly) not so old as their fence but it was rusted in places and had become loose and probably, if they could locate the gate, they could force the gate open, and step inside.

Hello! We are your neighbors on East Crescent Drive.

We don't want to disturb you but . . . We are concerned . . .

The husband held back now. The husband was having second thoughts about his mission now that the alarming noises seemed to have ceased.

Again the wife said maybe they should turn back?

It seemed an extreme measure, to approach their neighbors' house from the rear, like trespassers. To come up to their neighbors' house from the rear, uninvited.

For this would be *trespassing* and Crescent Lake Farms expressly forbade *trespassing*.

The children called. One by one, in sequence.

As if the calls were planned.

First, Carrie. Then Tim. Then Ellen.

The husband told them that things were fine, more or less. Except for the God-damned *neighbors-through-the-trees.*

The wife told them that things were fine, more or less. Except for the neighbors they'd never met, across the median on West Crescent Drive.

"For God's sake—Mom, Dad! Don't you have anything else to talk about except the neighbors?"

Their children were exasperated with them. Laughed at them. The husband was furious, and the wife was deeply wounded.

"But—you don't know what it's like, with these people. Your father is under such strain, I'm worried about his health."

"What about your health, Mom? We're worried about *you*."

And: "If you're unhappy there, you can move. The house is much too large for two people. The maintenance must be out of sight, especially in the winter . . . Mom? Are you listening?"

No. She wasn't listening.

Yes. She was listening, politely.

Into one of those retirement villages? Your father would never survive.

They explained that they were not unhappy in their house, which they loved. In fact they were *very happy*.

Only just upset, at times. By their *neighbors-through-the-trees*.

<hr />

"The Jesters! God damn them."

Another party on the back terrace. From late afternoon until past midnight.

Amplified rock music. Throbbing notes penetrating the dense thicket of trees. The Jesters were thrumming with life: there was no avoiding the Jesters who penetrated the very air.

The wife returned from her chemo treatment ashen-faced, staggering. Fell onto a bed and tried to sleep for three hours during which time she tried not to be upset by the amplified music-through-the-trees and by her own nausea. The husband had shut himself in his *home office*.

Crack!—crack! Crack-crack-crack!

(Was it gunfire? From the Jesters' property?)

Hunting was forbidden in Crescent Lake Farms. As were firecrackers, fireworks—any kind of noisy activity that was a *disturbance of the peace and privacy of one's neighbors*.

Middle of the night, uplifted voices. Waking the husband and the wife from their troubled sleep.

The adult Jesters were arguing with one another, it seemed. A man's voice sharp as a claw hammer, a woman's voice sharp as flung nails. At 3:20 A.M.

(Were the children involved in the argument? This wasn't clear, initially.)

(Yes, at least one of the children was crying. A forlorn sound like that of a small creature grasped in the jaws of an owl, being carried to the uppermost branches of a tree to be devoured.)

"We have to speak with them. This can't continue."

"We should file a complaint. That might be more practical."

"With the Homeowners Association? Nobody there gives a damn."

"With the township police, then. 'Disturbing the peace'—'suspicion of child abuse.'"

"No! The Jesters could sue, if we made such allegations and couldn't prove them."

"Then we should speak with them. Maybe we can work something out." The wife paused, trying to control her voice. She was very shaken, and close to tears. "They're decent people, probably. They don't realize how disturbing they are to their neighbors. They will listen to reason..."

In their bedroom, in the night. The husband saw that the wife was ashen-faced, and trembling; the wife saw, with a pang of love for him, a despairing sort of love, that the husband was looking strained, older than his age; beneath his eyes, bruised-looking shadows. Yet he tried to smile at her. He took her hand, squeezed the fingers. He was like an actor who has forgotten his lines, yet will make his way through the scene, eyes clutching the eyes of his fellow actor, the two of them stumbling together.

"I'm so sorry this is happening to us. Now you're retired, you should be spared any more stress. I wish I knew what to do."

"Don't be ridiculous. It isn't up to you. I should be more forceful. We can't let our lives be ruined by the Jesters."

It was quiet now. The terrible quarrel had flared up, like wild fire, and abruptly ceased. There had been a sharp noise like the shutting of a door.

Tentatively the husband and the wife lay back down in their bed, the wife huddling in the husband's arms. By slow degrees they drifted into sleep.

※

Slap-slap-*slap*. The boys had returned to their basketball practice, early-morning. The dogs were barking. Someone shouted words that were nearly distinct—*Don't! God damn you.*

※

"If you're coming with me, come on."

"But, are you sure . . ."

"We have no choice! We'll talk with them, and if they don't cooper-ate we'll file a formal complaint with the township police."

Bravely the husband spoke. The wife hurried to keep up with him, headed for their car. She saw that the husband had shaved hastily and that tiny blood-nicks shone in his jaws.

The husband always drove. The wife sat beside him, sometimes clutching at the dashboard when the husband drove quickly and errati-cally and spoke as he drove, distracted.

The husband was saying that there have been "primitive cultures" in which the populace cut down trees year after year—decade after decade—until at last there was but a single tree remaining on the island—(evidently, these were "island aboriginals")—and this tree, they cut down.

Then, there were no more trees. The people were amazed.

Amazed and mystified. *For there had always been trees.*

Where had the trees gone? Had demons cast a spell? The belief of centuries was, *there had always been trees.*

The husband said grimly, "You do not question inherited beliefs. That is blasphemy, and blasphemy will get you killed."

The husband laughed, "Yet: where are the trees?"

The wife had no idea what the husband was talking about. She had missed his initial remarks, as they'd climbed into their car, in haste and yet in determination.

She thought *Does he mean, we have no idea what will happen to us next? Or does he mean—we can alter our future, before it's too late?*

The husband drove along East Crescent Lake Drive, and at Juniper Road he turned right; a half mile north on Juniper, and a right turn onto a smaller road, then another small road, then West Crescent Drive.

"These houses are beautiful. And the landscaping . . ."

The wife spoke admiringly. The wife was very nervous, both of the husband's driving, which was too fast for the circumstances, and of their impending destination,

The husband said, "West Crescent isn't any different than East Crescent. The houses are no more beautiful here. The landscaping is similar. In fact, some of the houses are identical with houses on our road. Look—that Colonial? It's a replica of the Colonial a few doors down from us."

The wife wasn't so sure. This Colonial had dark green shutters; the Colonial on East Crescent Lake Drive had dark red shutters.

They came to 88 East Crescent Drive. The road curved as their road did, and the cul-de-sac resembled theirs. To their surprise, the mailbox at the Jesters' house was made of white brick and stainless steel, exactly like their own, but the Jesters' mailbox door was opened, and the interior of the mailbox crammed with what looked like an accumulation of rain-soaked junk mail.

Growing in a little patch at the base of the mailbox were ugly, coarse-flowering weeds. In a little patch at the base of their mailbox the wife had planted marigolds as she did every year.

"Oh my God! Look."

"What is . . ."

To their astonishment, the house they believed to belong to the Jesters resembled their own, though not precisely. It was a sprawling country house of weathered shingleboard, large, with a horseshoe driveway like their own, but badly cracked and weedy. The elegant plantings in the Jesters' lawn had been allowed to grow wild. Rotted tree limbs lay scattered in the weedy grass.

The husband and the wife were stunned. The husband and the wife were nearly speechless. For it seemed that the Jesters' house had been damaged in some way, and was boarded up.

"Do you think—no one lives here?"

"That isn't possible . . ."

The husband had parked their car at the curb. Cautiously now they were making their way up the driveway, staring.

Waiting for a dog to rush at them, barking. . . . Two dogs.

It was so; the shingleboard house was shut up. Seemingly abandoned. No one lived here, or had lived here in a while. There was a dark stain across half the façade, like scorch.

It *was* scorch—smoke damage.

As the husband and the wife approached the house, they saw that there was a faded-yellow tape around it, at least so far as they could see. On the tape were repeated DO NOT ENTER BY ORDER OF HECATE TOWNSHIP FIRE DEPT.—DO NOT ENTER BY ORDER OF HECATE TOWNSHIP FIRE DEPT.—in black, badly faded.

The fire could not have been recent. But how was this possible?

Boldly the husband approached the house, stooping beneath the yellow tape. The wife protested, "Wait! Where are you going? It's a violation of the law . . ."

"No one is here. No one is watching."

"But—maybe it's dangerous."

(It might not have been correct, that no one was watching. Just outside the cul-de-sac, at 86 East Crescent Drive, there was a large putty-colored French Provincial house with numerous glittering windows. And a vehicle parked in the driveway.)

The husband approached the front door, stepping on debris on the stoop. As if to ring the doorbell, though obviously there was no one inside the wreck of a house.

They could see now that fire damage was considerable. From the road, it had not been so evident. Much of the house had collapsed, at the rear; downstairs windows were boarded up, somewhat carelessly; part of the roof, burnt through, had collapsed. The wife was shivering in the midsummer heat. *Did anyone die in the fire? How many?* The wife did not want to think *Was it arson? And when?* Beside the heavy oak door there were inset windows, of stained glass, which were partly broken but not boarded up; through these, the husband and the wife stared into the house, into a foyer with a silly, forlorn-looking crystal chandelier, a badly stained tile floor, miscellaneous overturned furniture.

A chair lying on its side. A crooked mirror, reflecting what looked like mist, or gas. Smoke stains like widespread black wings on the once-white wall.

A smell of something terrible, like burnt flesh.

"Please! Let's leave."

"No one can see us."

"People have died here. You can tell. Please let's *leave.*"

The husband laughed at the wife, irascibly. In the reflected light from the stained glass his skin was unnaturally mottled, rubefacient; his eyes narrowed with thought, a kind of frightened animal cunning. His nostrils widened and contracted as if, like an animal, he was sniffing the air for danger.

The wife pulled at his arm and he threw off her hand. But he relented, and followed her back to their car.

The wife saw that the husband had parked the car crookedly at the curb. It was a large gleaming new-model Acura, a beautiful silvery-green color, yet parked so carelessly it looked clownish. The husband saw this too and drew in his breath sharply.

"What the hell? I didn't park the car like this."

"You must have."

"I said, *I did not.*"

"Then who did?"

"You drove."

"I did not drive! You drove."

"You drove, and you parked the car like a drunken woman or a—a senile woman. Lucky we aren't in town, you'd have a ticket."

"But I didn't drive here. I would never have driven here. I didn't even bring my handbag, with my driver's license."

"Driving without a license! That's *points* on your license."

The wife was deeply agitated. The smell of the burnt house and what had burnt inside it was still in her nostrils. Badly she wanted to flee home and lie down on the bed and hide her face and sleep but in the corner of her eye she saw a figure approaching her and the husband, from the house across the cul-de-sac. A white-haired woman, genteel, with kindly eyes, in gardening clothes, on her head a wide-brimmed straw hat. On her hands, gloves. The wife saw that the white-haired woman had been tending to roses bordering the driveway of her house, a striking red-brick Edwardian with a deep front lawn. Obviously, the white-haired woman had, like the wife, a gardener-helper who came at least once a week to till the soil for her and take out the worst of the weeds.

"Excuse me! Hello."

The white-haired woman removed her soiled gloves, smiling at the husband and the wife. Hers was a beautiful ruin of a face, soft as a leather glove; her nose was thin, aristocratic. Her small mouth was pale primrose-pink.

"Are you—by any chance—considering that house? I mean—to buy?"

"To *buy*? The house isn't in any condition to be inhabited."

"Yes. But it could be rebuilt and repaired."

"And it isn't for sale anyway, so far as we can see. Is it?"

"I wouldn't know. I mean—it might be listed with a realtor. Realtor's signs aren't allowed in Crescent Lake Farms."

The white-haired woman smiled at them wistfully. She went on to say how hopeful they all were, on West Crescent Drive, that someone would buy the house soon, and restore it. "What a beautiful house it was! This is all such a shame and a—tragedy."

"Why? What happened?"

"The fire was—wasn't—an accident. So the investigators ruled."

"Who set the fire, if it wasn't an accident? One of the sons?"

Seeing that the husband was eager to know, the white-haired woman became cautious. She backed away, though with a polite smile.

"No one knows. Not definitely."

"*Was* there a son? A teenager?"

"There's an investigation—ongoing. It's been years now. I don't know anything more."

"You must know if they died in the fire? Someone did die—yes?"

"Who?"

"Who? The Jesters, of course. *How many of them died in the fire?*"

The husband was speaking harshly. The wife was embarrassed of his vehemence, with this gracious stranger. She tugged at his arm, to bring him back to himself.

" 'The Jesters'? I don't understand."

"What was the name of the family who lived here?"

"I—don't remember. I have to leave now."

The white-haired woman turned quickly away. That so gracious a person would turn her back on fellow residents of Crescent Lake Farms was astonishing to the wife though the husband grunted as if such rude behavior only confirmed his suspicions.

"Let's go. 'The Jesters' are taboo, it seems."

The husband drove. At the intersection of West Crescent Drive with a smaller road called Lilac Terrace he turned left, thinking to take a shortcut to Juniper, and home; but Lilac Terrace turned out, as the wife might have told the husband, to be a dead end. NO OUTLET.

After some maneuvering, the husband and the wife returned home to 88 East Crescent Drive. In their absence, the house had remained unchanged.

⅊

Next morning at dawn they were awakened by—what was it?—a battery of shots—*crack crack crack CRACK.*

The wife sat up in panic thinking that the roof of the house was collapsing upon them.

The husband swung his legs out of bed in panic thinking that someone had entered the house, to shoot them.

They went to the window which was a floor-to-ceiling window with a balcony, rarely used, outside. Because of the Jesters' unpredictable noises, the husband and the wife no longer opened this window even on cool summer nights.

The husband's face was mottled with rage, and fear. The wife thought *I will comfort him all the days of our lives.*

It was the morning of July 4. The Jesters were celebrating early.

THE DEVIL AND DR. TUBEROSE

John Herdman

Dr. Marcus Tuberose was being victimised. Whether it was because he had a poetic temperament, or because of his present difficult domestic circumstances, or because of the machinations of Dr. Philip Pluckrose, his rival and enemy, or whether all these factors were fatally combining to discredit and disadvantage him was not yet clear. An artistic sensibility, he well knew, was not a recommendation in the world of academic departmental politics; rather it was a focus of jealousy, suspicion, and mistrust. Dr. Tuberose did not flaunt his superiority in the very least; but neither on the other hand did he attempt hypocritically to conceal it. He knew his worth, and he knew that some day that worth would be recognised. But his openness in this respect did put him at a disadvantage, he was well aware of that. He did not conceal that from himself, not at all.

The fact that he had recently been deserted by his wife, Malitia, did not help either. The break-up of a marriage might no longer be in itself a social embarrassment, but in this case the circumstances, the particular and special circumstances . . . Dr. Tuberose was not unconscious of the fact that there were people who did not scruple to laugh at him behind his back. People were like that, and academics in particular were like that. Dr. Tuberose knew that he had not always made himself popular. He spoke his mind when it would be against his conscience to keep silent, and that was not a worldly-wise thing to do. But he thanked God that worldly wisdom had never been a part of his make-up. He was also not adept at currying favour in high places, unlike certain successful departmental politicians he could think of. It was amazing, he always thought, how intelligent people were so easily taken in by flattery. But then vanity was a powerful force, a more powerful force than intelligence, or disinterested commitment, a much stronger force than honesty or intellectual integrity . . . that was the way the world was, the way it had always been.

Ever since it had become known that Professor McSpale was to spend the coming academic year at the University of Delaware, a certain sentence had kept revolving and repeating itself in Dr. Tuberose's head. He had not exactly composed it, it had come as it were unbidden and without his full consent. These things happened to people of a poetic sensibility, of an intuitive temperament, they were not altogether under conscious control. "Marcus Aurelius Tuberose, M.A., B. Litt., Ph. D., has been appointed Acting Head of the Department of English Literature for the academic year 1988–89." That was the little sentence, or jingle. It was silly, he knew—he was even a little ashamed of it, deep down. But, after all, the message which it contained communicated an essential truth. The formal recognition which that sentence would represent, should it ever emerge from the mind of Dr. Tuberose into outer reality, would be no more than he deserved. He did not expect it or ask for it, he disdained to canvas it or tout for it or flatter for it, but he was too honest to hide from himself the simple fact that he deserved it. Not that he wanted it, no, but simply that he deserved it.

A month ago it had seemed to him that it was really going to happen. Things were looking good, he felt, he was not blind to the impression that there were certain factors in his favour, certain realities which it would be foolish to ignore, unrealistic, in a sense, to disregard... Then had come the day of the departmental meeting. Dr. Tuberose had arrived early, but Philip Pluckrose was there before him, and so, strange to say, was Professor McSpale. Dr. Tuberose did not like the smell of that. They were huddled deep in conversation when he entered, McSpale expatiating assertively but in low, almost conspiratorial tones, Pluckrose nodding vehemently, but with a look of fawning obsequiousness that was quite revolting. When Tuberose entered the room they ceased their confabulations quite suddenly, even blatantly, as if scorning to conceal the truth that they had been saying things that were not for his ears, things that were almost certainly to his direct disadvantage.

The decision as to the appointment of the Acting Head of Department was, as it turned out, deferred until the next meeting. Tuberose did not like that, it was clear to him that it meant that whatever understanding was being worked out between McSpale and Pluckrose required time to be brought to fruition, that it was unscrupulously being given time, and that time was therefore on the side of his enemies. During the course of that afternoon, he was frequently aware of Professor McSpale directing at him, from under his coarse, tangled, greying eyebrows, a quite peculiar look. It was a look that, thinking about it afterwards, he found it very hard to analyse. It was a look of scorn, perhaps, of hard, cold scorn, and there was something insolently defiant about it, something altogether blatant. It seemed to say that power was going to be exercised, directly and shamelessly, that justice and right were going to be disregarded, trampled upon, set altogether at nought, that this was wrong, yes, certainly, but it was going to happen all the same, and there was nothing whatever that Dr. Tuberose could do about it, not this time. This, Tuberose realised, was the price of integrity, this was the cost of speaking one's mind.

Ever since that meeting the attitude of condescending friendliness which Philip Pluckrose customarily adopted towards him had become more odiously bland, and at the same time more unconcealedly tinctured with genial contempt. On one occasion he had even had the effrontery to pretend to commiserate with Tuberose about his domestic misfortune. 'You'll have to come and have a meal with Polly and I,' he had fawned with his customary grammatical insensibility, 'and if there is anything we can do to help, Marcus, you know we're always at the end of the phone . . .'—and so on and so on; it would be embarrassing to record all the banal, gloating hypocrisies that oozed from his lips and hung heavily in the air like halitosis.

But Dr. Tuberose's nature was not of the kind that lies down meekly under persecution. He had, of course, the clean bright shield of conscious integrity with which to defend himself, but he had something else, too, something more tellingly substantial, an eloquent expression of his worth that would be hard for anyone simply to ignore, even the hardened careerists of the department, to whom intellectual distinction was apparently such a contemptible irrelevance in the primitive struggle for place, power, and personal advantage. This secret weapon was his new lecture course on the Romantic Imagination, which was to form the nucleus, the matrix, of his projected work on this well-worn topic. Already, in spite of himself, Dr. Tuberose could hear phantom phrases from future critical comments on this embryonic work of genius flitting restlessly about his brain: 'allusive, learned, lucid, and perspicacious'; 'the daring taxonomies of Tuberose'; 'as Tuberose has seminally suggested'; and so on and so forth.

Everything, however, depended on the success of the lecture course, really everything. Dr. Tuberose was now in such a position and of such an age that if he didn't go up, he could only go down—or even out. Things being as they were in the academic world, it was either promotion or early retirement, Tuberose knew that. Since the most recent departmental meeting he was aware, too, that the odds were stacked heavily against him. But the lecture course might yet change all that. There were some things that simply couldn't be disregarded, even by the English department, one had to believe that, or else life could hold no meaning.

In the early hours of the morning of the day, a Friday, on which he was due to deliver his first lecture in the series, Dr. Tuberose awoke in his lonely bed moaning and groaning from a most appalling nightmare. He had entered through the sliding doors of the main arts building of the university, his lecture notes in his briefcase, to find himself, without surprise, in the chamber of the House of Commons. A vast crowd composed of students, newspaper correspondents, internationally famous critics, and even a few well-known movie stars was wedged closely in the benches and thronging eagerly in the aisles, jostling for position, manifesting every symptom of impatient excitement, awaiting in breathless anticipation some crucial public announcement. As the bewildered Tuberose mingled with the throng, an official in the shape of a Himalayan bear advanced towards the Speaker's chair, followed by Professor McSpale in the garb of the Lord Chancellor. The Himalayan bear banged three times on the ground with his ceremonial staff and called for silence. Professor McSpale, instantly picking out Tuberose among the seething press, fixed him for a terrible moment with a baleful eye flashing with a most hellishly malignant lustre. Then he averted his gaze, and drawing from among the folds of his gown a slip of paper, read out in clear and ringing tones: "Philip Endymion Pluckrose, M.A., D. Phil., has been appointed Acting Head the Department of English Literature for the academic year 1988–89."

A wild cheer rose up, and almost instantly every eye was turned upon Dr. Tuberose with open, wicked mockery, while raucous laughter burst out and jeers, whistles, and catcalls smote upon his ears. He dropped his head in shame and struggled to leave, but no one would let him pass; instead they shoved and shouldered him provocatively while heaping upon him vague but deadly insults. Then Professor McSpale pointed to him with his long, lank, skinny finger, slapped the Himalayan bear on the rump, and shouted, "Go get him, Spielberg!" The crowd instantly parted, and the bear charged down the aisle towards Dr. Tuberose with slavering fangs, and there was nowhere for him to flee. Its teeth were not a hair's-breadth from his throat when the unhappy scholar awoke in the pitiable condition already indicated. For the remainder of that night he tossed and turned hopelessly as fragments of his lecture, the announcement by Professor McSpale, the superior smile of Pluckrose, the teeth of the Himalayan bear, and the inscrutable eyes of a certain Chinese waiter mingled and coalesced in the fevered jumble of his imagination.

It may be imagined that Dr. Tuberose entered the lecture hall considerably unnerved. He was made of stern stuff, however, Marcus Aurelius Tuberose was not a man of jelly, and in spite of every setback he remained quietly but ruthlessly determined to do himself justice, to acquit himself with honour, to put all his cards squarely on the table, to show up Pluckrose for what he was. In this first lecture he was plunging right into the very heart of the matter, addressing Coleridge's distinction between Fancy and Imagination. As he warmed to his subject he began to be stirred and even exalted by his own eloquence, and he was soon confident that he had his audience eating out of the palm of his hand. The tables were turned, Pluckrose was a dead letter—even in the impetuous onrush of his discourse that consciousness was shining at the back of his mind. And then a terrible thing happened.

"We have, above all, to ask ourselves," Dr. Tuberose was saying as he reached what he thought of as the high point of his lecture, "what exactly Coleridge meant by 'Imagination.' We have to be clear about this before we can proceed any further. Did he mean by 'Imagination' a permanent, universal faculty of the human mind, equally possessed by all? Or did he mean by it what we nowadays usually understand the term to mean, namely a mere image-forming capacity, an ability to image to ourselves facts and possibilities and potentialities outside immediate reality, a capacity which different people possess in differing and variable degrees? Do we all possess Imagination in the same way in which we all possess two arms and two legs?"

Dr. Tuberose paused impressively and looked around at his audience. He was about to continue when he noticed a hand raised about three-quarters of the way up the lecture hall, to his right, near a side-entrance. To his irritation, and with a certain sinking of the heart, he saw that it belonged to an unhealthy-looking young man in a wheelchair, the lower moiety of whose person was concealed by a travelling-rug.

"Yes?" he snapped impatiently, in a way which he hoped indicated that interruptions were not scheduled for this lecture course.

"Excuse me," came back at him the weak but at the same time asser-tive tones of the student in the wheelchair, "but it is not true that we all possess two arms and two legs."

Dr. Tuberose frowned and traversed the rostrum once or twice, look-ing at his feet.

"Let me rephrase that," he resumed. "Do we all possess Imagination in the same way in which we all possess a head?" He paused again. "Or am I once again assuming too much? Is there anyone here without a head?"

This sally was met with a horrified, stunned silence.

"So," said Dr. Tuberose complacently, "we all have heads." He paused yet again. "But perhaps there is among us some smart-ass with *two* heads, who would like to exploit his—or, I had no doubt better add, her—misfortune in order to score a debating point off me?"

At this, signs of disorder began to manifest themselves in the lecture hall: there was some laughter of a nervous kind, but also more ominous stirrings and mutterings. Dr. Tuberose raised his voice.

"I can see that I shall have to make a diversion, in order to attempt to establish the distinction between essence and accident. The essence of a thing refers to that which it is in itself, its inner, universal condition; its accidents refer to that which has befallen it accidentally, that, in other words, which has *happened* to it. The essence of a thing is undisturbed by its accidents."

"It wasn't an accident!" shouted the student in the wheelchair, "I was born without legs!"

"You misunderstand me!" yelled back Dr. Tuberose, "you misunderstand me deliberately and maliciously! That you were born without legs is an accident, essentially you have legs! I will not be provoked! I will not be persecuted!"

Scarcely aware of what he was doing, shaking with fury but also close to tears, he began gathering up his papers and stuffing them into his briefcase. There was a vague consciousness in him that he was crossing some kind of Rubicon, that he was recklessly hurling himself forward into a region whence there is no return, but he did not care, the ardour and impetuosity of his temperament carried him onwards and could not be withstood; and then he was right, right beyond a shadow of doubting, persecuted and provoked and buffeted by the tempests of ill-fortune, but right, right, right ... The students were too shocked to move or speak, they sat on in wide-eyed amazement, although a few were tentatively standing up, it was hard to say why. Dr. Tuberose tore out of the lecture hall, made straight for the staff toilet, and plunged his head in a basin of cold water.

He could just not account for this unprovoked attack. He was aware that he was liberal even to a fault, entirely confident that his record was irreproachable. He had always, as it happened, had particularly compassionate feelings and views about the treatment of the limbless. Had he not, as a matter of fact, been directly responsible, through his forceful eloquence at a crucial meeting of the University Council, for the installation of ramps and electrically-operated sliding doors throughout the lecture block—was it not through his caring vigilance that the very ramp existed by which his assailant had ascended to his commanding position above Dr. Tuberose? And was this his reward? More, had he not agitated, unsuccessfully it was true but sincerely, for the removal from the University Library of all shelves higher than three feet from the ground? And how was he now rewarded?

But when at length he emerged from the toilet, everything became instantly and chillingly clear. Little groups of students from his truncated lecture were standing around in animated conversation, there was a general buzz of excited gossip and speculation, there was seriousness and there was laughter, there was a little hilarity but perhaps a great deal more righteous indignation. Around the student in the wheelchair a particularly large and vocal group had gathered, and among them, with a lunge of panic, a stab of recognition, and at the same time a detached, ironical insight, a kind of sigh of inevitability, he identified the little Mephistophelean beard and the brown corduroy jacket of Philip Endymion Pluckrose. Tuberose realised now, with a calm certainty, that all this had been planned long ago. A student had been suborned, his lecture course deliberately sabotaged, and it was, of course, precisely this that McSpale had been plotting with Pluckrose on the afternoon of the departmental meeting.

Tuberose gazed at his enemy with a disgust too deep for words. Pluckrose always looked to him as if he were in disguise, like a spy in a bad comedy film of the fifties. The ascetic cut of his meagre, jet-black hair suggested a renegade monk of the Renaissance, despatched on some obscure and dubious mission to a distant court—an aspiring poisoner, perhaps; while his black trimmed beard gave the impression of being hooked over his ears. The truth, thought Tuberose, was that Pluckrose *was* in disguise: hiding himself, masking the truth of his own malice and hopeless mediocrity, poisoning the minds of the young, poisoning the wells of truth, poisoning them all against Tuberose, the righteous one, the disinterested one, the man of integrity. Pluckrose the poisoner.

There had to be a confrontation, Tuberose knew that, but not yet. Now was not the time. The students were incensed, they had been stirred up against him, bought by Pluckrose, and he could hope for no justice there. But tonight he would speak out—yes, tonight at Cowperthwaite's party. Everybody in the department would be there, everybody who counted, anyway, with one crucial exception. McSpale, he knew, had been obliged to refuse the invitation, or at least had made some excuse, and that was greatly in the favour of Dr. Tuberose. Without McSpale, Pluckrose was nothing, a mere paper tiger, a hand puppet from which the hand had been withdrawn, essentially just a limp rag. In fact, to call Pluckrose a limp rag was to flatter him.

When Tuberose had said what he had to say, Pluckrose would be finished, it would be totally out of the question that he could become Acting Head of the Department, he would be obliged instead to apply for early retirement, and he would be lucky if he got that, very lucky indeed. In fact, he would be much more likely to be up before the University disciplinary committee, a fate normally reserved for only the most hopeless drunks, and he might even have to leave the country. And then, of course, Tuberose would come into his own. His worth would be recognised, his disinterested and fearless exposure of Pluckrose would be widely discussed and favourably assessed, integrity would win through, truth would prevail and poetic sensibility be vindicated, he would be appointed Acting Head of Department, the idea of a personal Chair would be mooted, his book on the Romantic Imagination would be praised by George Steiner, he would succeed McSpale, and so on and so forth. . . .

What happened to Dr. Tuberose between the truncation of his lecture and the time of his arrival at the Cowperthwaites' party I do not know. He was known not to be a heavy drinker, and had he over-indulged himself on this occasion it would have been quite out of character. On the other hand, a man of his delicate frame, and of a constitution unaccustomed to alcohol, might, I suppose, have been more affected than another by a little Dutch courage. But those present at the party all agreed that Dr. Tuberose did not really appear to be drunk. It is more likely that his susceptible and excitable temperament was agitated by his horribly disturbed night, by the most unfortunate incident which had interrupted so inauspiciously the first in his series of lectures, and by the rather fevered speculations outlined above. He had, besides, been under considerable strain for some time past as a result of his unfortunate domestic circumstances; and that, really, is as much as can be usefully suggested as likely to throw light on what follows.

Everybody enjoyed the little gatherings given once or twice a year by Cowperthwaite and his lovely wife, Aminta. Cowperthwaite was a remarkable man. His favourite word was "teleological," though he was pretty keen also on "ontological," "epistemological," and "taxonomy." He was always calling his children "darling" and his wife "sweetheart," and sometimes he would even address the family dog, Demiurge, as "darling." Aminta was not quite as intelligent as her husband, though not, of course, by any means unintelligent. Perhaps for this reason, she was a stabilising influence on the wilder flights of Cowperthwaite's speculative conjectures. She spoke to him habitually in a teasing tone which conveyed that for all his little weaknesses there was really no one in the world quite so wonderful as he. That is not to say that he was not at times an embarrassment to her: when on one dire occasion that evening he spoke of the "Heraclitean flux," her reaction was such as to suggest that she had mistaken that ontological phenomenon for a form of dysentery.

Demiurge, who is to play a not unimportant part in this tale of truth, was a cross between a spaniel and a corgi, something that can't possibly be imagined until it has been seen. As to his name, he was the victim of some obscure academic joke, a fate which, along with his appearance, probably contributed to his habitual look of shame, as if he were the author of some vile mess on the carpet which was perpetually the subject of discussion. Though known familiarly in the household as "Demmy," he seemed to know that this was merely a diminutive, and to live in constant fear that the guilty secret of his full name would be revealed to visitors; as, indeed, it often was, thanks to his master's keenness to tell the story attached to the name, which displayed his genial intelligence to especial advantage.

I wish I could describe the wit and urbanity and the relaxed intellectual authority which marked the tone of that memorable evening: the talk of contemporary film, of child abuse, of advanced social theory, of construction and deconstruction, of Adorno and Jürgen Habermas, of "the Frenchman, Derrida" (whose name I personally would have pronounced "Dereeda," but whom all of that company, and certainly correctly, called "Derry Dah"); and at the same time the common touch, the homely aspersions on the Thatcher Government, the substitution of the word "Jockish" for "Scottish," and other little foibles to which it would be unpardonably bad taste to draw attention; and then the sense almost of an extended family, united in benignity and complacency of feeling, in the best sense: all this I would love to be able to depict. But my talents are not equal to the task—I lack the qualifications. Certain it is that anyone who had strayed by chance among those excellent people, lacking a doctorate or at the absolute minimum a very good honours degree, would have felt diffident and tongue-tied in the extreme; indeed even with these recommendations, but lacking the easy fluency which knows how to deploy difficult and complex, obscure and advanced ideas with geniality and deceptive simplicity and unostentatious control, such a person might have felt distinctly inferior and out of place.

The delightful atmosphere which I have just haltingly attempted to convey was already well established when Dr. Tuberose made his entry. He was unaccompanied, embarrassingly so, for when his wife had left him five months previously it had soon emerged that she was living with a Chinese waiter in Burntisland. Cowperthwaite and Aminta, in fact, had invited him partly out of sympathy and fellow-feeling, for Adrian, their seventeen-year-old son, was living with another Chinese waiter in Tollcross. When Dr. Tuberose came in they were all discussing Rudolf Steiner play-groups. As Tuberose advanced into the room with an intent but somehow abstracted look on his sensitive little face, a knowing, almost scornful little smile playing about the corners of his mouth, and an exalted expressiveness in his light grey eyes, the guests turned towards him with genial, welcoming expansiveness. Dr. Tuberose nodded vaguely at his acquaintances, his eyes flickering over the company, searching for Pluckrose. At that moment, an amazing incident occurred.

Demiurge, who up to that moment had been dozing comfortably beside the fire, having decided that the conversation, fascinating though it doubtless was, was way above his head, now suddenly sat up, the hair rising along his back, and staring at Tuberose with every sign of venomous hostility, growled at him in the most menacing manner, and even started to yap in a pitch of hellish stridency, advancing towards Tuberose and then backing away again as if uncertain whether the situation called for attack or defence. Tuberose, quite unnerved, retreated against a sideboard, and Cowperthwaite in complete consternation abandoned the drinks he had been pouring and hastened over, crying, "Demmy! Demmy! What is it, darling? You know Uncle Marcus! It's only Uncle Marcus, Demmy, he won't hurt you, sweetheart!"

Demiurge, however, was not to be pacified so easily. He was now yapping furiously and pertinaciously, and as it were with a growing confidence in the justice of his cause; Dr. Tuberose had retreated within a protective ring of guests, utterly taken aback but conscious of a dawning recognition that something was afoot, that there was more here than met the eye. Sterner measures were clearly required, and now Cowperthwaite rapped out, "Demiurge!" in a tone of warning, and with a rising emphasis on the final syllable.

The uttering of this shameful name had an instantaneous effect on the poor animal. With an appearance of great fright he shot off with his tail between his legs and slumped abjectly on the hearthrug; it was really impossible not to feel sorry for him. He now lay unmoving with his head between his paws, and soon commenced making ostentatious snuffling noises and settling his lips, as if he had never had any other thought in his head but to prepare for sleep. It was all a show, however. Shortly he began once more to cast furtive glances at Dr. Tuberose, and once the commotion had died down a little and he was no longer an object of scrutiny, he kept following 'Uncle Marcus' with his eyes, with an unfathomable gaze that spoke volumes, but in some unknown tongue.

The party had no sooner settled back into normality than the telephone rang. Cowperthwaite left the room to answer it, and after a brief absence returned and called over to Aminta, 'That was Phil Pluckrose, sweetheart. He sends his apologies, they won't be coming. It seems McSpale needed to see him very urgently about something.' Dr. Tuberose was at this moment in conversation with a psychiatrist whom he had always known simply as "Justin's Daddy." Justin's Daddy had a club foot, for which reason he had been called "Dr. Goebbels" at school, which just goes to show how cruel children can be; and a few unpleasant people still referred to him by that name, not of course in his hearing. Justin's Daddy, who had met Dr. Tuberose socially on two or three previous occasions, had suddenly become interested in him when, a few minutes previously, he had overheard him say to Cowperthwaite, "Did you notice how McSpale kept staring at me during the Department meeting? There was an awful depth and malignancy in his eye . . ." ("Oh, dear," Aminta had interrupted with sweet concern, "has he got cancer?") Now, when the news about Pluckrose was announced, Dr. Tuberose broke off in midsentence and his poetic face at once took on a horrified, haunted, harried look, a look which caused Justin's Daddy to observe him with an almost professional concern. But no one else noticed.

The company was artistically dispersed all round the room, chatting expansively. The subject of conversation was the reading given the previous Saturday evening by the poet Brechin of his epic work, "The Old Dying Sheep."

"I take it that it is intended as an allegory of the fate of the artist in a materialistic society," observed Robin Dross-Jones, who wrote a very highly regarded newspaper column, "Vermicular Viewpoint."

"Yes, but the symbolism can be understood at a number of different levels," responded Cowperthwaite sagaciously. "We could also, for instance, assume the old dying sheep to be Scotland."

"And surely there's a rather impudent, tongue-in-cheek allusion to the motif of the young dying god?" suggested someone else.

"Indeed," said Cowperthwaite, "why not? The image means all of these things, of course, and at the same time none of them. Finally, perhaps, it's about himself that Brechin is speaking," he closed, magisterially. There was a great deal of affirmatory grunting and vehement nodding of heads.

"Brechin was completely legless last time I saw him," remarked Robin Dross-Jones.

"Legless?" cried Dr. Tuberose suddenly, in terrible agitation. 'Did you say legless?'

The creator of "Vermicular Viewpoint" stared at him. "Yes, legless," he replied. 'You know...drunk.'

"Ah," said Dr. Tuberose, relieved, but at the same time still suspicious.

"But that was after his mother's funeral, dear," said Florrie Dross-Jones.

"My mother was always belittling me," put in Dr. Tuberose wildly, "devaluing me, casting aspersions on me! 'I'm sorry for your wife,' she would say, 'if you ever get one.' I always remember that, I can never forget it! What a thing to say to a child: 'I'm sorry for your wife, if you ever get one.'"

"Oh, dear," said Aminta, faintly.

"And now, you see," continued Dr. Tuberose relentlessly, "she is living with a Chinese waiter in...in...Burntisland. Not that I have anything against the Chinese, who are an industrious little people. The man has legs, so far as I am aware, and not by accident. Yes, he has legs, and everything else that he needs to betray me!" He looked around the room and was vaguely aware of the terrible embarrassment and consternation which he was causing. "I'm sorry," he said, and passed his hand over his eyes. "This is the price I have to pay for having the sensibility of a poet."

No one said anything. After a quite long and very awkward silence, they all, as if by a prearranged signal, began talking about where they had been and what they were doing when Kennedy was assassinated.

"I was still at school," said Aminta, and for some reason this was greeted with howls of urbane laughter. "I can't remember what I was doing—I expect I was doing my sums."

"I think I was cutting my toenails," said Dr. Tuberose. "It's a strange thing, you know, but I have rather coarse feet. My hands are sensitive and artistic, but my feet are rather solid and coarse and peasant-like."

Demiurge, who had been keeping his own counsel for some time, now growled most threateningly at Dr. Tuberose. Cowperthwaite at once went over to the dog and tried to quieten him.

"Come on, Urgie-Purgie, who loves his daddy?" he coaxed gently.

But whoever loved his daddy, it didn't appear to be Urgie-Purgie. He sat up, staring at Dr. Tuberose, and began once more to yap in a frightened but at the same time a challenging and even provocative tone. Dr. Tuberose sprang to his feet in a dawning epiphany: he had just understood something. This was not Demiurge. This was not the Demiurge he knew, not the dog whose long floppy ears he had fondled when he was a puppy, no, no, no: this was, on the contrary, Philip Endymion Pluckrose, M.A., D. Phil.!

This insight did not represent quite such a remarkable imaginative leap on the part of Dr. Tuberose as might at first appear. For, you see, he had already realised, quite suddenly that afternoon, that Pluckrose was the devil. The truth had dawned on him after it had struck him outside the lecture hall how Mephistophelean, even Luciferian, was Pluckrose's little black beard: it flashed on him then that he was not just metaphorically but literally in disguise, that he was in fact the devil! As he mulled over his dream of the previous night, it was quite clear to Dr. Tuberose that the official in the form of a Himalayan bear whom McSpale had set on him could only be Pluckrose, that is, the devil, in another disguise. McSpale was God the Father, or more strictly (since Dr. Tuberose was a man of sophisticated literary sensibility) he was a symbolic projection of God the Father; and he was testing Dr. Tuberose by giving Satan power over him for a season, as he had done many years before with his servant

Job. How perfectly it all fitted into place! How ever had he failed to see it before! He was being tested and proved like gold, and he must not be found wanting. And now Pluckrose the devil had come to him in yet another disguise, in the form of Demiurge the dog, and he must stand up to him and confront him boldly.

Dr. Tuberose was now completely fearless. He advanced towards Demiurge with his left hand in his trouser pocket, a glass of wine in the other sensitive instrument, his head slightly on one side in an almost effeminate attitude, and a complacent, knowing smirk on his small, re-fined features.

"Do you imagine that I am stupid, Pluckrose?" he commenced qui-etly, utterly in control of himself. The dog stopped yapping and stared in astonishment. "Do you think you can fool *me*? You can appear as a dog or a Himalayan bear or as King Kong, if you choose, it's entirely up to yourself. You are being used, Pluckrose, don't you realise that? You are no more than an instrument. Every dog has his day, and you have had yours. The future is mine. Justice will prevail, truth will prevail. You are yesterday's man, Pluckrose. In fact, if you only knew it, you were yesterday's man yesterday. I know who you are. But perhaps you don't know who McSpale is ... I shall be Acting Head of the Depart-ment! It has been decided and ordained!"

Dr. Tuberose's calm tone had been giving way during the course of this harangue to one of inspired, prophetic conviction, and now this in turn was converted into righteous fury. Dr. Tuberose cast his glass to the floor, dropped to his knees, and faced Demiurge nose to nose.

"Mongrel trash!" he cried impetuously. "I'll cut off your legs, you mongrel trash! Dog of hell!"

Demiurge backed away from the raging madman, howling with ter-ror. The ruin of a noble mind is always pitiful; but this was a terrible reversal to behold, the man in the role of the beast! But now the Cow-perthwaites' twelve-year-old daughter, who had been standing listening by the door, rushed forward fearlessly, gathered up Demiurge in her arms, and ran out with him, crying, "Never mind, Demmy! Never mind, my poor little Semi-semi-demiurge! Pay no attention to the silly, bad man!"

Cowperthwaite had already gone into a huddle with Justin's Daddy; they were talking eagerly, excitedly but in hushed tones. Dr. Tuberose found himself sitting bemusedly on a three-legged stool, in calm of mind, all passion spent; Florrie Dross-Jones had given him a Perrier water, which she said was very good for the digestion. Fragments of conversation reached Dr. Tuberose from the group clustering around Justin's Daddy over by the door.

"I can arrange for him to be admitted tonight..."

"We'd better start phoning for a taxi right away, it'll take ages on a Friday night..."

"It's all right, we've ordered one already, you can take that, we can wait..."

"Poor man!"

"Phil Pluckrose'll have to take over his lecture course."

"Out of the question with all his departmental responsibilities."

"That's not till next year. Phil's the only one..."

"Oh, no, Angela Mulhearn could do it very competently. It's well within her field of interest."

"Should we let Malitia know, do you think?"

"Good God, no!"

"Better phone his GP, perhaps. I think it's Gebbie."

"No, no, there's no problem there, he can be taken in tonight."

"No, no, I cannot be taken in!" cried Dr. Tuberose suddenly. "You can take me in, if you understand me, but I cannot be taken in. I know a hawk from a handsaw."

"Don't worry, Marcus, Justin's Daddy is going to take you home; he'll give you something to make you sleep, you'll be fine in the morning!"

"I see, you want me to go with Dr. Goebbels here? Well, that's all right! Legs eleven—bingo! And not by accident. Yes, the legs of a Chinese waiter, with a club foot at one end and betrayal at the other!"

"It's funny, you very seldom see a club foot nowadays," said Aminta, in the general confusion quite forgetting about Justin's Daddy. Then she suddenly remembered! "Oh, dear! But it's wonderful what they can do nowadays," she added vaguely.

The door-bell rang. "That's the taxi!" everybody shouted at once.

"I'll let the driver know you're coming," said Robin DrossJones eagerly, and rushed down the stair.

Dr. Goebbels took Dr. Tuberose gently but very firmly by the elbow and steered him towards the front door; he let himself be taken, offering no resistance. Everyone was crowding around him with looks and words of sympathy and concern, but Dr. Tuberose was no longer in need of sympathy or concern, for he had understood it all. Everything had suddenly become crystal-clear to him; and though it would be impossible to put into words the full depth and comprehensiveness of his understanding, there was no mistaking its reality, for his eyes glowed with exaltation, a smile of triumph played about his sensitive little mouth, and his whole being was suffused with a light of wonderful self-approbation.

At the head of the stair he turned and faced the assembled company once more, gazing at them as if from an immense height.

"I declare this meeting adjourned!" he cried with tremendous authority. "As Acting Head of Department, I declare this meeting adjourned."

PHANTOMS

Steven Millhauser

THE PHENOMENON. The phantoms of our town do not, as some think, appear only in the dark. Often we come upon them in full sunlight, when shadows lie sharp on the lawns and streets. The encounters take place for very short periods, ranging from two or three seconds to perhaps half a minute, though longer episodes are sometimes reported. So many of us have seen them that it's uncommon to meet someone who has not; of this minority, only a small number deny that phantoms exist. Sometimes an encounter occurs more than once in the course of a single day; sometimes six months pass, or a year. The phantoms, which some call Presences, are not easy to distinguish from ordinary citizens: they are not translucent, or smoke-like, or hazy, they do not ripple like heat waves, nor are they in any way unusual in figure or dress. Indeed they are so much like us that it sometimes happens we mistake them for someone we know. Such errors are rare, and never last for more than a moment. They themselves appear to be uneasy during an encounter and swiftly withdraw. They always look at us before turning away. They never speak. They are wary, elusive, secretive, haughty, unfriendly, remote.

———— ☙ ————

EXPLANATION #1. One explanation has it that our phantoms are the auras, or visible traces, of earlier inhabitants of our town, which was settled in 1636. Our atmosphere, saturated with the energy of all those who have preceded us, preserves them and permits them, under certain conditions, to become visible to us. This explanation, often fitted out with a pseudoscientific vocabulary, strikes most of us as unconvincing. The phantoms always appear in contemporary dress, they never behave in ways that suggest earlier eras, and there is no evidence whatever to support the claim that the dead leave visible traces in the air.

———— ☙ ————

HISTORY. As children we are told about the phantoms by our fathers and mothers. They in turn have been told by their own fathers and mothers, who can remember being told by their parents—our great-grandparents—when they were children. Thus the phantoms of our town are not new; they don't represent a sudden eruption into our lives, a recent change in our sense of things. We have no formal records that confirm the presence of phantoms throughout the diverse periods of our history, no scientific reports or transcripts of legal proceedings, but some of us are familiar with the second-floor Archive Room of our library, where in nineteenth-century diaries we find occasional references to "the others" or "them," without further details. Church records of the seventeenth century include several mentions of "the devil's children," which some view as evidence for the lineage of our phantoms; others argue that the phrase is so general that it cannot be cited as proof of anything. The official town history, published in 1936 on the three hundredth anniversary of our incorporation, revised in 1986, and updated in

2006, makes no mention of the phantoms. An editorial note states that "the authors have confined themselves to ascertainable fact."

⁂

HOW WE KNOW. We know by a ripple along the skin of our forearms, accompanied by a tension of the inner body. We know because they look at us and withdraw immediately. We know because when we try to follow them, we find that they have vanished. We know because we know.

⁂

CASE STUDY #1. Richard Moore rises from beside the bed, where he has just finished the forty-second installment of a never-ending story that he tells each night to his four-year-old daughter, bends over her for a good-night kiss, and walks quietly from the room. He loves having a daughter; he loves having a wife, a family; though he married late, at thirty-nine, he knows he wasn't ready when he was younger, not in his doped-up twenties, not in his stupid, wasted thirties, when he was still acting like some angry teenager who hated the grown-ups; and now he's grateful for it all, like someone who can hardly believe that he's allowed to live in his own house. He walks along the hall to the den, where his wife is sitting at one end of the couch, reading a book in the light of the table lamp, while the TV is on mute during an ad for vinyl siding. He loves that she won't watch the ads, that she refuses to waste those minutes, that she reads books, that she's sitting there, waiting for him, that the light from the TV is flickering on her hand and upper arm. Something has begun to bother him, though he isn't sure what it is, but as he steps into the den he's got it, he's got it: the table in the side yard, the two folding chairs, the sunglasses on the tabletop. He was sitting out there with her after dinner, and he left his sunglasses. "Back in a sec," he says, and turns away, enters the kitchen, opens the door to the small screened porch at the back of the house, and walks from the porch down the steps to the backyard, a narrow strip between the house and the cedar fence. It's nine thirty on a summer night. The sky is dark blue, the fence lit by the light from the kitchen window, the grass black here and green over there. He turns the corner of the house and comes to the private place. It's the part of the yard bounded by the fence, the side-yard hedge, and the row of three Scotch pines, where he's set up two folding chairs and a white ironwork table with a glass top. On the table lie the sunglasses. The sight pleases him: the two chairs, turned a little toward each other, the forgotten glasses, the enclosed place set off from the rest of the world. He steps over to the table and picks up the glasses: a good pair, expensive lenses, nothing flashy, stylish in a quiet way. As he lifts them from the table he senses something in the skin of his arms and sees a figure standing beside the third Scotch pine. It's darker here than at the back of the house and he can't see her all that well: a tall, erect woman, fortyish, long face, dark dress. Her expression, which he can barely make out, seems stern. She looks at him for a moment and turns away—not hastily, as if she were frightened, but decisively, like someone who wants to be alone. Behind the Scotch pine she's no longer visible. He hesitates, steps over to the tree, sees nothing. His first impulse is to scream at her, to tell her that he'll kill her if she comes near his daughter. Immediately he forces himself to calm down. Everything will be all right. There's no danger. He's seen them before. Even so, he returns quickly to the house, locks the porch door behind him, locks the kitchen door behind him, fastens the chain, and strides to the den, where on the TV a man in a dinner jacket is staring across the room at a woman with pulled-back hair who is seated at a piano. His wife is watching. As he steps toward her, he notices a pair of sunglasses in his hand.

THE LOOK. Most of us are familiar with the look they cast in our direction before they withdraw. The look has been variously described as proud, hostile, suspicious, mocking, disdainful, uncertain; never is it seen as welcoming. Some witnesses say that the phantoms show slight movements in our direction, before the decisive turning away. Others, disputing such claims, argue that we cannot bear to imagine their rejection of us and misread their movements in a way flattering to our self-esteem.

HIGHLY QUESTIONABLE. Now and then we hear reports of a more questionable kind. The phantoms, we are told, have grayish wings folded along their backs; the phantoms have swirling smoke for eyes; at the ends of their feet, claws curl against the grass. Such descriptions, though rare, are persistent, perhaps inevitable, and impossible to refute. They strike most of us as childish and irresponsible, the results of careless observation, hasty inference, and heightened imagination corrupted by conventional images drawn from movies and television. Whenever we hear such descriptions, we're quick to question them and to make the case for the accumulated evidence of trustworthy witnesses. A paradoxical effect of our vigilance is that the phantoms, rescued from the fantastic, for a moment seem to us normal, commonplace, as familiar as squirrels or dandelions.

CASE STUDY #2. Years ago, as a child of eight or nine, Karen Carsten experienced a single encounter. Her memory of the moment is both vivid and vague: she can't recall how many of them there were, or exactly what they looked like, but she recalls the precise moment in which she came upon them, one summer afternoon, as she stepped around to the back of the garage in search of a soccer ball and saw them sitting quietly in the grass. She still remembers her feeling of wonder as they turned to look at her, before they rose and went away. Now, at age fifty-six, Karen Carsten lives alone with her cat in a house filled with framed photographs of her parents, her nieces, and her late husband, who died in a car accident seventeen years ago. Karen is a high school librarian with many set routines: the TV programs, the weekend housecleaning, the twice-yearly visits in August and December to her sister's family in Youngstown, Ohio, the choir on Sunday, dinner every two weeks at the same restaurant with a friend who never calls to ask how she is. One Saturday afternoon she finishes organizing the linen closet on the second floor and starts up the attic stairs. She plans to sort through boxes of old clothes, some of which she'll give to Goodwill and some of which she'll save for her nieces, who will think of the collared blouses and floral-print dresses as hopelessly old-fashioned but who might come around to appreciating them someday, maybe. As she reaches the top of the stairs she stops so suddenly and completely that she has the sense of her own body as an object standing in her path. Ten feet away, two children are seated on the old couch near the dollhouse. A third child is sitting in the armchair with the loose leg. In the brownish light of the attic, with its one small window, she can see them clearly: two barefoot girls of about ten, in jeans and T-shirts, and a boy, slightly older, maybe twelve, blond-haired, in a dress shirt and khakis, who sits low in the chair with his neck bent up against the back. The three turn to look at her and at once rise and walk into the darker part of the attic, where they are no longer visible. Karen stands motionless at the top of the stairs, her hand clutching the rail. Her lips are dry and she is filled with an excitement so intense that she thinks she might burst into tears. She does not follow the children into the shadows, partly because she doesn't want to upset them, and partly because she knows they are no longer there. She turns back down the stairs. In the living room she sits in the armchair until nightfall. Joy fills her heart. She can feel it shining from her face. That night she returns to the attic, straightens the pillows on the couch, smooths out the doilies on the chair arms, brings over a small wicker table, sets out three saucers and three teacups. She moves away some bulging boxes that sit beside the couch, carries off an old typewriter, sweeps the floor. Downstairs in the living room she turns on the TV, but she keeps the volume low; she's listening for sounds in the attic, even though she knows that her visitors don't make sounds. She imagines them up there, sitting silently together, enjoying the table, the teacups, and the orderly surroundings. Now each day she climbs the stairs to the attic, where she sees the empty couch, the empty chair, the wicker table with the three teacups. Despite the pang of disappointment, she is happy. She is happy because she knows they come to visit her every day, she knows they like to be up there, sitting in the old furniture, around the wicker table; she knows; she knows.

EXPLANATION #2. One explanation is that the phantoms *are not there*, that those of us who see them are experiencing delusions or hallucinations brought about by beliefs instilled in us as young children. A small movement, an unexpected sound, is immediately converted into a visual presence that exists only in the mind of the perceiver. The flaws in this explanation are threefold. First, it assumes that the population of an entire town will interpret ambiguous signs in precisely the same way. Second, it ignores the fact that most of us, as we grow to adulthood, discard the stories and false beliefs of childhood but continue to see the phantoms. Third, it fails to account for innumerable instances in which multiple witnesses have seen the same phantom. Even if we were to agree that these objections are not decisive and that our phantoms are in fact not there, the explanation would tell us only that we are mad, without revealing the meaning of our madness.

OUR CHILDREN. What shall we say to our children? If, like most parents in our town, we decide to tell them at an early age about the phantoms, we worry that we have filled their nights with terror or perhaps have created in them a hope, a longing, for an encounter that might never take place. Those of us who conceal the existence of phantoms are no less worried, for we fear either that our children will be informed unreliably by other children or that they will be dangerously unprepared for an encounter should one occur. Even those of us who have prepared our children are worried about the first encounter, which sometimes disturbs a child in ways that some of us remember only too well. Although we assure our children that there's nothing to fear from the phantoms, who wish only to be left alone, we ourselves are fearful: we wonder whether the phantoms are as harmless as we say they are, we wonder whether they behave differently in the presence of an unaccompanied child, we wonder whether, under certain circumstances, they might become bolder than we know. Some say that a phantom, encountering an adult and a child, will look only at the child, will let its gaze linger in a way that never happens with an adult. When we put our children to sleep, leaning close to them and answering their questions about phantoms in gentle, soothing tones, until their eyes close in peace, we understand that we have been preparing in ourselves an anxiety that will grow stronger and more aggressive as the night advances.

⚭

CROSSING OVER. The question of "crossing over" refuses to disappear, despite a history of testimony that many of us feel ought to put it to rest. By "crossing over" is meant, in general, any form of intermingling between us and them; specifically, it refers to supposed instances in which one of them, or one of us, leaves the native community and joins the other. Now, not only is there no evidence of any such regrouping, of any such transference of loyalty, but the overwhelming testimony of witnesses shows that no phantom has ever remained for more than a few moments in the presence of an outsider or given any sign whatever of greeting or encouragement. Claims to the contrary have always been suspect: the insistence of an alcoholic husband that he saw his wife in bed with *one of them*, the assertion of a teenager suspended from high school that a group of phantoms had threatened to harm him if he failed to obey their commands. Apart from statements that purport to be factual, fantasies of crossing over persist in the form of phantom-tales that flourish among our children and are half-believed by naïve adults. It is not difficult to make the case that stories of this kind reveal a secret desire for contact, though no reliable record of contact exists. Those of us who try to maintain a strict objectivity in such matters are forced to admit that a crossing of the line isn't impossible, however unlikely, so that even as we challenge dubious claims and smile at fairy tales we find ourselves imagining the sudden encounter at night, the heads turning toward us, the moment of hesitation, the arms rising gravely in welcome.

CASE STUDY #3. James Levin, twenty-six years old, has reached an impasse in his life. After college he took a year off, holding odd jobs and traveling all over the country before returning home to apply to grad school. He completed his coursework in two years, during which he taught one introductory section of American History, and then surprised everyone by taking a leave of absence in order to read for his dissertation (*The Influence of Popular Culture on High Culture in Post–Civil War America, 1865–1900*) and think more carefully about the direction of his life. He lives with his parents in his old room, dense with memories of grade school and high school. He worries that he's losing interest in his dissertation; he feels he should rethink his life, maybe go the med-school route and do something useful in the world instead of wasting his time wallowing in abstract speculations of no value to anyone; he speaks less and less to his girlfriend, a law student at the University of Michigan, nearly a thousand miles away. Where, he wonders, has he taken a wrong turn? What should he do with his life? What is the meaning of it all? These, he believes, are questions eminently suitable for an intelligent adolescent of sixteen, questions that he himself discussed passionately ten years ago with friends who are now married and paying

mortgages. Because he's stalled in his life, because he is eaten up with
guilt, and because he is unhappy, he has taken to getting up late and
going for long walks all over town, first in the afternoon and again at
night. One of his daytime walks leads to the picnic grounds of his
childhood. Pine trees and scattered tables stand by the stream where he
used to sail a little wooden tugboat—he's always bumping into his past
like that—and across the stream is where he sees her, one afternoon in
late September. She's standing alone, between two oak trees, looking
down at the water. The sun shines on the lower part of her body, but her
face and neck are in shadow. She becomes aware of him almost immediately, raises her eyes, and withdraws into the shade, where he can no
longer see her. He has shattered her solitude. Each instant of the encounter enters him so sharply that his memory of her breaks into three
parts, like a medieval triptych in a museum: the moment of awareness,
the look, the turning away. In the first panel of the triptych, her shoulders are tense, her whole body unnaturally still, like someone who has
heard a sound in the dark. Second panel: her eyes are raised and staring
directly at him. It can't have lasted for more than a second. What stays
with him is something severe in that look, as if he's disturbed her in a
way that requires forgiveness. Third panel: the body is half-turned away,
not timidly but with a kind of dignity of withdrawal, which seems to
rebuke him for an intrusion. James feels a sharp desire to cross the
stream and find her, but two thoughts hold him back: his fear that the
crossing will be unwelcome to her, and his knowledge that she has disappeared. He returns home but continues to see her standing by the
stream. He has the sense that she's becoming more vivid in her absence,
as if she's gaining life within him. The unnatural stillness, the dark
look, the turning away—he feels he owes her an immense apology. He
understands that the desire to apologize is only a mask for his desire to
see her again. After two days of futile brooding he returns to the stream,
to the exact place where he stood when he saw her the first time; four
hours later he returns home, discouraged, restless, and irritable. He

understands that something has happened to him, something that is probably harmful. He doesn't care. He returns to the stream day after day, without hope, without pleasure. What's he doing there, in that desolate place? He's twenty-six, but already he's an old man. The leaves have begun to turn; the air is growing cold. One day, on his way back from the stream, James takes a different way home. He passes his old high school, with its double row of tall windows, and comes to the hill where he used to go sledding. He needs to get away from this town, where his childhood and adolescence spring up to meet him at every turn; he ought to go somewhere, do something; his long, purposeless walks seem to him the outward expressions of an inner confusion. He climbs the hill, passing through the bare oaks and beeches and the dark firs, and at the top looks down at the stand of pine at the back of Cullen's Auto Body. He walks down the slope, feeling the steering bar in his hands, the red runners biting into the snow, and when he comes to the pines he sees her sitting on the trunk of a fallen tree. She turns her head to look at him, rises, and walks out of sight. This time he doesn't hesitate. He runs into the thicket, beyond which he can see the whitewashed back of the body shop, a brilliant blue front fender lying up against a tire, and, farther away, a pick-up truck driving along the street; pale sunlight slants through the pine branches. He searches for her but finds only a tangle of ferns, a beer can, the top of a pint of ice cream. At home he throws himself down on his boyhood bed, where he used to spend long afternoons reading stories about boys who grew up to become famous scientists and explorers. He summons her stare. The sternness devastates him, but draws him, too, since he feels it as a strength he himself lacks. He understands that he's in a bad way; that he's got to stop thinking about her; that he'll never stop thinking about her; that nothing can ever come of it; that his life will be harmed; that harm is attractive to him; that he'll never return to school; that he will disappoint his parents and lose his girlfriend; that none of this matters to him; that what matters is the hope of seeing once more the phantom lady who will look harshly at him and turn away; that he is weak, foolish, frivolous; that such words have no meaning for him; that he has entered a world of dark love, from which there is no way out.

⸮ⸯ

MISSING CHILDREN. Once in a long while, a child goes missing. It happens in other towns, it happens in yours: the missing child who is discovered six hours later lost in the woods, the missing child who never returns, who disappears forever, perhaps in the company of a stranger in a baseball cap who was last seen parked in a van across from the elementary school. In our town there are always those who blame the phantoms. They steal our children, it is said, in order to bring them into the fold; they're always waiting for the right moment, when we have been careless, when our attention has relaxed. Those of us who defend the phantoms point out patiently that they always withdraw from us, that there is no evidence they can make physical contact with the things of our world, that no human child has ever been seen in their company. Such arguments never persuade an accuser. Even when the missing child is discovered in the woods, where he has wandered after a squirrel, even when the missing child is found buried in the yard of a troubled loner in a town two hundred miles away, the suspicion remains that the phantoms have had something to do with it. We who defend our phantoms against false accusations and wild inventions are forced to admit that we do not know what they may be thinking, alone among themselves, or in the moment when they turn to look at us, before moving away.

⸮ⸯ

DISRUPTION. Sometimes a disruption comes: the phantom in the supermarket, the phantom in the bedroom. Then our sense of the behavior of phantoms suffers a shock: we cannot understand why creatures who withdraw from us should appear in places where encounters are unavoidable. Have we misunderstood something about our phantoms?

It's true enough that when we encounter them in the aisle of a supermarket or clothing store, when we find them sitting on the edges of our beds or lying against a bed-pillow, they behave as they always do: they look at us and quickly withdraw. Even so, we feel that they have come too close, that they want something from us that we cannot understand, and only when we encounter them in a less frequented place, at the back of the shut-down railroad station or on the far side of a field, do we relax a little.

⚜

EXPLANATION #3. One explanation asserts that we and the phantoms were once a single race, which at some point in the remote history of our town divided into two societies. According to a psychological offshoot of this explanation, the phantoms are the unwanted or unacknowledged portions of ourselves, which we try to evade but continually encounter; they make us uneasy because we know them; they are ourselves.

⚜

FEAR. Many of us, at one time or another, have felt the fear. For say you are coming home with your wife from an evening with friends. The porch light is on, the living room windows are dimly glowing before the closed blinds. As you walk across the front lawn from the driveway to the porch steps, you become aware of something, over there by the wild cherry tree. Then you half-see one of them, for an instant, withdrawing behind the dark branches, which catch only a little of the light from the porch. That is when the fear comes. You can feel it deep within you, like an infection that's about to spread. You can feel it in your wife's hand tightening on your arm. It's at that moment you turn to her and say, with a shrug of one shoulder and a little laugh that fools no one: "Oh, it's just one of them!"

⚜

PHOTOGRAPHIC EVIDENCE. Evidence from digital cameras, camcorders, iPhones, and old-fashioned film cameras divides into two categories: the fraudulent and the dubious. Fraudulent evidence always reveals signs of tampering. Methods of digital-imaging manipulation permit a wide range of effects, from computer-generated figures to digital clones; sometimes a slight blur is sought, to suggest the uncanny. Often the artist goes too far, and creates a hackneyed monster-phantom inspired by third-rate movies; more clever manipulators stay closer to the ordinary, but tend to give themselves away by an exaggeration of some feature, usually the ears or nose. In such matters, the temptation of the grotesque appears to be irresistible. Celluloid fraud assumes well-known forms that reach back to the era of fairy photographs: double exposures, chemical tampering with negatives, the insertion of gauze between the printing paper and the enlarger lens. The category of the dubious is harder to disprove. Here we find vague shadowy shapes, wavering lines resembling ripples of heated air above a radiator, half-hidden forms concealed by branches or by windows filled with reflections. Most of these images can be explained as natural effects of light that have deceived the credulous person recording them. For those who crave visual proof of phantoms, evidence that a photograph is fraudulent or dubious is never entirely convincing.

⚕

CASE STUDY #4. One afternoon in late spring, Evelyn Wells, nine years old, is playing alone in her backyard. It's a sunny day; school is out, dinner's a long way off, and the warm afternoon has the feel of summer. Her best friend is sick with a sore throat and fever, but that's all right: Evvy likes to play alone in her yard, especially on a sunny day like this one, with time stretching out on all sides of her. What she's been practicing lately is roof-ball, a game she learned from a boy down the block. Her yard is bordered by the neighbor's garage and by thick spruces running along the back and side; the lowest spruce branches bend down to the grass and form a kind of wall. The idea is to throw the tennis ball, which is the color of lime Kool-Aid, onto the slanted garage roof and catch it when it comes down. If Evvy throws too hard, the ball will go over the roof and land in the yard next door, possibly in the vegetable garden surrounded by chicken wire. If she doesn't throw hard enough, it will come right back to her, with no speed. The thing to do is make the ball go almost to the top, so that it comes down faster and faster; then she's got to catch it before it hits the ground, though a one-bouncer isn't terrible. Evvy is pretty good at roof-ball—she can make the ball go way up the slope, and she can figure out where she needs to stand as it comes rushing or bouncing down. Her record is eight catches in a row, but now she's caught nine and is hoping for ten. The ball stops near the peak of the roof and begins coming down at a wide angle; she moves more and more to the right as it bounces lightly along and leaps into the air. This time she's made a mistake—the ball goes over her head. It rolls across the lawn and disappears under the low-hanging spruce branches not far from the garage. Evvy sometimes likes to play under there, where it's cool and dim. She pushes aside a branch and looks for the ball, which she sees beside a root. At the same time she sees two figures, a man and a woman, standing under the tree. They stare down at her, then turn their faces away and step out of sight. Evvy feels a ripple in her arms. Their eyes were like shadows on a lawn. She backs out into the sun. The yard does not comfort her. The blades of grass seem to be holding their breath. The white wooden shingles on the side of the garage are staring at her. Evvy walks across the strange lawn and up the back steps into the kitchen. Inside, it is very still. A faucet handle blazes with light. She hears her mother in the living room. Evvy does not want to speak to her mother. She does not want to speak to anyone. Upstairs, in her room, she draws the blinds and gets into bed. The windows are above the backyard and look down on the rows of spruce trees. At dinner she is silent. "Cat got your tongue?" her father says. His teeth are laughing. Her mother gives her a wrinkled look. At night she lies with her eyes open. She sees the man and woman standing under the tree, staring down at her. They turn their faces away. The next day, Saturday, Evvy refuses to go outside. Her mother brings orange juice, feels her forehead, takes her temperature. Outside, her father is mowing the lawn. That night she doesn't sleep. They are standing under the tree, looking at her with their shadow-eyes. She can't see their faces. She doesn't remember their clothes. On Sunday she stays in her room. Sounds startle her: a clank in the yard, a shout. At night she watches with closed eyes: the ball rolling under the branches, the two figures standing there, looking down at her. On Monday her mother takes her to the doctor. He presses the silver circle against her chest. The next day she returns to school, but after the last bell she comes straight home and goes to her room. Through the slats of the blinds she can see the garage, the roof, the dark green spruce branches bending to the grass. One afternoon Evvy is sitting at the piano in the living room. She's practicing her scales. The bell rings and her mother goes to the door. When Evvy turns to look, she sees a woman and a man. She leaves the piano and goes upstairs to her room. She sits on the throw rug next to her bed and stares at the door. After a while she hears her mother's footsteps on the stairs. Evvy stands up and goes into the closet. She crawls next to a box filled with old dolls and bears and elephants. She can hear her mother's footsteps in the room. Her mother is knocking on the closet door. "Please come out of there, Evvy. I know you're in there." She does not come out.

⁂

CAPTORS. Despite widespread disapproval, now and then an attempt is made to capture a phantom. The desire arises most often among groups of idle teenagers, especially during the warm nights of summer, but is also known among adults, usually but not invariably male, who feel menaced by the phantoms or who cannot tolerate the unknown. Traps are set, pits dug, cages built, all to no avail. The non-physical nature of phantoms does not seem to discourage such efforts, which sometimes display great ingenuity. Walter Hendricks, a mechanical engineer, lived for many years in a neighborhood of split-level ranch houses with back-yard swing sets and barbecues; one day he began to transform his yard into a dense thicket of pine trees, in order to invite the visits of phantoms. Each tree was equipped with a mechanism that was able to release from the branches a series of closely woven steel-mesh nets, which dropped swiftly when anything passed below. In another part of town, Charles Reese rented an excavator and dug a basement-sized cavity in his yard. He covered the pit, which became known as the Dungeon, with a sliding steel ceiling concealed by a layer of sod. One night, when a phantom appeared on his lawn, Reese pressed a switch that caused the false lawn to slide away; when he climbed down into the Dungeon with a high-beam flashlight, he discovered a frightened chipmunk. Others have used chemical sprays that cause temporary paralysis, empty sheds with sliding doors that automatically shut when a motion sensor is triggered, even a machine that produces flashes of lightning. People who dream of becoming captors fail to understand that the phantoms cannot be caught; to capture them would be to banish them from their own nature, to turn them into us.

EXPLANATION #4. One explanation is that the phantoms have always been here, long before the arrival of the Indians. We ourselves are the intruders. We seized their land, drove them into hiding, and have been careful ever since to maintain our advantage and force them into postures of submission. This explanation accounts for the hostility that many of us detect in the phantoms, as well as the fear they sometimes inspire in us. Its weakness, which some dismiss as negligible, is the absence of any evidence in support of it.

THE PHANTOM LORRAINE. As children we all hear the tale of the Phantom Lorraine, told to us by an aunt, or a babysitter, or someone on the playground, or perhaps by a careless parent desperate for a bedtime story. Lorraine is a phantom child. One day she comes to a tall hedge at the back of a yard where a boy and girl are playing. The children are running through a sprinkler, or throwing a ball, or practicing with a hula hoop. Nearby, their mother is kneeling on a cushion before a row of hollyhock bushes, digging up weeds. The Phantom Lorraine is moved by this picture, in a way she doesn't understand. Day after day she returns to the hedge, to watch the children playing. One day, when the children are alone, she steps shyly out of her hiding place. The children invite her to join them. Even though she is different, even though she can't pick things up or hold them, the children invent running games that all three can play. Now every day the Phantom Lorraine joins them in the backyard, where she is happy. One afternoon the children invite her into their house. She stares with wonder at the sunny kitchen, at the carpeted stairway leading to the second floor, at the children's room with the two windows looking out over the backyard. The mother and father are kind to the Phantom Lorraine. One day they invite her to a sleepover. The little phantom girl spends more and more time with the human family, who love her as their own. At last the parents adopt her. They all live happily ever after.

<hr />

ANALYSIS. As adults we look more skeptically at this tale, which once gave us so much pleasure. We understand that its purpose is to overcome a child's fear of the phantoms, by showing that what the phantoms really desire is to become one of us. This of course is wildly inaccurate, since the actual phantoms betray no signs of curiosity and rigorously withdraw from contact of any kind. But the tale seems to many of us to hold a deeper meaning. The story, we believe, reveals our own desire: to know the phantoms, to strip them of mystery. Fearful of their difference, unable to bear their otherness, we imagine, in the person of the Phantom Lorraine, their secret sameness. Some go further. The tale of the

Phantom Lorraine, they say, is a thinly disguised story about our hatred of the phantoms, our wish to bring about their destruction. By joining a family, the Phantom Lorraine in effect ceases to be a phantom; she casts off her nature and is reborn as a human child. In this way, the story expresses our longing to annihilate the phantoms, to devour them, to turn them into us. Beneath its sentimental exterior, the tale of the Phantom Lorraine is a dream-tale of invasion and murder.

***

OTHER TOWNS. When we visit other towns, which have no phantoms, often we feel that a burden has lifted. Some of us make plans to move to such a town, a place that reminds us of tall picture books from childhood. There, you can walk at peace along the streets and in the public parks, without having to wonder whether a ripple will course through the skin of your forearms. We think of our children playing happily in green backyards, where sunflowers and honeysuckle bloom against white fences. But soon a restlessness comes. A town without phantoms seems to us a town without history, a town without shadows. The yards are empty, the streets stretch bleakly away. Back in our town, we wait impatiently for the ripple in our arms, we fear that our phantoms may no longer be there. When, sometimes after many weeks, we encounter one of them at last, in a corner of the yard or at the side of the car wash, where a look is flung at us before the phantom turns away, we think: now things are as they should be, now we can rest awhile. It's a feeling almost like gratitude.

***

EXPLANATION #5. Some argue that all towns have phantoms, but that only we are able to see them. This way of thinking is especially attractive to those who cannot understand why our town should have phantoms and other towns none; why our town, in short, should be an exception. An objection to this explanation is that it accomplishes nothing but a shift of attention from the town itself to the people of our town: it's our ability to perceive phantoms that is now the riddle, instead of the phantoms themselves. A second objection, which some find decisive, is that the explanation relies entirely on an assumed world of invisible beings, whose existence can be neither proved nor disproved.

⚬

CASE STUDY #5. Every afternoon after lunch, before I return to work in the upstairs study, I like to take a stroll along the familiar sidewalks of my neighborhood. Thoughts rise up in me, take odd turns, vanish like bits of smoke. At the same time I'm wide open to striking impressions—that ladder leaning against the side of a house, with its shadow hard and clean against the white shingles, which project a little, so that the shingle-bottoms break the straight shadow-lines into slight zigzags; that brilliant red umbrella lying at an angle in the recycling container on a front porch next to the door; that jogger with shaved head, black nylon shorts, and an orange sweatshirt that reads, in three lines of black capital letters: EAT WELL/KEEP FIT/DIE ANYWAY. A single blade of grass sticks up from a crack in a driveway. I come to a sprawling old house at the corner, not far from the sidewalk. Its dark red paint could use a little touching up. Under the high front porch, on both sides of the steps, are those crisscross lattice panels, painted white. Through the diamond-shaped openings come pricker branches and the tips of ferns. From the sidewalk I can see the handle of an old hand mower, back there among the dark weeds. I can see something else: a slight movement. I step up to the porch, bend to peer through the lattice: I see three of them, seated on the ground. They turn their heads toward me and look away, begin to rise. In an instant they're gone. My arms are rippling as I return to the sidewalk and continue on my way. They interest me, these creatures who are always vanishing. This time I was able to glimpse a man of about fifty and two younger women. One woman wore her hair up; the other had a sprig of small blue wildflowers in her hair. The man had a long straight nose and a long mouth. They rose slowly but without hesitation and stepped back into the dark. Even as a child I accepted phantoms as part of things, like spiders and rainbows. I saw them in the vacant lot on the other side of the backyard hedge, or behind garages and tool sheds. Once I saw one in the kitchen. I observe them carefully whenever I can, I try to see their faces. I want nothing from them. It's a sunny day in early September. As I continue my walk, I look about me with interest. At the side of a driveway, next to a stucco house, the yellow nozzle of a hose rests on top of a dark green garbage can. Farther back, I can see part of a swing set. A cushion is sitting on the grass beside a three-pronged weeder with a red handle.

THE DISBELIEVERS. The disbelievers insist that every encounter is false. When I bend over and peer through the openings in the lattice, I see a slight movement, caused by a chipmunk or mouse in the dark weeds, and instantly my imagination is set in motion: I seem to see a man and two women, a long nose, the rising, the disappearance. The few details are suspiciously precise. How is it that the faces are difficult to remember, while the sprig of wildflowers stands out clearly? Such criticisms, even when delivered with a touch of disdain, never offend me. The reasoning is sound, the intention commendable: to establish the truth, to distinguish the real from the unreal. I try to experience it their way: the movement of a chipmunk behind the sun-lit lattice, the dim figures conjured from the dark leaves. It isn't impossible. I exercise my full powers of imagination: I take their side against me. There is nothing there, behind the lattice. It's all an illusion. Excellent! I defeat myself. I abolish myself. I rejoice in such exercise.

YOU. You who have no phantoms in your town, you who mock or scorn our reports: are you not deluding yourselves? For say you are driving out to the mall, some pleasant afternoon. All of a sudden—it's always sudden—you remember your dead father, sitting in the living room in the house of your childhood. He's reading a newspaper in the armchair next to the lamp table. You can see his frown of concentration, the fold of the paper, the moccasin slipper half-hanging from his foot. The steering wheel is warm in the sun. Tomorrow you're going to dinner at a friend's house—you should bring a bottle of wine. You see your friend laughing at the table, his wife lifting something from the stove. The shadows of telephone wires lie in long curves on the street. Your mother lies in the nursing home, her eyes always closed. Her photograph on your bookcase: a young woman smiling under a tree. You are lying in bed with a cold, and she's reading to you from a book you know by heart. Now she herself is a child and you read to her while she lies there. Your sister will be coming up for a visit in two weeks. Your daughter playing in the backyard, your wife at the window. Phantoms of memory, phantoms of desire. You pass through a world so thick with phantoms that there is barely enough room for anything else. The sun shines on a hydrant, casting a long shadow.

EXPLANATION #6. One explanation says that we ourselves are phantoms. Arguments drawn from cognitive science claim that our bodies are nothing but artificial constructs of our brains: we are the dream-creations of electrically charged neurons. The world itself is a great seeming. One virtue of this explanation is that it accounts for the behavior of our phantoms: they turn from us because they cannot bear to witness our self-delusion.

⌘

FORGETFULNESS. There are times when we forget our phantoms. On summer afternoons, the telephone wires glow in the sun like fire. Shadows of tree branches lie against our white shingles. Children shout in the street. The air is warm, the grass is green, we will never die. Then an uneasiness comes, in the blue air. Between shouts, we hear a silence. It's as though something is about to happen, which we ought to know, if only we could remember.

⟡

HOW THINGS ARE. For most of us, the phantoms are simply there. We don't think about them continually, at times we forget them entirely, but when we encounter them we feel that something momentous has taken place, before we drift back into forgetfulness. Someone once said that our phantoms are like thoughts of death: they are always there, but appear only now and then. It's difficult to know exactly what we feel about our phantoms, but I think it is fair to say that in the moment we see them, before we're seized by a familiar emotion like fear, or anger, or curiosity, we are struck by a sense of strangeness, as if we've suddenly entered a room we have never seen before, a room that nevertheless feels familiar. Then the world shifts back into place and we continue on our way. For though we have our phantoms, our town is like your town: sun shines on the house fronts, we wake in the night with troubled hearts, cars back out of driveways and turn up the street. It's true that a question runs through our town, because of the phantoms, but we don't believe we are the only ones who live with unanswered questions. Most of us would say we're no different from anyone else. When you come to think about us, from time to time, you'll see we really are just like you.

ON JACOB'S LADDER

Steve Stern

❧

"Spin, little spider, spin," the corporal called down in his guttural sing-song. He was attempting—to no effect whatever—to twirl the rope with which he'd lowered Toyti into the chimney. Braced against the warm walls of the flue, the boy ignored Corporal Luther's efforts at sabotage; he was after all harmless, the corporal, a laughingstock among his fellows, and his lame jokes and taunts were merely the way he tried to disguise his fear of scaling the smokestack. It was on account of his cowardice and generally unfit condition that Untersturmführer Stroop had assigned him repeatedly to this exercise in humiliation. Then other guards and even kapos would gather to observe his fat rump toiling up the iron rungs behind his charge, whose nimbleness was a torment that the tub-of-guts Luther took as a personal offense.

The little yid should by all rights have been dead already—hadn't the corporal lost a small fortune in wagers on that score? The shelf life, so to speak, of climbing boys in the camp was ordinarily measured in minutes, but this one had survived, even thrived at the task; which was why Luther, smug in his use of a Jewish locution, had christened him Toyti. And Toyti—since he was no longer able to remember his real name—was who he'd become. There was in fact a whole world he no longer remembered, though bits of it sometimes came back to him like objects under water that never surface far enough to recognize. The guards called him Toyti as well, as did the other prisoners, who viewed him as a creature whose intimacy with the machinery of death gave him the status of an honorary corpse. He took a peculiar pride in his status, which endured long after so many of his fellow inmates had disappeared. Generations of them had joined the ranks of the officially dead, their torched bones pulverized and sprinkled over the gardens and orchards beyond the high-voltage fence, while Toyti continued to master the game of survival.

"Hey, little spider," shouted Luther, still asthmatically panting, "you know how the sausage-makers of Rott—*hunh*—they claim to use every part of the pig but the oink? Well, here we use every part of the yid—*hunh*—but the oy." His wheezy laugh like a trodden concertina reverberated in the square chimney shaft.

Toyti had heard the joke before ad nauseam, to say nothing of the endless threats and complaints that accompanied their climbing excursions. He knew that Luther looked forward to the day when the stunted sweep would be overcome by the heat and fumes, and instead of hauling up a spider he would reel in a dead fish. That was after all the purpose of the rope, not to protect the boy but to prevent his becoming an obstruction. Hence the wire ruff like a ballerina's skirt that encircled his chest along with the rope, so that in the event he was no longer capable of scraping residue from the tiles, his very body could still serve as a cleaning instrument. It was another example of the efficiency for which Luther and his kind had such affection, but Toyti had cheated them all by making the chimneys his element.

By now he'd descended far enough into the flue that Luther's barbs were barely audible anymore. The bloated corporal was in any case an amateur at abuse compared to the death's head soldiers that supervised the work details to which Toyti had been attached before his transfer to the crematoria. His back still bore the stripes from their quirts, his head the ache from the heels of their patent leather boots grinding his face into the mud. Their dogs had sunk their fangs into his ankles as he shoveled drek from a latrine overflowing from a thousand cases of dysentery; they snapped at him as he dragged stumps and lugged stones to no purpose other than breaking a body in which the spirit no longer resided. For these endeavors he was rewarded each evening with a bowl of soup abob with drowning vermin and a mealy potato from which even his empty gut revolted. His eyes drooled a murky sap, his limbs brittle as twigs, and during that notable morning selection when the oberführer called his number, he groaned in relief that he would soon be delivered from the onus of his days. But rather than sent to the gas he was dispatched (owing no doubt to his pint size and advanced puniness) to sweep the chimney of one of the incineration centers. At the time he would have preferred to lie down and die. But when he was hoisted by the disgruntled corporal onto the rusted rungs that protruded from the smokestack wall, something happened; because his spent limbs, never athletic or especially strong, seemed to welcome the opportunity to clamber up the ladder. In no time at all he had risen to an altitude at which the poison stench of the camp was dispersed by crisp breezes, and the jaunty marches the slave orchestra played were no longer a mockery. He could see beyond the barbed wire and the towers to the woods and cultivated fields, the feather-soft rolling hills, but even more pleasing than the view from the crown of the chimney was the sense of safety he felt once he was lowered into the shaft.

So it seemed that Toyti had a vocation. The work was of course no less taxing than the drudgery he had previously endured, but it was essential. If the flues were not regularly scoured of the crust of chemical condensation that the burning bodies deposited on the ceramic tiles, the chimneys were in danger of catching fire, and such an event could have devastating consequences for the otherwise seamless operation of the camp. Therefore, diminutive boys saddled with an ungainly utility belt—from which depended a whisk broom, putty knife, and hammer—boys wearing the ridiculous wire collar and the rope wound beneath their arms were dangled like plumb bobs into the smoky conduits. There they had to chip, scrape, and dust with a feverish activity in order to complete the job before succumbing to the heat and the choking atmosphere. It was true that the furnaces were extinguished during the cleaning, but the work of the crematoria was a twenty-four-hour-a-day enterprise, so the Reich could not afford to take a building out of commission for very long. As a result, the flues were never given time to cool. Such conditions had caused the asphyxiation if not the roasting alive of his predecessors, and Toyti himself was scalded head to toe; his char-broiled flesh—where it wasn't uniformly coated in soot—had turned the color of coral, and only vestigial patches remained of his ocher hair. (It was a startling countenance that had the virtue of discouraging the kapos from using him as they did the other boys.) But Toyti's aptitude for sweeping chimneys, and his peculiar habit of outliving the task, had earned him a semi-permanent situation in the lager.

Transferred from the lice-ridden barracks, he was given a berth above the incineration hall, in an attic room penetrated by pipes like pneumatic tubes through which the gas pellets were dropped from the roof. His rations were improved: he was allowed a quarter loaf of black bread a day along with a dollop of coal tar margarine, and on Sundays fifty grams of wurst. He was careful, however, to eat only enough to assuage his hunger, since any increase in the size of his spindly frame could result in his becoming ineligible for an occupation Toyti lived to resume.

Why? "Because I'm ensuring the Jews a clear passage to heaven," he told himself, though he never believed it for an instant.

Due to the constant accumulation of creosote and fatty deposits, the cleaning rotation was ongoing, but there could be lapses between of several days. During that time Toyti was expected to lend his energies to facilitating the business of cremation, though his assistance in that area was negligible. He was negligible, he understood, in everything but his function as sweep. Still he helped sort the clothing that the victims left behind on numbered hooks in the undressing room, often finding scraps of food that could be bartered for various indulgences. He found jewelry secreted in their shoes and the folds of their garments, treasures that must be turned over as property of the Reich on pain of being tossed into the furnaces one's self. With a rag masking his face, he moved among the tangled bodies, pink and dappled with seagreen spots, that were brought up in the lift from the basement chamber. Often they had to be pried apart like braided cheeses, and once Toyti had seen, between a lady's legs, the just emerging head of a child. He sheared off the hair of the women, which would be woven into socks for the crews of submarines, and cracked the jaws of the deceased to extract their gold teeth; he removed rings from fingers and sometimes, when the rings were stubborn, the fingers themselves. He stood beside the pit where the corpses were burned when the furnaces became glutted, while the guards laughed at the rude noises the pyre emitted, how the men's penises came to attention in the flames. He hosed out the blood and shit from the artificial showers, their walls stained an azure blue from the Zyklon gas, like a mural of the sky that someone had begun and abandoned. But for these tasks anyone would do, and whole units of Sonderkommandos had come and gone since Toyti had been reassigned to the killing centers. He knew well enough that it was only for the sake of his skill in the chimneys that he was kept on this side of oblivion.

Far above Luther was shouting something about a spider tangled in its own web, something about the cold, to which Toyti paid no special heed. But as he scraped, brushed, and chiseled toward a depth that was the point of no return for so many before him, he encountered an obstacle in his way. This had never happened before. While the sludge that caked the insulation could often be bulbous and dense, there was never so much of it that it interfered with his descent; but this was something else, an authentic obstruction. The sulfurous square of light high over his head gave no help in identifying the blockage, but as Toyti holstered his tools and ran his hands along the dry, lath-like surfaces, he was satisfied that what lay in his path were bones. It was a skeleton, curled up but—as best he could judge—wholly intact and belonging to a creature no larger in fact than himself. Blindly he described with his calloused fingers the human-shaped configuration of limbs, stroking here a knotted knee joint, there a vertebra, a collarbone. As he proceeded in his inspection, he discovered an irregularity beyond the skeleton's natural frame, from which jutted a pair of appendages comprised of a cartilage as fragile as jackstraws. Toyti handled the twin protrusions, one of them crimped to accommodate the shaft's right angle, the other unfolded to allow a fully extended wing.

He recoiled, thinking he'd come upon the upshot of one of those monstrous experiments the doctors performed on the inmates of Block 10. But how could it have gotten lodged here in the flue? Gingerly Toyti began again to trace its contours, feeling a warmth suffuse his body that had nothing in common with the residual heat from the furnaces. This was a warmth that inspired visions: a clockwork marionette wobbling across a damson carpet in a room whose walls were lined with books. He stroked a shinbone and saw a slender lady seated at a crow-black piano; stroked a rib and felt the silken tongue of a spaniel lapping his chin in a garden where he hunted snails; he touched a knuckle and saw, as if lit by lightning, a bearded gentleman in a top hat cradling a scroll. The bones were an instrument for evoking images and sensations, the sensations causing a stir in the pit of his stomach, which curdled and convulsed until Toyti had to undo his trousers and empty his bowels on the spot. Then his head was light as a bubble and floating, his body dangling like a jellyfish in the inky air. He jammed his feet and spine against the tiles to catch himself and shuddered from a vicious impulse to kick the thing from its perch. When the impulse passed, he pulled the rope off over his head and looped it in turn around the skeleton's rib cage, pulling it tight. "What a joke this will be on Luther!" thought Toyti. But who was he kidding? Having resolved to salvage the bones at whatever cost, he feared that the joke was on him.

He yanked at the tether, which was the signal for the treble-chinned guard to begin hauling up his burden, but instead of becoming abruptly taut, the rope tumbled down the shaft on top of him.

"Corporal Luther?" cried Toyti, but there was no answer.

Ordinarily such an event would not have greatly concerned him. Agile in his narrow domain, he could inchworm his way up the vertical duct with relative ease. Of course today's ascent would be somewhat encumbered by his new acquisition. Then there was a further development: for as Toyti embraced the skeleton with the intent of lifting it out of the chimney's throat, the heat from the furnaces below, which were supposedly inoperative, had begun to intensify. Moreover, though he struggled from his nearly upended attitude to dislodge the bones, they remained obstinately wedged in place. Toyti tried again to wrench them free from their station, while the thickening smoke caused his lungs to constrict, his smarting eyes to flood with tears. He coughed and gasped for air, yowled from the scorching tiles, so hot now they'd begun to blister his flesh. Then he made his mightiest effort yet to wrestle his prize from its fixed position, and this time he did manage to jar it loose, but its weight—who would have thought that such a small parcel of bones could weigh so much?—tugged Toyti from his own precarious purchase, and losing his balance he pitched headlong after the angel into the abyss.

⚭

Down below Corporal Luther, a fat baker tending his oven, opened a muffle to see if all the clattering meant that his strategy had met with success.

THE PANIC HAND

Jonathan Carroll

I'd just finished going through a time in life when one day bled into the next. Nothing worked, nothing smelled good, nothing smiled, nothing fitted. Even my feet grew a little, for some mysterious reason, and I had to buy three pairs of new shoes. Figure that. Maybe my body was trying to burst out of its old, failed skin like a snake and form a new one.

In the middle of this black mess I met Celine Davenant. She lived in Munich, five easy hours away from Vienna on the train. With her beautifully smooth and reassuring voice, she worked reading the news on an English language radio station up there.

On Friday evenings after work I'd hurry over to the Westbahnhof and catch 'The *Rosenkavalier*' to Munich. That really was the name of the train.

Sometimes Celine came to Vienna, but made no bones about the fact she didn't like the city one bit. I told her the train trip was a pleasure for me and I looked forward to it. So we silently agreed for the time being

to leave things as they were: she'd meet the train at the Munich Haupt-
bahnhof at eleven-thirty and our weekend would begin there amidst
startled pigeons, travellers, the jerk and hoots of trains.

My first excited trip West, I made the mistake of buying a first-class
ticket. But even there, the compartment was crowded with weekend
people and their many bags. What I subsequently learned was to buy a
second-class seat, arrive early, and go directly to the dining car. If I sat
there until the town of AttnangPuchheim, the train would have emptied
and, strolling back to second class, I could have my pick of empty places.

The arrangement worked out well, particularly because the railroad
served good food. It was delightful to sit eating by those large windows
and watch the Austrian countryside slide by. Perchtoldsdorf, St Pölten,
Linz. Stationmasters in red caps waved. Farmers in old pick-up trucks,
blank-faced. Unmoving people stood frozen at small stations, rural
crossings, in the middle of who cares, watching us dick by. Dogs barked
silently. I often saw deer grazing. Rabbits darted zigzags across open
fields.

It took me away from my life; it took me closer to Celine.

***

What is the name of that pink and white lily that smells so strongly of
pepper and spice. I can't remember, but it's one of my favourites. When
they entered the dining car that evening it was the first thing I noticed.
Both of them were wearing that marvellous flower in their hair. Maybe
it was the second thing I noticed: it was hard not to be wide-eyed about
their uniquely different beauty.

The woman was tall and splendid. She looked as if she'd been an
actress earlier, or at least held perfect champagne glasses and looked out
of high windows at the Manhattan or Paris skyline. Now in her late
thirties or early innings of forty, she'd come through the game strong
and unimpeded. If there were lines on her face they made her look sex-
ier, more knowing. The flower behind her ear said she had a sense of

humour, could give the world a smile. The flower behind her daughter's ear said here was an attentive, pleased mother. A rare combination.

The girl had the same russet-coloured hair and wide round eyes as her mother. At least I assumed it was the mother. They looked too much alike—senior and junior versions of the same great face. The face the girl would grow into in twenty years if she had luck.

I spent a good portion of every day thinking about Celine and how things would work out between us. I wanted them to work out and was hoping she did too. We hadn't talked about long-range plans because that sort of discussion comes after you have surveyed the new lands of your relationship and given long thought to where you want to drive in the first permanent posts.

We liked many of the same things, couldn't get enough of each other in bed but, best of all, knew there was almost always something to talk about. Very few quiet spaces in our time together, and if they came, it was only because we were savouring the silent hum of contentment that is the real electricity of love.

When I started thinking about Celine, almost nothing could distract me. And I *was* thinking about her when the mother and daughter came into the dining car. So it shocked me to realize all thoughts of my friend had disappeared while I watched these two stunners cross . . . to my table.

"Do you mind if we sit here?"

The car was about a third full and there were a number of empty tables. Why did they want to sit here? I am a good-looking man and women generally like me, but they don't cross rooms for me. Particularly when they looked like this one.

"Please." I half stood and gestured to the empty chairs. I could smell the flowers in their hair. The little girl was blushing and smiling and wouldn't look at me. Snatching the chair out so hard that it almost tipped over, she had to grab it with two hands at the last moment.

The mother laughed and put her hands to her cheeks. "Poor Heidi.

She wanted to make such a good impression on you. She saw you walk down the platform at the station and actually jumped out of the train to see which car you went into. She made us wait till now so we wouldn't look too eager."

The girl looked daggers at her mother; her secrets were being told, laughed at. I didn't think that was funny and tried to tell her with a smile and a small, friendly shrug. She was sunburn-red and wouldn't look at me after one fast, furtive glance.

Mama shook her head, still smiling, and put out her slim hand. "I'm Francesca Pold. This is my daughter, Heidi. And you are . . . ?"

I said my name and shook the woman's warm hand. She held on a few seconds too long. I looked into her eyes to see if she was telling me something with that, but saw only, "Wouldn't *you* like to know!" there. Her smile spread and she sat down.

Hmmmm.

"What are you reading? *Albanian Wonder Tales*? That sounds interesting." Without asking, she picked it up, opened it, and started reading aloud. " 'Whether you believe it or doubt it no matter. May all good things come to you who listen!' "

Both mother and daughter burst out laughing. The laughter was exactly the same except that one was high and young, the other deep and more experienced. It was charming.

"What a funny way to start a story! Are they fairy tales?" She put the book down on the table and the girl picked it right up.

"Yes. I like to read them. It's a hobby."

The woman nodded. Her expression said she fully approved. I'd scored points.

"What do you do for a living?"

"I sell computers to the East bloc."

"You sell computers and read fairy tales? A well-rounded man."

"That's nice to say, but it's probably only a bad case of arrested development."

That got a chuckle and another approving smile.

She raised a hand for the waiter and one swept down on the table like a hawk. The world can be divided between people who can get a waiter's attention and those who can't.

Those who *can* have only to raise a tired or lazy finger and waiters lift their heads as if some secret radio signal has suddenly been beamed out on their private frequency. They arrive seconds later.

Those who can't resort to finger-snapping and other embarrassing things, but it does no good. They are unheard, invisible. They might as well rot. Francesca Pold got waiters. It wasn't surprising.

The two of them ordered and our chat continued. The girl pretended to be deeply involved in my fairy-tale book, but I often saw it slip down and her eyes—all attention and interest—watch carefully. Beautiful eyes. Large and smart, they had a kind of liquidness to them that made you think she was on the verge of crying. Yet that very quality made them more singular and attractive.

The mother was a gabber and, although what she said was mostly interesting, it was easy to tune in and out on her monologue. More and more I found myself looking at the daughter. When their food came, I saw my chance.

"What's your favourite subject in school, Heidi?"

"Ma-ma-math-e-ma-ma-matics." Her jaw trembled up and down.

"Is that what you want to do when you get older?"

She shook her head and, pointing at me, smiled. "C-C-C Computers."

She had a torturous, machine-gun stutter that grew worse as she got more excited. But it was also very plain she wanted to talk to me. Her mother made no attempt to interrupt or explain what Heidi said, even when some word or phrase was largely unintelligible. I liked that. They'd obviously worked it out between them and, handicapped as she was, the girl would grow up in a world where she was used to fighting her own battles.

I'd already had dinner but joined them for dessert when I saw how big and fresh the strawberries were they ordered. The three of us sat there and spooned them up while the sky lost the rest of its day. It was completely dark outside when we got up from the table.

'Where are you sitting?'

I smiled. "You mean what class am I in? Second, I'm afraid."

"Good, so are we! Do you mind if we sit with you?"

I liked to look at the woman, but was growing tired of her motor-mouth. More and more looks passed between Heidi and me. I would have happily sat alone with the girl and her stutter for the rest of the trip to Munich (they were going there too), if that had been possible.

Despite being able to call waiters, Francesca appeared to have the mistaken idea that beauty also means licence to go on about anything, ad infinitum. I pitied her daughter having to put up with it every day of her life.

But what could I say: no, I don't want to sit with you? I could have, but it would've been rude and essentially wrong. We would sit together and Francesca would talk and I'd try to make Heidi's ride a little more pleasant.

As usual, most of the compartments were empty. Once settled, Francesca reached into her purse and took out a pack of cigarettes. That was surprising because she hadn't smoked at all till then. The brand was unfiltered Camels and she drew smoke way down into her lungs. While she puffed, Heidi and I talked about computers and the things she was doing with them at school. The girl knew a lot and I wondered what she would do with this skill when she grew older. That's one of the nice things about working with computers—you don't have to *say* a word to them and they'll still do your bidding. Even if Heidi retained her stutter in later life, computers would be a good thing for her to pursue because she could do wonderful, productive things without uttering a word.

To be young and suffer the kind of affliction she carried on her tongue must have been as bad, in its way, as having a case of the worst acne. Only pimples usually go away when we get older. Stuttering stays around and doesn't pay much heed to a person's birth-date or self-esteem.

She tried so damned hard to speak. No matter what subject we were discussing, there was something she wanted to say, but her words came out so slowly and painfully that at times I literally forgot what we'd been discussing after watching Heidi strain her way through the sentences.

Once when we were discussing computer games she got completely hung up on the title of her favourite and her mother had to come in and help.

"The game she likes so much is called Panic Hand. Have you ever played?"

"No, I've never even heard of it."

The girl tried explaining how it worked, but when none of it came out the right way, gave up and slumped in her seat. I knew she was about to cry. She'd tried but lost another game to her inner enemy: in living contrast to her gorgeous mother who had only to sit there and carry on her own boring, unending monologue.

But even mother was silent a while. The girl looked out through the window, flushed and tight-lipped, while Francesca smiled at me and smoked one cigarette after the other.

Suddenly Heidi looked at me and said, "Don't you th-th-think ciga-rette s-s-s-smo—king is c-c-c-c-ool? I d-d-d-do."

I shrugged. "Tried it when I was younger but never got the hang of it. I think it looks good in the movies."

Hearing this mild rebuff, the girl cringed down into her seat as if I'd hit her. Was she *that* sensitive?

I was looking at her and trying to catch her eye and wink when her mother said, "I'd like to sleep with you. I'd like to sleep with you right now. Right here."

"What did you say?" I looked at Francesca. She had her hand on her blouse and was unbuttoning it.

"I said I want to sleep with you. Here."

"And what about your daughter?"

"She'll go out in the corridor. We can pull the curtain." Her hand continued to climb down the buttons.

"No."

The blouse was open and a nice lilac frilly bra showed through against the stark white of her secret skin in there.

"Look, Francesca. Just wait, huh? Christ. Think about your daughter!"

The woman looked at the girl, then back at me. "You can sleep with her too. Would you rather that? I can leave!" She laughed high and fully, winked at Heidi, then began to button herself back up. "See, honey, sometimes you don't need me. You just have to find a computer man."

"Hey, just stop." I finally had the presence of mind to stand up and start for the door.

"D-d-d-d-don't go, please!" The girl grabbed my arm and held on hard. Her face was fear and shame. She got up out of her seat and put her arms around my neck. "Please don't go, please! I'll m-m-m-m-make her g-g-g-g-go aw-wa-wa-wa-wa-way!"

I hugged her back and, slowly easing her arms from around my neck, pushed her back into her seat at the same time. When I had her there, I turned to Francesca. Who wasn't there. Who wasn't anywhere. I was standing with my back to the door, so there was no way she could have gotten around me to get out.

Torn between a strong urge to get the hell out of there, and big curiosity to know what was going on, I more or less froze where I was and waited for something to decide the next move.

The train began to slow and the loudspeaker announced that we were pulling into Rosenheim, the last stop before Munich. I sat down. Heidi slid over next to me. Then she did something so erotic and wrong that I shiver to think of it, even now. Very gently, she took my hand and slid it under her skirt, between her legs. It was there a milli-second before I tried to pull it away. But couldn't because she held it there and she was much, *much* stronger than I. That power, more than where my hand rested, was what scared me. What was she, eleven? Twelve? No twelve-year-old had that much strength.

When she spoke it was in a very normal, un-stuttering girl's voice. "Didn't you like her? Tell me what you like and I'll make it for you. I promise. Whatever you want!"

"What are you doing, Heidi? What are you doing?"

Her hand tightened on my arm. It was so, so strong. "Didn't you think she was cool? The colour of her hair and the way she smoked those Camels? That's how I'll do it. That's what I want to be like when I'm old. That's how I'm going to make myself." Her eyes narrowed. "You don't believe me? You don't think she was cool? That's what I'll be like and every man will want me. They'll all want to touch me and listen to me talk. I'll have lots of stories and things. I'll be able to say whatever I want."

"Why can't you say it now?"

She squeezed my hand till I cried out. "Because I stutter! You heard! You think I was *kidding around*? I can't help it."

Trying to prise her hand off mine, I gave up. "Why can you talk normally now?"

"Because your hand's there. Men are going to want me all the time then because I'll talk like her. I'll be beautiful and I'll talk beautifully."

"You made her?"

Her hand loosened a little. She looked at me, wanting a reaction. "Yes. You don't like her? All men like her. They always want her. Whenever she asks, they say yes. And if they want her then they'll want me too. 'Cause that's what I'll be like."

I had two choices—to play along and pretend or tell the truth and hope . . .

'She talks too much.' Heidi stopped squeezing my hand but kept it where it was.

"What do you mean?"

"She talks too much. She's boring."

"B-B-B-oring?"

"Yes. She talks about herself too much and a lot of it isn't interesting. I stopped listening to her. I was paying more attention to you."

"Why? You didn't think she was pretty?"

"Pretty but dull."

"The other men didn't think that! They always wanted her! They always took her!"

"Not all men are the same. I like a woman to be interesting."

"More than pretty?" It was as if she were asking me things from a questionnaire. I had little choice but to answer her.

In fact, the rest of the way to Munich she questioned me about 'Francesca.' How did I like her voice? What about her body? What was wrong with her stories? Would I have wanted to sleep with her if she'd been alone?

I never found out who the woman . . . 'was.' I did not want to make the girl angrier or more upset than she was, for obvious reasons. I answered her questions as best I could and, believe me, there were a great many. I answered her right into the Munich train station where she stood up as the train was slowing and told me she had to go. Nothing more, nothing else. Sliding the glass door open, she gave me one last small smile and was gone.

What do I think happened? I think too many things. That she had an idea for the perfect woman she wanted to be and created her out of her unhappiness to take her place until she could grow into her adult skin. But she was young and made mistakes. What the young think is cool or sexy we grown-ups often smile at. That's one thought. Or she was a witch playing her own version of 'Panic Hand,' a game I naturally looked for but never found. Or . . . I don't know. It sounds completely dumb and helpless, but I *don't* know. I'm sorry if you're unsatisfied.

I saw her one last time. When I got off the train I saw her running down the platform and into the arms of a nice-looking couple who were delighted to see her. The man wouldn't put her down and the woman kept giving her kisses. She never turned around once. I kept my distance.

But I walked far behind them and was glad she didn't see me. Then there was Celine. And look who came with her so late at night! Fiona. The wonderful Fiona—Celine's daughter.

MORIYA

Dean Paschal

He's VERY mechanically minded.

Oh?

Yes. It's scary at times. How so?

There is a darkness to mechanical objects that he is a bit too quick to appreciate and understand.

(The elderly lady turned ahead of them down a long hall and the mother and the boy followed. The three of them turned again, passing a shelf covered with whiskey bottles and a mahogany cabinet which the boy noticed was full of wine and single-malt scotch.)

In that case (the elderly lady said) I have something—something mechanical—that he might like to see. The girl next door wanted to see it this morning, so it's already wound.

The boy to whom the two grown women are impolite enough to be indirectly referring is fourteen years old and is following them through a Victorian-looking house on his first day in New Orleans. He is to take six weeks of intensive French lessons in a special summer program for adolescents in a school on Jackson Avenue. The elderly woman is a moderately distant friend of his mother's who is going to put him up and who is leading both of them now into a parlor tinkling with prisms and light.

Indeed, the idea of "something mechanical" immediately had this boy's interest. Just as immediately, he saw it and was disappointed. Enough so, that it was difficult to fully conceal his disappointment. The mechanical thing was a clock. It was a glass clock in the center of a marble table. It was ticking steadily. The clock had an exposed mechanism, a pendulum weighted with dual glass tubes full of mercury, but otherwise was of a rather familiar style and unremarkable. There were some other antiquated objects in the room, some family pictures in ornate, somewhat brassy-looking shadow-box frames, a spinet-style piano, two medallion sofas facing one another beneath a third medallion on the ceiling. Indeed, there was something of a medallion "theme" to the entire center of the parlor. It is unlikely that the boy would have known or noticed this. He was, after all, mechanically, not architecturally, minded. On the left-hand sofa, however, there was something he *did* notice, couldn't help but, a doll, a virtually life-sized doll, not a "'baby" doll either but a doll representing an adolescent girl, a girl in her mid-adolescence, perhaps. Had she been standing up she might have been over four feet high, perhaps well over. She was wearing a nineteenth-century, European, many-buttoned, fin-de-siècle dress, a maroon velvet jacket, and some high-topped black shoes. She had been positioned so that she was looking somewhat wistfully out of a long French window, one elbow on the arm of the sofa.

There was a black ribbon with a medallion on it around her neck.

(The boy went dutifully to the clock.)

We think a Swiss clockmaker made it, the woman continued. It's from 1892, over a hundred years old at this point.

The boy looked at the beveled glass, the spattering of color on the marble tabletop, the mercury-filled tubes, and stood there waiting for the woman to say something more about it. Actually, though, he knew the theory of the tubes himself. Heat causes metal to expand, and the pendulum, being metal, will lengthen, lowering the center of gravity and therefore slowing the clock—not much, of course, infinitesimally, as a matter of fact, but when one is counting seconds over months or years the differences become significant, then profound. The mercury in the tubes is confined so that it can only expand upward, *raising* the center of gravity so the effects cancel.

(Well, he thought, standing patiently, politely, at the table, at least he could show off his knowledge.)

Is this the original key? he said.

What?

It was only then that the boy realized that the woman was looking at neither him nor the clock.

Oh, that, she said. Not *that*. I know nothing about that. That's new, for us anyway. That was at an estate sale last year. Sit down.

Ma'am?

Sit down. Here. The woman patted the sofa beside her, rubbed the red velvet flirtatiously, made room between herself and the boy's mother.

This woman, with her well-applied makeup and at least one facelift, was elegant in the slightly decadent manner of the best-preserved of sixty-year-old females. She was the sort of woman who can successfully squeeze the last remnants of sensuality out of age, possessing still the power of crossed legs in cocktail dresses, knowing well the uses of black chiffon, gold jewelry, French perfume, and alcohol. In fact, bringing a fourteen-year-old into a parlor tinkling with such temptations might have given many a mother pause. But this particular woman had a husband she was still moderately crazy about, a handsome lawyer with an alcoholic nose who was a member of one of the old-line Mardi Gras krewes and a fixture at Galatoire's on Friday. (In fact, the husband was there now, this being a Friday.) So that particular story is possibly over before it starts.

Wait, the woman said, facing the other sofa now.

The doll continued looking out the window. The clock continued ticking on its table.

The boy sat down, began waiting, leaned forward slightly.

It may take a while. Would you like a Coca-Cola?

The boy was equally puzzled by both sentences.

He was still facing the sofa. He had already noticed that the two sofas were not quite identical. The one the doll was on was slightly longer and had darker, somewhat different-looking woodwork. He was beginning to make other comparisons. But at that moment the doll began to turn. She began to turn toward him, slowly, as he watched, though not so slowly as to be unlifelike. It was as though she had been interrupted in the midst of a daydream. Her brilliant hazel eyes were not fixed, not what they call "doll-like"; they moved independently of her head and slightly in advance of it, giving an effect the realism of which was uncanny. Her hazel-colored eyes were crystalline, maybe literally. There was no movement of her mouth, which, like her face, was ceramic, or ivory, or alabaster, and *was* doll-like, though the lips were full and there was a feeling and even a glimpse of natural teeth. She moved her elbow and left hand from the armrest and crossed both hands (politely?) in her lap. She was wearing long white gloves which, had her jacket been removed, would have proved to extend past her elbows. She moved her right hand and tugged on the fabric of her left glove as though to straighten it or exorcise some ghost of disorder.

Then she looked at the boy again, directly at him, through him. There could have been no more steadfast stare. The most saucy and impudent thirteen-year-old that has ever taken the perilous step of trying the effects of lipstick on a stepfather could not have had such a gaze. The doll had a breathtaking face, not innocent, but breathtaking: high cheekbones, shadowy eyes, dark hair that seemed real. His own gaze flinched down somewhat to the black-and-white medallion around her neck. Her breasts were so well formed, her blouse so tucked in as to give a sense of suspended breathing.

The woman was talking to his mother now.

It's the only one like it we've ever seen. It's Swiss, we think. It stayed in the attic for decades in a cedar-lined box. It was in my husband Eric's family. Eric's grandfather would have had to know something about it, since this was his house and furniture. Eric himself says he had never seen it before. His grandfather never mentioned the thing, had forgotten about it, perhaps, or perhaps kept it a secret deliberately, since he had three daughters in addition to his son. Maybe he wanted to avoid a fight. We didn't find it till a few months ago. The year 1892 was stamped on—actually burned into—the wood of the box. It was in an alcove under an unbelievable number of blankets.

(The women, of course, are talking around the boy again.)

The crank is in that case, the woman said, pointing to a narrow leather box. There are a number of movements it goes through randomly, *sometimes* randomly, sometimes not. I'm not sure that we've seen them all as yet. It seems, at times, that where you touch it very much affects the internal program. You may touch it, if you like.

The boy came closer but could hear no sound of clockwork. The doll's eyes had not moved, her head had not moved, still she seemed to be following him. He grasped the tips of her gloved fingers, tremulously, as though shaking hands, as though saying hello.

After a moment, the doll turned slightly and looked up at him. Her eyes, once again, slightly leading the movement. It was impossible to believe it was coincidental.

It will run for days, the woman said. The spring must be enormous. It *feels* enormous when you wind it.

What's her name?

My God! You're the second person who has asked that today! Actually, we haven't named her. Or maybe we have. My husband and I have begun calling her "the doll." You can name her if you like.

(The boy was still waiting, still holding the doll's hand.)

Can you stop her? he said. Her motion, I mean. Is it possible to shut her off?

(Outside the house, he heard the shriek of a young girl's voice next door.)

Yes, there's a little wheel in the back of her neck, just under the ribbon.

The boy went behind her, behind the sofa, and rested both his hands on the doll's shoulders. Her eyelashes were almost assuredly real, her hair too, human, straight, long and luxurious. It seemed he could smell a trace of perfume. He looked down at the fabric of her dress, felt the little wheel beneath the ribbon.

Interesting, the woman said. See what I mean? (The woman was talking to the boy's mother now.) I've never seen her do that before.

The doll was turning around to look at the boy. She succeeded, too, to a surprising degree, finishing by staring up at him, her neck arched slightly.

❧

During the first week, the boy attempted to make a complete catalog of the doll's movements. She seldom moved as much as she had the first day. Sometimes she would go a full hour or two without any motion of any kind. He would come into the parlor in the afternoon or evening and watch her and wait. Her activity was completely unpredictable: five minutes, thirty minutes, forty-seven and a half minutes between movements. Then she might do a lot, an entire series of things, as though bored by the long inactivity—straighten a glove, adjust her knees, slap at an invisible fly. The most elaborate thing she could do was the following: put both hands down, curl her knuckles slightly, and lift her entire body a fraction of an inch to the right. But before that motion was ever repeated, she would move to the left again, so that there was no overall change in position. Often she would fold her hands together, waiting; and from that position move her eyes, alone, so as to look slowly around the room. (Literally, she seemed very much to *look* at something for a while, then at something else.) Occasionally she would look down at the floor for quite a period of time, so that one would be very tempted to say, "This little doll once had a little dog."

Her eyes themselves, the boy noticed, seemed as though they should be able to close, the lids seemed to be hinged, or *potentially* hinged, but they never did, or he never saw them do it. They never blinked, even. He could hear her ticking only by holding his ear directly on her body, but anyplace on it would work—her back, for instance, or one of her shoulders. There was quite a *presence* in the sound, not a slow tick . . . tick . . . tick . . . tick . . . like a clock, but something faster, shorter, more breathless and passionate: a tic-tic-tic-tic-tic-tic-tic-tic-tic, full in its own way, of the quality of construction, of the click of micrometers, of the precise cut of lathes, of the tempering of steel for shafts and mainsprings.

The boy had other concerns, of course. Before leaving home, he had had daydreams that there might be some girl in New Orleans waiting just for him. But those dreams did not pan out. All the girls were older. He was literally the youngest individual in his class. Most of the girls had boyfriends with driver's licenses. They were friendly enough but definitely not interested in any fourteen-year-old "mechanically minded" boy. On several occasions he hunted for but did not find the girl next door, nor, for that matter, did he ever hear her again.

Under the circumstances, the question that became paramount for him was how long the doll would run. It dawned on him that it might be somewhat difficult to tell. The doll might continue to *tick* long after she had stopped moving because it should take less energy to do that. In fact, every day, after class, he would wonder, has she stopped already?

He began to leave things in her hands, little bits of paper, to see if she had moved in his absence. Infinitesimal, these pieces of paper were, some of them virtually the size of lint. He would find them later, on the sofa, on the armrest, on the floor beneath her feet. After a while he began writing tiny messages on them. To camouflage, as far as possible, what he was doing, he would write very small, so that what she ended up holding was an unreadable blob of ink. But in each case *he* knew what he had written and was pleased to think she did as well.

Hello.

Thinking of you.

Sleep well.

Or:

I think you're beautiful.

Will try to dream of Switzerland for your sake.

(He would find the messages on the cushion of the sofa, on the armrest, on the floor beneath her feet.)

The boy *did* try to dream of Switzerland for her; and, in order to get a focus for his dream, saturated himself with ideas and images of the area from two sets of encyclopedias in the house: pictures of the Alps, of cows, of cheese, of Zurich and Bern. He thought that perhaps she might come *alive* for him in a dream.

(And, as he began to learn more French, he tried speaking to her.)

Je t'aime.

On the sofa sometimes, unmoving for hours, he would stare at her, trying to saturate his brain with her beauty. Her hazel eyes were so realistic it was impossible to believe she was not seeing him too, watching him, waiting for something.

Nothing came of the dreams, though. That is, they did not happen.

In truth, the two of them didn't get much time absolutely alone together. Other things would intervene. The maid would come in. The husband would enter with his pipe, the wife with her cigarettes, or both, simultaneously. They seemed mainly to smoke in that room. The boy noticed one evening that the doll was looking directly at the husband as he fiddled with his pipe, and he suddenly realized he was feeling something very like jealousy.

One afternoon, while waiting for the doll to move, he began looking at the family pictures in the shadow-box frames. He noticed there was a resemblance, a definite resemblance, between this doll and certain of the women in the pictures. He thought they might be the wives. The maid came on Tuesdays and Thursdays and he began to ask her questions. She knew the answers to most of them, and the woman eventually provided him with the rest. He found that the daughters in the family had something of a resemblance, passed on, no doubt, genetically; but what he had guessed initially was the truth. The real resemblance was to the wives.

The boy opened the leather box, looked at the crank with its mahogany handle, lifted it up, set it back. There were some spare buttons for the blouse, a long Allen wrench with a T-shaped handle, some regular wrenches too, three screwdrivers, a button hook. (There was also an impression of these things crushed into the velvet lining of the top of the box.)

How long could the spring *last*? he wondered. It was already more than "days," as the woman had suggested. It was "weeks" now, past two, and well into a third. But then it quit. The boy came home one afternoon and found his last message (unread?) in her hand. The doll had run down. She was stopped, frozen, dead, caught in the middle of a motion. It was a most unnatural-looking position for her, her eyes on the floor, her neck in the process of a turn. Seeing it, he immediately understood the importance of a little-appreciated role and function of funeral directors, who have as their responsibility the final, strictly physical disposition of a human body: the adjusting of hands and feet, the closing of eyes, the stopping of life at a node.

The boy felt strongly that the doll shouldn't be left like this. Did they even notice, the man and woman? Why *didn't* they? Maybe they weren't really looking at her. He decided he would rewind her himself. He decided he would fix the problem.

It would be three days before he could do that, though. The man and woman were going to dinner at Commander's Palace on Saturday.

Afterward they were going to a party in the French Quarter. He would
have two full hours at least, maybe more, maybe considerably more.

(In the meantime, she sat there, gathering infinitesimal dust.)

Saturday evening he waited a full twenty minutes after they left. Then
he waited another ten in case they had forgotten something. Finally he
went into the parlor, locked the doors, closed the curtains, and opened
the box of tools. He saw the mahogany handle, the black velvet lining,
noted, in passing almost, that the top section of the box (where the images
of the tools were crushed) was somewhat thicker than it had to be. He
realized the velvet lining of the case might hold or conceal something,
might, in fact, fold down (*did* fold down, he discovered with the aid of a
bent paper clip). What he saw immediately inside was a certificate.

The certificate had a name, *Moriya*, printed in ornate black script at
the top. There was some more writing too, near that, in a smaller, different script: Austral Kraftwerk, Prague. Then there was a paragraph of
print and some handwritten specifications in an antique and purple-
looking ink in a series of printed blanks. The writing might have been
German, might have been Czech. He did not know. He had had two
years of Latin and now, of course, a smattering of French. But he had no
idea. Austral Kraftwerk, Prague. What he saw now was that the design
on the medallion on the doll's neck was the trademark for the company.
Not one word of the writing was meaningful to him. There was a serial
number and part of a decorative scroll around the edge of the certificate.
One of the bottom corners of the scroll had been torn off. He thought
there might once have been an engraved picture of the doll in that corner. If so, it had been torn off. Why had it been torn off?

The boy thought that there might have been such a picture because
there was something *else* engraved on the other corner, something totally
unexpected: the sofa! But of course! The sofa was part of the doll! Not
connected, obviously, but a platform for it, as it obviously had to be.

Probably the doll had to be placed at the end of it, at the far left end, too. There might be things inside it, magnets, for instance, that allowed the doll to orient herself. Who, then, in this family had known to put her there? Someone was not telling the whole truth here.

Well, well, well, he thought. So, then, the doll's name was Moriya.

"Moriya," he said, coming around in front and looking at her, touching her fingertips.

But she continued to look dead to him, distorted; and, of course, there was no movement of her eyes.

Still, the boy realized, it was very possible that only *he* knew the rest of the story. This doll had not been made in Switzerland; she had been made in Prague. His hands were slightly tremulous now as he began to undress her. He was worried, at first, about how to handle her arms; but her maroon velvet jacket unhooked in the back, came off immediately, he discovered. He unlaced the back of the dress, which also came apart easily. The dress had innumerable pleats and revealed underneath what he would have called a black corset, but which the woman, outside of the house now, would have known was a bustier. The boy saw that he didn't have to remove that. There was a hole in the fabric itself in the low back. As a precaution, though, before he inserted the crank, he moved the wheel in her neck to the "off" position. He inserted the short, stubby, but rather massive crank and began to turn it. He was expecting a heavy sound like click . . . click . . . click. What he heard instead had more of a roaring quality and feel. He wound it on and on, tighter and tighter: ten, twelve, fifteen, twenty, thirty, a total of forty times before the spring began to feel really tight to him. At the end he relaxed the crank very carefully to be sure the ratchet would hold. Then he turned the wheel in her neck and watched as she completed the turn she had begun days ago. She came to rest in a position he had seen many times before, her eyes slightly averted. Was she being shy? Flirtatious?

Disheveled now, her jacket down, her young back showing, what he saw was the breathtaking, incredible modeling of her scapulas and vertebrae. Her skin was not ceramic, but what was it? Ivory? Alabaster? It was something that looked like ivory to him. It was slightly warm-feeling. He saw the dark bustier, the stunning shoulder blades, the pleated cloth hanging off her right shoulder, and all of a sudden the temptation became too great for him.

He began to undo the front of her dress.

The little fabric-covered buttons were somewhat difficult to manip-ulate. He saw it would be rather easy to break one. The doll's breasts were not overly large. Her nipples were of a deeper hue than her lips. Her pigments were getting darker, it seemed, in the more caudal direc-tion (a word he would not have known but a principle he might have appreciated). What he noticed about the breasts was that they were not unfinished. The doll's breasts, like her back, were perfect; they were not just forms and armatures for fabric; they were meant to be seen. He began to see very clearly now; this doll was not designed around a dress. She was designed around a nude body.

The doll's nipples were of a rubbery material, darkly pink. Where the rubber came together centrally, it could be pulled and teased apart. It dawned on him that something might be hidden beneath the rubber. Screws, perhaps. This might be the way to take off the front of the doll.

The boy was well familiar with the deviousness of mechanical constructions. In disassembling such things as vacuum cleaners, ra-dios, televisions, and lawn mowers, he had learned long ago (virtually in kindergarten, in fact) that the innocent-looking moldings and chrome strips frequently hid the mounting attachments for a motor or chassis. This was wildly different, of course; yet, all things considered, it was right up his alley. He turned the doll off, ran to the kitchen, and got a flashlight. With the light, he looked carefully as he pried gently into the rubber nipples with the tip of the button hook. No, there were no screw heads. The holes went deeper, though, so maybe something else would fit. The Allen wrench, perhaps. It was possible that he was on the right track. Another thought, though, was beginning to bother him. Would a dress of this era normally lace in the back and *button* in front? He had no idea.

It seemed this doll's clothes were made to be taken off quickly.

Behind him, on the marble table, the clock continued to tick. The boy was taking rather more time with all of this than he realized. And now, in his rush to get the flashlight, he had left the door to the parlor unlocked.

He took the T-shaped Allen wrench out of the case and tried to insert it directly through the rubber in the right nipple. He was not successful. He met resistance immediately. Still, to be thorough, he tried it in the left as well. It went in. Not a little. It went in the full length of the shaft.

With one hand on her back and one hand on the T-shaped handle, he now had a decision to make: whether or not to turn the wrench. The doll's eyes were still averted. This could possibly cause her body to spring open. He might not be able to get her back together again. There was no clue as to what was going to happen. He waited several seconds, thinking, deliberating, resting his full palm flat against her bare back. Then the doll's eyes began to move. They moved upward a matter of millimeters and began to drift steadily to the right toward him. It was a move he had never seen her make before. Finally her eyes met his, not exactly but almost. He leaned down to intersect her gaze. It was impossible to believe she was not seeing him, talking to him, begging him silently. He took a quick breath and turned the handle clockwise. Nothing happened. Absolutely nothing. He met complete resistance. (Actually, he was almost relieved to find it.) Then (being very thorough again) he turned the handle the other way.

Something clunked deep within the interior of the doll. Deep within the doll, he heard something rather heavy-sounding move into another position.

The boy listened quickly, almost desperately, holding his ear to her bare shoulder. There was no change whatsoever in the noise (tic-tic-tic-tic-tic-tic-tic-tic-tic). Then again, maybe there *was*. Maybe the ticking was faster now.

The boy held the Allen wrench in his hand, waiting, but nothing happened. He sat down beside her; still nothing. He looked at the clock on the table. Fifteen minutes, he thought.

He waited beside her, the doll with her breasts bared, her black bustier open. She seemed to be looking toward but not directly at the clock. A woman ignoring you might look in such a direction. Suddenly the boy remembered the unlocked door. He jumped up, ran to lock it, sat down again.

He should be safe anyway, he thought, should have plenty of time. They should still be at Commander's Palace now. He should have plenty . . . hours, maybe. On the other hand, what if they dropped by *here* on the way to the Quarter.

Fifteen minutes, he thought.

But it didn't take that long.

After six minutes of ticking, the doll blinked. Actually, what the doll did was a good deal more than a blink; it was slower, and more prolonged:

She fully closed and opened her eyes.

Then she began to move her right hand. The doll moved her right hand forward and set it down rather firmly near the boy's knee and began to pull along his leg and thigh. She did not stop. She pulled steadily and directly into his crotch and stayed there for a long time. What she was doing now was evidently not unintentional. She was steadily moving her hand. The boy did not know whether to look at her or not. He could barely see her dark and tender lashes. Then he felt her hand on his shoulder. The doll had changed positions somewhat; she had put her gloved hand on his left shoulder and leaned into him. This was an entirely different, beseeching, sort of movement. In a human being you would say that what was wanted now was a kiss; the girl—or lady— wants a kiss. In a doll, of course, you could not say that—not accurately, that is. But the boy said it anyway. He kissed her. He kissed her on her mouth. The doll's mouth was not unpleasant-feeling. Her mouth was electrifying. She looked up, seemed to lock onto his eyes. He felt more and more pressure in her kiss, more and more and more of the pressure. Then he realized what was happening.

The doll was climbing on top of him. The boy fell the full length of the sofa, and her sudden, unexpected heaviness was upon him. Her dark hair fell completely over both of them. By helping her slightly he got her legs on the sofa too, and centered in his groin area. She was as heavy as a small sack of fertilizer. Altogether the sensation was unexpected, weird, and magical; she *felt* real. Not that he had ever felt a girl in this situation. But then again there was no object that had ever felt like *this*. Her balance was perfect. He had already been phenomenally, wildly turned on by the kiss alone. With this extra activity, he was reaching unprecedented heights (or lengths). But he didn't feel any receptacle for what had now grown between them. Steadily, powerfully, the doll began to grind against him. Her searching eyes locked firmly onto his. He felt desperately, but her groin was perfectly smooth. He inserted his hand down beneath her clothes to make absolutely sure. There was nothing. She continued to pin him with her mouth and grind against him. What must such a doll have *cost?* was almost his last thought before he exploded into his own underwear. She ground into him for another full minute, then stopped, leaving him with her weight and the warm, soapy stickiness.

Je t'aime, the boy said. J'ai la tête de la mécanique.

The doll's eyes remained closed, as though sleeping. The boy put his hand on the back of her head. He stayed on the sofa an additional ten minutes, feeling her satisfying weight, the slight vibration of her body, all fear of being discovered gone, the glass clock on the table steadily ticking, all centers of gravity in the room perfectly balanced now. The boy waited another five minutes, even afterward, vaguely curious, vaguely thinking something else might happen. But nothing did.

At last the boy sat up, then sat *her* up and turned her off. Her dress was still more or less in place. But he wanted to take a closer look at her groin area. There was nothing there, nothing. The area was perfectly smooth, sexless in a way, an ivory groin. No, wait a minute. There was *something*, but it was not a part of her. There was something *written*, embroidered in the cloth of her underpants (they didn't really look like panties to him, but it was the last garment before her bare body). The writing was in script in dark letters, a phrase in Latin: *Talis umbras mundum regnant.*

The boy smiled and said it aloud, musingly. So the sole use, thus far, in his life of two full years of Latin was to understand the message written on a doll's underpants. He began to put the doll back together. He checked carefully for stains. All was fine, perfect; no stains, nothing. Finally, with the Allen wrench, he set her back to the clockwise position, waited a moment, looking.

The doll suddenly opened her eyes.

He kissed her and turned off the light.

❧

Have you thought of a name for her?

No.

(This was three days later, in the parlor, where the boy was sitting after class, studying a list of verbs. The woman had come in to retrieve a pack of cigarettes from a carton.)

The boy was shocked at how quickly he had been able to lie, to think of all the unknowns and ramifications and know the name he now had for her, *her* name in fact, could never be said. It was one of those moments in life in which he knew for sure that he was developing the adult mind.

I think "the doll" is a perfectly fine name, he said, watching the woman.

The woman fished a pack of cigarettes from a carton. (Even *she* resembled the doll; could she possibly not *see* that?)

Who thought of putting her on the sofa? the boy said.

Oh? You think she looks good there?

Yes.

My husband.

⁂

Four times, and four times only, the boy and Moriya were able to inter-sect. During the last two, the boy was bare from the waist down and Moriya was almost perfectly nude. By diligently searching up and down Magazine Street, he had found a filling station with a condom machine in the restroom. He had bought several; they were a bit large, of course; still, they simplified certain worries—not so *much* of a problem, after all, for a fourteen-year-old, but enough for staining a sofa or a dress.

All through the days that followed, the boy had more energy than he had ever had in his life. He felt more *alive*. He would watch Moriya in the afternoon light, the saucy, impudent, perfectly beautiful face, the risqué and hungry mouth, cherish the memory and anticipation of her ivory groin grinding into his. In the actual sexual encounters, it helped to know, now, exactly what was going to happen, when her hand was going to move, when she was going to need assistance with her feet.

Since the boy now knew where Moriya was *really* from, he decided to try the trick of the dream again. It worked, too, this time, and magnifi-cently. (But once, and once only.) He sneaked a heavy volume of the en-cyclopedia to bed with him and read the entire article about Prague, twice through, completely, just before turning out the light. Sure enough, during the night she came to him. Or, more correctly, *he* went to her. He went to Prague. He and Moriya were suddenly walking across the Charles Bridge together. She was tracing the veins in his hand with her gloved hand.

Then they were in a café, each with a glass of wine.

I have a *secret*, she said.

(There was a light heaviness to her voice; it was precisely articulate, as though English were her third or fourth language.)

What? he said.

She was bubbling over with excitement.

But she would not tell him.

I know a *secret!* she said again, later. She came around the little table and sat on his lap, dangling her feet above the ceramic tiles. She pressed the tips of her fingers into his cheeks, head to head, nose to nose, her eyes locked onto his, to fix and center his vision. There was an incredible glow of energy around her. She leaned forward as though to whisper something, but licked his ear instead.

Interestingly, the boy's dream was not set in 1892, not in the era of gaslights and horses, the era of her construction, but in a strange and intermediate time. It would have had to have been somewhere in the 1930s, just before the Second World War. There were only a few cars, very dark, dusty. But what cars! What magnificent machines! He saw a fair number of Mercedes, a couple of Rolls-Royces (the great roadsters and dual-cowled phaetons), a Bugatti, an Invicta, a Hispano-Suiza. The cars were parked on the stone bridges, the stone streets, the horses clopping by them. The greatest cars of the twentieth century, covered with dust from the road.

It was a mechanically minded dream.

But four times, and four times only, the two of them had together. Not that that was absolutely all the possible chances. It was because on the last chance something disastrous happened.

The man and woman were going to another party (in Covington, this time, across Lake Pontchartrain and the causeway).

The boy knew he would have plenty of time.

Thirty minutes after they'd left, he had the doll perfectly nude. But with such a luxury of time, he began to look at her more carefully. On her flanks now, he saw several other places for the Allen wrench to insert, a total of six of them, between her arms and her waist. This had to be the way to get inside her. The boy's curiosity began to get the better of him. There was so much she could *do,* and he couldn't begin to imagine how. He simply had to *see* firsthand what was going on. He quickly removed six long machine screws with hexagonal insert heads and set them on the marbletopped table. He managed to get his fingernails into a seam in her back and then, with the smallest screwdriver, pry her alabaster skin up carefully, very carefully, so as not to crack it. He had to break a sort of suction. He could scarcely pull the skin off. This doll had probably not been opened in a hundred years. He saw some green felt, some brass gears, some shafting; then, suddenly, an incredible surprise: wires! Electrical wires! Yellow, cotton-covered wires! Bundles of them, everywhere, even attached to her back through a very odd-looking detachable connector. There was a flywheel between the doll's shoulder blades. It was not spinning, though, and would not spin even when he released the control in her neck. He suspected some chunks of unmachined metal that he saw near the flywheel might be magnets, and tested one of them with the blade of the screwdriver:

It was all he could do to pull it away again.

A magnet indeed, a very powerful magnet! What he was looking at was a dynamo. This doll generated her own electricity! There were several copper discs attached to the underside of her skin. He saw a number of others inside too, maybe an eighth of an inch thick, maybe thicker, and a couple of inches in diameter. For what? Capacitance effects? Probably not, at least not in this era. On the other hand, thermocouples were a definite possibility. Thermocouples were really old, he knew; he had seen a book from the 1880s that had them in it. Thermocouples would be sensitive to heat too, or to *changes* in heat. So she *could* know when and where she was being touched.

There was absolutely no dust, though. The doll's body might have been sealed yesterday. Only the dullness of the brass and some corrosion of the bearings revealed her true age. So moisture itself can enter, the boy thought (or perhaps it simply condensed inside her). He saw shafts with differential gearing and hard-rubber wheels pressing against discs to give integrals and derivatives of motion. Along her flanks and in the back side of her breasts there were areas where lead had been cast to give the proper weight distribution. All of this was so much more elaborate than he could have dreamed. There were banks of wire-wound resistors in what appeared to be a series of Wheatstone bridges, arranged, perhaps, in a sort of decision tree. (Wouldn't you need to *amplify* the current, though? Maybe not.) What must such a doll have *cost?* he thought. Her movements themselves were powered by the spring; but many of the decisions were evidently electromechanical. Not all of them, though, because he saw a cylindrical stack of metal discs with slots, like in a music box, tiny relays, strain gauges, electromagnetic clutches. The doll had to be pushing the absolute *limits* of the technology of the era. Still, the great majority of the time everything was evidently disengaged; she sat there ticking steadily, declutched and waiting.

(Tic-tic-tic-tic-tic-tic-tic-tic-tic.)

The boy sat the doll up and put her, very carefully now, in the counterclockwise position, since the motions were continuous there and he knew what they would be. The flywheel of the dynamo suddenly began to spin. He could slow it, stop it, though, by touching the escapement wheel. The escapement was finer-toothed than a clock's. Every time he put his finger down on the wheel, the doll's hand would stop. If he let it go, it would run. It would run, then stop, run, then stop. Tic-tic-tic-tic ... tic-tic ... He was watching the part of the movement where she would normally grab for his shoulder. But this time there was going to be no shoulder for her to grab. With his finger he had complete control of her: tic-tic-tic ... tic-tic ... tic-tic. She moved now an inch, now a quarter of an inch, now a matter of millimeters. Something seemed to have been filtered out of the movement, though. Something very real but difficult to describe. What? Well. *Something.* Passion, maybe. It seemed to be passion.

Was passion some function of time?

She would run, then stop, run, then stop: tic-tic-tic-tic ... tic-tic. Her movements had become somewhat jerky at this speed. The boy was

utterly fascinated. He found himself watching the tremor of her gloved hand. Had he inadvertently *aged* the doll? He touched her again and again, letting her move only incrementally. Tic . . . tic . . . tic . . . . tic . . . .
. . . . tic

At that moment the escapement wheel sheared off. It sheared completely off and dropped deep within the mechanism. What was left of the little shaft began to spin furiously. The gloved hand of the doll shot eight inches in less than a second. The boy's sense of panic could not have been greater had there been an artery spurting blood across the room. He quickly grabbed at the other control in her neck, stopped the motion, stopped the shaft, his heart pounding furiously.

Oh my God!

He couldn't get to the wheel. It had fallen deep inside. He could not reach it within the labyrinth of machinery. The boy tilted the doll, shook her a little, righted her. There was a tinkling springy noise as the wheel fell down and lodged somewhere near the bottom. It would take a major disassembly to get to it now and would do no good whatsoever since the shaft itself was broken.

There was absolutely no way to put the wheel back.

The boy stood there, terrified. In desperation, he tried inserting the wrench and turning her back to the clockwise position. He thought there possibly might be a second escapement for that position. (Just possibly.) At the same time, he knew in his heart that that would never be true. Absolutely knew, even before he turned the wrench. It was impossible. And yet there *was*. He heard it as soon as he released the control. There was indeed another escapement ticking more deeply inside her. He waited, sat her up, her back still open, waited, waited (tic-tic-tic). Suddenly she began to move. The normal position seemed to be OK. The boy held his ear close to her shoulder. (Tic-tic-tic-tic-tic-tic-tic.) The sound was exactly the same as always. The normal position was OK, or seemed to be. He began sealing her shut again.

After all, he thought, perhaps no one *knew* about the other position.

Working furiously, he began to put Moriya back together. The precision of this doll's construction was absolutely unbelievable. He had to wait to let air escape before the two halves would seal together. He was virtually spinning the Allen wrench now, his hands moving as accurately as a surgeon's. Soon there was no trace whatsoever of his entering, no felt showing, no misalignment. It was all snug, tight, perfect.

The boy began to dress her, then to lace up her bustier. He had a sense that his time was limited, that something *else* was about to go wrong. He laced up the back of her dress, missed one position and had to start again. The normal position was OK, he thought, and perhaps no one knew about the other. Or if they did, they might assume they had broken her themselves. He straightened her dress, began to hook her velvet jacket. Get her dressed! Get her *dressed! Hurry!* he thought. The normal position is OK, he told himself (or *was* telling himself) until a question brought him up short in his thoughts:

Exactly which position was normal?

He finished hooking up her velvet jacket and quickly turned out the light.

⁂

There had been absolutely no need to rush. It was several hours before the man and woman returned. Still, afterward, for three full days, the boy worried himself sick about the doll. Why? Because of the escapement wheel. How could he be sure it was completely out of the way? For all possible movements, that is. It might still strip a gear or cause something to short-circuit. The boy studiously avoided entering the parlor. He didn't want to be physically in the same room if something within Moriya began to grind and malfunction. Each day before class, he looked in to see whether or not she had moved. When he was home, he went past the parlor doorway, nervously, almost hourly. Had she changed position? Yes. No. Maybe. Yes. (Yes, indeed.) The doll seemed to be running perfectly. Still, he could not study for worrying. All he thought of in class now was Moriya, alone, in that parlor, initiating each perilous new motion. Three days, four days, five days, six. She should have gone through most of her program now. The man and woman would go into the parlor, leave it, notice nothing, say nothing. Mostly, though, Moriya sat there all alone. The boy would watch her from the hall. He too noticed absolutely nothing. Indeed, it seemed absolutely nothing had changed.

But in those days of worry and despair, he began to see the doll in a new light, as something of an agent, ambassador, and spy. What kind of reasoning had gone into her? What was she all about? Her design was more than clever; it was *demonic* in its brilliance, compulsive in its perfection; perhaps the work of some famously dirty-minded old clockmaker from the Austral Kraftwerk in Prague who had sent her into the world in search of fourteen-year-old boys. From this point of view, the boy saw that he had been set up, framed, completely. There was nothing necessarily gentle or bright here. What dark imperatives was this doll fulfilling? The boy could imagine a shop with lathes and drill presses, wires and electromagnets, petticoats and steel filings—pipes too, and cheese, micrometers, and tankards of beer. What was *he* thinking of (the clockmaker) when he had designed her? Was he dreaming of the sex himself? And if so, with whom? Was it *his* hand that found its way up your leg? After all, the message on the underwear was not from her but from the clockmaker: *Talis umbras mundum regnant.* That was a message from the clockmaker, wasn't it?

The feeling did not last long. Another feeling soon replaced it in the boy's heart. The new feeling was loneliness, a bottomless loneliness, the most abject loneliness imaginable. He went through a daily agony. It was as though *he* were broken, not she. He would stand at the door, watch her adjust her position, straighten her glove, scratch an invisible fly off a sleeve. She was trapped now. *He* was trapped without her. His misery and guilt became unbearable. After dinner one evening, he realized he simply had to go in to see her again. Cautious, shy, nervous, he tucked his shirttail in, actually checked his appearance in a mirror before he went through the door. He sat down on the opposite sofa with his French book as though nothing had happened. He waited there nervously. *Why* was he nervous? What was this, silliness? Superstition? She was a *toy*, wasn't she? At last the doll began to turn and look directly at him. He held his breath as her eyes met his. Then he saw her, truly saw her, for the first time in a week. Her face. He had forgotten it. He had *not* forgotten it. He had . . . He went numb inside.

He went.

Then she continued her turn beyond him, seemed at last to be looking at something out the door. She adjusted her glove, became motionless once more.

She did not move again for two hours.

She was trapped now. *He* was trapped without her. The doll did not look at him again. She seemed to avert her eyes.

The boy's dream of Prague came back to him. What secret could she have had? What could it have possibly been? That she loved him? That she was pregnant? What could it have been?

It was an agony to remember it. It was simply too painful to think about.

There was nothing now, nothing. The doll would adjust her gloves, straighten them, fold her hands, look up, look down, and just about break his heart.

I have insulted her, he thought, with these thoughts of a clockmaker. He had met *her* in Prague, or at least had met something that very much *seemed* to be her. They had talked. She had talked *to* him. *She* was not bound by those wires. There was something, a shadow of something, within her that got beyond everything, beyond the gears, the shafts, the magnets—an umbra, so to speak; *umbras*, the plural would be. Was that her secret? Was that what she had wanted and not wanted to tell him? *Talis umbras mundum regnant.* ("Such shadows rule the world.") He could not have had that dream without her.

Did she say she *knew* a secret or *had* a secret?

His memory of the dream was already fading.

And then his French course was over.

And then there was the afternoon he came to visit her for the last time. He felt the briefest flush of hope when he entered the room. Everything was not perfectly gloomy. What can be broken can be fixed, he thought. What can be broken can be fixed. There was a dimension to all of this he had to ignore, a reality, if you will. But a balance wheel can be reattached, a shaft can be machined, from scratch if necessary. Still, it would be too late for him. The normal, or maybe *not* the normal, part of the doll still worked perfectly. The other could be fixed. But not for him, never for him, fixed or not, *that* was gone forever. He would never be in this parlor again, never have another chance, never be on the sofa with this girl, never feel her pressure against him, never see her close her eyes like a kitten to sleep.

The dangling prisms weighed heavily on his soul. The doll sat on her sofa, perfectly motionless. He stood there, watching her, breathing mainly out of his mouth. "Je t'aime," he said quietly.

It had been impossible, over the days, not to see longing, then reproach, then anger in those eyes.

He would leave tomorrow. He told her that. (Out loud, in fact.) He waited, waited a long time. She did not move.

Je t'aime. I love you, he said again, finally.

The doll still did not move. She continued staring out the window. She did not believe him anymore.

The boy picked up some papers that he had left in the parlor and walked toward the front of the house. He heard, outside, in another world, another block, the shriek of some children. On the spur of the moment, he decided to go out onto the front porch. He saw the streetlamps, the live oaks, stood there quietly, glum and melancholy. There was a solid hedge of boxwood in front of him and to his right.

The loveliness of the afternoon was almost but not completely lost on him.

Did she say I have or I *know?* he thought.

Strange, in six weeks, he had scarcely been on this porch. He stood there patiently in the late-afternoon light, looking out at the enormous hedge. Whatever life held for him, whatever *waited* for him, lay beyond it now. There was an immense stillness, a perfect quietness to the tiny leaves. He had learned some French in this town, some other things. Well, it would pass. Time itself would pass.

Passion was some function of time.

THE PUPPETS

Jean-Christophe Duchon-Doris

Translated by Edward Gauvin

Dear Mistress Mine,

Do you remember?

I was, I believe, the first to see him, his naïve smile light on his lips as a bird perched on a laundry line, his features so fine he looked like a wax doll. He stood back from the crowd, the collar of his frock coat turned up, his beautiful white hands folded before him.

I saw him, his eyes half-closed, savoring the intense sweetness of that late October afternoon as he might a steaming, oversugared cup of tea brought close to his lips. His gaze played, delighted, over the fringe of red and gold gleaming through the foliage, dallied with the lightly dancing ribbons dangling from the nannies' hats—navy blue and crimson ribbons fluttering in the wind, shivering in the air. He relished—I could tell—the reverberating laughter of the children on the benches, their funny faces, the sudden jolting motions of their spring-loaded bodies, and just like me, he relished the soft, lazy smell of vanilla that set one purring.

He was daydreaming, Mistress, but evidently that wasn't why he'd come. What gave him away was the slight nervous quiver in his eyebrow whenever his gaze fell on our tiny theater. "Commedia dell'arte," he must have murmured as he read the gilded letters graven on the pediment of our proscenium. Did he deplore our Punchinello's over-exaggerated deformities—his extravagant hump, that breast-plate too tightly bowed over his belly, too glittery with false gold? Or was it our compeer Punch's impossible face, his malformed nose, his mocking mouth—in short, his troublemaker's manner—that upset the man? When the town constable made his entrance, our visitor quite clearly took the side of order against whimsy.

And so, once the curtain had fallen to applause, and the children, with their nannies, had deserted the benches, I was not surprised to see him reflexively turn down his frock coat collar and come sit mere inches from the stage.

I couldn't resist.

"Uh-oh!" said I, rushing out from behind the curtain. "Trouble's a-brewing!"

Another slight quiver of his brow tipped me off to his surprise. It was clear he wasn't expecting a puppet of my demeanor: beautifully colored eyes of pastel blue, a finely drawn pretty little face, a dress of white chiffon that left my arms and shoulders bare, and last but not least, my pride and joy, the bosom that earns me a few whistles every time I make an entrance.

"Can't you see the show's already over?" I emphasized my commoner's accent, that raucous voice I take from you, which—despite whatever notions my physique imposes—defends me from ridicule. "No doubt it's because you're a policeman. You lot are always so ill-informed."

He couldn't help but smile. Oh, Mistress, you can't know how much I savor such smiles when I bring them to men's mouths! Sincere smiles that escape them and give me, a wooden puppet, the fleeting illusion that I could be their beloved.

"Would you be so kind, Mademoiselle, as to tell Monsieur Lippi that Commissioner Costa would like a word with him?"

"Monsieur Lippi is a great artiste, and quite exhausted at the moment—" Before I could finish, he abruptly rose, rounded the proscenium, and swept the curtain curtly aside, exposing our undefended rear.

Old Lippi, busy putting away the props, briefly blocked his view of us. But Mistress, I saw the commissioner's gaze dive straight for me, stop at the right hand that donned me, then move slowly back up your arm.

Oh! how silly he looked, Mistress! The look of a child upset by the world's complications once you'd turned around and he realized you were every inch my replica. Together, we burst out in a great guffaw that scattered the birds. Judging by the exact spot where his gaze got bogged down, he seemed surprised to find your breasts no less brazen than my own.

"Dear Papa, I do believe Monsieur the Commissioner has just paid a handsome homage to your talents as a sculptor." And to highlight the resemblance, you brought me up beside your face.

"Mistress," said I, straightening up, "didn't I say Monsieur was rather fetching?"

"You're so right, darling Francesca," you replied, advancing on him while staring shamelessly into his eyes. "He's quite charming with his green eyes and little sideburns."

"And his little mustache, Mistress? Isn't his little mustache ravishing?"

"What do you want, sir?" Old Lippi asked. "We have permission from the Prefecture, and all our plays were vetted—"

The commissioner had to back up to answer your father. "Your puppet plays are precisely what I wished to speak with you about, Monsieur Lippi. I've received several reports from the Prefecture testifying to the fact that you rarely stick to the script, and that such strayings are sometimes disrespectful of the authorities."

We returned to the assault. "How well-spoken he is, Francesca!"

"Yes, Mistress, and his lips are so appetizing when they shape themselves around words!"

Old Lippi gave us a murderous glare, as if to flay us with a plane. How well he knew, poor old man—from having been led around by the hand all his life by the moppets he'd made—just what spectacles we could make.

"Please forgive her, Monsieur Commissioner. She has no manners. She was raised on the road with puppets as her only friends. How can you expect her to take anything seriously?"

"You're going to have to, Mademoiselle," the other man replied in his most serious voice. "I have strict orders. From now on you must keep a closer eye on your puppets' chatter."

What a funny man! You and I exchanged complicit smiles. I knew quite well what you had in mind, and when you put me away in my box, I made no protest; at most, I settled myself so that, with my head propped up, I could watch the rest of the scene. Quick as a falling curtain, you kissed him greedily on the mouth. No doubt fearing some perfidy, he made a valiant attempt to escape, to push you far away, but when he realized it was no mere stage kiss, his determination seemed to desert him. I watched him flap his arms a few more times for the sake of form, like a marionette with his strings cut, cast a worried glance at your father, and finally surrender completely to the warm, frolicsome insistence you pitted against him. A shiver even ran through Punchinello's hump.

"And have you, pet," you said greedily, "any strict orders about that?"

And you burst out in that laugh, that terrible laugh you sometimes lend me, which I send thundering out over the trestles of our little theatres.

How fetching he was, at a loss, trying comically to wipe his mouth with his sleeve, casting desperately about for some magic trick to reclaim his composure.

"I'll be back tomorrow," he finally said in a trembling voice. "Please be so kind as to have your scripts ready. If you wish to alter certain scenes, we can discuss it."

Poor little thing! That wasn't what he should have said. I wanted to whisper a few rejoinders to him from deep in my cardboard box, to warn him that not reacting more firmly to that kiss had left his authority rickety. But I kept quiet, Mistress, for I make it a point of honor never to speak without your permission.

He said no more, only stepped back with a sheepish air, almost smacking his head on the lamp and stumbling into our trunk. He managed to extricate himself at last. His beautiful green eyes seemed to crack like glass. He gave an awkward wave and then, to keep from turning his back to us, fled around the side of our little theatre.

I barely had time to leap out before the curtains and call to him. "Commissioner!"

He turned and saw me. I added, "My mistress was quite clear, Monsieur. You kiss very well. Come back whenever you want."

Do you remember, Mistress, how the next day a fine rain fell on Paris? We were both in our rooms on the Rue Traversine, saddened that rainy days forced our theatre to close. You were patching my dress, concentrating on the needle's *paso doble*. I was dreaming about the commissioner. I pictured him walking through the empty park, his frock coat collar turned up to keep icy water from running down his neck. The sand that Monsieur Alphand's road-menders spread along the paths must have stuck to the soles of his shoes. He too must have been sad, uncertain, seeing but not noticing the pretty ripples raindrops made in the ornamental ponds. I wondered if he knew our address, knew where the Rue Traversine was, if he'd ever before come to this neighborhood of Italian emigrants, rag and bone men, and Romagnols, made up of miserable alleyways—Rue Fresnel, Rue Saint-Victor, Rue du Bon-Puits, Rue d'Arras—that crews clearing the way for the Rue Monge were already laying low.

"Did you hear a knock, Francesca?" you asked me all of a sudden, rising.

It was him, looking like a bird fallen from its nest, sopping as soup-dipped bread, trying to hold his head stiffly enough to give off the look of authority his duties required.

When he saw it was just the two of us, he grew frightened and made as if to turn back.

"How nice of you to come, dear," you said mockingly, and I saw him shiver at the sound of our raucous accent, our greasy, almost oily voice.

You were wearing a dress that flattered your waist and underlined the triumphant beauty of your breasts. I have one just like it, and I know, from having seen the state it puts Punchinello in, how great its powers over men are. And when you went to put me in my box, how stunningly well you wore it, sticking your chest out, swaying your hips. Little chance now the fellow would leave.

"My father is away for a few hours."

"It doesn't matter," he said. "I'll come back."

But he didn't move.

"If you've come for the plays, you won't need him, my pet. There they are. I'm the one who writes them; Papa can't even read."

He took a step toward the pile of pamphlets, giving in to his desire to stay. His long white hand seized the first script and, since you were cleverly blocking the way to the room's only chair, and he wished to avoid all contact, he settled on the low bed with an indiscreet squeal of springs.

His beautiful green eyes flickered like candleflames, wavering between watching you and starting to read. He must have feared, for a moment, you might sit down beside him, then immediately regretted that you didn't, so ridiculous did he seem, his head no higher than your thighs, skimming the booklets too feverishly to truly seem interested in them.

Outside, it started raining even harder. Torrents of water hammering the tin roofs hid a quiet, almost mechanical background hum. And as you were both suddenly solemn, deeply focused, still—from time to time you merely brushed back an unruly lock of hair, while he, sparing with his motions, let his head sway to the ostensible rhythms of reading, turning the page only with infinite caution—you might have been mistaken for a pair of clockwork creatures. Stark light from the sky lit your faces, seeming to freeze time, while your springs ever so gently wound down like figures on a music box.

"Multiple complaints," he said, suddenly breaking the silence, "make mention of the fact that you've openly criticized the Prefect of the Seine's public works policy."

"What would you think of such a policy if it had hounded your theatre from the Boulevard du Temple and now threatened to expropriate you?" Your voice no longer held a trace of irony, and that intrigued him.

"It is not for me to judge."

"But surely, dear, you have your own opinion?"

"I obey. And the orders I received were to see that your puppets did not stray from the scripts approved by the Prefecture."

"I don't think you understand." You crossed to the dresser, plucked me from the depths of my box, and went back to him. You yourself seemed surprised by the heaviness in your every gesture. "Here—take Francesca and look at her. Is she a threat to the Empire?"

I shivered at the touch of his white hands.

"She's beautiful," he said. My rosewood must have blushed mahogany. "Astonishing how much she looks like you."

"Papa claims he made her first, and conceived me in her image only after. But look closely. Concentrate. At first, you'll see nothing but a bit of wood and cloth. Then, if your soul isn't dead yet, stifled under bundles of official bulletins, the doll will reveal itself to you, and you'll no doubt find it a pretty plaything."

"It's a very beautiful puppet."

You took me back and returned me to my box. My cheeks were flushed with pride.

"If you knew how to look, you'd see she's much more than that. She too has a soul, feelings, her own character. Plaything? I am every bit as much a plaything as she. Woman? She is every bit as much a woman as I. But I'm not sure you have the talent to lend puppets life."

You knelt before him, your great blue eyes staring deep into his, your bosom his entire horizon.

"But you do, my ... dear," said he, instantly regretting the liberty, "and so I must keep an even closer eye on them."

"How can you say such things with a straight face? Keeping an eye on puppets—doesn't that seem ridiculous to you? Besides, they do what they want, you know. You must give them their head."

"Come now, Mademoiselle—these are inert objects that belong to you. Keep them under control!"

"My pet, do you think we're always in control of what belongs to us? Would you like an example?" And so saying, you placed your hand resolutely at the exact spot where his trousers betrayed a pretty bulge.

He leapt backwards, but your blue eyes kept him firmly ensnared.

"Oh my!" you said, reaching out again, "I see the animal is himself the Prefect of the Seine's zealous servant ... better yet, a propaganda agent for the Grands Travaux!"

And since he didn't understand, you took pleasure in dexterously undoing his buttons and freeing one of the prettiest puppets I ever did see.

"*Oui, oui,*" you went on—I thought to hear the slightest tremble in your voice—"an excellent propaganda agent ... long as the Rue La Fayette, broad as the Rue de Rivoli, and finely adorned as the new opera house! Is it also pointless as the Parc Monceau and tedious as the new view leading to the Louvre?"

There was a moment of silence. You watched him, never breaking your smile, your hand flattering his firmness, your eyes seeking his. He was at a loss for what to do in his imprisonment, wavering between ridiculous flight and adventurous abandon. The downpour had stopped. A fine rain had begun to beat at the windows, and one could make out drops clinging to the panes, as curious as I was about what would happen next.

His puppet filled me with wonder. I found him madly charming, with his crimson pink head, that virility in full, unassuming flower, his air of Lamartine mixed with Saint-Just. And my resemblance to you gave me reason to believe the homage he paid you was meant for me as well.

"He's too darling! We'll call him Jack-a-dandy, shall we? Why, he's so quiet—is he shy? Perhaps he's embarrassed to be naked before us?" And, with your free hand, you took up the sewing kit you'd set aside when the commissioner arrived. Then, one after the next, you pulled out ribbons, gold braid, bits of silk trimming, and reveled in dressing up Jack-a-dandy, decking him out in diverse attire. From time to time, as much to rekindle the flame as to reward the submissive mannequin, you granted him furtive caresses that made my little wooden heart pound.

"That's enough!" Costa suddenly cried. His voice was hoarse and his tone firm.

Without taking his eyes from you, he seized you by your shoulders and laid you on the parquet, amidst the contents of your overturned sewing kit. You on the floor, and me in my box—now we were in the same position. And like you, passive and consenting, I waited, breathless, my eyes half-closed. Furiously, he rummaged through your drawers; he fumbled through your layers of lace. It was as if he were facing massive waves, battling frothing tides. But when Jack-a-dandy got too close, you sat up halfway and, seizing his hand, folding his last two fingers, so that only thumb, index, and middle finger remained upright, like a puppeteer, you whispered, indicating me with your chin: "I am as much a plaything as she . . ."

And as you hid your head in your arms, he abruptly understood, and brought his white hand to your proffered thighs as a swan might have brought his head. With the same delicacy, to make the illusion complete, he tugged your skirt back down over his forearm with his other hand.

Poor Jack-a-dandy was nodding sadly. I blew him a kiss and, since even voyeurs have their tact, I gave my box a little kick so the cover came down.

The rain, too, had stopped, demure.

It was several days before we saw the commissioner again. I found you dreamy, and wondered which, of the two of you, was the puppeteer and which the puppet. And then one morning, a policeman brought word. Costa had sent him.

Mademoiselle,

We have received other complaints, and I note with disappointment that you ever more openly defy the Empire's authority. I have been reprimanded for it. I am ordered to arrest the guilty parties, or else face the consequences for an irresoluteness incompatible with my profession. You know I have something of a weakness for you. But I am here to obey the orders of my superiors, hard as they may be to understand. For so many things escape us, so many tiny mechanisms have their part in the world's working smoothly, so many regulations are necessary to maintain its fragile balance. I am charged with seeing that a few of these are followed. I do not judge them; I only apply them. I beg of you—do not force my hand.

Commissioner Costa

The letter had you seeing red. We had to make reply. You managed to convince us easily, we puppets. And though Old Lippi was against it, as a former supporter of the *République* he had to give in to the majority: we had to push our provocation farther. The consequences weren't long in coming.

One fine morning, I saw him from behind my curtain again. He had quietly stationed himself and his men back from the audience, waiting for the show to end. He carried himself the same as that first day: his frock coat collar turned up, a smile riding lightly on his lips, his beautiful white hands folded before him. It was as if nothing had happened.

If, when he approached, I popped out as I'd done before, it was to prolong, just for a little while, the illusion that everything was starting all over again. He seemed relieved to see me; a great weight lifted from him, reassured, for my presence dispelled misunderstandings, testified to the fact that we knew (you first, with me at the end of your arm) that all this was but a play like any other, already written long ago.

"Bonjour, Monsieur Commissioner."

"Bonjour, Francesca."

"We were expecting you earlier. My mistress was at wit's end for ways to make you return."

"Here I am."

"How is Jack-a-dandy?"

I saw him go pale. But casting a glance at the constables, he saw they hadn't noticed, and realized they couldn't catch the reference.

"He's quite miserable," he said with a smile, "for he's no policeman and so couldn't care less about affairs of state. Come. Time to do our duty."

He signaled to his men to follow him, and rounded the proscenium. Old Lippi was waiting for him there, resigned, almost offering up his wrists. You hurriedly set me down on the sideboard next to Punchinello and stepped between them.

"So, my dear commissioner. Come to do your job?" Your aggressive tone caught him off guard, such a contrast was it with my own good humor.

"Mademoiselle, I've come to arrest those who attack the Empire. You hardly left me any choice."

"Indeed, you couldn't do otherwise. You're a policeman, and can't help it, darling. A puppet like Punchinello . . . you and he both, manipulated."

"True," he said, as calm as you were cross. "But as I believe you once told me, I, like Punchinello, while respecting my script and scrupulously executing my orders, am only doing exactly as I please."

He solemnly drew from his frock coat pocket a pair of handcuffs and, dangling them from two fingers over his head, shook them so they shimmered in the sun.

He stepped forward, and without abandoning his gravity, turned to us. "Monsieur Punchinello, Mademoiselle Francesca, you have slandered the Emperor, ridiculed his institutions, and in so doing, compromised the nation's greater interests. I am forced to arrest you. Please come with me, and don't put up a fight."

As we didn't move, he turned to his men. "Seize them!"

But since the constables hadn't understood, and made ready to arrest you and your father, he added in a peremptory tone that brooked no reply, "No, not them! The puppets!"

We let ourselves be taken away. Punchinello found the joke funny and as for me, Mistress, I was moved to tears, aware that this was my finest role, my finest hour—that at last we had dissolved into a single soul.

"As for you, Mademoiselle," he continued in the same curt tone, not a bit flustered by the beautiful smile you aimed at him, "I cannot recommend strongly enough that in the future you'd best choose your company more wisely. For now, leave this city at once, before my orders become more specific."

And without a care for the constables' whispers, he found the courage to turn his back on you and walk briskly off, holding us in his hands: Punchinello and me, each in the hoop of a handcuff.

Wherever you are, Mistress mine, do you remember it all? Do you remember your little Francesca? What is left of those days gone by?

Sometimes I see Commissioner Costa again. Maybe you know he left the police two years ago, dismissed after an arrest that didn't go the way his superiors would have liked.

We often speak of you. It must be said that my arrest had few consequences. They'd forgotten to build prisons for puppets, and so I was allowed to leave with Costa. I've lost track of Punchinello. The poor fellow's probably sleeping in some drawer back at headquarters. Lazy as he is, he must quite like it there; I'm sure one of these days some hand, seduced by that abominable mug, will take him from his hiding place. As you know, I myself wasn't always immune to his charms.

For now, I've set up home with Jack-a-dandy. He's a charming and very attentive boy. Every night I surround him with the softness of my dress, and we make love as best we can. Sometimes I wonder if it isn't you he's loving, through me.

What a frivolous letter this is! I'm writing you at your address on the Rue Traversine—naturally, without hope of ever reaching you, since that street vanished three months ago in the construction and clearing along the Rue Monge. It was Costa who insisted. He said that in a world of puppets, anything could happen. I believe that above all, the poor boy wanted this letter to prove that, contrary to what you might believe, he too can lend life to puppets, and as a result, make them speak.

As if I needed him . . .

Adieu, Mistress mine,

Francesca

OLD MRS. J

Yoko Ogawa

❦

My new apartment was in a building at the top of a hill. From my window, there was a wonderful view of the town spread out like a fan below and the sea beyond. An editor I knew had recommended the place.

The hill was planted with fruit: a few grapevines and some peach and loquat trees. The rest was all kiwis. The orchards belonged to my landlady, Mrs. J, but she was elderly and lived alone, and she apparently left the trees and vines to themselves. There was no sign of laborers working the orchard, and the hill was always quiet. Nevertheless, the trees were covered with beautiful fruit.

The kiwis in particular grew so thick that on moonlit nights when the wind was blowing, the whole hillside would tremble as though covered with a swarm of dark green bats. At times I found myself thinking they might fly away at any moment.

Then one day I realized that all the kiwis had disappeared from one section of the orchard, though I had seen no one picking them. After a few days the branches were again covered with tiny new fruit. Since I was in the habit of writing at night and sleeping until almost noon, it was possible I had simply missed the workers.

The building was three stories tall and U-shaped. In the center was a spacious garden, with a large eucalyptus tree for shade when the sun was too bright. Mrs. J grew tomatoes, carrots, eggplants, green beans, and peppers, which she shared with her favorite tenants, I assumed.

Her apartment was directly across the courtyard from mine. A single curtain hung in her window; the other was missing and she seemed to be in no hurry to replace it. Whenever I looked up from my desk, I would see that orphaned curtain.

From what I could tell, Mrs. J led a quiet, monotonous life. As I was getting up each day, I could see her through the window sitting down in front of her TV, wearily eating her lunch. If she happened to spill something, she would wipe it up with the tablecloth or her sleeve. After lunch, she would pass the time knitting or polishing pots or simply napping on the couch. And by the evening, when I was at last beginning to get down to work, I would see her changing into a worn-out nightgown and crawling into bed.

I wondered how old she was. Well past eighty, I imagined. She was unsteady on her feet and was constantly bumping into chairs or knocking over something on the table. In the garden, however, she was a different woman; she seemed years younger and much more at ease when she was watering or staking the plants, or plucking insects with her tweezers. The clicking of her shears as she harvested her crop echoed pleasantly through the courtyard.

A stray cat turned out to be the reason for my first gift of vegetables from Mrs. J.

"Nasty thing!" she screamed, brandishing a shovel. I spotted a cat slinking off toward the orchard. It looked nearly as old as Mrs. J and seemed to be suffering from a skin disease.

I opened the window and called out that she should spread pine needles around the beds, but in response she just turned and walked toward me, apparently still quite angry.

"I can't stand them!" she said. "They dig up the seeds I've just planted, leave their smelly mess in the garden, and then have the nerve to make that terrible racket."

"Pine needles around the beds would keep them away," I repeated.

"Why do you suppose they insist on coming here and ignore all the other yards? I'm allergic to the hair. It gives me sneezing fits."

"Cats hate prickly things," I persisted. "So pine needles—"

"Someone must be feeding them on the sly. If you see anyone leaving food out, would you mind telling them to stop?" As she made this last request, she came marching into my apartment through the kitchen door. Having finished her diatribe against cats, she looked around with poorly disguised curiosity, studying my desk and the cupboard and the glass figurines on the windowsill. "So, you're a 'writer,'" she said, as though she found the word difficult to pronounce.

"That's right."

"Nothing wrong with writing," she said. "It's nice and quiet. A sculptor used to live in this apartment. That was awful. I nearly went deaf from all the pounding." She tapped on her ear and then went over to the bookcase and began reading out titles as she traced the spines with her finger. Yet she got them all wrong—perhaps she was losing her eyesight, or simply did not know how to read.

Mrs. J was extremely slender. Her face was narrow and her chin long and pointed. She had a flat nose, and her eyes were set widely apart in a way that gave the middle of her face a strange blankness. When she spoke, her bones seemed to grind together with each word, and I feared that her dentures might drop out of her head.

"What did your husband do?" I asked.

"My husband? He was nothing but a lousy drunk. I've had to manage for myself, living off the rents from the building, and the money I earn giving massages." Bored with the bookcase, she next went to my word processor and tapped gingerly at a key or two, as though it were a dangerous object. "He gambled away everything I made and didn't even have the decency to die properly. He was drunk and went missing down at the beach."

"I'd love to get a massage when you have time," I said, eager to change the subject for fear she would go on forever about her husband. "I sit all day and my neck gets terribly stiff."

"Of course," she said. "Whenever you like. There's some strength left in these old hands." Then she cracked her knuckles so loudly I thought she might have broken her fingers. As she left, she gave me five peppers she had just picked from her garden.

⁂

When I got up the next day, the whole courtyard was covered with pine needles. They were scattered from the trunk of the eucalyptus to the storage shed—everywhere except in the vegetable beds themselves.

I overheard from my window one of the tenants ask about the needles, and Mrs. J explained that they were to keep the cats away. "Cats hate pine tar," she said. "My grandmother taught me that years ago when I was a girl." I wondered whether she had ever been a girl; somehow I felt she had been an old woman from the day she was born.

One evening, Mrs. J had a visitor—apparently a rare occasion. A large, middle-aged man appeared at her apartment. The moon, full and orange, lit up her window more brightly than ever. The man lay down on the bed, and she sat on top of him.

At first I thought she was strangling him. She appeared to have much greater strength than I had realized; she had pinned him down with her weight, and gripped the back of his neck with her powerful hands. It seemed as though he were withering away while she grew more powerful, wringing the life from his body.

The massage lasted quite a long time. The darkness between our two windows was filled with the smell of pine needles.

Mrs. J began to come to my apartment quite often. She would have a cup of tea and chatter on about something—the pain in her knee, the high price of gas, the terrible heat—and then go home again. In the interest of preserving good relations with my landlady, I did my best to be polite. And with each visit she brought more vegetables.

She also began receiving letters and packages for me when I was out.

"This came for you," she'd say, arriving at my door almost before I'd had time to put down my purse. Just as I could see everything that went on in her apartment, she missed nothing that happened in mine. "A delivery truck brought it this afternoon," she added.

"Thank you," I said. "It looks like a friend has sent me some scallops. If you like, I'll bring some over for you later."

"How kind of you! They're my favorite."

But I nearly became ill when I opened the package: the scallops were badly spoiled. The ice pack had long since melted, and they were quite warm. When I pried open a shell with a knife, the scallop and viscera poured out in a liquid mass.

I checked the packing slip and found that they had been sent more than two weeks earlier.

<hr />

"Look at this!" Mrs. J called as she came barging into my apartment one day.

"What is it?" I asked. I was in the kitchen making potato salad for dinner.

"A carrot," she said, holding it up with obvious pride.

"But what a strange shape," I said, pausing over the potatoes. It was indeed odd: a carrot in the shape of a hand.

It was plump, like a baby's hand, and perfectly formed: five fingers, with a thick thumb and a longer finger in the middle. The greens looked like a scrap of lace decorating the wrist.

"I'd like you to have it," Mrs. J said.

"Are you sure?" I said. "Something this rare?"

"Of course," she said, and put her lips close to my ear to whisper: "I've already found three of them. This one is for you. But don't mention it to anyone; some people might be jealous." I could feel her moist breath. "Is that potato salad?" she added. "Then my timing is perfect: a carrot is just the thing!" She laughed with delight.

I sensed the lingering warmth of the sun as I washed the flesh of the carrot. Scrubbing turned it bright red. I had no idea where to insert the knife, but I decided it would be best to begin by cutting off the five fingers. One by one, they rolled across the cutting board. That evening, my potato salad had bits of the pinkie and the index finger.

The next day, a strong wind blew all through the afternoon and deep into the night. Whirlwinds swept down the hillside and through the orchard. I could sense the trembling of the kiwis.

I was in the kitchen, reading over a manuscript I had recently completed. Whenever I finish a piece, I always read it aloud one last time. But that night I was probably reading to muffle the howl of wind blowing through the branches of the fruit trees.

When I looked up at the window over the sink, I caught sight of a figure in the orchard. Someone was running down the steep slope in the dark. I could see only the back, but I could tell that the person was carrying a large box. When the wind died for a moment, I could even hear the sound of footsteps on the grass. At the bottom of the hill, the figure emerged into the circle of light under a streetlamp and I could see that it was Mrs. J.

Her hair was standing on end. A towel she had tucked into her belt fluttered in the wind, threatening to blow away at any moment. The bottom of the carton she carried was bulging from the weight of its contents. The load was clearly too heavy for a woman of Mrs. J's size, but she seemed to manage it without much difficulty. Eyes front, back straight, she balanced the load with amazing skill—almost as if the box had become a part of her.

I went to the window and stared out. A stronger gust of wind blew through the trees and for a moment Mrs. J lost her footing, but she quickly recovered and moved on. The rustling of the kiwis grew louder.

Mrs. J went into the abandoned post office at the foot of the hill. I had passed it from time to time when I was out for a walk, but I had no idea what it was being used for now or that it belonged to my landlady.

When she finally came back to her apartment, the sea was beginning to brighten in the east. She got undressed with apparent relief, gargled, pulled a comb through her hair, and put on her old nightgown.

She was once again the Mrs. J I knew—the one who bumped into furniture on the way from the bathroom to her bed, who had trouble simply buttoning her dress. I returned to my reading, the manuscript damp now from the sweat on my palms.

Many more hand-shaped carrots appeared in the days that followed. Even after everyone in the building had received one, there were several left over. Some were long and slender, like the hands of a pianist; others were sturdier, like those of a lumberjack. There were all sorts: swollen hands, hairy hands, blotchy hands . . .

Mrs. J harvested them with great care, digging around each carrot and pulling gently on the top to extract it, as though the loss of a single finger would have been a great tragedy. Then she would brush away the soil and hold the carrot up in the sunlight to admire it.

"You're terribly stiff," Mrs. J said. I tried to reply, but she had me so completely in her grip that I could manage nothing more than a groan.

I lay down on the bed, as she had instructed, my face buried in a pil-

low, naked except for a towel around my waist. Then she climbed on my
back and pinned me down with tremendous force.

"You sit all day. It's not good for you." She jabbed her thumb into
the base of my neck, boring into the flesh. "Look here, it's knotted up
like a ball." I tried to move, to squirm free of the pain, but she had me
clamped down tight with her legs, completely immobilized.

Her fingers were cold and hard, and seemed to have no trace of skin
or flesh on them. It was as though she were massaging me with her
bones.

"We've got to get this loosened up," she said. The bed creaked and
the towel began to slide down my hips. Her dentures clattered. I was
afraid that if she went on much longer, her fingers would scrape away my
skin, rip my flesh, crush my bones. The pillow was damp with saliva,
and I wanted to scream.

"That's right. Stand just a little closer together. Now, big smile!"

The reporter's voice echoed through the courtyard as he focused his
camera. Perhaps he thought Mrs. J was hard of hearing. "Hold the carrot just a bit higher . . . by the greens so we can see all five fingers. That's
it, now don't move."

We were posing right in the middle of the vegetable bed, the reporter trampling on pine needles as he positioned himself for the shot.
The other tenants peered curiously from their windows.

I tried to smile, but I couldn't. It was all I could do to keep my eyes
open in the blinding sunlight. My mouth, my arms, my eyes—everything
seemed to be coming apart and I felt terribly awkward. And thanks to
the massage, I hurt all over.

"Pretend you're saying something to each other. Just relax . . . and
turn the carrot this way . . . It's all about the carrot!"

Mrs. J had done her best to dress up for the occasion. She had put
on lipstick and wrapped a scarf over her head. The hem of her dress

came almost to her ankles, and she wore a pair of old-fashioned high heels instead of her usual sandals.

But the scarf only emphasized her narrow face, the lipstick had smeared, and somehow her formal dress and heels seemed to clash with the carrots.

"Make us look good," she told the reporter. "In all my years, I've never once been in the newspaper." She let out a husky laugh, and her smile pinched up the wrinkles around her eyes.

The article ran in the regional section of the paper the next morning: CURIOUS CARROTS! HAND-SHAPED AND FRESH FROM GRANNY'S GARDEN!

Chest thrust forward to compensate for her slight frame, Mrs. J stood, listing a bit to the right as her high heel dug into the earth; and though she had laughed during much of the photo session, in the picture she looked almost frightened. But the carrot cradled in her hands was perfect.

I stood next to her, holding a carrot of my own. In the end, I had managed a smile of sorts, but my eyes looked off in a random direction and I was clearly tense and uncomfortable.

The carrots appeared even stranger in the photograph, like amputated hands with malignant tumors, dangling in front of us, still warm from the earth.

⁂

"Did you ever meet her husband?" the inspector asked. "No, I just moved into the building," I answered. "Did she tell you he was dead?" asked another officer.

"Yes, she said he had been drinking and had fallen into the sea and died . . . Or maybe she just said that he was missing. I don't really remember. We weren't really very close . . ."

I glanced out at the courtyard. Mrs. J's apartment was empty. The single curtain fluttered in the window.

"Any little detail could be helpful. Did you notice anything suspicious?" said a young policeman, bending down to meet my gaze. "Anything at all?"

"Suspicious?" I said. "Suspicious . . . Once, in the middle of the night, I saw someone running down through the orchard . . . carrying a heavy box. They took it into the post office, the abandoned one at the bottom of the hill."

❧

The post office was searched and found to contain a mountain of kiwis. But when the fruit was cleared out, it revealed only the mangy body of a cat. Then a backhoe was brought in to turn up the garden, releasing a suffocating odor of pine needles. The tenants at their windows covered their noses.

As the sun fell behind the trees in the orchard, the shovel uncovered a decomposing body in the vegetable patch. The autopsy confirmed that it was Mrs. J's husband and that he had been strangled. Traces of his blood were found on her nightgown.

The hands were missing from the corpse, and they never turned up, even after the whole garden had been searched.

WHITEWORK

Kate Bernheimer

—◆—

The cottage into which my companion had broken, rather than allow me, in my desperately wounded condition, to pass a night in the thick-wooded forest, was one of those miniaturized and hand-carved curiosities from the old German folktales that make people roll their eyes in scorn. This, despite the great popularity of a collection of German stories published the very same year of my birth! As to the justifiability of this scornful reaction: I cannot abide it, nor can I avoid it by altering the facts. This is where I found myself: in a fairy-tale cottage deep in the woods. And I had no use of my legs.

When we came upon the cottage we were certain, by its forlorn appearance, that it had long ago been abandoned to the wind and the night, and that we would be perfectly safe. Or rather, my dear companion was certain of this. As for me, I was certain of nothing—not even of my own name, which still eludes me.

There were but few details for my enfeebled mind to record, as if the cottage had been merely scribbled into existence by a dreamer's hand. Tiny pot holders hung from the wall in the kitchen, beside tiny dish towels embroidered with the days of the week. In each corner of each room was tucked an empty mousetrap—open and ready but lacking bait. At the entryway, on a rusted nail, hung a minuscule locket, along with a golden key. As to whether the locket ever was opened, and what it contained, I have conveniently misplaced any knowledge. About the key I will not presently speak.

My companion placed me onto a bed, though I would not know it was a trundle bed until morning. I had only vague notions as to how we had arrived at the cunningly thatched cottage, but I believe we had walked through the forest in search of safety. Perhaps we sought some gentle corner where we would not perish at the hands of those who pursued us. Or had we been banished, from a kingdom I no longer recall?

The room in which my companion put me to bed was the smallest and least furnished of all. It lay, strangely enough, down a long hallway and up a stairway—I say "strangely" because the house was so diminutive from outside. I realized, upon waking in the morning, that I lay in a turret. Yet from outside, no curved wall was visible. With its thatched roof the house had resembled a square Christmas package, a gift for a favorite stuffed rabbit—a perfect dollhouse of a cottage, the sort I had painstakingly, as a child, decorated with wallpaper, curtains, and beds.

Though there was scarcely any furniture in this turret room, the sparse pieces were exactly correct—nothing more, nothing less: the trundle bed, empty and open; and the walls bedecked with no other ornamentation or decoration save whitework, the same sampler embroidered with the same message over and over. It was embroidered in French, which I do not speak: *Hommage á Ma Marraine*. In the center of each piece of linen was sewn an image of a priest holding two blackbirds, one on each hand. The edges of all the whitework were tattered, and some even had holes. To these white-on-white sewings, my foggy mind immediately fastened, with an idiot's interest—so intently that when my dear companion came up to the turret with a hard roll and coffee for breakfast, I became very angry with him for interrupting my studies.

What I was able to discern, looking about me, while nibbling the roll after my companion had left, was that some of the whitework contained a single gold thread as the accent over the *a*. Why the gold thread was used, I had no idea, and in considering this detail, along with the remarkable fact that blackbirds had been so expertly depicted in white, I finally asked my companion to return to the room. I called him and called him before he returned—disconcertingly, for it seemed he had returned only by accident, to fetch my empty teacup—and when he took the cup from my hand he gazed into it for a very long time without speaking a word.

At last, he closed the shutters of the windows tight; which was my wish, as it allowed me to see the whitework more clearly: I find I see better in the dark. A candle in the shape of a bluebird sat on the floor beside the bed, and I lit it, and turned it just-so, toward the wall. Luminous! I felt I had not, in many years, experienced such nocturnal bliss—even though the broad daylight shone outside the curtained windows, at least a day as broad as a day may shine in a deep and thickly wooded forest where real and grave danger does lurk.

This activity transfixed me for hours upon hours and days upon days.

In time, my companion and I so well established ourselves in the cottage that soon we felt that we had lived there our entire lives. I presume we had *not* lived there our entire lives; yet of the event that drove us into the forest to the cottage I cannot speak, and not only because I cannot recall it. But I can tell you that we had so well established ourselves in this cottage that I was shocked one morning to discover, under my feather pillow, a miniature book that had not been there before. It proposed to criticize and describe the whitework on the walls.

Bound in black velvet, with a pink ribbon as a placeholder, the volume fit precisely in the palm of my hand, just as if it had been bound for me to hold there. Long—long I read, and devoutly, devotedly I gazed. Rapidly and gloriously the hours flew by and then the deep midnight came. (Not that I knew the day from night with the curtains so tightly drawn.) The bluebird was guttering—just a puddle of blue now, with yellow claws fashioned from pipe cleaners protruding from the edges of the blue puddle. I reached my hand out to try to build the wax once more into the form of a bird, but I achieved merely a shapeless mass of color. Regardless, the candlelight flamed up and shone more brightly than ever upon the black velvet book with onionskin pages.

In my zeal to illumine the onionskin, the better to learn about *Ma Marraine* and so on, I had, with the candle's light, also illumined the corners of the room, where sat the mousetraps. Yes, this turret had corners— quite a remarkable thing, as the room was a circle. If I failed to perceive the corners before, I cannot explain ... truly this architectural marvel of corners was a marvel inside a marvel, since even the turret itself was not visible from outside.

With the corners of the room thus illumined, I now saw very clearly in one corner, behind a mousetrap, a very small portrait of a young girl just ripening into womanhood. I don't know how that phrase comes to me—"ripening into womanhood"—for I would prefer simply to describe the portrait as a very small portrait of a young lady. But, to continue, I could not look at the painting for long. I found I had to close my eyes as soon as I saw the portrait—why, I have no idea, but it seems to be that my injury, rather than being limited to my crippled legs, had crept inward to my mind, which had become more ... impulsive or secretive, perhaps. I forced my eyes back on the portrait again.

It was nothing remarkable, more a vignette than an exposition. The girl was depicted from top to bottom, smudged here and there, fading into the background, reminiscent somehow of the *Kinder- und Hausmärchen* yes, you could describe her portrait as an illustration. She was a plain girl, not unlike me. Her eyes were sullen, her hair lank and unwashed, and even in the face and shoulders you could see she was undernourished—also not unlike me. (It is not my intention to plead my case to you or to anyone else, now or in the future; I merely note the resemblance.)

Something about the girl's portrait startled me back to life. I had not even realized what a stupor I'd lain in, there in the turret, but looking into her sullen eyes, I awoke. My awakening had nothing to do with the girl herself, I believe, but rather with the bizarre execution of this portrait, this tiny portrait—no bigger than that of a mouse, yet life-size. And it was painted entirely white upon white, just like the embroidery on the walls.

Though I felt more awake and alive than ever before, I found that I was also suddenly overcome with sadness. I don't know why, but I do know that when my companion brought me my nightly black coffee, I sent him away for a pitcher of blueberry wine. I asked for him also to bring me a pink-flowered teacup. My needs felt at once more urgent and delicate, and thankfully he was able to find articles in the cupboards that satisfied them.

For quite some time, drinking the wine, I gazed at the portrait of the sullen girl staring out of miniature eyes. At length, wholly unsatisfied with my inability to decipher the true secret of the portrait's effect (and apparently unaware that I very nearly was standing), I fell into the trundle. I turned my frustrated attentions back to the small book I had found under the pillow. Greedily, I turned its onionskin pages to the girl's portrait. "Flat, unadorned," the page read. The rest of the description was missing—everything except a peculiar exclamation for an encyclopedia to contain:

SHE WAS DEAD!

"And I died." Those are the words that came to my head. But I did not die then, nor did I many days and nights later, there in the forest, where I lived with my companion quite happily—not as husband and wife, yet neither as siblings: I cannot quite place the relation.

Soon, of course, I thought of nothing else but the girl in the painting. Nightly my companion brought me a teacup of blueberry wine, and nightly I drank it, asked for another, and wondered: *Who was she? Who am I?* I expected no answer—nay, nay, I did not wish for one either. For in my *wonder* I possessed complete satisfaction.

It was of no surprise to me, so accustomed to confusions, that one morning I awoke to find the painting vanished—and not only the painting but all the little priests with the little birds from the walls. No whitework, no turret, no companion. No blueberry wine. I found myself in a different small and dark room, again on a bed (not a trundle). An old woman and a doctor sat by my side.

"Poor dear," the old woman murmured. She added that I would do well to take courage. As you may imagine, the old woman and doctor were at once subjected to the greatest of my suspicions; and as I subjected them privately, I also protested publicly, for I knew I had done nothing to lose all I had learned to love there in that mysterious prison or home. No: I should have been very happy to be lame and blurred, to have my companion bring me teacups of wine at night, and in the morning my coffee and rolls. I never minded that the rolls were so tough to the bite that my teeth had become quite loose in their sockets, as loose as my brain or the bluebirds in the forest when their nests are looted by ravens.

Cheerfully, the doctor spoke over my protests. He said that my prognosis relied on one thing, and one thing alone: to eliminate every gloomy idea. He pointed toward a room I had not noticed before. "You have the key to the Library," he said. "Only be careful what you read."

STONE ANIMALS

Kelly Link

❧

Henry asked a question. He was joking.

"As a matter of fact," the real estate agent snapped, "it is."

It was not a question she had expected to be asked. She gave Henry a goofy, appeasing smile and yanked at the hem of the skirt of her pink linen suit, which seemed as if it might, at any moment, go rolling up her knees like a window shade. She was younger than Henry and sold houses that she couldn't afford to buy.

"It's reflected in the asking price, of course," she said. "Like you said."

Henry stared at her. She blushed.

"I've never seen anything," she said. "But there are stories. Not stories that I know. I just know there are stories. If you believe that sort of thing."

"I don't," Henry said. When he looked over to see if Catherine had heard, she had her head up the tiled fireplace, as if she were trying it on, to see whether it fit. Catherine was six months pregnant. Nothing fit her except for Henry's baseball caps, his sweatpants, his T-shirts. But she liked the fireplace.

Carleton was running up and down the staircase, slapping his heels down hard, keeping his head down and his hands folded around the banister. Carleton was serious about how he played. Tilly sat on the landing, reading a book, legs poking out through the railings. Whenever Carleton ran past, he thumped her on the head, but Tilly never said a word. Carleton would be sorry later and never even know why.

Catherine took her head out of the fireplace. "Guys," she said. "Carleton, Tilly. Slow down a minute and tell me what you think. Think King Spanky will be okay out here?"

"King Spanky is a cat, Mom," Tilly said. "Maybe we should get a dog, you know, to help protect us." She could tell by looking at her mother that they were going to move. She didn't know how she felt about this, except she had plans for the yard. A yard like that needed a dog.

"I don't like big dogs," said Carleton, six years old and small for his age. "I don't like this staircase. It's too big."

"Carleton," Henry said. "Come here. I need a hug."

Carleton came down the stairs. He lay down on his stomach on the floor and rolled, noisily, floppily, slowly, over to where Henry stood with the real estate agent. He curled like a dead snake around Henry's ankles. "I don't like those dogs outside," he said.

"I know it looks like we're out in the middle of nothing, but if you go down through the backyard, cut through that stand of trees, there's this little path. It takes you straight down to the train station. Ten-minute bike ride," the agent said. Nobody ever remembered her name, which was why she had to wear too-tight skirts. She was, as it happened, writing a romance novel, and she spent a lot of time making up pseudonyms, just in case she ever finished it. Ophelia Pink. Matilde Hightower. LaLa Treeble. Or maybe she'd write gothics. Ghost stories. But not about people like these. "Another ten minutes on that path and you're in town."

"What dogs, Carleton?" Henry said.

"I think they're lions, Carleton," said Catherine. "You mean the stone ones beside the door? Just like the lions at the library. You love those lions, Carleton. Patience and Fortitude?"

"I've always thought they were rabbits," the real estate agent said. "You know, because of the ears. They have big ears." She flopped her hands and then tugged at her skirt, which would not stay down. "I think they're pretty valuable. The guy who built the house had a gallery in New York. He knew a lot of sculptors."

Henry was struck by that. He didn't think he knew a single sculptor.

"I don't like the rabbits," Carleton said. "I don't like the staircase. I don't like this room. It's too big. I don't like *her*."

"Carleton," Henry said. He smiled at the real estate agent.

"I don't like the house," Carleton said, clinging to Henry's ankles. "I don't like houses. I don't want to live in a house."

"Then we'll build you a tepee out on the lawn," Catherine said. She sat on the stairs beside Tilly, who shifted her weight, almost imperceptibly, toward Catherine. Catherine sat as still as possible. Tilly was in fourth grade and difficult in a way that girls weren't supposed to be. Mostly she refused to be cuddled or babied. But she sat there, leaning on Catherine's arm, emanating saintly fragrances: peacefulness, placidness, goodness. *I want this house*, Catherine said, moving her lips like a silent-movie heroine, to Henry, so that neither Carleton nor the agent, who had bent over to inspect a piece of dust on the floor, could see. "You can live in your tepee, and we'll invite you to come over for lunch. You like lunch, don't you? Peanut butter sandwiches?"

"I don't," Carleton said, and sobbed once.

But they bought the house anyway. The real estate agent got her commission. Tilly rubbed the waxy stone ears of the rabbits on the way out, pretending that they already belonged to her. They were as tall as she was, but that wouldn't always be true. Carleton had a peanut butter sandwich.

The rabbits sat on either side of the front door. Two stone animals sitting on cracked, mossy haunches. They were shapeless, lumpish, patient in a way that seemed not worn down, but perhaps never really finished in the first place. There was something about them that reminded Henry of Stonehenge. Catherine thought of topiary shapes, *The Velveteen Rabbit*, soldiers who stand guard in front of palaces and never even twitch their noses. Maybe they could be donated to a museum. Or broken up with jackhammers. They didn't suit the house at all.

"So what's the house like?" said Henry's boss. She was carefully stretching rubber bands around her rubber-band ball. By now the rubber-band ball was so big, she had to get special extra-large rubber bands from the art department. She claimed it helped her think. She had tried knitting for a while, but it turned out that knitting was too utilitarian, too feminine. Making an enormous ball out of rubber bands struck the right note. It was something a man might do.

It took up half of her desk. Under the fluorescent office lights it had a peeled red liveliness. You almost expected it to shoot forward and out the door. The larger it got, the more it looked like some kind of eyeless, hairless, legless animal. Maybe a dog. A Carleton-sized dog, Henry thought, although not a Carleton-sized rubberband ball.

Catherine joked sometimes about using the carleton as a measure of unit.

"Big," Henry said. "Haunted."

"Really?" his boss said. "So's this rubber band." She aimed a rubber band at Henry and shot him in the elbow. This was meant to suggest that she and Henry were good friends and just goofing around, the way good friends did. But what it really meant was that she was angry at him. "Don't leave me," she said.

"I'm only two hours away." Henry put up his hand to ward off rubber bands. "Quit it. We talk on the phone, we use e-mail. I come back to town when you need me in the office."

'You're sure this is a good idea?" his boss said. She fixed her reptilian, watery gaze on him. She had problematical tear ducts. Though she could have had a minor surgical procedure to fix this, she'd chosen not to. It was a tactical advantage, the way it spooked people.

It didn't really matter that Henry remained immune to rubber bands and crocodile tears. She had backup strategies. She thought about which would be most effective while Henry pitched his stupid idea all over again.

Henry had the movers' phone number in his pocket, like a talisman. He wanted to take it out, wave it at the Crocodile, say, Look at this! Instead he said, "For nine years, we've lived in an apartment next door to a building that smells like urine. Like someone built an entire building out of bricks made of compressed red pee. Someone spit on Catherine in the street last week. This old Russian lady in a fur coat. A kid rang our doorbell the other day and tried to sell us gas masks. Door-to-door gasmask salesman. Catherine bought one. When she told me about it she burst into tears. She said she couldn't figure out if she was feeling guilty because she'd bought a gas mask, or if it was because she hadn't bought enough for everyone."

"Good Chinese food," his boss said. "Good movies. Good bookstores. Good dry cleaners. Good conversation."

"Tree houses," Henry said. "I had a tree house when I was a kid."

"You were never a kid," his boss said.

"Three bathrooms. Crown moldings. We can't even see our nearest neighbor's house. I get up in the morning, have coffee, put Carleton and Tilly on the bus, and go to work in my pajamas."

"What about Catherine?" The Crocodile put her head down on her rubber-band ball. Possibly this was a gesture of defeat.

"There was that thing. Catherine's whole department is leaving. Like rats deserting a sinking ship. Anyway, Catherine needs a change. And so do I," Henry said. "We've got another kid on the way. We're going to garden. Catherine'll teach ESL, find a book group, write her book. Teach the kids how to play bridge. You've got to start them early."

He picked a rubber band off the floor and offered it to his boss. "You should come out and visit some weekend."

"I never go upstate," the Crocodile said. She held on to her rubber-band ball. "Too many ghosts."

***

"Are you going to miss this? Living here?" Catherine said. She couldn't stand the way her stomach poked out. She couldn't see past it. She held up her left foot to make sure it was still there and pulled the sheet off Henry.

"I love the house," Henry said.

"Me too," Catherine said. She was biting her fingernails. Henry could hear her teeth going click, click. Now she had both feet up in the air. She wiggled them around. Hello, feet.

"What are you doing?"

She put them down again. On the street outside, cars came and went, pushing smears of light along the ceiling, slow and fast at the same time. The baby was wriggling around inside her, kicking out with both feet like it was swimming across the English Channel, the Pacific. Kicking all the way to China. "Did you buy that story about the former owners moving to France?"

"I don't believe in France," Henry said. *"Je ne crois pas en France."*

"Neither do I," Catherine said. "Henry?"

"What?"

"Do you love the house?"

"I love the house."

"I love it more than you do," Catherine said, although Henry hated it when she said things like that. "What do you love best?"

"That room in the front," Henry said. "With the windows. Our bedroom. Those weird rabbit statues."

"Me too," Catherine said, although she didn't. "I love those rabbits."

Then she said, "Do you ever worry about Carleton and Tilly?"

"What do you mean?" Henry said. He looked at the alarm clock: it was 4:00 A.M. "Why are we awake right now?"

"Sometimes I worry that I love one of them better," Catherine said. "Like I might love Tilly better. Because she used to wet the bed. Because she's always so angry. Or Carleton, because he was so sick when he was little."

"I love them both the same," Henry said.

He didn't even know he was lying. Catherine knew, though. She knew he was lying, and she knew he didn't even know it. Most of the time she thought that it was okay. As long as he thought he loved them both the same and acted as if he did, that was good enough.

"Well, do you ever worry that you love them more than me?" she said. "Or that I love them more than I love you?"

"Do you?" Henry said.

"Of course," Catherine said. "I have to. It's my job."

⚭

She found the gas mask in a box of wineglasses, and also six recent issues of *The New Yorker*, which she still might get a chance to read someday. She put the gas mask under the sink and the *New Yorkers* in the sink. Why not? It was her sink. She could put anything she wanted into it. She took the magazines out again and put them into the refrigerator, just for fun.

Henry came into the kitchen, holding silver candlesticks and a stuffed armadillo, which someone had made into a purse. It had a shoulder strap made out of its own skin. You opened its mouth and put things inside it, lipstick and subway tokens. It had pink gimlet eyes and smelled strongly of vinegar. It belonged to Tilly, although how it had come into her possession was unclear. Tilly claimed she'd won it at school in a contest involving doughnuts. Catherine thought it more likely Tilly had either stolen it or (slightly preferable) found it in someone's trash. Now Tilly kept her most valuable belongings inside the purse to keep them safe from Carleton, who was covetous of the previous things—because they were small and because they belonged to Tilly—but afraid of the armadillo.

"I've already told her she can't take it to school for at least the first two weeks. Then we'll see." She took the purse from Henry and put it under the sink with the gas mask.

"What are they doing?" Henry said. Framed in the kitchen window, Carleton and Tilly hunched over the lawn. They had a pair of scissors and a notebook and a stapler.

"They're collecting grass." Catherine took dishes out of a box, put the bubble wrap aside for Tilly to stomp, and stowed the dishes in a cabinet. The baby kicked like it knew all about bubble wrap. "Whoa, Fireplace," she said. "We don't have a dancing license in there."

Henry put out his hand, rapped on Catherine's stomach. *Knock, knock.* It was Tilly's joke. Catherine would say, "Who's there?" and Tilly would say, "Candlestick's here." "Fat Man's here." Box. Hammer. Milkshake. Clarinet. Mousetrap. Fiddlestick. Tilly had a whole list of names for the baby. The real estate agent would have approved.

"Where's King Spanky?" Henry said.

"Under our bed," Catherine said. "He's up in the box frame."

"Have we unpacked the alarm clock?" Henry said.

"Poor King Spanky," Catherine said. "Nobody to love except an alarm clock. Come upstairs and let's see if we can shake him out of the bed. I've got a present for you."

The present was in a U-Haul box exactly like all the other boxes in the bedroom, except that Catherine had written HENRY'S PRESENT on it instead of LARGE FRONT BEDROOM. Inside the box were Styrofoam peanuts and then a smaller box from Takashimaya. The

Takashimaya box was fastened with a silver ribbon. The tissue paper inside was dull gold, and inside the tissue paper was a green silk robe with orange sleeves and heraldic animals in orange and gold thread.

"Lions," Henry said.

"Rabbits," Catherine said.

"I didn't get you anything," Henry said.

Catherine smiled nobly. She liked giving presents better than getting presents. She'd never told Henry because it seemed to her that it must be selfish in some way she'd never bothered to figure out. Catherine was grateful to be married to Henry, who accepted all presents as his due; who looked good in the clothes she bought him; who was vain, in an easygoing way, about his good looks. Buying clothes for Henry was especially satisfying now, while she was pregnant and couldn't buy them for herself.

She said, "If you don't like it, then I'll keep it. Look at you, look at those sleeves. You look like the emperor of Japan."

They had already colonized the bedroom, making it full of things that belonged to them. There was Catherine's mirror on the wall, and their mahogany wardrobe, their first real piece of furniture, a wedding present from Catherine's great-aunt. There was their serviceable queen-size bed with King Spanky lodged up inside it, and there was Henry, spinning his arms in the wide orange sleeves, like an embroidered windmill. Henry could see all of these things in the mirror, and behind him, their lawn and Tilly and Carleton, stapling grass into their notebook. He saw all of these things and he found them good. But he couldn't see Catherine. When he turned around, she stood in the doorway, frowning at him. She had the alarm clock in her hand.

"Look at you," she said again. It worried her, the way something, someone, *Henry*, could suddenly look like a place she'd never been before. The alarm began to ring and King Spanky came out from under the bed, trotting over to Catherine. She bent over, awkwardly—ungraceful, ungainly, so clumsy, so fucking awkward; being pregnant was like wearing a fucking suitcase strapped across your middle—put the alarm clock down on the ground, and King Spanky hunkered down in front of it, his nose against the ringing glass face. And that made her laugh again. Henry loved Catherine's laugh. Downstairs, their children slammed a door open, ran through the house, carrying scissors, both Catherine and Henry knew, and slammed another door open and were outside again, leaving behind the smell of grass. There was a store in New York where you could buy a perfume that smelled like that.

Catherine and Carleton and Tilly came back from the grocery store with a tire, a rope to hang it from, and a box of pancake mix for dinner. Henry was online, looking at a JPEG of a rubber-band ball. There was a message, too. The Crocodile needed him to come into the office. It would be just a few days. Someone was setting fires, and there was no one smart enough to see how to put them out except for him. They were his accounts. He had to come in and save them. She knew Catherine and Henry's apartment hadn't sold; she'd checked with their listing agent. So surely it wouldn't be impossible, not impossible, only inconvenient.

He went downstairs to tell Catherine. "That *witch*," she said, and then bit her lip. "She called the listing agent? I'm sorry. We talked about this. Never mind. Just give me a moment."

Catherine inhaled. Exhaled. Inhaled. If she were Carleton, she would hold her breath until her face turned red and Henry agreed to stay home, but then again, it never worked for Carleton. "We ran into our new neighbors in the grocery store. She's about the same age as me. Liz and Marcus. One kid, older, a girl, um, I think her name was Alison, maybe from a first marriage—potential babysitter, which is really good news. Liz is a lawyer. Gorgeous. Reads Oprah books. He likes to cook."

"So do I," Henry said.

"You're better looking," Catherine said. "So do you have to go back tonight, or can you take the train in the morning?"

"The morning is fine," Henry said, wanting to seem agreeable. Carleton appeared in the kitchen, his arms pinned around King Spanky's middle. The cat's front legs stuck straight out, as if Carleton were dowsing. King Spanky's eyes were closed. His whiskers twitched Morse code. "What are you wearing?" Carleton said.

"My new uniform," Henry said. "I wear it to work."

"Where do you work?" Carleton said, testing.

"I work at home," Henry said. Catherine snorted.

"He looks like the king of rabbits, doesn't he? The emperor of Rabbitaly," she said, no longer sounding particularly pleased about this.

"He looks like a princess," Carleton said, now pointing King Spanky at Henry like a gun.

"Where's your grass collection?" Henry said. "Can I see it?"

"No," Carleton said. He put King Spanky on the floor, and the cat slunk out of the kitchen, heading for the staircase, the bedroom, the safety of the bedsprings, the beloved alarm clock, the beloved. The beloved may be treacherous, greasy-headed, and given to evil habits, or else it can be a man in his late forties who works too much, or it can be an alarm clock.

"After dinner," Henry said, trying again, "we could go out and find a tree for your tire swing."

"No," Carleton said regretfully. He lingered in the kitchen, hoping to be asked a question to which he could say yes.

"Where's your sister?" Henry said.

"Watching television," Carleton said. "I don't like the television here."

"It's too big," Henry said, but Catherine didn't laugh.

<hr />

Henry dreams he is the king of the real estate agents. Henry loves his job. He tries to sell a house to a young couple with twitchy noses and big dark eyes. Why does he always dream that he's trying to sell things?

The couple stare at him nervously. He leans toward them as if he's going to whisper something in their silly, expectant ears. It's a secret he's never told anyone before. It's a secret he didn't even know that he knew. "Let's stop fooling," he says. "You can't afford to buy this house. You don't have any money. You're rabbits."

⚮

"Where do you work?" Carleton said in the morning when Henry called from Grand Central.

"I work at home," Henry said. "Home where we live now, where you are. Eventually. Just not today. Are you getting ready for school?"

Carleton put the phone down. Henry could hear him saying something to Catherine. "He says he's not nervous about school," she said. "He's a brave kid."

"I kissed you this morning," Henry said, "but you didn't wake up. There were all these rabbits on the lawn. They were huge. King Spanky—sized. They were just sitting there like they were waiting for the sun to come up. It was funny, like some kind of art installation. But it was kind of creepy, too. Think they'd been there all night?"

"Rabbits? Can they have rabies? I saw them this morning when I got up," Catherine said. "Carleton didn't want to brush his teeth this morning. He says something's wrong with his toothbrush."

"Maybe he dropped it in the toilet, and he doesn't want to tell you," Henry said.

"Maybe you could buy a new toothbrush and bring it home," Catherine said. "He doesn't want one from the drugstore here. He wants one from New York."

"Where's Tilly?" Henry said.

"She says she's trying to figure out what's wrong with Carleton's toothbrush. She's still in the bathroom," Catherine said.

"Can I talk to her for a second?" Henry said.

"Tell her she needs to get dressed and eat her Cheerios," Catherine said. "After I drive them to school, Liz is coming over for coffee. Then

Kelly Link

388

we're going to go out for lunch. I'm not unpacking another box until you get home. Here's Tilly."

"Hi," Tilly said. She sounded as if she was asking a question.

Tilly never liked talking to people on the telephone. How were you supposed to know if they were really who they said they were? And even if they were who they claimed to be, they didn't know whether you were who you said you were. You could be someone else. They might give away information about you and not even know it. There were no protocols. No precautions.

She said, "Did you brush your teeth this morning?"

"Good morning, Tilly," her father (if it was her father) said. "My toothbrush was fine. Perfectly normal."

"That's good," Tilly said. "I let Carleton use mine."

"That was very generous," Henry said.

"No problem," Tilly said. Sharing things with Carleton wasn't like having to share things with other people. It wasn't really like sharing things at all. Carleton belonged to her, like the toothbrush. "Mom says that when we get home today, we can draw on the walls in our rooms if we want to, while we decide what color we want to paint them."

"Sounds like fun," Henry said. "Can I draw on them, too?"

"Maybe," Tilly said. She had already said too much. "Gotta go. Gotta eat breakfast."

"Don't be worried about school," Henry said.

"I'm not worried about school," Tilly said.

"I love you," Henry said.

"I'm real concerned about this toothbrush," Tilly said.

He closed his eyes only for a minute. Just for a minute. When he woke up, it was dark and he didn't know where he was. He stood up and went over to the door, almost tripping over something. It sailed away from him in an exuberant, rollicking sweep.

According to the clock on his desk, it was 4:00 A.M. Why was it always 4:00 A.M.? There were four messages on his cell phone, all from Catherine.

He went online and checked train schedules. Then he sent Catherine a fast e-mail:

Fell asleep @ midnight? Missed trains. Awake now, going to keep on working. Pttng out fires. Take the train home early afternoon? Still lv me?

Before he went back to work, he kicked the rubber-band ball back down the hall toward the Crocodile's door.

Catherine called him at 8:45.

"I'm sorry," Henry said.

"I bet you are," Catherine said.

"I can't find my razor. I think the Crocodile had some kind of tantrum and tossed my stuff."

"Carleton will love that," Catherine said. "Maybe you should sneak in the house and shave before dinner. He had a hard day at school yesterday."

"Maybe I should grow a beard," Henry said. "He can't be afraid of everything all the time. Tell me about the first day of school."

'We'll talk about it later," Catherine said. "Liz just drove up. I'm going to be her guest at the gym. Just make it home for dinner."

At 6:00 P.M. Henry e-mailed Catherine again. "Srry. Accidentally started avalanche while putting out fires. Wait up for me? How ws 2nd day of school?" She didn't write him back. He called and no one picked up the phone. She didn't call.

He took the last train home. By the time they reached the station, he was the only one left in his car. He unchained his bicycle and rode it home in the dark. Rabbits pelted across the footpath in front of his bike. There were rabbits foraging on his lawn. They froze as he dismounted and pushed the bicycle across the grass. The lawn was rumpled; the bike went up and down over invisible depressions that he supposed were rabbit holes. There were two short, fat men standing in the dark on either side of the front door, waiting for him, but when he came closer, he remembered that they were stone rabbits. "Knock, knock," he said.

The real rabbits on the lawn tipped their ears at him. The stone rabbits waited for the punch line, but they were just stone rabbits. They had nothing better to do.

The front door wasn't locked. He walked through the downstairs rooms, putting his hands on the backs and tops of furniture. In the kitchen, cut-down boxes leaned in stacks against the wall, waiting to be recycled or remade into cardboard houses and spaceships and tunnels for Carleton and Tilly.

Catherine had unpacked Carleton's room. Night-lights in the shapes of bears and geese and cats were plugged into every floor outlet. There were little low-watt table lamps as well—hippo, robot, gorilla, pirate ship. Everything was soaked in a tender, peaceable light, translating Carleton's room into something more than a bedroom: something luminous, numinous, a cartoony midnight church of sleep.

Tilly was sleeping in the other bed.

Tilly would never admit that she sleepwalked, the same way that she would never admit that she sometimes still wet the bed. But she refused to make friends. Making friends would have meant spending the night in strange houses. Tomorrow morning she would insist that Henry or Catherine must have carried her from her room, put her to bed in Carleton's room for reasons of their own.

Henry knelt down between the two beds and kissed Carleton on the forehead. He kissed Tilly, smoothed her hair. How could he not love Tilly better? He'd known her longer. She was so brave, so angry.

On the walls of Carleton's bedroom, Henry's children had drawn a house. A cat nearly as big as the house. There was a crown on the cat's head. Trees or flowers with pairs of leaves that pointed straight up, still bigger, and a stick figure on a stick bicycle, riding past the trees. When he looked closer, he thought that maybe the trees were actually rabbits. The wall smelled like Froot Loops. Someone had written HENRY is A RAT FINK! HA HA! He recognized his wife's handwriting.

"Scented markers," Catherine said. She stood in the door, holding a pillow against her stomach. "I was sleeping downstairs on the sofa. You walked right past and didn't see me."

"The front door was unlocked," Henry said.

"Liz says nobody ever locks their doors out here," Catherine said. "Are you coming to bed, or were you just stopping by to see how we were?"

"I have to go back in tomorrow," Henry said. He pulled a tooth-brush out of his pocket and showed it to her. "There's a box of Krispy Kreme doughnuts on the kitchen counter."

"Delete the doughnuts," Catherine said. "I'm not that easy." She took a step toward him and accidentally kicked King Spanky. The cat yowled. Carleton woke up. He said, "Who's there? Who's there?"

"It's me," Henry said. He knelt beside Carleton's bed in the light of the Winnie-the-Pooh lamp. "I brought you a new toothbrush."

Carleton whimpered.

"What's wrong, spaceman?" Henry said. "It's just a toothbrush." He leaned toward Carleton and Carleton scooted back. He began to scream.

In the other bed, Tilly was dreaming about rabbits. When she'd come home from school, she and Carleton had seen rabbits sitting on the lawn as if they had kept watch over the house all the time that Tilly had been gone. In her dream they were still there. She dreamed she was creeping up on them. They opened their mouths, wide enough to reach inside like she was some kind of rabbit dentist, and so she did. She put her hand around something small and cold and hard. Maybe it was a ring, a diamond ring. Or a. Or. It was a. She couldn't wait to show Carleton.

Her arm was inside the rabbit all the way to her shoulder. Someone put their hand around her wrist and yanked. Somewhere her mother was talking. She said—

"It's the beard."

Catherine couldn't decide whether to laugh or cry or scream like Carleton. That would surprise Carleton, if she started screaming, too. "Shoo! Shoo, Henry—go shave and come back as quick as you can, or else he'll never go back to sleep."

"Carleton, honey," she was saying as Henry left the room, "it's your dad. It's not Santa Claus. It's not the big bad wolf. It's your dad. Your dad just forgot. Why don't you tell me a story? Or do you want to go watch your daddy shave?"

Catherine's hot-water bottle was draped over the tub. Towels were heaped on the floor. Henry's things had been put away behind the mirror. It made him feel tired, thinking of all the other things that still had to be put away. He washed his hands, then looked at the bar of soap. It didn't feel right. He put it back on the sink, bent over and sniffed it, and then tore off a piece of toilet paper, used the toilet paper to pick up the soap. He threw it in the trash and unwrapped a new bar of soap. There was nothing wrong with the new soap. There was nothing wrong with the old soap either. He was just tired. He washed his hands and lathered up his face, shaved off his beard, and watched the little bristles of hair wash down the sink. When he went to show Carleton his brand-new face, Catherine was curled up in bed beside Carleton. They were both asleep. They were still asleep when he left the house at five thirty the next morning.

***

"Where are you?" Catherine said.

"I'm on my way home. I'm on the train." The train was still in the station. They would be leaving any minute. They had been leaving any minute for the last hour or so, and before that, they had had to get off the train twice, and then back on again. They had been assured there was nothing to worry about. There was no bomb threat. There was no bomb. The delay was only temporary. The people on the train looked at each other, trying to seem as if they were not looking. Everyone had their cell phones out.

"The rabbits are out on the lawn again," Catherine said. "There must be at least fifty or sixty. I've never counted rabbits before. Tilly keeps trying to go outside to make friends with them, but as soon as she's outside, they all go bouncing away like beach balls. I talked to a lawn specialist today. He says we need to do something about it, which is what Liz was saying. Rabbits can be a big problem out here. They've probably got tunnels and warrens all through the yard. It could be a problem. Like living on top of a sinkhole. But Tilly is never going to forgive us. She knows something's up. She says she doesn't want a dog anymore. It would scare away the rabbits. Do you think we should get a dog?"

"So what do they do? Put out poison? Dig up the yard?" Henry said. The man in the seat in front of him got up. He took his bags out of the luggage rack and left the train. Everyone watched him go, pretending they were not.

"He was telling me they have these devices, kind of like ultrasound equipment. They plot out the tunnels, close them up, and then gas the rabbits. It sounds gruesome," Catherine said. "And this kid, this baby has been kicking the daylights out of me. All day long it's kick, kick, jump, kick, like some kind of martial artist. He's going to be an angry kid, Henry. Just like his sister. Her sister. Or maybe I'm going to give birth to rabbits."

"As long as they have your eyes and my chin," Henry said.

"I've gotta go," Catherine said. "I have to pee again. All day long it's the kid jumping, me peeing, Tilly getting her heart broken because she can't make friends with the rabbits, me worrying because she doesn't want to make friends with other kids, just with rabbits, Carleton asking if today he has to go to school, does he have to go to school tomorrow, why am I making him go to school when everybody there is bigger than him, why is my stomach so big and fat, why does his teacher tell him to act like a big boy? Henry, why are we doing this again? Why am I pregnant? And where are you? Why aren't you here? What about our deal? Don't you want to be here?"

"I'm sorry," Henry said. "I'll talk to the Crocodile. We'll work something out."

"I thought you wanted this, too, Henry. Don't you?"

"Of course," Henry said. "Of course I want this."

"I've gotta go," Catherine said again. "Liz is bringing some women over. We're finally starting that book club. We're going to read *Fight Club*. Her stepdaughter, Alison, is going to look after Tilly and Carleton for me. I've already talked to Tilly. She promises she won't bite or hit or make Alison cry."

"What's the trade? A few hours of bonus TV?"

"No," Catherine said. "Something's up with the TV."

"What's wrong with the TV?"

"I don't know," Catherine said. "It's working fine. But the kids won't go near it. Isn't that great? It's the same thing as the toothbrush. You'll see when you get home. I mean, it's not just the kids. I was watching the news earlier, and then I had to turn it off. It wasn't the news. It was the TV."

"So it's the downstairs bathroom and the coffeemaker and Carleton's toothbrush and now the TV?"

"There's some other stuff as well, since this morning. Your office, apparently. Everything in it—your desk, your bookshelves, your chair, even the paper clips."

"That's probably a good thing, right? I mean, that way they'll stay out of there."

"I guess," Catherine said. "The thing is, I went and stood in there for a while and it gave me the creeps, too. So now I can't pick up e-mail. And I had to throw out more soap. And King Spanky doesn't love the alarm clock anymore. He won't come out from under the bed when I set it off."

"The alarm clock, too?"

"It does sound different," Catherine said. "Just a little bit different. Or maybe I'm insane. This morning, Carleton told me that he knew where our house was. He said we were living in a secret part of Central Park. He said he recognizes the trees. He thinks that if he walks down that little path, he'll get mugged. I've really got to go, Henry, or I'm going to wet my pants, and I don't have time to change again before everyone gets here."

"I love you," Henry said.

"Then why aren't you here?" Catherine said victoriously. She hung up and ran down the hallway toward the downstairs bathroom. But when she got there, she turned around. She went racing up the stairs, pulling down her pants as she went, and barely got to the master bedroom bathroom in time. All day long she'd gone up and down the stairs, feeling extremely silly. There was nothing wrong with the downstairs bathroom. It was just the fixtures. When you flushed the toilet or ran water in the sink. She didn't like the sound the water made.

Several times now, Henry had come home and found Catherine painting rooms, which was a problem. The problem was that Henry kept going away. If he didn't keep going away, he wouldn't have to keep coming home. That was Catherine's point. Henry's point was that Catherine wasn't supposed to be painting rooms while she was pregnant. Pregnant women were supposed to stay away from paint fumes. Catherine had solved this problem by wearing the gas mask while she painted. She had known the gas mask would come in handy. She told Henry she promised to stop painting as soon as he started working at home, which was the plan. Meanwhile, she couldn't decide on colors. She and Carleton and Tilly spent hours looking at paint strips with colors that had names

like Sangria, Peat Bog, Tulip, Tantrum, Planetarium, Galactica, Tea
Leaf, Egg Yolk, Tinker Toy, Gauguin, Susan, Envy, Aztec, Utopia, Wax
Apple, Rice Bowl, Cry Baby, Fat Lip, Green Banana, Trampoline, Fingernail. It was a wonderful way to spend time. They went off to school,
and when they got home, the living room would be Harp Seal instead of
Full Moon. They'd spend some time with that color, getting to know it,
ignoring the television, which was haunted (*haunted* wasn't the right word,
of course, but Catherine couldn't think what the right word was), and
then a couple of days later, Catherine would go buy some more primer
and start again. Carleton and Tilly loved this. They begged her to re-
paint their bedrooms. She did.

She wished she could eat paint. Whenever she opened a can of paint,
her mouth filled with saliva. When she'd been pregnant with Carleton,
she hadn't been able to eat anything except olives and hearts of palm
and dry toast. When she'd been pregnant with Tilly, she'd eaten dirt
once in Central Park. Tilly thought they should name the baby after
a paint color—Chalk, or Dilly Dilly, or Keelhauled. Lapis Lazulily.
Knock, knock.

Catherine kept meaning to ask Henry to take the television and put
it in the garage. Nobody ever watched it now. They'd had to stop using
the microwave as well, and a colander, some of the flatware, and she was
keeping an eye on the toaster. She had a premonition, or an intuition. It
didn't feel wrong, not yet, but she had a feeling about it. There was a
gorgeous pair of earrings that Henry had given her—how was it possible to be spooked by a pair of diamond earrings?—and yet. Carleton
wouldn't play with his Lincoln Logs, and so they were going to the
Salvation Army, and Tilly's armadillo purse had disappeared. Tilly
hadn't said anything about it, and Catherine hadn't wanted to ask.

Sometimes, if Henry wasn't coming home, Catherine painted after
Carleton and Tilly went to bed. Sometimes Tilly would walk into the
room where Catherine was working, Tilly's eyes closed, her mouth open,
a tourist-somnambulist. She'd stand there with her head cocked toward

Catherine. If Catherine spoke to her, she didn't answer, and if Catherine took her hand, she would follow Catherine back to her own bed and lie down again. But sometimes Catherine let Tilly stand there and keep her company. Tilly was never so attentive, so *present*, when she was awake. Eventually she would turn and leave the room and Catherine would listen to her climb back up the stairs. Then Catherine would be alone again.

Catherine dreams about colors. It turns out her marriage was the same color she had just painted the foyer. Velveteen Fade. Leonard Felter, who had had an ongoing affair with two of his graduate students, several adjuncts, two tenured faculty members, brought down Catherine's entire department, and saved Catherine's marriage, would make a good lipstick or nail polish. Peach Nooky. There's the Crocodile, a particularly bilious Eau de Vil, a color that tastes bad when you say it. Her mother, who had always been disappointed by Catherine's choices, turned out to have been a beautiful, rich, deep chocolate. Why hadn't Catherine ever seen that before? Too late, too late. It made her want to cry.

Liz and she are drinking paint, thick and pale as cream. "Have some more paint," Catherine says. "Do you want sugar?"

"Yes, lots," Liz says. "What color are you going to paint the rabbits?"

Catherine passes her the sugar. She hasn't even thought about the rabbits, except which rabbits does Liz mean, the stone rabbits or the real rabbits? How do you make them hold still?

"I got something for you," Liz says. She's got Tilly's armadillo purse. It's full of paint strips. Catherine's mouth fills with water.

Henry dreams he has an appointment with the exterminator. "You've got to take care of this," he says. "We have two small children. These things could be rabid. They might carry plague."

"See what I can do," the exterminator says, sounding glum. He stands next to Henry. He's an odd-looking, twitchy guy. He has big ears. They contemplate the skyscrapers that poke out of the grass like obelisks. The lawn is teeming with skyscrapers. "Never seen anything like this before. Never wanted to see anything like this. But if you want my opinion, it's the house that's the real problem—"

"Never mind about my wife," Henry says. He squats down beside a knee-high art deco skyscraper and peers into a window. A little man looks back at him and shakes his fists, screaming something obscene. Henry flicks a finger at the window, almost hard enough to break it. He feels hot all over. He's never felt this angry before in his life, not even when Catherine told him that she'd accidentally slept with Leonard Felter. The little bastard is going to regret what he just said, whatever it was. He lifts his foot.

The exterminator says, "I wouldn't do that if I were you. You have to dig them up, get the roots. Otherwise, they just grow back. Like your house. Which is really just the tip of the iceberg lettuce, so to speak. You've probably got seventy, eighty stories underground. You gone down on the elevator yet? Talked to the people living down there? It's your house, and you're just going to let them live there rent-free? Mess with your things like that?"

"What?" Henry says, and then he hears helicopters, fighter planes the size of hummingbirds. "Is this really necessary?" he says to the exterminator.

The exterminator nods. "You have to catch them off guard."

"Maybe we're being hasty," Henry says. He has to yell to be heard above the noise of the tiny, tinny, furious planes. "Maybe we can settle this peacefully."

"Hemree," the interrogator says, shaking his head. "You called me in because I'm the expert, and you knew you needed help."

Henry wants to say, "You're saying my name wrong." But he doesn't want to hurt the undertaker's feelings.

The alligator keeps on talking. "Listen up, Hemreeee, and shut up about negotiations and such, because if we don't take care of this right away, it may be too late. This isn't about home ownership, or lawn care, Hemreeeeee, this is war. The lives of your children are at stake. The happiness of your family. Be brave. Be strong. Just hang on to your rabbit and fire when you see delight in their eyes."

He woke up. "Catherine," he whispered. "Are you awake? I was having this dream."

Catherine laughed. "That's the phone, Liz," she said. "It's probably Henry, saying he'll be late."

"Catherine," Henry said. "Who are you talking to?"

"Are you mad at me, Henry?" Catherine said. "Is that why you won't come home?"

"I'm right here," Henry said.

"You take your rabbits and your crocodiles and get out of here," Catherine said. "And then come straight home again."

She sat up in bed and pointed her finger. "I am sick and tired of being spied on by rabbits!"

When Henry looked, something stood beside the bed, rocking back and forth on its heels. He fumbled for the light, got it on, and saw Tilly, her mouth open, her eyes closed. She looked larger than she ever did when she was awake. "It's just Tilly," he said to Catherine, but Catherine lay back down again. She put her pillow over her head. When he picked Tilly up, to carry her back to bed, she was warm and sweaty, her heart racing as if she had been running through all the rooms of the house.

He walked through the house. He rapped on walls, testing. He put his ear against the floor. No elevator. No secret rooms, no hidden passageways.

There wasn't even a basement.

Tilly has divided the yard in half. Carleton is not allowed in her half, unless she gives permission.

From the bottom of her half of the yard, where the trees run beside the driveway, Tilly can barely see the house. She's decided to name the yard Matilda's Rabbit Kingdom. Tilly loves naming things. When the new baby is born, her mother has promised that she can help pick out the real names, although there will only be two real names, a first one and a middle. Tilly doesn't understand why there can only be two. *Oishii* means delicious in Japanese. That would make a good name, either for the baby or for the yard, because of the grass. She knows the yard isn't as big as Central Park, but it's just as good, even if there aren't any pagodas or castles or carriages or people on roller skates. There's plenty of grass. There are hundreds of rabbits. They live in an enormous underground city, maybe a city just like New York. Maybe her dad can stop working in New York and come work under the lawn instead. She could help him, go to work with him. She could be a biologist, like Jane Goodall, and go and live underground with the rabbits. Last year her ambition had been to go and live secretly in the Metropolitan Museum of Art, but someone has already done that, even if it's only in a book. Tilly feels sorry for Carleton. Everything he ever does, she'll have already been there. She'll already have done that.

Tilly has left her armadillo purse sticking out of a rabbit hole. First she made the hole bigger, then she packed the dirt back in around the armadillo so that only the shiny, peeled snout poked out. Carleton digs it out again with his stick. Maybe Tilly meant him to find it. Maybe it was a present for the rabbits, except what is it doing here, in his half of the yard? When he lived in the apartment, he was afraid of the armadillo purse, but there are better things to be afraid of out here. But be careful, Carleton. Might as well be careful. The armadillo purse says don't touch me. So he doesn't. He uses his stick to pry open the snap mouth, dumps out Tilly's most valuable things, and with his stick pushes them one by one down the hole. Then he puts his ear to the rabbit hole so that he can hear the rabbits say thank you. Saying thank you is polite. But the rabbits say nothing. They're holding their breath, waiting for him to go away. Carleton waits, too. Tilly's armadillo, empty and smelly and haunted, makes his eyes water.

Someone comes up and stands behind him. "I didn't do it," he says. "They fell."

But when he turns around, it's the girl who lives next door. Alison. The sun is behind her and makes her shine. He squints. "You can come over to my house if you want to," she says. "Your mom says. She's going to pay me fifteen bucks an hour, which is way too much. Are your parents really rich or something? What's that?"

"It's Tilly's," he says. "But I don't think she wants it anymore."

She picks up Tilly's armadillo. "Pretty cool," she says. "Maybe I'll keep it for her."

Deep underground, the rabbits stamp their feet in rage.

❧

Catherine loves the house. She loves her new life. She's never understood people who get stuck, become unhappy, can't change, adapt. So she's out of a job. So what? She'll find something else to do. So Henry can't leave his job yet, won't leave his job yet. So the house is haunted. That's okay. They'll work through it. She buys some books on gardening. She plants a rosebush and a climbing vine in a pot. Tilly helps. The rabbits eat off all the leaves. They bite through the vine.

"Shit," Catherine says, when she sees what they've done. She shakes her fists at the rabbits on the lawn. The rabbits flick their ears at her. They're laughing, she knows it. She's too big to chase after them.

"Henry, wake up. Wake up."

"I'm awake," he said, and then he was. Catherine was crying. Noisy, wet, ugly sobs. He put his hand out and touched her face. Her nose was running.

"Stop crying," he said. "I'm awake. Why are you crying?"

"Because you weren't here," she said. "And then I woke up and you were here, but when I wake up tomorrow morning you'll be gone again. I miss you. Don't you miss me?"

"I'm sorry," he said. "I'm sorry I'm not here. I'm here now. Come here."

"No," she said. She stopped crying, but her nose still leaked. "And now the dishwasher is haunted. We have to get a new dishwasher before I have this baby. You can't have a baby and not have a dishwasher. And you have to live here with us. Because I'm going to need some help this time. Remember Carleton, how fucking hard that was."

"He was one cranky baby," Henry said. When Carleton was three months old, Henry had realized that they'd misunderstood something. Babies weren't babies—they were land mines, bear traps, wasp nests. They were a noise, which was sometimes even not a noise but merely a listening for a noise; they were a damp, chalky smell; they were the heaving, jerky, sticky manifestation of not-sleep. Once Henry had stood and watched Carleton in his crib, sleeping peacefully. He had not done what he wanted to do. He had not bent over and yelled in Carleton's ear. Henry still hadn't forgiven Carleton, not yet, not entirely, not for making him feel that way.

"Why do you have to love your job so much?" Catherine said.

"I don't know," Henry said. "I don't love it."

"Don't lie to me," Catherine said.

"I love you better," Henry said. He does, he does, he does love Catherine better. He's already made that decision. But she isn't even listening.

"Remember when Carleton was little and you would get up in the morning and go to work and leave me all alone with them?" Catherine poked him in the side. "I used to hate you. You'd come home with take-out, and I'd forget I hated you, but then I'd remember again, and I'd hate you even more because it was so easy for you to trick me, to make things okay again, just because for an hour I could sit in the bathtub and eat Chinese food and wash my hair."

"You used to carry an extra shirt with you, when you went out," Henry said. He put his hand down inside her T-shirt on her fat, full breast. "In case you leaked."

"You can't touch that breast," Catherine said. "It's haunted." She blew her nose on the sheets.

Catherine's friend Lucy owns an online boutique, Nice Clothes for Fat People. There's a woman in Tarrytown who knits stretchy, sexy argyle sweaters exclusively for NCFP, and Lucy has an appointment with her. She wants to stop off and see Catherine afterward, before she has to drive back to the city again. Catherine gives her directions and then begins to clean house, feeling out of sorts. She's not sure she wants to see Lucy right now. Carleton has always been afraid of Lucy, which is embarrassing. And Catherine doesn't want to talk about Henry. She doesn't want to explain about the downstairs bathroom. She had planned to spend the day painting the wood trim in the dining room, but now she'll have to wait.

The doorbell rings, but when Catherine goes to answer it, no one is there. Later on, after Tilly and Carleton have come home, it rings again, but no one is there. It rings and rings, as if Lucy is standing outside, pressing the bell over and over again. Finally Catherine pulls out the wire. She tries calling Lucy's cell phone but can't get through. Then Henry calls. He says that he's going to be late.

Liz opens the front door, yells, "Hello, anyone home?! You've got to see your rabbits, there must be thousands of them. Catherine, is something wrong with your doorbell?"

⚜

Henry's bike, so far, was okay. He wondered what they'd do if the Toyota suddenly became haunted. Would Catherine want to sell it? Would resale value be affected? The car and Catherine and the kids were gone when he got home, so he put on a pair of work gloves and went through the house with a cardboard box, collecting all the things that felt haunted. A hairbrush in Tilly's room, an old pair of Catherine's tennis shoes. A pair of Catherine's underwear that he found at the foot of the bed. When he picked them up he felt a sudden shock of longing for Catherine, like he'd been hit by some kind of spooky lightning. It hit him in the pit of the stomach, like a cramp. He dropped the underwear in the box.

The silk kimono from Takashimaya. Two of Carleton's night-lights. He opened the door to his office, put the box inside. All the hair on his arms stood up. He closed the door.

Then he went downstairs and cleaned paintbrushes. If the paintbrushes were becoming haunted, if Catherine was throwing them out and buying new ones, she wasn't saying. Maybe he should check the Visa bill. How much were they spending on paint anyway?

Catherine came into the kitchen and gave him a hug. "I'm glad you're home," she said. He pressed his nose into her neck and inhaled. "I left the car running—I've got to pee. Would you go pick up the kids for me?"

"Where are they?" Henry said.

"They're over at Liz's. Alison is babysitting them. Do you have money on you?"

"You mean I'll meet some neighbors?"

"Wow, sure," Catherine said. "If you think you're ready. Are you ready? Do you know where they live?"

"They're our neighbors, right?"

"Take a left out of the driveway, go about a quarter of a mile, and they're the red house with all the trees in front."

But when he drove up to the red house and went and rang the doorbell, no one answered. He heard a child come running down a flight of stairs and then stop and stand in front of the door. "Carleton? Alison?" he said. "Excuse me, this is Catherine's husband, Henry. Carleton and Tilly's dad." The whispering stopped. He waited for a bit. When he crouched down and lifted the flap of the mail slot, he thought he saw someone's feet, the hem of a coat, something furry? A dog? Someone standing very still, just to the right of the door? Carleton, playing games. "I see you," he said, and wiggled his fingers through the mail slot. Then he thought maybe it wasn't Carleton after all. He got up quickly and went back to the car. He drove into town and bought more soap.

Tilly was standing in the driveway when he got home, her hands on her hips. "Hi, Dad," she said. "I'm looking for King Spanky. He got outside. Look what Alison found."

She held out a tiny toy bow strung with what looked like dental floss, an arrow the size of a needle.

"Be careful with that," Henry said. "It looks sharp. Archery Barbie, right? So did you guys have a good time with Alison?"

"Alison's okay," Tilly said. She belched. "'Scuse me. I don't feel very good."

"What's wrong?" Henry said.

"My stomach is funny," Tilly said. She looked up at him, frowned, and then vomited all over his shirt, his pants.

"Tilly!" he said. He yanked off his shirt, used a sleeve to wipe her mouth. The vomit was foamy and green.

"It tastes horrible," she said. She sounded surprised. "Why does it always taste so bad when you throw up?"

"So that you won't go around doing it for fun," he said. "Are you going to do it again?"

"I don't think so," she said, making a face.

"Then I'm going to go wash up and change clothes. What were you eating, anyway?"

"Grass," Tilly said.

"Well, no wonder," Henry said. "I thought you were smarter than that, Tilly. Don't do that anymore."

"I wasn't planning to," Tilly said. She spit in the grass.

When Henry opened the front door, he could hear Catherine talking in the kitchen. "The funny thing is," she said, "none of it was true. It was just made up, just like something Carleton would do. Just to get attention."

"Dad," Carleton said. He was jumping up and down on one foot. "Want to hear a song?"

"I was looking for you," Henry said. "Did Alison bring you home? Do you need to go to the bathroom?"

"Why aren't you wearing any clothes?" Carleton said.

Someone in the kitchen laughed, as if they had heard this.

"I had an accident," Henry said, whispering. "But you're right, Carleton, I should go change." He took a shower, rinsed and wrung out his shirt, put on clean clothes, but by the time he got downstairs, Catherine and Carleton and Tilly were eating Cheerios for dinner. They were using paper bowls, plastic spoons, as if it were a picnic. "Liz was here, and Alison, but they were going to a movie," Catherine said. "They said they'd meet you some other day. It was awful—when they came in the door, King Spanky went rushing outside. He's been watching the rabbits all day. If he catches one, Tilly is going to be so upset."

"Tilly's been eating grass," Henry said.

Tilly rolled her eyes. As if.

"Not again!" Catherine said. "Tilly, real people don't eat grass. Oh, look, fantastic, there's King Spanky. Who let him in? What's he got in his mouth?"

King Spanky sits with his back to them. He coughs and something drops to the floor, maybe a frog, or a baby rabbit. It goes scrabbling across the floor, half-leaping, dragging one leg. King Spanky just sits there, watching as it disappears under the sofa. Carleton freaks out. Tilly is shouting, "Bad King Spanky! Bad cat!" When Henry and Catherine push the sofa back, it's too late, there's just King Spanky and a little blob of sticky blood on the floor.

∽∾

Catherine would like to write a novel. She'd like to write a novel with no children in it. The problem with novels with children in them is that bad things will happen either to the children or else to the parents. She wants to write something funny, something romantic.

It isn't very comfortable to sit down now that she's so big. She's started writing on the walls. She writes in pencil. She names her characters after paint colors. She imagines them leading beautiful, happy, useful lives. No haunted toasters. No mothers no children no crocodiles no photocopy machines no Leonard Felters. She writes for two or three hours, and then she paints the walls again before anyone gets home. That's always the best part.

∽∾

"I need you next weekend," the Crocodile said. Her rubber-band ball sat on the floor beside her desk. She had her feet up on it, in an attempt to show it who was boss. The rubber-band ball was getting too big for its britches. Someone was going to have to teach it a lesson, send it a memo.

She looked tired. Henry said, "You don't need me."

"I do," the Crocodile said, yawning. "*I do.* The clients want to take you out to dinner at the Four Seasons when they come in to town. They want to go see musicals with you. *Rent. Phantom of the Cabaret Lion.* They want to go to Coney Island with you and eat hot dogs. They want to go out to trendy bars and clubs and pick up strippers and publicists and performance artists. They want to talk about poetry, philosophy, sports, politics, their lousy relationships with their fathers. They want to ask you for advice about their love lives. They want you to come to the weddings of their children and make toasts. You're indispensable, honey. I hope you know that."

"Catherine and I are having some problems with rabbits," Henry said. The rabbits were easier to explain than the other thing. "They've taken over the yard. Things are a little crazy."

"I don't know anything about rabbits," the Crocodile said, digging her pointy heels into the flesh of the rubber-band ball until she could feel the red rubber blood come running out. She pinned Henry with her beautiful, watery eyes.

"Henry." She said his name so quietly that he had to lean forward to hear what she was saying.

She said, "You have the best of both worlds. A wife and children who adore you, a beautiful house in the country, a secure job at a company that depends on you, a boss who appreciates your talents, clients who think you're the shit. You *are* the shit, Henry, and the thing is, you're probably thinking that no one deserves to have all this. You think you have to make a choice. You think you have to give up something. But you don't have to give up anything, Henry, and anyone who tells you otherwise is a fucking rabbit. Don't listen to them. You can have it all. You *deserve* to have it all. You love your job. Do you love your job?"

"I love my job," Henry says. The Crocodile smiles at him tearily. It's true. He loves his job.

When Henry came home, it must have been after midnight, because he never got home before midnight. He found Catherine standing on a ladder in the kitchen, one foot resting on the sink. She was wearing her gas mask, a black cotton sports bra, and a pair of black sweatpants rolled down so far that he could see she wasn't wearing any underwear. Her stomach stuck out so far she had to hold her arms at a funny angle to run the roller up and down the wall in front of her. Up and down in a V. Then fill the V in. She had painted the kitchen ceiling a shade of purple so dark, it almost looked black. Midnight Eggplant.

Catherine had recently begun buying paints from a specialty catalogue. All the colors were named after famous books—*Madame Bovary, Forever Amber, Fahrenheit 451, The Tin Drum, A Curtain of Green, 20,000 Leagues Under the Sea*. She was painting the walls *Catch-22*, a novel she'd taught over and over again to undergraduates. It had gone over pretty well. The paint color was nice, too. She couldn't decide if she missed teaching. The thing about teaching and having children was that you always ended up treating your children like undergraduates and your undergraduates like children. There was a particular tone of voice. She'd even used it on Henry a few times, just to see if it worked.

All the cabinets were fenced around with masking tape, like a crime scene. The room stank of new paint.

Catherine took off the gas mask and said, "Tilly picked it out. What do you think?" Her hands were on her hips. Her stomach poked out at Henry. The gas mask had left a ring of white and red around her eyes and chin.

Henry said, "How was the dinner party?"

"We had fettuccine. Liz and Marcus stayed and helped me do the dishes."

("Is something wrong with your dishwasher?" "No. I mean, yes. We're getting a new one.")

She had had a feeling. It had been a feeling like déjà vu, or being drunk, or falling in love. Like teaching. She had imagined an audience of rabbits out on the lawn, watching her dinner party. A classroom of rabbits, watching a documentary. Rabbit television. Her skin had felt electric.

"So she's a lawyer?" Henry said.

"You haven't even met them yet," Catherine said, suddenly feeling possessive. "But I like them. I really, really like them. They wanted to know all about us. You. I think they think that either we're having marriage problems or that you're imaginary. Finally I took Liz upstairs and showed her your stuff in the closet. I pulled out the wedding album and showed them photos."

"Maybe we could invite them over on Sunday? For a cookout?" Henry said.

"They're away next weekend," Catherine said. "They're going up to the mountains on Friday. They have a house up there. They've invited us. To come along."

"I can't," Henry said. "I have to take care of some clients next weekend. Some big shots. We're having some cash-flow problems. Besides, are you allowed to go away? Did you check with your doctor—what's his name again, Dr. Marks?"

"You mean, did I get my permission slip signed?" Catherine said. Henry put his hand on her leg and held on. "Dr. Marks said I'm shipshape. That was his exact word. Or maybe he said tiptop. It was something alliterative."

"Well, I guess you ought to go then," Henry said. He rested his head against her stomach. She let him. He looked so tired. "Before Golf Cart shows up. Or what is Tilly calling the baby now?"

"She's around here somewhere," Catherine said. "I keep putting her back in her bed and she keeps getting out again. Maybe she's looking for you."

"Did you get my e-mail?" Henry said. He was listening to Catherine's stomach. He wasn't going to stop touching her unless she told him to.

"You know I can't check e-mail on your computer anymore," Catherine said.

"This is so stupid," Henry said. "This house isn't haunted. There isn't any such thing as a haunted house."

"It isn't the house," Catherine said. "It's the stuff we brought with us. Except for the downstairs bathroom, and that might just be a draft, or an electrical problem. The house is fine. I love the house."

"Our stuff is fine," Henry said. "I love our stuff."

"If you really think our stuff is fine," Catherine said, "then why did you buy a new alarm clock? Why do you keep throwing out the soap?"

"It's the move," Henry said. "It was a hard move."

"King Spanky hasn't eaten his food in three days," Catherine said. "At first I thought it was the food, and I bought new food and he came down and ate it and I realized it wasn't the food, it was King Spanky. I couldn't sleep all night, knowing he was up under the bed. Poor spooky guy. I don't know what to do. Take him to the vet? What do I say? Excuse me, but I think my cat is haunted? Anyway, I can't get him out of the bed. Not even with the old alarm clock, the haunted one."

"I'll try," Henry said. "Let me try and see if I can get him out." But he didn't move. Catherine tugged at a piece of his hair and he put up his hand. She gave him her roller. He popped off the cylinder and bagged it and put it in the freezer, which was full of paintbrushes and other rollers. He helped Catherine down from the ladder. "I wish you would stop painting."

"I can't," she said. "It has to be perfect. If I can just get it right, then everything will go back to normal and stop being haunted and the rabbits won't tunnel under the house and make it fall down, and you'll come home and stay home, and our neighbors will finally get to meet you and they'll like you and you'll like them, and Carleton will stop being afraid of everything, and Tilly will fall asleep in her own bed, and stay there, and—"

"Hey," Henry said. "It's all going to work out. It's all good. I really like this color."

"I don't know," Catherine said. She yawned. "You don't think it looks too old-fashioned?"

They went upstairs and Catherine took a bath while Henry tried to coax King Spanky out of the bed. But King Spanky wouldn't come out. When Henry got down on his hands and knees and stuck the flashlight under the bed, he could see King Spanky's eyes, his tail hanging down from the box frame.

Out on the lawn the rabbits were perfectly still. Then they sprang up in the air, turning and dropping and landing and then freezing again. Catherine stood at the window of the bathroom, toweling her hair. She turned the bathroom light off, so that she could see them better. The moonlight picked out their shining eyes, the moon-colored fur, each hair tipped in paint. They were playing some rabbit game like leapfrog. Or they were dancing the quadrille. Fighting a rabbit war. Did rabbits fight wars? Catherine didn't know. They ran at each other and then turned and darted back, jumping and crouching and rising up on their back legs. A pair of rabbits took off in tandem, like race-horses, sailing through the air and over a long curled shape in the grass. Then back over again. She put her face against the window. It was Tilly, stretched out against the grass, Tilly's legs and feet bare and white.

"Tilly," she said, and ran out of the bathroom, wearing only the towel around her hair.

"What is it?" Henry said as Catherine darted past him and down the stairs. He ran after her, and by the time she had opened the front door, was kneeling beside Tilly, the wet grass tickling her thighs and her belly, Henry was there, too, and he picked up Tilly and carried her back into the house. They wrapped her in a blanket and put her in her bed, and because neither of them wanted to sleep in the bed where King Spanky was hiding, they lay down on the sofa in the family room, curled up against each other. When they woke up in the morning, Tilly was asleep in a ball at their feet.

***

For a minute or two last year, Catherine thought she had it figured out. She was married to a man whose specialty was solving problems, salvaging bad situations. If she did something dramatic enough, if she fucked up badly enough, it would save her marriage. And it did, except that once the problem was solved and the marriage was saved and the baby was conceived and the house was bought, then Henry went back to work.

She stands at the window in the bedroom and looks out at all the trees. For a minute she imagines that Carleton is right, and they are living in Central Park and Fifth Avenue is just right over there.

Henry's office is just a few blocks away. All those rabbits are just tourists.

***

Henry wakes up in the middle of the night. There are people downstairs. He can hear women talking, laughing, and he realizes Catherine's book club must have come over. He gets out of bed. It's dark. What time is it anyway? But the alarm clock is haunted again. He unplugs it. As he comes down the stairs, a voice says, "Well, will you look at that!" and then, "Right under his nose the whole time!"

Henry walks through the house, turning on lights. Tilly stands in the middle of the kitchen. "May I ask who's calling?" she says. She's got Henry's cell phone tucked between her shoulder and her face. She's holding it upside down. Her eyes are open, but she's asleep.

"Who are you talking to?" Henry says.

"The rabbits," Tilly says. She tilts her head, listening. Then she laughs. "Call back later," she says. "He doesn't want to talk to you. Yeah. Okay." She hands Henry his phone. "They said it's no one you know."

"Are you awake?" Henry says.

"Yes," Tilly says, still asleep. He carries her back upstairs. He makes a bed out of pillows in the hall closet and lays her down across them. He tucks a blanket around her. If she refuses to wake up in the same bed that she goes to sleep in, then maybe they should make it a game. If you can't beat them, join them.

Catherine hadn't had an affair with Leonard Felter. She hadn't even slept with him. She had just said she had, because she was so mad at Henry. She could have slept with Leonard Felter. The opportunity had been there. And he had been magical somehow: the only member of the department who could make the photocopier make copies, and he was nice to all of the secretaries. Too nice, as it turned out. And then, when it turned out that Leonard Felter had been fucking everyone, Catherine had felt she couldn't take it back. So she and Henry had gone to therapy together. Henry had taken some time off work. They'd taken the kids to Disney World. They'd gotten pregnant. She'd been remorseful for something she hadn't done. Henry had forgiven her. Really, she'd saved their marriage. But it had been the sort of thing you could only do once.

If someone had to save the marriage a second time, it would have to be Henry.

Henry went looking for King Spanky. They were going to see the vet; he had the cat cage in the car, but no King Spanky. It was early afternoon, and the rabbits were out on the lawn. Up above, a bird hung, motionless, on a hook of air. Henry craned his head, looking up. It was a big bird, a hawk maybe? It circled, once, twice, again, and then dropped like a stone toward the rabbits. The rabbits didn't move. There was something about the way they waited, as if this were all a game. The bird cut through the air, folded like a knife, and then it jerked, tumbled, fell, the wings loose.

The bird smashed into the grass and feathers flew up. The rabbits moved closer, as if investigating.

Henry went to see for himself. The rabbits scattered, and the lawn was empty. No rabbits, no bird. But there, down in the trees, beside the bike path, Henry saw something move. King Spanky swung his tail angrily, slunk into the woods.

When Henry came out of the woods, the rabbits were back guarding the lawn again and Catherine was calling his name. "Where were you?" she said. She was wearing her gas mask around her neck, and there was a smear of paint on her arm. Whiskey Horse. She'd been painting the linen closet.

"King Spanky took off," Henry said. "I couldn't catch him. I saw the weirdest thing—this bird was going after the rabbits, and then it fell—"

"Marcus came by," Catherine said. Her cheeks were flushed. He knew that if he touched her, her skin would be hot. "He stopped by to see if you wanted to go play golf."

"Who wants to play golf?" Henry said. "I want to go upstairs with you. Where are the kids?"

"Alison took them into town, to see a movie," Catherine said. "I'm going to pick them up at three."

Henry lifted the gas mask off her neck, fitted it around her face. He unbuttoned her shirt, undid the clasp of her bra. "Better take this off," he said. "Better take all your clothes off. I think they're haunted."

"You know what would make a great paint color? Can't believe no one has done this yet. Yellow Sticky. What about King Spanky?" Catherine said. She sounded like Darth Vader, maybe on purpose, and Henry thought it was sexy: Darth Vader, pregnant with his child. She put her hand against his chest and shoved. Not too hard, but harder than she meant to. It turned out that painting had given her some serious muscle. That will be a good thing when she has another kid to haul around.

"Yellow Sticky. That's great. Forget King Spanky," Henry said. "He's great."

※

Catherine was painting Tilly's room Lavender Fist. It was going to be a surprise. But when Tilly saw it, she burst into tears. 'Why can't you just leave it alone?' she said. "I liked it the way it was."

"I thought you liked purple," Catherine said, astounded. She took off her gas mask.

"I hate purple," Tilly said. "And I hate you. You're so fat. Even Carleton thinks so."

"Tilly!" Catherine said. She laughed. "I'm pregnant, remember?"

"That's what you think," Tilly said. She ran out of the room and across the hall. There were crashing noises, the sounds of things breaking.

"Tilly!" Catherine said.

Tilly stood in the middle of Carleton's room. All around her lay broken night-lights, lamps, broken lightbulbs. The carpet was dusted in glass. Tilly's feet were bare and Catherine looked down, realized that she wasn't wearing shoes either. "Don't move, Tilly," she said.

"They were haunted," Tilly said, and began to cry.

※

"So how come your dad's never home?" Alison said.

"I don't know," Carleton said. "Guess what? Tilly broke all my night-lights."

"Yeah," Alison said. "You must be pretty mad."

"No, it's good that she did," Carleton said, explaining. "They were haunted. Tilly didn't want me to be afraid."

"But aren't you afraid of the dark?" Alison said.

"Tilly said I shouldn't be," Carleton said. "She said the rabbits stay awake all night, that they make sure everything is okay, even when it's dark. Tilly slept outside once, and the rabbits protected her."

"So you're going to stay with us this weekend," Alison said.

"Yes," Carleton said.

"But your dad isn't coming," Alison said.

"No," Carleton said. "I don't know."

"Want to go higher?" Alison said. She pushed the swing and sent him soaring.

When Henry puts his hand against the wall in the living room, it gives a little, as if the wall is pregnant. The paint under the paint is wet. He walks around the house, running his hands along the walls. Catherine has been painting a mural in the foyer. She's painted trees and trees and trees. Golden trees with brown leaves and green leaves and red leaves, and reddish trees with purple leaves and yellow leaves and pink leaves. She's even painted some leaves on the wooden floor, as if the trees are dropping them. "Catherine," he says. "You have got to stop painting the damn walls. The rooms are getting smaller."

Nobody says anything back. Catherine and Tilly and Carleton aren't home. It's the first time Henry has spent the night alone in his house. He can't sleep. There's no television to watch. Henry throws out all of Catherine's paintbrushes. But when Catherine gets home, she'll just buy new ones.

He sleeps on the couch, and during the night someone comes and stands and watches him sleep. Tilly. Then he wakes up and remembers that Tilly isn't there.

The rabbits watch the house all night long. It's their job.

Tilly is talking to the rabbits. It's cold outside, and she's lost her gloves. "What's your name?" she says. "Oh, you beauty. You beauty." She's on her hands and knees. Carleton watches from his side of the yard.

"Can I come over?" he says. "Can I please come over?"

Tilly ignores him. She gets down on her hands and knees, moving even closer to the rabbits. There are three, one of them almost close enough to touch. If she moves her hand slowly, maybe she can grab one by the ears. Maybe she can catch one and train it to live inside. They need a pet rabbit. King Spanky is haunted. He spends most of his time outside. Her parents keep their bedroom door shut so that King Spanky can't get in.

"Good rabbit," Tilly says. "Just stay still. Stay still."

The rabbits flick their ears. Carleton begins to sing a song Alison has taught them, a skipping song. Carleton is such a girl. Tilly puts out her hand. There's something tangled around the rabbit's neck, like a piece of string or a leash. She wiggles closer, holding out her hand. She stares and stares and can hardly believe her eyes. There's a person, a little man, sitting behind the rabbit's ears, holding on to the rabbit's fur and the piece of knotted string with one hand. His other hand is cocked back, like he's going to throw something. He's looking right at her—his hand flies forward and something hits her hand. She pulls her hand back, astounded. "Hey!" she says, and she falls over on her side and watches the rabbits go springing away. "Hey, you! Come back!"

"What?" Carleton yells. He's frantic. "What are you doing? Why won't you let me come over?"

She closes her eyes, just for a second. Shut up, Carleton. Just shut up. Her hand is throbbing and she lies down, holds her hand up to her face. Shut. Up.

Wake up. Wake *up*. When she wakes up, Carleton is sitting beside her. "What are you doing on my side?" she says, and he shrugs.

"What are you doing?" he says. He rocks back and forth on his knees. "Why did you fall over?"

"None of your business," she says. She can't remember what she was doing. Everything looks funny. Especially Carleton. "What's wrong with you?"

"Nothing's wrong with me," Carleton says, but something is wrong. She studies his face and begins to feel sick, as if she's been eating grass. Those sneaky rabbits! They've been distracting her, and now, while she wasn't paying attention, Carleton's become haunted.

"Oh yes it is," Tilly says, forgetting to be afraid, forgetting her hand hurts, getting angry instead. She's not the one to blame. This is her mother's fault, her father's fault, and it's Carleton's fault, too. How could he have let this happen? "You just don't know it's wrong. I'm going to tell Mom."

Haunted Carleton is still a Carleton who can be bossed around. "Don't tell," he begs.

Tilly pretends to think about this, although she's already made up her mind. Because what can she say? Either her mother will notice that something's wrong or else she won't. Better to wait and see. "Just stay away from me," she tells Carleton. "You give me the creeps."

Carleton begins to cry, but Tilly is firm. He turns around, walks slowly back to his half of the yard, still crying. For the rest of the afternoon, he sits beneath the azalea bush at the edge of his side of the yard and cries. It gives Tilly the creeps. Her hand throbs where something has stung it. The rabbits are all hiding underground. King Spanky has gone hunting.

⚓

"What's up with Carleton?" Henry said, coming downstairs. He couldn't stop yawning. It wasn't that he was tired, although he was tired. He hadn't given Carleton a good-night kiss, just in case it turned out he was coming down with a cold. He didn't want Carleton to catch it. But it looked like Carleton, too, was already coming down with something.

Catherine shrugged. Paint samples were balanced across her stomach like she'd been playing solitaire. All weekend long, away from the house, she'd thought about repainting Henry's office. She'd never painted a haunted room before. Maybe if you mixed the paint with a little bit of holy water? She wasn't sure: what was holy water anyway? Could you buy it? "Tilly's being mean to him," she said. "I wish they would make some friends out here. He keeps talking about the new baby, about how he'll take care of it. He says it can sleep in his room. I've been trying to explain babies to him, about how all they do is sleep and eat and cry."

"And get bigger," Henry said.

"That too," Catherine said. "So did he go to sleep okay?"

"Eventually," Henry said. "He's just acting really weird."

"How is that different from usual?" Catherine said. She yawned. "Is Tilly finished with her homework?"

"I don't know," Henry said. "You know, just weird. Different weird. Maybe he's going through a weird spell. Tilly wanted me to help her with her math, but I couldn't get it to come out right. So what's up with my office?"

"I cleared it out," Catherine said. "Alison and Liz came over and helped. I told them we were going to redecorate. Why is it that we're the only ones who notice everything is fucking haunted around here?"

"So where'd you put my stuff?" Henry said. "What's up?"

"You're not working here now," Catherine pointed out. She didn't sound angry, just tired. "Besides, it's all haunted, right? So I took your computer into the shop, so they could have a look at it. I don't know, maybe they can unhaunt it."

"Well," Henry said. "Okay. Is that what you told them? It's haunted?"

"Don't be ridiculous," Catherine said. She discarded a paint strip. Too lemony. "So I heard about the bomb scare on the radio."

"Yeah," Henry said. "The subways were full of kids with crew cuts and machine guns. And they evacuated our building for about an hour. We all went and stood outside, holding on to our laptops like idiots, just in case. The Crocodile carried out her rubber-band ball, which must weigh about thirty pounds. It kind of freaked people out, even the firemen. I thought the bomb squad was going to blow it up. So tell me about your weekend."

"Tell me about yours," Catherine said.

"You know," Henry said. "Those clients are assholes. But they don't know they're assholes, so it's kind of okay. You just have to feel sorry for them. They don't get it. You have to explain how to have fun, and then they get anxious, so they drink a lot and so you have to drink, too. Even the Crocodile got drunk. She did this weird wriggly dance to a Pete Seeger song. So what's their place like?"

"It's nice," Catherine said. "You know, really nice."

"So you had a good weekend? Carleton and Tilly had a good time?"

"It was really nice," Catherine said. "No, really, it was great. I had a fucking great time. So you're sure you can make it home for dinner on Thursday."

It wasn't a question.

"Carleton looks like he might be coming down with something," Henry said. "Here. Do you think I feel hot? Or is it cold in here?"

Catherine said, "You're fine. It's going to be Liz and Marcus and some of the women from the book group and their husbands, and what's her name, the real estate agent. I invited her, too. Did you know she's written a book? I was going to do that! I'm getting the new dishwasher tomorrow. No more paper plates. And the lawn-care specialist is coming on Monday to take care of the rabbits. I thought I'd drop off King Spanky at the vet, take Tilly and Carleton back to the city, stay with Lucy for two or three days—did you know she tried to find this place and got lost? She's supposed to come up for dinner, too—just in case the poison doesn't go away right away, you know, or in case we end up with piles of dead rabbits on the lawn. Your job is to make sure there are no dead rabbits when I bring Tilly and Carleton back."

"I guess I can do that," Henry said.

"You'd better," Catherine said. She stood up, with some difficulty, and came and leaned over his chair. Her stomach bumped into his shoulder. Her breath was hot. Her hands were full of strips of color. "Sometimes I wish that instead of working for the Crocodile, you were having an affair with her. I mean, that way you'd come home when you're supposed to. You wouldn't want me to be suspicious."

"I don't have any time to have affairs," Henry said. He sounded put out. Maybe he was thinking about Leonard Felter. Or maybe he was picturing the Crocodile naked. The Crocodile wearing stretchy red rubber sex gear. Catherine imagined telling Henry the truth about Leonard Felter. I didn't have an affair. Did not. Is that a problem?

"That's exactly what I mean," Catherine said. "You'd better be here for dinner. You live here, Henry. You're my husband. I want you to meet our friends. I want you to be here when I have this baby. I want you to fix what's wrong with the downstairs bathroom. I want you to talk to Tilly. She's having a rough time. She won't talk to me about it."

"Tilly's fine," Henry said. "We had a long talk tonight. She said she's sorry she broke all of Carleton's night-lights. I like the trees, by the way. You're not going to paint over them, are you?"

"I had all this leftover paint," Catherine said. "I was getting tired of just painting with the rollers. I wanted to do something fancier."

"You could paint some trees in my office, when you paint my office."

"Maybe," Catherine said. "Ooof, this baby won't stop kicking me." She lay down on the floor in front of Henry and lifted her feet into his lap. "Rub my feet. I've still got so much fucking paint. But once your office is done, I'm done with the painting. Tilly told me to stop it or else. She keeps hiding my gas mask. Will you be here for dinner?"

"I'll be here for dinner," Henry said, rubbing her feet. He really meant it. He was thinking about the exterminator, about rabbit corpses scattered all across the lawn, like a war zone. Poor rabbits. What a mess.

⚓

After they went to see the therapist, after they went to Disney World and came home again, Henry said to Catherine, "I don't want to talk about it anymore. I don't want to talk about it ever again. Can we not talk about it?"

"Talk about what?" Catherine said. But she had almost been sorry. It had been so much work. She'd had to invent so many details that eventually it began to seem as if she hadn't made it up after all. It was too strange, too confusing, to pretend it had never happened, when, after all, it *had* never happened.

⚓

Catherine is dressing for dinner. When she looks in the mirror, she's as big as a cruise ship. A water tower. She doesn't look like herself at all. The baby kicks her right under the ribs.

"Stop that," she says. She's sure the baby is going to be a girl. Tilly won't be pleased. Tilly has been extra good all day. She helped make the salad. She set the table. She put on a nice dress.

Tilly is hiding from Carleton under a table in the foyer. If Carleton finds her, Tilly will scream. Carleton is haunted, and nobody has noticed. Nobody cares except Tilly. Tilly says names for the baby, under her breath. Dollop. Shampool. Custard. Knock, knock. The rabbits are out on the lawn, and King Spanky has gotten into the bed again, and he won't come out, not for a million haunted alarm clocks.

Her mother has painted trees all along the wall under the staircase. They don't look like real trees. They aren't real colors. It doesn't look like Central Park at all. In among the trees, her mother has painted a little door. It isn't a real door, except that when Tilly goes over to look at it, it is real. There's a doorknob, and when Tilly turns it, the door opens. Underneath the stairs, there's another set of stairs, little dirt stairs, going down. On the third stair, there's a rabbit sitting there, looking up at Tilly. It hops down, one step, and then another. Then another.

"Rumpelstiltskin!" Tilly says to the rabbit. "Lipstick!"

Catherine goes to the closet to get out Henry's pink shirt. What's the name of that real estate agent? Why can't she ever remember? She lays the shirt on the bed and then stands there for a moment, stunned. It's too much. The pink shirt is haunted. She pulls out all of Henry's suits, his shirts, his ties. All haunted. Every fucking thing is haunted. Even the fucking shoes. When she pulls out the drawers, socks, underwear, handkerchiefs, everything, it's all spoiled. All haunted. Henry doesn't have a thing to wear. She goes downstairs, gets trash bags, and goes back upstairs again. She begins to dump clothes into the trash bags.

She can see Carleton framed in the bedroom window. He's chasing the rabbits with a stick. She hoists open the window, leans out, yells, "Stay away from those fucking rabbits, Carleton! Do you hear me?"

She doesn't recognize her own voice.

Tilly is running around downstairs somewhere. She's yelling, but her voice gets farther and farther away, fainter and fainter. She's yelling, "Hairbrush! Zeppelin! Torpedo! Marmalade!"

The doorbell rings.

<hr>

The Crocodile started laughing. "Okay, Henry. Calm down."

He fired off another rubber band. "I mean it," he said. "I'm late. I'll be late. She's going to kill me."

"Tell her it's my fault," the Crocodile said. "So they started dinner without you. Big deal."

"I tried calling," Henry said. "Nobody answered." He had an idea that the phone was haunted now. That's why Catherine wasn't answering. They'd have to get a new phone. Maybe the lawn specialist would know a house specialist. Maybe somebody could do something about this. "I should go home," he said. "I should go home right now." But he didn't get up. "I think we've gotten ourselves into a mess, me and Catherine. I don't think things are good right now."

"Tell someone who cares," the Crocodile suggested. She wiped at her eyes. "Get out of here. Go catch your train. Have a great weekend. See you on Monday."

So Henry goes home, he has to go home, but of course he's late, it's too late. The train is haunted. The closer they get to his station, the more haunted the train gets. None of the other passengers seem to notice. It makes Henry sick to his stomach. And, of course, his bike turns out to be haunted, too. It's too much. He can't ride it home. He leaves it at the station and he walks home in the dark, down the bike path. Something follows him home. Maybe it's King Spanky.

Here's the yard, and here's his house. He loves his house, how it's all lit up. You can see right through the windows, you can see the living room, which Catherine has painted Ghost Crab. The trim is Rat Fink. Catherine has worked so hard. The driveway is full of cars, and inside, people are eating dinner. They're admiring Catherine's trees. They haven't waited for him, and that's fine. His neighbors: he loves his neighbors. He's going to love them as soon as he meets them. His wife is going to have a baby any day now. His daughter will stop walking in her sleep. His son isn't haunted. The moon shines down and paints the world a color he's never seen before. Oh, Catherine, wait till you see this. Shining lawn, shining rabbits, shining world. The rabbits are out on the lawn. They've been waiting for him, all this time, they've been waiting. Here's his rabbit, his very own rabbit. Who needs a bike? He sits on his rabbit, legs pressed against the warm, silky, shining flanks, one hand holding on to the rabbit's fur, the knotted string around its neck. He has something in his other hand, and when he looks, he sees it's a spear. All around him, the others are sitting on their rabbits, waiting patiently, quietly. They've been waiting for a long time, but the waiting is almost over. In a little while, the dinner party will be over and the war will begin.

TIGER MENDING

Aimee Bender

꧁꧂

My sister got the job. She's the overachiever, and she went to med school
for two years before she decided she wanted to be a gifted seamstress.
(What? they said, on the day she left. A surgeon! they told her. You could
be a tremendous surgeon! But she said she didn't like the late hours, she
got too tired around midnight.) She has small motor skills better than
a machine; she'll fix your handkerchief so well you can't even see the
stitches, like she became one with the handkerchief. I once split my lip,
jumping from the tree, and she sewed it up, with ice and a needle she'd
run through the fire. I barely even had a scar, just the thinnest white
line.

So of course, when the two women came through the sewing school,
they spotted her first. She was working on her final exam, a lime-colored
ball gown with tiny diamonds sewn into the collar, and she was fully
absorbed in it, constructing infinitesimal loops, while they hovered
with their severe hair and heady tree-smell—like bamboo, my sister

said—watching her work. My sister's so steady she didn't even flinch, but everyone else in class seized upon the distraction, staring at the two Amazonian women, both six feet tall and strikingly beautiful. When I met them later I felt like I'd landed straight inside a magazine ad. At the time, I was working at Burger King, as block manager (there were two on the block), and I took any distraction offered me and used it to the hilt. Once, a guy came in and ordered a Big Mac, and for two days I told that story to every customer, and it's not a good story. There's so rarely any intrigue in this shabberdash world of burger warming; you take what you can get.

But my sister was born with supernatural focus, and the two women watched her and her alone. Who can compete? My sister's won all the contests she's ever been in, not because she's such an outrageous competitor, but because she's so focused in this gentle way. Why *not* win? Sometimes it's all you need to run the fastest, or to play the clearest piano, or to ace the standardized test, pausing at each question until it has slid through your mind to exit as a penciled-in circle.

In low, sweet voices, the women asked my sister if she'd like to see Asia. She finally looked up from her work. Is there a sewing job there? They nodded. She said she'd love to see Asia, she'd never left America. They said, Well, it's a highly unusual job. May I bring my sister? she asked. She's never traveled either.

The two women glanced at each other. What does your sister do?

She's manager of the Burger Kings down on 4th.

Their disapproval was faint but palpable, especially in the upper lip. She would simply keep you company?

What we are offering you is a position of tremendous privilege. Aren't you interested in hearing about it first?

My sister nodded lightly. It sounds very interesting, she said. But I cannot travel without my sister.

This is true. My sister, the one with that incredible focus, has a terrible fear of airplanes. Terrible. Incapacitating. The only way she can relax on a flight is if I am there, because I am always, always having some kind of crisis, and she focuses in and fixes me and forgets her own concerns. I become her ripped hemline. In general, I call her every night, and we talk for an hour, which is forty-five minutes of me, and fifteen minutes of her stirring her tea, which she steeps with the kind of Zen patience that would make Buddhists sit up in envy and then breathe through their envy and then move past their envy. I'm really really lucky she's my sister. Otherwise no one like her would give someone like me the time of day.

The two Amazonian women, lousy with confidence, with their ridiculous cheekbones, in these long yellow print dresses, said OK. They observed my sister's hands quiet in her lap.

Do you get along with animals? they asked, and she said, Yes. She loved every animal. Do you have allergies to cats? they asked, and she said, No. She was allergic only to pine nuts. The slightly taller one reached into her dress pocket, a pocket so well hidden inside the fabric it was like she was reaching into the ether of space, and from it her hand returned with an airplane ticket.

We are very happy to have found you, they said. The additional ticket will arrive tomorrow.

My sister smiled. I know her; she was probably terrified to see that ticket, and also she really wanted to return to the diamond loops. She probably wasn't even that curious about the new job yet. She was and is stubbornly, mind-numbingly, interested in the present moment.

When we were kids, I used to come home and she'd be at the living room window. It was the best window in the apartment, looking out, in the far distance, on the tip of a mountain. For years, I tried to get her to play with me, but she was unplayable. She stared out that window, never moving, for hours. By night, when she'd returned, I'd usually injured myself in some way or other, and I'd ask her about it while she tended to me; she said the reason she could pay acute attention now was because of the window. It empties me out, she said, which scared me. No, she said, to my frightened face, as she sat on the edge of my bed and ran a washcloth over my forehead. It's good, she said. It makes room for other things.

Me? I asked, with hope, and she nodded. You.

We had no parents by that point. One had left, and the other died at the hands of a surgeon, which is the real reason my sister stopped medical school.

That night, she called me up and told me to quit my job, which was what I'd been praying for for months—that somehow I'd get a magical phone call telling me to quit my job because I was going on an exciting vacation. I threw down my BK apron, packed, and prepared as long an account of my life complaints as I could. On the plane, I asked my sister what we were doing, what her job was, but she refolded her tray table and said nothing. Asia, I said. What country? She stared out the porthole. It was the pilot who told us, as we buckled our seat belts; we were heading to Kuala Lumpur, straight into the heart of Malaysia.

Wait, where's Malaysia again? I whispered, and my sister drew a map on the napkin beneath her ginger ale.

During the flight, I drank Bloody Marys while my sister embroidered a doily. Even the other passengers seemed soothed by watching her work. I whispered all my problems into her ear and she returned them back to me in slow sentences that did the work of a lullaby. My eyes grew heavy. During the descent, she gave the doily to the man across the aisle, worried about his ailing son, and the needlework was so elegant it made him feel better just holding it. That's the thing with handmade items. They still have the person's mark on them, and when you hold them, you feel less alone. This is why everyone who eats a Whopper leaves a little more depressed than they were when they came in.

At the airport curbside, a friendly driver picked us up and took us to a cheerful green hotel, where we found a note on the bed telling my sister to be ready at six A.M. sharp. It didn't say I could come, but bright and early the next morning, scrubbed and fed, we faced the two Amazons in the lobby, who looked scornfully at me and my unsteady hands—I sort of pick at my hair a lot—and asked my sister why I was there. Can't she watch? she asked, and they said they weren't sure. She, they said, might be too anxious.

I swear I won't touch anything, I said.

This is a private operation, they said.

My sister breathed. I work best when she's nearby, she said. Please.

And like usual, it was the way she said it. In that gentle voice that had a back to it. They opened the car door.

Thank you, my sister said.

They blindfolded us for reasons of security, and we drove for more than an hour, down winding, screeching roads, parking finally in a place that smelled like garlic and fruit. In front of a stone mansion, two more women dressed in printed robes waved as we removed our blindfolds. These two were short. Delicate. Calm. They led us into the living room, and we hadn't been there for ten minutes when we heard the moaning.

A bad moaning sound. A real bad, real mournful moaning, coming from the north, outside, that reminded me of the worst loneliness, the worst long lonely night. The Amazonian with the short shining cap of hair nodded.

Those are the tigers, she said.

What tigers? I said.

Sssh, she said. I will call her Sloane, for no reason except that it's a good name for an intimidating person.

Sloane said, Sssh. Quiet now. She took my sister by the shoulders and led her to the wide window that looked out on the land. As if she knew, instinctively, how wise it was to place my sister at a window.

Watch, Sloane whispered.

I stood behind. The two women from the front walked into view and settled on the ground near some clumps of ferns. They waited. They were very still-minded, like my sister, that stillness of mind. That ability

I will never have, to sit still. That ability to have the hands forget they are hands. They closed their eyes, and the moaning I'd heard before got louder, and then in the distance, I mean waaaay off, the moaning grew even louder, almost unbearable to hear, and limping from the side lumbered two enormous tigers. Wailing as if they were dying. As they got closer, you could see that their backs were split open, sort of peeled, as if someone had torn them in two. The fur was matted, and the stripes hung loose, like packing tape ripped off their bodies. The women did not seem to move, but two glittering needles worked their way out of their knuckles, climbing up out of their hands, and one of the tigers stepped closer. I thought I'd lose it; he was easily four times the first woman's size, and she was small, a tiger's snack, but he limped over, in his giantness, and fell into her lap. Let his heavy striped head sink to the ground. She smoothed the stripe back over, and the moment she pierced his fur with the needle, those big cat eyes dripped over with tears.

It was very powerful. It brought me to tears, too. Those expert hands, as steady as if he were a pair of pants, while the tiger's enormous head hung to the ground. My sister didn't move, but I cried and cried, seeing the giant broken animal resting in the lap of the small precise woman. It is so often surprising, who rescues you at your lowest moment. When our mother died in surgery, the jerk at the liquor store suddenly became the nicest man alive, and gave us free cranberry juice for a year.

What happened to them? I asked Sloane. Why are they like that?

She lifted her chin slightly. We do not know, but they emerge from the forests, peeling. More and more of them. Always torn at the central stripe.

Do they ever eat people?

Not so far, she said. But they do not respond well to fidgeting, she said, watching me clear out my thumbnail with my other thumbnail.

Well, I'm not doing it.

You have not been asked.

They are so sad, said my sister.

Well, wouldn't you be? If you were a tiger, unpeeling?

Sloane put a hand on my sister's shoulder. When the mending was done, all four—women and beasts—sat in the sun for at least half an hour, tigers' chests heaving, women's hands clutched in their fur. The day grew warm. In the distance, the moaning began again, and two more tigers limped up while the first two stretched out and slept. The women sewed the next two, and the next. One had a bloody rip across its white belly.

After a few hours of work, the women put their needles away, the tigers raised themselves up, and without any lick or acknowledgment, walked off, deep into that place where tigers live. The women returned to the house. Inside, they smelled so deeply and earthily of cat that they were almost unrecognizable. They also seemed lighter, nearly giddy. It was lunchtime. They joined us at the table, where Sloane served an amazing soup of curry and prawns.

It is an honor, said Sloane, to mend the tigers.

I see, said my sister.

You will need very little training, since your skill level is already so high.

But my sister seemed frightened, in a way I hadn't seen before. She didn't eat much of her soup, and she returned her eyes to the window, to the tangles of fluttering leaves.

I would have to go find out, she said finally, when the chef entered with a tray of mango tartlets.

Find out what?

Why they unpeel, she said. She hung her head, as if she was ashamed of her interest.

You are a mender, said Sloane, gently. Not a zoologist.

I support my sister's interest in the source, I said.

Sloane flinched every time I opened my mouth.

The source, my sister echoed.

The world has changed, said Sloane, passing a mango tartlet to me, reluctantly, which I ate, pronto.

It was unlike my sister to need the cause. She was fine, usually, with just how things were. But she whispered to me, as we roamed outside looking for clues, of which we found none, she whispered that she felt something dangerous in the unpeeling, and she felt she would have to know about it in order to sew the tiger suitably. I am not worried about the sewing, she said. I am worried about the gesture I place inside the thread.

I nodded. I am a good fighter, is all. I don't care about thread gestures, but I am willing to throw a punch at some tiger asshole if need be.

We spent the rest of the day outside, but there were no tigers to be seen—where they lived was somewhere far, far off, and the journey they took to arrive here must have been the worst time of their lives, ripped open like that, suddenly prey to vultures or other predators, when they were usually the ones to instill fear.

We slept that night at the mansion, in feather beds so soft I found them impossible to sleep in. Come morning, Sloane had my sister join the two women outside, and I cried again, watching the big tiger head at her feet while she sewed with her usual stillness. The three together were unusually productive, and sewn tigers piled up around them. But instead of that giddiness that showed up in the other women, my sister grew heavier that afternoon, and said she was sure she was doing something wrong. Oh no, said Sloane, serving us tea. You were remarkable.

I am missing something, said my sister. I am missing something important.

Sloane retired for a nap, but I snuck out. I had been warned, but really, they were treating me like shit anyway. I walked a long distance, but I'm a sturdy walker, and I trusted where my feet went, and I did not like the sight of my sister staring into her teacup. I did not like the feeling it gave me, of worrying. Before I left, I sat her in front of the window and told her to empty herself, and her eyes were grateful in a way I was used to feeling in my own face but was not accustomed to seeing in hers.

I walked for hours, and the wet air clung to my shirt and hair. I took a nap inside some ferns. The sun was setting, and I would've walked all night, but when I reached a cluster of trees, something felt different. There was no wailing yet, but I could feel the stirring before the wailing, which is almost worse. I swear I could hear the dread. I climbed up a tree and waited.

I don't know what I expected—people, I guess. People with knives, cutting in. I did not expect to see the tigers themselves, jumpy, agitated, yawning their mouths beyond wide, the wildness in their eyes, and finally the yawning so large and insistent that they split their own back in two. They all did it, one after the other—as if they wanted to pull the fur off their backs, and then, amazed at what they'd done, the wailing began.

One by one, they left the trees and began their slow journey to be mended. It left me with the oddest, most unsettled feeling.

I walked back when it was night, under a half moon, and found my sister still at the window.

They do it to themselves, I whispered to her, and she took my hand. Her face lightened. Thank you, she said. She tried to hug me, but I pulled away. No, I said, and in the morning, I left for the airport.

THE BLACK SQUARE

Chris Adrian

Henry tried to pick out the other people on the ferry who were going to the island for the same reason he was. He wasn't sure what to look for: black Bermuda shorts, an absence of baggage, too-thoughtful gazing at the horizon? Or just a terminal, hangdog look, a mask that revealed instead of hiding the gnarled little soul behind the face? But no one was wearing black, or staring forlornly over the rail. In fact, everyone was smiling. Henry looked pretty normal himself, a man in the last part of his young middle age dressed in plaid shorts and a T-shirt, a dog between his legs and a duffel bag big enough to hold a week's clothes at his side.

The dog was Bobby's, a black Lab named Hobart, borrowed for the ostensible vacation trip to make it less lonely. It was a sort of torture to have him along, since he carried thoughts of Bobby with him like biting fleas. But Henry loved Hobart as honestly as he had ever loved anything or anybody. And, in stark opposition to his master, the dog seemed to love Henry back. Henry was reasonably sure he would follow him, his paws fancy-stepping, through the black square. But he wasn't going to ask him to do that. He had hired an old lady to bring Hobart back to Cambridge at the end of the week.

He reached down and hugged the dog around the neck. Hobart craned his neck back and licked Henry's face. A little girl in enormous sunglasses, who'd skibbled over twice already since they'd left Hyannis, did it again, pausing before the dog and holding out her hand to him. "Good holding out your hand for the doggie to sniff!" her mother called out from a neighboring bench, and smiled at Henry. "What's his name?" the girl asked. She hadn't spoken the other two times she'd approached.

"Blackheart's Grievous Despair," Henry said. Hobart gave up licking her hand and started to work on her shoe, which was covered in the ice cream she'd been eating a short while before.

"That's stupid," the girl said. She was standing close enough that Henry could see her eyes through the sunglasses, and tell that she was staring directly into his face.

"So are you," he said. It was one of the advantages of his present state of mind, and one of the gifts of the black square, that he could say things like this now, in part because his long sadness had curdled his disposition, and in part because all his decisions had become essentially without consequence. He wasn't trying to be mean. It was just that there wasn't any reason anymore not to say the first thing that came into his mind.

The little girl didn't cry. She managed to look very serious, even in the ridiculously oversized sunglasses, biting on her lower lip while she petted the dog. "No," she said finally, "I'm not. *You* are. You are the *stupidest*." Then she walked away, calmly, back to her mother.

He got surprises like this all the time these days, ever since he had decided to give up his social filters. A measured response from a five-year-old girl to his little snipe, a gift of flowers from his neighbor when he'd told her he didn't give a flying fuck about the recycling, a

confession of childhood abuse from his boss in response to his saying she was an unpleasant individual. The last was perhaps not so
surprising—every unpleasant individual, himself included, had a bevy
of such excuses that absolved them of nothing. But there was something
different about the world ever since he had discovered the square and
committed himself to it. *People go in,* someone had written on the Black
Square Message Board, which Henry called up over his bed every night
before he went to sleep, *but have you ever considered what comes OUT of it?* Most
of those who wrote there were a different sort of freak from Henry, but
he thought the writer might mean what he wanted him to mean, which
was those sort of little daily surprises, and more than that a funny sense
of carefree absolution. Once you had decided to go in (he didn't sub-
scribe to the notion, so popular on the board, that the square called you
or chose you) things just stopped mattering in the way that they used to.
With the pressure suddenly lifted off of every aspect of his life, it had
become much easier to appreciate things. *So many wonderful things have come
to me since I accepted the call,* someone wrote. *It's too bad it can't last.* And someone replied, *You know that it can't.*

The girl's mother was glaring now, and looked to be getting ready to
get up and scold him, which might possibly have led to an interesting
conversation. But it didn't seem particularly likely, and one surprise a
day was really enough. Henry got up and walked to the bow of the ferry.
Hobart trotted ahead, put his paws up on the railing, and looked back
at him. The island was just visible on the horizon. Henry sat down behind the dog, who stayed up on the rail, sniffing at the headwind and
looking back every now and then. Henry laughed and said, "What?"
They sat that way as the island drew nearer and nearer. The view was
remotely familiar—he'd seen it countless times when he was a little
boy—though it occurred to him as he stared ahead that he had the same
feeling, coming up on the island, that he used to get facing the other
way and approaching the mainland: he was approaching a place that was
strange, exciting, and a little alien, though it was only the square that

made it that way now. Nantucket in itself was ordinary, dull, and familiar. *You are especially chosen*, a board acquaintance named Martha had written, when he'd disclosed that he had grown up on the island. *Fuck that*, he
had written back. But as they entered the harbor, he hunkered down
next to the dog, who was going wild at the smells rolling out from the
town and the docks. "Look, Hobart," he said. "Home."

⚏

Those who ascribed a will or a purpose to it thought it was odd that the
square should have chosen to appear on Nantucket, one of the least
important places on the planet, for all that the island was one of the
richest. Those same people thought it might have demonstrated a sense
of humor on the square's part to appear, of all the places it could have,
in the middle of a summer-mansion bathroom, where some grotesquely
rejuvenated old lady, clinging to her deluxe existence, might have stepped
into it accidentally on her way out of the tub. But it had appeared on the
small portion of the island that was still unincorporated, in a townie
commune that had been turned subsequently into a government-sponsored
science installation and an unofficial way station for the ever-dwindling
and ever-renewing community of people who called themselves Black
Squares.

Every now and then someone posted a picture of a skunk or a squirrel on the board, with a caption naming the creature Alpha or Primo or
Columbus, and calling it the first pioneering Black Square. It was true
that a number of small animals, cats and dogs and rabbits and even a
few commune llamas, went missing in the days before the square was
actually discovered by a ten-year-old boy who tried to send his little
sister through it. Around her waist she wore a rope that led to her brother's hand; he wasn't trying to kill her. He had been throwing things in
all day, rocks and sticks and one heavy cinder block, and finally a rabbit
from the eating stock. His mother interrupted him before he could send
his sister through. He had put a helmet on her, and given her a flashlight,

sensing, as the story went on the board, that there was both danger and discovery on the other side.

There followed a predictable series of official investigations, largely muffled and hidden from the eyes of the public, though it seemed that from the first missing rodent there was mention of the square on the boards. The incorporated portion of the island wanted nothing to do with it. Once the government assured them that it would be a very closely supervised danger, they more or less forgot about it, except to bemoan the invasion of their island by a new species of undesirable, one that didn't serve them in their homes or clubs. The new arrivals had a wild, reckless air about them, these people who had nothing to lose, and they made one uncomfortable, even if they did spend wildly and never hung around for very long. The incorporated folks hardly noticed the scientists, who once the townies had been cleared out never left the compound until they departed for good within a year, leaving behind a skeleton crew of people not bothered by unsolvable mysteries.

By then it had become obvious that there was nothing to be learned from the square—at least nothing profitable in the eyes of the government. It just sat there, taking whatever was given to it. It refused nothing (*And isn't it because it loves everyone and everything perfectly, that it turns nothing and no one away?* Martha wrote), but it gave nothing back. It emitted no detectable energy. No probe ever returned from within it, or managed to hurl any signal back out. Tethers were neatly clipped, at various and unpredictable lengths. No official human explorer ever went through, though an even dozen German shepherds leaped in obediently, packs on their backs and cameras on their heads. The experiments degraded, from the construction of delicate listening devices that bent elegantly over the edge of the square to the government equivalent of what the boy had been doing: tossing things in. The station was funded eventually as a disposal unit, and the government put out a discreet call across the globe for special and difficult garbage, not expecting, but not exactly turning away, the human sort that inevitably showed up.

Henry had contracted with his psychiatrist not to think about Bobby. "This is a condition of your survival," the man had told him, and Henry had not been inclined to argue. There had been a whole long run of better days, when he had been able to do it, but it took a pretty serious and sustained effort, and exercised some muscle in him that got weaker, instead of stronger, the more he used it, until he succumbed to fatigue. Now it was a sort of pleasure not to bother resisting. It would have been impossible, anyway, to spend time with Bobby's dog and not think of him, though he loved the dog quite separately from Bobby. It was a perfectly acceptable indulgence, in the long shadow of the square, to imagine the dog sleeping between them on their bed, though Hobart hadn't been around when they were actually together. And it was acceptable to imagine himself and Bobby together again—useless and agonizing, but as perfectly satisfying as worrying a painful tooth. It was even acceptable to imagine that it was he and Bobby, and not Bobby and his Brazilian bartender husband, who were about to have a baby together, a little chimera bought for them from beyond the grave by Bobby's fancy dead grandma.

Yet Bobby wasn't all he thought about. It wasn't exactly the point of the trip to torture himself that way, and whether the square represented a new beginning or merely an end to his suffering, he wasn't trying to spend his last days on the near side of the thing in misery. He was home, after all, though Nantucket Town did not feel much like home, and he didn't feel ready, at first, for a trip to the old barn off Polpis Road. But there was something—the character of the light and the way the heat seemed to hang very lightly in the air—that though unremembered, made the island feel familiar.

He showed the dog around. It was something to do; it had never been his plan to go right to the square, though there were people who got off the ferry and made a beeline for it. Maybe they were worried that they might change their mind if they waited too long. Henry wasn't worried about changing his mind or chickening out. The truth was he had been traveling toward the thing all his life, in a way, and while the pressure that was driving him toward it had become more urgent since he came to the island, he still wasn't in any particular hurry to jump in. There were things to say good-bye to, after all; any number of things to be done for the last time. He had spent his last sleepless night in Cambridge in a bed-and-breakfast down the street from where Bobby lived with his bartender, lying on the bed with his hands behind his head, staring at the ceiling and enumerating all those things he'd like to do one last time. He wasn't organized enough to make a list, but he'd kept a few of them in his head. It turned out to be more pleasant to do them with the dog than to do them alone, and more pleasant, in some ways, to do them for the dog instead of for himself. Last meals were better enjoyed if Hobart shared them with him—they ate a good deal of fancy takeout in the hotel room, Henry sitting on the floor with his back against the bed, Hobart lying on his belly with his face in a bowl resting between his legs. Henry made a tour of some dimly remembered childhood haunts, rediscovering them and saying good-bye to them at the same time: a playground on the harbor, a pond that he thought was Miacomet but might have been Monomoy, and finally the beach at Surfside.

He had pictures of himself at that beach on his phone, taken by his father during Henry's very well-documented childhood. He was his father's last child, and the only one from his second marriage. His brothers were all much older than him, born when their father had been relatively poor, when he still made his living, despite his Haverford education and his well-received first book, playing piano in bars. Henry came in well after that, when there was money for cameras and camcorders and time, attention, and interest to take a picture of the baby every day. He had thumbed through them in bed the night before, showing them to Hobart, who somehow got conditioned to yawn every time he saw a picture of Henry at the beach with a bucket and a shovel. It was a less melancholy pastime, and less pathetic, to look at old pictures of himself, instead of pictures of himself and Bobby, though he did that, too, late into the night, with Hobart's sleeping head on his chest.

They spent the morning making their way slowly down the beach by throws of a rubber football the size of a child's fist. Henry had a reasonably good arm: once or twice he threw the ball far enough that Hobart disappeared around a dune to go in search of it. He daydreamed considerably as they went, and thought indulgently of Bobby as Hobart leaped and galumphed and face-planted into the sand. He had to be persuaded every time to give up the ball, running back as if to drop it at Henry's feet, then veering away and playing a prancing, high-stepping keep-away until Henry caught him around the neck and pulled open his jaws. It made him a defective sort of retriever, and it doubled the work of play with him, but Henry didn't mind it.

He laughed at the dog, and thought of his father laughing behind the camera at him, and thought of something Bobby had said to him more than once. He'd accused Henry of being unable to delight in him, and had said that this was part of the reason that Henry had never been properly able to love him, or anybody, really. Bobby had said deflating things like that all the time—he'd kept an arsenal of them always at hand and ready to spoil any occasion—and the Bobby in Henry's head still kept up a running commentary years after they broke up. But it had been fair, for Bobby to say he was delightless, a million years before, when Henry had been an entirely different person, selfish and self-loathing and more in love with his own misery than with the man who wanted to marry him.

All that had changed. It was far too late to make any difference with Bobby, but now he was the sort of person who couldn't help but take pleasure in the foolish exuberance of a clumsy black Lab. "Look, Bobby," he said quietly as Hobart raced after the football. "Look at him go." He shook his head at himself, and sat down, then lay down on his back with his knees bent and his arms thrown out at his sides, staring up at the sky for a while before he closed his eyes. "I'm tired, Hobart," he said, when the dog came back and started to lick his face. "Sit down and relax for a minute." But the cold nose kept pressing on his eyelids, and the rough tongue kept dragging across his cheek and nose and lips. He swatted at the dog's head, and grabbed his collar, and reached with his other hand to scratch the Lab's neck.

In another moment his face was being licked from the other side. When Henry opened his eyes he discovered that this was Hobart. The dog he had been petting was someone else entirely, another black Lab, but with a face that was much pointier (and frankly less handsome) than Hobart's. The owner came trotting up behind him. He was standing in front of the sun. Henry only registered his hairy chest and baseball cap before the man asked him, "Why are you making out with my dog?"

<hr>

One heard various stories about Lenny. He was alternately from San Francisco, or Houston, or Pittsburgh, or Nantucket, or someplace no one had ever heard of. He was a teenager, or an old man, or in his middle age. He was perfectly healthy, or terminally ill. He was happily married, or heartbroken and bereft. He was a six-foot-eight black man or he was a diminutive honky. He might not even have been the first one to go through. It was only certain that he'd been the first to announce that he was going, and the founding poster on what became the Black Square Message Board. As the first official Black Square (the anonymous individuals who might have passed in before him, as well as the twelve German shepherds, together held that title unofficially) he had become something of a patron saint for everyone who proposed to go after him. *Lenny knows* was a fairly common way to preface a platitude on the board, and his post, *this is not a suicide,* had become a motto of sorts for the whole group. The post had a *ceci n'est pas une pipe* quality about it, but it was consistent with what became the general attitude on the board, that the square offered an opportunity to check into another universe as well as the opportunity to check out of this one. *He should have said, This is not merely a suicide*, Martha wrote. Not everything she wrote was stupid, and Henry was inclined to agree with her on this count. There was an element of protest to Lenny's leap into the square: it was a fuck-you to the ordinary universe the likes of which it had not previously been possible to utter. By entering into the square you could express your disdain for the declined world, so far fallen, to some people's minds, from its potential for justice and beauty, as effectively as you could by blowing your head off, but instead of just dying, you might end up someplace else, someplace different—indeed, someplace full of people just like you, people who had leaped away from their own declined, disappointing lives.

⁂

The pointy-nosed Lab's name was Dan; his master's name was Luke. Henry ought not to have talked to him beyond saying "Sorry!" Meeting yet another handsome, witty, accomplished fellow who was utterly uninteresting on account of his failure to be Bobby was not part of the plan for his last days on the near side of the square. Henry tried to walk away, but the dogs were already fast friends, and Hobart wouldn't come. The man was smiling and looking at Henry in a particular way as Henry tugged on Hobart's collar. He was short and muscled-up and furry, and had a pleasant, open face. Henry was trying to think of something inappropriate to say, but nothing was coming to mind. The man stuck out his hand and introduced himself. Henry, his left hand still on Hobart's collar, stuck out his own, shifting his balance as he did, so when Hobart lunged at his new friend he pulled Henry over. Henry ought to have let go of the stranger's small, rough, appealing palm—he thought as he squeezed it harder that it felt like a blacksmith's palm, and that it went along nicely with the man's blacksmith build—but he gripped it harder as he fell, and pulled the other man over on top of him. They were momentarily a pile of bodies, human and canine, Luke on Henry on Hobart, with Dan on top of all of them. Henry got a paw in his face, and a dog nail scratched his cheek, and his face was pressed hard into Luke's chest. Luke smelled like coffee and salt, and tasted salty too, when Henry thought he had accidentally tasted the sweat on the man's hairy chest, but it turned out that it was his own blood on his lip, trickling from the scratch.

The injury, though it wasn't totally clear which dog had inflicted it, prompted profuse apologies and an invitation to dinner. Henry felt sure he should have declined. All his plans aside, he knew that he wasn't going to be interested in this man as certainly as he knew that the sun got a little colder every day, or that eventually the whole island would be incorporated as surely as Hilton Head or Manhattan, and that the rich folk would have to ferry in their household help from Martha's Vineyard. It was inevitable. But he considered, as he wiped the blood off his face and listened to Luke apologize, that he might be overlooking another gift of the square, and that it didn't matter that loving Bobby had ruined him, and smothered in the cradle any possible relationship with any other man. He had no future with anyone, but he had no future at all. That took the pressure off of dinner. And it was something else to say good-bye to, after all: dinner with a handsome man.

"Sometimes I kind of like being the only homo in a ten-mile radius," Luke said while they were eating. "Or almost the only one." Henry had asked what had possessed him to come to Nantucket for a vacation. When Henry cocked his head at that, Luke asked him the same question.

"Something similar," Henry said, reaching down to pet Hobart's head, a gesture that was becoming his new nervous tic. They were sitting outside at a restaurant in 'Sconset, both dogs at their feet and a bowl of clams between them. Dan was just as well-behaved as Hobart was. They both sat staring up at the sky or at another table, or staring intently into each other's eyes, leaning forward occasionally to sniff closer and closer, touching noses and then touching tongues before going back to looking distracted and disinterested until they started it all over again with a sudden glance. Henry and Luke took turns saying, "I think they like each other."

"I was born here," Henry added. Luke was smiling at him—he seemed to be one of those continuous smilers, the sort of people that Henry generally disliked (Bobby, until he had left, had always appeared perpetually troubled), but there was something sad, or at least resigned, in Luke's smile that Henry found appealing.

"I didn't think anybody was born on Nantucket," Luke said. "I thought people just magically appeared here once they made enough money."

"They do," Henry said. "Sort of. There's a ceremony. You claw your way naked through a pool of coins and they drape you in a white robe and everyone chants, 'One of us! One of us!' But if you're poor you just get squeezed out of a vagina and they put your name on a plaque in the hospital."

"You have a plaque?"

"Sure. Henry David Conroy. May 22, 1986."

"I figured you were special," Luke said, managing to smile differently, more warmly and more engagingly and more attractively. Henry looked away. It was part of his problem that flattering attention from handsome men only made him more sad, and made him feel Bobby's rejection more achingly and acutely. The handsomer the man, and the more flattering the attention, the greater his sadness. To date, anybody else had only discovered in miserable degrees how thoroughly and hopelessly they were not Bobby. But there was always that homunculus in Henry, weakly resistant to the sadness, that protested in a meek little voice whenever he said good-bye early, or declined an invitation up to someone's apartment. Proximity to the square made it a little bolder, and Henry thought he could hear it shouting something about saying good-bye to sucking on a nice cock.

Henry took a clam and looked at the dogs. They were looking away from each other now, but he said it anyway. "Look at that. They really like each other, don't they?"

"They sure do," Luke said.

———————— ❧ ————————

Because of my mother, somebody wrote. Half the messages on the farewell board were unsigned. You were only supposed to post your final notes there, but this was a rule that was impossible to enforce, since anybody could retire one ID and come back with a new one. And you were supposed to limit yourself to just one reason, either by prioritizing, or, more elegantly, by articulating a reason that contained all other possible reasons. While *Because of my mother* could be unpacked at length, there was something crude, or at least unsophisticated, about it. *Because of incorporation* was its political equivalent: it contained a multitude of reasons, all the accumulated disappointments of the past decade for the people who cared to mourn the dashed hopes of the early part of the century. But it was less subtle and less mysterious than *Because I believe,* into which one could read a richer sort of disappointment, one that was tempered with hope that something besides oblivion lay on the other side of the square. This sort of post could be crude as well: *Because I want to see Aslan* was its own common type. Still, there was something pleasing about these notes which looked forward through the square and saw something or someone waiting there, Aslan in Narnia, Dejah Thoris on Barsoom, or more private kings in more particular kingdoms. *Because I have suffered enough* was less appealing than *Because I wish to suffer differently.*

Most mysterious and most mundane of all were the last posts of the lovelorn. They were neither necessarily hopeful nor despairing. *Because of Alice* could mean anything in a way that *Because of my mother* generally could not—Alice might be hero or villain, after all, but all mothers were villains on the board. *Because of Louise, Because of Juliet, Because of John, Because of Alan and Wanda and Bubbles*—that one seemed like cheating to Henry, though he liked it for the possibility that Bubbles might be a chimpanzee, and for the likelihood that the circumstances driving the poster through the square must be uniquely weird and horrible. *Because of George, Because of Althea, Because of you. Because I broke his heart, Because she broke my heart. Because of Bobby.*

⁂

Henry took Luke and the dogs out to the old barn. There were pictures of that, too, taken back when it had been Henry's home. Henry had called them up on the ceiling and they had all looked at them, even the dogs. It was hardly a first-date activity, to share your distant past this way, though he'd done it with Bobby, the two of them sitting in an overpriced café in Cambridge with their phones on the table, excitedly trading pictures of their dead brothers and fathers. That had felt like showing each other their scars, part of the process of recognition by which they came independently to understand that, while it was probably too early to say they were meant for each other, they were at least very lucky to have collided. It was a less intimate revelation to show pictures of himself at five years old, naked except for a little cowboy hat and boots, to a man he had fucked three times in the twelve hours he had known him, but it was still a startling bit of progress. He hadn't been interested in that sort of thing—the moving-on that his friends and shrinks and Bobby himself had encouraged him to do—largely because it seemed both impossible and unnecessary. Trying to not be in love with Bobby was like trying to not be gay anymore, or like annulling the law of gravity by personal decree. It was ridiculous to try, and anyway gayness and gravity, for whatever sadness or limitation they might generate, felt right. Henry still wasn't interested in moving on, but there was something about his pending encounter with the square that made it feel like this was something else, similar in form but not in substance to getting over it at last, since he was about to make a permanent attestation to his devotion to Bobby, and to his objection to the end of their relationship.

"This is okay," he said to Hobart, the only other one of the four still awake after the slide show. Luke and his dog had fallen asleep before it finished, and now the man's head was on Henry's chest. "This is okay," Henry said again, staring down his nose at Luke's face. He was doing a whistling sort of snore, in through the nose, out through the mouth. "I'm not making out with your dog," Henry said quietly. "He's throwing up into my mouth." He wondered why he couldn't have thought to say that two days before. Hobart crawled up the bed and added his head to the empty side of Henry's chest. It was a little hard to breathe, but he still fell asleep that way.

The barn was in as much of a state of ruin as the law would allow. No one had lived there for five years, and no one sanely inclined to keep it up had lived there for fifteen. A friend of his father's, a crazy cat lady who kept birds instead of cats, had moved in after his father had died, and after she died Henry had left it empty, never visiting and only paying now and then to have it painted when the nearest neighbor complained that it was starting to look shabby in a way that was no longer picturesque. All the nearest neighbors were eventually eaten up by incorporation, and there were mansions all around now in the near distance, but Henry had never sold the place in spite of offers that grew both more generous and more threatening. He'd left it to Bobby with instructions never to sell, which he probably wouldn't—Bobby was not exactly a friend of incorporation—but who knew. Maybe he and the Brazilian would want to make another baby together, and Bobby's grandma had only been good for one.

⁂

"You used to live here?" Luke asked in the morning. "All the time?"

"All the time," Henry said. "It's why my manners are so atrocious." They were standing in what remained of the living room. A pair of squirrels were staring at them from a rafter above. The dogs were staring back. "It was fine," Henry said. "It was great, actually. As much as I remember. It doesn't have anything to do with . . . it."

"Yeah. Mine neither," Luke said. They had started talking about the square during breakfast. Henry wasn't the one to bring it up. Out of nowhere and all of a sudden Luke had asked him what he was going to wear when he went through. "Shorts," Henry had said, not thinking to deny it, or even ask how Luke knew he was a Square.

"I brought a parka," Luke said.

"Because you think it will be cold?" Henry asked.

"Because I like the parka," Luke said. "It's my favorite piece of clothing. It's puffy but not too puffy." A silence followed, not entirely awkward. They were eating in the room, on the bed, and had just moved the plates to the floor for the dogs to finish up. Henry was still trying to decide what to say next when Luke reached over for his cock, and what followed felt like a sort of conversation. Henry had always thought that having someone's cock in your mouth ought to provide you with some kind of insight on them, though this hadn't ever been the case. Staring into someone's eyes while he pounded on their ass made him feel infinitely remote from them, except of course for Bobby, and maybe it was the extraordinary intimacy he had achieved doing such things with Bobby that spoiled it with everyone else. But there was something revealing in the exchange between him and Luke. Luke was holding on to him too tightly, and he was holding on too tightly to Luke, and Henry thought he heard notes of agonized sadness in both their voices when they cried out at each other as they came. By the end of it Henry felt as if they had communicated any number of wordless secrets, and that he had a deep, dumb understanding of why Luke was going through the square, and felt sure that Luke felt the same way, and it seemed all of a piece with the whole process that it would fuck things up by asking if this was true.

"I was such a happy kid," Luke said. "Not one single thing about my childhood was fucked up. I always wanted to put that on my gravestone, if I was going to have a gravestone."

"Mine would say . . ." Henry started, and then thought better of it.

"What?" He had been going to say, *He made bad choices.*

"*Poodle,*" he said. "Just, *Poodle.* And let people wonder what that meant, except it wouldn't mean anything." Luke put an arm around him.

"I like you," he said. "I *like* you." The way he stressed the *like* made it sound as if he hadn't liked anybody for a while.

"I like you, too," Henry said, feeling stupid and exalted at the same time. It changed nothing, to like somebody. It didn't change anything at all about why he was here, or what he was going to do. He could like somebody, and say good-bye to liking somebody, in the same way he was saying good-bye to ice cream and gingersnaps and blow jobs and the soft fur on the top of Hobart's head. It didn't change the past, or alter any of the choices he had made, or make him into a different person. It didn't change the fact that it was too late to do anything but proceed quietly and calmly through the square.

The dogs were taking turns leaping and barking uselessly at the squirrels. "I *like* you," Henry said again, trying to put the same charming emphasis on the word that Luke had, but it only came out funny, his voice breaking like he was thirteen, or like he was much sadder or more overcome than he actually was. Luke gathered him closer in his arms, and pressed his beard against Henry's beard, and Henry was sure this man was going to say something that would be awkward and delightful and terrifying, but after five minutes of squeezing him and rubbing their faces together but never quite kissing all he said was "You're *cuddly.*"

⁂

Some days I'm into, Martha wrote, *and some days I'm through. But I'm never not going.* Everybody had those days, when the prospect of going into the square, with no expectation of anything but oblivion on the other side, was more appealing than the prospect of passing through it to discover a new world where pain was felt less acutely, or less urgently, or even just differently, although most people liked to pretend that they were only interested in the latter destination. These were not suicides, after all. But how many people would pass through, Henry wondered, if it were in fact a guaranteed passage to Narnia? He wasn't sure that nuzzling with Aslan would make him any less troubled over Bobby, or that topping Mr. Tumnus's hairy bottom would dispel any unwanted memories. Living beyond Bobby, beyond the pain and delight of remembering him, beyond the terrible ironies of their failed almost-marriage, required something more than the promise of happiness or relief. It could only be done someplace farther away than Narnia, and maybe even someplace farther away than death, though death, according to the deep illogic that had governed all Henry's actions since he and Bobby had broken up beyond any hope of reconciling, was at least a step in the right direction. When he had made his drunken attempt to hang himself all Henry had been thinking about was getting away from Bobby, from loving him and hurting over him and from the guilt of having hurt him, but when he actually settled his weight down on the telephone cord around his neck and let himself begin to be suspended by it, some monstrously naive part of him felt like he was accelerating back toward his old lover. Killing himself, as he tried to kill himself, felt like both a way forward and a way back.

He blacked out ever so gently—he'd chosen to hang himself for the sheer painless ease of it—and he felt sure that he was traveling, felt a thrill at having made what seemed like a reportable discovery, that death was falling. This seemed like tremendously important news, the sort of thing that might have validated his short-lived and undistinguished scientific career. He thought how sad it was that he wasn't going to be able to tell Bobby— It's all right after all, he would have said, that our brothers are dead and our fathers are dead because death is only *falling*. And at the same time he thought, I'll tell him when I see him.

He woke up with a terrible headache, lying among the shoes on his closet floor, all his neatly pressed work clothes on top of him and splinters from the broken closet bar in his hair. He spent the night there because it seemed like this was the place he had been heading all his life, and the dreary destined comfort of it gave him the best night's sleep he'd had in months. When he woke again all the desperate intoxications of the night before had worn off, and he only felt pathetic, failed suicides being the worst sort of losers in anybody's book, his own included. He stayed in there through the morning—he'd wet himself as he lay unconscious, and did it again without much hesitation—feeling afraid to go out into what seemed now like a different world. It was early evening before growing boredom forced him to look at his phone. He'd sent a text to Bobby—*I'm so sorry*—and received no reply.

⁑

Henry went walking at dusk with Luke along the fence around the station where the square was housed. The dogs went quietly before them, sniffing at the grass that poked around the chain link but neither one ever finding a place to pee. When they came into view of the concrete shed, Dan barked softly at it, but Hobart only lay down and appeared to go to sleep. Henry and Luke stared silently for a while, holding hands.

"How did you know I came to Nantucket for this?" Henry asked.

"I don't know," Luke said. "Same way I knew you were gay, I guess. Squaredar."

"Huh," Henry said. "I didn't know with you until you asked. And then I knew." This seemed like a terribly lame thing to say. He was reminded of all his late conversations with Bobby, before Bobby had ended their long fruitless talk about whether or not they should try being together again by marrying the Brazilian, when hapless unrequited love of the man had kept Henry from making a single articulate point.

"And you didn't know I was gay until I came in your mouth."

"I'm slow," Henry said. "But that doesn't make you gay. Hundreds and hundreds of straight guys have come in my mouth. Hundreds and hundreds and hundreds." It suddenly occurred to him that holding hands they would be too big to fit through the square.

They were quiet for a little while, until Luke heaved a big sigh and said, "There it is." His tone was somehow both reverential and disappointed.

"You couldn't have thought it would be bigger," Henry said. "Everybody knows how big it is."

"No. I just thought I would feel something . . . different. If I close my eyes I can't even tell it's there."

"Well," Henry said. "Maybe it's just a hole."

Luke shook his head. "Look," he said, and pointed. Someone was approaching the shed. Luke raised a little pair of binoculars to his eyes and made an odd noise, a grunt and a laugh and also something sadder than either of those noises, and handed the glasses to Henry. It was a woman wearing a short, sparkling dress. "I don't think it's very practical to go through in heels," Henry said.

"Makes it difficult to leap properly," Luke said. "She's probably just going to fall in, which isn't right at all."

Henry put the binoculars down. "Why do you think she's going?"

Luke shrugged. " 'Cause she's too pretty for this world." He took the glasses back from Henry, who gave them up gladly, not wanting to watch her pass through the door.

"Let's go," Henry said.

"Hold on," Luke said, still watching. "She's stranded here from another dimension, and thinks this might be the way back."

"Or some dead person told her to do it," Henry said. "To be with them again. Let's go."

"Just a minute," Luke said, and lifted his head like Hobart sniffing at the harbor smells, cocking his head and listening. Henry turned and walked away, whistling for Hobart to follow him, but the dogs stayed together, sitting next to Luke, all of them sniffing and listening. Henry

kept walking, and shortly they all came bounding up behind him. Luke
caught him around the shoulders and pulled him close. "She's gone," he
said matter-of-factly. "Did you feel it?"

All through dinner Henry wanted to ask the question that he knew
he shouldn't, the question that probably didn't need to be answered, and
the one that he felt intermittently sure would be ruinous to ask. But it
wasn't until later, as Luke lay sweating on top of him, that he couldn't
resist anymore, and he finally asked it. "How come?" he said into Luke's
shoulder.

"What?"

"How come you're going through?"

"It's complicated," he said. "Why are you going?"

"It's complicated," Henry said.

"See?"

"Yeah. Dumb question," Henry said. Though in fact his reason for
going through no longer seemed very complicated at all. If it was simple
that didn't make it any less powerful, but crushing hopeless loneliness
was something Henry suddenly felt able to wrap his arms around even
as he wrapped his arms around Luke. "I'm lonely" did no sort of justice
to what he'd suffered in the past two years, and yet he could have said it
in answer and it would have been true. It seemed suddenly like it might
be possible that loneliness did not have to be a crime punishable by
more and more extreme loneliness, until a person was so isolated that he
felt he was being pushed toward a hole in the world.

"Not dumb. Not dumb." Luke kissed the side of Henry's neck each
time he said it. "You're *cuddly*."

"I was going to go tomorrow," Henry said. "That was my date.
That's what I paid for. But I was thinking of changing it."

"Really?"

"Really. It's not going anywhere, right? It'll be there next week. And
the next week. It's kind of nice, you know, how it's always there, not going anywhere. Nice to know you could always just go in, whenever you

want. But that you don't have to, yet, if you want to go to the beach tomorrow instead. Or if you want to play tennis, instead, or before. Tennis, and then in you go. Unless you want to make pancakes first."

"I don't think Hal gives refunds," Luke said. Hal was the guard who took semi-official bribes to look the other way while people took one-way trips into the shed.

"I don't mind," Henry said. "It's just money. When were you going?"

A long silence followed. Henry was afraid to ask again, because he couldn't imagine that Luke hadn't heard him. But Luke only lay there, dripping less and less and breathing more and more deeply, until Henry decided that he was asleep. Henry was almost falling asleep himself, for all that the unanswer was a disappointment, when Luke spoke, not at all sleepily, into his shoulder. "Next week," he said. "Around then."

Then he really did fall asleep, and Henry stayed awake, thinking of the week to come, and the one after that, and the one after that, and of repairs to the barn, and sex among the power tools, and the dogs frolicking, and of Bobby wondering what happened to his wonderful fucking dog, and whether Hobart would be sad if he never went back to Cambridge. Henry fell asleep not any less sad, or any less in love with Bobby, but surprised in a way that did nothing to satisfy his cynicism'. Nantucket, he thought before he slept, and two dogs, and a good man asleep on him. It was all relatively all right.

How a two-hundred-pound man could roll off of him and get dressed in the dark and take his parka out of a closet full of rattling wire hangers without waking him up Henry never could figure. He left a note. *You are lovely but the square is lovelier.* It was pinned to Dan's collar. Both dogs stared at Henry impatiently while he sat on the bed with the note in his hands, probably wondering when they were going to go out, or be fed, or be played with, or even acknowledged when they licked his hands or jumped up on the bed to nuzzle his chest. Dan eventually peed in the corner, and then joined Hobart to lie at Henry's feet, both of them wagging their tails, then staring up at him with plaintive eyes, then eventually falling asleep as the morning turned into the afternoon. Henry finally dozed himself, the note still in his hand, maintaining the posture of sad shock he felt sure he was going to maintain forever, and did not dream of Bobby or Luke or the square or his brother or his father or the frolicking dogs or of the isle of Nantucket sinking into the sea. When he woke up he stood and stretched and rustled up his phone from where it had got lost amid the sheets. Then he called the old lady, sure he was going to tell her there was an extra dog for her to bring to Cambridge until he left her a message saying he would bring Hobart back himself.

FOUNDATION

China Miéville

❧

You watch the man who comes and speaks to buildings. He circles the houses, looking up from the sidewalks, from the concrete gardens, looking down at the supports that go into the earth. He enters every room, taps windows and wiggles ill-fitted panes, he prods at plaster, hauls into attics. In the basements he listens to supports, and all the time he whispers.

The buildings whisper back, he says. He works in brownstones, in tenements, banks and warehouses across the city. They tell him where their faultlines run. When he's done he tells you why the crack is spreading, why the wall is damp, where erosion is, what the cost will be to fix it or to let it rot. He is never wrong.

Is he a surveyor? A structural engineer? He has no framed certificates but a thick portfolio of references, a ten-year reputation. There are cuttings about him from across America. They have called him the house-whisperer. He has been a phenomenon for years.

When he speaks he wears a large and firm smile. He has to push his words past it so they come out misshapen and terse. He fights not to raise his voice over the sounds he knows you cannot hear.

"Yeah no problem but that supporting wall's powdering," he says. If you watch him close you will see that he peeps quickly at the earth, again and again, at the building's sunken base. When he goes below, into the cellar, he is nervy. He talks more quickly. The building speaks loudest to him down there, and when he comes up again he is sweating below his smile.

When he drives he looks to either side of the road with tremendous and unending shock, taking in all the foundations. Past building sites he stares at the earthmovers. He watches their trundling motion as if they are some carnivore.

<hr>

Every night he dreams he is where air curdles his lungs and the sky is a toxic slurry of black and black-red clouds that the earth vomits and the ground is baked to powder and lost boys wonder and slough off flesh in clots and do not see him or each other though they pass close by howling without words or in a language of collapsing jargon, acronyms and shorthands that once meant something and now are the grunts of pigs.

He lives in a small house in the edges of the city, where once he started to build an extra room, till the foundations screamed too loud. A decade later there is only a hole through striae of earth, past pipes, a pit, waiting for walls. He will not fill it. He stopped digging when a dark, thick and staining liquid welled up from below his suburban plot, clinging to his spade, cloying, unseen by any but him. The foundation spoke to him then.

In his dream he hears the foundation speak to him in its multiple voice, its muttering. And when at last he sees it, the foundation in the tight-packed hot earth, he wakes retching and it takes moments before he knows he is in his bed, in his home, and that the foundation is still speaking.

—we stay

—we are hungry

Each morning he kisses good-bye the photograph of his family. They left years ago, frightened by him. He sets his face while the foundation tells him secrets.

In a midcity apartment block the residents want to know about the crack through two of their floors. The man measures it and presses his ear to the wall. He hears echoes of voices from below, travelling, rising through the building's bones. When he cannot put it off anymore, he descends to the basement.

The walls are grey and wet-stained, painted with a little graffiti. The foundation is speaking clearly to him. It tells him it is hungry and hollow. Its voice is the voice of many, in time, desiccated.

He sees the foundation. He sees through the concrete floor and the earth to where girders are embedded and past them to the foundation.

A stock of dead men. An underpinning, a structure of entangled bodies and their parts, pushed tight, packed together and become architecture, their bones broken to make them fit, wedged in contorted repose, burnt skins and the tatters of their clothes pressed as if against glass at the limits of their cut, running below the building's walls, six feet deep below the ground, a perfect runnel full of humans poured like concrete and bracing the stays and the walls.

The foundation looks at him with all its eyes, and the men speak in time.

—we cannot breathe

There is no panic in their voices, nothing but the hopeless patience of the dead.

—we cannot breathe and we shore you up and we eat only sand

He whispers to them so no one else can hear.

"Listen," he says. They eye him through the earth. "Tell me," he says. "Tell me about the wall. It's built on you. It's weighing down on you. Tell me how it feels."

—it is heavy, they say, and we eat only sand, but at last the man coaxes the dead out of their solipsism for a few moments and they look up, and close their eyes, all in time, and hum, and tell him, it is old, this wall built on us, and there is rot halfway up its flank and there is a break that will spread and the sides will settle.

The foundation tells him everything about the wall and for a moment the man's eyes widen, but then he understands that no, there is no danger. Untreated, this wall will only slump and make the house more ugly. Nothing will collapse. Hearing that he relaxes and stands, and backs away from the foundation which watches him go.

"You don't have to worry about it," he tells the residents' committee. "Maybe just fix it up, smooth it down, that's all you have to do."

⁂

And in a suburban mall there is nothing to stop expansion onto waste ground, and in the character house the stairs are beyond repair, and the clocktower has been built using substandard bolts, and the apartment's ceiling needs damp-proofing. The buried wall of dead tells him all these things.

Every home is built on them. It is all one foundation, that underpins his city. Every wall weighs down upon the corpses that whisper to him with the same voice, the same faces, ripped-up cloth and long-dried blood and bodies torn up and their components used to fill gaps between bodies, limbs and heads stowed tidily between men bloated by gas and spilling dust from their cavities, the whole and partial dead concatenated.

Every house in every street. He listens to the buildings, to the foundation that unites them.

⁂

In his dream he tramps through land that swallows his feet. Missing men shuffle in endless, anxious circles and he passes them by. Syrupy-thick liquid laps at him from just below the dust. He hears the foundation. He turns and there is the foundation. It is taller. It has breached the ground. A wall of dead-men bricks as high as his thighs, its edges and its top quite smooth. It is embedded with thousands of eyes and mouths that work as he approaches, spilling rheum and skin and sand.

—we do not end, we are hungry and hot and alone

Something is being built upon the foundation.

There have been years of petty construction, the small schemes of developers, the eagerness of people to improve their homes. Doggedly he makes the foundation tell him. Where there is no problem he passes that on, or where there is a small concern. Where problems are so great that building will be halted early on he tells that, too.

It is nearly a decade that he has been listening to buildings. It is a long time till he finds what he has been looking for.

The block is several storeys high, built thirty years before from shoddy concrete and cheap steel by contractors and politicians who got rich on the deficiencies. The fossils of such corruption are everywhere. Mostly their foundering is gradual, doors sticking, elevators failing, subsidence, over years. Listening to the foundation, the man knows something here is different.

He grows alarmed. His breath is short. He murmurs to the buried wall of dead, begging them to be sure.

The foundation is in swampland—the dead men can feel the ooze rising. The basement walls are crumbling. The supports are veined, infinitesimally, with water. It will not be long. The building will fall.

"Are you sure?" he whispers again, and the foundation looks at him with its countless dust-thick and haemorrhaged eyes and says yes. Trembling, he stands and turns to the caretaker, the housing manager.

"These old things," he says. "They ain't pretty, and they weren't well built, and yeah you're going to get damp, but you've got nothing to worry about. No problem. These walls are solid."

He slaps the pillar beside him and feels vibrations through to the water below it, through the honeycomb of its eroded base, into the foundation where the dead men mutter.

※

In the nightmare he kneels before the wall of torn-up flesh. It is chest-high now. The foundation is growing. It is nothing without a wall, a temple.

He wakes crying and stumbles into his basement. The foundation whispers to him and it is above the ground now; it stretches into his walls.

※

The man has weeks to wait. The foundation grows. It is slow, but it grows. It grows up into the walls and down, too, extending into the earth, spreading its base, underpinning more and more.

Three months after he visited the high-rise he sees it on the local news. It looks like someone who has suffered a stroke; its side is slack, tremulous. Its southern corner has slumped and sandwiched on itself, opening up its flesh to forlorn half-rooms that teeter at the edge of the air. Men and women are hauled out on stretchers.

Figures flutter across the screen. Many dead. Six are children. The man turns the volume up to drown out the whispers of the foundation. He begins to cry and then is sobbing. He hugs himself, croons his sadness; he holds his face in his hands.

"This is what you wanted," he says. "I paid you back. Please, leave me alone. It's done."

In the basement he lies down and weeps on the earth, the foundation beneath him. It looks up from its random gargoyle poses. It blinks dust out of its dead eyes and watches. Its stare burns him.

"There's something for you to eat," he whispers. "God, please. It's done, it's done. Leave me alone. You have something to eat. I've paid it back. I've given you something."

In the smogged dream he keeps walking and hears the static calls of lost and lonely comrades. The foundation stretches out across flattened dunes. It whispers in its choked voice as it has since that first day.

∽

He helped build the foundation. A long way away. Between two foreign countries, while borders were in chaos. He had come through. First Infantry (Mechanized). In the last days of February, ten years ago. The conscripted opposition, hunkered down in trenches in the desert, their tools poking out through wire, sounding off and firing.

The man and his brigade came. They patted down the components vigorously, mixed up the cement with a half-hour pounding, howitzers and rockets commingling grit and everything else stacked in the sunken gutters of men like pestles and mortars, pasting everything into a good thick red base. The tanks came with their toylike motion, gunstalks rotating but silent. They did their job with other means. Plows mounted at their fronts, they traced along the lines dug in the dirt. With humdrum efficiency they shunted the hot sand into the trenches, pouring it over the contents, the mulch and ragged soup and the men who ran and tried to fire or to surrender or to scream until the desert dust gushed in and encased them and did its job, funnelling into them so their sounds were choked and they became frantic, then sluggish and still, packed the thousands down together with their friends and the segments of their friends, in their holes and miles of dugout lines.

Behind the tanks with their tractor-attachments M2 Bradleys straddled the lines of newly piled-up sand where protrusions showed the construction unfinished, the arms and legs of men beneath, some still twitching like insects. The Bradleys hosed the building site with their

7.62 mms, making sure to shove down all the material at the top, anything that might get out, making it patted down.

And then he had come behind, with the ACEs. Armored Combat Earthmovers, dozers with the last of the small-arms pinging against their skins. He had finished off the job. With his scoop, he had smoothed everything away. All the untidy detritus of the building work, the sticks and bits of wood, the sand-clogged rifles like sticks, the arms and legs like sticks, the sand-blasted heads that had tumbled slowly with the motion of the earth and now protruded. He flattened all the projections from the ground, smeared them across the dirt and smeared more dirt across them to tidy them away.

On the 25th of February in 1991, he had helped build the foundation. And as he looked out across the spread-out, flattened acres, the desert made neat, wiped clean for those hours, he had heard dreadful sounds. He had seen suddenly and terribly through the hot and red-set sand and earth to the dead, in their orderly trenches that angled like walls, and intersected and fanned out, that stretched for miles, like the plans not of a house or a palace but a city. He had seen the men made into mortar, and he had seen them looking at him.

⚭

The foundation stretched below everything. It spoke to him. It would not be quiet. In his dream or out.

He thought he would leave it behind him in the desert, in that unnatural flat zone. He thought the whispering would dissipate across the thousands of miles. He had come home. And then his dream had started. His purgatory of well fires and bloody sky and dunes, where his dead comrades were lost, made feral by loneliness. The others, the foundation, the other dead, were thousands strong. They were endless.

—morning of goodness, they whispered to him in their baked dead voices. morning of light

—praise be to god

—you built us so

—we are hot and alone. we are hungry. we eat only sand. we are full of it. we are full but hungry. we eat only sand

He had heard them nightly and tried to forget them, tried to forget what he had seen. But then he dug a pit in his yard, to put down a foundation for his house, and he had found one waiting. His wife had heard him screaming, had run out to see him scrabbling in the hole, bloodying his fingers to get out. Dig deep enough, he told her later, though she did not understand, it's there already.

A year after he had built it and first seen it, he had reached the foundation again. The city around him was built on that buried wall of dead. Bone-filled trenches stretched under the sea and linked his home to the desert.

He would do anything not to hear them. He begged the dead, met their gaze. He prayed for their silence. They waited. He thought of the weight on them, heard their hunger, at last decided what they must want.

"Here's something for you," he shouts, and cries again, after the years of searching. He pictures the families in the apartment tumbling down to rest among the foundation. "There's something for you; it can be over. Stop now. Oh, leave me alone."

He sleeps where he lies, on the cellar floor, walked across by spiders. He goes to his dream desert. He walks his sand. He hears the howling of lost soldiers. The foundation stretches up for countless thousands of yards, for miles. It has become a tower in the charred sky. It is all the same material, the dead, only their eyes and mouths moving. Little clouds of sand sputter as they speak. He stands in the shadow of the tower he was made to build, its walls of shredded khaki, flesh and ochre skin, tufted with black and dark red hair. From the sand around it oozes the same dark liquid he saw in his own yard. Blood or oil. The tower is like a minaret in Hell, some inverted Babel that reaches the sky and speaks only one language. All its voices still saying the same, the words he has heard for years.

The man wakes. He listens. For a long time he is motionless. Everything waits.

When he cries out it starts slow and builds, growing louder for long seconds. He hears himself. He is like the lost American soldiers in his dream.

He does not stop. Because it is day, the day after his offering, after he gave the foundation what he thought it hankered for, after he paid it back. But he can still see it. He can still hear it, and the dead are still saying the same things.

They watch him. The man is alone with the foundation, and he knows that they will not leave.

He cries for those in the apartment that fell, who died for nothing at all. The foundation wants nothing from him. His offering means nothing to the dead in their trenches, crisscrossing the world. They are not there to taunt or punish or teach him, or to exact revenge or blood-price, they are not enraged or restless. They are the foundation of everything around him. Without them it would crumble. They have seen him, and taught him to see them, and they want nothing from him.

All the buildings are saying the same things. The foundation runs below them all, fractured and made of the dead, and it is saying the same things.

—we are hungry. we are alone. we are hot. we are full but hungry

—you built us, and you are built on us, and below us is only sand

GOTHIC NIGHT

Mansoura Ez Eldin

Translated by Wiam El-Tamami

His departure came without explanation.

His destination was remote, he said, uttering a series of ominous sounds—the name of a city I had never heard of before. His leaving seemed a matter of fate. In an instant I could see the city he set out for, with its ashen streets.

There are no colours save for the grey that cloaks much of the place, alongside surreptitious strokes of black and white. Throngs of people walk slowly in the faded streets, wearing grim expressions and staring at a still point ahead. A leaden silence bears down on everything.

There he walks, lost in thought. And I, outside the scene, peer at him worriedly, sensing the arrival of a giant with a black coat, sullen face, and heavy footsteps. Suddenly, chaos reigns: people run in every direction, trying to escape.

―――――※―――――

I feel the earth shake under the footfalls of the man in the black coat. I know he appears on the streets from time to time, stepping powerfully with the aid of his ebony cane. His sightless eyes shift over the faces ahead, until they fall on one that will restore his vision. He points his finger at the face, and its owner vanishes from existence. The giant returns to his blindness, awaiting his next victim.

―――――※―――――

This time, however, there was only the anticipation of his coming, and the tremors that accompany him wherever he goes. Within minutes, those who were running realized they had been duped, and went back to walking as before.

―――――※―――――

I scanned the throngs and found him walking with the same slow steps. I looked closer, in search of that cunning-fox expression that characterises him, but I could not see it. He adjusted the black scarf around his neck, raising his head to the sky like someone startled by raindrops on a dry day, then returned to his daydreaming.

―――――※―――――

He has been exploring the city since his arrival, wandering its streets without stopping. He wrote to me excitedly that it is a city of the world: "Every conceivable language is here. No nationalities, no differences. You don't even need to speak to communicate your thoughts!" In the year that followed, his letters became less frequent and said nothing about this city of his—the city that seemed somehow out of this world.

※

Some time later, he went back to writing about the city: long letters that contained nothing personal—no information about him, no questions about me. Just extensive passages about this city that bears no resemblance to the cities I know, written in ornate script with small, carefully-drawn characters and an exaggerated attention to style.

※

He wrote: they called it the city of eternal sun. Its sun set only after the last inhabitant slept, and rose before the first got up. They were all deprived of the night. They were not even aware of its existence.

※

There was no giant then, or faded streets, or people running. Just the perennial day and a fierce, barely-setting sun. The streets of the city resemble each other so closely they are like infinite replicas of the same street. Its Gothic architecture inspires awe: spired towers and prominent arches; stark, imposing squares; screaming gargoyles with eyes wide open in horror; and gardens—more akin to woods—pooling out along the city's periphery.

※

These are the same woods from which the giant with the sightless eyes emerged—except, at the time, he was not blind, and his expression was suffused with seduction rather than sullenness. He moved about lightly then, speaking of a beautiful thing called *night*; he had read about it in the books piled high in his cabin in the woods and heard about it from the fishermen in the neighbouring lake.

They said they had seen it in other cities, while working on big fishing boats in faraway seas. He closes his seductive eyes and speaks of the night as though he can see it: "A great darkness that not even a thousand lanterns can dispel—only soften it slightly, imbuing it with even greater beauty." He moistens his lower lip with his tongue, savouring the idea of *night*.

He left the city of the sun in search of the night. He walked for hundreds of miles; days and weeks passed, then years. He asked all those he met, describing it in words that were muddled and unsure.

With the passage of time he began to lose hope—but he kept on his path defiantly, not once looking behind him. He walked for he knew not how long, picking fruit from trees and drinking spring water, until he found himself on the way back to his city.

He recognised it by its tall spires and crystal domes that reflect the sun's rays, giving rise to a galaxy of brilliant suns. He could not tear his eyes away from their frightening luminescence, until he began to feel the light seeping away. The closer he came, the dimmer they became. At first, he did not understand what he was experiencing; he assumed that the lights of the world around him were slowly fading out. Only when he was submerged in total darkness did he realise that he had finally fulfilled his quest. He had met the night face-to-face. He was overjoyed, for now he would carry his own private night back to the city of the sun.

The remaining distance, short though it was, was the most difficult in his long journey. He stumbled and circled the city walls several times before he could get in. When he finally entered, the city people were astonished by the sight of this scowling giant with dark clothes and lumbering steps. They discovered that, with his return, their city had been transformed into another: a pallid place, caught between a day that had left never to return, and a night that refused to arrive.

In the next letter my friend appeared to have forgotten about his last one, repeating everything he had already said, with minor adjustments, before continuing the story. The giant with the snuffed-out eyes retreated to his cabin in the woods for a long time, during which he did not utter a single word, instead listening to the sighing of the trees, the twittering of the birds, and the roar of the wind when it blew. When he tired of his solitude and his silence, he took to the streets with heavy footsteps that shook the ground beneath—leaning on his ebony cane, sheltering behind his blind and sullen stare, and armed with his experience in listening to nothingness. His eyes shift over the faces ahead until they fall on one that has the power to restore his vision. He points his finger, and its owner vanishes from existence. The giant tries to gather in all the details of the new world around him before he is plunged into darkness once again—but to no avail. He returns, despondent, to his cabin and his waiting.

The city with its Gothic soul takes root in my mind. Its identical streets and imposing squares inhabit me. I dream about the gargoyles on its buildings' facades, and awaken feeling like someone who has roamed its paths. I get up at dawn, weighed down by what I've seen. The giant moves in my mind, his expression transformed once again from sullenness to seduction, as though inviting me to follow him.

I read and re-read my friend's letters. I pore over the elegant script with its precisely-penned characters, and I think of how much he has changed. He no longer bears any resemblance to the person he once was. The city seems to have performed some mysterious black magic on him, driving him to write without emotion, without purpose, without stopping. I send him letters asking how he is, what he's doing, whether or not he is planning to return. He does not utter a single word in response to my questions, but continues to write about the city that has cast its spell on him, transforming him into an eye that captures the details of its surroundings and a hand that records them tirelessly.

I thought: I will follow his lead. Instead of letters steeped in questions that he skips over as though they weren't there, I began to write about my city. An invented city that lies between mountains clad in lush green plants and trees, and a relentlessly raging sea that films the air with the scent of iodine and whose waves, every morning, spit thick layers of salt upon the beach. Built entirely on the precipice that sweeps down from the mountains to the raging sea, the houses of the city appear to be in eternal freefall. Its people are caught in a neverending battle with gravity: they walk slowly in ascent or descent, fearful of falling from this great height to the crashing waves below.

I composed a letter for every one I received from him, not commenting on what he'd written or asking about him, and he—as always—appeared to have not even read mine. Then I begin to write without pause, long letters preoccupied with details and penned with care. I send some and neglect to send most, until I stop corresponding with him altogether, intent only on inking hundreds of letters that I stack high here and there throughout my house.

———— ❦ ————

I write, ignoring my aching fingers and the pain in my hunched back, blurring the lines between my city and his, between the Gothic architecture with its squares and screaming faces and the perilous precipice with its houses resisting eternal freefall; between his giant with the black coat and blind eyes and the people I see when I open my window, walking cautiously up and down.

———— ❦ ————

I re-read my letters, strewn all around me; I contemplate my ornate script with its small, carefully-drawn characters and exaggerated attention to style, and I think of how much I've changed. I emerge from my house, surrounded by plants and thick tangled trees, and come, in shock, upon my city with its grey streets and stark squares and the leaden silence bearing down on everything. Closing my eyes, I succumb to the darkness, and the scene opens up silently before me. I see throngs of people moving slowly, staring at a still point ahead . . . I see him walking, lost in thought . . . and I hear, loud in my ears, the thud of heavy footsteps. Could it be coming from me?

REINDEER MOUNTAIN

Karin Tidbeck

⎯⎯⎯⎯

Cilla was twelve years old the summer Sara put on her great-grandmother's
wedding dress and disappeared up the mountain. It was in the middle of
June, during summer break. The drive was a torturous nine hours, interrupted much too rarely by bathroom- and ice cream-breaks. Cilla was
reading in the passenger seat of the ancient Saab, Sara stretched out in
the back seat, Mum driving. They were travelling northwest on gradually narrowing roads, following the river, the towns shrinking and the
mountains drawing closer. Finally, the old Saab crested a hill and rolled
down into a wide valley where the river pooled into a lake between two
mountains. Cilla put her book down and looked out the window. The
village sat between the lake and the great hump of Reindeer Mountain,
its lower reaches covered in dark pine forest. The mountain on the other
side of the lake was partly deforested, as if someone had gone over it
with a giant electric shaver. Beyond them, more shapes undulated toward the horizon, shapes rubbed soft by the ice ages.

"Why does no one live on the mountain itself?" Sara suddenly said, pulling one of her earphones out. Robert Smith's voice leaked into the car.

"It's not very convenient, I suppose," said Mum. "The hillside is very steep."

"Nana said it's because the mountain belongs to the vittra."

"She would." Mum smirked. "It sounds much more exciting. Look!"

She pointed up to the hillside on the right. A rambling two-storey house sat in a meadow outside the village. "There it is."

Cilla squinted at the house. It sat squarely in the meadow. Despite the faded paint and angles that were slightly off, it somehow seemed very solid. "Are we going there now?"

"No. It's late. We'll go straight to Aunt Hedvig's and get ourselves installed. But you can come with me tomorrow if you like. The cousins will all be meeting to see what needs doing."

"I can't believe you're letting the government buy the land," said Sara.

"We're not letting them," sighed Mum. "They're expropriating."

"Forcing us to sell," Cilla said.

"I know what it means, smartass," muttered Sara and kicked the back of the passenger seat. "It still blows."

Cilla reached back and pinched her leg. Sara caught her hand and twisted her fingers until Cilla squealed. They froze when the car suddenly braked. Mum killed the engine and glared at them.

"Get out," she said. "Hedvig's cottage is up this road. You can walk the rest of the way. I don't care who started," she continued when Cilla opened her mouth to protest. "Get out. Walk it off."

They arrived at Hedvig's cottage too tired to bicker. The house sat on a slope above the village, red with white window frames and a little porch overlooking the village and lake. Mum was in the kitchen with Hedvig.

They were having coffee, slurping it through a lump of sugar between their front teeth.

"I've spoken to Johann about moving him into a home," said Hedvig as the girls came in. "He's not completely against it. But he wants to stay here. And there is no home here that can handle people with . . . nerve problems. And he can't stay with Otto forever." She looked up at Cilla and Sara and smiled, her eyes almost disappearing in a network of wrinkles. She looked very much like Nana and Mum, with the same wide cheekbones and slanted grey eyes.

"Look at you lovely girls!" said Hedvig, getting up from the table.

She was slightly hunchbacked and very thin. Embracing her, Cilla could feel her vertebrae through the cardigan.

Hedvig urged them to sit down. "They're store-bought, I hope you don't mind," she said, setting a plate of cookies on the table.

Hedvig and Mum continued to talk about Johann. He was the eldest brother of Hedvig and Nana, the only one of the siblings to remain in the family house. He had lived alone in there for forty years. Mum and her cousins had the summer to get Johann out and salvage whatever they could before the demolition crew came. No one quite knew what the house looked like inside. Johann hadn't let anyone in for decades.

⚮

There were two guest rooms in the cottage. Sara and Cilla shared a room under the eaves; Mum took the other with the threat that any fighting would mean her moving in with her daughters. The room was small but cosy, with lacy white curtains and dainty furniture, like in an oversized doll's house: two narrow beds with white throws, a writing desk with curved legs, two slim-backed chairs. It smelled of dried flowers and dust. The house had no toilet. Hedvig showed a bewildered Cilla to an outhouse across the little meadow. Inside, the outhouse was clean and bare, with a little candle and matches, even a magazine holder. The rich scent of decomposing waste clung to the back of the nose.

Cilla went quickly, imagining an enormous cavern under the seat, full of spiders and centipedes and evil clowns.

When she got back, she found Sara already in bed, listening to music with her eyes closed. Cilla got into her own bed. The sheets were rough, the pillowcase embroidered with someone's initials. She picked up her book from the nightstand. She was reading it for the second time, enjoying slowly and with relish the scene where the heroine tries on a whalebone corset. After a while she took her glasses off, switched off the lamp, and lay on her back. It was almost midnight, but cold light filtered through the curtains. Cilla sat up again, put her glasses on, and pulled a curtain aside. The town lay tiny and quiet on the shore of the lake, the mountain beyond backlit by the eerie glow of the sun skimming just below the horizon. The sight brought a painful sensation Cilla could neither name nor explain. It was like a longing, worse than anything she had ever experienced, but for what she had no idea. Something tremendous waited out there. Something wonderful was going to happen, and she was terrified that she would miss it.

Sara had fallen asleep, her breathing deep and steady. The Cure trickled out from her earphones. It was a song Cilla liked. She got back into bed and closed her eyes, listening to Robert sing of hands in the sky for miles and miles.

※

Cilla was having breakfast in the kitchen when she heard the crunch of boots on gravel through the open front door. Mum sat on the doorstep in faded jeans and clogs and her huge grey cardigan, a cup in her hands. She set it down and rose to greet the visitor. Cilla rose from the table and peeked outside. Johann wasn't standing very close to Mum, but it was as if he was towering over her. He wore a frayed blue anorak that hung loose on his thin frame, his grime-encrusted work trousers tucked into green rubber boots. His face lay in thick wrinkles like old leather, framed by a shock of white hair. He gave off a rancid, goat-like odour that made Cilla put her hand over her nose and mouth. If Mum was bothered by it, she didn't let on.

"About time you came back, stå'års," he said. He called her a girl. No one had called Mum a girl before. "It's been thirty years. Did you forget about us?"

"Of course not, Uncle," said Mum. "I just chose to live elsewhere, that's all." Her tone was carefully neutral.

Johann leaned closer to Mum. "And you came back just to help tear the house down. You're a hateful little bitch. No respect for the family."

If Mum was upset, she didn't show it. "You know that we don't have a choice. And it's not okay to talk to me like that, Johann."

Johann's eyes softened. He looked down at his boots. "I'm tired," he said.

"I know," said Mum. "Are you comfortable at Otto's?"

Cilla must have made a noise, because Johann turned his head toward her. He stuck out his hand in a slow wave. "Oh, hello there. Did you bring both children, Marta? How are they? Any of them a little strange? Good with music? Strange dreams? Monsters under the bed?" He grinned. His teeth were a brownish yellow.

"You need to go now, Johann," said Mum.

"Doesn't matter if you move south," Johann said. "Can't get it out of your blood." He left, rubber boots crunching on the gravel path.

Mum wrapped her cardigan more tightly around herself and came inside.

"What was that about?" Cilla said.

"Johann has all sorts of ideas."

"Is he talking about why we have so much craziness in the family?"

"Johann thinks it's a curse." She smiled at Cilla and patted her cheek. "He's very ill. We're sensitive, that's all. We have to take care of ourselves."

Cilla leaned her forehead against Mum's shoulder. Her cardigan smelled of wool and cold air. "What if me or Sara gets sick?"

"Then we'll handle it," said Mum. "You'll be fine."

⚮

What everyone knew was this: that sometime in the late nineteenth century a woman named Märet came down from the mountain and married Jacob Jonsson. They settled in Jacob's family home, and she bore him several children, most of whom survived to adulthood, although not unscathed. According to the story, Märet was touched. She saw strange things, and occasionally did and said strange things, too. Märet's children, and their children in turn, were plagued by frail nerves and hysteria; people applied more modern terms as time passed.

Alone of all her siblings, Cilla's mother had no symptoms. That was no guarantee, of course. Ever since Cilla had been old enough to understand what the story really meant, she had been waiting for her or Sara to catch it, *that*, the disease. Mum said they weren't really at risk since Dad's family had no history of mental illness, and anyway they had grown up in a stable environment. Nurture would triumph over nature. Negative thinking was not allowed. It seemed, though, as if Sara might continue the tradition.

⚮

Sara was sitting under the bed covers with her back to the wall, eyes closed, Robert Smith wailing in her earphones. She opened her eyes when Cilla shut the door.

"Johann was here." Cilla wrinkled her nose. "He smells like goat."

"Okay," said Sara. Her eyes were a little glazed.

"Are you all right?"

Sara rubbed her eyes. "It's the thing."

Cilla sat next to her on the bed, taking Sara's hand. She was cold, her breathing shallow; Cilla could feel the pulse hammering in her wrist. Sara was always a little on edge, but sometimes it got worse. She had said that it felt like something horrible was about to happen, but she couldn't say exactly what, just a terrible sense of doom. It had started about six months ago, about the same time that she got her first period.

"Want me to get Mum?" Cilla said as always.

"No. It's not that bad," said Sara, as usual. She leaned back against the wall, closing her eyes.

Sara had lost it once in front of Mum. Mum didn't take it well. She had told Sara to snap out of it, that there was nothing wrong with her, that she was just having hysterics. After that, Sara kept it to herself. In this, if in nothing else, Cilla was allowed to be her confidante. In a way, Mum was right: compared to paranoid schizophrenia, a little anxiety wasn't particularly crazy. Not that it helped Sara any.

"You can pinch me if it makes you feel better." Cilla held out her free arm. She always did what she could to distract Sara.

"Brat."

"Ass."

Sara smiled a little. She looked down at Cilla's hand in hers, suddenly wrenching it around so that it landed on her sister's leg.

"Why are you hitting yourself? Stop hitting yourself!" she shouted in mock horror.

There was a knock on the door. Mum opened it without waiting for an answer. She was dressed in rubber boots and a bright yellow raincoat over her cardigan. "I'm going to the house now, if you want to come."

"Come on, brat," said Sara, letting go of Cilla's hand.

⚭

The driveway up to the house was barely visible under the weeds. Two middle-aged men in windbreakers and rubber boots were waiting in the front yard. Mum pointed at them.

"That's Otto and Martin!" Mum waved at them through the window.

"I thought there were six cousins living up here," said Sara.

"There are," said Mum. "But the others aren't well. It's just Otto and Martin today."

They stepped out into cold, wet air. Cilla was suddenly glad of her thick jeans and knitted sweater. Sara, who had refused to wear any of the (stupid and embarrassing) sweaters Mum offered, was shivering in her black tights and thin long-sleeved shirt.

The cousins greeted each other with awkward hugs. Otto and Martin were in their fifties, both with the drawn-out Jonsson look: tall and sinewy with watery blue eyes, a long jaw, and wide cheekbones. Martin was a little shorter and younger, with fine black hair that stood out from his head like a dark dandelion. Otto, balding and with a faraway look, only nodded and wouldn't shake hands.

This close, the old house looked ready to fall apart. The red paint was flaking in thick layers, the steps up to the front door warped. Some of the windowpanes were covered with bits of white plastic and duct tape.

Mum waved toward the house. "Johann's not with you?"

Martin shrugged, taking a set of keys from his pocket. "He didn't want to be here for this. All right. We'll start with going through the rooms one by one, seeing what we can salvage. Otto has pen and paper to make a list."

"You haven't been in here until now?" said Mum.

"We've been cleaning a little. Johann only used a couple of the rooms, but it was bad. The smell should be bearable now."

Otto opened the door. Johann's unwashed stench wafted out in a sour wave. "You get used to it." He ducked his head under the lintel and went inside.

Johann had used two rooms and the kitchen on the ground floor. Neither Cilla nor Sara could bring themselves to enter them, the stench of filth and rot so strong it made them gag. By the light coming in through the door, Cilla could see piles of what looked like rags, stacks of newspapers, and random furniture.

"There was a layer of milk cartons and cereal boxes this high on the floors in there," said Martin, pointing to his knee. "The ones at the bottom were from the seventies."

"I don't think he ate much else," Otto filled in. "He refuses to eat anything but corn flakes and milk at my house. He says all other food is poisoned."

Otto, Martin, and Mum looked at each other. Mum shrugged. "That's how it is."

Otto sucked air in between pursed lips, the quiet *.jo* that acknowledged and ended the subject.

The smell wasn't as bad in the rest of the house; Johann seemed to have barricaded himself in his two rooms. The sitting room was untouched. Daylight filtered in through filthy windowpanes, illuminating furniture that looked hand-made and ancient: cabinets painted with flower designs, a wooden sofa with a worn seat, a rocking-chair with the initials O.J. and the date 1898.

"It looks just like when we were kids," said Mum.

"Doesn't it?" said Otto.

Cilla returned to the entryway, peering up the stairs to the next floor. "What about upstairs? Can we go upstairs?"

"Certainly," said Martin. "Let me go first and turn on the lights." He took a torch from his pocket, lighting his way as he walked up the stairs. Sara and Cilla followed him.

The top of the stairs ended in a narrow corridor, where doors opened to the master bedroom and two smaller rooms with two beds in each.

"How many people lived here?" Cilla peered into the master bedroom.

"Depends on when you mean," Martin replied. "Your grandmother had four siblings altogether. And I think there was at least a cousin or two of theirs living here during harvest, too."

"But there are only four single beds," said Sara from the doorway of another room.

Martin shrugged. "People shared beds."

"But you didn't live here all the time, right?"

"No, no. My mother moved out when she got married. I grew up in town. Everyone except Johann moved out."

"There are more stairs over here," said Sara from further away.

"That's the attic," said Martin. "You can start making lists of things up there." He handed Cilla his torch, a pen, and a sheaf of paper. "Mind your step."

<hr />

The attic ran the length of the house, divided into compartments. Each compartment was stacked with stuff: boxes, furniture, old skis, kick-sleds, a bicycle. The little windows and the weak light bulb provided enough light that they didn't need the torch. Cilla started in one end of the attic, Sara in the other, less sorting and more rooting around. After a while, Mum came upstairs.

"There's a huge chest here," said Sara after a while, pushing a stack of boxes to the side.

Cilla left her list and came over to look. It was a massive blue chest with a rounded lid, faded and painted with flowers.

"Let me see," said Mum from behind them.

Mum came forward, knelt in front of the chest, and opened it, the lid lifting with a groan. It was filled almost to the brim with neatly folded white linen, sprinkled with mothballs. In a corner sat some bundles wrapped in tissue paper.

Mum shone her torch into the chest. "This looks like a hope chest." She carefully lifted the tissue paper and uncovered red wool. She handed the torch to Cilla, using both hands to lift the fabric up. It was a full-length skirt, the cloth untouched by vermin.

"Pretty," said Sara. She took the skirt, holding it up to her waist.

"There's more in here," said Mum, moving tissue paper aside. "A shirt, an apron, and a shawl. A whole set. It could be Märet's."

"Like what she got married in?" said Cilla.

"Maybe so," said Mum.

"It's my size," said Sara. "Can I try it on?"

"Not now. Keep doing lists." Mum took the skirt back, carefully folding it and putting it back into the chest.

Sara kept casting glances at the chest the rest of the morning. When Cilla caught her looking, Sara gave her the finger.

Later in the afternoon, Mum emptied a cardboard box and put the contents from the hope chest in it. "I'm taking this over to Hedvig's. I'm sure she can tell us who it belonged to."

⚘

After dinner, Mum unpacked the contents of the hope chest in Hedvig's kitchen. There were six bundles in all: the red skirt with a marching bodice, a red shawl, a white linen shift, a long apron striped in red and black, and a black purse embroidered with red flowers. Hedvig picked up the purse and ran a finger along the petals.

"This belonged to Märet." Hedvig smiled. "She showed me these once, before she passed away. That's what she wore when she came down from the mountain," she said. "I thought they were gone. I'm very glad you found them."

"How old were you when she died?" said Sara.

"It was in twenty-one, so I was fourteen. It was terrible." Hedvig shook her head. "She died giving birth to Nils, your youngest great-uncle. It was still common back then."

Cilla fingered the skirt. Out in daylight, the red wool was bright and luxurious, like arterial blood. "What was she like?"

Hedvig patted the purse. "Märet was . . . a peculiar woman," she said eventually.

"Was she really crazy?" Cilla said.

"Crazy? I suppose she was. She certainly passed something on. The curse, like Johann says. But that's silly. She came here to help with harvest, you know, and she fell in love with your great-grandfather. He didn't know much about her. No one did, except that she was from somewhere northeast of here."

"I thought she came down from the mountain," Cilla said.

Hedvig smiled. "Yes, she would say that when she was in the mood."

"What about those things, anyway?" Sara said. "Are they fairies?"

"What?" Hedvig gave her a blank look.

"The vittra," Cilla filled in helpfully. "The ones that live on the mountain."

"Eh," said Hedvig. "Fairies are cute little things that prance about in meadows. The vittra look like humans, but taller and more handsome. And it's *inside* the mountain, not on it." She had brightened visibly, becoming more animated as she spoke. "There were always stories about vittra living up there. Sometimes they came down to trade with the townspeople. You had to be careful with them, though. They could curse you or kill you if you crossed them. But they had the fattest cows, and the finest wool, and beautiful silver jewellery. Oh, and they liked to dress in red." Hedvig indicated the skirt Cilla had in her lap. "And sometimes they came to dance with the local young men and women, even taking one away for marriage. And when a child turned out to have nerve problems, they said it was because someone in the family had passed on vittra blood . . ."

"But did you meet any?" Sara blurted.

Hedvig laughed. "Of course not. There would be some odd folk showing up to sell their things in town, but they were mostly Norwegians or from those *really* small villages up north where everyone's their own uncle."

Sara burst out giggling.

"Auntie!" Mum looked scandalized.

Hedvig waved a hand at her. "I'm eighty-seven years old. I can say whatever I like."

"But what about Märet?" Cilla leaned forward.

"Mother, yes." Hedvig poured a new cup of coffee, arm trembling under the weight of the thermos. "She was a bit strange, I suppose. She really *was* tall for a woman, and she would say strange things at the wrong time, talk to animals, things like that. People would joke about vittra blood."

"What do you think?" said Sara.

"I think she must have had a hard life, to run away from her family and never speak of them again." Hedvig gently took the skirt from Cilla and folded it.

"But the red . . ."

Hedvig shook her head and smiled. "It was an expensive colour back then. Saying someone wore red meant they were rich. This probably cost Märet a lot." She put the clothes back in the cardboard box and closed it.

Cilla stayed up until she was sure everyone else had gone to bed. It took ages. Sara wrote in her journal until one o' clock and then took some time to fall asleep, Robert Smith still whining in her ears.

The cardboard box was sitting on the kitchen sofa, the silk paper in a pile next to it. Cilla lifted the lid, uncovering red wool that glowed in the half-dawn. The shift and the skirt were too long and very tight around the stomach. She kept the skirt unbuttoned and rolled the waist-line down, hoisting it so the hem wouldn't trip her up. She tied the apron tight around her waist to hold everything up, and clipped the purse onto the apron string. The bodice was too loose on her flat chest and wouldn't close at the waist, so she let it hang open and tied the shawl over her shoulders.

It was quiet outside, the horizon glowing an unearthly gold, the rest of the sky shifting in blue and green. The birds were quiet. The moon was up, a tiny crescent in the middle of the sky. The air was cold and wet; the grass swished against the skirt, leaving moisture pearling on the wool. Cilla could see all the way down to the lake and up to the moun-tain. She took her glasses off and put them in the purse. Now she was one of the vittra, coming down from the mountain, heading for the river. She was tall and graceful, her step quiet. She danced as she went, barefoot in the grass.

A sliver of sun peeking over the horizon broke the spell. Cilla's feet were suddenly numb with cold. She went back into the house and took everything off again, fished her glasses out, and folded the clothes into the cardboard box. It was good wool; the dew brushed off without soaking into the skirt. When Cilla slipped into bed again, it was only a little past two. The linen was warm and smooth against the cold soles of her feet.

They returned to the family house the following day. Sara decided that wading through debris in the attic was stupid and sulked on a chair outside. Cilla spent the day writing more lists. She found more skis, some snowshoes, a cream separator, dolls, a half-finished sofa bed, and a sewing table that was in almost perfect condition.

Johann showed up in the afternoon. Martin and Otto seemed to think he was going to make a scene, because they walked out and met him far down the driveway. Eventually they returned, looking almost surprised, with Johann walking beside them, his hands clasped behind his back. When Cilla next saw him, he had sat down in a chair next to Sara. Sara had a shirtsleeve over her nose and mouth, but she was listening to him talk with rapt attention. Johann left again soon after. Sara wouldn't tell Cilla what they'd spoken about, but her eyes were a little wider than usual, and she kept knocking things over.

When they returned to Hedvig's house, Sara decided to try on Märet's dress. On her, the skirt wasn't too long or too tight; it cinched her waist just so, ending nearly at her ankle. The bodice fit like it was tailor-made for her as well, tracing the elegant tapering curve of her back from shoulder to hip. She looked like she'd just stepped out of a story. It made Cilla's chest feel hollow.

Sara caught her gaze in the mirror and made a face. "It looks stupid." She plucked at the skirt. "The red is way too bright. I wonder if you could dye it black? Because that would look awesome."

Cilla looked at her own reflection, just visible beyond Sara's red splendour. She was short and barrel-shaped, eyes tiny behind her glasses. There were food stains on her sweater. "*You* look stupid," she managed.

Mum was scrubbing potatoes in the kitchen when Cilla came downstairs.

"Who's getting the dress, Mum? Because Sara wants to dye it black."

"Oh ho?" said Mum. "Probably not, because it's not hers."

"Can I have it?" Cilla shifted her weight from foot to foot. "I wouldn't do anything to it."

"No, love. It belongs to Hedvig."

"But she's *old*. She won't use it."

Mum turned and gave Cilla a long look, eyebrows low. "It belonged to her *mother*, Cilla. How would you feel if you found my wedding dress, and someone gave it away to some relative instead?"

"She has everything else," Cilla said. "I don't have anything from great-gran."

"I'm sure we can find something from the house," said Mum. "But not the dress. It means a lot to Hedvig. Think of someone else's feelings for a change."

Sara came down a little later with the same request. Mum yelled at her.

Maybe it was because of Mum's outburst, but Sara became twitchier as the evening passed on. Finally she muttered something about going for a walk and shrugged into her jacket. Cilla hesitated a moment and then followed.

"Fuck off," Sara muttered without turning her head when Cilla came running after her.

"No way," said Cilla.

Sara sighed and rolled her eyes. She increased her pace until Cilla had to half-jog to keep up. They said nothing until they came down to the lake's shore, a stretch of rounded river stones that made satisfying billiard-ball noises under Cilla's feet.

Sara sat down on one of the larger rocks and dug out a soft tenpack of cigarettes. She shook one out and lit it. "Tell Mum and I'll kill you."

"I know." Cilla sat down next to her. "Why are you being so weird? Ever since you talked to Johann."

Sara took a drag on her cigarette and blew the smoke out through her nose. She shrugged. Her eyes looked wet. "He made me understand some things, is all."

"Like what?"

"Like I'm not crazy. Like none of us are." She looked out over the lake. "We should stay here. Maybe we'd survive." Her eyes really were wet now. She wiped at them with her free hand.

Cilla felt cold trickle down her back. "What are you on about?"

Sara rubbed her forehead. "You have to promise not to tell anyone, because if you tell anyone bad stuff will happen, okay? Shit is going to happen just because I'm telling *you*. But I'll tell you because you're my little sis." She slapped a quick rhythm on her thigh. "Okay. So it's like this—the world is going to end soon. It's going to end in ninety-six."

Cilla blinked. "How would you know?"

"It's in the newspapers, if you look. The Gulf War, yeah? That's when it started. Saddam Hussein is going to take revenge and send nukes, and then the U.S. will nuke back, and then Russia jumps in. And then there'll be nukes everywhere, and we're dead. Or we'll die in the nuclear winter, 'cause they might not nuke Sweden, but there'll be nothing left for us." Sara's eyes were a little too wide.

"Okay," Cilla said, slowly. "But how do you *know* all this is going to happen?"

"I can see the signs. In the papers. And I just . . . know. Like someone told me. The twenty-third of February in ninety-six, that's when the world ends. I mean, haven't you noticed that something's really really *wrong?*"

Cilla dug her toe into the stones. "It's the opposite."

"What." There was no question mark to Sara's tone.

"Something wonderful," Cilla said. Her cheeks were hot. She focused her eyes on her toe.

"You're a fucking idiot." Sara turned her back, demonstratively, and lit a new cigarette.

Cilla never could wait her out. She walked back home alone.

⸎

On midsummer's eve, they had a small feast. There was pickled herring and new potatoes, smoked salmon, fresh strawberries and cream, spiced schnapps for Mum and Hedvig. It was past ten when Cilla pulled on Sara's sleeve.

"We have to go pick seven kinds of flowers," she said.

Sara rolled her eyes. "That's kid stuff. I have a headache," she said, standing up. "I'm going to bed."

Cilla remained at the table with her mother and great-aunt, biting her lip.

Mum slipped an arm around her shoulder. "Picking seven flowers is an old, old tradition," she said. "There's nothing silly about it."

"I don't feel like it anymore," Cilla mumbled.

Mum chuckled gently. "Well, if you change your mind, tonight is when you can stay up for as long as you like."

"Just be careful," said Hedvig. "The vittra might be out and about." She winked conspiratorially at Cilla.

At Hedvig's dry joke, Cilla suddenly knew with absolute certainty what she had been pining for, that wonderful *something* waiting out there. She remained at the table, barely able to contain her impatience until Mum and Hedvig jointly decided to go to bed.

Mum kissed Cilla's forehead. "Have a nice little midsummer's eve, love. I'll leave the cookies out."

Cilla made herself smile at her mother's patronizing remark, and waited for the house to go to sleep.

She had put the dress on right this time, as well as she could, and clutched seven kinds of flowers in her left hand—buttercup, clover, geranium, catchfly, bluebells, chickweed, and daisies. She stood at the back of the house, on the slope facing the mountain. It was just past midnight, the sky a rich blue tinged with green and gold. The air had a sharp and herbal scent. It was very quiet.

Cilla raised her arms. "I'm ready," she whispered. In the silence that followed, she thought she could hear snatches of music. She closed her eyes and waited. When she opened them again, the vittra had arrived.

They came out from between the pine trees, walking in pairs, all dressed in red and white: the women wore red skirts and shawls and the men long red coats. Two of them were playing the fiddle, a slow and eerie melody in a minor key.

A tall man walked at the head of the train, dressed entirely in white. His hair was long and dark and very fine. There was something familiar about the shape of his face and the translucent blue of his eyes. For a moment, those eyes stared straight into Cilla's. It was like receiving an electric shock; it reverberated down into her stomach. Then he shifted his gaze and looked beyond her to where Sara was standing wide-eyed by the corner of the house in her oversized sleeping T-shirt. He walked past Cilla without sparing her another glance.

The beautiful man from the mountain approached Sara where she stood clutching the edge of the rain barrel. He put a hand on her arm and said something to her that Cilla couldn't hear. Whatever it was, it made Sara's face flood with relief. She took his hand, and they walked past Cilla to the rest of the group. The fiddle players started up their slow wedding march, and the procession returned to the mountain. Sara never looked back.

⚍

Cilla told them that Sara must have taken the dress, that she herself had gone to bed not long after the others. She told them of Sara's doomsday vision and her belief that she could tell the future by decoding secret messages in the newspaper. When the search was finally abandoned, the general opinion was that Sara had had a bout of psychotic depression and gone into the wild, where she had either fallen into a body of water or died of exposure somewhere she couldn't be found. Up there, you can die of hypothermia even in summer. Cilla said nothing of the procession, or of the plastic bag in her suitcase where Märet's dress lay cut into tiny strips.

She kept the bag for a long time.

MUZUNGU

C. Namwali Serpell

Isabella was nine years old before she knew what white meant. White in the sense of being a thing, as opposed to not being a thing. It wasn't that Isa didn't know her parents were white. Of course with her mother, this was largely a matter of conjecture. A layer of thick dark hair kept Sibilla's face a mystery. And even though as she aged, this blanket of hair turned grey, then silver, then white, a definite movement toward translucence, Isa never could properly make out her mother's features. More distinct were Sibilla's legs, tufts of fur running like a mane down each thick shin, and her strange laugh, like large sheets of paper being ripped, then crumpled. Isa's father, the Colonel, was white, but it often seemed as if pink and grey were battling it out on his face. Especially when he drank.

Her parents had settled into life in Zambia the way most expats do. They drank a lot. Every weekend was another house party, that never-ending expatriate house party that has been swatting mosquitoes and swimming in gin and quinine for more than a century. Sibilla floated around in a billowy Senegalese boubou, sending servants for refills and dropping in on every conversation, distributing laughter and ease amongst her guests. Purple-skinned peanuts had been soaked in salt water and roasted in a pan until they were grey; they cooled and shifted with a whispery sound in wooden bowls. There were Tropic beer bottles scattered around the veranda, marking the table and the concrete floor with their damp semi-circular hoof prints. Full or empty? Once the top is off a Tropic bottle, you can't tell because the amber glass is so dark. You have to lift it to check its weight. Cigars and tobacco pipes puffed their foul sweetness into the air. Darts and croquet balls went in loopy circles around their targets, loopier as the day wore on. The Colonel sat in his permanent chair just beyond the shade of the veranda, dampening with gin the thatch protruding from his nostrils, occasionally snorting at some private or overheard joke. His skin was creased like trousers that had been worn too long. Budding from his arms were moles so large and detached they looked ready to tumble off and roll away into the night. And as though his wife's hairiness had become contagious, his ears had been taken over by hair—the calyx whorl of each had sprouted a bouquet of whiskers. The Colonel liked to drink from the same glass the entire day, always his favorite glass, decorated with the red, white, and green hexagons of a football. As his drunkenness progressed, the glass got misty from being so close to his open mouth, then slimy as his saliva glands loosened, then muddy as dirt and sweat mixed on his hand. At the end of the evening, when Isa was sent to fetch her father's glass, she often found it beneath his chair under a swarm of giddy ants, the football spattered like it had been used for a rainy day match.

Isa had no siblings and when the other expatriate children were around she was frantic and listless in turns. Today, she began with frantic. Leaving the grown-ups outside propping their feet on wooden stools and scratching at their sunburns, Isa marched three of the more hapless children inside the house and down the long corridor to her bedroom.

There, she introduced them to her things. First to her favorite book, *D'Aulaires' Book of Greek Myths*. Second to the live, broken-winged bird she'd found in the driveway. Third, and finally, to Doll.

"And this is my doll. She comes from America. She has an Amurrican accent. Her name is Doll."

Bird and Doll lived together in an open cardboard box. Isabella stood next to the box with her chin lifted, her hand pointing down to the box. Due to the scarcity of imported goods in Lusaka, Isa was allowed only one doll at a time, and this one had gone the way of all dolls: tangled-haired–patchy–bald. Forever smiling Doll, denied a more original name by her fastidious owner, sat with her legs extended, her right knee bent at an obtuse and alluring angle. From Doll's arched left foot a tiny plastic pink stiletto dangled. Her perforated rubber head tilted to one side. She seemed interested and pleasant. Bird, also on its way to bald, cowered as far away from Doll as possible, looking defeated. Isa poked at it with her finger. The bird skittered lopsidedly around the box until, cornered, it uttered a vague chirp. Alex and Stephie, prompted by Isabella, applauded this effort. But Emma, the littlest, thinking that the doll rather than the bird had made the sound, burst into startled tears. She had to be soothed (by Stephie) and corrected (by Isa). Isa was annoyed. So, she sat them down in a row on her bed and taught them things that she knew. About fractions and about why Athena was better than Aphrodite. About the sun and how it wasn't moving, we were. But soon enough, Emma's knotted forehead and Alex's fidgeting began to drive Isa to distraction. Then came the inevitable tantrum, followed by a dark sullen lull. The other three children hastened from the room in a kind of daze. Isa sat next to the cardboard box and cried a little, alternately stroking Doll's smiling head and Bird's weary one.

When she'd tired of self-pity, Isa went to the bathroom and carefully closed and locked the door. She took off her shoes and climbed onto the edge of the bathtub, which faced a wall about two feet away. Only by standing on the edge of the tub could she see herself in the mirror on the wall, which hung at adult height. She examined her grey eyes, closing each of them in turn to see how she looked when blinking. She checked her face for hair (an endless, inevitable paranoia) and with a cruel finger pushed the tip of her nose up. She felt it hung too close to her upper lip. Then Isa let herself fall into the mirror, her own face rushing toward her, her eyes expanding with fear and perspective. At the last minute, she reached out her hands and stopped herself. She stayed in this position for a moment, angled across the room, arms rigid, hands pressed against the mirror, nose centimeters from it. Then, bored of her face, she jumped down and explored the floor. She unraveled the last few squares of toilet paper from its roll and wrapped it around her neck. Then she opened the cardboard cylinder from the toilet paper roll into a loose brown curlicue—a bracelet. She discovered some of her mother's torn OB wrappers, which twisted at each end like candy wrappers. She stood them on their twists to make goblets for Doll.

Eventually drunken guests started lining up outside the bathroom, knocking at the door with tentative knuckles and then flat palms and then clenched fists. Isa emerged, head high and neck at full extension, her OB goblets balanced on an outstretched hand like a tray. Bejeweled with toilet paper, she strolled past the line of full-bladdered guests. She gave Doll the goblets, modeled the jewelry for Bird. But Isa's heavily curtained bedroom was too cold to play in alone. Reluctantly, she removed her makeshift jewelry—too childish for her mother to see—and rejoined the party outside. As she marched outside in her marigold dress, she glanced at the other children running around making pointless circles and meaningless noises in the garden. She avoided them, choosing instead to be pointedly polite to their parents, who were still sitting in a half-circle on the veranda, insulting each other. There was something excessive about her attentiveness as she shoved snack platters under the noses of perfectly satiated guests and refilled their mostly full beer glasses, tilting both bottle and glass to minimize the foam, just like the Colonel taught her.

Finally her mother, annoyed, told her to sit down over by Ba Simon, the gardener. He was standing at the far end of the veranda, slapping varieties of dead animal onto the smoking brai. He reached down to pat Isa on the head, but she ducked away from his hand, ignoring his eyes and his chuckle. The saccharine smell of the soap he used mingled with the smell of burnt meat. Ba Simon was singing softly under his breath. He'd probably picked up some nasty song from the shabeen, Isa thought emphatically, repeating in her head a condemnation that she'd heard a thousand times from Ba Gertrude, the maid. There are three kinds of people in the world: people who unconsciously sing along when they hear someone else singing, people who remain respectfully or irritably silent, and people who start to sing something else. Isa began singing the Zambian national anthem. Stand and sing of Zambia, proud and free. Land of work and joy and unity. Eventually Ba Simon gave up on his quiet song, smiling down at Isa and shaking his head while he flipped steaks he wouldn't get to eat. Ashes from the brai drifted and spun like the children playing in the garden. Isa watched the other children with a detached revulsion, her elbows on her knees, cheeks cradled in her hands, ashes melting imperceptibly onto the pale shins below the hem of her marigold dress. Stephie was sitting in a chair, depriving a grown-up of a seat, reading a book. Isa was scandalized. It was her mythology book! She stared at Stephie for a while and then decided to forgive her because her nose had a perfect slope. Unlike Winnifred, whose nose was enormous and freckled, almost as disgusting as the snot bubbling from Ahmed's little brown one. The two of them were trying to play croquet under the not-so-watchful eye of Aunt Kathy. Younger than most of the adults at the party, Aunt Kathy always spent the day chain smoking and downing watery Pimm's cups and looking through everyone, endlessly making and unmaking some terribly important decision. Isa found her beautiful, but looking at her for too long sometimes made her feel like there were too many things that she didn't know yet.

Emma, who had cried about Doll, was all smiles now, sitting

cross-legged by herself and watching something, probably a ladybug, crawl along her hand. Emma was so small. Isa tried to remember being that small, but the weight of her own elbows on her knees made it hard to imagine. The ladybug was even smaller. What was it like to be that small? But anyway, how could Emma have been so afraid of Doll when she clearly wasn't afraid of insects, which everyone knew could bite and were much more disgusting? Isa had once retched at the sight of a stray cockroach in the sink, but it had been a pretend retch because she'd heard at school that cockroaches were supposed to be disgusting. Horribly, Isa's pretend retch had become real and had burned her throat and she'd felt ashamed at having been so promptly punished by her body for lying. But enough time had passed to transform the feeling of disgust at herself into disgust about small crawling creatures. She watched as Emma turned her cupped hand slowly like the Queen of England waving at everyone on the television. The ladybug spiraled down her wrist, seeking edges, finding curves. Emma giggled. Isa swallowed, looked away.

Far off in the corner of the garden, there was a huddle of boys crouching, playing with worms or cards or something. Isa watched them. Every once in a while, the four boys would stand up and move a little further away and then huddle down again, like they were following a trail. They were inching this way along the garden wall, toward where it broke off by the corner of the house. Around that corner was the guava tree Isa climbed every afternoon after school. Isa got curious. And then she got suspicious. She stood up, absently brushing ashes from her dress instead of shaking them off and accidentally streaking the yellow with grey. She noticed and bit her lip and squeezed her left hand with her right, caught between her resolve to do good and her need to change her dress. But the adults were roaring with laughter and slumping with drunkenness. Whatever inappropriate behavior was taking place in the garden, it was up to her to fix. She started running across the garden, looking behind her to make sure no one followed. When she was close, she stopped herself and began stalking the boys, holding her breath.

She tiptoed right up to their backs and peered over their shoulders. At first she couldn't see much of anything, but then she realized that they were huddled around a thick-looking puddle. It was mostly clear but, as Jumani pointed out in a hushed whisper, there were spots of blood in it. Isa's eyes widened. Blood in her own garden? She winced a little and looked back at the party: Emma was interrupting Stephie's quiet read; Winnifred's freckles were pooling into an orange stain in the middle of her forehead as she concentrated on the next croquet hoop; Ahmed, snot dripping dangerously close to his open mouth, stared back at Isa, but he seemed sunstruck rather than curious. She glared warningly at him and turned back around. The boys, oblivious to her presence, had disappeared around the corner. She followed and found them squatting at the foot of the guava tree, her guava tree, with its gently soughing leaves, its gently sloughing bark. She circled the mysterious puddle and walked toward them with purpose, abandoning all efforts at being sneaky. But the boys were too fascinated with whatever they saw to notice her. A whining and a rustling from under the tree drowned the sounds of her approach. Isa peered over their shoulders, her throat tight. Lying on its side, surrounded by the four boys, was Ba Simon's dog. She was a ridgeback, named thus because of a tufted line down the back where the hairs that grew upward on either side of the spine confronted each other. At the bottom of this tiny mane, just above the tail, was a little cul-de-sac of a cowlick. Ba Simon had named the dog Cassava because of her color, though Isa thought Cassava's yellowish white fur was closer to the color of the ivory horn that her father had hung on the living room wall. But today her fur was crusted over with rust. Her belly, usually a grey suedish vest buttoned with black teats, was streaked dark red.

Isa's first thought was that these boys had poisoned Cassava and were now watching her die a slow miserable death under the guava tree. But then she saw that the side of Cassava's head was pivoting back and forth along the ground. Isa stepped to the left and saw an oblong mass quivering under the eager strokes of Cassava's long pink tongue. The thing was the color of the ice at the top of milk bottles from the fridge, cloudy and clear. From the way it wobbled, it seemed like it was made of jelly, maybe more like the consistency of gravy that had been in the fridge too long. It was connected by a pink cord to a slimy greenish black lump.

The boys were whispering to each other and just then Jumani made to touch the lump with a stick. Isa jumped forward and said, "No!" in a hushed shout. Cassava whined a little and licked faster, her tail sweeping weakly in the dust. The boys turned to Isa, but before she could say anything, the oblong thing jerked a little and Isa inhaled sharply with fright. She pointed at it, her eyes and mouth wide open. The boys turned back to look. Where Cassava was insistently licking, there was a patch along the oily surface through which they could just glimpse a grey triangle. It was an ear. Isa took her place beside the boys, sitting in the dust, her precious marigold dress forgotten.

Perhaps out of fear, perhaps out of reverence, the boys didn't touch Cassava until she had burst the wobbling sac and licked away all of the clear fluid inside it. Occasionally there was a tobacco-tainted breeze from around the corner. Sometimes laughter would flare up, crackling down to Sibilla's chortle. But the grown-ups didn't come. At first the children whispered their speculations, but soon they were all watching in silence, gasping only once when the outer skin finally burst, releasing a pool that crept slowly along the ground.

There it was, lying in a patch of damp dirt, trembling as Cassava's tongue grazed along its sticky body. It was the size of a rat; it was hairy and pink; its face was a skull with skin. Below its half-closed pink eyelids, the eyes were blue-black and seemed almost see-through. But that was just the sunlight dappling through the guava leaves and reflecting off their shiny surface; the children looked closer and saw the eyes were opaque and dead. The boys became restless. Cassava was still licking, but nothing was happening; the mystery was revealed, the thing was dead, what else was there to see? They got up and left, already knocking about for other ways to pass the long afternoon. Awed and resolved to maintain her dignity and her difference from the boys, Isa decided to stay, silently shaking her head when Jumani offered her a hand up. She was so absorbed in watching that hypnotic tongue rocking the corpse back and forth that she didn't notice the girl until she spoke.

"He et oh the bebbies? Eh-eh, he et them," the girl asked and answered. Isa looked around and saw nothing. Laughter fell from the sky. Isa looked up into the tree and saw Ba Simon's daughter sitting up in a wide crook, her little head hanging to one side as she smirked down upon the world. Chanda was about six or seven, close enough to Isa's age, but they weren't allowed to play together because of an unspoken agreement between Ba Simon and Sibilla. The two girls had been caught making mudpies together once when they were younger and had been so thoroughly scolded by their respective parents that even to look at each other felt like reaching a hand toward an open flame. Isa's entrance into primary school had made their mutual avoidance easier, as had her innate preference for adult conversation and her recently acquired but deeply held feelings about the stained men's T-shirt that Chanda wore every day as a dress.

Isa glared at Chanda's laughing face.

"He ate what? Anyway, it's a her," she replied with hesitant indignation. She gathered some strength in her voice. "Obviously," she said. Chanda was expertly descending from the crook of the tree, flashing a pair of baggy but clean pink panties on the way down. Isa abruptly decided that Chanda had been secretly climbing the guava tree during school hours and that she had stolen the panties off the clothesline.

As she carefully lowered herself to the ground, Chanda said: "His stomach has been very row. And then pa yesterday? He was just cryingcrying the ho day. Manje ona, jast look: he et the bebby."

Isa was horrified, then dubious. "How do you know?"

Chanda, now standing with her feet planted a little apart, her hands resting on her haunches in imitation of Ba Gertrude, nodded knowingly.

"Oh-oh? Jast watch." Her voice trembled nevertheless.

Cassava hadn't stopped licking the stillborn. Her tongue maintained its rhythm and her mouth appeared to have moved closer to the dead-eyed skull. Isa shuddered and scrambled to her feet. Suddenly, mustering all her courage, she stretched her leg out and with her bare foot kicked the dead puppy as hard as she could away from Cassava. It tumbled away into the dust, a guava leaf trailing from it like an extra tail. Cassava growled ominously.

"Did she do that yesterday too?" Isa demanded, reaching behind her for Chanda's hand. Chanda was silent. Cassava scudded her distended torso across the ground toward the puppy. Isa quickly glanced back at Chanda's face, which, in reflecting her own fear, terrified her even more. Cassava wheezed and growled at the same time. Her legs twitched.

"Let's go," Isa suggested breathlessly.

Their hands still clasped, the two girls ran away, Cassava baying behind them. Isa felt buoyed by her fear, like it had released something in her, and she let her legs run as fast as they wanted, relishing the pounding of her feet on the dusty path to the servants' quarters. It had been a long time since Isa had visited this concrete building at the back of the garden. When she had been a very little girl, like Emma, there had been an emergency when her father had drunk too much from his bleary glass. There hadn't been anyone among the expats to take care of her when the Colonel had tumbled to the ground, football stein clutched unbroken in his hand. So that night, while her mother veiled up and drove the Colonel to the hospital, Isa had gone with Ba Simon to his home for supper. They'd eaten nshima and delele, the slimy okra dish that reminded her of the shimmery snail trails on the garden wall. Ba Simon had been as kind and as chatty as usual, but it had gotten cold and the servants' quarters had been very dark and smelly. Isa had been grateful to hear the soft shuffle of her mother's hair on the floor when she came to fetch her that night.

Isa stopped running abruptly. Her left foot had stepped on a small but sharp rock. Her halt jolted Chanda, who still held her hand. With the pain in her foot, Isa suddenly felt an arrow of real fear piercing her exhilaration, deflating her back into her sulky self. The vegetable patch behind the servants' quarters was just visible beyond the avocado tree. She lifted her foot and examined the sole. It wasn't bleeding, but there was a purple dot where the rock had dented it. As she put her foot down she remembered Cassava and turned back to look at how far they'd run. The garden was huge and encompassed a small maize field, which Isa could glimpse just beyond the mulberry trees with their slight branches and their stained roots. She really ought to go and tell mummy about the dog.

When she turned back to tell Chanda exactly that in her most grown-up voice, Isa found herself surrounded by three other small children. There was a little boy who looked just like Chanda, and two slightly younger girls, toddlers, who looked just like each other. Isa stared at them. She'd never seen twins before. They stood with their hands clasped behind their backs, their bellies sticking forward like they were pretending to be pregnant. Isa sometimes played this game in the bath herself, pushing her belly out as far as it could go until her breath ran out, but this did not seem to be what the little girls were doing. A picture of Cassava's low stomach from the previous week flashed through Isa's head. One of the girls was probing around her mouth with her tongue and the other was making stuttery noises that Chanda apparently understood because she replied, pointing at Isa and shaking her head. The little boy was staring at Isa and smiling broadly. He stepped forward and held out his hand, making the same upward-turned tray that Isa had made for Doll's goblets. Isa shook her head and stepped back, unsure. Chanda implored, "Bwela. Come. Come." She pointed at the servants' quarters to show where Isa was meant to come. There was blue smoke and the sound of splashing water coming from around back. Isa relented.

They walked together toward the building, which was low to the ground and had no door, just a gap in the façade. There were also no windows, just square grids drilled into the concrete here and there for ventilation. As they approached, the little boy ran to the back shouting something. A young woman whom Isa had never seen before appeared from around the corner carrying a metal pot, her wrists and hands wet. She wore a green chitenge and an old white shirt, but Isa immediately noticed that she wasn't wearing a bra: you could see the shape of her breasts and the dark outline of her nipples. The woman smiled at Isa and waved and as she approached, said, "Muli bwanji?" Isa knew this greeting and replied in an automatic whisper, without smiling, "Bwino." The woman shook Isa's hand and Isa noticed that she didn't bend at the knee or touch her right elbow with her left hand as blacks usually did with her. Halfway through the handshake, Isa suddenly realized that she herself was supposed to be deferential. She hurried to bend her knees, but they seemed to be locked and she managed only a jerky wobble.

The woman lifted her head, sniffing the air imperiously. Then she turned to Chanda and demanded something. Chanda shrugged and ran up the three stairs into the servants' quarters, dribbling a forced giggle behind her. "Ach," the woman said and sucked her teeth. She walked back to the rear of the house to finish her washing. Halfway there she turned and gestured to Isa that she should follow Chanda into the quarters. Isa gingerly made her way up the steps and into the velvet darkness beyond the doorway. The concrete floor wasn't dirty—it was polished to a slippery shine—but the dust on her bare feet rasped as she stepped inside. The place had a strong coppery smell of fried kapenta mixed with a tinge of woodsmoke. As Isa moved further in, the smell took on an acrid note that she dimly recognized as pee. It was so dark that she couldn't see anything except for the gold grid on the floor where the sunlight had squeezed through the ventilation grill. The fuzzy squares seemed more radiant for having been through that concrete sieve. Isa walked toward them. The patch of latticed light traveled up her body as she moved into it and eventually glowed on her stomach. It was like being in church or on Cairo Road. She held her hand in front of it and the light made her hand glow like the orange road lamps . . .

A chuckle from the corner interrupted her reverie. Isa looked around, her heart thudding, but she still couldn't see anything. She stood still and concentrated her eyes on the darkness, willing them to adapt. She could just make out three figures sitting in the corner. There was a young woman, younger than the one outside, an old woman, and Chanda, who sat cross-legged, fiddling with an ancient cloth doll with a vaguely familiar shape. Isa worked out that it was the faceless ghost of the Doll who had preceded Doll; she felt a little shocked that it should be here and then even more shocked that she should have forgotten it to such a fate.

She walked toward the women, who were mumbling to each other. Only then did Isa notice the baby sitting on the young woman's lap. In fact—she moved closer—the child was sucking on the woman's breast. Isa knew about breastfeeding, but she'd never seen it before. She couldn't tell whether the baby was a boy or a girl; it had short hair and was naked except for a cloth diaper. She wanted to turn away, but she couldn't stop looking at the way the child's lips moved and the way the breast hung, oblong and pleated like a rotten pawpaw. The women continued to deliberate while Chanda, who was responsible for this intrusion, for this straying, sat staring at Isa, absently twisting the doll's dirty arm as though to detach it.

The child started crying: not the wailing of a newborn, but an intelligent sobbing. Isa stared at it and then realized that it was staring back. Its mother lifted it and began bouncing it up and down on her lap. After a moment, the old woman began laughing, a rattling laugh that devolved into coughing and then rose back up again to the heights of gratified amusement. She said something. Then the young woman began to laugh too and finally Chanda joined in with a somewhat forced high-pitched trill.

"What?" Isa asked. "What?" she demanded.

But they kept on laughing and then the woman stood up and held the baby in front of her. Isa stared at its sobbing face, distorted with wet concentric wrinkles like its nose was a dropped stone rippling a dark pool. The child began to scream, wriggling its little body as its legs kicked. Was she supposed to take the child in her arms? The room echoed with laughter and wailing.

Isa shouted "What? What?" again.

The laughing woman kept shoving the child at Isa's face in jerks until their noses suddenly touched.

"Muzungu," the woman said.

As though at the flip of a switch, Isa began to cry. Her breath hitching on every corner of her young-girl chest, she turned and ran out of the room, tripping down the steps in her haste. As she ran past the mulberry trees, the beat of her feet released a flock of birds from their boughs. They fluttered past her and flickered above her bobbing head, their wings a jumble of parentheses writing themselves across the sky.

The night brought the breeze and the mosquito candles. The guests waned in number and spirit. When she'd had enough, Sibilla planted bristling kisses upon their cheeks and sent them to navigate the intricacies of Lusaka's geography and their drunken dramas on their own. Colonel Corsale was still in the garden, dozing on his chair, one hairy hand holding his football glass clasped to his belly, the other dangling from the armrest, swaying like a hanging man. In the early days, Sibilla used to drag her husband to bed herself. But over the years, his boozing had swollen more than just his ankles. These days, she told Ba Simon to do it.

"A-ta! I'm not carrying the cornuto to bed. The man's earlobes are fat," she'd grumble, leaving her husband to the night, the breeze, and the mosquitoes. Isa wandered around the yard, yawning, picking up Tropic bottles of various weight under Ba Simon's direction. She hadn't told anyone about the dog yet, or about all the inhabitants of the servants' quarters—did they realize how many people lived there?—or about the laughing. She felt tired and immensely old, old in a different way from the times she played teacher to the other children. Old like her father was old, a shaggy shambling old, an old where you'd lost the order of things and felt so sad that you simply had to embrace the loss, reassuring yourself with the lie that you hadn't really wanted all that order to begin with.

Ba Simon was singing something spiritual, not in English, while sweeping the porch, but Isa could barely muster the energy to gainsay his song with her own. She only got halfway through "Baby you can drive my car" before she collapsed on the grass beside her father's chair. The wicker creaked in rhythm with his snoring. She put her fingers in his dangling hand and he muttered something.

"Papa?" she asked softly. "Dormendo?"

She only spoke Italian to him when she was very very tired. The international school she attended had compressed all her thoughts into English, but some of her feelings remained in the simple Italian her parents had used on her as a toddler.

"I went to the servants' quarters," she said.

The Colonel's whiffling snore continued. Isa slapped a mosquito away from her shin. She stood up and walked over to Ba Simon, who was vigorously scrubbing the grill.

"What does muzungu mean?" she asked, sitting on her stool.

He kept humming for a second.

"Where did you hear that word?" he asked.

Isa didn't reply.

Ba Simon hesitated. Then he made a face and said, "Ghost!" He waved his hands about. "Whoooo! Like that katooni you are always watching." He smiled and moved closer to her with his hands still waving. "Caspah Caspah the shani-shani ghost," he sang in the wrong key.

"Whoooo!" she giggled back at Ba Simon in spite of herself and they chatted about nothing for a few minutes. Ba Simon wasn't very bright, she thought and then forgot. But Ba Simon noticed her thought even though she hadn't said it and soon enough, he told her to go to bed. When she looked back from the doorway to the house, Ba Simon was just getting ready to carry her father to bed. His body was pitched awkwardly over the Colonel, his face contorted, his long stringy arms planted beneath the Colonel's neck and knees. But when he saw Isa turn back, the strain on Ba Simon's face dissolved instantly into a smile.

"Go," he whispered, and she did.

HAUNTING OLIVIA

Karen Russell

❧

My brother, Wallow, has been kicking around Gannon's Boat Graveyard for more than an hour, too embarrassed to admit that he doesn't see any ghosts. Instead, he slaps at the ocean with jilted fury. Curse words come piping out of his snorkel. He keeps pausing to readjust the diabolical goggles.

The diabolical goggles were designed for little girls. They are pink, with a floral snorkel attached to the side. They have scratchproof lenses and an adjustable band. Wallow says that we are going to use them to find our dead sister, Olivia.

My brother and I have been making midnight scavenging trips to Gannon's all summer. It's a watery junk yard, a place where people pay to abandon their old boats. Gannon, the grizzled, tattooed undertaker, tows wrecked ships into his marina. Battered sailboats and listing skiffs, yachts with stupid names—*Knot at Work* and *Sail-la-Vie*—the paint peeling from their puns. They sink beneath the water in slow increments, covered with rot and barnacles. Their masts jut out at weird angles. The marina is an open, easy grave to rob. We ride our bikes along the rock wall, coasting quietly past Gannon's tin shack, and hop off at the derelict pier. Then we creep down to the ladder, jump onto the nearest boat, and loot.

It's dubious booty. We mostly find stuff with no resale value: soggy flares and UHF radios, a one-eyed cat yowling on a dinghy. But the goggles are a first. We found them floating in a live-bait tank, deep in the cabin of *La Calavera*, a swamped Largo schooner. We'd pushed our way through a small hole in the prow. Inside, the cabin was rank and flooded. There was no bait living in that tank, just the goggles and a foamy liquid the color of root beer. I dared Wallow to put the goggles on and stick his head in it. I didn't actually expect him to find anything; I just wanted to laugh at Wallow in the pink goggles, bobbing for diseases. But when he surfaced, tearing at the goggles, he told me that he'd seen the orange, unholy light of a fish ghost. Several, in fact, a school of ghoulish mullet.

"They looked just like regular baitfish, bro," Wallow said. "Only deader." I told my brother that I was familiar with the definition of a ghost. Not that I believed a word of it, you understand.

Now Wallow is trying the goggles out in the marina, to see if his vision extends beyond the tank. I'm dangling my legs over the edge of the pier, half-expecting something to grab me and pull me under.

"Wallow! You see anything phantasmic yet?"

"Nothing," he bubbles morosely through the snorkel. "I can't see a thing."

I'm not surprised. The water in the boat basin is a cloudy mess. But I'm impressed by Wallow's one-armed doggy paddle.

Wallow shouldn't be swimming at all. Last Thursday, he slipped on one of the banana peels that Granana leaves around the house. I know. I didn't think it could happen outside of cartoons, either. Now his right arm is in a plaster cast, and in order to enter the water he has to hold it above his head. It looks like he's riding an aquatic unicycle. That buoy-ancy, it's unexpected. On land, Wallow's a loutish kid. He bulldozes whatever gets in his path: baby strollers, widowers, me.

For brothers, Wallow and I look nothing alike. I've got Dad's blond hair and blue eyes, his embraceably lanky physique. Olivia was equally Heartland, apple cheeks and unnervingly white teeth. Not Wallow. He's got this dental affliction which gives him a tusky, warthog grin. He wears his hair in a greased pompadour and has a thick pelt of back hair. There's no accounting for it. Dad jokes that our mom must have had dalliances with a Minotaur.

Wallow is not Wallow's real name, of course. His real name is Waldo Swallow. Just like I'm Timothy Sparrow and Olivia was—is—Olivia Lark. Our parents used to be bird enthusiasts. That's how they met: Dad spotted my mother on a bird-watching tour of the swamp, her beauty magnified by his 10x binoculars. Dad says that by the time he lowered them the spoonbills he'd been trying to see had scattered, and he was in love. When Wallow and I were very young, they used to take us on their creepy bird excursions, kayaking down island canals, spying on blue her-ons and coots. These days, they're not enthusiastic about much, feathered or otherwise. They leave us with Granana for months at a time.

Shortly after Olivia's death, my parents started travelling regularly in the Third World. No children allowed. Granana lives on the other side of the island. She's eighty-four, I'm twelve, and Wallow's fourteen, so it's a little ambiguous as to who's babysitting whom. This particular summer, our parents are in São Paulo. They send us postcards of bullet-pocked favelas and flaming hillocks of trash. "'GLAD YOU'RE NOT HERE! xoxo, the 'Rents.'" I guess the idea is that all the misery makes their marital problems seem petty and inconsequential.

"Hey!" Wallow is directly below me, clutching the rails of the lad-der. "Move over."

He climbs up and heaves his big body onto the pier. Defeat puddles all around him. Behind the diabolical goggles, his eyes narrow into slits.

"Did you see them?"

Wallow just grunts. "Here." He wrestles the lady-goggles off his face and thrusts them at me. "I can't swim with this cast, and these bitches are too small for my skull. You try them."

I sigh and strip off my pajamas, bobbling before him. The elastic band of the goggles bites into the back of my head. Somehow, wearing them makes me feel even more naked. My penis is curling up in the salt air like a small pink snail. Wallow points and laughs.

"Sure you don't want to try again?" I ask him. From the edge of the pier, the ocean looks dark and unfamiliar, like the liquid shadow of something truly awful. "Try again, Wallow. Maybe it's just taking a while for your eyes to adjust . . ."

Wallow holds a finger to his lips. He points behind me. Boats are creaking in the wind, waves slap against the pilings, and then I hear it, too, the distinct thunk of boots on wood. Someone is walking down the pier. We can see the tip of a lit cigarette, suspended in the dark. We hear a man's gargly cough.

"Looking for buried treasure, boys?" Gannon laughs. He keeps walking toward us. "You know, the court still considers it trespassing, be it land or sea." Then he recognizes Wallow. He lets out the low, mournful whistle that all the grown-ups on the island use to identify us now.

"Oh, son. Don't tell me you're out here looking for . . ."

"My dead sister?" Wallow asks with terrifying cheer. "Good guess!"

"You're not going to find her in my marina, boys."

In the dark, Gannon is a huge stencil of a man, wisps of smoke curling from his nostrils. There is a long, pulsing silence, during which Wallow stares at him, squaring his jaw. Then Gannon shrugs. He stubs out his cigarette and shuffles back toward the shore.

"All right, bro," Wallow says. "It's go time." He takes my elbow and gentles me down the planks with such tenderness that I am suddenly very afraid. But there's no sense making the plunge slow and unbearable. I take a running leap down the pier—

"Ayyyyiii!"

—and launch over the water. It's my favorite moment: when I'm one toe away from flight and my body takes over. The choice is made, but the consequence is still just an inky shimmer beneath me. And I'm flying, I'm rushing to meet my own reflection— Gah!

Then comes the less beautiful moment when I'm up to my eyeballs in tar water, and the goggles fill with stinging brine. And, for what seems like a very long time, I can't see anything at all, dead or alive.

When my vision starts to clear, I see a milky, melting light moving swiftly above the ocean floor. Drowned moonbeams, I think at first. Only there is no moon tonight.

❦

Olivia disappeared on a new-moon night. It was exactly two years, or twenty-four new moons, ago. Wallow says that means that tonight is Olivia's unbirthday, the anniversary of her death. It's weird: our grief is cyclical, synched with the lunar cycles. It accordions out as the moon slivers away. On new-moon nights, it rises with the tide.

Even before we lost my sis, I used to get uneasy when the moon was gone. That corner of the sky, as black as an empty safe. Whatever happened to Olivia, I hope she at least had the orange residue of sunset to see by. I can't stand to think of her out here alone after nightfall.

The last time we saw Olivia was at twilight. We'd spent all day crab-sledding down the beach. It's the closest thing we island kids have to a winter sport. You climb into the upended exoskeleton of a giant crab, then you go yeehaw slaloming down the powdery dunes. The faster you go, the more sand whizzes around you, a fine spray on either side of your crab sled. By the time you hit the water, you're covered in it, grit in your teeth and your eyelids, along the line of your scalp.

Herb makes the crab sleds—he guts the crabs and blowtorches off the eyestalks and paints little racer stripes along the sides. Then he rents them down at Pier 2, for two dollars an hour, twelve dollars for a full day. The three of us had been racing down the beach all afternoon. We were sunburned, and hungry, and loused up with sea bugs. Wallow had stepped on a sea urchin and broken his fall on more urchins. I wanted Jiffy Pop and aloe vera. Wallow wanted prescription painkillers and porno. We voted to head over to Granana's beach cottage, because she has Demerol and an illegal cable box.

Olivia threw a fit. "But we still have half an hour on the sled rental!" A gleam came into her eyes, that transparent little-kid craftiness. "You guys don't have to come with me, you know."

Legally, we did. According to official Herb's Crab Sledding policy, under-twelves must be accompanied by a guardian—a rule that Herb has really cracked down on since Olivia's death. But neither Wallow nor I felt like chaperoning. And Olivia was eight and a half, which rounds up to twelve. "Stick to the perimeter of the island," Wallow told her. "And get that crab sled back before sundown. Any late fees are coming out of your allowance."

"Yeah, yeah," she assured us, clambering into the sled. The sun was already low in the sky. "I'm just going out one last time."

We helped Olivia drag the sled up the white dunes. She sat Indian style in the center of the shell, humming tunelessly. Then we gave her a final push that sent her racing down the slopes. We watched as she flew out over the rock crags and into the foamy water. By the time we'd gathered our towels and turned to go, Olivia was just a speck on the horizon. Neither of us noticed how quickly the tide was going out.

Most people think that tides are caused by the moon alone, but that is not the case. Once a month, the sun and the moon are both on the same side of the globe. Then the Atlantic kowtows to their conglomerate gravity. It's the earth playing tug-of-war with the sky.

On new-moon nights, the sky is winning. The spring tide swells exceptionally high. The spring tide has teeth. It can pull a boat much farther than your average quarter-moon neap tide. When they finally found Olivia's crab sled, it was halfway to Cuba, and empty.

※

"What do you see, bro?"

"Oh, not much." I cough. I peer back under the surface of the water. There's an aurora borealis exploding inches from my submerged face. "Probably just plankton."

When I come up to clear the goggles, I can barely see Wallow. He is silhouetted against the lone orange lamp, watching me from the pier. Water seeps out of my nose, my ears. It weeps down the corners of the lenses. I push the goggles up and rub my eyes with my fists, which just makes things worse. I kick to stay afloat, the snorkel digging into my cheek, and wave at my brother. Wallow doesn't wave back.

I don't want to tell Wallow, but I have no idea what I just saw, although I'm sure there must be some ugly explanation for it. I tell myself that it was just cyanobacteria, or lustrous pollutants from the Bimini glue factory. Either way, I don't want to double-check.

I shiver in the water, letting the salt dry on my shoulders, listening to the echo of my breath in the snorkel. I fantasize about towels. But Wallow is still watching me, his face a blank oval. I tug at the goggles and stick my head under for a second look.

Immediately, I bite down on the mouthpiece of the snorkel to stop myself from screaming. The goggles: they work. And every inch of the ocean is haunted. There are ghost fish swimming all around me. My hands pass right through their flat bodies. Phantom crabs shake their phantom claws at me from behind a sunken anchor. Octopuses cartwheel by, leaving an effulgent red trail. A school of minnows swims right through my belly button. Dead, I think. They are all dead.

"Um, Wallow?" I gasp, spitting out the snorkel. "I don't think I can do this."

"Sure you can." Squat, boulder-shouldered, Wallow is standing over the ladder, guarding it like a gargoyle. There's nowhere for me to go but back under the water.

Getting used to aquatic ghosts is like adjusting to the temperature of the ocean. After the initial shock gives way, your body numbs. It takes a few more close encounters with the lambent fish before my pulse quiets down. Once I realize that the ghost fish can't hurt me, I relax into something I'd call delight if I weren't supposed to be feeling bereaved.

I spend the next two hours pretending to look for Olivia. I shadow the spirit manatees, their backs scored with keloid stars from motorboat propellers. I somersault through stingrays. Bonefish flicker around me like mute banshees. I figure out how to braid the furry blue light of dead coral reef through my fingertips, and very nearly giggle. I've started to enjoy myself, and I've nearly succeeded in exorcising Olivia from my thoughts, when a bunch of ghost shrimp materialize in front of my goggles, like a photo rinsed in a developing tray. The shrimp twist into a glowing alphabet, some curling, some flattening, touching tails to antennae in smoky contortions.

Then they loop together to form words, as if drawn by some invisible hand:

G-L-O-W-W-O-R-M G-R-O-T-T-O.

We thought the Glowworm Grotto was just more of Olivia's make-believe. Olivia was a cartographer of imaginary places. She'd crayon elaborate maps of invisible castles and sunken cities. When the Glowworm Grotto is part of a portfolio that includes Mt. Waffle Cone, it's hard to take it seriously.

I loved Olivia. But that doesn't mean I didn't recognize that she was one weird little kid. She used to suffer these intense bouts of homesickness in her own bedroom. When she was very small, she would wake up tearing at her bedspread and shrieking, "I wanna go home! I wanna go home!" Which was distressing to all of us, of course, because she was home.

That said, I wouldn't be surprised to learn that Olivia was an adoptee from some other planet. She used to change into Wallow's rubbery yellow flippers on the bus, then waddle around the school halls like some disoriented mallard. She played "house" by getting the broom and sweeping the neon corpses of dead jellyfish off the beach. Her eyes were a stripey cerulean, inhumanly bright. Dad used to tell Olivia that a merman artisan had made them, out of bits of sea glass from Atlantis.

Wallow saved all of her drawings. The one labelled "Glowerm Groto" is a sketch of a dusky red cave, with a little stick-Olivia swimming into the entrance. Another drawing shows the roof of the cave. It looks like a swirly firmament of stars, dalmatianed with yellow dots.

"That's what you see when you're floating on your back," Olivia told us, rubbing the gray crayon down to its nub. "The Glowworm Grotto looks just like the night sky."

"That's nice," we said, exchanging glances. Neither Wallow nor I knew of any caves along the island shore. I figured it must be another Olivia utopia, a no-place. Wallow thought it was Olivia's oddball interpretation of Gannon's Boat Graveyard.

"Maybe that rusty boat hangar looked like the entrance to a cave to her," he'd said. Maybe. If you were eight, and nearsighted, and nostalgic for places that you'd never been.

But, if the Glowworm Grotto actually exists, that changes everything. Olivia's ghost could be there now, twitching her nose with rabbity indignation— "But I left you a map!" Wondering what took us so long to find her.

When I surface, the stars have vanished. The clouds are turning red around their edges. I can hear Wallow snoring on the pier. I pull my naked body up and flop onto the warm planks, feeling salt-shucked and newborn. When I spit the snorkel out of my mouth, the unfiltered air tastes acrid and foreign. The Glowworm Grotto. I wish I didn't have to tell Wallow. I wish we'd never found the stupid goggles. There are certain things that I don't want to see.

When we get back to Granana's, her cottage is shuttered and dark. Fat raindrops, the icicles of the Tropics, hang from the eaves. We can hear her watching *Evangelical Bingo* in the next room.

"Revelation 20:13!" she hoots. "Bingo!"

Our breakfast is on the table: banana pancakes, with a side of banana pudding. The kitchen is sticky with brown peels and syrup. Granana no longer has any teeth left in her head. For the past two decades, she has subsisted almost entirely on bananas, banana-based dishes, and other foods that you can gum. This means that her farts smell funny, and her calf muscles frequently give out. It means that Wallow and I eat out a lot during the summer.

Wallow finds Olivia's old drawings of the Glowworm Grotto. We spread them out on the table, next to a Crab Shack menu with a cartoon map of the island. Wallow is busy highlighting the jagged shoreline, circling places that might harbor a cave, when Granana shuffles into the kitchen.

"What's all this?"

She peers over my shoulder. "Christ," she says. "Still mooning over that old business?"

Granana doesn't understand what the big deal is. She didn't cry at Olivia's funeral, and I doubt she even remembers Olivia's name. Granana lost, like, ninety-two million kids in childbirth. All of her brothers died in the war. She survived the Depression by stealing radish bulbs from her neighbors' garden, and fishing the elms for pigeons. Dad likes to remind us of this in a grave voice, as if it explained her jaundiced piti-lessness: "Boys. Your grandmother ate pigeons."

"Wasn't much for drawing, was she?" Granana says. She taps at stick-Olivia. "Wasn't much for swimming, either."

Wallow visibly stiffens. For a second, I'm worried that he's going to slug Granana in her wattled neck. Then she raises her drawn-on eye-brows. "Would you look at that—the nudey cave. Your grandfather used to take me skinny-dipping there."

Wallow and I do an autonomic, full-body shudder. I get a sudden mental image of two shelled walnuts floating in a glass.

"You mean you recognize this place, Granana?"

"No thanks to this chicken scratch!" She points to an orange dot in the corner of the picture, so small that I hadn't even noticed it. "But look where she drew the sunset. Use your noggins. Must be one of them coves on the western side of the island. I don't remember exactly where."

"What about the stars on the roof?"

Granana snorts. "Worm shit!"

"Huh?"

"Worm shit," she repeats. "You never heard of glowworms, Mr. Straight-A Science Guy? Their shit glows in the dark. All them coves are covered with it."

We never recovered Olivia's body. Two days after she went missing, Tropical Storm Vita brought wind and chaos and interrupted broadcasts, and the search was called off. Too dangerous, the Coast Guard lieutenant said. He was a fat, earnest man, with tiny black eyes set like watermelon seeds in his pink face.

"When wind opposes sea," he said in a portentous singsong, "the waves build fast."

"Thank you, Billy Shakespeare," my father growled under his breath. For some reason, this hit Dad the hardest—harder than Olivia's death itself, I think. The fact that we had nothing to bury.

It's possible that Olivia washed up on a bone-white Cojímar beach, or got tangled in some Caribbean fisherman's net. It's probable that her lungs filled up with buckets of tarry black water and she sank. But I don't like to think about that. It's easier to imagine her turning into an angelfish and swimming away, or being bodily assumed into the clouds.

Most likely, Dad says, a freak wave knocked her overboard. Then the current yanked the sled away faster than she could swim. In my night terrors, I watch the sea turn into a great, gloved hand that rises out of the ocean to snatch her. I told Wallow this once, hoping to stir up some fraternal empathy. Instead, Wallow sneered at me.

"Are you serious? That's what you have nightmares about, bro? Some lame-ass Mickey Mouse glove that comes out of the sea?" His lip curled up, but there was envy in his voice, too. "I just see my own hands, you know? Pushing her down that hill."

The following evening, Wallow and I head over to Herb's Crab Sledding Rentals. Herb smokes on his porch in his yellowed boxers and a threadbare Santa hat, rain or shine. Back when we were regular sledders, Wallow always used to razz Herb about his getup.

"Ho-ho-ho," Herb says reflexively. "Merry Christmas. Sleigh bells ring, are ya listening." He gives a halfhearted shake to a sock full of quarters. "Hang on, nauticats. Can't sled without informed consent."

Thanks to the Olivia Bill, new island legislation requires all island children to take a fourteen-hour Sea Safety! course before they can sled. They have to wear helmets and life preservers, and sign multiple waivers. Herb is dangling the permission form in front of our faces. Wallow accepts it with a genial "Thanks, Herb!" Then he crushes it in his good fist.

"Now wait a sec . . ." Herb scratches his ear. "I, ah, I didn't recognize you boys. I'm sorry, but you know I can't rent to you. Anyhow, it'll be dark soon, and neither one of you is certified."

Wallow walks over to one of the sleds and, unhelmeted, unjacketed, shoves it into the water. The half shell bobs there, one of the sturdier two-seaters, a boiled-red color. He picks up a pair of oars, so that we can row against the riptides. He glares at Herb.

"We are going to take the sled out tonight, and tomorrow night, and every night until our parents get back. We are going to keep taking it out until we find Olivia." He pauses. "And we are going to pay you three hundred and seventy-six dollars in cash." Coincidentally, this is the exact dollar amount of Granana's Social Security check.

Herb doesn't say a word. He takes the wad of cash, runs a moistened finger through it, and stuffs it under his Santa hat. He waits until we are both in the sled before he opens his mouth.

"Boys," he says. "You have that crab sled back here before dawn. Otherwise, I'm calling the Coast Guard."

Every night, we go a little farther. Out here, you can see dozens of shooting stars, whole galactic herds of them, winking out into cheery oblivion. They make me think of lemmings, flinging themselves over an astral cliff.

We are working our way around the island, with Gannon's Boat Graveyard as our ground zero. I swim parallel to the beach, and Wallow follows along in the crab sled, marking up the shoreline that we've covered on our map. "X" marks all the places where Olivia is not. It's slow going. I'm not a strong swimmer, and I have to paddle back to Wallow every fifteen minutes.

"And just what are we going to do when we find her?" I want to know.

It's the third night of our search. We are halfway around the island, on the sandbar near the twinkling lights of the Bowl-a-Bed Hotel. Wallow's face is momentarily illuminated by the cycloptic gaze of the lighthouse. It arcs out over the water, a thin scythe of light that serves only to make the rest of the ocean look scarier.

"What exactly are we going to do with her, Wallow?"

This question has been weighing on my mind more and more heavily of late. Because let's just say, for argument's sake, that there is a Glowworm Grotto, and that Olivia's ghost haunts it. Then what? Do we genie-in-a-bottle her? Keep her company on weekends? I envision eternal Saturday nights spent treading cold water in a cave, crooning lullabies to the husk of Olivia, and shudder.

"What do you mean?" Wallow says, frowning. "We'll rescue her. We'll preserve her, uh, you know, her memory."

"And how exactly do you propose we do that?"

"I don't know, bro!" Wallow furrows his brow, flustered. You can tell he hasn't thought much beyond finding Olivia. "We'll . . . we'll put her in an aquarium."

"An aquarium?" Now it's my turn to be derisive. "And then what? Are you going to get her a kiddie pool?"

It seems to me that nobody's asking the hard questions here. For example, what if ghost-Olivia doesn't have eyes anymore? Or a nose? What if an eel has taken up residence inside her skull, and every time it lights up it sends this unholy electricity radiating through her sockets?

Wallow fixes me with a baleful stare. "Are you pussying out, bro? She's your sister, for Christ's sake. You telling me you're afraid of your own kid sister? Don't worry about what we're going to do with her, bro. We have to find her first."

I say nothing. But I keep thinking: It's been two years. What if all the Olivia-ness has already seeped out of her and evaporated into the violet welter of clouds? Evaporated, and rained down, and evaporated, and rained down. Olivia slicking over all the rivers and trees and dirty cities in the world. So that now there is only silt, and our stupid, salt-diluted longing. And nothing left of our sister to find.

On the fourth night of our search, I see a churning clump of ghost children. They are drifting straight for me, all kelped together, an eyeless panic of legs and feet and hair. I kick for the surface, heart hammering.

"Wallow!" I scream, hurling myself at the crab sled. "I just saw—I just—I'm not doing this anymore, bro, I am not. You can go stick your face in dead kids for a change. Let Olivia come find us."

"Calm it down." Wallow pokes at the ocean with his oar. "It's only trash." He fishes out a nasty mass of diapers and chicken gristle and whiskery red seaweed, all threaded around the plastic rings of a six-pack. "See?"

I sit huddled in the corner of the sled, staring dully at the blank surface of the water. I know what I saw.

The goggles are starting to feel less like a superpower and more like a divine punishment, one of those particularly inventive cruelties that you read about in Greek mythology. Every now and then, I think about how much simpler and more pleasant things would be if the goggles conferred a different kind of vision. Like if I could read messages written in squid ink, or laser through the Brazilian girls' tankinis. But then Wallow interrupts these thoughts by dunking me under the water. Repeatedly.

"Keep looking," he snarls, water dripping off his face.

On the fifth night of our search, I see a plesiosaur. It is a megawatt behemoth, bronze and blue-white, streaking across the sea floor like a torpid comet. Watching it, I get this primordial déjà vu, like I'm watching a dream return to my body. It wings toward me with a slow, avian grace. Its long neck is arced in an S-shaped curve; its lizard body is the size of Granana's carport. Each of its ghost flippers pinwheels colored light. I try to swim out of its path, but the thing's too big to avoid. That Leviathan fin, it shivers right through me. It's a light in my belly, cold and familiar. And I flash back to a snippet from school, a line from a poem or a science book, I can't remember which:

There are certain prehistoric things that swim beyond extinction.

I wake up from one of those naps which leach the strength from your bones to a lightning storm. I must have fallen asleep in the crab sled. Otherworldly light goes roiling through an eerie blue froth of clouds.

Wallow is standing at the prow of the sled. Each flash of lightning limns his bared teeth, the hollows of his eyes. It's as if somebody up there were taking an X-ray of grief, again and again. .

"I just want to tell her that I'm sorry," Wallow says softly. He doesn't know that I'm awake. He's talking to himself, or maybe to the ocean. There's not a trace of fear in his voice. And it's clear then that Wallow is a better brother than I could ever hope to be.

We have rowed almost all the way around the island. In a quarter of an hour, we'll be back at Gannon's Boat Graveyard. Thank merciful Christ. Our parents are coming back tomorrow, and I can go back to playing video games and feeling dry and blameless.

Then the lighthouse beacon sweeps out again. It bounces off an out-cropping of rocks that we didn't notice on our first expedition. White sequins of light pop along the water.

"Did you see that? That's it!" Wallow says excitedly. "That's gotta be it!"

"Oh. Excellent."

We paddle the rest of the way out in silence. I row the crab sled like a condemned man. The current keeps pushing us back, but we make a quiet kind of progress. I keep praying that the crags will turn out to be low, heaped clouds, or else a seamless mass of stone. Instead, you can tell that they are pocked with dozens of holes. For a second, I'm relieved—nobody, not even string-beany Olivia, could swim into such narrow openings. Wallow's eyes dart around wildly.

"There has to be an entrance," he mutters. "Look!"

Sure enough, there is a muted glow coming from the far end of a salt-eaten overhang, like light from under a door.

"No way can I fit through there," I gasp, knowing immediately that I can. And that the crab sled can't, of course. Which means I'll be going in to meet her alone.

What if the light, I am thinking, is Olivia?

"It's just worms, bro," Wallow says, as if reading my mind. But there's this inscrutable sadness on his face. His muddy eyes swallow up the light and give nothing back.

I look over my shoulder. We're less than half a mile out from shore, could skip a stone to the mangrove islets; and yet the land draws back like a fat swimmer's chimera, impossibly far away.

"Ready?" He grabs at the scruff of my neck and pushes me toward the water. "Set?"

"No!" Staring at the unlit spaces in the crags, I am choked with horror. I fumble the goggles off my face. "Do your own detective work!" I dangle the goggles over the edge of the sled. "I quit."

Wallow lunges forward and pins me against the side of the boat. He tries to spatula me overboard with his one good arm, but I limbo under his cast.

"Don't do it, Timothy," he cautions, but it is too late.

"This is what I think of your diabolical goggles!" I howl. I hoist the goggles over my head and, with all the force in my puny arms, hurl them to the floor of the crab sled.

This proves to be pretty anticlimactic. Naturally, the goggles remain intact. There's not even a hairline fracture. Stupid scratchproof lenses.

The worst part is that Wallow just watches me impassively, his cast held aloft in the air, as if he were patiently waiting to ask the universe a question. He nudges the goggles toward me with his foot.

"You finished?"

"Wally!" I blubber, a last-ditch plea. "This is crazy. What if something happens to me in there and you can't come in after me? Let's go back."

"What?" Wallow barks, disgusted. "And leave Olivia here for dead? Is that what you want?"

"Bingo!" That is exactly what I want. Maybe Granana is slightly off target when it comes to the Food Pyramid, but she has the right idea about death. I want my parents to stop sailing around taking pictures of

Sudanese leper colonies. I want Wallow to row back to shore and sleep through the night. I want everybody in the goddam family to leave Olivia here for dead.

But there's my brother. Struggling with his own repugnance, like an entomologist who has just discovered a loathsome new species of beetle.

"What did you say?"

"I said I'll go," I mumble, not meeting his eyes. I position myself on the edge of the boat. "I'll go."

So that's what it comes down to, then. I'd rather drown in Olivia's ghost than have him look at me that way.

⚏

To enter the grotto, you have to slide in on your back, like a letter through a mail slot. Something scrapes my coccyx bone on the way in. There's a polar chill in the water tonight. No outside light can wiggle its way inside.

But, sure enough, phosphorescent dots spangle the domed roof of the grotto. It's like a radiant checkerboard of shit. You can't impose any mental pictures on it—it's too uniform. It defies the mind's desire to constellate randomness. The Glowworm Grotto is nothing like the night sky. The stars here are all equally bright and evenly spaced, like a better-ordered cosmos.

"Olivia?"

The grotto smells like salt and blood and bat shit. Shadows web the walls. I try and fail to touch the bottom.

"Oliviaaa?"

Her name echoes around the cave. After a while, there is only rippled water again, and the gonged absence of sound. Ten more minutes, I think. I could splash around here for ten more minutes and be done with this. I could take off the goggles, even. I could leave without ever looking below the surface of the water, and Wallow would never know.

"Oli—"

I take a deep breath, and dive.

Below me, tiny fish are rising out of golden cylinders of coral. It looks like an undersea calliope, piping a song that you can see instead of hear. One of the fish swims right up and taps against my scratchproof lenses. It's just a regular blue fish, solid and alive. It taps and taps, oblivious of the thick glass. My eyes cross, trying to keep it in focus.

The fish swims off to the beat of some subaqueous music. Everything down here is dancing—the worms' green light and the undulant walls and the leopard-spotted polyps. Everything. And following this fish is like trying to work backward from the dance to the song. I can't hear it, though; I can't remember a single note of it. It fills me with a hitching sort of sadness.

I trail the fish at an embarrassed distance, feeling warm-blooded and ridiculous in my rubbery flippers, marooned in this clumsy body. Like I'm an impostor, an imperfect monster.

I look for my sister, but it's hopeless. The goggles are all fogged up. Every fish burns lantern-bright, and I can't tell the living from the dead. It's all just blurry light, light smeared like some celestial fingerprint all over the rocks and the reef and the sunken garbage. Olivia could be everywhere.

NOTES

Page 2   The list of definitions of "uncanny" and "canny": *Dictionary of the Scots Language* http://www.dsl.ac.uk/

Page 2   *general uncanny ugliness and horror and pain*: Henry James. *The Turn of the Screw* (London: Henry James, Everyman, J.M. Dent, 1993): 4.

Page 2   *beautiful hand*: ibid: 4.

Page 2   *utmost price*: ibid: 3.

Page 3   *transforming the concerns of art, literature, film*: Nicholas Royle. *The Uncanny* (New York: Routledge, 2003): 27.

Page 3   *belonging to the house*: Sigmund Freud, translated by David

McClintock. "The Uncanny" in *The Uncanny* (New York: Penguin Group USA, 2003): 126.

Page 4   *private*: ibid: 130.

Page 4   *secret*: ibid: 130.

Page 4   *concealed*: ibid: 129.

Page 4   *the uncanny is a 'province' still before us*: Nicholas Royle. *The Uncanny* (New York: Routledge, 2003): 27.

Pages 4–5   When something that should have remained hidden . . . foreign to ourselves: these are not exact quotes, but paraphrased and compiled from:

Nicholas Royle. *The Uncanny* (New York: Routledge, 2003): 1–2.

Sigmund Freud, translated by David McClintock. "The Uncanny" in *The Uncanny* (New York: Penguin Group USA, 2003): 135–51.

Page 6   *The uncanny that we find in fiction*: Sigmund Freud: 155.

Page 6   *In a sense, then, [the fiction writer] betrays us*: ibid: 157.

Page 7   *little box . . . of no remarkable character*: Edgar Allan Poe. "Berenice," *Complete Tales and Poems* (New York: Vintage, 1975): 647.

Page 7   To make strange, to defamiliarize. Paraphrased from Victor Shklovsky, translated by Lee T. Lemon and Marion

J. Reis. "Art as Technique" in *Russian Formalist Criticism: Four Essays* (Lincoln: University of Nebraska Press, 1965): 13.

Page 8 *devouring blaze of lights*: Edith Wharton. "Pomegranate Seed" in *The Ghost Stories of Edith Wharton* (New York: Charles Scribner's Sons, 1973): 200.

Page 8 *the uncertain hold of a ship*: Franz Kafka, translated by Michael Hofmann. "The Stoker," in *Metamorphosis and Other Stories* (Penguin Group, 2007): 58.

Page 9 *If you wish to guess what our ancestors felt*: Virginia Wolff. "The Supernatural in Fiction," in *Granite and Rainbow: Essays* (New York: Harcourt Brace Jovanovitch, 1975): 63.

Page 9 *ruins, or moonlight, or ghosts*: ibid: 63.

Page 9 *But what is it that we are afraid of?*: ibid: 63.

Page 11 *against the kingdom of the quotidian*: Bruno Schulz, translated by Jerzy Ficowski. *The Street of Crocodiles* (New York: Penguin USA, 1997): 21.

ABOUT THE AUTHORS

CHRIS ADRIAN is the author of three novels: *Gob's Grief*, *The Children's Hospital*, and *The Great Night*, and a collection of short stories, *A Better Angel*. He lives in New York, where he works as a pediatric oncologist.

<hr>

ROBERT AICKMAN [1914–1981] was born in London into a literary family and sustained in his early writing efforts by his mother's encouragement. Originally trained as an architect, he ultimately made his way into work in the literary and performing arts and became a major figure in English canal-system conservation and restoration. Over the span of this multi-faceted career, he published nearly fifty "strange stories"—his own term for his work—and is today considered one of the modern masters of weird fiction. Fritz Leiber called him "weatherman of the unconscious." Among Aickman's other published works are two novels (*The Late Break-fasters* and *The Model*), two volumes of memoir (*The Attempted Rescue* and *The*

River Runs Uphill), and two books on the canals of England (*Know Your Waterways* and *The Story of Our Inland Waterways*). Aickman's story in this volume, "The Waiting Room," appeared in his first solo collection, *Dark Entries: Curious and Macabre Ghost Stories,* in 1964.

⁂

JOAN AIKEN (1924–2004) was born in Rye, Sussex, England, into a literary family: her father was the poet and writer Conrad Aiken; and her siblings, the novelists Jane Aiken Hodge and John Aiken. Aiken herself began writing at the age of five, and her first collection of stories, *All You've Ever Wanted,* was published in 1953. After her first husband's death, Aiken supported her family by copyediting at *Argosy* and working at an advertising agency before turning to writing fiction full-time. She went on to write for *Vogue, Vanity Fair,* and many other magazines. She wrote over a hundred books and is perhaps best known for the dozen novels in the Wolves of Willoughby Chase series. She won the Guardian and Edgar Allan Poe awards for fiction and in 1999 she received an MBE from the Queen for her services to children's literature. "The Helper" was originally published in Aiken's 1979 collection, *A Touch of Chill* (Gollancz), and was reprinted in 2011 in the posthumous collection *The Monkey's Wedding and Other Stories* (Small Beer Press).

⁂

AIMEE BENDER is the author of five books, including *The Girl in the Flammable Skirt* and *The Particular Sadness of Lemon Cake.* The most recent, *The Color Master,* was recently named a *New York Times* Notable Book of 2013. "Tiger Mending" was inspired by a painting by Amy Cutler of the same name. The image and even tattoos of it are findable online.

⁂

KATE BERNHEIMER is the author of the story collection *Horse, Flower, Bird* (Coffee House Press, 2010, with illustrations by Rikki Ducornet) and a novel trilogy that concluded recently with *The Complete Tales of Lucy Gold* (FC2, 2011). *How a Mother Weaned a Girl from Fairy Tales*, a new story collection, was published by Coffee House Press in 2014. She has also edited the World Fantasy Award–winning *My Mother She Killed Me, My Father He Ate Me: Forty New Fairy Tales* (Penguin, 2010) and *xo Orpheus: Fifty New Myths* (Penguin, 2013), among other books.

※

AMBROSE BIERCE (1842–1914?) was born in Horse Cave, Ohio, and spent most of his childhood in Indiana. He fought in several of the major battles of the American Civil War and after the war headed west, settling in San Francisco, where in the years to come he would establish his reputation as one of the nation's best—and fiercest—journalistic satirists. All the while he continued to produce and publish stories ranging from the realistic to the supernatural and macabre. Among his best-known works are the Civil War stories published in *Tales of Soldiers and Civilians* (1891), and *The Devil's Dictionary* (1906). "One of Twins" was originally published in *The San Francisco Examiner* on October 28, 1888, and was included in Bierce's 1893 collection of supernatural tales, *Can Such Things Be?* In the last two decades of his life, Bierce suffered a series of personal tragedies, including the deaths of two of his children, and in 1909 he ended his relationship with *The San Francisco Examiner* and began to travel. In some of his last correspondence he suggested he might go to Mexico, and the postscript of his last known letter, dated December 26, 1913, and purportedly sent from Chihuahua, Mexico, says only this: "As to me, I leave here tomorrow for an unknown destination."

※

MARJORIE BOWEN (GABRIELLE MARGARET VERE CAMPBELL LONG, 1885–1952) was born on Hayling Island, Hampshire, England. A self-taught writer who availed herself of libraries and museums from an early age, Bowen supported her family through the writing of more than 150 volumes ranging from tales of the weird and supernatural, historical novels, and mysteries to biography and popular history. She composed under several pen names, including Joseph Shearing and George Preedy. Although her work has fallen into obscurity, she was greatly admired by critics and writers of her day, including Graham Greene and Rebecca West. Greene, who read Bowen's first novel, *The Viper of Milan*, when he was fourteen years old, considered it one of the great influences on his own writing career.

JONATHAN CARROLL has written twenty books and lives in Vienna, Austria.

ANTON CHEKHOV (1860–1904) was born in Taganrog, in the Russian Empire, the son of a grocer and the grandson of a serf. A practicing physician for most of his writing life, he once said, "Medicine is my lawful wife and literature is my mistress." Until his death from tuberculosis at the age of forty-four, he produced several hundred short stories, novellas, and works for the stage, among them such classic works as "The Lady with the Pet Dog" and "In the Ravine" and the plays *Uncle Vanya*, *The Cherry Orchard*, *Three Sisters*, and *The Seagull*. "Oysters," written in 1884 when Chekhov was in medical school, is almost hallucinatory in its evocation of an impoverished and hungry child's first encounter with an unfamiliar word—and an equally unfamiliar food. *Fames*, a term that appears early in the story, is Latin for "hunger." Uncannily, twenty years after this story was published, Chekhov's body was returned to Moscow by train from Badenweiler, Germany, in a freight car labeled "For Oysters Only."

JEAN-CHRISTOPHE DUCHON-DORIS Trained as a lawyer and now a judge in Marseilles, Jean-Christophe Duchon-Doris is the author of three story collections and seven novels. He is chiefly known for his popular literary historical mysteries featuring, in one instance, a Perrault copycat killer; and in another, Napoléon's chef Antonin Carême, who is credited with inventing haute cuisine. The stories in Duchor-Doris' Goncourt-winning *Les Lettres du Baron* (Juillard, 1994), an interconnected collection, take the form of dead letters to addresses that Baron Georges-Eugène Haussmann's renovations erased from Paris.

⚙

MANSOURA EZ ELDIN is an Egyptian journalist and author of short stories and novels. Her work has been translated into a number of languages, including an English translation of *Maryam's Maze* (AUC Press, 2007). In 2009, the Beirut39 project selected Ez Eldin as one of the 39 best Arab authors below the age of forty. In 2010, her second novel, *Beyond Paradise*, was shortlisted for the prestigious Arabic Booker Prize and was translated into German (Unions Verlag, 2011) and Italian (Piemme, 2011). Ez Eldin's third novel, *The Emerald Mountain*, was out at the beginning of 2014 and her collection of short stories *The Path to Madness* won the award of the best Egyptian collection of short stories in 2013.

⚙

JOHN HERDMAN was born in Edinburgh, Scotland, and educated there and at Magdalene College, Cambridge, where he read English and later took his Ph.D. He is a novelist, short story writer, and literary critic. His fiction includes *A Truth Lover* (1973), *Pagan's Pilgrimage* (1978), *Imelda and Other Stories* (1993), *Ghostwriting* (1996), and *The Sinister Cabaret* (2001), and his most recent story collection is *My Wife's Lovers* (2007). As a critic he has published a study of Bob Dylan's lyrics, *Voice Without Restraint* (1982) and *The Double in Nineteenth-Century Fiction* (1990), as well as much work on modern Scottish literature. *Another Country* (2013) is a memoir of literary-political life in Scotland in the 1960s and 1970s. John Herdman is a former Creative Writing Fellow at Edinburgh University and now lives with his wife in Edinburgh, Scotland.

FELISBERTO HERNÁNDEZ (1902–1964) was born in Montevideo, Uruguay. A talented (and self-taught) pianist, he began playing in the silent-screen movie theaters when he was twelve years old and later toured the small concert halls of Uruguay and Argentina. He married four times, published seven books, and died, impoverished, in 1964. His short stories went largely unnoticed during his lifetime, but his fiction has had a profound influence on many great twentieth-century authors, including Julie Cortásar, Italo Calvino, and Gabriel Garcia Márquez. The latter once wrote: "If I hadn't read the stories of Felisberto Hernández in 1950, I wouldn't be the writer I am today." "The Usher" is part of the collection *Piano Stories*, reissued by New Directions Publishing in January 2014.

ERNST THEODOR AMADEUS HOFFMANN (1776–1822) Born in Königsberg, Prussia, Hoffmann was not only an accomplished writer of hallucinatory tales blurring the lines between the quotidian and the fantastic but also a composer, conductor, music critic, theater director, and set designer. A civil servant by day, he lost several governmental posts due to his habit of making fun of the authorities in print. He died at the age of forty-six, paralyzed in his legs and hands, dictating his last story and telling jokes to his friends. He has influenced writers from Dostoyevsky to Barthelme and beyond. "The Sand-Man," which first appeared in his book *Nachtstücke* (Night Pieces), vol. 1, is discussed at length in Freud's 1919 essay "*The Uncanny.*"

SHIRLEY JACKSON (1916–1965) wrote more than one hundred novels, short stories, and plays, including the iconic "The Lottery." In her works she often explored themes of psychological turmoil, isolation, prejudice, and the inequity of fate. Many of Jackson's works take place in the small, xenophobic towns of New England, where she and her husband, Professor Stanley Edgar Hyman, wrote and taught. Her major works include the novels *We Have Always Lived in the Castle* and *The Haunting of Hill House*, now regarded as "the quintessential haunted house tale." Dorothy Parker called Jackson "unparalleled as a leader in the field of beautifully written, quiet, cumulative shudders." The Library of America recently honored Jackson by publishing an anthology of her literary works, edited by Joyce Carol Oates. The Jackson family has been carefully combing through the voluminous material that their mother had left behind—fifty-two cartons containing nearly seventy-five hundred items, which are archived at the Library of Congress. "Paranoia" is one of the previously unpublished stories that the Jackson family found; its publication in *The New Yorker* in August 2013 represented the first time that Jackson had been published in the magazine in sixty years.

⚜

FRANZ KAFKA (1883–1924) is best known for such stories as *Metamorphosis,* "The Hunger Artist," and "In the Penal Colony," as well as the novels *The Trial* and *The Castle.* Critic Erich Heller once described him as "the creator of the most obscure lucidity in the history of literature," and it is perhaps no accident that the term "Kafkaesque"—however misused—has so thoroughly entered the daily lexicon. Born into a Jewish family in Prague, Kafka studied at German-language schools and Charles University, earning a law degree there in 1906. An insurance official for most of his life, he pursued his writing late at night. "The Stoker" (1913) is one of the few of Kafka's works to see publication during his lifetime and is the first chapter of his projected novel, *Amerika/The Man Who Disappeared.* That this novel and many other of Kafka's works are with us today we owe to his friend Max Brod, who found himself unable to fulfill

Kafka's final wish: the destruction of all his unpublished and unfinished manuscripts.

⚭

KELLY LINK is the author of the story collections *Stranger Things Happen, Magic for Beginners,* and *Pretty Monsters,* as well as the founder, with her husband, Gavin J. Grant, of Small Beer Press. A fourth collection of stories, *Get in Trouble,* is forthcoming from Random House in 2015.

⚭

H. P. LOVECRAFT [HOWARD PHILLIPS LOVECRAFT, 1890–1937] is widely recognized as one of the most significant horror writers of the twentieth century. Lovecraft created the "Cthulhu Mythos," a sprawling universe populated by insane, indifferent, and unknowable horrors. Lovecraft freely lent his creation to his many protégés and correspondents, among them Robert Howard (creator of Conan the Barbarian) and Robert Bloch (author of *Psycho*). Lovecraft also penned *Supernatural Horror in Literature,* one of the first substantive examinations of the horror genre. In this seminal essay, Lovecraft wrote, "The oldest and strongest emotion of mankind is fear, and the oldest and strongest kind of fear is fear of the unknown." Lovecraft died in poverty in 1937, but today his influence can be felt widely in popular culture and in the work of many of the finest contemporary writers of the weird and the supernatural.

⚭

HENRI-RENÉ-ALBERT-GUY DE MAUPASSANT [1850–1893] is considered a founding father of the modern short story. In a legendary dozen-year creative run from 1880 to his death, Maupassant penned more than three hundred short stories, of which just over a tenth are fantastical, as well as six novels, starting with *Une Vie* (A Woman's Life). He was raised by his mother, who risked the then-public shame of divorce to escape his abusive father. At the age of eighteen, he saved Swinburne from drowning, for which the English poet, among other displays of gratitude, introduced him to that macabre artifact a dried human hand, which Maupassant later came to own and which features in no fewer than three of his tales. Flaubert took the author under his wing as a protégé. "On the Water" dates from the March 1876 issue of *Le Bulletin Français*, under the title "In a Dinghy," and in 1881 was collected in the author's first book of stories, *La Maison Tellier*. At a time when river life was favored by leisured society, Maupassant himself was an avid boater and a regular at the floating café La Grenouillère, depicted by both Monet and Renoir.

CHINA MIÉVILLE is the award-winning author of several novels, including *The City & the City*, *Embassytown*, and *Railsea*, and of various short stories. His nonfiction includes the book *Between Equal Rights*, a study of international law; and the essay "London's Overthrow," on London after the riots of 2011.

STEVEN MILLHAUSER is the author of twelve works of fiction, including *Edwin Mullhouse: The Life and Death of an American Writer*, *Martin Dressler: The Tale of an American Dreamer*, and, most recently, *We Others: New and Selected Stories*. His work has appeared in *Tin House*, *McSweeney's*, *The New Yorker*, *Harper's*, and other publications. His story "Eisenheim the Illusionist" was the basis of the 2006 film *The Illusionist*. He teaches at Skidmore College and lives in Saratoga Springs, New York.

JOYCE CAROL OATES is a recipient of the National Humanities, Medal, the National Book Critics Circle Ivan Sandrof Lifetime Achievement Award, the *Chicago Tribune* Lifetime Achievement Award, the National Book Award, and the PEN/Malamud Award for Excellence in Short Fiction and has been nominated for the Pulitzer Prize. She is the Roger S. Berlind Distinguished Professor of the Humanities at Princeton University and has been a member of the American Academy of Arts and Letters since 1978.

YOKO OGAWA is the author of more than twenty works of fiction and non-fiction, including the story collection *Revenge: Eleven Dark Tales*, in which "Old Mrs. J" appears. Her novels include *The Diving Pool*, *The Housekeeper and the Professor*, and *Hotel Iris*. Her fiction has won every major Japanese literary award and has appeared in *The New Yorker*, *A Public Space*, and *Zoetrope*. Her novel *The Housekeeper and the Professor* was adapted into a film, *The Professor's Beloved Equation*. She lives in Ashiya, Japan, with her husband and son.

DEAN PASCHAL, originally from Albany, Georgia, now lives in New Orleans, where he works as an emergency room physician. "Moriya," included in this volume, was his first published story and was reprinted in *The Best American Short Stories 2003*. He has a book of short stories, *By the Light of the Jukebox*, which was brought out by Ontario Review Press in 2002—the stories in which have appeared in many anthologies, including *The Pushcart Prize*, Press 53's *Surreal South*, Norton's *New Sudden Fiction*, and Portals Press' *Something in the Water*. His novel, *The Frog Surgeon*, was released in September of 2013 by Portals Press, New Orleans.

EDGAR ALLAN POE [1809–1849] was born to traveling actors in Boston and, after their deaths, raised by John and Frances Allan of Richmond, Virginia. He published his first book, *Tamerlane*, at the age of eighteen. After a brief period at West Point, Poe began his lifelong work as a writer, magazine editor, and critical reviewer for literary magazines. Widely acknowledged as the inventor of the modern detective story, a pioneer of modern science fiction, and the nation's first great literary critic, Poe also helped usher the gothic tale into the modern era by shifting its settings from ancient castles to houses, libraries, and schools and by bringing a terrifying psychological realism to the horror story. "Berenice"——one of his most violent and disturbing stories——first appeared in 1835 in *The Southern Literary Messenger* and was later included in volume 2 of *Tales of the Grotesque and Arabesque*, volume 1 of which contained such well-known stories as "The Fall of the House of Usher," "William Wilson," and "MS Found in a Bottle." Poe died at the age of forty, under mysterious circumstances, in Baltimore, Maryland.

KAREN RUSSELL is the author of three books, including the story collections *St. Lucy's Home for Girls Raised by Wolves* (2006) and *Vampires in the Lemon Grove* (2013). Her novel, *Swamplandia*, was a finalist for the 2012 Pulitzer Prize and was included in the *New York Times'* Ten Best Books of 2011. Her short fiction has appeared in such publications as *The Best American Short Stories*, *The New Yorker*, *Granta*, *Zoetrope*, and *Oxford American*. Recipient of a 2013 MacArthur Foundation grant, she lives in New York and has taught writing and literature at several universities and colleges, including Columbia University, Williams College, Bard College, and Bryn Mawr.

BRUNO SCHULZ [1892–1942] was born into a family of cloth merchants who owned a shop on the market square of Drohobycz. Schulz rarely left the town; although the town itself would pass in his lifetime from Austrian, to Polish, to Soviet, and to Nazi jurisdiction. Schulz became an art teacher there, at his old school. He wrote his stories there, mythologized accounts of his own childhood, which recount the progressive illness of his aging father and the family's descent into financial ruin, stories populated by outré relatives and townspeople who testify richly to a way of life now gone, swept away in the Holocaust. Schulz would be murdered in the town in which he was born, by a Nazi officer who reportedly then went to a colleague to say, "You shot my Jew, so I have shot yours." Schulz's fame rests on his talents as both a visual artist and a writer. He first gained fame in 1922, when his *Book of Idolatry*, a collection of stylish and erotic *cliché-verre* pictures, was presented in Warsaw and L'vov. But it is his two volumes of short stories, *Cinnamon Shops and Other Stories* and *Sanatorium Under the Sign of the Hourglass*, that have gained him immortality and a reputation as the greatest modern prose stylist of the Polish language.

C. NAMWALI SERPELL was born in Zambia in 1980 and moved to the United States when she was eight. She is an assistant professor in the English Department at the University of California, Berkeley. Her creative work has appeared in *Callaloo, The Believer, Bidoun, Tin House, The Caine Prize Anthology,* and a collection, *Should I Go to Grad School?* Her first short story, "Muzungu," appeared in *The Best American Short Stories 2009* (ed. Alice Sebold) and was short-listed for the 2010 Caine Prize for African Writing. In 2011 she won a Rona Jaffe Foundation Writers' Award for women writers, on the basis of excerpts from a novel in progress. She lives in San Francisco.

STEVE STERN grew up in Memphis, Tennessee. His books include *The Frozen Rabbi,* a novel, and *The Wedding Jester,* a collection of stories for which he received the National Jewish Book Award. *The Book of Mischief: New and Selected Stories* was published by Graywolf Press in 2012. He has received fellowships from the Guggenheim and Fulbright foundations.

KARIN TIDBECK is the award-winning author of *Jagannath* and *Amatka*. She lives and works in Malmö, Sweden, where she makes a living as a freelance teacher and consultant on all things fictional and interactive. She writes in Swedish and English and has published short stories and poetry in Swedish since 2002 and English since 2010. Her publication history includes *Weird Tales*, *Tor.com*, *Lightspeed Magazine*, and the anthologies *Steampunk Revolution* and *The Time Travelers Almanac*.

***

EDITH WHARTON [EDITH NEWBOLD JONES, 1862–1937] published over forty volumes of fiction, nonfiction, and poetry over the course of her distinguished writing career and won the Pulitzer Prize in 1921 for her novel *The Age of Innocence*. Acclaimed for her keenly observed fictional chronicles of upper-class New York society, Wharton moved to France in 1907 and lived there until the end of her life. She was awarded the Cross of the French Legion of Honor for her philanthropic work in that country during World War I. Along with her friend and mentor Henry James, Wharton had an abiding interest in the psychological ghost story. "Pomegranate Seed" originally appeared in *The Saturday Evening Post* on April 25, 1931. It was subsequently included in Wharton's collection of short fiction *The World Over* (1936) and reprinted in her collection *Ghosts*, published the year of her death. In Wharton's preface to *Ghosts*, she remarked that "the teller of supernatural tales should be well frightened in the telling; for if he is, he may perhaps communicate to his readers the sense of that strange something undreamt of in the philosophy of Horatio."

ABOUT THE TRANSLATORS

J. T. (JOHN THOMAS) BEALBY (1858–1944) (ERNST THEODOR AMADEUS HOFF-MANN'S "THE SAND-MAN") Born in England and educated at Cambridge, J. T. Bealby translated an 1885 volume of Hoffmann's stories, *Weird Tales*. A prolific writer and editor, Bealby edited the collected Dryburgh edition of *The Waverley Novels* of Sir Walter Scott, contributed to several editions of the *Encyclopedia Britannica* (collaborating on some items with noted anarchist Peter Kropotkin), edited *The Scottish Geographical Magazine*, and translated other works on a variety of subjects, including books about travel and explorations. He moved to British Columbia in 1907 and two years later published the classic *Fruit Ranching in British Columbia*, part memoir and part manual for prospective immigrants.

⁂

JOHN CURRAN DAVIS (BRUNO SCHULZ'S "THE BIRDS") was born in North East England and went at an early age to London to seek his fortune. He found instead an array of unconnected occupations from building work to political campaigning. In the wake of the Fall of Communism, John went to Poland, first as a mature student and later as a teacher of English, and there became fascinated by Polish language and literature.

—— ⚜ ——

WIAM EL-TAMAMI (MANSOURA EZ ELDIN'S "GOTHIC NIGHT") grew up in a yellow place where nothing grows and has been traveling since. She has lived in Kuwait, England, and Vietnam and is currently based in Egypt, where she writes, translates short stories and poetry, edits novels, cooks, explores, revolts, and tries to rest her itchy feet. Her work has been featured in *Granta, Banipal, Jadaliyya, Alif*, and several anthologies. In 2011 she was awarded the Harvill Secker Young Translators' Prize for her translation of "Gothic Night."

—— ⚜ ——

CONSTANCE GARNETT (1861–1946) (CHEKHOV'S "OYSTERS") was one of the first English translators of nineteenth-century Russian literature. At the age of eighteen she won a scholarship to Newnham College, Cambridge, and in 1883 she moved to London, where she began to work in publishing. Her career as a translator began when she was introduced to the Russian exile Felix Volkhovsky, with whom she studied Russian. The first to translate Chekhov and Dostoyevsky into English, Garnett also translated the complete works of Turgenev and Gogol and the major works of Tolstoy. Altogether she produced over seventy English-language volumes of Russian literary works.

—— ⚜ ——

EDWARD GAUVIN (DUCHON-DORIS' "THE PUPPETS" AND MAUPASSANT'S "ON THE WATER") is the winner of the John Dryden Translation prize. A Clarion alum, he has received fellowships and residencies from the NEA, the

Fulbright Program, PEN England, PEN America, the Centre National du Livre, and the Lannan Foundation. His volume of Georges-Olivier Châteaureynaud's selected stories, *A Life on Paper* (Small Beer, 2010), won the Science Fiction & Fantasy Translation Award and was shortlisted for the Best Translated Book Award. Other publications have appeared in *The New York Times*, *Tin House*, *Conjunctions*, and *The Southern Review* and elsewhere. The contributing editor for Francophone comics at *Words Without Borders*, he writes a bimonthly column on the Francophone fantastic at *Weird Fiction Review*.

LUIS HARSS (FELISBERTO HERNÁNDEZ'S "THE USHER") is a bilingual writer who has translated works by Julio Cortázar, José María Arguedas, and other Spanish American novelists and Sor Juana Inés de la Cruz's *Dream*.

MICHAEL HOFMANN (FRANZ KAFKA'S "THE STOKER") is the author of six books of poetry and dozens of translations from the German, including works by Hans Fallada, Ernst Jünger, Franz Kafka, Wolfgang Koeppen, Joseph Roth, and Wim Wenders. Recent publications include a book of essays, *Where Have You Been?* and an edition of Gottfried Benn, *Impromptus: Selected Poems and Some Prose* (both from Farrar, Straus and Giroux). He teaches at the University of Florida.

STEPHEN SNYDER (YOKO OGAWA'S "OLD MRS. J") teaches Japanese literature at Middlebury College. In addition to translating the work of Yoko Ogawa, he has also translated works by Kenzaburō Ōe, Ryū Murakami, Natsuo Kirino, and Miri Yu.

ACKNOWLEDGMENTS

Anthologies don't arrive like Venus—let alone oysters—on the half shell, and this one is indebted to a long line of storytellers, teachers, scholars, students, family, and friends. My first thanks go to the late Francisca Rodriguez of Alhambra, California, who closed the curtains of our suburban home in the early sixties and told me ghost stories of the San Gabriel Valley, forever changing my picture of that suburban landscape and all places to follow. I am grateful to my amazing mother, Jeanne Sandor, who made readers of us all, and to my three older brothers, Jon, Richard, and David, who let me stay up late in the 1960s to watch *The Innocents, The Haunting,* and *The Picture of Dorian Gray.* Thanks, guys.

It was Rory Watson, poet and professor emeritus of University of Stirling in Scotland, who introduced me to the tales of E. T. A. Hoffmann and who answered my letter-out-of-the-blue all these years later, to talk about the Scottish uncanny. John McNamara of the University of

Houston helped me track down the origins of the word itself. Steven Millhauser gave this project a much-appreciated boost of encouragement early on and continued to lend his support throughout, and Joyce Carol Oates offered support, wisdom, and practical guidance at several key junctures along the way. Several literary compadres pointed the way to uncanny authors new to me, helped me through rough passages, offered valuable second opinions, and helped write the author bios of the dead. I give heartfelt thanks to them all: Jane Sandor, Deborah Eisenberg, Kelly Link, Michael Hofmann, Edward Gauvin, Patrick J. Clarke, Suzanne Berne, Susan Jackson Rodgers, Murray Weiss, and Matthew Burriesci.

I am indebted to Christopher Golden, Kate Bernheimer, Ellen Datlow, Gavin Grant, Jeff VanderMeer, Ray Russell, and S. T. Joshi for answering my questions so generously, and equally indebted to a small host of angels in the World of Permissions, for kindness to a greenhorn.

Thanks to the Oregon State University College of Liberal Arts and the School of Writing, Literature, and Film for a research grant and time to develop this project and to my comrades in the School—and particularly in the MFA Program—for being the best friends and colleagues a person can rightly hope for. Nor would this anthology exist if it weren't for the adventurous spirit of the MFA and MA students at Oregon State University, who have been going down the rabbit hole of the uncanny with me over the last several years. Two of that tribe deserve a special shout-out for their generous reading assistance: Patrick J. Clarke, composer, and Jon Ross, writer. To yet another OSU MFA alum, Adam Michaud, I owe thanks for the Herculean effort of transcribing squirrelly uncanny reprints.

Colleen Mohyde of The Doe Coover Agency helped me shape this idea into a viable proposal and has been a wonderful supporter for many years. Michael Homler at St. Martin's Press took a chance on this project, then emanated great calm, patience, and fortitude in the aftermath. Thank you both.

My beloved daughter, Hannah, has my eternal admiration for the way she put up with terrifying stories and equally terrifying midges on bleak, beautiful Rannoch Moor in the Scottish Highlands and has grown up to be such an intrepid reader and person of the world. And finally, my deepest gratitude goes to my husband, Tracy Daugherty, who has been living with the *Unheimliche* in the house ever since we met and who has always been there to help incubate a dream.

The editor with friends

COPYRIGHT ACKNOWLEDGMENTS

ABOUT THE EDITOR

Marjorie Sandor is the author of four books, most recently *The Late Interiors: A Life Under Construction* (Skyhorse/Arcade, 2011). Her story collection *Portrait of My Mother, Who Posed Nude in Wartime* (Sarabande Books), won the 2004 National Jewish Book Award in Fiction, and an essay collection, *The Night Gardener: A Search for Home* (The Lyons Press), won the 2000 Oregon Book Award for literary nonfiction. Her work has appeared in such journals as *The Georgia Review, AGNI, The Hopkins Review*, and the *Harvard Review* and has been anthologized in *Best American Short Stories, Pushcart Prize, Twenty Under Thirty*, and elsewhere. She lives in Corvallis, Oregon, and is on the faculty of the Oregon State University MFA Program in Creative Writing, and Pacific Lutheran University's low-residency MFA Program. She has been teaching courses on the uncanny in literature for the past decade.